ALL THE SKIES SO HUNGRY

TRANSPLANTED
BOOK TWO

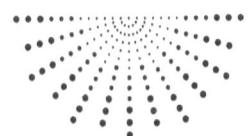

EMMIE CHRISTIE

For Daniel -
My husband, best friend,
and fight scene outliner.

THE EXPEDITION

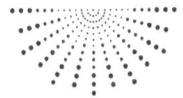

Saida had snuck away from the training expedition.

A grin pulled at Alesio's mouth as he scanned the retinue of eleven travelers, ten of them rookies on the world of Touch. No flash of crimson hair met his gaze; no skulking form hid behind anyone else.

Of course she waited till the afternoon. He held up a hand, signaling a pause for the other members of their expedition. "This is a good spot for a break, here at the pod shelters. Let me drop my shield and you all can get some magic exposure."

Touch's Glass Sea lay before them, a vast, shallow body of water stretching to the horizon like an enormous mirror for a god to check their eyeliner in. Pod shelters shaped like teardrops dotted the openness nearby. Everyone perched or knelt on some rocks above the shallow water. Alesio dropped his shield, the large area of Touch magic that he'd formed around them out of water. They all tensed, and some winced, as the pressure of the water and the cold caress of late fall's salty breeze on their faces intensified.

Alesio breathed in, grateful for the reprieve. Keeping up that large a shield for the last two hours had drained the strength from both his body and his magic. Water didn't require much magic for short periods, but he had to keep feeding the shield the entire time instead of Shaping it into a permanent object, as he could with solid materials like wood or stone.

Sometimes part of the shield would drop, even though he fed it magic anyway, and he concentrated to shore up the chinks when they appeared. He'd done this for the past year for longer and longer stints with larger areas—the first time he'd couldn't hold a shield for himself longer than a few minutes.

He stretched and rolled his neck, surreptitiously sniffing under his arms through his silver skintight suit the Touchians called the buoy. On Touch, any loose clothing abraded the skin or allowed wind or water to penetrate, so most locals and visitors wore the traditional suit. Touchians had Shaped the suit's material with tiny veins of a type of lightweight crystal found in the rocks here. The resulting garment wicked away moisture, including sweat, so that people didn't have to change out of their suits as often and expose themselves to the potency of brisk air.

The buoy could also balloon with air if he so chose, letting him float if he wanted on the shallow sea. He didn't smell like a barrel of nonflowers, but after an entire day of travel, he'd smelled worse.

"Alright, I'm gonna go answer some calls of nature," he told the group. "Don't wander anywhere while I'm gone. I don't want to have to fish anyone out of a depth."

The other explorers murmured assent, many adding a few words in the effusive language of yawns. Most of them hailed from the world of Sound and had suffered from a five-hour time jump when they had teleported to this part of Touch three days ago. Alesio had learned a trick from Saida on how to adjust to the new world's time faster; he just stayed awake till evening arrived and slept hard that night. Most of the others hadn't followed their example.

Linia, a piper from Sound, the sponsor for the expedition, sat crisscrossed, flipped open a little umbrella, and held it against the slight wind. "You mean you're just going to leave us? What if we're attacked by some horrifying fish-person? Or what if that giant Wave thing comes and sweeps us away?"

"Would that I were so lucky."

"What was that?"

"The Summit Wave is due today or tomorrow. That's kind of why you're on this trip, so you can learn the signs and manage to avoid it, remember? That's how you earn your safety certificates for this world. It's the deadliest thing here."

Muey, a native Touchian and their official guide, had stayed upright and squared her shoulders. She wore the traditional buoy suit and, like most other Touchians, she'd spent most of her life wading through shallow water, so her calf muscles bulged the size of his head, and, he guessed, had the same density as rocks. "Most importantly, we're here to scope out the big, new kind of magic the foxan is sensing. That is why my people have agreed to these expeditions, not just because otherworlders want to gawk at the Summit. It is the foxan's will."

"Stand down, Muey," Alesio said. "We know your feelings on Saida and the others."

"I would not so casually use any of the foxans' first names."

Alesio clicked his teeth together and tried not to clench them. He'd learned to ration such reactions along with his magic, or he'd develop headaches. "Can anyone tell me the signs of the Summit Wave?"

A young Scentian named Paras raised her hand. "Five hours from impact, the wind will rise, and small waves will appear on the Glass Sea."

"Correct. And two hours from impact? Quickly, so I don't add to the water level?"

Paras blushed, the red scarlet on her pale skin. In the Scentians' world of enhanced smells, they tended to hide such calamitous matters as bodily functions. "You can see it in the distance, but it's hard to tell at first because it'll resemble a mountain or a cloud."

"Good. And we have pod shelters right here, so if we see it at the two-hour mark, we're good and safe." Alesio strolled to the nearest pod shelter and waded around it.

Whoever had constructed the gray enclosures had bolted them into the ground with iron bars, and the lower end of their teardrop shape always faced the way the Summit Wave flowed, ensuring that the mountain-sized wave would not tear them out of their holdings. He rounded the pod shelter to the higher end, which rose above his head, and as soon as it hid him from view of the others, he crouched, settling into a fighting stance and keeping his center of gravity low. He didn't have to pee, but he preferred to have privacy in his ongoing game of hide and seek with Saida.

He breathed in and out and accessed his new magic that had *texture.*

Just six months ago he hadn't known where to find it, but had gravitated towards his Sound magic, the magic he'd known his whole life. Now, though, he located his Touch magic with ease: he Received it, conceptualizing it as an actual room inside himself.

A slight rippling sensation let him know he'd entered a place where time slowed down to a crawl; a room with squares of wallpaper, and each square had a different surface. One square, his boots, felt rubbery, and another, the air, felt cold. Lower down on the wall, a larger section, the sand, had a gritty surface. He searched lower for the wet one and located it at the bottom. He imagined laying his palm against that, and the water around him responded.

Concentrating, he Shaped from that square on the wall little ships of water, molding them with his imagined hands. If he used more force and time on the ships, he could solidify the water to ice, so they kept their form a bit longer, but then they wouldn't sail as fast.

Several minutes seemed to pass, but he knew the process happened in less than a moment. Before he'd begun visualizing his magic inside of himself, he'd created Sound knives with half-formed thoughts. But now, he could Shape his magic with so much more precision and purpose.

He ended up with three water ships and returned from his magic room—the jarring sensation of leaving the time dilation of his magic room sending shivers down his spine—and sent the ships out around him. He had meant to Shape five, but two of the ships didn't respond. Crafting intricate shapes instead of simple shields required more effort, time, and magic. He directed one ship around the edge of the pod shelter he hid behind, and the second and third to the other pod shelters. In the back of his mind, he continued to send a low flow of magic energy into them to keep them afloat.

He smiled, happy that he had a better knowledge of magic now. Over the course of the last year, the Council had tasked magic users from each world to create shared basic terminology for how magic worked. Most everyone agreed that magic use had two distinct stages. Receiving referred to an internal stage, when people pulled magic from the Primal Plane into their specific world, transforming it into one of the Sensory magics.

Everyone experienced Receiving; humans, foxans, and fox-persons alike could savor the enhanced sweetness of star melons on Taste or gasp at the overwhelming lavender sunrises on Vison. Unless, of course, they had some sort of disability like Alesio's partial deafness, which had its drawbacks but also its benefits.

The second stage, which the Council and the group of magic users had voted to call 'Shaping,' referred to using the magic they had Received to create external changes, like Shaping the water ships. Fewer humans could Shape magic, and foxans and fox-people couldn't at all, and so far, just he could Shape two kinds of magic. It meant that somewhere, in the centuries before the Severing—that apocalyptic era when the Hunger had cut off the five Sensory worlds from the Primal Plane, where raw magic originated—he had ancestors from a different world.

The ships wobbled, creating ripples in the smooth Glass Sea. He tried to level out their sailing, but the second ship grew instead, sending out more ripples. He'd already used a lot of magic today keeping the water shield up. He hadn't used enough to fear draining himself, but he would need to conserve most of what he had left, just to be safe.

He surveyed his wobbling Touch magic ships with a resigned air. He *could* have used Sound magic but Touch magic manifested stronger on the Touch world. Besides, Saida had established the rule that he had to use Touch magic to find her, "or you'll find me too fast!"

She was right. Even on Touch, he'd find her in a moment with

Sound magic. Hearing her breathe, that little catch in her throat when she heard his voice—with Saida, it didn't matter where they were, he could find her.

During their game, though, worry waved at him from far off, like a face in the audience he couldn't quite see because of the lights on stage. He scanned the corners of the shelters for more than just Saida.

Seven months ago, a report of an underground cage match had surfaced on Touch, and he brooded over the probability that Clef, his old tormentor and the old shadow leader of the straits, had spread the appalling practice. He'd instituted cage matches in Flock, the other Soundian city, after all, and built up a network of fighters there who called themselves shrikers. He had eluded capture ever since the Reconnection a year before, but that didn't mean he laid low. Clef schemed in the same manner that a shrike hunted: without stopping, and with an eye for malicious vengeance.

Clef had likely fled to Flock. Hestafon, Anthem's leader and the delegate for Sound, had sent many search parties there over the past several months, but had forbidden Alesio to go. The shrikers hated Alesio as a renowned cage fighter from Anthem and Hestafon worried they would incite a riot.

With his newfound fame as the Voice of Reconnection, and the fact that artists had plastered sketches of his face all over Sound and Touch to advertise for his performances at the two Cadenzas—the original, and the new one built in the caves on Touch—Alesio couldn't necessarily argue with Hestafon's assessment. He didn't want to cause more strife in the city, either. But sounddamn it, how else could he search for Clef?

Just play the game, Alesio. Don't bring it up again when you're both trying to have fun. She already had too much to think about, with her newfound difficulty hearing magical voices. Which terrified him even more. He needed to protect her from threats both outside and in. At least he had practice with the first. But how could he help her with something he couldn't hear and didn't know if it was real or a realistic outcome of her condensed loneliness for 300 years? At least with his partial deafness, if someone spoke too quiet on his bad side, he could just ask them to speak louder.

Just play the game. I just need to distract her enough that it stops bothering her, even for just a little while.

His first ship rounded the edge. No Saida there. The second wavered in the water and paused. The farther away he tried to control magic, the more difficult it became.

The third ship sailed around another pod shelter about ten yards away and bumped against something soft on its far end.

Alesio didn't need to use Sound magic to hear Saida's gasp, then a muffled *"Sounddamn it!"* and splashing. He ducked, keeping his profile low, and sprinted across the gap, while trying to keep his splashing down to a minimum. By the time he rounded the taller, wider end of the teardrop shaped enclosure, she had disappeared, leaving nothing but ripples in her wake.

SAIDA LINGERED around the curve of the pod shelter, her heart skittering in her chest like a bellbug in a butter churn.

The fear of reaching hands tried to grasp at her throat, but it didn't have the same effect as it used to. Not when the excitement of Alesio's hands consumed her and filled her with anticipation for more of that tingling sensation. She'd waited all day for this, for when she could choose her approach. She shifted her lower body to her strong foxan hind legs, peeked around the curve—

Ah! The way his gaze snagged on her lips, and how even as his dark brown eyes deepened almost to black, he waited for her to move first!

She pivoted to face him and crashed into him like the Summit Wave. He fell backwards, laughing, meeting her lips with his, and they tangled into each other. On Touch, it felt like electricity, like lightning had bolted down and now sizzled in her stomach. He drew back for a moment, and she whimpered at the absence, but then he cupped her face in both hands and dragged his thumb over her bottom lip. She closed her eyes and sucked in a breath as the sensation zinged through her whole body.

"You waited till the later part of the day on purpose." He leaned forward, stopping just before their lips touched. "To ensure I had to conserve my magic use."

She craned her head around to his left ear, his partially deaf side, and a little into the water. "Maybe."

"Deplorable."

"I think you mean adorable."

His gaze shifted to her ears, his smile fading. His thoughts had shifted to The Problem. It hit her all over again, that sense of loss, that void in her mind.

It had begun at a slow pace, so slow that at first, she hadn't noticed it. But over the last few weeks, she had lost her ability to sense overgrowths, those too-dense areas of magic that needed trimming. Then, her magic trimmings had stopped speaking to her, those bits and bobs of trimmed magic that either refused to transplant to a new world or couldn't yet.

A few days later, thirteen vivid spots of powerful, already transplanted magic, had risen all over the five Sensory worlds, potent enough to break through her blunted senses. One of the thirteen magical beacons radiated from inside Anthem itself: the Epitaph of St. Rina's cathedral. That meant the other twelve bright spots were also likely Epitaphs, or foxans who had died and transplanted into the world of their choosing.

Saida lifted her paws to her foxan ears where she imagined her magical voices used to speak to her, like an inner ear, now deaf.

What if this part of the Glass Sea needed trimming, but she couldn't sense it?

On instinct, she searched for the loud thrumming of the powerful magic that had pulled at her for the last few days. A strong magic filled her mouth with the taste of basil and thyme, and some other herb she couldn't place. Taste magic mixed with Touch magic, a sign that the foxan who had transplanted had merged with magic from both worlds. She swallowed.

What if even the powerful Epitaphs winked out for her?

Alesio skated his lips over her collarbone over her silver Touchian suit, and the sensation brought her back. She wished she wore just her foxan clothing, the fur shorts and shirt she could control, so she could inch it lower. She wore a truncated buoy suit to allow her to shift without trouble, which wrapped just her chest and torso. Heat pooled in her core, and she almost stopped breathing. The course hairs of his beard, grown longer on the expedition than he'd usually allow, tickled her skin, raising gooseflesh in their wake.

"Hmmm," Alesio said. "I may be part deaf, but it sounds like your heartbeat's sped up."

He'd lived with the partial deafness his whole life and she was obsessing over something that had happened for a few weeks. The heat in her stomach curdled into shame.

"Oh, I said the wrong thing, didn't I?" He pulled in a breath through his teeth. "I'm . . . I'm never sure how to help. I'm sorry."

"You don't need to worry about it."

"But I care about you. Worry's a part of the package."

She trailed her fingers on his neck. He pushed forward so that her hand furrowed into the small hairs of his nape, and she shifted her fingernails to claws, grazing them around to his jawline so that he shivered.

This was Touch. The same world where Carn had imprisoned her and assaulted her. She and Alesio had gone on a few short expeditions in Touch the last few months and established contacts with some of the locals, but those trips hadn't lasted longer than a few days.

And she couldn't stop wondering. *Fantasizing.* They hadn't gone much beyond kissing yet, but now, images flashed through her mind. Being bare in the shallows. Alesio using Touch magic on her skin.

"Saida?"

She blinked. He tilted his dark head at her, then smirked. "Your heartbeat just sped up to thirty-second notes."

"You . . ." she licked her lips, inches away from his. "You're wrong, you know. You always know how to help."

"Is this helping?" His eyes half-closed and he kissed the sides of her mouth, inching to the center. Her eyes rolled back in her head. The magic of Touch reverberated through her, back and forth, back and forth, like the clapper of a bell. He didn't use Touch magic *on* her, but he didn't have to.

"It is taking him a long time to raise that water level." Muey's voice drifted over to them.

Saida gave a muffled, "No, don't—"

Alesio sang two quick low notes. A bubble of Sound magic surrounded them, pushing sound outward. A Sound shield. "—stop," Saida finished, gasping. "Nooooo, don't stop!"

"Muey, come back!" Paras said from somewhere.

The ache of his absent hands gripped her like a vise, both pain and pleasure mixing, and she mewled her frustration into his mouth.

Alesio stroked her hair with his physical hands and chuckled low in his throat. "That's not the last time, Starlight," he whispered, and pulled her to her feet along with him. She stumbled, her core pulsing.

"Muey?" Paras's voice and sounds of her splashing through the ankle-deep water increased and she rounded the curve of the pod shelter.

Saida didn't care. She'd waited all day for their rendezvous. She tilted her face up and leaned towards him. He cupped the back of her head with one hand and reveled in the easy strength in his stocky frame, his well-muscled arms. He slanted his mouth over hers and she clung to him, asking him with her body to hold her closer. He did.

"Muey, where did you—oooh my!" Paras's cheeks bloomed a deep crimson, and her blonde hair seemed even lighter in comparison.

Saida and Alesio broke apart.

"I'm so—I'm sorry, I didn't mean, uh, I was looking for Muey!"

"Haven't seen her," Alesio said. "We'll be over in a minute."

"Right." Paras stared at them.

Heat suffused through Saida. Alesio's wet hair had spiked up in the back from where she'd apparently thrust her hands in and kneaded it like she sometimes did to particularly blankets. He focused on her lips, his own puffy.

Muey's voice sounded from behind them. "There are little waves on the Glass, foxan."

She and Alesio spun around.

The Touchian stepped from behind the next pod shelter farther in and gestured around them. "If you want to find the magic before the Summit Wave finds us, we must make haste."

Saida glanced to the side. Wavelets and dimples marred the clear surface of the water that the Touchians called the Glass Sea, and the breeze had chilled, slowing the petulant pulse inside her core. She sighed and, snaking her hand inside Alesio's, slogged back towards the others, Paras and Muey following behind them.

———

THEY TRAVELED FOR TWO HOURS, following Saida's sense of the large transplant, or Epitaph, as she'd begun calling it. It called to her, thrumming through her with a strong and consistent rhythm. On this world, it manifested as a drumbeat in her chest, merged with the taste of basil, so basil throbbed into her mouth with each beat.

All the transplants she'd created over the centuries emitted varying amounts of power. They tended to have less than overgrowths, but radiated a much more stable and unwavering power, binding the origin magic of the trimming with the new place they settled into. Epitaphs emanated a stable strength larger than most overgrowths, and this one was no exception.

Saida found herself pulling at the hairs in her braid.

"Are they all what I think they are?" She'd asked her parents. She replayed Falrie's words from a year before about the identity of St. Rina's cathedral: a foxan that had transplanted themself, their last act of binding the worlds together. And, two weeks ago, they had flared up as one of the thirteen strong magical energies calling to her across the worlds.

"We don't know for sure," Darrow had said.

"But it's likely," Falrie had added.

"Did you . . . did you know any of them?"

They hadn't. Some of their memories had returned from their lives before the Severing. They remembered random, small things, like what sweetbread they used to buy, but they couldn't tell her if they'd bought it in the Cloves, or if the Cloves had even existed back then. Around 800 years of remaining full shifted foxans and trying to forget everything didn't reverse in the space of one year. Some things she wished would change tended to remain the same.

Saida loped through the deeper water as part foxan, on four legs, to keep out of the wind a little bit more, which had picked up, misting a cold, annoyingly consistent spray on the explorers' faces. A paper-thin sheet of ice had formed on the surface as the afternoon had waned, so they had to break through each time they stepped, and little ice chunks bobbed on the surface behind in the expedition's wake like awakened fish. Winter would arrive soon on this part of Touch.

Alesio had ceased protecting them with his Touch shield, preserving his magic in case of emergencies. Muey could use Touch magic too, but with the Summit approaching, they should save energy wherever possible.

Muey strode closer to her, matching her bounding pace with the strength of her muscular legs. Saida tensed. Her anxiety around exploring this world may have decreased, and she'd even considered asking Alesio to use Touch magic on her, but she didn't know if she'd ever relax around a Touchian. Not after what Carn had done.

"I do not mean to question your guidance, foxan, but are you sure the magic is near?"

"Sounds like you're questioning her guidance," Alesio said on her other side.

She shifted a bit taller and elbowed him with foxan elbows.

"Yes. I am sorry." Muey scanned the way ahead. "We have two hours before the Summit. We could still reach the pod shelters if we turned back now. I ask, as the Epitaph may seem close because you say its signal is strong, but mayhap it is not. Again, I am sorry for my presumptions on your abilities being restricted in any way."

Saida hadn't considered that possibility, like a mountain might seem close due to its size but could take hours more to reach its base.

She pursed her lips, which in her more foxan form, meant she bared her fangs. The beating of the drums had quickened, and the taste of basil thundered in her mouth. "Well, that might be the case. But even if we don't find the magic before the Summit Wave hits, I've saved my teleport today just in case. I'd rather travel for as long as we can, so I can portal to that point at a later day."

Muey inclined her head. "As you wish."

Alesio reached out and scratched Saida's head. She leaned into it, his touch grounding, a balm to her nerves.

Until a new thought popped in her head. Maybe because it had happened just over a year ago, she found herself recalling the time Watthe had shown up right before the Summit Wave, and they had almost drowned, all because she hadn't used her items to teleport. How would Alesio respond if he knew she still missed her magic items? Ever since the Epitaphs had begun resonating with strong magic, she had nursed a dream of one day talking again with her magic friends, Goosefeather and Tricksy Stone. She'd given them up, yes, but what if they could somehow communicate in a new way, as these Epitaphs seemed able to do? But she'd traded Tricksy Stone to the rich pipers so Alesio could sing at the Cadenza. If she wanted them back, would he feel that she didn't care about him?

Did missing Tricksy Stone mean she *didn't* care about him?

She blinked. Alesio had said something. "What was that?"

"I asked if you are alright." He glanced back at where Muey waded now alongside Paras. He had bent his knees a little, lowering his center of gravity to better power through the shallow water, as the Touchian did. The effortless grace he managed it spoke of his time as a cage fighter. "How is it, being around her?"

Touchians tended to treat foxans with eerie reverence, believing that they guided people to their next lives after they passed. One of the pods of Touchians had once captured Saida and kept her captive for several years, under the guise of worshipping her.

"It's . . . she's respectful, at least." The wind skated across the icing sea, chilling her even through her fur and the Touchian suit. "Hasn't asked me to follow her into any alleys or tried to tie me to an altar of worship."

"Quite a high bar you've set there."

She cocked an eyebrow at him. "I have to keep it low or certain singers tend to trip over the key change."

He gasped and placed a hand over his heart. "You wound me! I would *never* miss a key change!" His lips quirked up and distracted her with their softness, and that heat they'd built together by the pod shelters flared back up in her like fanned flames. "You've learned so much about music these past few months. Are you practicing singing in secret? Aha! I figured it out! Your fondest wish is to become the five worlds' most famous performer, mobbed by crowds and shouted at by random strangers!"

She snorted. "I *fondly* wish you would handle those crowds."

Alesio bowed low over her hand and bent an elegant leg, belying his stocky frame with a quick flick of his wrist as if flaring an invisible cape. "In that case, oh foxan, how about I lead our expedition in a marching song, so everyone slogs a little faster?"

"If it means you'll stop talking like that."

Alesio did an about face and addressed the others. "Alright, everyone, some of you may not know this one, but it's easy to catch on to the chorus! Match your feet to the rhythm and let's jog!"

OH, bend your ears to the brandy now
    And hear the tale of Vundin town
    Where young lad Foro fought the shrikes
    That drove the Vundins underground.

A SHRIKE HUNT! A shrike hunt!
    Keep your knives at home!
    Strike first! Strike first!
    Or you'll become its home!

· · ·

CHAPTER 1

OH, bend your ears to the brandy, friends,
 For Foro filed down each edge
 And sharp corner inside Vundin,
 And then sang up a mighty hedge!

A SHRIKE HUNT! A shrike hunt!
 Keep your knives at home!
 Strike first! Strike first!
 Or you'll become its home!

THE SHRIKES DOVE with piercing shrieks,
 To spike brave Foro on their beaks,
 Or throw him on the sharpest thing,
 And build a nest for their chicks to feast.

A SHRIKE HUNT! A shrike hunt!
 Keep your knives at home!
 Strike first! Strike first!
 Or you'll become its home!

BUT CLEVER FORO SANG A COVER, high,
 Trapping the shrikes inside,
 Then slipped into the underground,
 And waited till the shrikes had died.

A SHRIKE HUNT! A shrike hunt!
 Keep your knives at home!
 Strike first! Strike first!
 Or you'll become its home!

. . .

THE EXPLORERS all marched closer together, keeping to the quick rhythm of the song, splashing more in the deepening water.

"I've always hated that song." Linia panted a little from the exertion. Her late forties had come to call, and though slim and somewhat taller, she didn't have much muscle mass. "It's so gruesome! And untrue. There's no town named Vundin."

"Not that we know of," Paras said. Two bright spots colored her cheeks as she drove her short body onward. "Someone had to inspire the story, right? On Scent, we have a saying. 'You find the stink by going upriver.' You might find Vundin on your world someday, on an expedition like this."

Saida decided that she liked Paras. Though the woman had issues with open displays of affection, she always responded first to Saida or Alesio's questions about how to survive.

Linia scoffed. "It's obviously about Flock. Everyone knows the shrikers run that city."

"Flock is the other city on Sound, is it not?" Paras asked. "Why would shrikes nest there? I thought they were quite violent birds. Unless I misunderstood the song."

"They don't," Alesio said, his mouth twisting. "Linia is talking about a group of fighters in Flock who named themselves the shrikers. Those who fought in the cage matches."

Saida gripped his hand. Clef had forced him to fight one of those men last year, a Flockian named Brezeek. The old strait's leader had threatened Alesio's father if he didn't give in and fight like he had most of his young life in the cage matches. He still bore the weight of those bouts and upbringing like internal gravity shifts; simple things like the way he kept himself lower to the ground, as if ready to pivot on his heel at the whistle of a Sound knife, or how he still practiced holding his breath.

"So, it's a dangerous city?" Paras asked.

"I wouldn't go there," one of the other expedition members said, a man from the straits. "That's where Clef went to ground, I'd bet twenty whole notes. He controlled both cities from the shadows before . . ." he trailed off, glancing at Alesio.

Paras furrowed her brow. She followed the man's gaze and opened her mouth to ask another question but then seemed to stop herself.

Alesio clenched Saida's hand. He jogged faster, away from the others, creating a wake of water behind him, and Saida sprinted to keep up. She wiggled her fingers in his, and he blinked, and slowed down so everyone could catch up to him.

"I hope we find something useful on these outings, not a town full of dead birds," Linia said. "Something like the jewel that revolves in the Cadenza." She gave a sidelong glance at Saida, flipping her light brown hair over her shoulder. "I'll pay a handsome price to have one of those beauties lighting up my living room."

Saida breathed through her nose to slow the angry words simmering in her throat. "That's not how the magic works."

Linia puffed her words as she propelled herself forward. "You might find. That the right price. Will be magical enough for you. To make it happen." She paused to catch her breath. "Like how me and my associates helped build another Cadenza right here on Touch, I just want a better quality of life for everyone."

Saida re-decided that she disliked Linia. The wind gusted on all their faces like a slap, and she opened her mouth to say something, but Muey beat her to it.

"You should not speak to the foxan in such a manner, Noisemaker."

"Someone pinch me," Alesio said. "I must be dreaming that there's something Muey and I agree on." He narrowed his eyes at Linia. Though he had a high, sweet tenor when he sang, his speaking voice pitched lower, more like what someone might expect from his solid frame and barrel-thick chest. "Just because you paid a shit load of notes to the Council to be here doesn't mean you decide what we do."

Linia simpered, the wrinkles around her mouth deepening, showing that her face knew the expression well. "Why, Voice of Reconnection, that's not a very . . . diplomatic thing to say. I'll remind you that I sponsored this expedition."

"I expect that is the Summit Wave?" Paras said.

They all swung their heads to her, then to where she pointed.

A veritable mountain had appeared in the sky behind them, backlit by the larger, hazy purple world of Vision in the sky.

"Correct," Muey said. The Touchian glanced at Saida, opened her mouth, then shut it. The wind gusted harder, and the water had risen to their knees.

"We're almost there," Saida said. The Epitaph drummed in her chest so loud and filled her mouth with the taste of basil with such intensity, she wondered that the others couldn't feel it or taste it. But she used to feel that way about magic in general, and now, she couldn't sense anything beyond the Epitaph. She couldn't even sense Alesio's silver voice magic any longer, though listening to it still soothed her.

"Let's go." Muey gestured for Saida to lead the way, and everyone stopped talking as the massive, unsettling wave chased them with the inevitability of a sunset. Saida dashed ahead, keeping her longer human legs, now, and tried to pinpoint where the Epitaph's magic drew her to. It had to be close. It had to be.

On, and on, and still they hadn't found it in twenty minutes. Twenty-five. Everyone kept glancing backwards. The Summit Wave roared close, now, and the Glass Sea had risen to their thighs, slowing their progress. The chill spray stung their faces.

"Saida," Alesio said. "Do you want to portal—"

"There!" Saida pointed. A gray outline of a cave had appeared ahead in the mist.

They all shaded their eyes and wiped their faces.

"It's in there!" Saida said.

"Muey!" Alesio shouted. "Get us over there!"

"Right away," Muey said, and raised her arms in a fluid, graceful gesture.

The water around each of the explorers rose so they fell backwards, and it supported them. She pushed her hands forward, and the water raced towards the cave like liquid sleds. Off to her left, Linia screeched, and Saida whooped even as the mist needled into her and the spray thrown up by Muey's magic whipped across her arms.

They upended next to the cave. The Summit Wave had chased

them just as quick, if not quicker, than Muey's water sleds had carried them. They had maybe ten minutes. But the cave mouth had a sheer face, a smooth covering over it.

"It's a protected cave," Muey said. "Someone used Touch magic to seal it to keep it from flooding." She closed her eyes and reached for the smooth rock, as did Alesio.

"Where's Linia?" Paras asked.

Saida frowned and scanned the group. No Linia. She whipped her head and squinted behind them. Linia had slogged back about thirty yards, goggling at the towering Summit Wave.

"Get it open," Saida said to Alesio and Muey. "I've got her."

She waded out towards the piper, setting her jaw. She trusted Alesio and Muey to do their part. Meanwhile, she had to do hers.

"Linia!"

The woman jerked her head, then said something, but the roar of the wave drowned out her words. Her face and hands sported lurid red whiplash marks.

"Linia! Get over here!" The waves lapped up over their chests. "It's too dangerous now!"

"—something—up—"

"Linia!" The needle-like pain had intensified, the cold sharpening it like a whetstone. Without a full buoy suit like the others, it affected her stronger, piercing her foxan fur.

Watthe had touched her here with his horrible mass of hands, and Carn—so different, so different from Alesio's gentle magic. She flinched.

She didn't let those memories stop her anymore. She was ready to make new ones. Better ones.

She slogged closer. They had five minutes. Less. Any longer than two or three more minutes and the water would rise too high for them to reach the cave in time. "Linia! *Linia!*"

"There's someone up there!" Linia screamed. "Someone is *riding the wave!*"

Saida squinted up but the water in her eyes muddled everything. She rubbed them with her arm, reached Linia, and grabbed her.

"Are you trying to die out here? Come *on!*"

Linia let Saida pull her, and then she blinked and seemed to register the danger. She almost fell over as she fought through the waves.

Muey and Alesio Shaped the stone like taffy, stretching it out and to the side to open a way. The other Soundians huddled outside, waiting for it to open. Paras tried to wade out to help Saida, but the buffeting waves knocked her slight frame back.

Saida cursed as a large wave almost knocked her off her feet. She coughed from the spray.

Had Alesio and Muey opened the way yet? If not, she would need to portal them all away in the next minute.

There! They had staggered through to the hollow space behind the stone!

She called up a portal, dragged Linia's slight body through it, and stumbled through the cave opening. Everyone herded inside, water rushing in around their ankles along with foam as waves crashed against the sides of the cave.

A gray wall of water roared closer, and closer. As the last person ducked through, Alesio and Muey trudged backwards, Shaping the rock back over the entrance layer by layer, their arms shaking. The stone flowed back into place.

The Summit Wave broke like the bones of gods overhead.

2

THE QUESTION

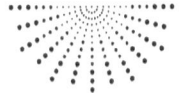

S aida was safe. She was safe.

Just a few more seconds and the Wave would have crushed her.

Alesio brought out his torch and flint from his waterproof pack. With trembling hands, he struck the flint a few times on the cave wall. Sparks flew and lit the torch, illuminating the dark of the musty cave.

He rushed over, his hands hovering over her, checking for gashes, for blood. "Saida. Saida, can you hear me?"

She groaned; her voice hoarse from screaming in the intensity of the wave.

"You don't have to speak. Can you move alright?"

She rolled over and sat up. Touch rashes, or abraded, irritated skin from Touch magic, marred her legs, arms, and reddish-brown cheeks and upper neck above her shortened buoy suit's collar, where the spray of the Wave had lashed her. She smirked even as she winced and held her hand to her human face. "Dying . . . for a kiss."

Alesio held his breath at the first word, then rolled his eyes. He pecked her on the lips then scrabbled through his pack with one hand while holding the torch with the other. Muey crouched and handed him the balm he searched for. Alesio afforded the Touchian a quick, grateful smile, then turned to Saida. "Here, this should help."

Linia began sobbing on the ground.

Alesio clenched his jaw. "Linia." He kept his voice low, imagining himself on stage, controlling his breathing. "What do you think would happen if we lost Saida?"

Linia raised her head, her pastel blue eyes teary. Loud red Touch rashes covered her face. Her straight brown hair lay plastered against her scalp and the neck of her buoy suit. "There was someone riding the wave. The top of it. I had to go and look."

He ground his teeth and kept his fists balled at his sides with effort. He had to convince his body he performed a difficult song, so he didn't give into the urge of punching Linia in the face. "You put us all in danger over a *hallucination?*"

"I almost drowned, too. But none of you seem to care." She propped herself against the cave wall and fished in her own pack for the balm.

Alesio closed his eyes. *Performance ended. Breathe.*

Paras and the other Soundians had plopped down as well and begun lathering it on their faces and hands, the few areas their buoy suits had left exposed. Muey hovered near Saida until Alesio barked at her to check the seal on the cave.

They'd both almost drained themselves, Shaping that sheer face of rock. He hadn't had much magic left, so Muey had had to do most of it, Shaping the stone to warp inward, like a door, and then closing that door after them.

He smoothed some more balm on Saida's neck. She pushed herself against his hand, a *murr* sound resonating in her throat like a giant cat, a sound he had learned meant "more." She'd changed so much in just a year, how she had overcome her fear of human touch. Well, his, anyway. He was so damn proud of her.

She followed his hands with slitted foxan eyes in a way that heated his cheeks. In the first four months of their relationship, she had wanted simple, slow kisses. Sometimes she still half-reached for him, then pulled back.

He hadn't minded. She had a lot of traumas to work through. He would go as fast or as slow as she liked. The last week or so, though, things between them had sped up, almost like she had had to lay a foundation before she could trust her own attraction, but once she had, she was ready to build. He cupped the back of her neck and trailed kisses along her hairline, up to her ear, and down her neck again. She clutched at him, and the way she gasped and the *murring* sound caught in her throat was like a song he was learning how to play.

Sound, but he loved this woman. Last year, he'd all but given up hope of ever amounting to anything, scrabbling for notes to feed his father and himself while begging for any scrap of attention from the pipers. He'd even considered returning to Clef just to feel valued. Then she'd crashed into his life like a carmine lightning bolt, opening his mind to other worlds and a stronger dream of performing for the one person in the audience who cared. Singing for Saida gave him the strongest thrill he'd ever experienced.

He had to keep her safe. He loved exploring the worlds with her, searching for the Epitaphs with her, but he'd tagged along for other reasons, too. He couldn't leave her to travel alone, not with so many dangers out there that could harm her.

The box that called itself 'the Hunger' that had ordered Watthe around still hunkered inside of the Primal Plane spouting its horrible little mantra about the rest of it 'coming soon.' The box had caused the Severing in the first place over 800 years ago, and if that thing represented a larger . . . Hunger, it could Sever the Planes again. Or do something even worse.

They didn't understand how it had managed to cut the link between the Planes the first time, so he had no way of knowing what it could do with more power. However, judging by its own De Capo mantra and its obsession with foxan magic, it probably had something do with absorbing Saida, her parents, and the new little foxan, Tener.

And then, of course, there was Clef.

Clef had threatened Alesio's father over and over growing up, forcing Alesio to continue fighting in the cage matches. But Saida had transplanted Watthe, the being that Clef had begun to worship. That, coupled with the fact that she and Alesio had become a couple . . . the target on her back had grown to a size that terrified him.

Outside dangers abounded, but he worried for her mental stability too. She'd endured so much for so long and had even made friends with her*self* by pouring parts of herself into magic items, so they could talk to her.

He still didn't really understand that. Had she truly heard voices from the magic, or had she imagined them in her isolation?

And, of course, he hadn't helped things. He'd run off, angry at her for not using those magic items to save herself from the Summit Wave. He'd cut her off, and in doing so, had cut her remaining tie to her sanity. She'd forgotten . . . everything, for a brief time. She'd forgotten her own name. She'd picked herself back up, but what if she hadn't? What if she'd just drifted into another world, and forgotten everything and everyone she'd ever known? Her parents had experienced permanent memory loss from the trauma of the Severing, and Saida had enough trauma to fill a depth.

What if she loses her memory again in the future?

"You're shaking." Saida laid a hand on his forearm, her blue-black galaxy eyes searching his, her foxan ears flicking forward in question.

He brushed wetness from her cheek with the back of his hand. "It took a lot of magic to close the cave."

He had almost drained himself doing it. Saida's voice sounded a little muffled, and her touch on his arm seemed lighter than normal.

Alesio waved his hand to get Muey's attention. "You said this cave was protected. What did you mean by that?"

Muey flicked her gaze over to them, scanning how Saida nestled against him, his legs and arms wrapped around hers. Her lips pursed. "It's a testament to the ancient times. Before we built the pod shelters, our ancestors lived in caves below the ground to avoid the Summit and sealed off the openings with Touch magic each time it occurred."

Alesio glanced at Saida. She stared where the light of the torch faded, and the darkness of the cave began, as if a sound bubble surrounded her and she couldn't hear any of their words. They didn't know how deep this cave stretched, but if ancient Touchians had lived here, at least they didn't have to worry about running out of air while waiting out the Summit Wave.

She tensed in his arms, and shifted herself from part foxan, back to human in just a few seconds, almost like her sense of self flickered in his arms.

"Are you cold? You were so close to the Summit."

"A little."

He wrapped himself around her like a flower closing for the night, cupping her hands in his and blowing warm air on them. The cave maintained a warmer temperature than the outside, even before the Summit had turned everything frigid. Saida stilled for a few moments, though her gaze drifted back to the dark part of the cave, her foxan ears pricked forward.

"Is everyone ready?" She scanned the group. "I want to reach the Epitaph today, if everyone is still okay."

"Whatever the foxan wishes, I will do," Muey said.

Linia huffed and pushed herself up. "I can continue, I suppose. We're already here. And I'd still like to try and find a piece of that magic."

Saida didn't even address that, though Alesio glared at the piper. He hated that she had bought her way here, and that the Council had allowed it, even encouraged it.

"I'm alright after putting that balm on," Paras said, smoothing another layer on her arms.

"Then let's go!" Saida bounded up and out of Alesio's arms. She dug the torch from her pack and held it to Alesio's, giving him a quick smile and a lingering brush against his shoulder. He drank in her touch, trying not to grip her fingers back, trying not to show how *much* he craved her closeness.

The Question had burned inside him for a long while now, but he hadn't dared voice it, for fear of scaring her. He didn't want her to feel caged in by him.

She led the way further into the cave, which sloped downwards. The shadows danced on the gray walls like the butterflies in his stomach before a big performance. Red striations mixed with the gray rock underfoot, camouflaging the reddish-brown-skinned Saida, illuminated by the red and orange torchlight. He inched closer to her.

Behind them, Paras's voice sounded muffled in the close quarters. "Muey, your world is so beautiful. But it's also very . . . it's a lot."

"It is all I knew for my whole life," Muey said. "It is not so bad once you know what to expect."

The ground sloped a little steeper, and they had to brace themselves against the sides one at a time, where a crumbling wooden railing jutted out. When one of the Soundians brushed it with their fingers, it crumbled to dust, and Linia screeched as she almost toppled over.

Alesio glared at her. "Maybe don't advertise our presence here for everything within fifty miles. We don't know what's in here."

"Nothing," Linia said, brushing off her silver suit and grimacing at the dust. "Obviously no one's lived in here for eons."

They continued descending. *How far down does it go?* He shuddered and squinted in the darkness. What if they found a depth, one of those blue-black sea pockets in this closed off, ancient cave? He brushed his fingers against the sides of the cave and felt a faint pressure back, like he'd grown even thicker calluses than he already had. His sense of touch had dulled. That meant he'd almost drained that part of himself; he didn't have any Touch magic left to Shape breathing spheres for the group. He checked inside that room full of texture. The walls had smoothed. He wouldn't know where to reach to affect any specific area.

Whenever he reached this point of magical exhaustion, it confused him. Raw, Primal magic still rippled *behind* the wall. He could sense it, though not in any specific sense like Touch or Sound. But he couldn't Receive it; the room wouldn't let him.

The Council and the group of magic users had agreed to use the term 'draining' after much debate. It referred to when someone spent too long in the time dilation or tried to Shape too much. Everyone needed a base amount of Received magic to stay in their bodies, like people needed a certain amount of water to function. If someone drained themselves, they lost that foundation and became desensitized to their origin of Sensory magic. Even their ability to experience normal senses could fade, leaving them squinting to see or straining to hear, depending on which magic they had lost. At its worst, the loss of connection also induced a kind of restless panic, a need to Receive that they could not remedy without time for the magic to refill. He didn't have that symptom, thankfully.

On the other end of the magic spectrum, they had discovered and named the sensation of 'flooding.' When Receiving—pulling the magic through from the Primal Plane into the room inside himself—he and the group of magic users had found they could flood themselves with too *much* magic, which they couldn't Shape at all, even with the time dilation helping. Most people became overstimulated and shaky and had to sit or lay down to let the magic absorb and leave their body. In severe cases they could fall unconscious, as their body couldn't handle so much magic flowing through it.

He'd practiced honing his Shaping skills with both Touch and Sound. He'd never had issues with flooding, or pulling too much magic through, but he did with draining.

The two torches cast dim light over the ruins of a few houses ahead of them. Saida gasped and dashed forward in human form.

"Hey!" He sprinted after her, almost tripping over the ground as it leveled out. "What—"

The ceiling opened above them, and the walls stretched far and wide, the flickering torchlight two pinpricks in an expanse of obscurity. His "what" would have boomed in the space if the Summit Wave didn't drown everything out. Its roar had lessened as they wended down, but in the large space, it thundered even louder.

What would the Summit Wave sound like on Sound? He shuddered to imagine such auditory power. It sounded like one never-ending explosion.

The light of Saida's torch had shrunk, and her form had faded into the darkness. He dashed after her. "Saida, wait! Please!"

Her torch halted. He sipped in controlled bursts of air to keep his legs pumping, catching up to her. She tilted her head at him. Her foxan ears flickered with uncertainty, her eyes wide, and for a moment, he had the overwhelming fear that she didn't recognize him, that her recent issues with losing the voices in magic and her ability to sense most magic had tumbled all the way to memory loss.

"What's wrong?" She stepped into his arms, the light skipping the furrows in her brow. Even in her human form, she felt so slight and tenuous, like a strong wind might shove her over. "You sounded scared." They had to shout to hear each other, and she peered into his eyes. "Oh! I'm sorry. I didn't realize you'd lost so much magic."

"It's not that. You ran on ahead. We don't know what's in here, Saida. There could be water swanseize overgrowths or something."

He wanted to say more. No, he wanted to ask her The Question. It roiled in his stomach like a bad piece of hotrat. They hadn't had alone time in the last few days, and he hadn't anticipated that becoming an issue beyond how much they craved to kiss and touch each other. He hadn't anticipated the Question growing in his chest like an overgrowth, choking everything else.

She rose on her tiptoes and bunted her cheek against his, her smooth skin sliding against the bristles on his face. He'd tried shaving with his trusty physical knife he always kept on his person and the reflection of the Glass Sea, but the odd angle had put him off. He disliked his disheveled appearance, but she didn't seem to mind it. "It's just that I could sense the Epitaph. It's right here." She gestured with the torch.

The light illuminated a trellis of live foliage among all the rocks and crumbling wood. Even with Alesio's reduced sensory input, it had a strong smell, a fresh green herb scent with a slight tinge of sweetness. He blinked. "How is that—how is it still growing in the dark? Without soil?"

"It's magic," Saida said. "It's a garden. It must have been how they grew crops in here to feed their village."

They trailed around it. The trellis extended like a wall all the way around, except for one archway opening. They crept inside. The taste of that herb filled his mouth even more, and the same herb filled the trellis walls, whereas other plants grew on the inside. The torchlight illuminated the oblong leaves with pointed tips. *Basil.* He recognized it from his forays into the Cloves where they sold fresh herbs daily.

"Is it—is it speaking to you?"

According to Falrie, when foxans died, they transplanted into different worlds and merged their raw Primal magic with that world's magic. Saida believed the strong magic sources they searched for were all foxan transplants.

He didn't know what she expected from the Epitaph, as every time he'd tried to ask, she'd changed the subject. But he could hazard a guess that she hoped the strength of their magic would mean she would hear their voices.

She pressed her forehead against one of the trellises, her head disappearing into the greenery. Had she heard him over the Wave?

The other members in their group trotted up to them. "Why'd you run off like that?" Paras asked, not quite loud enough, but Alesio could read lips. "Is everything alright?"

Alesio gestured to Saida. He shepherded them a little way off so they wouldn't distract her.

"Is she trimming some magic? That garden looks magical," Linia said. "Though I hoped for something more gem-like."

Alesio leveled his gaze at Linia. "We've been over this, so I don't want to keep telling you. She won't trim this magic. She does that to overgrowths, the kind that has too much energy in one place. This one's already transplanted."

"She's not going to take *anything*? Isn't it giving off a huge magical energy? Doesn't that mean it's an overgrowth?"

Alesio pinched the bridge of his nose, not sure how to explain all the intricacies of Saida's magical gardening and the reasoning for each trimming. He wasn't sure all the time. The other expedition members murmured among themselves.

Paras motioned them all over, not bothering to try and shout over the crashing of the Summit Wave. The petite Scentian pointed at the side of one of the few stone houses. Someone had carved a series of hands near the bottom, each using different gestures.

Muey squatted and brushed her hand over the carvings. "This is ancient Touchian writing!"

"Can you read it?" Alesio asked, darting a glance back at Saida, who still concentrated on the wall of verdigris like a moth engrossed in the study of light.

"Not well . . ." Muey traced the hand symbols and closed her eyes. "This word right here is 'city.' This one is 'journey', and this one . . ." Her words devolved into half-mumbles. Paras knelt beside her, and Muey's gaze did not waver.

Linia brushed an area on the floor clean with her hands and knelt there. After a moment, Alesio sat crisscrossed, picking at his buoy to dislodge the scrap that had ridden up his ass. The wet material did not extricate easily, and he had to grip a larger section and yank. It lifted from his skin with a sucking sound, then snapped back down.

The sensation probably would have given him quite the Touch rash if he hadn't almost drained himself, but now, it just felt like someone had whipped him with a towel, and he stopped himself from yelping. Linia watched this endeavor as if she'd never had clothing ride up in her life and could not fathom his boorish behavior. A year ago, such a reaction might have mortified him, especially from someone with such a pedigree, but now, he simply smacked his own ass and gave her his shit-eating grin. "Just killing the bellbugs. We sat in a nest."

Her eyes widened and she bolted to her feet, squinting at the ground. He laughed, and she glared at him. She sniffed and sought asylum on the far side of the torch lit space.

"I'm not sure what this means," Muey said. The wall and the Epitaph had enthralled the others. "Sedella? Maybe it's the name of something."

Paras brushed her hand against the ancient carving, copying Muey. She squinted at them, her blonde hair falling over her shoulder, but then shrugged and surveyed the other houses.

Alesio's attention drifted back to Saida. She'd stilled, as if by quieting herself enough, she'd latch on to whatever frequency the Epitaph spoke on. He understood that. He'd done the same when he'd worked as a guard at St. Rina's. They'd had to keep quiet, there, to preserve the sanctified silence in the place dedicated to the God of Sound. Sometimes, the richness of the ringing bells had reverberated through his feet. Now, he knew he'd felt traces of Touch magic.

He had a faint idea of the gravity of her loss. He'd drained himself of Sound magic just once, and a restless, aching absence had overtaken him, had driven him to a mindless run in the city. Saida's voice in his ear had rung like a distant bell. He just wanted to reconnect to that faded part of himself, prodding at the empty spot like the gap left by a lost tooth. He had understood nothing except panic in those horrible moments. Almost an hour had passed till Saida's voice rang through clear again.

If his limited experience with loss of magic felt anything like her ongoing one, it worried him. Even if he didn't believe magic voices spoke to her, the loss of them in her own head had still wounded her. What if she lost even more of herself? What if she started to lose her memory of their relationship in her extensive lifespan? He had to protect her from that. He had to find a way to bond himself to her closer, so that she wouldn't drift away, a way to transplant himself into her life.

"Aha!" Muey shot upright. Everyone's heads twitched toward her. "It's an account of a family who left this place to find 'where they grab,' or . . . perhaps 'harness the Wave.' Here, it reads: 'It will be a hard trip because we must reach the suthen'—I believe that's an old word for southern, 'suthen portal in one week. But the suthen portal will transport us close to Sedella, where they harness the Wave and have'— I'm not sure of this word — 'increasers. Finally, the . . . lun . . . have come to us at last.'"

"I thought you said you couldn't translate it very well," Alesio said.

Muey blinked. "I could not read it at once as the elders could. I had to study it for several minutes."

"Muey, that was amazing!" Paras trotted over and studied the wall again. Muey grinned at the Scentian, her rigid face cracking like a mold.

"I wonder if this strange city is still there?" Linia had busied herself with brushing dirt away from her, succeeding in uncovering more dirt.

"I would love to know this as well," Muey said.

Saida trudged over to them, her shoulders slumped, her foxan ears drooping. Alesio sprang up and wrapped his arms around her.

"Nothing." She produced no sound, but he read her lips. "All I can sense is that it's radiating consistent magic, like a kind of signal. But I don't understand it. There are no words."

"Hey, it's okay." Her lips trembled, and he blocked her from view of the others. "Maybe it just needs to . . . wait a little bit. And now, you can always portal here anytime you like, to check."

She bounced her head up and down and smiled up at him in such a bereft way, her lips a bow rosined with ruddy anguish. The Question burned in his chest, and in his throat, and all the way to his tongue. It sizzled on his lips. He leaned closer and whispered in her foxan ear. "Saida . . . do you want to live with me?"

Her eyes widened and she stepped back. "What?"

Sounddamn it.

He'd known she'd react this way. She'd needed several months before they'd even kissed. He understood why; her past with Carn provided more than enough reason, but she also had a restless soul. She didn't like staying in one place.

Each of the four times she'd stayed over at his house this month, he'd lain down and waited, and she'd crept in next to him as a foxan with the hesitation and surreptitiousness of twilight. Then, after several seconds, she'd shifted parts of herself to human one at a time and nestled against his chest. The last time they'd kissed while in his bed, though outside of it, they'd done that and much more.

"I'm just a little worried about you." He stepped closer so their words remained quiet enough for privacy, angling his good ear towards her. "With what's happened with your powers, and Clef still at large, I just . . . I want to stick close. To make sure you're alright."

She didn't step away again, but she curved her shoulders in the manner of a rolled up bellbug and flicked her ears back.

He clenched his hands, stopping himself from reaching out for her. He needed to salvage this, to lessen the importance, so hopefully she'd feel less pressure. Like throwing the lever on a gravity shift. "I just don't want you to — I want to help you. You know, while I'm still young enough to keep you out of trouble."

Her head shot up, almost clipping his chin. He bit his lip. He'd tried to say that last part as a joke. But jokes always had a transplant of truth in them.

"Alesio," she whispered. "We'll age at the same time, now. I'm sure of it."

He swallowed. Nodded.

The Reconnection had supposedly done much more than invigorate the worlds' magic. The foxans had explained that the Primal Plane sending magic through to the Sensory worlds would extend the human lifespan to centuries, the same length as the foxans'. Something about the renewal of magic rehydrating desiccated individual links to the humans' own life forces. He couldn't see such links—and neither could the foxans, for that matter. Saida's parents had based their conjectures on vague memories they'd had from before the Severing, but the effects had begun to show all the same in those on the edges of life. Babies had stayed basically the same age as they had since the Reconnection. Those old enough to cast a shadow death's door and even grip its handle still cleaved to their lives with a tenacity belying their blue-veined hands.

This phenomenon had come with a set of new concerns, of course, for now mothers had to nurse for much longer. Pregnant people had to remain pregnant longer. Those who had expected to gasp their last at a 'normal' age and had composed their peace with the afterlife now had to postpone that acceptance.

But would this mystical delay in aging continue at this pace? What if it slowed, or stopped for twenty, thirty, or even fifty years? Everything had happened so fast, and they still didn't understand much about how magic worked at a base level. He could grow old while Saida remained aging at her current leisurely rate.

When he'd first found out Saida's age—300 some years old, or thirtyish in foxan years—he'd reacted to the startling gap, but he hadn't considered how a long-term relationship would work with someone like Saida if his lifespan remained that of a normal human. Not until it had dawned on him several months ago.

They'd lounged on a grassy hill on an expedition in Taste, outside the salt-flats, and she'd said something about how she used to just lie and count the trees in Between at a mere eighty years old. And it had hit him like a Sound knife. He could someday reach eighty, while she remained thirty-five or forty. Even if her memory remained intact, why would she stay with someone who looked old enough to be her father? Or her grandfather?

Now, a part of him shook its head and ssked at him. *He* was worried about the future? Someone who had scolded his own father about losing sight of the immediate landscape of the present, like having enough food to eat, because he couldn't stop worrying about the hazy mountain ahead?

But Alesio had entered a different stage of life. He didn't have to scrape for his and his father's survival any longer. Was it any wonder that his mind had flipped to study the horizon, squinting for any possible danger, when the present had transformed into such a wondrous place? He just wanted to safeguard their happiness, when so many things could snatch it away.

Regardless, the time and place did not lend themselves for such a discussion. He'd already tipped his hand to Saida that he worried about her, about their relationship, which she didn't seem thrilled about.

"I'm sorry," he said, still holding his breath. He could do that for several minutes, now, while speaking, spending his Sound magic in tiny increments. "You don't have to move in. Only if you want to."

"Of course I want to." She flicked her gaze up at him, then rose on her tiptoes and rubbed her cheek against his.

SAIDA WOKE UP BEFORE ALESIO, nestled against him like a curtsy flower, a common weed that grew in the Sound wilds, named for how their yellow bright petals bent as if in respect to the sun, so their blooms often folded in on each other. She pried herself from his warmth with regret and levered on her elbows to peer at him.

In the dark of the cave, the planes of his face showed in grays and blacks to her foxan eyes: the sweet way he reached for her absence, his eyelids twitching, about to open, the tilt of his mouth. She stroked his dark hair, and he sighed at her touch, and she stayed there till his breathing evened back out.

She didn't want to light a torch and risk waking anyone, so she shifted to foxan, her ears flicking to catch any noise, padding on her calloused vulpine toes with slow, light steps around the rocky terrain and the sleeping expedition members. Her half buoy suit crinkled as her torso shrank, rubbing against her with an irritating sensation. She considered shucking herself out of it, but that seemed more trouble than it was worth.

She maneuvered around a broken, crumbling building and back to the Epitaph. The trellis wall seemed to rustle at her approach. Its strong basil taste thudded on her tongue, and its steady beat drummed in her chest, a savory sonata. She snuck around to the archway entrance on the left and slipped inside, surrounded by the trellis walls and the various plants of the interior.

The taste of potatoes, lingering in the ground and waiting for harvest, landed on her tongue. Tomatoes awaited her, ripe on the vine, and a strange kind of mustard-yellow lettuce. The basil acted as a kind of barrier, keeping their magic locked inside the garden, so the crops never molded or decomposed no matter how long they waited for harvest. A strong transplant, for sure. And they had waited for a long, long time. The magic thrummed, and she imagined their words: *Come and eat! We have so much! The lettuce has many more leaves underneath! We have fifty tomatoes in our vines, ready to pop out whenever it's time!*

But she had no idea what they might be really saying.

Had she imagined all their voices? Even the magic trimmings she'd kept in her den, and the ones she'd transplanted? What about Saltfall? What about Winter Lightning?

She scratched around one of the potato plants and sniffed at it, trying to sense it better. *What are you saying? Do you remember who you are? Do you remember who you were . . . before?*

No answer. She settled back on her hind legs and curled her tail around herself, pulling at the human hairs in her braid. She wished she could talk to Goosefeather about Alesio, and what he had said. Goosefeather had known how to speak in a gentler, softer way. They would've known how to answer.

Do you want to live with me?

"Of course I want to," she murmured.

The wall of basil rustled as in answer. She extended her claws and etched patterns in the dirt of the garden, relishing how the ground stretched and honed the ends, musing on human pleasures as she dallied in a foxan one.

She loved cuddling Alesio, kissing Alesio, letting Alesio hold her. She loved the heat, the craving, the closeness. She'd loved exploring that new side of herself and opening herself up like a flower that needed a whole year to bloom. She did want to be with him. She did.

Do you want to live with me?

She flicked the dirt off her claws. Her paws trembled. She shifted them to hands and clenched them into fists. "I do want to!" She hissed. "Why don't I want to?"

To make sure you're alright.

He worried about her so much. He kept ruminating on the aging process, about possibly growing old before her. She'd tried to reassure him that the magic had already begun in that regard. Before she'd lost her ability to sense magic, she had sensed it, and so had her parents, that the worlds' connection to the Primal Plane had raised the humans' vitality levels.

By living in environments rich in magic, the humans absorbed that magic. Babies and children had stopped growing in that absurd, almost visible way from week to week. This had alarmed and upset many people, which confused Saida. To her, how humans shot up like daylilies and then faded just as fast had always seemed the unnatural state.

Do you want to live with me?

She wished she could talk to Tricksy Stone just one more time. Tricksy Stone might have known why she couldn't sense magic any more or hear magic voices. They had had a knack for telling her if she forgot something, or what to do when she hesitated. The part that she had poured into Tricksy Stone had merged back to herself when her friend had transplanted and sometimes, their dry wit emerged in the patterns of some of her thoughts or her banter with Alesio. They had said *we are you,* and that held true. If she'd imagined them, if the voices had never existed except in her head, well, at least they belonged their anyway.

But now that their unique voices had merged with her once again, becoming a part of her mind instead of existing in an object outside of her, she had trouble identifying what they would've said to her. Or rather, what she would've said to herself. And now she'd promised Alesio she'd move in with him. Share a space with him. Stay with him, even if her future self might not always want such a thing.

Why not? She imagined the transplant asking.

"Well, I don't have a great track record with consistency."

"Why are you saying that to a potato?"

Saida spun. Linia sidled up to her, kneeling next to her, holding a torch for light. Saida fell back on her rear, almost crushing the potato plant.

"It's still early. Aren't you tired?" Saida asked, scrambling to her feet and shifting to more human. Her absorption in trying to speak to the magic had plugged her normal ears.

"Still not used to the time change. And when I'm up, I'm up." Linia eyed the potato that Saida had knelt in front of, then brushed more dirt from around it. "So, that's all there is to this magic, then? Root vegetables?"

"What do you mean, 'that's all there is?' What are you talking about? This garden is self-replenishing. It could feed an entire village for generations. It *did*." Saida gestured towards the crumbling wooden structures in the shadowy darkness of the cave.

"Hm, well, it didn't stop them from relocating, though," Linia said. "To that other city, or whatever that puffed up Touchian said."

Saida bit her lip.

"What I don't understand is why these big magics started radiating energy. Haven't they been here for ages and ages? Will they start other magics that you can trim and perhaps sell?"

"I wouldn't just sell you a magic trimming, Linia. I would have to try and transplant it in your home, and it might not want to. They decide where to settle down, not me."

Linia tapped her lips with a finger. "But in your time where you lived in the tiny Between world, some people say that you kept magic trimmings for yourself, without transplanting them."

Saida tasted blood. She'd grown foxan fangs without realizing it and bit down on her lips. "They were my *friends*."

The piper tilted her head, and the edges of her lips crinkled.

"Saida?" Alesio's silver-toned tenor called out. It echoed now, in the large open cave, without the Summit Wave to drown everything out.

"Over here," she called back.

A torch lit in the darkness, and the tap, tap, tap of quick steps reverberated through the cavern. Alesio rounded the edge of the Epitaph's archway, Paras and Muey trailing behind him. His forehead creased, then he glanced at Linia. "Didn't expect to see you up and about."

Linia shrugged her thin shoulders and smiled her coy smile. While the wrinkles around her mouth showed the evidence of many such smiles, her eyes did not have almost any accompanying wrinkles. "The cave isn't the most pleasant of accommodations. I simply asked when our fox-person here could teleport us back. I am most in need of a hot bath and clothes that don't reek of salt-water."

Paras yawned and stretched, rubbing at her eyes. Sleep and sweat had tangled her hair and darkened it with grease. She and Muey's lighter skin tones showed up easier in the dim light. "Are we heading back, then? I'm ready for some fresh air."

Saida straightened. The consistent drumbeat and taste of the various crops in the Epitaph still drew her, but as with St. Rina, she had no way of understanding what they said. Or, rather, if they said anything at all.

Closing her eyes, she searched for any portals nearby, those wandering spaces that answered her when she called them. She could sense them again, now, as her internal clock had reset as well. Saida had stayed on Touch for long enough that her internal clock had adapted to the rise and fall of the sun on this world. Sometimes, now that she often traveled through multiple worlds which had different time zones, she had to wait for her internal clock to tell her when her portals recharged instead of waiting for the sun to rise.

There. One roamed underground, around the edge of the Epitaph. It swam up through the rock like a fish and breached in front of them, opening a doorway to where Saida asked it: Anthem.

"Everyone, hold your breath," she reminded them.

They all filed inside without hesitation. Before Alesio's voice magic had transplanted to the Primal Plane and reconnected it to the Sensory, the worlds had all drifted more and more apart. While teleporting, she had had to hold her breath for over a minute, and towards the end, the worlds had all almost snapped apart. Now, though, she and the people she guided through the portals never had to hold their breath longer than a few seconds. Everyone stepped through to the other side, blinking at the brightness of the daylight after the darkness of the cave.

Something darkened the heavens, as large as the other two Sensory worlds of Vision and Taste in Touch's sky. No planet or moon occupied the space, rather a hole in space, like someone had shut off the sun in that spot. Dots appeared inside the spherical oblivion like islands in a vast sea. The void seemed to wrench at the very air, creating a warped corona half as wide as itself of rippling clouds and blue skies, twisting like a cloth.

"I HAVE ARRIVED," the entity said. "I HAVE COME TO CONSUME YOU ALL! RUN AND FEAR, LITTLE MAGICS, RUN AND FEAR! YOU HAVE NOWHERE TO HIDE!"

All the air seemed to leave Saida's lungs. Sweat broke out on her forehead and palms.

The Hunger had come.

3

THE HUNGER

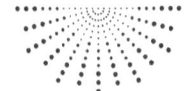

Alesio stepped through Saida's portal into a composition scored by chaos.

She'd deposited them in the market area surrounding the Portal Station on Anthem. At least a hundred people crowded the streets, some of them gushing towards the raised platform of with its shimmering circle of portals like packed fish in a stream. Some people had jammed sound cloths in their ears, a Soundian's natural defense against magic, and to block the Hunger's voice. "RUN AND FEAR! YOU HAVE NOWHERE TO HIDE! I HAVE ARRIVED—"

Beside Alesio, Saida's ears flattened, and the whites of her eyes showed. She remained in her human form with effort, her face a grimace, shivering in the cold of Anthem's winter. Late fall had arrived on Touch, but here, the wind cut like a Sound knife. Linia, Paras, and the other Soundians cowered in Muey's shadow, who stood tall and unmoving. That made sense to him. People born in a world where a cliff-sized wave roared past once a week had to develop a powerful mettle.

"Saida!" Alesio gripped her arm and bent to whisper in her ears. "Go to my house!" He'd bought it mainly for its proximity to the Portal Station.

She shook her head, her foxan fangs poking out of her lips. "I want to help!"

A large man running past clipped her, and she stumbled into Alesio. He caught her and steadied her, glaring at the man's receding back. He didn't have any sound cloths on him, but he had something better. He descended into his Sound room, tracing the wall papered over with bars of panic, and Shaped his breath into a Sound shield to surround their group.

Both the shouting humans and the booming voice from the sky silenced. The others straightened, lifting their hands from their ears. The absence of one sense seemed to magnify their vision, drawing their gaze towards that twisting whirlpool above them. Same as on Touch, the entity grabbed at the heavens and seemed to suck the color upwards, bending the clouds and the very air. Alesio couldn't sense any severing of the world's magic yet, but maybe that would come later.

Paras broke from the group and dashed towards the portal to Taste. She'd want to return to her village on Scent, but a direct departure portal from Sound to Scent didn't exist, so she'd arrive in Taste's Portal Station first, then use the departure portal to Scent from there.

The Soundians from the expedition scattered into the city. A family of four raced up to the dais, the father shoving past Tak, his friend and the Portal Station's lone guard, who reeled and sprawled on the ground.

Alesio and Saida ran to help Tak back up. They pulled him off the dais and to the surrounding marketplace. Blood trickled down the older gentleman's temple.

"Tak! How long has this been happening?"

"Three hours," Tak said, his voice hoarse from shouting. "They didn't come for the portals first, but after that *thing* kept talking . . ." He waved Alesio's concerned hands away and pointed back at the Portal Station. "I rebuffed most everyone until the people panicked and swarmed the dais. A few minutes ago, three ran through to Vision!"

Alesio cursed. Most citizens of Anthem had received their travel training for the Cloves on Taste; the incredible food and large population surged its popularity. Vision's gravity shifts, however, made it the most dangerous world to visit, especially without training. Almost no one had received travel certificates there; most had no idea how to stay safe.

Someone ran through Alesio's Sound shield, a young woman clutching at her dress to stop from tripping. She slowed, her mouth open in surprise. Then, like the rest, her face turned upwards. She screamed and exited the Sound bubble, sprinting towards the dais and the shimmering circle of portals.

Maybe I could form some sort of barrier around the Vision portal.

"Muey!" The Touchian guide had started towards the portal that led to Touch. "Muey! Help me!"

"Many people just passed through! They could drown in a depth!" She disappeared, vanishing through the portal.

"Sounddamn it," he muttered. If they could cut off access to the portals first, it would limit how many people they'd need to find and save later.

What would Clef do in all this chaos? He would take advantage of the distractions. He'd probably known this would happen since he served the Hunger.

But Alesio couldn't worry about what he couldn't control. He had to stay in the moment. He descended to his Touch magic room, running his hands along the walls and searching for something he could use as solid material. His fingers grazed a patch of gravel from the street, and he began to Shape with it, molding it with his hands into a low wall around the portal leading to Vision.

Maybe he could have with Muey's help. The cave wall on Touch, before the Summit Wave hit, had needed almost all their magic, combined, and they had done it quickly. But on Sound, Touch magic was less efficient. He couldn't Receive enough magic to Shape it in time—not without draining himself in that moment. Shaping solid material instead of air or water paid the price of time, as well.

His magic room shuddered, the time distortion rippling as if trying to dilate further and give him more of a gap but failing.

Time passed outside the magic room. Reality overlaid on his vision like a shadow, and even as the wall he Shaped crept up around the Vison portal, four men raced up to the dais as if in slow motion. Saida and Tak tried to block them, but the men shoved them aside. Two of the men kicked at the wall and it crumbled, not having enough density yet.

He ascended from the magic room back into reality and tried to grab the men, but they wrenched out of his grasp and vanished through the Vision portal.

"*Sounddamn!*" So much had already gone awry.

"Saida!" Darrow, Saida's father, dashed up to them on human legs, though his upper half had shifted to all foxan. He threw his shorter foxan arms around his daughter. "I'm so glad you're safe!"

"Where's Mom and Tener?" Saida hugged her father back.

"They went to Vision. We split up fifteen minutes ago to try and help with the panic. They both still have their portals to get people out." Darrow whined, a foxan sound Alesio knew from Saida that indicated fear or worry. "But . . . you know how she gets with crowds. Especially crowds like this."

"I'll go through to Vision to help them," Alesio said. "Maybe I can craft some softer ground in case people fall off a gravity shift."

"I'll stay here and help Dad," Saida said.

Is it because of what I said last night?

Alesio kissed her on the cheek. "Stay safe."

She bobbed her head and hugged him. He closed his lips against the petty words rising in his throat like vomit— *"Don't put yourself in danger just because you want distance from me,"* and ducked through the portal to Vision, and the tiny village of Lavoa.

Color blared bright and bitter here, reflecting a pearly sheen off the light snow dusting the dirt streets. The sun had risen to its full height in Anthem, but here it had just stumbled out of bed, and the Lavoa didn't have hundreds of buildings to dull the sharp wind.

He let down his Sound shield to save his Received magic. If he used too much of one type, the other reservoir of magic decreased as well, though not as quickly. As soon as he did, the Hunger's repeated mantra thundered in his ears. "I HAVE COME TO CONSUME YOU ALL! RUN AND FEAR, LITTLE MAGICS—"

Alesio shivered. At least the voice didn't have the same increased effect as it did on the Sound world.

Here, though, the stark image of the Hunger abused the eye. It contrasted with the lavender heavens not in the manner of color clashing against color, but color collapsed in on itself, a shade that shouldn't have existed, a hue that felt like the corpse of gray. Masses of darker gray floated inside the rotating grayish void like algae in a pond. Its rotation pulled at everything around it, slurping the skies into its whirlpool throat. He blinked and rubbed his eyes, the afterimage of it burned on the inside of his eyelids.

The foxans had built Lavoa's Portal Station in the middle of the village square, as requested by the villagers themselves. Posted signs warned of gravity shifts in certain directions, and to stay on the assigned path.

Alesio counted at least twenty people dashing willy-nilly outside the designated safety areas. Locals huddled inside their houses, avoiding that horrific nightmare in the sky. Such a difference in reaction from the two different worlds; yet it made sense. The overwhelming sound had penetrated even through sound cloths and had driven people out of their homes in Sound, searching for any escape from the never-ending chant, but the people on Vision could hide inside their homes from the revolving maw that marred their sky. The worlds of Taste, Touch, and Scent probably had even less trouble, considering that the Hunger had not used those senses to terrorize people. At least, not that Alesio could tell.

On the other side of Lavoa, Falrie and Tener wrangled a group trying to push out into the Vision-wilds.

On his side of the village, a gradual gravity shift had appropriated four people. It sloped back down on a gentle grade, but farther out, past where the village ended, a switchback gravity shift had seized a group of at least seven, who now milled in abject terror along its route, the fear-inducing image of the Hunger bearing down on them.

Alesio knew that gravity shift. It ended with the gravity yanking upward and falling a fair distance into the sky. The shimmer showing the shift gleamed and rippled in the air, but they probably didn't know what that shine signified. They had already stumbled into the first gravity shift.

"Stop!" he shouted up at them, pushing the air of his words with a bit of Sound magic so they could hear him from farther off. "You're going to fall!"

A few of them paused. Distance shrouded their features from him, though a few of them looked short. Children, or teens, maybe. He dashed towards them, using a simple gravity shift in front of him that ended after a few steps to climb higher in the sky. "Go back!" he shouted again, trying to speak to all of them. "It's not safe here!"

Two of the figures didn't listen, the shortest ones. They followed the switchback, and the gravity shift yanked them upwards like puppets on strings, their shouts thin but echoing in the cold winter air. They fell several feet into the hill above them.

The other five figures stopped. Alesio gritted his teeth and Shaped a burst of air with Touch magic so that he could step on it for just a moment, which allowed him to reach a different gravity shift with a steep grade upwards. He slid on his rear into the sky, then stopped himself at the end, windmilling his arms so that he didn't touch the gravity shift on his right, which would have sent him spiraling sideways.

Instead, he grabbed above him and to the left, at the shimmer there, which yanked his arm up. With a grunt, he hauled himself up onto the ledge, which extended at a straight line parallel to the ground, and leading closer to the kids that had fallen.

"Hold on, hold on!" He shouted at them. "Stay there! Don't move!"

Sobbing sounds drifted on the wind. One of the children stood back up, but the other remained crumpled on the "ground" of the upside-down hill. If they moved out of that shift they could fall to the real ground. He picked his way along the thin, parallel shift as fast as he dared. The real ground waited at least fifty feet below. A light drift of snow had padded the shift, slicking it.

The five others that had stopped, seeing the two kids fall, shouted up to him. The wind snatched their words and buffeted him as if at war with the gravity, trying to shove him sideways.

The first kid, a little boy of about ten, reached out to him. "What's happening, Mister? Why is everything upside down?"

"It's okay, it's okay! Just don't—"

The wind howled, pushing him from behind, now, and he swore and fell to his knees, gripping the slender gravity shift like a balance beam. The snow numbed the tips of his fingers and stung his palms.

The boy stumbled backwards from the onslaught and toppled outside of the small gravity shift. The air yanked him sideways, slamming him into the side of a different shift a few feet away, one without much dirt to show its surface. He hit his head on the side of the shift and went limp.

Alesio growled, descending in his magic room. He didn't have time to create anything fancy or permanent. He Shaped a sail of air, puffing outward, with handles for him to grip. He grabbed on but had to remain in his Touch magic room to keep re-fashioning the handles, which disintegrated every moment he touched them. Those few seconds seemed to last almost an hour. The wind pushed him along the gravity shift like an arrow shot from a bow. He let the air magic fall just in time to stumble onto the gravity shift, so that he fell up a foot or two, and landed on his face next to the second kid, a little girl, younger, maybe seven or eight years old.

Her mouth dropped open. Her leg twisted the wrong way, and tears stained her face.

"I know it hurts," Alesio said. "I'm gonna check on your friend."

"He's my brother."

"Got it. Don't let the wind move you, okay? Hold onto the grass. Dig your fingers in the dirt."

"O-okay."

Alesio crept to the edge of the gravity shift, bracing and

positioning himself so he would land next to the unconscious boy. The shift yanked him sideways, and he let it. He landed on his side with a grunt.

He climbed to his feet. Next to him, the little girl laying on the snowy ground resembled a bellbug climbing a white wall.

He checked the boy's pulse. Shallow but still breathing. He released his held breath in a whoosh of relief.

Now, to get them back down.

He couldn't carry two kids back along the thin gravity shift. He could try to Shape some sort of platform to reach the switchback gravity shift below them, but he didn't want to chance his Touch magic disintegrating under their feet.

Alesio checked below them. The two foxans had emigrated back to the Portal Station at the center of Lavoa, far below them and a little way off. From his perspective, it seemed like he could just walk down to the ground, as his gravity oriented sideways in the sky. But the shift ended in front of them, a tell-tale glimmer showing that an open box of gravity held him and the little girl. He dug some snow from the thin layer that had accumulated here and threw it in front of him. The glimmer caught it and pulled it in an arch further into the sky, towards the Hunger.

Not going that way.

He pursed his lips and used his Sound magic to push his message down to Falrie and Tener. Thankfully, Sound magic didn't have to follow the rules of Vision magic, of gravity, and it glided straight down to the ground where he aimed it. He spoke in thin, forceful bursts, not creating Sound knives, but more like Sound ships that flew. "Help. Portal. Two kids."

The words sailed to them and their faces turned upwards, reddish brown against the white of the swirling snow. One of them headed upwards, using the same track that Alesio had, climbing the little platform, then leaping as a foxan towards the steep graded shift and sliding upwards.

It was Tener, which worried Alesio somewhat, him being just a kid himself. The young foxan trundled along the horizontal path towards them, hunkering down when the wind shoved at his slight form. While waiting, Alesio gathered the boy in his arms, inhaled a deep breath, and jumped back to where the little girl lay sprawled. His gravity reoriented so that once more, the real ground became his sky. The little boy groaned in his arms but remained still.

Someone shouted from below. Alesio twitched at the sound. More people, ten or more adults, had stumbled into the switchback gravity shift, leaving footprints in the loose snow. It was one of the more dangerous shifts around Lavoa, broad and near the edge of the village. The locals had posted signs everywhere to help visitors avoid it, but signs didn't work when people didn't stop to read.

Alesio shouted down at them, but they ran in fear, not understanding why their world had tilted into the sky, closer to that thing they wanted to escape! They shouldered past the first group, who shouted at them and tried to stop them. They ran straight into the gravity shift and dropped upwards.

Tener, a few feet away on the horizontal gravity shift, threw his slender arms wide. A portal appeared above them and underneath the falling group, but small.

Three of the people fell outside of the portal. Two missed the shift on their left, the opposite side of the little box the unconscious boy had fallen into. The gravity on that side had no shifts to them, and they kept falling up. The third adult, a man, slammed into Alesio and knocked the little boy out of his arms.

The boy's body slid away from him, teetering near the edge, while the man kept rolling and slid off, screaming. The gravity tugged the man up into the sky, following the other two adults.

"Can't—hold it—much longer!" Tener shouted.

Alesio tried to reach the boy as he shouted at the little girl behind him. "Jump up! Up into that circle!"

She cried out as she stepped onto her broken leg, stumbling. She couldn't jump. Cursing, Alesio pivoted to her, grabbed her little body, and hurled her into the portal just before it closed, thanking the Sound that foxan portals worked on both sides.

The unconscious kid slipped sideways in the snow.

"No!" Alesio screamed.

The kid fell into the same gravity shift as the adults. It yanked him up, and up, and up. He didn't stop falling, but another kind of gravity pulled him towards the revolving lavender air, into that horrific gray hole.

4
THE COUNCIL MEETING

Verrity swam to her appointed Council seat, a stump that
floated in the raw magic of the Primal Plane like fruit seeds
in jam. One of the Touchians had Shaped them with Touch
magic to help fashion the semblance of a meeting area in the vast
emptiness here. She paddled her arms and kicked her legs to propel
herself through the thick air, which she could somehow still breathe.
It slid into her lungs like water but filled them in an oddly more
satisfying way than normal air. She still sometimes coughed as a
reaction to the sensation.

Before the Reconnection, the Primal Plane used to absorb a person
if they loitered too long in one place, like a living swamp. The
Reconnection had directed all the pent-up magic back into the
Sensory Plane, but that hadn't fixed everything. Saida and the other
foxans had toiled over the past year to smooth out the rest of the
stuck magic bits. Now, the Primal Plane had no distinctions between
ground and air. All of it shone with a wheat yellow light, like a soft
sunrise before the sun crests the horizon.

Transplants from the five Sensory worlds provided a bit of
variation or perspective in this vague yellow space, seemingly
floating: a stretch of grass a few yards long that indicated a slight

gravity shift, a salt rubbing from Taste, a seashell that sang whenever someone passed it, and others, perhaps twenty or so overall. Past these odd decorations hanging in the soft yellow area close to the Portal Station, the Primal Plane seemed to stretch into forever.

The Primal Plane's magic, itself, overwhelmed in a more general way than Sensory magic. The magic didn't shout too loud, shine too bright, or create an intense flavor or smell, but she did develop headaches like whenever she stepped onto Sound and didn't stuff a sound cloth in her ears. Primal magic affected peoples' minds rather than through their senses. She pressed her hands to her temples.

The past twelve hours hadn't exactly been strewn with nonflowers. Shouts had woken her and much of the village up in the infant hours of the night. Time ran several hours ahead in the two larger cities of the Cloves and Anthem, and the sun had already illuminated the horror there. Thank the Senses a straight Sound-Scent portal didn't exist yet, but many Soundians and a few Tastians had panicked and shoved their way through to Tremain from Taste-Scent, searching for somewhere safe from the horrifying hole of obscurity that had appeared in every world's sky. Most of the crowds consisted of Soundians, more panicked because of the relentless voice that had chanted for several hours straight, magnified on the world of Sound. The relentless booming chants had finally stopped in the late afternoon.

Verrity had run ragged trying to protect the crop fields near the portal, which Tremain had just planted with potatoes and baza beans, but it hadn't done much good. Yashalis had called the Council meeting after the people of Anthem and the Cloves had fatigued themselves.

Verrity passed Saida, who half-dozed on the log seat to the side of the Council and gave a little wave. The foxan's eyes opened for a moment and brightened as she waved back, her gestures slower in the resistance of the magic all around them. Huge bags draped under her eyes and that of Alesio's, the Voice of Reconnection. Hadn't they been on an expedition the past few days? And then they had also helped with the fallout of that . . . thing.

Verrity didn't want to look up. She didn't want to consider what it meant. She and the people of Tremain couldn't find the time or energy to process their own terror, not when the tidal forces of the large cities had washed over them, bringing their unmanaged body odor and mud and blood on their shoes.

She reached her seat and settled—though she could have "sat" without the help of the stump because of the magic's density—and glanced around. Two of the other seven Council members had already shown up to the emergency meeting. Xen, the delegate for Touch, sat two stumps away. An older man, he kept his shoulder-length graying hair in a high ponytail, and the form-fitting silver suit of the Touch people contrasted his normal upper frame with the large leg muscles awarded to those who waded through water their entire lives.

Falrie, the foxan representative and Saida's mother, coiled on the stump to Verrity's left, her smaller foxan legs tucked under her. She snored softly.

The Portal Station shimmered, and Yashalis, the Council leader and delegate for Vision, shuffled through. She slid her feet forward instead of picking them up, a method Verrity now knew the old woman used because of the strange gravity on Vision and tapped her cane in front of her. The gravity shifted on her world, so she had a continual habit of testing the way ahead to ensure it would not change.

A few minutes later one of the foxans dashed through the portal, the young one named Tener, in their human form. They had darker brown skin rather than the reddish brown of the other foxans, and black freckles spotted their cheeks and the area around their eyes. They had glossy, wavy black hair that curled around their ears. Verrity didn't quite understand how foxan age worked, because Saida's parents had reached their late 800s or early 900s even though they had the outward appearance and energy of people in their sixties.

Meanwhile, Tener had emerged from the Primal Plane just last year, but they bounced and chattered like a seven-year-old. The foxan vaulted through the Primal magic's thick viscosity with the confidence of someone who hadn't gained a healthy fear of the ground.

Something interested her about the young foxan. Verrity's Scent magic worked in the Primal Plane, as did all the other Sense magics, so she could sense that Tener didn't emanate either a feminine or a masculine hormone, but a third that hovered somewhere in between. They dressed in a loose-fitting shirt and dark pants and perched next to Saida on the bench, still bouncing, and shifted just their ears, which formed on top of their head in tall, pointed foxan form, poking through their wavy hair. Their ears, too, stuck out wider and larger than Saida's or her parents, even more when compared to their small face. Verrity didn't know if all young foxans had huge ears, or if Tener had just ended up different from the other three.

Did Saida or the other foxans know Tener's gender? They had more masculine features, but Verrity knew more than anyone how appearances could lie.

Regardless, she shouldn't say anything. Tener might not even have figured it out, yet. They were very young.

Next to the overactive young one, Saida had laid her head on Alesio's shoulder and closed her eyes. Alesio had laid his head on hers and every so often fluttered his eyes open, peering at the circle of delegates. Tener swung their feet back and forth on the log next to them. They'd never attended a Council meeting before.

Is it alright for them to be here? We're dealing with serious issues, not anything a child should listen to.

She stopped herself from worrying further. Before she'd met Saida, Verrity had never met a foxan or even a fox-person. It had taken her an embarrassing amount of time to reconcile her image of a mindless, snarling beast-thief and the fox-people and foxans she'd actually met. Even more shame had waylaid her when she'd realized she had more in common with some of them than other humans. Saida, after all, had charged into her world and said those life-changing words, as if she'd known Verrity her whole life: *We can't always help how we feel. You must've pulled yourself through something terrible.*

Verrity reached for her own scent, her little ritual: female, as it had remained from four years old, different from what people expected from her face and body. Of course, back on Scent, everyone had known her gender, since they could all scent her, too. Even they had done double takes every now and again. The experience had so demoralized her that up until last year, she had doubted her ability to scent herself.

Now, she gazed at the other delegates and marveled at how far she had emotionally traveled from hovering in the back in Tremain's big barn, both wishing someone would notice her and terrified they would.

After Watthe had Consumed Mother Rean and a few others in Tremain last year, Verrity had stepped up to manage the fields. Then, she'd just kept doing it, and no one had minded, so long as she oversaw the rotation, planting, and maintenance of the crops. They had begun calling her Mother Verrity several months ago. Then, around the same time, the foxans had begun installing the Portal Stations in each world, and she'd worked with Saida because most of the 278 people of Tremain didn't want to travel and didn't want citizens from other worlds to travel to them. They didn't like outsiders. They'd only agreed to having a Portal Station because they *did* like the food from the Cloves and traded goods for it.

She never would have imagined she'd have become someone so important as a Council delegate, representing not just her home village of Tremain, but the other tiny community named Suln that an expedition on Scent had discovered about a week's walk east of Tremain. It had less than fifty people, all disinterested in exploring the other worlds—they hadn't even known that Tremain existed—and regarded outsiders with much suspicion. After she had visited with Paras a few months ago and brought good tasting things from the Cloves, they had agreed to establish a trade every few months "for more of those olos." However, it had still shocked her when all the Scentians had voted for her to represent them on the Council.

When things became more manageable here, she hoped one of the foxans could portal to Suln to check on it. The foxans hadn't had time yet to create Portal Stations for other cities beyond one for each world. The otherworlder stampede had not impacted Flock,

Suln, or Liranel, but that isolation also cost those towns any mass aid.

The minutes ticked past as they waited for the last two delegates representing Taste and Sound. Of course *those* two were late.

"—in an uproar!" The two men bustled through the portal one after the other. Balt, the Tastian delegate, swept his arms around, the gesture more dramatic in the slowness of the thick Primal magic. "What am *I* supposed to do? Throw a cruffin at it? They're all demanding I stop it from coming any closer—"

"Balt," Yashalis said from the seat facing them all. "Stop yammering like a bird that lost its feathers. Sit, both of you."

Hestafon lifted his chin as he propelled to his seat. He wore dark purple pants and a torn white jacket, his iconic matching purple bows drooping on his lapels. A dusting of blonde stubble had started on his large chin.

Verrity raised her eyebrows. The piper had never attended a Council meeting in such a disheveled state, but then again, she hadn't had time to change out of the random outfit she'd thrown on when the chaos had begun; an older pale olive skirt that had always reminded her of the contents of a stomach, and a brown blouse that strained around her shoulders and armpits. Why did she even still *have* that blouse?

"I'll have you know," Hestafon said to Yashalis, "I was quite busy calming down the crowds outside the Portal Station. Not something you would know anything about in Vision." He reached his stump, three away from Verrity. He rummaged in his pocket and produced a small cloth tied with a ribbon, which he untied to reveal a caramel drop. He popped the sweet in his mouth.

Verrity gritted her teeth. She glanced to the side, towards Alesio. The stocky, muscled singer had clenched his jaw and balled his hands at his sides. The people of Sound had nominated him for the Council first, but he had declined. Verrity wished he hadn't. She'd preferred him over Hestafon.

She could understand why he'd declined, though. From the way his pheromones had deepened to that musk, he had fallen nose over toes for the foxan who slouched against him. They made quite the striking pair; the lithe, red-brown woman with the v-shaped face, foxan ears, and slitted eyes, folded next to the bulky, dark-brown man with large, muscled arms. Alesio brushed the foxan's lips with his fingertips, and her pink tongue darted out and licked his fingers.

Verrity looked away, a flush rising in her cheeks. In Tremain, couples did not even hold hands in public, to avoid raising their pheromones in front of others. Otherworlders had no such qualms.

Yashalis raised her hand. "This meeting is in session. I will call on each of you for a status report, and if there are any injuries." She paused, staring at Falrie, who still lay curled on her stump. Tener left their log and tapped her on the shoulder.

"Yes. Of course, I'd love some eggsssss—" Falrie peered up at Tener, her slitted foxan eyes dilating. "What is it, dear?"

"The humans want to talk now," Tener whisper shouted.

Falrie straightened and shifted to her more human side. She had long brown hair streaked with gray flowing down her back, and wrinkles showed at the corners of her eyes and mouth. Her back legs remained foxan instead of human, making her shorter than everyone else. Foxans had trouble shifting everything over to human. In this form, Falrie's age seemed more apparent: over eight and a half centuries. Much older than Yashalis, the oldest-looking member of the Council.

Yashalis tapped her cane on her own stump. "Sound first."

Hestafon rose, probing at his teeth with his tongue. "The hysteria has decreased. Word has spread that, um, that *thing* is everywhere, on all the worlds." He coughed and swayed a bit on his feet. "Darrow is at Anthem's Portal Station. The foxans escorted Soundians and stopping them from stampeding through the Portal Station. The crowds outside the station just calmed down enough for me to leave. So far, it seems we have fifty-four people with minor cuts and bruises, thirteen with broken limbs or other major wounds, and four people dead, who, um, fell into the sky on Vision. We have a missing count of six, but I expect that will rise."

By the Senses. Verrity couldn't imagine handling a city with around twenty-five hundred people in it. She did some quick math in her head. The Hunger had injured or killed seventy-seven people altogether on Anthem. Over a fourth of Tremain's entire population.

Yashalis bowed her head. "That is most unfortunate. And we don't know anything about how Flock is doing?"

Hestafon shook his head.

Yashalis's shoulders rose and fell as she inhaled a large breath. "Scent?"

Verrity jolted up from the stump. Their stares crawled on her body like lice. Not for the first time, she wished she could use Sound magic to pitch her voice higher. Or just that she wore the dress she preferred to at these meetings, the one that propped up her small breasts better, and fell in flattering, loose layers around her. She straightened to her full height, regardless. "Our village is managing as best it can. The children are scared, of course, but the adults are keeping them inside for now. Our crops are all damaged, and the stampede injured two village men, incurring a broken arm and a bruised rib. Much of the damage stemmed from people milling around because our departure portals lead back to Anthem or the Cloves, both of which they'd already either arrived from or gone through, of course."

"Thank you, Verrity," Yashalis said. "Touch?"

FALRIE YAWNED as the delegate from Touch—she didn't remember his name—stood and spoke. He had white hair and muscular legs for a human.

"The sun rose for our pod cluster just four hours ago." Touchians lived in small clusters of constructed shelters called pods, scattered over several miles. "We also endured stampedes in the night but suffered no damage as we kept everyone inside the shelters, and our crops remain in the caverns. The stampede overwhelmed our Portal Station, and many left the marked path. No injuries or damage to report on our side, though we did find a Tastian who drowned in a depth. They fell in the dark, and . . . there's a reason we tell visitors they must learn how to swim." He paused. "Also, resentful rumors are spreading about humans from other worlds."

Yashalis pressed her mouth into a thin line. "I know of what you speak but explain this to the Council."

The Touch delegate's eyes flicked to Falrie, and back again. "Some say that humans in the other worlds and their lack of foxan worship have led us to judgment. Some are sure we are all doomed and have requested guiding ceremonies from the foxans, so they might pass without barriers to the next life."

The Tastian delegate, Balt—Falrie remembered that one's name, because it rhymed with salt, and she liked salt—let out a guffaw. "Ridiculous. Absolutely ridiculous." He glanced at Falrie, opened his mouth as if to say something further, then closed it.

Falrie shifted her ears to foxan, laying them flat. She agreed with the heavyset human. What drivel these humans thought up! Guiding souls to the afterlife? She couldn't even guide them out of their own panicked, *living* crowds.

The other delegates shifted in their seats. The humans of Taste, Scent, and Sound did not worship foxans; on the contrary, their long-held beliefs stipulated that foxans stole magic and possessions. Such prejudices ran deep and had only recently been challenged when Saida, along with Alesio, had saved the worlds from Watthe last year. Humans on these worlds had just started warming to the idea that foxans didn't steal humans' voices, their pies, or various magics. The idea that humans should *worship* foxans was quite the leap for them.

Falrie didn't fear those kinds of humans as much as the cultists on Touch, those extremists who deified foxans and who had kidnapped her daughter, Saida, years ago. On the worlds of Touch and Vision, people revered foxans as a kind of conduit to the gods, or perhaps as little gods themselves, and some of them possessed aggression as well as fervor. The human man who had held Saida captive had died, but others in his cluster of pods on Touch had known about her imprisonment and done nothing to help her. They had believed her as a kind of good luck charm for their community. That more such fanatics existed, even if they acted respectful, lifted Falrie's hair on the back of her neck.

Maybe I'm a little cranky from being up all night.

Saida still slept, her head lolling in that human's lap. It was just as well. She needed her rest.

The old crone leader of the human delegates stood to signify she would speak for Vision. "Our people sustained one minor injury. Most of Lavoa stayed inside their homes. We do not run on our world; we train that behavior away at a young age. When the crowds stampeded through our Portal Station, they saw the thing hung in our sky as well and continued straight through to Tremain on Scent.

"However, too many Soundians funneled through at one point, much as they must have on Touch, and the gravity shifts caught a few. One village man caught someone falling upwards on a gravity shift past his balcony and managed to pull them to safety. Others were not so lucky. As mentioned, one child and three adults fell into the sky and were lost. Six others sustained injuries such as broken ankles and wrists, which we have managed to send back to Anthem. Gravity shifts are not to be trifled with."

The Council leader pressed her fingers against her temples. "Beyond that, our people requested multiple times for me to ask the foxans for guiding ceremonies in case of their demise. Many fear that if we step on the wrong gravity shift leading into the sky, we could also end up falling towards . . ." she paused and tilted her head up. The others followed her gaze.

In the Primal Plane, the five planets showed overhead in a star pattern: Vision, large and hazy lavender, Taste, mid-sized, a mixture of bronze and dark blue cobalt, Touch, the smallest world and all azure, and Sound and Scent, both interspersed with emerald and sapphire, Scent a tad smaller. That thing, that *absence* in the sky, loomed above all of them like a sixth planet comprised of nothing except for a strange gray void and those islands dotting it throughout. "Falrie, what do you say to this request? Is this something that you and the other foxans are amenable to?"

It's a bunch of ratwash. But Saida wanted to help the humans, and she couldn't deny her daughter's wishes when Saida had worked so hard alone for three hundred years. Falrie stiffened her spine. "I will consider it. I do not speak for the others."

"I'll help, too," Tener said, his voice uncharacteristically monotone.

Falrie set her teeth. She'd have to speak to him later. He was much too young for such a thing. Senses, he was much too young to have witnessed the violence of the past day.

Yashalis nodded to both the foxans and sat back down. A heavy silence reigned until the Council leader said, "Taste?"

Balt heaved himself to his feet. He had a bit of extra weight on him, a sign of authority and prestige in the Cloves. "Finally. Well, everyone, it's what you'd expect. The Cloves are in chaos. We do not have pod shelters or caverns to hide away in. The sunlight reflects off the salt-flats, which makes that *thing* stand out even more. It appeared in broad daylight for us—not in the night when everyone slept. My bakery had one of its windows broken by a looter. We don't have as many citizens as Anthem, but we have enough that the panic spread. The Soundians created more chaos, upending carts of food, and causing general mayhem. As head chef of the Cloves and their leader, I demand recompense from Anthem to repair the damage."

The snooty delegate from Sound crossed his arms. Someone must have torn one of the bows on his lapel and he frowned at it. "If the Cloves promise the same for the damage done from their citizens."

Falrie raised her eyebrows. *Huh. I thought those two were friends.*

"This is the not the time for such demands, Balt," The Council leader said. What was her name? Damn her faulty memory. Was it too much to ask that her mind retain *new* information? Was she to be cursed with memories that flowed in and out of her like a hole in a damn? "We are still in a crisis. Our priority is to stop the panic and help the already injured. What is the tally so far for your wounded and dead?"

"I don't know how I should know that yet," Balt said.

The Council leader—her name started with a "Y", right? — narrowed her eyes.

". . . *But* I would hazard a guess it is around . . . nine or ten . . .

broken arms. And legs. I don't know if anyone's died. Well, I guess now I know someone drowned on Touch."

Falrie may not have cared much for humans, but such callous indifference to the leader's own people set her on edge. She bared foxan teeth, shifting her foxan clothes and human skin back into her speckled gray fur with apricot stripes across her back and face.

Tener popped up with enough force that he floated in the Primal magic. His foxan ears, huge on top of his smaller head, swiveled towards the Tastian. "Do you know *anything?*"

"How rude!" Balt sputtered. "You should speak better to your elders!"

Tener did need to learn restraint in some ways. He didn't understand the need or the know-how to fade into the background on the streets of Anthem—indeed, he often drew attention to himself on purpose! But in a Council meeting with six humans total, he shouldn't have to fear speaking.

Tener balanced on the log on human legs, hands on his hips. Falrie recognized the posture as hers. "I saw people fall into the sky, and lots more got hurt on other worlds, or hurt other people."

Falrie swallowed a sudden lump in her throat. Tener had reacted first to Alesio's request for aid, bounding up the gravity shift before she had thought to stop him. And then, those other humans had mucked everything up, forcing Tener to use his portal before they'd managed to retrieve the other, unconscious child.

She hadn't birthed Tener like she had Saida. But he was her son in her heart, and she'd already failed Saida in so many ways. She wanted to do better by Tener. She wanted to protect him from the harshness of the worlds.

And she'd already allowed him to witness four people fall to their deaths.

"Why is that my fault?" Balt crossed his arms.

"It's not your fault, Balt," Y said. "But it is your responsibility. It's sad that a child can see that, yet you can't."

Balt muttered something to himself.

Y steepled her wrinkled fingers. "I move that, after things settle down, we build emergency barriers, first and foremost on Anthem, that can close access temporarily to its departure portals. Xen, can you spare any of your Touch magic users to help with this?"

Xen—the Touch delegate with the muscled legs the size of a young swanseize—bowed his head. "I will ask."

Y swiveled to the snooty delegate for Sound. "Hestafon, can you spare anyone to check on Flock?"

Thank the Senses she's reminding me of all these names.

Hestafon hesitated. "We may not be able to send anyone for at least a few days. Everyone is very . . . on edge in Anthem, and Flock is known for being less than welcoming."

Y tapped her chin with a bony finger. Falrie wished someone would say the Council leader's name. "They will still need assistance though, yes? Maybe a foxan could help check on them. Falrie? Would you or one of the other foxans be willing to help?"

Falrie clenched her jaw, shifting back into human, again except for her back legs, and stood. Her brindled fur receded except for where she changed it into the shape of clothing, a long-sleeved shirt and close-fitting trousers with the same speckled gray. She had to shift to human, to alter her thoughts just a little. The very idea of visiting a city full of spiteful humans—already upset that they didn't have a Portal Station, let alone one marinating in fear from the Hunger—made her want to sprint out of there.

Tener's mouth opened. She spoke before he could. "Darrow could check on the city."

Guilt weighed on her. Volunteering her partner for danger? But as hazardous as Flock was, something even worse needed doing and she couldn't have any of them tag along with her. Not her husband. Not her new son, naïve and so trusting. Not her poor daughter, who'd already suffered enough horror to last her a lifetime.

She paused. "I move that we speak now on the topic of the entity."

She spoke with a strong, clear voice, keeping her fear of humans in the back of her throat. Skulking to avoid attention worked well—until the attention spotted you. Showing fear while on display attracted human fear and hatred, because it confirmed what they already thought about foxans and fox-people. She didn't remember much from before she'd hidden in Between for centuries. But she remembered that.

Y sighed. "Yes, it is time. I know you checked on the box sometime during the night. Are there any clues that they are linked to the entity? Did it try to hurt or affect you in any way?"

The box wedged in another area of the Primal Plane had chanted the same mantra for the past year, ever since Saida and Alesio had reconnected the Sensory and Primal Planes. The words had seared themselves into Falrie's brain. *I've teleported from far away, much farther than you simple beings could comprehend! The box I sent is just a single brick from the world of my body! I will arrive soon!*

Falrie had gone to check on the box before the others had even thought about it. She hadn't wanted to, of course. That box represented everything she'd feared for over 800 years. The violence of humans. The sudden and terrible detachment from the Primal Plane. The drying up of the magic that rejuvenated everyone and everything.

But even more than her fear, she hadn't wanted Tener or Saida near the box, or Darrow for that matter. Her husband had had trouble acclimating in a different way than her. He had more . . . physical trouble, since he couldn't usually shift his face to human. He had always stayed more often as a foxan in Between than she had, so that made sense to her.

Somehow, though, he seemed less afraid overall of humans and the worlds, which made *no* sense to her. It would terrify her if she couldn't shift her face in a crowd full of humans. He seemed able to shift better emotionally, as if all his ability to change had channeled into his heart and mind.

She couldn't do that. Her world, for 800 and some years, had consisted of her relationships with Darrow, Pell, and Saida. Her identity had chipped away, her memories had sanded down to a terrible smoothness, with just the unchanging sky and the small forest where she snagged the birds and the little lake where she caught the fish and the desert where she sunned herself, and time had passed her like the clouds of Between: unhurried, unvarying, drifting without cease.

When she'd left Between—a year ago, now—it had shocked her, jarred her out of that numbness somewhat, but she still felt slow. Dazed. Unattached to the worlds she walked through. Even sleeping in the Primal Plane hadn't helped. All the while, Darrow had seemed to pull ahead of her, walking faster, his foxan face flexible, able to laugh and joke with Tener and Saida, while hers remained so often like a mask. Sometimes, it felt he changed faster than she could follow. In changing himself, he'd changed their relationship, which had in turn changed her. He hadn't asked her permission to do that. Who was she when *they* changed? She felt hollowed out underneath, and all she had left was this hard exterior she could not let drop, or she'd collapse like one of those Consumed in a horrible melting sludge.

The Council waited for her to respond, their faces polite, yet growing impatient. She wet her human lips.

She breathed in the thick air. It felt like her mind gained muscle, somehow, when she did that.

Straight back. Project strength. "The box has not said anything new. However, it has changed. The box is not . . . it is a tiny version of the Hunger in the sky. It pulled at me when I got too close."

Everyone on the Council began to speak at once.

"So, it's true!"

"What are we going to do? What can we do against it?"

"Didn't it say it wants to consume us all? Will it *eat* our worlds?"

"Yeah, Balt, it just needs some spices, and it'll pop us in like dumplings—"

Y banged her cane on the side of her stump several times. "Stop it, all of you! By the Senses, it's like you've never been threatened by a cannibalistic sky before."

Silence had a turn to speak at her comment, then they all chuckled. Falrie grinned. Yasha—Yashalis! That was her name! Maybe her memory wasn't completely shot.

"Now," Yashalis said, "I'd say that is good enough evidence that yes, this thing," she pointed up with her cane, "Is what the box called 'the Hunger.' Falrie, remind us. What did the box do when it first arrived?"

"It caused the Severing." Falrie twitched her human nose, paused, then rubbed at it with the back of her hand. She didn't ever want to think about the Severing. That time had left her with nothing but pure terror that overrode her practiced facade. "The box appeared on the Primal Plane and stopped the flow of magic from the Primal to the Sensory." She had told the story many times in the past year, and her words had a rote tone. "It also caused great fear in myself and my husband, as it preferred foxan magic, our Primal magic, and we hid in Between. We now know that it tried to choke out all the Sensory magic and ferment the Primal Plane's raw magic, to twist into a giant overgrowth that it wanted to consume."

"But it failed," Xen said. "The foxan Saida reconnected the Planes by transplanting Sensory magic back into the Primal Plane. Why would it still want our magic when it's no longer fermenting?"

Could the Hunger separate our Planes again? Now that all of it is here, not just a 'single brick'...

Fear. The pure kind that made her want to cower and cringe into the nearest shadow. Falrie forced herself to keep her back straight, though her ears did flatten on top of her head. She'd shifted them back to foxan at some point.

When Falrie didn't respond, everyone's gaze swung to Saida, who had stirred awake in the last exchange with all the shouting.

"What? Did someone ask a question?" Saida yawned.

Tener repeated the question in one of his loud whispers. Saida straightened and tottered upright, keeping hold of Alesio's hand.

"The Hunger could try another Severing," Saida said in a slow, sleepy voice. Beside her, Alesio jerked back awake. "That seems far within their ability."

Murmurs from everyone started again. Saida bulled ahead, ignoring them. *Good girl. Project strength.* Even though her words terrified Falrie. "Or they might just consume us before then, out of spite, or just that they are hungry and don't care if we aren't fermented, twisted magic like they prefer. We don't know. We need to stop them before either of those things happen."

"How do you propose accomplishing something so outlandish?" Hestafon pressed his hands to his temples. "Can you teleport to it?"

Falrie snorted. *Humans.* They had no understanding of how teleportation worked. Foxans had no natural link to that thing in the sky like they did with the Sensory and Primal Planes.

"No." Saida picked at the end of her braid, which she'd wrapped around her waist, and used it to cover another yawn. "But the Epitaphs might give us an answer. They're ancient beings from before the Severing, even. They might tell us how to stop the Hunger."

Because I for sure can't remember anything. And neither can Darrow.

Balt sniffed. "You mean the dead foxans you've been trying to find? Yeah, seems like they have would have a lot say."

Saida shifted, showing her fangs to Balt.

"They recently began emanating a strong magical energy," Falrie said. "Thirteen of them across the worlds. They very well might be able to tell us something."

She neglected to mention that her daughter had had trouble over the past few weeks hearing any magics, transplanted or not. Right before the Epitaphs began to emanate all that power, of course. But she had faith that Saida would work through that issue.

Yashalis banged her cane on her stump. "I agree that any avenue we can pursue that might give us answers is a good one. That being said," the Council leader inclined her head to Saida, "We should pursue more than one. Anyone else have ideas?"

Alesio stood alongside Saida, rubbing at his eyes. "Finding Clef would answer some questions. Watthe and the Hunger transformed him, after all. He must know something. A weakness, maybe. A way to injure it or drive it away." He paused. "If I'm allowed to search Flock, I think I could find him." He jutted his chin at Hestafon, locking eyes with him. The singer's chest swelled as he inhaled.

Why is he puffing up like a ruffled swanseize? . . . Oh. Right. At some point over the past year, the Soundian delegate had forbidden Alesio to visit that dangerous city.

Yashalis looked to Hestafon. The Soundian coughed and held his hand to his chest, as if checking his own heartbeat, and glanced around at the others.

"That will be fine," he said. "Just . . . keep a low profile."

Alesio grinned, and somehow the dark circles under the human's eyes fashioned a menacing expression. "I'm from the straits, remember? I was born low."

Hestafon shifted his weight from one foot to the other and avoided Alesio's burning gaze.

A charged moment of silence passed. Everyone watched the two Soundians, the ever-changing colors and patterns of the Primal magic around them.

So, both of our significant others will head into that terrible city.

The Scent delegate stood, breaking the tension. She had the square jaw and broad shoulders of a human male but obviously identified as female. She wore a dress, grew her hair long, and moved her hands with a delicate grace. "What about questioning the box again?"

"Hah!" Balt rolled his eyes. "We've tried that already!"

Falrie focused on the Scentian delegate. Someone who thought like she did! Why chase answers over all the worlds when they had a link to the Hunger right here?

And, as much as it terrified her, she should step up to do it. She needed to protect her family, when she'd failed at it so spectacularly before.

Yashalis glared at Balt. "Go on, Verrity. Explain your reasoning."

Verrity! Finally, Falrie had all the names of those present.

"Well." Verrity swallowed. "Yes, we've tried it, but—well—" she pitched her voice higher and cleared her throat. Falrie cocked her head. Did humans sometimes wish that they could shift in some ways? "We haven't tried after that thing appeared, right? Maybe now that the rest of it is here, it will respond to questions, or maybe even, um, threats."

"Threats!" Xen covered his face with a hand. "What in the name of the Senses could we threaten it with?"

Verrity looked down.

"We stopped its main tool, Watthe, didn't we?" Falrie raised his chin at Xen. "I'm sure it didn't expect that. It doesn't know what we can or can't do."

Yashalis raised her cane and pointed it. "Verrity, you and Falrie interrogate the box. Everyone else, focus on helping the wounded and finding those still missing. We will meet again in a few days to check on the crises on Sound and Taste, and I'll expect updates from these plans."

Falrie clenched her fists. She had asked for this, senses take her.

Strength. Project strength.

She kept her ears from flattening and nodded assent.

THE PARENTS

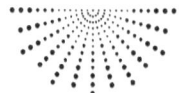

Saida slipped through Alesio's front door, wearing her soft foxan foot pads to stay quiet, and her human hands to twist the knob. She and the other foxans had all agreed to meet today to catch up after all the chaos. Saida shut the front door behind her and joined Tener and her parents on the porch.

Tener had grown *a lot.*

His body had climbed to a level with her shoulder, and his legs and arms swung like pendulums. A few days ago, he'd appeared nine or so, but now, he had the height of a fifteen or sixteen-year-old human, or a hundred fifty to hundred sixty-year-old in foxan years.

Even with the Reconnection fueling his development, such rushed maturity alarmed her. It couldn't be *healthy,* growing up so fast. And what about his mind? Had it kept pace with his body?

"Whoa," she said. "Um, Tener, you feeling alright?"

His head hung down like one of Lavoa's levers that altered the direction of a gravity shift. "I should ask *you* that. Your bo—uh, hmm. Never mind."

She shut her mouth with a click, her gaze flicking behind Tener to Falrie and Darrow. They nodded and shrugged, as if to say, *"Yeah, we know it's weird, but what are we supposed to do about it?"*

Tener also seemed less enthusiastic than his normal self, not bouncing around like a bellbug in a butter churn. Alesio had mentioned something about him and Tener failing to rescue four humans, one of them a child, who had fallen into the sky on Vision. She couldn't help but wonder if that loss had somehow triggered his sudden departure from the world of childhood.

She lifted her hand and patted his shoulder. "What is it? Were you going to say something?"

"That . . . your hair-fur is all messy. Like a swanseize licked you."

Still with the melancholy tone. Maybe she could distract him. Saida shifted her hand to a paw, licked it, then dashed at Tener. "Guess I'll have to make sure you match!"

Tener shrieked and ran around, giggling, his voice cracking back into that of a nine-year-old. *So, he hasn't quite caught up to his body yet.*

At that age, Saida, remembered, everything was new and exciting. She'd felt all grown up one minute and crying at something silly the next.

Still, even compared to human maturity, Tener's change had happened lightning quick.

Saida seized him and rubbed her wet paw backwards, so his chestnut-brown fur stuck up. He squealed and wriggled out of her grasp. She released him and he trotted over to her parents.

"Is Alesio coming?" Darrow quirked a gray eyebrow at her. Both her parents had trouble keeping all of themselves shifted, but Darrow had had more obvious trouble than Falrie, as he often struggled to shift his muzzle to a human nose and mouth, and the four reddish-brown stripes that he had as a foxan remained on his cheeks. Tall and thin with a scruffy gray beard, he wore an offensively lemon-yellow sweater and tan pants over his foxan fur clothing, she suspected to keep out the cold of Anthem's winter. The yellow had the unfortunate effect of highlighting the yellow-green bruise on his jaw.

"He's still sleeping. I left a note."

"Humans." Falrie licked the back of her human hand, blinked, and shifted it to her paw. "How they can sleep more than a few hours at a time is beyond me."

Darrow ruffled the back of her neck. "Didn't someone sleep in today longer than her usual? A whole fifteen minutes?"

Falrie swatted her partner's hand away. She wore her human form as well, except for her paws and legs, the areas she struggled to shift. Thunder-gray streaked her long, straight brown hair, and the bags under her eyes resembled bruises. She wore foxan clothes, a long-sleeved fur shirt and close-fitting fur trousers, both brown with speckled gray.

"We all had to work hard." Saida sighed, surveying the empty street. Two days had passed since the Hunger had twisted everyone's sky, and the panicked crowds on Sound had dispersed late that first night, most of them retreating to their homes and hiding behind shuttered windows. The Hunger had stopped chanting sometime during the first day. Saida and Alesio had stumbled over to a meeting for the Council, slept a few hours, then spent the next day tracking down missing people.

As if to discourage any lingering panic, a snowstorm had blown through last night, sticking to the streets and leaving a few inches piled on roofs. Everyone still watched the skies with trepidation, but the void-shaped planet hadn't loomed any closer or resumed its inexorable mantra.

Tener's black freckles contrasted with his chestnut cheeks a little more than usual, a sign that he, too, had suffered a little fatigue from the past few days. His subdued manner saddened her, and she chucked him under the chin. "Want to visit Auntie Naya on Taste? We could buy some cinnamon olos on the way."

"Olos?" Tener's ears perked up. "It's warmer on Taste, too!"

Darrow shrugged. "I'd like to see Naya. Before I head out to Flock later today."

"You're going to Flock?" Saida asked.

"Per Council instructions. You were sleeping."

Saida chewed on that. The Soundian city didn't have a Portal Station yet, so of course the Council wanted a foxan to teleport to the citizens after the Hunger had appeared. She opened her mouth, then remembered that Tener was there and closed it.

"Don't worry," Darrow said to her. "I'll keep a lookout for Clef."

Saida offered him a weak smile. "Alesio will appreciate it." She paused. "Well, you might see him there. He said he has to check something first, but he'll probably go there."

Tener tilted his head to the side, glancing between her, Falrie, and Darrow. Falrie studied Alesio's house, avoiding Saida's gaze.

Saida understood her mother's mixed emotions. They couldn't leave Flock to fend for themselves. Plus, Darrow might flush out some information on Clef. On the other paw, the city retained a group of humans who called themselves shrikers, after the murderous, carnivorous birds. The line between protecting a few loved ones versus having compassion for the many was a thin one sometimes.

"Mom?" Tener asked, shining his bright eyes on Falrie.

"We'll go to Taste," Falrie said slowly. "We need to check on the Cloves anyway."

Tener bounced up on foxan hind legs, high in the air. "Yes! I love Auntie Naya! She gives the best hugs!" He grabbed Falrie's hands and hopped in shorter bursts, his earlier gloom forgotten.

Falrie played along for a few moments before stopping, protesting that her knees couldn't handle such abuse. "But we should go through at the Portal Station to save our teleports for the day. Just in case."

They left Alesio's house, heading towards the Portal Station. His newfound fame as the Voice of Reconnection had garnered him quite a few fans and a tidy profit whenever he performed. He'd bought the house a few months ago, securing a location smack in the middle of Anthem, close to both the Portal Station and the Drinks De Capo. He had bought it with them both in mind.

After a few minutes, they arrived at the Portal Station, where she and the other foxans had installed four departure portals: three leading to a different world and one to the Primal Plane, and three arrival portals: two that led from other worlds, and one that led from the Primal Plane. Saida and the other foxans had created Portal Stations on each world, so people could flow with ease from one world to another.

Maybe a little too easily, Saida thought. The merged transplants twisted with ribbons of light into giant, round, shimmering mirrors. Each of them emanated echoes of the magic they led toward or away from. Saida and the other foxans had agreed to focus on Anthem the most at first, as it had the largest population center, and so the Portal Station here mixed with three different magics from the arrival portals: the taste of salt, the touch of wind, and the vision of light swirling throughout the station itself.

The permanent portals did not allow people to view the other side, like foxan portals did, but when all the magics blended on the dais, it tended to generate a revitalizing sensation for humans, much like the Primal Plane did for foxans. Those ribbons of light showed for everyone, visible, living magic, and the blend of the transplants created a sensation of well-being, energy, and vitality. Indeed, Hestafon had placed guards at the station in Anthem because people had kept crowding on the dais and creating bottlenecks. But the echoes of the blended magic flowed for several streets beyond the Portal Station, diffusing out into the city. Saida believed that the energy from the Portal Stations would lengthen the humans' lifespans, like in the days before the Severing.

Because of this refreshing effect, people loitered around the station even when not queuing in line, and vendors had set up shops around the dais, hoping to capture the interest of tourists from other worlds. Corner singers crooned the praises of various vendors, some of them with signs boasting of the items within. They passed sellers and their corner singers peddling flutes, chocolates, rice, and violas, and those were just the ones who sang loud enough to pierce the general cacophony of Anthem's hustle and bustle. She'd learned how to transfer the constant commotion to the back of her mind, but here, near the Portal Station, the people packed in like sand, filling up all possible space.

Saida and the rest of them queued at Sound-Taste, and at least twenty or so Soundians waited ahead of them. To the left, Sound-Touch had five people waiting, and to the right, Sound-Vision had no one. Vision still had the smallest amount of people in it, and so few Soundians traveled there. Most people from Anthem preferred to visit the other largest city, the Cloves on Taste. Also, on Vision, the Hunger in the sky clashed so stark and visceral, people flinched every time they glanced up. The gravity shifts had scared even more off from traveling there, at least for now.

"Saida! How high can you jump?" Tener crouched and leapt into the air, the highest he'd gone so far, then landed with a thump on the street. The last ten or so people in line jerked to stare at the group of foxans, murmuring.

The ghost of fear, of needing to hide, washed over Saida, but she swallowed and squared her shoulders, staring back at them, and the citizens looked away first.

Saida grinned and leapt. "This high!"

"Get your papers out," a voice called from the front of the line. "The faster you show your safety certs, the faster you go through."

The people in front of them fumbled in pockets and pulled out slips of papers showing the signatures from a foxan and a Tastian guide confirming they had already ventured on a guided expedition to Taste. The frigid wind picked up, howling like shrikes and pricking any exposed skin. Everyone they clutched their papers so as not to lose them and waited for the gust to pass. Saida shivered and grew her foxan fur all over under her human clothes, as her father already had.

When they reached the front of the line, Tak, Alesio's friend who used to work as a security guard with him at St. Rina's, checked people through, and Muey did the same for people filing through to Sound-Touch. The Touchian's towering form reminded Saida that in the panic, she'd never signed the peoples' safety certificates who'd gone on that expedition to Touch. *Whoops.* She'd have to let the Council know, so they could track the people down and sign their slips.

Though, Tak wore a bandage on his head and his arm in a sling, and that made her wonder. What was the point of safety certificates? The system hadn't helped when the Hunger had appeared. The Soundians had just overrun the departure portals in a panic for several hours.

"Tak," Falrie said as he waved them forward. "Why aren't you resting at home?"

He flashed the group of foxans his bright, mustachioed grin and shifted his arm in his sling. "The same reason you all aren't, I imagine. We return to what's familiar to block out what we don't understand." He grimaced. "Even if it was, uh, overwhelming, it's still guard duty."

"You need more guards at the station," Falrie murmured. "Just in case. I'll talk to the Council."

Tak shrugged and waved them through. "Couldn't hurt, I suppose. Though, I'm of the mind that bringing in some barriers to close off the Portal Station would be a grand idea."

"Some Touchians will help build those barriers, I believe." Falrie lowered her voice. "We just need to tend to the wounded first, now that we've found the missing."

Saida winced. The day before, she and Darrow had located three of the six missing Soundians in the Sound wilds, unharmed except for some scratches, while Falrie, Alesio, and Tener had located the other three in Vision. Two had died from falling a great height off a gravity shift to the ground, and one remained in critical condition. That meant six Soundians had died altogether, counting the four that had fallen into the Hunger the day before that. All of them had died on Vision.

Tak sighed, the handles of his salt and pepper mustache blowing upwards. "We all do what we can when we can, eh?"

Tener tugged on Saida's hand, giving her an encouraging smile, his black hair bringing out the freckles on his cheeks and the luster of his dark-brown eyes. "C'mon! C'mon!"

Had he heard Falrie's comment? The young foxan hadn't shied from the grisly facts at the Council meeting, but she didn't want to expose him to more tragedy if she could help it.

They bounded through the departure portal together, Falrie and Darrow trailing behind. At their age, they couldn't handle running down to the dregs of their strength, and the invigorating magic of the Portal Station didn't work on foxans like it did on humans.

The portal deposited them right outside the Cloves, the several small villages on Taste connected in one place, surrounded by a wall. The warmth of spring suffused through them, relaxing them, and the sun shone down from high in the sky. They had left Anthem's midmorning for midday, here. A light, buttery flavor floated on the air.

"What is that, Saida?" Tener stuck out his tongue, tasting the air, shifting his face into a foxan muzzle and jaw, though he kept his human hair and ears.

Saida shifted her foxan fur back into human skin under her human clothes. "That's baked purpatoes!" She jiggled Tener's hand in hers.

"The purple potatoes from Vision? I can't wait to try them!"

They passed through to the city without incident, the guard letting them through with a curt nod. The various food stalls so prevalent in the Cloves had suffered from the appearance of the Hunger, as well, but a few had popped back up. They navigated to the purpato stand first, following the strongest taste on the wind. Some of the Tastians had crept back out of their houses, and they narrowed their eyes at the group of foxans.

How long will until they accept us? Saida wondered. *How long before we are treated the same on all the worlds?*

Tener had asked why the secret pathways existed on Taste and Sound and had seemed confused by the concept of distrust based on race. She hadn't had the heart to describe the years of abuse from humans, though she told him never to portal alone to any world. The discrimination had decreased, as the portals had forced at least some of the humans to interact with foxans and fox-people, dispelling the rumors that they stole magic. She no longer feared open, sunlit streets, but pockets of hatred still existed in the shadow places on each world. Not to mention that the humans on Touch and Vision still worshipped foxans. No world held true safety for their kind.

"It's so soft! And salty! And buttery!"

She blinked back to the present. Tener had bitten into the purpato they had purchased and closed his eyes in bliss.

Darrow bought more, offering them to Saida and Falrie. Falrie refused. The baked vegetable shone a richer color than the rest of the world around them, displaying its Vision magic, and it tasted a little better on Taste than it would have on Vision. "Look!" Darrow said. "Mine looks a little like a bird! See its eyes, and this bit is the beak?"

"Whoa!" Tener stared at the purple vegetable.

"Let's get going," Falrie said.

Saida had to agree with her mother. She still didn't like staying in one spot for too long, not in public. They left the purpato vendor, searching for cinnamon olos, which they found without issue. The olo vendor had the longest line around with twenty or more people already waiting. Darrow and Tener jumped in line, while Falrie and Saida waited on the side.

As they waited, Falrie's eyes flicked around her at every movement. Then, as if something had grabbed her gaze and pulled, she tilted her head up. Falrie's eyes glazed over, like when she used to lose her memory back in Between. Saida followed her stare.

The Hunger loomed next to the hazy, purple circle of Vision like a giant ashen bruise on the thigh of the heavens, like the sky had banged its leg against a cosmic table. Saida squinted at the Hunger. *Did it have that nub sticking out like a little arm before?*

Saida looked back down, then bumped her hip against Falrie's. "Gonna fall asleep on us?"

Falrie blinked, her gaze de-glazing. "Nothing a few more hours rest won't fix."

Saida studied Tener's gangly form. "I've been meaning to ask you, or Darrow. Um . . ."

"About Tener's growth spurt?"

Saida exhaled. "I know it's the magic of the Reconnection, but that was *fast*."

"You hid your surprise much better than we did. And no, we didn't see it happen. I woke up on the Primal Plane, in our usual clump, and there he was." She sighed. "I might have screamed. Poor Darrow had his claws out and scratched the boy before he realized."

"But is he okay? Is it . . . healthy for him?"

"Dear, I have no idea. Everything moves too fast for me, nowadays." Falrie's voice had a strained quality, like a stretching piece of yarn. "Time is strange for us. It stands still like a stone for centuries, then morphs to liquid, to water, and flows and changes everything in moments."

"It's been hard for you lately," Saida said. "Adjusting."

Darrow and Tener inched forward, still at the back of the line. Tener chattered with someone behind them.

"I know I wasn't always there for you," Falrie said. "I want to stop anything else bad from happening to either of you."

Saida laid her arm around her mother's shoulder. "You don't have anything to make up for. It's enough that you're here with me now."

Falrie hugged her daughter back, then licked the back of her hand and smoothed it over her long, dark graying human hair, fixing a few fly-aways. "So." She drew out the word. "Speaking of things happening to you. When are you moving in with that singer of yours?"

Saida blinked. The taste of the purpato lingered in the air. "W-what? Did Alesio tell you?"

"Tell me? No one needs to tell me. Dear, you slept over last night again." She raised an eyebrow. "That's what, the fourth time this month?"

Heat rose in Saida's cheeks. "Something like that." *Fifth.*

Falrie gave her a look. Saida slept on whatever world she had traveled to, or back on the Primal Plane with the other foxans. Healthy Primal magic refreshed them; they had chosen to sleep there instead of the tiny hallway world of Between. Saida experienced it, too, but it affected the older foxans more, giving them more energy and focus.

"The expeditions start early," Saida said. "It's more efficient."

"You don't need to defend yourself. With how much you two enjoy each other's company, I assumed you would move in when he bought the house. While I may be averse to change, even I can tell where water will flow." Falrie's eyes darted around to the various vendors, at the people in line in front of and behind Tener and Darrow. "Your father and I, while we disliked the smallness of Between, enjoyed our seclusion together. It was . . . it was the most peaceful of our lives. I'm sure it will be much the same for you both."

Saida's cheeks heated even more. "I'm sure," she murmured.

"Darrow was just telling me that Alesio joked with him a few months ago about portaling in some furniture. Shelves, and a place for clothes, or something human like that. Do you know, Darrow did it? A fine use of a portal we can use once a day, in my opinion."

Tener pointed at another vendor's wares and yipped. Darrow barked a foxan laugh from his muzzle.

Falrie pursed her lips, the faint reddish stripes on the bare skin of her cheeks pulling down. "He should be quieter. At least to teach Tener not to draw attention."

Saida hesitated. "Probably."

The flow of people in the stalls increased as the day warmed. Tener and Darrow moved up in the line, Darrow restraining the younger foxan from leaping upwards again with a gentle hand on his shoulder.

Falrie clicked her tongue. "This is taking too long." She marched forward and grabbed Tener's hand, dragging him out of line as he protested.

"Dear," Darrow said, trailing behind. "We were almost at the front."

"We don't have all day," Falrie said. She lowered her voice and hissed at the wilted Tener. "Straighten up and follow me. Don't make a scene in front of the humans."

ALESIO WOKE up in his own bed for the first time in weeks. He groaned and rolled over, reaching for Saida. His hands found empty space.

She left?

Panic jolted him upright and his legs twisted in his sheets. He fell off the bed and Shaped a slipshod Touch shield, so he didn't smash his nose on the wooden floor. The invisible magic caught him, but in his sleepy state he formed it just from his chest upwards, so he succeeded in smacking his shoulder while the rest of him slumped to the ground. The magic dissipated.

"Ow."

After a few seconds of bemoaning his rough wake up, he struggled to his feet and rubbed his eyes. "Saida? Are you here?"

A note rested on the bedside table. She'd written, in her sloppy handwriting, "Went owt with Parenz and Tennr. Hav a god day."

He smiled. Her spelling had improved the past couple months. He'd convinced her that reading and writing was like talking to magic, because it involved communication through an object.

Alesio glanced out the window, gauging the time from the sun, avoiding the unsettling void in the sky off to the right, squinting at how the light reflected off the light snow on the ground. It was . . . late morning. They'd stumbled into bed late last night after finding the rest of the missing Soundians on separate worlds. *When did she leave? Did she sleep enough?*

She'd curled next to him, but he'd passed out so fast he didn't recall anything beyond his head hitting the pillow.

The image of that little boy falling into the Hunger echoed in his mind like the visible toll of a bell. If only he'd reacted quicker and used his magic to grab the kid somehow. After the incident, he'd dashed through the various worlds as if in a dream, trying to help soothe the crowds, almost draining himself again. After several hours, the Hunger had stopped repeating its mantra, which had done wonders to calm people down.

When he'd fought Watthe in the Primal Plane, he had somehow pulled in more magic than he ever had before and Shaped it without issue. He didn't know how he'd done that without flooding or draining himself.

I need to figure out my magic so I can protect her better. What if that had been her, falling into the sky?

Right now, though, he needed water. And food. When had he eaten last? He tottered to the water keg in the kitchen, drinking straight from the tap, and considered options for breakfast. A stack of Tastian tortillas moldered on his counter next to a pile of fresh aliberries from Vision. Saida must have left, returned with the berries, and left again.

He popped a handful in his mouth. Sometimes he wished he lived on Taste, but not on days when he wanted to rush a meal. Doing that on Taste would overwhelm him and he'd end up spluttering.

His silver buoy suit lay crumpled on the floor. Even with its special material, it had stiffened from dried sweat and smelled terrible. He picked it up with two fingers and tossed it in the bin to wash later, when he would have ample time to scrub the stink out. He ran a quick bath in the metal basin and groomed his beard in front of the Sounds-blessed mirror, trimming it to his customary neat swath on his chin and an accompanying line along his jaw. He pulled on one of his newer clothing sets that Saida had picked out for him: a silvery shirt, which she said matched the quality of his Sound magic, and black pants lined with goose feathers for the cold.

Refreshed, he strode outside. He paused to appreciate his home for a few moments, a cheery little log house with a red-tiled roof and a bright-red painted door. He'd purchased it a few months ago, dipping into his savings for the first time since becoming the Voice of Reconnection and performing at the Cadenza. He'd searched for one in the middle of Anthem, near Mona's pub, and close to the Portal Station. That way Saida could stay over whenever she liked in between their expeditions, if she didn't want to stay with her parents and Tener, who tended to sleep in the Primal Plane.

The town had calmed, though some people still clustered on the street, pointing at the sky. Alesio walked at a quick pace, wanting to check on his father after the chaos, and almost slipped twice in the snow. He reached the Drinks De Capo in a few minutes. Mona and his father ate traditional bowls of rice for breakfast at a table near the bar. As he tended to do, Alesio angled his right side through the door first, so his good ear picked up sound.

"Alesio!" Luca, his father, stood, holding out his arms. His eyes had whitened almost completely from cataracts, but he knew the rhythm of his son's steps.

Alesio stepped into his father's embrace. He'd already checked the bar yesterday, but just for a few moments. "Did you have any property damage?"

Mona, the bar owner, tipped her head at the back door, her strawberry blonde swinging above her shoulders. "Someone tried to force the alley door open, but no real damage. People shouted a lot about going to Taste."

Mona had housed Luca and helped him recover from a Sound knife wound last year, and after a while, the two of them had struck up a relationship. It still seemed strange to Alesio, but it had allowed him to stop worrying about his father's health and wellbeing. If he *had* to trust someone with that responsibility, he'd have picked Mona himself, though a part of him sometimes missed his father depending on him.

"Did you find the missing Soundians?" His father asked, sitting back down with a grunt.

"Saida and Darrow found three wandering around the Sound wilds. That group was fine." Alesio hesitated. "Falrie, Tener, and I found the other three on Vision. Two . . . two of them didn't make it."

A heavy silence descended.

"Well. Shit," Mona said.

"I still don't understand what's so terrifying." His father scouted for his spoon with his hands and ate more rice, speaking once he'd swallowed. "And whenever I ask, no one can describe it."

"You asked exactly one person, Luca," Mona said. "And I told you; it's like a giant well, sucking all the water in and twisting it around and around. Except, it's in the sky."

Alesio shrugged, letting his father feel his shoulders rise and fall. "That's the best description I've heard so far."

"By the Senses. What a strange thing." His father scraped his spoon in the bowl, missing the remaining few grains. "Are people . . . changing again?"

"No one's walking around with holes in their chests, if that's what you mean, but the box Watthe carried around has warned us for a while now that 'something' is coming."

"Any word of Clef?" His father's face showed no sign of tension beyond the wrinkles of his forehead, like he tried to appear nonchalant.

Alesio shook his head, holding his breath to strengthen his lungs and train his Sound magic to last longer. "Not since the last sighting on Touch. We're lucky him and his goons didn't show up in the chaos."

Seven months had passed since they'd last heard a whisper of Clef's whereabouts. Someone had started an underground cage match ring—literally underground, in one of the caves on Touch. But Alesio couldn't shake the suspicion that Clef had bigger schemes planned. The old strait's leader wouldn't accept the loss of his power and influence in Anthem without cooking up a revenge plot. The Council had sent many search parties to find him, to no avail. And now, Alesio had obtained Hestafon's approval to visit Flock himself.

His mouth dried as that fact hit home. He hadn't had time to think about it before this, what with the search for the rest of the missing Soundians yesterday, and the exhaustion throughout. But now, he could go whenever he liked. He just needed to check in on some other leads, first.

Something bothered him about Hestafon and how he had hesitated at the Council meeting to approve Alesio's request. Alesio had been several notes short of a song at the time, but the Soundian delegate had seemed agitated, maybe because of the chaos . . . and maybe not. What if Hestafon hadn't wanted him to search for Clef in Flock for a different reason?

Mona scooped up her bowl and Luca's, heading behind the bar to wash them. Luca rubbed at his shoulder where one of Clef's lackeys had once sung a Sound knife into his flesh, probably feeling the ache where it had sunk in.

Alesio's thoughts sped up as he contemplated. As the Soundian delegate for the Council, Hestafon could have rigged the searches to avoid Clef, or even have warned the strait's leader beforehand. Alesio wouldn't have known *because* of Hestafon forbidding him entry, citing the unrest and how Flockians distrusted Alesio as a cage fighter from

Anthem. The possibility had churned in the back of Alesio's mind for months, but he couldn't ignore it any longer.

Hestafon could be working with Clef.

Why had Alesio ignored the signs, though? Why hadn't he just disobeyed Hestafon's order? Saida could have portaled him to Flock at any time in a moment. He could have gone in disguise, kept his head down. He probed at the dissonance in his brain, and that part of him flinched.

He knew why.

The straits of Anthem had raised Alesio, yes. But he knew the rules there, the ins and outs of how to survive. He knew how many sixteenth notes it took to bribe a hostel owner to slide his father a few more potatoes in the stew. He knew to avoid the lower half east side on Monday nights when the bar owner on Twelfth Street dumped his waste, and the smell reverberated for several streets over. He knew the faces and names of all the cage fighters he'd fought and some he had not. He knew which of them curdled danger in their hearts like sour milk, and which ones Clef had pressed into his service through blackmail or threats of violence and who hadn't wanted to fight any more than Alesio had.

He'd started to learn the piper side of Anthem, too, which possessed a more subtle but just as calculating menace. Some of the Cadenza performers influenced the piper side, but above even them, there were the backers, the sumptuously wealthy people like Linia, musicians and performers from long ago who had retired and now moved the current entertainers like pieces on a game board. He supposed he should be grateful that the people had elected Hestafon instead of her—though he suspected she and the three others of her status that Alesio knew about, those who owned the Cadenza, had somehow manipulated the people to vote that way.

Flock, on the other hand, he didn't know at all. He had some skills that transferred, like how to slip money in a handshake, but he didn't know the territory. The people. Though he despised Linia and all the privilege she represented, he agreed with her opinion on Flock. He'd adjusted to traveling to new worlds with Saida and learning them alongside her, but the second largest Soundian city made his spine shudder like tales of those giant hundred-legged eels that lived deep in the Sound caves. The one time he'd gone to the city, before Hestafon had forbidden him, it had reminded him of a nightmare version of the straits, like someone had warped his childhood memories into something unrecognizable. As if, he should have known where this or that street led, or which bar was safe till which time, but he didn't. The shrikers had roamed the streets like a murmuration of menace, in swarms of two or three at a time, but always watching, managing the places of business and enacting monthly tolls from homes. They had taken to tattooing the bird on their arms.

A figurehead held "power" there, a proxy for the shrikers, who had asked the Council more than once this past year for a Portal Station of their own. The Council and Hestafon had staved them off for now, saying that each world needed an established Portal Station first. Alesio shuddered to think of Flockians slinking into any of the other worlds, or Anthem, with such ease. Flock needed cleaning up first, and he wasn't looking forward to it.

Alesio's insides twisted. Hestafon hadn't stopped him. Not really. He'd stopped himself.

A few seconds of silence had passed. It felt like he'd descended into one of his magic rooms and time had slowed. Mona had just finished washing and drying the bowls and setting them on a shelf, and his father had lowered his arm from his old shoulder wound that Clef's thugs had inflicted on him.

Resolve and shame flooded through him. He and Saida had beaten Clef together. But Clef loved using Alesio's loved ones against him. The strait's old leader had forced Alesio to fight in the cage matches for years by threatening to hurt his father. When Alesio had stood up to him, Clef had kidnapped Luca and held him at knifepoint.

Now that Alesio had Saida in his life, the strait's leader had yet another target he could aim at. Considering that Saida had transplanted Watthe, who he had worshipped, he had several reasons to try and kill her—if he'd retained his autonomy.

86

Clef could also have evolved into more of an extension of the Hunger's will, like one of the Consumed. Either way, Clef's existence put Saida in danger, considering how the box had fixated on consuming foxan magic.

I have to find him before he hurts her.

"Dad . . . I'm going to search for him again. Hestafon approved me to search in Flock."

His father stiffened. The silence in the bar heightened, the static in the ears increasing.

"Just be smart," His father said. "Keep your sound rags close."

Alesio sucked in a surprised breath. Before everything in his life had changed, his father would have tried to stop him from going anywhere near the underground leader of the straits. And he would have had the right to. Alesio had almost given in to the lure of the cage matches, to Clef's scheming. His voice had echoed in Alesio's head since childhood with both the persistence and menace of a corner singer at two in the morning. *You're mine. You'll never escape this. Don't you want this?*

Now that he had the fame he'd always craved, what Clef offered had lost its appeal. Audiences all over the worlds screamed his name at the same time he'd stopped needing them to. He just wanted enough strength to protect the voices that mattered.

"Don't just look in Flock." Mona dried a mug and set it on a shelf with the others in a tidy row. "Also, the city isn't as dangerous as you all seem to think."

Alesio raised his eyebrows while Luca said, "Do tell?"

She jutted out her chin. "I get all kinds in the De Capo, dearest. Just because people come from the same song doesn't mean they have the same key signature. You should know that more than anyone."

Alesio frowned. "I've seen the corruption, Mona. The city's rampant with shrikers."

She unfolded a sound cloth and set to buffing the bar. "Well, then. You seem to have the world figured out. But think about it, Alesio. He could be anywhere. *I* think it makes more sense for him to be holed up somewhere in the wilds on a different world."

Mona had a sharp eye and had seen how Clef had abused him over the years, perhaps even better than he'd let slip to his father in his later teens. She probably hoped he would search everywhere else first but the most dangerous, by convincing him that Flock was somehow not dangerous. He opened his mouth to argue again, but Luca shook his head at him and mouthed, "not now."

"That could be," Alesio said.

"How is Saida taking all this?" Mona slipped back behind the bar, tapped some ale, watered it down, and slid it in front of Alesio with a casual, practiced ease, then leaned her elbows on the bar. "Drink and calm down. Sounddamn, you look like you just had a fight with one of those swan things from Scent."

"You mean a swanseize?"

"Whatever."

He peered down and blinked; his hands shook. Thinking about Clef and Flock did this to him sometimes. He tipped the ale-water to his lips before she awarded him a curt nod and returned to buffing the bar.

She cared for him, but she hadn't ironed the wrinkles out of her all-purpose brusqueness into maternal coddling since she and his father had become a couple. He appreciated that. His mother had died when he was two, but her role still felt sacred to him.

Alesio gulped the diluted alcohol down and set the mug on the table. "She's doing alright, I think. It was just a lot after the expedition, you know? We were already tired."

"She still missing those magic voices of hers?" Luca tapped his ear.

"More than she lets on." He and the foxans had kept the secret of Saida's lost ability to hear and speak with magic, but most everyone knew the tale of how she had sacrificed her two magical friends last year. "I wish I knew if her losing them was actually a good thing in the long run. She's so messed up about it. But . . . maybe it'll help her heal. Move on. Make real friends." He shook his head. "I don't know how to help her, I guess. And I don't want to push her away by saying she shouldn't miss them. It makes sense that she does."

That, and it seemed speaking and hearing magic related to her ability to trim and transplant overgrowths. The other foxans didn't hear or speak with magic and it hadn't hindered them from trimming or transplanting. But when people lost something or someone dear to them, they tended to lose more than just that one person or thing. Everything was connected, after all. Roots tangled with other roots underground.

Mona shrugged. "Have you asked her what she thinks is good for *her*?"

He paused, thinking back over the days on the expedition, replaying their conversation in the cave. It seemed so long ago already. "Not . . . not recently."

"Well, then." Mona bent to wipe the floor with a sound cloth where a single drip from the ale barrel had marred her perfect floor, then regarded the barrel as if admonishing it for such heinous actions.

He fiddled with the mug handle, that conversation in the cave echoing in his head. "I did ask her to move in."

Mona and his father both raised their eyebrows, the motion loud as trumpets. On his father it had the effect of showing more of the cataracts in his eyes. Alesio had hoped that the Reconnection would have reversed his father's condition, or slowed it, but that hadn't happened. It seemed the magic that decelerated aging didn't apply to disease or other medical issues.

"Took you long enough." Mona gestured for the empty mug, and he slid it back across to her. "You've had that room ready for her for what, three months now?"

"Four." He cleared his throat. "But she wasn't ready, before. She's still . . . I don't know. She still has a lot to work out. And I haven't showed her the room yet."

"But she said yes? Eh? Eh?" His father grinned and elbowed him.

Alesio rolled his eyes. "I didn't know you could mature backwards."

"Oh, it's a thing." Mona squinted at the table and polished it with her sound cloth, her short hair swaying around her face. "If you were a woman, you'd know that already."

"So, you're off to see her, then?" His father raised his arm to pat him on the back and would have missed if Alesio didn't step into the touch.

"I need to find her. She left with the other foxans and didn't say where to meet up after."

Mona inspected the table again and huffed her approval. "Well, where does she go, if she's not with you?"

"Lately?" He laughed. "It's kind of ironic. She likes to hang out at the Cadenza."

6
THE PLACE OF YOU

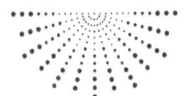

Naya threw open the door and beamed at Tener's eager face. She wore an off-white long sleeve shirt tucked into a pair of brown trousers. Red-brown fur peeked out from her wrists and ankles. She stared at Tener's new and tall form no longer than a few extra seconds.

"Well, if it isn't the biggest of all the troublemakers! What was your name again?" The fox-person scratched the three thin pumpkin-orange stripes on the sides of her foxan muzzle. "Tango? Tender?" She bent in front of Tener and slitted her eyes. "Tasty?"

The young foxan giggled and leapt into Naya's arms as a full foxan —smaller, but still quite a bit larger than the last time he'd done this feat. "It's Tener! You know that, Auntie Naya!"

Naya *whoofed* from his increased weight, then swung him inside, holding him under the arms, and blew on his furry belly. "Oooh, he's Tasty! Num num num!"

"No, Auntie Naya!" Tener squirmed and squealed. "It's Tener! And I'm not a he, I'm a they!"

Saida blinked and cocked her head. *Huh.* Tener did seem more like a they in the way they walked and talked, with neither a feminine nor masculine air, but hovering somewhere in between. Had that happened after his—*their*—growth spurt?

"Ah, I see you now." Naya set them down. He—*they* had hunched a little, and their eyes darted around the room. It struck Saida how young they looked, like they'd shifted emotionally, if not physically, back to nine years old.

Naya stuck out her hand and shook their paw. "Nice to meet you, Tener."

Saida squeezed through the door and peeked behind Naya as if waiting in line. "I want to meet them too!"

Tener straightened, giggled, and shook Saida's outstretched hand. Falrie and Darrow lined up behind her, smiling at Tener and shaking their paw.

They all filed inside Naya's home. The lack of a bed implied she slept elsewhere. The barrier of flour sacks she kept around the edges of the small home softened the taste of her existence to the humans around her and cloaked her.

"When did you know you were a they?" Darrow asked, perching on a flour sack.

Tener shrugged. "I think I always knew. I tried to be a boy, but it made me feel bad. Then I tried to be a girl, and that didn't feel good either. But I wanted to be sure. I haven't seen any other theys before. But then I saw Verrity at the Council, and she sort of looks like a he or a they, but she is a she. You can just tell. And that made me think it's okay to not be a he either if I don't think that I am." Their face was flushed. "I'm glad you all think it's okay, too."

"Well," Saida said, "All magic are theys, you know. At least, that's how they always seemed to me." *Before I stopped sensing them.*

"Really? For truly?"

"Really for truly."

"Ah! Then I'm not the only one!" Tener hopped up on the flour sack barrier and cavorted along it like a newborn calf in a meadow.

"Retract your claws!" Falrie called out. "Don't poke holes in the bags!"

"Ah, it's alright," Naya said. "They're only here to mask my fox-personness, anyway."

"Well!" Falrie said. "Things are never dull with hi-*them* around." She coughed and turned to Naya, giving her a hug and lowering her voice. "It's good to see you."

Tener paused mid-cavort. "We were gonna bring you olos, Auntie, but . . ."

"The line was too long." Falrie disengaged from the embrace, her eyes glimmering with unshed tears.

"Wraps around the block sometimes!" Naya hugged Darrow next.

Saida had to swallow a lump in her throat, too, seeing them all together. The three stripes down Naya's nose, along with the red-brown fur on her arms and legs, had distinguished her as Pell's descendent. Of course, all the fox-people descended from ancient foxans and human pairings from long before Saida's time, but Naya's patterns displayed Pell's without doubt.

She wished for the hundredth time that Pell could have met her. He had asked Saida, over and over, where his daughter Gemma had disappeared to, forgetting she had long since passed away. When the Hunger's box had disconnected magic from the Planes, fox-people and humans' lives had shortened to eighty or ninety years old, instead of 800 or 900. Saida had hoped that finding Pell's descendent would ease some of his memory loss and grief, but Watthe had killed him before he'd had a chance to meet Naya.

Tener babbled about Taste, and Sound, about how much they liked rolling around on Touch so that they tingled all over, and something about pretty strings, their huge dark eyes animated in their face.

"Wait, what was that?" Naya asked.

"Our strings are so pretty! Between you and Mom and me and Dad and Saida."

"Strings?" Saida checked her human clothing for unraveling threads.

"Not *that* kind of string, silly! Your glowing ones!"

The adult foxans and Naya all glanced at each other.

"Tener? Are you saying we have something glowing that's connecting us?"

Tener ducked their head and traced the ground with their foot. "I'm sorry. I keep saying and being things that make you all look at me strange."

"It's alright," Darrow said. "We don't mean to make you feel bad, Tener. We were just surprised. Can you tell us more?"

The young foxan stared at the ground. "They connect everyone. But no one else can see them. I asked Mom before, and she didn't understand. And then, I tried to tell a little human girl, but she just looked at me weird. I meant to stop asking after that, but my mouth said things before I said it could." Their head shot up. "But I really do see them!"

"When did you ask me . . . oh." Falrie covered her face with one hand. "Last week, you did say something about strings. I thought you were talking about chasing a string."

"What do these strings look like?" Saida asked. "Do we have more than one?"

Tener held their hands behind their back and their gaze zipped from person to person. "They glow! Like . . . um, like sunrises! We all have lots. Humans do too. And they come out of us all over, but the most glowy ones come from here." They pointed at their chest.

"Fascinating," Falrie murmured. "That's maybe . . . maybe something I heard about when I was small. Darrow? Do you remember what this sight is called?"

"Bondsight." Darrow stared at Tener. "It was called bondsight. Just a few foxans had it."

Tener nodded. "That feels like the right name."

"What does it mean?" Saida asked her father. "Does it . . . do anything?"

Darrow exhaled a long breath. "I'm—I don't remember. I just know it was special."

Tener beamed.

Naya gestured at her torso. "So, these threads, are they brighter when people are closer to each other?" She acted like she pulled on a string, walking towards Tener. "Like this?"

"U-huh! And when they love each other more!"

Amazement passed through Saida at first, then a shadow of fear. She covered it up by ruffling the young foxan's big ears. "That's incredible, Tener!"

The rest of them asked more questions, but Tener didn't know anything else beyond what they'd already explained.

"So, Saida." Naya groaned, hauled Tener up under their arms, counted to three, and flung them onto the flour sacks. Tener landed on all fours and screeched in delight. "Did you find the Epitaph, before all the madness the other night?"

"We found it," Saida said. "But I still couldn't sense what it said." She plucked at the hairs in her braid. "And I still can't sense magic outside of Epitaphs, at all."

"Ah." Naya folded her legs under her and knelt on her feet. Tener tested the bounciness, or lack thereof, of the flour sacks beside her. "I'm sorry to hear that."

"Didn't your group also find something else, though?" Darrow plopped on one of the flour sacks and stretched his human legs, yawning, his tongue curling over his pointed foxan teeth.

"We found an old Touchian text carved into a stone wall. It said something about another city called Sedella. The people moved their settlement on Touch there, or at least they tried to."

Darrow frowned. "That name sounds familiar." He blinked, then shook his head. "Sorry. Nothing I can remember. Falrie?"

Her eyes had glazed over, and her eyelids drooped. "Maybe it was before our time."

That could be, or their memories are too spotty. Just reconnecting the flow of magic to the Sensory worlds hadn't repaired their withered memories. The Severing would have happened in the time of their youth, perhaps in their 100's. They had lived out the prime of their lives in the Between, enjoying life as a couple and giving birth to Saida the old-fashioned way somewhere in their 500's. But their isolation and instinctive fear of the box had gouged perhaps permanent holes in their minds.

Tener jiggled in place, perusing the older foxans' serious faces, then dashed along the flour sack barrier on their four foxan legs. "Can't catch me!"

Saida took the bait, letting her parents rest for a bit. She chased Tener around Naya's house, and bits of flour puffed up in the air. Saida caught them and they rolled around on the floor in their foxan forms. Flour coated them both. Tener's dark eyes juxtaposed against their flour-covered face.

Through the tangle of Tener's limbs, she could see Darrow and Falrie holding human hands.

Tener broke away from Saida and raced for the door. "I'm gonna get some olos! Can't stop me!"

Darrow heaved himself to his feet. "Let me."

"Tener," Falrie called. "Stay here and sit down for a bit. You know better than to go running off."

Darrow paused halfway up, then sat back down.

Tener scanned back and forth between them, then drooped. Were they looking at her parents' bond? Something pressed on her chest, a sadness she couldn't place.

Falrie pursed her lips, and Darrow leaned forward like he wanted to say something but stopped himself. His hands shifted to paws, and his face shifted back to foxan, his beard disappearing from his muzzle.

"Well," Naya said. "Seeing as how you didn't eat any olos, how about I get my aliberry scones out of the cupboard?"

ALESIO AMBLED into the Cadenza under a sense of déjà vu, his footsteps echoing up to the high arched ceiling. The outer atrium remained empty. The scheduled musicians wouldn't perform for hours yet. Someone had posted a notice on the front doors, announcing that after tonight, the Cadenza would close. He had a feeling they would remain closed until either the Hunger left the sky or the pipers that ran the city adjusted to the sight of it. The echoes of the great concert hall possessed the same abject hollowness as last year when Watthe had brutalized the citizens of Anthem, creating a host of dead followers called Consumed who wandered the streets.

He opened the doors to the main concert area. Velvet-covered seats faced a grand stage, and the ceiling soared, so that any sound echoed in the space tenfold. Sound magic woven into the performances here could wring tears from the most hardened cage fighters. And high up, shining down on it all, a brilliant light rotated, its light ever changing. One might see shapes in it if they let their eyes half-close. A flower blooming, then folding up for the night. The wind ruffling the branches in a tree. A bird unfurling its wings.

Saida arched back on one of the velvet seats in the middle of the auditorium, her V-shaped face angled upwards. She must have just spoken, because whispered echoes of her voice slipped past him like fish in the sea on his bad side. "... better ... what if ..."

Alesio jogged down the slanted, carpeted aisle towards her, relieved that he had guessed right. "Hey."

She blinked, the slits of her blue-black eyes reflecting the changing light. "Oh. Hi."

"Any luck?"

She swallowed and straightened on the seat. "No. Nothing." She unwound the ends of her braid. She almost never let it fully down or it would drag a bit on the floor and cutting it would cut her tail in foxan form. "How did you know I was here?"

Alesio sank into the seat next to her, staring up at the ever-changing light. Something in the way she held herself stopped him from draping his arm around her shoulders. "Well, you come here the second we get back from an expedition, like clockwork." He puffed the tiniest bit of Sound magic at her face, and it lifted some of the flyaway hairs away from her cheek. "You've become like the Summit wave. Very punctual. I'm beginning to think my earlier theory about you training to become a famous singer is true."

"I—I come to your house, too."

He paused. "I didn't say you didn't."

"And you're performing tonight. I just wanted to beat the crowds."

As if to prove her point, the doors swung open. Foret, wearing a maroon silk suit as always, strode down towards the stage and stopped a few feet from them. "Ah. It's good you're already here. I worried you might be too fatigued to perform, in all the, uh, tumult."

Alesio pivoted. "Not at all. People need music the most in times like these, after all."

"Very good." Foret's cheeks puffed out as if playing his titular instrument, the trumpet. The Cadenza had employed him decades earlier as one of their main performers, and he had soared high in favor and wealth, renowned for his legendary lung strength and the purity of his high tones. After he had retired, he'd bought a share in the Cadenza and, therefore, had claimed his place alongside Linia, Peggio, and Jupen. Altogether, these four owned not just the Cadenza, but all of Anthem through their various holdings and influence, and as such, belonged to the peak echelon of wealth and power in the Sensory Plane. Technically, they also owned the Cadenza built in Touch, as well, and he had a contract to perform there once every few months. Hestafon might have had some power as the surface leader of Anthem and its delegate to the other worlds, but nothing happened in the city unless one of the four owners sponsored it.

Of the four, Foret managed the Cadenza's day-to-day business, scheduling, and advertising. They could have hired someone to do such mundane tasks, but he seemed to enjoy the bustling and schmoozing. The other three preferred staying out of the public eye, though Linia, of course, had sponsored the expedition to Touch and had even come along, surprisingly enough. Peggio and Jupen, though they'd attended Alesio's audition, had otherwise stayed out of sight. The private boxes high up on the right side reserved for them on performance nights remained empty for often than not.

"I'll just check with the man at the box, then, to ensure the corner singers call out the playbill correctly." Foret puffed back towards the big main double doors.

Saida shifted to more foxan, growing her braid out so that it flipped up like a tail. "I'll be listening." She kissed him on the cheek.

"Saida—"

"I'm gonna go up to my spot before more people get here. Will you sing "The Space of You and Me?""

"When you ask with those big eyes, how could I say no?"

She grinned and scampered towards the side entrance that led up to her private box, which he'd negotiated for her after she'd exchanged Tricksy Stone for his audition, and he was left wondering how he could soften the ache in her eyes when she wouldn't talk to him about what she had lost.

Her magic will come back to her. He wanted it for her, even if he didn't know if it would help her heal or not. Was that selfish of him?

He waited behind the curtain as people trickled in and settled in their seats, all of them pipers. Though the Cadenza had opened its doors to straiters on Alesio's request, most still wouldn't set foot on this side of Anthem.

The opening musician played an instrumental piece of "Waves of Gold" on the Cadenza organ, as tradition dictated. The flutist Ravina played next, a middle-aged woman with a talent for clear, precise fingering and lighthearted, happy songs. She performed a rendition of "Three Ways You Irk Me" that relaxed the whole audience, the true purpose of the night.

Alesio wished he could use the night to perform at the Drinks De Capo instead. More straiters had panicked than pipers. The pipers had huddled in their large houses, cushioned from the Hunger's booming voice because of their strategic trees and lines of bushes planted around their neighborhoods. Adding to that, since Alesio had announced that he owed his start to Mona's bar, it had become a huge tourist attraction almost equaling the Cadenza itself and would have drawn plenty. He could have helped a fair amount of straiters relax and forget their anxiety with music. But he had a standing promise to play here once a month and exhaustion had dulled his memory. He didn't even have his mandolin, which did worry him a bit. He couldn't cover the fatigue and stress in his voice from the past few days without an instrument.

Ravina finished her set and strode off the stage.

"Nice job, Ravina," he said.

"—has a stain on it." She brushed past him, head high. He missed the first part of her words, unable to read her lips very well in the dimness backstage, but he could guess.

"Ah." He pulled at his shirt and located the offending mark: a blue blot, probably from the aliberries he'd eaten that morning. He had ways of fixing that. He rummaged through the box of props and accessories near the stage and discovered a purple silk necktie, which he affixed to his collar. "Better?"

Ravina had reclined on the chaise backstage. Her eyes flicked up and scanned him. She pursed her lips. He grinned.

He stepped out onto the stage, and the audience clapped. While other Cadenza mainstay performers might not relish having a straiter in their midst, the pipers at large had accepted him.

But he didn't need the pipers' admiration anymore. Maybe that explained why even with a rough voice, no instrument, and a stained shirt, his nerves did not assail him.

He would've *preferred* not to perform that way. He adored smart, trim clothing, especially vests, with their versatility and class—but he didn't panic without all the niceties.

Also, he had a lot more fun when he didn't strive to impress everyone at every moment. He just wanted one person's esteem tonight.

He squinted up and to the left towards Saida's box. The lights blinded him to anything past the stage, of course.

He filled his lungs and began a rollicking ditty that most pipers wouldn't have heard: a tongue-in-cheek piece about a lady who preferred peaches over pickles, and how she often licked her fingers clean. A few gasps echoed, but a few snorts of laughter, too, which he counted as a victory for this crowd.

After that, he sang one of the oldest songs that everyone knew regardless of where they lived, even those from Flock: "The Rhythm of the Street," which consisted of all choruses, beginning slow and gathering speed with each one, the people stomping in time with the rhythm.

. . .

THE STREET, how it trips!
How it stumbles, how it slips!
How it staggers by the pub,
How it lurches and it stubs!

THE STREET, how it plods!
How it trudges, how it slogs!
How it lumbers in its timbre,
How it wishes it could canter!

THE STREET, how it strolls!
How it saunters under soles!
How it wanders and meanders,
How it longs to take a gander!

THE STREET, how it stamps!
How it marches, how it tramps!
How it matches those with boots,
How it strides along on routes!

THE STREET, how it trots,
How it jogs without a thought!
How it holds a steady gait,
How it rolls and does not wait!

THE STREET, how it sprints!
How it dashes in the wind!
How it darts, how it races,

How hard to keep the pace is!

THE STREET, how it blurs!
How it flashes so assured!
How it—

THE SONG SPED TOO FAST for the audience to keep up and they dissolved in a rolling fit of merriment. Alesio bowed with a flourish. He'd accomplished true laughter a precious few times here at the Cadenza. He wished he could see Ravina's face.

The stomping from the song traveled up his foot to his left ear. The audience participation had generated Touch magic ready for him, already Received and ready for Shaping if he so desired. He hadn't tried using Touch magic while performing yet; he felt it might distract him from the sound of the performance, but maybe he'd try someday.

"Alright, everyone. For my last song, let's bring it down a notch." His voice had roughened a little, but it would work for what he had in mind.

The old ballad Saida had requested had remained her favorite for a while now. Mostly sung in straiter pubs, it had a strange, ethereal key, if there existed such a thing.

He sang in a lower register than the original composition called for, the roughness of his voice creating a smoky timbre. He Shaped his Sound magic as he did, entering his Sound room and Shaping the manic reverberations of "The Rhythm of the Street," tamping them down and pulling the magic into thin, diaphanous cloud-like Sounds, then releasing them.

He couldn't *sense* his magic outside of his magic rooms, like the foxans could, and Saida used to. But the effects of it showed as everyone hushed.

THE PLACE OF YOU, where you dwell

It turns me all a-tumble,
I look for you o'er time and dell
And each hour keeps me humble.

CAN I find the place of you,
Through all the spaces in between?
It's so far leaping from star to start
And keeping up beginnings.

EACH PLACE KEEPS PACE, space to space,
Across each stumbling sky,
Your place, it holds my weighted heart
And keeps it placed up high.

THE PLACE OF YOU, when you leave,
I cannot keep from aching,
I look for you twixt you and me,
And find you in the making.

ALESIO BOWED. Applause started in scattered pockets, though up and to the left, enthusiastic clapping told him Saida had liked it. The clapping grew as he bowed again, signaling he had finished with his set. He exited. To his amusement, Ravina had left.

The crowd still clapped, but they didn't do encores at the Cadenza. Something about it not being classy, or something pipist like that. But he didn't mind. He had missed performing and Shaping the magic in his voice to accomplish something artful instead of utilitarian or destructive, but now he just wanted to check on Saida.

Foret met him a few minutes later backstage, handing him his cut for the night from the ticket sales. Five whole notes. Enough to keep him in room and board at any average pub for at least a month, more than he knew what to do with. He'd bought his house, and his father lived with Mona at the Drinks De Capo now, so he didn't need money for rent any longer. Alesio just had to buy food and sometimes clothing for a new performance. He'd splurged on a few outfits at first, but now, it seemed wasteful when the straits remained in poverty, regardless of his efforts to push for more aid in the Council meetings. So, as he'd done for a while now, he pocketed the notes to donate to the fund for straits shelters. Not that they seemed to get built any faster.

He didn't wait for the piper audience to disperse. It wouldn't take long, considering everyone would scuttle back to their houses with the Hunger still appearing in their skies as their world turned, but patience eluded him. As soon as Foret left, he strode to the hallway backstage that led to the upper boxes, climbed the tiny velveted staircase, and jogged to the closest one, the one nearest the stage. A long curtain draped there.

"Saida."

She poked her head out around the curtain, her foxan ears pricked forward to catch his voice. "I loved that song!"

Alesio bent down and raised her chin, so her mouth tilted up. "I know, you're the one who asked me to sing it, silly!"

Saida giggled and drew him back with her into the box. He Shaped a sound bubble around them so they could talk as the audience milled around below them. As he drew closer to her, her gaze drifted up to the transplanted gemstone revolving above them, like a moth caught by a light. He stilled for few seconds.

She blinked, her eyes clearing from their haze. "Sorry. I'm—I'm just trying to cover all the possible solutions. They're not an Epitaph, but they were still very powerful."

"It's a good idea, to keep trying. We know even less about foxan magic than we do about human magic, and I can tell there's a lot more to Shaping and Receiving than I understand."

Alesio swept his gaze all around the concert hall, then back up to the transplant. He'd dreamed of performing here since childhood, of escaping the harsh life that Clef had crafted for him in the straits, of weaving a tapestry of Sound for an audience of thousands.

"It's so odd," he murmured.

"What?"

"How things change. Ever since I performed that night on Scent, my dream shifted . . . like that." He pointed up. "It's not just one shape anymore, wanting to perform for a big audience. I prefer singing for smaller groups now, because then I can tell the effect of my magic on individuals instead of a faceless crowd. It's funny, because the moment I lost my obsession with performing at the Cadenza, you became obsessed with it for a whole different reason."

She stiffened. "I'm not *obsessed* with it."

He quirked an eyebrow.

"I told you; I'm just here because of—"

"Saida, it's okay." He stopped himself from reaching for her, as her whole body had frozen like a rabbit watching a hawk, her foxan ears slanting backwards. *Let her come to you. Let her come to you, damn it.* "I know you miss them. Not just your ability to sense magic or hear their voices—but your old magic items."

Her lips trembled. "A little."

"A lot."

Tears shimmered in her dark blue eyes. "Is it wrong to hope they're not gone forever? When I sensed the Epitaphs' energy . . . I thought maybe . . . It's not that I don't care about you. I don't regret sacrificing them for you at all, I promise!"

"That doesn't mean it wasn't still hard."

The tears spilled over. He held out his arms, and she dove into them, burying her head in his chest. "It's—it's just that they were always there. They had distinct voices. And now—I can't always tell, you know? What thoughts are from them, or—or other parts of me. What parts are wise? What parts are comforting? What parts tell the truth?"

He spoke against the fur on her head. She'd shifted in his arms to the smallest version of herself, full-foxan. "I hate to be the bearer of bad news, but that's kind of what the rest of us have to figure out all the time."

"It's awful!"

He chuckled. "It really is."

She nestled against him, and his heart constricted, the fear that she would drift away from him settling for now.

"It's not wrong to miss them at all," he said. "They were a part of you for a long time. And I really, really do hope that the voices come back to you, and that they're good for you when they do." He hesitated. That was the edge of what he wanted to say.

"I might be wrong here," he continued, "But maybe you're not hearing voices anymore because you're healing, you know? From the loneliness?" She lay quiet against his chest. "I mean, didn't you say the last thing Tricksy Stone said to have 'no more walls between your thoughts'?"

"—have a good memory." She spoke against his chest, the words muffled. Her foxan ears, which had been flattened against him, popped out.

"And the whole moving in with me thing, if that's bothering you, you know it can wait, right? Like, however long you want. And we can live anywhere you want. Any world. It doesn't even have to be Sound."

The moment stretched forever.

"I really do want to live with you," she said.

He let out a breath.

"Also," she said, and swiveled, then pushed him against the side wall. "I've missed you performing these past few weeks." She brushed her hand along his arm, then rose on her toes to perch her chin on his shoulder. "Could you sing a song . . . just for me?"

He bent to hover his lips over hers, turning to frame her v-shaped chin with both hands. Such a delicate face, with those eyes like the night sky at dusk. "You must be some kind of fortune teller. I've been composing one for us. I've only worked on one verse so far, though."

"For us? For truly?" Her eyes reflected the light of Tricksy Stone's transplant, a mauve for now.

"For truly."

"Sing what you have so far!"

Her excitement for his art never failed to surprise and inspire him. His throat swelled and he had to inhale several deep breaths before he connected to his Sound magic.

YOU ARE MY BRIGHTEST PLACE,
Your name's a euphony,
Oh, you've transplanted me.

HE WHISPER-SANG, just for her, just in the bubble of Sound magic.

She linked her arms around his neck. She had her eyes closed. "Alesio. I can't sense it, but I know what your magic must be like right now. Silver ribbons, twisting all around us."

He kissed her, holding the back of her head with one hand and stroking down her side with the other. She pressed up against him, pushing him harder against the wall, and desire flared. Alesio ran his tongue along the seam of her lips how she liked, and she melted against him. He spun her around against the wall and did it again, holding one of her hands and her side, then spearing his tongue into her mouth. She whimpered, and he gave a low laugh as she then met his tongue with hers. She nipped his lip, then shrank down to her foxan form, and he stopped, as she tended to dislike sexual contact as a foxan. Saida scampered to one of the box's two seats and shifted back to human.

He sank into the other chair. "Was it too much?"

She cast her gaze down. "No. I wanted to try something."

Then she swung her legs over his, straddling him. His breath caught, and he had to check that the Sound bubble persisted. She skimmed her body up his torso, then back down. Flames of desire shot through him, and she grinned. "I thought you might like that."

"I do. I very much do."

She closed her eyes, and her foxan furred shirt with sleeves lowered, then withdrew down past her collarbone. He brushed the

107

backs of his knuckles over her bared skin, and her eyes rolled back. She inched the shirt lower, revealing the tops of her breasts, and he brushed down to where she'd shifted. She arched her back, moaning under her breath. His breath had shortened, which he shouldn't have an issue with, considering that he'd practiced holding his breath for up to twelve minutes in light movement, now. But this . . .

She'd stopped moving. He opened his eyes, not sure when he'd closed them. She shifted to foxan, and he gathered her in his arms. "Hey. Hey, are you okay?"

She ducked her head. "I'm just not sure, um . . ."

"It's alright. We'll do it when we're both ready, not just one." His pants had grown a bit tight already, but he ignored that. "Just checking. Was it something I did?"

"No! No." She fiddled with her tail, pulling at the fur there. He angled his good ear towards her. "It's almost . . . too good, you know? I'm afraid that. Um." She frowned.

"That it will stop feeling that way?"

"That I'll stop wanting it so much."

"Well, if that happens, you just tell me." He kissed her forehead. "I, for one, am enjoying the suspense."

"You sure?"

"The best songs don't rush the crescendo."

7
THE SISTERS

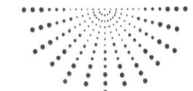

"Make sure the fieldworkers strew the whole area with nonflowers before they rake it, especially any areas that had blood soaked into it," Verrity said. "The scent sinks into the soil better than just spreading them after."

Paras slung a bag full of blush pink nonflowers over her shoulder. "Don't worry, I'll take care of things. You go and help the foxan."

The villagers flowed around them on their way to accomplish their morning tasks, carrying rakes, jars, and bags like Paras's. Nonflowers bloomed the best in spring, and they needed to gather some and dry the rest so that they would last throughout the year. A few villagers slid their eyes towards Verrity, then away again. No one spoke to her.

"And—oh! Don't forget to have the gatherers spread out while they're searching for nonflowers. We are over-picking a little on the east side of the village. I know no one except you likes to go north because of the Garden, but if people just go around—"

"Oh my Scents, did I turn into an otherworlder?" Paras elbowed her. "I *know*, Sis. I've watched you do all this for a year now."

Verrity sighed. Paras had spun story after story as they'd grown up about what wonders they might find if they just ventured a little further than the other villagers. When the worlds had opened, she'd wanted more than just the Anthem safety certificate she'd received for touring the city. The Council had outlawed visiting other worlds' wild lands without first training on the dangers of those worlds on an expedition with a foxan and learning the laws of that world's magic. She'd just returned from the trip to Touch and would want to explore it further now that she had her certificate.

Verrity didn't know how to soften what she had to say, so she just said it. "I'm afraid we need you here a little longer, before you set out on another trip."

Paras repositioned the bag on her other shoulder. Her short, slight body hid a strong core. Verrity bit back the jealousy that grew like a weed around her sister, with her pointed face and petite frame that shouted femininity. No one needed to sense her hormones to understand her gender.

Paras gave Verrity a wry smile. "What, I can't gallivant off into the sunset when all the worlds might end? Now you're just being mean, oh mighty Delegate."

Verrity rolled her eyes. "You know I'd trade places with you if I could."

"Go on, get to your thing with that foxan lady."

Verrity trekked around the fields surrounding Tremain, passing some citizens as they raked the top edge. Raos, their tracker, glanced at her, then his eyes slid away, his thundercloud-like hair hiding his expression.

The shift had begun awhile back, even before the Soundian mob had floated the villagers' attitude more to the surface. Even though Verrity's Council duties stole her away from them just once a week or so, they had begun to view her with growing suspicion, to see her as an otherworlder, because she worked with otherworlders. As if she had tracked a scent into their house and they all avoided her.

She didn't know the right thing to do. The village needed a Mother, but they also needed a liaison that they continued to trust, someone who would travel between the worlds and speak for them to the other world leaders. If she stepped down from her position as

Tremain's Mother while remaining their advocate on the Council, would the villagers even listen to her anymore? How could she call herself their delegate and pretend she represented them, if they didn't want her in that position?

But they *needed* her in that position. They needed to learn how to live with the fact that otherworlders existed, especially now with the Hunger in the sky above them. They had to learn to work together to stop the larger threat. If she bowed to their emotions, she left them without someone that would act to protect them from things bigger than losing a crop.

Or was she trying to hold onto both positions because she liked how they made her feel? She wouldn't have said being a delegate gave her a rush of confidence, but . . . she still felt stronger in herself than before. If she stepped down as Tremain's delegate or its leader, she might just wilt back down into that person who stayed in the background and never danced at the End of Harvest barn dance. Someone whose sole happiness squeezed from the rala nut. Someone who could never imagine standing in front of world leaders without shaking and checking the smoothness of her shave.

She didn't want to devolve into that version of herself again. Regardless of how she disliked Balt's misogyny or Xen's casual dismissals, she still liked herself better, standing in front of them as an equal. She wanted *more* of that self-assuredness, not less of it.

Perhaps she would step down from one or both positions once they dealt with the Hunger. She could assuage her conscience that way.

She'd arrived at Scent's Portal Station. It had two departure portals leading to Sound and Taste, and two arrival portals from Vision and Taste. A mixture of sweet aliberries baked into a pastry scintillated on her tongue, mixing with the swirling images dancing and shifting on the dais, of lavender skies and more vivid forests than the one here on Scent. The magic in a Portal Station always energized her and cleared her head.

Regardless of its charms, no one lingered here. No Scentians would travel even to Taste for a while and the massive flow of

Soundians to Scent had ceased. The few children in Tremain used to dawdle around it, until their parents had caught them avoiding their chores and forbid them to lay on the dais as they seemed to want to.

Verrity stepped through the Scent-Sound portal. The frigid winter wind sliced through the fabric of her thin dress, and she shivered.

"Verrity, right? The Council delegate?" Tak, one of Sound's Portal Station guards, waved her forward. He had a bandage on his head and wore his arm in a sling. She had her guide paper ready, but he waved her to step off the pedestal. "You're fine, I know you're certified."

She had left just after dawn in Tremain to meet with Falrie and interrogate the small Hunger. Early afternoon had arrived on Anthem, yet almost no one frequented the Portal Station or the streets outside. Most Soundians tended to stay up later at all the bars and concerts they hosted. Of course, her ears preferred it that way. Even the lone corner singer tuning their instrument twanged louder than Verrity liked.

Across the street, a store owner had just opened their doors and flicked a lantern on inside. A rose-pink dress with blue and pearl-gray flowers hung on a rod in the display window.

Verrity gravitated towards it, then stopped herself. She didn't have time for luxury. Falrie could arrive any moment.

"Ready for the rush?" She asked Tak.

"Ready as an audience at a Birri concert." He had a bowl of sticky rice, an Anthem staple, which he tucked into with a will.

"Um, what?"

He peeked over the rim of his bowl and swallowed. "Oh, sorry. Birri is a famous saxophone player. But she's always late to her own performances." He waved one hand. "It's just a saying here. I get bored. I like talking to people, don't you know?"

Verrity rubbed her arms to try and warm herself up, wanting to crane her neck to look at the dress in the store window. She hadn't anticipated waiting long in Anthem and hadn't thought to wear anything warmer.

She blinked. Tak apparently waited for an answer to his comment, looking at her with eyebrows raised.

"Um, I can't relate, to be honest. There are so many people I talk to now, on the Council, and it's hard to know what to say." She hesitated. "Do you ever miss when everything was simpler?"

Tak finished his rice bowl and tapped it three times, a tradition in Anthem. Something to do with honoring their Sound god. "Of course, my dear! Most everything was simpler back then, at least for me. I knew which side of Anthem to live on and which side to avoid. Who to stay away from." He set down his bowl and pulled out a harmonica from his pocket, blowing a few notes into it, like a test. He pulled out a cloth from his other pocket and wiped the instrument. "But once I started talking to people from the other worlds, I realized some of the things I thought were simple were never so; I'd just been deaf to the harmonies. Fox-people are not magic thieves, and straiters are not thugs. They are poor and need food and shelter and have few options to obtain them. Complexity is always present. If it isn't, we *simply* aren't looking hard enough."

"I guess . . . I guess that's true. The other worlds were always there. We just didn't know it."

"Exactly!" He blew another set of notes, higher this time. The music didn't seem enhanced in a special way like some performances in this world, though it did sound bright and happy and, of course, loud. "But then, the Portal Station did simplify some things."

At least he steered the conversation. She didn't have to imagine what he wanted her to say next. "What things?"

"Why, that all those new people felt the same as me! Overwhelmed. Scared. Fearful of what they didn't know. And then I thought, 'Well! If we're all afraid of the same thing, then we might have other things in common, too.' And so, I asked to guard the Station, to see if I can find more in common with people. More layers." He smiled at her, and Verrity couldn't help but smile back.

"Are you ready to go? You look cold."

Verrity jumped. Falrie had marched up to them at some point in her human form, except for her ears. She'd managed to shift her back legs this time, so her lanky frame rose a head higher than Verrity's.

"Ready as I'll ever be, I suppose." Verrity twisted her hands, then untwisted them to wave goodbye to the loquacious Tak.

Instead of traveling to the Primal Plane by way of the Portal Station, Falrie summoned a portal, calling it forth from the ground. They would travel to a different part of the Primal Plane than where the Portal Station led to, where the Council met. They fell through together and less than a second later, the density of un-Received magic clouded around them, buoying them to what might be called the ground. Falrie's portal closed, and the air warmed to a neutral degree, without a breath of wind.

Next to them, a permanent departure portal led the way back to Touch, created so foxans and humans could return to the Sensory Plane without having to wait a day for a foxan's teleportation to recharge.

Ahead of them, about fifty yards away, rose the tree Saida had transplanted Watthe into.

"We should establish what we want to find out." Falrie held up her fingers, ticking them off. "Number one: where it came from, so we can try and convince it to return there or chase it away somehow. Number two: how long it needs to 'consume' us, so we know how long we have before that happens. Number three: what we can do to slow it down or stop it. And number four: how it was made, so maybe, *maybe,* we can un-make it somehow." She paused. "Anything else you can think of?"

The foxan had that businesslike, confident attitude that reminded Verrity of the strong scent of pine in the crispness of winter. She shook her head.

"Alright then. What did you want to ask it?"

"Um, well, it seems very arrogant. If we could prick its pride, maybe it would give us information about itself."

Falrie's speckled gray foxan ears slanted backwards. "What if we anger it, and it gets closer, or tries to consume us?"

"I—I don't know. Maybe we shouldn't do that, then. What do you think we should do?"

"I like the idea of trying to get it to talk about itself. Maybe we just try a different method for that." Falrie inclined her head. "Follow my lead."

Verrity trailed behind the foxan, who padded up the gravity shift, which angled in a lazy loop about ten feet off the ground at its highest and ended a few yards away from the transplant tree.

"The box I sent is just a single brick from the world of my body! I will arrive soon!" It repeated the mantra as it had for the last year.

Just as Falrie had told the Council, the box was no longer a box. A square void squatted at the base of the Watthe-Tree. It reminded Verrity of a reflection of the sky in a lake, except that a reflection of the Hunger lay there. It twisted the roots of the tree and the ground around it, sucking everything towards itself like a weak gravity shift, including the two of them. What did the Hunger do to people in there?

"I've teleported from far away, much farther than you simple beings could comprehend! The box I sent—"

"You are so powerful, now," Falrie said. "We all want to worship you! Can you tell us how you became the way you are?"

The small void paused in its mantra. So far as Verrity knew, it had never done that before.

"—brick from the world of my body! I will arrive soon!"

"Oh, great and wonderful Hunger," Verrity said. The void paused again. "We pay homage to your altar, where you've deigned to set a brick of yourself in our inconsequential Plane. Can you tell us how to make you even more powerful?" *Meaning, what can we do to stop you from becoming more powerful, or at least slow you down?*

The void pulsed, a sound like heart palpitations. Was it . . . laughing? "You cannot trick me, simple beings, little bits of magic. I know you do not worship me."

Verrity almost stopped breathing. *It responded! I should try to keep this going!*

But no further words offered themselves to her mind. This extended far beyond communicating with otherworlders as a Council delegate.

Falrie shot a quick glance at Verrity, as if waiting for her to continue, then took over. "We are those who worship you. Old followers of Watthe. We have since learned that Watthe bent against you towards the end. We come here to right that wrong, and to beg your guidance on how long it might be before we are joined with you in the sky."

"You are not Consumed." The void vibrated in the roots of the Watthe-Tree. An angrier, stronger sound than the tremors from before. "You are not husks. You cannot build a cage to trap me with words. You are all doomed. You will all become Consumed, in the end. I've teleported from far away, much farther than you simple beings could comprehend!"

Falrie motioned for Verrity to follow her away from the void, back down the gravity shift. Trudging through the thick Primal Plane magic usurped some time, the ground gave way under their feet like the muddy banks of the river near Tremain. After a few hundred feet, Falrie stopped, and they turned to each other.

"It can respond!" Verrity said.

"Apparently." Falrie frowned, her tall foxan ears angled backwards. "But it seems quite intelligent. It can tell if we are "Consumed" or not."

"I'm so glad you kept trying to talk to it. I didn't know what else to say." Verrity chewed on her lower lip. "My sister would know what to say."

Falrie shrugged. "You're the one who got it to stop that infernal monologue."

"I guess so. Maybe Saida should come here, though. She transplanted them, after all, so she would understand them better."

Falrie paused and something glistened in her eyes. "Unfortunately, Saida has had trouble hearing magic lately."

"Oh." Verrity's mouth dropped open. "Oh, dear. I didn't know."

"We haven't exactly announced it to the public."

"Do you think it's because of . . ." Verrity jerked her head at the sky.

"We don't know, but that is the outlying variable." Falrie rubbed at her temples, tangling her hair in the process. She frowned and combed out the knot with her fingers. "She could always speak to and hear magic, even though Darrow and I never did and it didn't stop us from trimming overgrowths. But now that she can't hear them, she can't trim overgrowths either, for some reason." The foxan sighed. "I wish I knew what to do to help."

"You always know what to do. In the Council." Verrity bit her lip. "All the foxans do. Even Tener."

"You're not as observant as you think, if you think I have it all together."

Verrity blinked. "So . . . if even you're not sure what the best thing is, how do you *look* like you do?"

Falrie laughed. "It comes with responsibility. You move forward, even if you question yourself. Project strength when you don't feel it. Because no one knows what the right thing is, but someone must make decisions. We're just the ones who must make them."

Verrity stared at the Primal Plane, absorbing that along with all the magic floating around them.

As soon as Verrity left, Paras delegated all her duties to Ishira, who had shared the burden of sneaking those damn otherworlders food and supplies these last months. "I'll fix this," Paras said. "We can't keep feeding them. Not after the mob ruined our crop."

Ishira clutched Paras's hands, her mouth a grim line.

Her daughter, Miera, peeked at Paras behind her mother's skirt. "Will you make the bad people go away?"

Paras crouched down to the little girl's level. Ishira had wrapped her daughter's braided hair in a crown around her head, twined with nonflowers. "I'm gonna do my best."

She grabbed an overcoat to ward against the Anthem winter, crept to the Portal Station, waited an extra ten minutes—her anxiety mitigated by the refreshing energy the portals generated—and stepped through to Sound. She'd visited Anthem a few months back along with the most of Tremain, guided by a few locals to gain her safety certificate for the largest city on all the worlds. The rest of Tremain's villagers had huddled together and barely listened to the guide, but she had floated through the city and craned her neck to see down every street, absorbing every bit of information as a dusty field would absorb a summer rain.

The guard waved her on with half a glance, handing her two sound cloths as he skimmed her paper. Perhaps he recognized her from her recent expedition with Saida. "Stay in the city," he called after her.

As if they could do anything about it if she tried to leave. No walls surrounded Anthem. But she had a meeting with someone in the city.

The overall sound, of course, overpowered the smells, but Paras couldn't help but use both sound cloths for her nose instead of her ears, the cheap soap used to clean them stinging her sinuses. The foxans had assembled the Portal Station in the middle of Anthem, between the sides of straiter and piper.

Though frost lined the windowpanes and snow covered the ground, the children scuttled around in rags, a few of them smudged with dirt or maybe . . . something else. A few corner singers sang out: "Latest from the Council! We have plans to stop the Hunger!" She didn't see many adults, until she turned down the next street and encountered a line of people trudging towards one of the factories.

Right. Everyone here spends their time doing things in exchange for those things called notes. The concept of those little slips of paper to trade for food or goods had confused her the first time she'd visited. Why couldn't they just trade a few chicken eggs or potatoes for what they wanted?

Of course, most things wouldn't grow in the city. Whoever had built the houses had crammed them close enough that no one had a yard. The sludge in the streets, however, deserved the label of field— judging from her sensitive nose, it had plenty of uncovered fertilizer from the pack animals pulling things to the market. She doubted anyone had ever raked it clean.

A stumbling drunk exited a larger building on the corner, clutching a guitar. They set the instrument against the curb with a meticulousness that belied their inebriation, then promptly retched into the street. The sound and stench of it triggered Paras's gag reflex and she almost vomited as well.

Two people left the same bar a few moments later. They groaned at the sight of the drunk man. "Aw, Ibon," one of them said. "When'll you learn that three's your limit?"

"S'not," Ibon said. "I's just clearing my head, s'all."

"C'mon." The two of them grabbed the drunk man under his arms and dragged him off under Ibon's protestations, their eyes sliding over Paras, none too clearheaded themselves.

The encounter reminded Paras of that horrifying day when the three otherworlders had charged into Tremain's fields a couple months ago, one of them carrying a limp body in a bag, perhaps a dead person, over their shoulder.

Verrity had been off at a Council meeting, and the three otherworlders had demanded a hidden house and supplies of Ishira, the first person they'd found. Paras, overseeing the workers that day and hearing this, had rushed over and retorted that they could march themselves right back to the Portal Station.

One of them had said, *Clef said you might say that. He has an army of cage fighters, you know. And he'll kill every man, woman, and child in this piss-poor village—unless you hide us. And keep your mouths shut.*

They hadn't seemed the sharpest citruses in the basket, considering that if they had really wanted to hide themselves, they'd done a pitiable job by announcing it around so many villagers in the field. She'd almost said so to their faces, but then the name they'd threatened her with had registered.

Verrity had told her horror stories of this Clef. He'd served that giant shadow monster, the one that had Consumed Mother Rean last year. The Council had searched for him ever since he'd disappeared after the Reconnection, but he'd vanished. Stories had spread all over from Anthem into Tremain as well, stories of how he had directed Soundians to fight each other in brutal cage matches, and how he had a network of people forced to work for him out of fear for their own loved ones.

So, she'd done as they requested. She'd led them to the abandoned cabin past the Garden, kept her mouth shut, and told the others to do the same. When they'd expressed guilt over excluding Verrity from the situation, she'd explained how her sister would involve the Council and how Clef would murder them for doing so.

She strode on with a blank face, like she'd taught herself to do, keeping her darker emotions off her face, safe from her sister's empathic eyes in her mind. Those eyes that said, *You can trust me. I've been through enough to know.*

Walking helped. Moving helped, like it always did. She passed a few half-built houses with a strange, even-lined sediment instead of mud and straw. Verrity had mentioned something about Anthem trying to bridge the gap between the city's two sides. But the houses ended almost as soon as they'd begun.

Paras followed signs for the piper district, and the slurry-filled streets bloomed to clean brick shoveled of snow, and any children clung to their mothers or fathers. Someone had planted lines of trees between the houses and on the edges of busy streets to mute the mayhem of the marketplaces and the upscale bars with musicians on little stools tuning their instruments. She breathed a little easier, though a chill wind started up.

Where does their food come from? She didn't remember from her whirlwind tour of Anthem the last time around. Her excitement hadn't drowned out her overstimulation at all the sounds and the music displayed for them on every corner. She tried to follow the directions on the other piece of paper she had in her pocket, but she'd never aspired to much reading before, and she had to piece out the letters one by one. She followed the directions past a field where the snow lay in pretty drifts, with two large barns, each big enough to feed all of Tremain. As she passed, a few workers opened one of the barn doors, revealing gleaming bins of harvested wheat.

So, they did grow their own food here. But just on the piper side? Paras shook her head. She much preferred exploring open spaces and not worrying about why people did the things they did. She fumbled with the paper and tried to read out the next set of directions.

"Past the . . . harv . . . harvested fields. Take a left." Paras hurried on, her breath fogging in front of her like a visible scent. She didn't know how long she had before Verrity returned from her task with the foxan.

After a wrong turn, she followed a winding brick road that reminded her of Scent's wilds, removed from the loudness of the chaotic city. A thick hedge lined the road covered by a layer of glittering, untouched snow. Her footsteps echoed in the cold air. The path curved to the right and there in front of her loomed a house so large, Paras didn't know if she could call it a house. The closest thing in Tremain they had to this was the barn where they held their dances, but this was the farthest thing from a barn. Shapely columns of intricate stone buttressed a roofed wrap-around porch. The house resembled a cake with three distinct layers, each a little smaller than the one underneath. At the top, a golden rod pointed at the sky. This, Paras remembered from her first tour of Anthem, signified wealth and prosperity, the symbol of the pipers. They hadn't toured to this house, though.

She crept forward, trying to preserve the straightness of her back, and arrived at a stone gate, where a little bell hung. With trepidation hastened by the knowledge that she ran short on time, she rang it.

A guard popped out above the wall, peering down at her. "State your name and word of invitation."

"P-Paras. Um, the word she gave me was 'silence.'"

"You may pass." The guard disappeared behind the wall again, and for a moment, nothing happened.

Are they laughing at me behind the wall—

A crack in the stone appeared, and a door swung open. She slunk through it, and it shut behind her with a quiet snick. The guard had disappeared inside a small stone room on top of the wall. She guessed that indicated she should keep walking and not worry someone would whistle a Sound knife in her back.

She reached the massive wrap-around porch and raised her hand to knock, but it opened before she could. Inside, a staircase wound up and up, paired with a delicate lattice railing painted white. The ground gave a little under her work boots. A huge white rug with no end spanned the entire ground of the opening room, up the staircase, and the hallway next to the stairs. Someone must have stitched it together from several of the same animal.

A woman in a black silk dress stood there, holding out her hands. Paras didn't know what to do, but the woman pointed at her overcoat, and so Paras shrugged it off and gave it to her. The woman bowed, told her to remove her boots, and showed her to an adjoining room filled with chairs and a short table the height of Paras's knees. In here, too, a rug covered the floor, and even the walls. She felt surrounded by large animals, somehow, by a flock of swanseizes, perhaps, though swanseizes didn't live on Sound, at least that she knew. The rug muffled her footsteps. The woman in the silk dress gestured for her to sit, and Paras did. A fire roared in the hearth, heating the room. A different servant in all black carried in a tray of powdered pastries and poured tea into two transparent glasses.

Linia entered the room a few minutes later, after Paras had begun to sweat. She held her hair off her neck to cool herself.

"My dear, I'm so glad you could make it." The Soundian also wore all silk, so different from the silver buoy suit they had both worn on the expedition. Her white dress clung to her thin frame with a delicate elegance that made the skintight manner of the Touchian suit seem austere, and silver jewels sparkled at her throat and ears. "You haven't touched the sweets. Try them! They won't bite."

Paras reached for one of the pastries. "I can't stay. I have an hour, maybe, before I need to be back. So, we can talk about what you mentioned on the expedition."

Linia sipped tea from her glass. "Ah, well. Can't have your sister—or should I call her Mother Verrity? —knowing what you're up to? Probably for the best, or the Council would have a fit. It seems silly, considering what a terrible time we've had of it."

"It—it was terrifying—"

"What was terrifying?"

"Um." Paras swallowed the rest of the pastry. "Well, what everyone's been saying, of course. The huge hole in the sky. And then the people, trampling our crops."

"There it is." Linia set down her glass. It plinked on the tea set platter and the sound muffled in the fur-covered room. "I'm not afraid of some strange moon in the sky. I'm afraid of what happens when those addled by fear crash through my door."

Paras held the glass of tea in her hand, staring at the salmon-pink liquid inside. "Our fields had just sprouted, so we have to plant all over again."

Linia clucked her tongue. "That's a shame. And the Council refuses to do anything to stop them. They're all about 'papers' and 'expeditions to build empathy.' While people like you and I tremble in our homes and deal with the ramifications from those animals!"

Paras hesitated. "I wouldn't call them *animals*. I just . . . it's just frustrating. I just want to explore the other worlds. I want to keep doing the expeditions! But now, I have to stay and help plant the fields again." She sounded petulant even to her own ears, and she pressed her lips together.

"Ah," Linia said. "And there's the crux of it. It's only fair that some of those who destroyed your fields help plant it again. I have some in my employment more than willing to right those wrongs."

Paras hunched her shoulders, her blonde hair curtaining around her. Sweat trickled down her back. "Tremain wouldn't want help. They're even more scared of otherworlders now."

Linia tapped her chin. "What if I placed the offer before the Council? Then it's not just you convincing them, it's your sister, the Council member. She will see the benefit. It's for the good of your village, anyway, to ensure a plentiful harvest, and for you, so you could go on adventures." She paused. "The kind of adventure Verrity is having right now, in places like the Primal Plane."

"Verrity is helping the foxans keep us safe." The words flew out swift and defensive and rote. She'd felt what Linia had pointed out many times and had combatted it in her own head often enough that the words slipped out like a trained response. She didn't want to think about Verrity right now, how her sister had said *I wish we could trade places.* But then, why hadn't she? Why hadn't she asked Paras if she wanted to be the delegate, so Paras could be the one to visit those other places? Verrity had become the Mother of Tremain, why did she also have to be their village's representative to all those fascinating, explorable worlds?

My Ver, my Par, their mother used to say, in her singsong voice. *The very pair of daring!*

At six years old, Paras had pole vaulted across the mountain stream, soaring as high and as daring as a swanseize in spring, but the bank had crumbled under her, and she'd plummeted into the rushing water. At seven years old, Verrity had dashed in and dragged Paras out. When her sister didn't lock herself in her own mind about how others viewed her, she acted with confidence. That had always been their dynamic: Paras expended her bravery like it would sour if it stayed inside her, like fruit rotting on a counter, using it as soon as she had any, while Verrity saved hers over years, storing it in jars in a cellar in her heart, and only used it when she needed to save someone.

But if Verrity spent her precious bravery to drag Paras out of this mess using the Council, she could die. Clef could slaughter everyone in Tremain. The stream had grown too large to vault over. It would drag all of them down. Paras had to figure out a way that would keep them safe. She couldn't trade places with Verrity, not now.

In the room covered in white, silence pronounced itself louder. Linia sipped her tea. Her smile reminded Paras of the sharp-edged shells in Touch, hollow and delicate, and creases appeared around her lips like arrows pointing outwards.

Paras set her tea glass down. "Why do you care, anyway? Why would my adventuring do anything for you?" She paused. Linia had asked the foxan, Saida, about magic items back on the expedition. "You want me to find magic trimmings for you somehow, don't you?"

"Well, perhaps I would have a few days ago." Linia nibbled on a pastry. The powder sifted down onto her dress, but it disappeared white on white. "I wanted magical items to sell, to ensure my estate's safety. But now I have another way to do that. You remember that inscription the Touchian guide found inside the cavern?" Paras nodded. "The 'increaser' it mentioned, I believe, refers to an amplifier. It increases magical ability. That advanced city must have one, considering the inscription mentioned it. Just one exists that I know of, and Clef, the straiter leader, has it."

Paras winced.

"You see why I need one, then, in case of . . . extreme situations. I just want to protect myself, since the Council refuses to protect the person funding most of their expeditions." She raised an eyebrow plucked to perfection. "There is the bonus that, if you find me an amplifier, I could protect more than just my estate. I could protect the entire city of Anthem. I could make them return to their homes, instead of raiding yours."

Paras tried to keep her hands steady in her lap, beads of sweat running down her neck. Adventure, away from the monotony of the village, all while finding a way to protect it from Clef? She flushed with the fantasy of it.

"Of course, you must convince your sister without her catching on. I doubt the Council would allow me to search for what I want. Which is, of course, ridiculous, when I just want to protect myself and others." She gestured to the room. "I've gone to great lengths to soundproof my estate, but I can only do so much against a straiter leader with the entire straiter side of Anthem as a potential army."

"Why don't you go?" Paras trembled with the desire to say yes.

Linia sighed and brushed the white powder off her lap. "Though I had high aspirations to do so, after what happened on Touch, I . . . well, let's just say I no longer harbor any illusion to my desire for adventure." Those creases appeared again at her lips. "I need someone brave to go for me."

"I'll do it." The words spilled out before she could snatch them back. She'd wanted this her whole life, and she could protect Tremain at the same time.

And if the Hunger did consume their whole world, well, at least she would have done something fun before that happened.

"Wonderful!" Linia clapped her hands. "I'll handle the arrangements. Verrity should tell you the good news soon."

8

THE LUNNITES

S aida woke up curled into the crook of Alesio's arm, his shoulder her pillow, and lingered in the languorous feeling of relaxed, heavy muscles. She never, ever wanted to get up. Tricksy Stone's light shone in the dark of the concert hall, glistening above them like a tiny sun.

Alesio hadn't been upset about Tricksy Stone. He hadn't been angry that she missed her magic items. He'd voiced uncertainty if her hearing the voices would help her, but she could understand that. She didn't know, herself. But knowing that he didn't feel anger that she missed what she sacrificed for him had given her so much relief.

Then he had brought up her moving in again, in a way where he seemed to try to reduce the pressure of it. That had ironically increased the pressure for her, because she could tell it mattered to him that much more.

It would mean something different from spending the night once a week and kissing and cuddling before drifting off to sleep. It meant she would always return there, every day, and wake up to him every day, and explore the world of sensual sensation that waited for them—

—Why did she recoil from that idea?

She'd laid awake many times in the Primal Plane, huddled in the big foxan ball with her parents and Tener, wishing that she'd gone to Alesio's house, wishing that she nestled next to him. Why didn't her reaction to his question match how she felt about him?

What if I change my mind later, though? I can't even sense magic anymore. I'm always changing, more than just my body, but my emotions, too! What if I shift in how I feel about him? What if things don't work out between us, and I need to leave him because I get scared, or I don't like him anymore, and then I hurt him by leaving?

What they had done the night before flashed through her mind. She blushed, and the heat banished her thoughts like the sunrise herding the shadows of trees.

Alesio's forehead creased, and without opening his eyes, he buried his face next to her neck. His breath tickled and she squeaked.

"Hmmm." He snuggled his face in her neck and brushed his lips under her ear, his voice sleepy and husky. His clean-shaven face felt smooth except for his trimmed beard, the shorter hairs rougher. "What's this? Smells wonderful."

"Ale—sio!" She crimped her neck. "That tickles!"

He tugged on her earlobe with his lips. She giggled, light tingles running all through her. He skated his lips and teeth along her jaw, and she gasped, the tingles thickening to a stream of heat shooting through her core.

"A-Alesio!"

He swung his leg to her other side so that he hovered over her with effortless control. How was restrained power so attractive? He *could* push himself on her and pin her down—his chest might as well have been made of bricks, for all she could move him, but she never feared he would. He held himself back and waited for her cues. The control and the respect melted her insides like butter on a hot day.

He paused against her ear. Waiting for her to move first.

She turned her face to meet his lips and pushed up, pressing against him, and he groaned. His tongue flicked out and probed the seam of her lips. Heat pulsed inside her as if she'd grown a second heart made of fire. She opened her lips, but he licked them like frosting on a cake. She couldn't think and she wanted more. She wanted what they had done the other night. She nipped at his tongue, and he snickered. "Impatient, are we?"

She thrust her tongue at his lips, and he parted them for her. His tongue met hers in the way that she wanted, and they tasted each other. She *murred* deep in her throat. She hadn't made the strange vibration sound before a few months ago, hadn't even known she could, and now she couldn't seem to stop around him.

"I swear, that's my favorite sound." He pulled back and stared at her, at her mouth, and she stared back, wishing she could see the silver of his tenor, that base magic he created just by speaking.

She panted, rising to press herself against him. "Why is kissing with tongue so *fun?*"

He cupped the back of her head and lowered them both onto the seats. "Like this?"

He thrust his tongue into her mouth, and she almost screamed with pleasure. She arched her back, and he wrapped her waist with his other arm, pressing her to him. Pleasure crashed through her like waves breaking on rocks, and he thrust his tongue in her mouth back and forth, back and forth, and she writhed under him like the shore meeting the tide, and nothing, nothing, nothing else mattered.

Alesio jerked his head up. A few seconds later she heard the footsteps on the small, velveted staircase.

Alesio hummed a quick Sound bubble around them to contain their noise, but he could do nothing about the way their loud breathing and her little moans already echoed through the massive concert hall.

The footsteps stopped. "Ah, well, though I was right to check up here for you both, it seems I was also very, very *wrong* to check here."

Through the haze of sensation, Saida recognized the voice as Estro, the Cadenza's guard.

"When you are both presentable, you should come outside. Something has happened." The doors whispered closed, and in the amplification of the Cadenza, his muttered words sounded in their ears: "Probably gonna have to clean those seats."

As Estro's footsteps dwindled around them, they pulled apart. Saida's heart still pounded, and her body didn't understand why they had stopped. But the guard's words had punctured the glaze of sensation: *Something has happened.*

"What could it be now?" Alesio sighed and ran his hands through his mussed black hair. He helped Saida off the seats and they both straightened their rumpled clothing. He was wearing the silver shirt she'd told him matched the color of his magic, what he'd worn for the performance last night. "Can we get one day without something happening?"

"I wonder what it is." Saida pressed her hands to her lips. They buzzed, yearning for friction. She scrubbed her knuckles against them to stop the sensation. "Maybe more panicking citizens?"

"I hope not." He pressed a kiss to the top of her head.

She wanted to reach for him again but knew that she'd just lose herself in the song of his mouth and tongue. She placated herself with holding his hand as they proceeded outside the concert hall to the outside. The sun shone high and bright as they stepped out. They had slept in.

Then the quiet filtered through.

Anthem was not a quiet city, as the magic of the world amplified everything, but right now, not a whisper of someone hawking their wares in the street or even anyone playing an instrument sounded.

She blinked. A crowd surrounded the Cadenza. Many of them had foxan snouts. Some had fur poking out of their clothing at their wrists and necks. Their clothing, woven with plant fibers, blanketed their bodies, and some wore scarves around their necks. Some had tails, or ponytails like Saida's where their long hair transformed into a kind of tail with fur, wrapped in the same plant fibers. Over fifty fox-people bowed in front of the Cadenza, and they all chanted:

"Oh, Envoy of the Goddess, we pay homage!"

ONE OF THEM STEPPED FORWARD, a tall and broad-shouldered fox-person with foxan ears and long brown hair that swept into a tail, which he had gathered in a long headscarf and wrapped all the way down. Fur coated his cheeks like sideburns and wore simple trousers with reeds for a belt and a rough shirt that covered his arms. His bright green gaze flicked to Alesio and narrowed. "We ask to speak with the Envoy alone."

Hell, no.

"I'm probably not who you want to speak with," Saida said. "My mother is the foxan representative for the Council." She paused. "Are you all from Sound?"

"We wish to speak with you, the Envoy who reconnected the Planes."

A crowd of Soundians had also gathered around the fox-people like clouds caught on a mountaintop. Silence with this many people had quite a jarring effect.

"Oh. Well, I didn't do it alone. Alesio helped with his Sound magic. You might have heard his voice as the Voice of Reconnection last year?" She gestured at him. The one who had stepped forward pursed his lips into a thin line, scanning Alesio up and down. "If you want to speak with me, you can speak with him, too."

"This is acceptable," the fox-person said. "May we enter?"

Saida and Alesio glanced at Estro, who nodded. "Just a few."

The fox-person pivoted and spoke with a few other members of the group. Two others stepped forward, a woman with a foxan snout and burnt orange fur along her forehead, and another, older man with paws instead of hands and a grizzled, coarse beard who wore a long cloak knitted with plant fibers. They shivered in the frigid cold.

"This way." Saida motioned inside, and they trailed into the Cadenza behind her.

Is this some kind of trick? Will they try to kidnap her and worship her in that cult of theirs? Alesio met Estro's eyes and inclined his head at the crowd in a wordless: *watch them.*

Estro gave a measured nod and stayed outside. Everyone else filed inside, Alesio leading them to a side room where musicians warmed up their voices before performances.

Alesio readied his Sound magic. He didn't like this. He had to stop himself from setting his chair in front of Saida. Instead, he arranged their chairs so he and Saida faced all three of them, so he could read all their lips if he didn't catch all their words. Saida navigated to his right without him having to ask.

Fox-people can't use human magic, he reminded himself. *They can't sing a Sound knife at her or anything like that.*

Just because they had both human and foxan traits didn't mean anything. Saida shifted parts of herself all the time. Might one try to teleport her away? Or, the Sound forbid, could Clef have sent them?

He shook his head. That last one seemed a little far-fetched, considering they were fox-people.

The three of them bowed to Saida. The woman with the foxan snout situated on his far left spoke. She had a thin voice like a whistle, even harder for him to hear. "It is – honor to meet the Envoy – reconnected the Planes. We thank you."

"I just did what was necessary." Saida fiddled with her braid, perched on the stool by the piano. She'd started doing that more and more lately. "Now, who are you, and what do you want to talk about?"

"My name is Marik," the younger fox-man with the human facial features said. He pointed at the fox-woman and the older fox-man. "This is Etha, and he's Tosn. We are Lunnites from Touch. We want to help you find the Goddess Lunne."

Alesio frowned.

Saida shifted on her stool. "I . . . that's a lot to process. What are 'Lunnites?' What Goddess?"

Etha pointed at herself, then at the other two newcomers. "— Lunnites." Alesio didn't turn to her fast enough to catch the first part of Etha's sentence. "We descend from foxans, the Envoys of the Foxan Goddess Lunne. Others have called us 'fox-people.'"

"Oh," Saida said. "And . . . you want to find this Goddess? How do you do something like that?"

"We are loath to speak any more of our secrets in front of someone not of our race." Tosn, the older Lunnite, folded his paws back into the sleeves of his cloak.

"Aren't you descended from both human and foxan, though?" Alesio said. "So technically, humans are your race, too."

The three Lunnites glared at him loud and clear.

"We are not the same." Marik's tall, pointed ears flattened on top of his head.

"Didn't say that."

"Well," Saida said, "If you tell me whatever you know, you should know I will tell him whatever you say." She grasped his hand, and their three pairs of eyes zeroed in on the touch. "We are together, after all."

There was a pause.

"We will accept the Envoy's will." Tosn brought out something from a bag he carried, a rubbing of a stone carving with odd markings on it. "This script is ancient Lunnite, those foxans and their descendants before us who built the advanced city where call home. This stone speaks of our ancestors, along with other Lunnite civilizations across the worlds, trying to find a way to find the foxan Goddess, Lunne, herself. Sadly, we know no more about how, as time claimed most of the carvings in that city. And yet!"

He raised his arms and smiled at the close ceiling, his claws extending out. "The Goddess has smiled on us, as the Envoy reopened the portals, and we can now search for the ruins of other Lunnite cities across the worlds and find out how they searched for the Goddess!"

Alesio's mouth had dropped open, and he closed it with a click. The carving Muey had translated had mentioned an ancient, advanced city on Touch. "By the Sound."

Etha wrinkled her snout. "There is no Sound god. There – only Lunne."

"It's just a phrase, lady. I don't know if I believe in any god, let alone this one you just told us about."

Saida's eyes had glazed over. He chafed her hand, panic cutting through him like a Sound knife. "Hey. Hey, you okay?"

She refocused. Relief washed over him, and he swiveled back to the Lunnites, who glared at him again.

He gave them his "I don't care what you think" grin. "Well, if you're so excited about this, why didn't you come forward last year, when the Reconnection occurred?"

"It was . . . difficult to leave our hiding place." Tosn folded his paws back inside his cloak. It seemed a nervous tic. "We have a secret place on Touch to avoid the humans, as they have a manic, demented worship of both Lunnite and foxan kind. We have hidden ourselves for many generations."

"I understand," Saida said.

She alluded to Carn, a Touchian who had imprisoned Saida for five years under the guise of reverence for her foxan-ness and a twisted obsession for her. When she'd first told Alesio what Carn had done, she'd used the phrase, "he wouldn't stop petting me." About five months after she and Alesio had been together, she'd admitted what he'd suspected all along. Carn had assaulted her sexually.

Anger spiked inside of Alesio, and he controlled his breathing. At least the man was dead. Saida had ended up having to kill him to escape his psychological hold over her, which he had convinced her was love at the time.

Though Carn had acted alone, other Touchians had known about it and done nothing, and a few had used her in her captivity to point them towards magical areas and items. Alesio had asked pointed questions around Touch to find the others involved, and he had made it clear none of them would go anywhere near Saida. He'd also told the Council what they had done, and the Council had ruled that none of the extremists could become a delegate. Xen, the current delegate, hailed from a different shelter several miles from the pod cult that had imprisoned her, and though he had a definite worshipful attitude towards Saida and the other foxans, never once had he tried to use or confine her.

"—very concerned when the void appeared in our sky a few days ago." Etha hunched her shoulders. "We decided to overcome our apprehension, because now contacting the Goddess has become more of an urgent matter. She could stop this Hunger."

"What about the Epitaphs?" Saida leaned forward on her stool, her foxan ears pricking forward. "Do you know why they began emanating such strong magic energy? Do they speak to you?"

Marik cocked his head, his swathed hair-tail swinging over his shoulder and twitching upwards at the end. "Do they speak to *you?* How wondrous!"

Saida wilted on her stool. "No . . . no. I just hoped."

Alesio wished he could help her, but how could he protect her from her own grief? At least he'd asserted his concerns about the magic voices, and she hadn't seemed upset by that. She'd even agreed to live with him, though it had seemed a stretch for her. He didn't know what else to do to help her, and he *hated* that feeling of having nothing to give, of empty hands while someone he loved suffered in front of him. He should do something. Anything.

"They are strong magics," Tosn said. "I do not know if they can speak. I would believe they can. But we have not sensed such a thing yet. We will, of course, inform you if it changes."

Saida nodded, looking down, her braid morphing into more of a tail with fur instead of hair. The three Lunnites' eyes widened at her, then they all jerked their gazes away as if she had stripped bare in front of them.

The Lunnites waited for one of them to speak. He could do that, at least. "The Council will want to know about all this. Especially with what we found on Touch."

"—did you find?" Etha asked.

Alesio glanced at Saida, who still drooped on her stool. "We found the ruins of a Touchian village, down in a cave. A carving said the people there had left to search for a city called "Sedella." Is this the city you know of?"

The Lunnites glanced at each other. "It is the same," Tosn said.

Marik rose and bowed to Saida. He stood half a head higher than most fox-people at almost six feet, though Alesio had him beat by an inch or so. "If you wish to study these magics, we have one in our city. Would you like to visit?"

She jerked her head up, her eyes bright. "I sensed another weaker one on Touch, so I figured it would take weeks or months to reach. How did you travel here so fast?"

"We know the world of Touch well." Marik smiled at her. "We will show you the way."

Alesio jutted out his chin, his jaw flexing. He placed a hand on Saida's back. "Can we speak outside?"

She started. "What? Oh. Yes." She smiled at the Lunnites. "Just give us a minute, okay?"

They both sidled out of the small practice room back out to the main foyer. Alesio puffed out a Sound bubble so they could talk in privacy.

"I don't trust them," Alesio said. "I think they're hiding something."

Saida glanced back toward the practice room. "I don't believe the gibberish about the Goddess. But, Alesio, the other Epitaph! Maybe—I mean, I haven't heard St. Rina's voice. But the other Epitaphs might be stronger. Maybe I could hear them speak, and they might help us figure out what to do about the Hunger. Plus, we'd find out more about that strange city on Touch."

Alesio gnawed on the inside of his lip, still holding his breath. "I . . . I don't know. I don't understand how the Epitaphs could help us, even if they do—I mean, if you hear them again."

"They're old, Alesio. Ancient foxans older than my parents. They might have dealt with something like the Hunger before and chased it off. They for sure know more than we do."

"I don't like leaving you alone with these people. We don't know them, and they're a little too obsessed with foxans for my peace of mind."

He didn't say anything about the ugly jealousy that had roiled in his stomach. Marik's words had brightened her face while despondence took hold of her around Alesio. His petty jealousy wouldn't help, at all, so he hid it in the shadow of his first concern.

"I'll be fine," she said. "They're different from the cult. They're fox-people—I mean, Lunnites, I guess." She paused. "What if Naya came along? They'd probably accept her, she's another fox-person, or Lunnite, or whatever, after all."

Sounddamn it, that was a good idea.

What if you don't take care of yourself? What if you drift again, fracture again, and forget about me?

"Saida, are *we* alright?"

She rose on her tiptoes and kissed him on the cheek. "I know you want to protect me, so protect me in the way you feel is best. By finding Clef. I know you won't feel safe until then."

You *won't be safe until then.*

He bowed his head. "He'll have the advantage in Flock."

She searched his eyes as if he were new a world she'd teleported to, taking in the clouds, the darkness. She laid a hand on his arm. "I know what it is to avoid a place out of fear. Senses, I've avoided entire worlds before. And I don't like the idea of you going near Clef, either. But you can't let that fear stop you from doing what you know needs doing."

He hated this, that they had to separate to achieve their different goals. But she had her path, and he had his. He wouldn't let her tag along with him to hunt down Clef, at any rate. "If we're not together during the day, or if you have to travel with them for a while, we might not see each other for a while."

"I didn't forget." She tapped his arm. "I'm moving into your place tomorrow, okay?"

He smiled down at her. "That does help."

9
SEPARATE WAYS

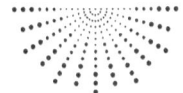

S aida, Naya, and Marik had lined up in the Portal Station in front of the Sound-Touch portal. They couldn't group more than two side by side, because the Touch magic users had built strategic barriers that controlled access to the portals.

The Council had agreed that Saida could hunt for clues about the strange, advanced cities, starting with the one on Touch called Sedella. From what Saida gathered, the Lunnites had hidden from humans for generations in Sedella's ruins. She'd searched for fox-people for so long, and they had their own *city*.

It's amazing the difference a few days can make, Saida thought. Just three days before, Soundians had shoved through the Portal Station in a panic. Now, almost no one lined up to leave. Anyone trying to leave Anthem didn't just have to wait in a simple line. They had to shuffle between two high, narrow wooden walls with gates that opened to the individual departure portals on the dais. The barriers also helped break the bitterness of the wind. Little flurries of snow had just started, sticking to everyone's cheeks and eyelashes.

Tener bounced in front of her, sticking out their lower lip. "But Saida, I don't want you to go! Who will I eat cinnamon olos with?"

They lowered their voice. "What if . . . what if our string starts to tear?"

Saida's throat swelled at the softness of their question, in volume and in content. She ruffled their huge, dark brown foxan ears. "It doesn't matter how far apart we are, okay? Nothing can change how much I love you."

Tener bobbed their head up and down, rubbing their ears against her hand. She laughed and scratched their ears. She bent closer to whisper, "Also, Alesio's dad is a big softie. He'll go with you for olos anytime you like."

"Really?" Tener's gaze shot to Alesio, who rechecked their packs behind them.

"She's right," Alesio said, trying not to stare at Tener. She'd explained to him before about Tener's startling growth spurt and that they seemed shy about it. "Unfortunately."

A few Soundians lined up behind them for the Touch portal. "What's the hold up?" one asked, a middle-aged woman with her hands on her hips, hauling a basket on her back stuffed with blank paper, a rare material on Touch.

Muey, the portal guard for Sound-Touch, said, "The Summit is close to the exit point. No passage till it passes. Five minutes."

The Lunnite, Marik, paced in front of the portal as if he wanted to leave right away and damn the Wave. Saida understood his urgency. She'd jumped at the chance to find a new Epitaph. Now that the time had come, though, exploring with a stranger who had announced he and the rest of his people considered her an intermediary for a Goddess made her jumpy in the bad kind of way. But she couldn't let Alesio know that, not when he already didn't like the situation. He stayed quiet as he fiddled with her bag, having packed and repacked it twice now as they waited.

The rest of the Lunnites crowded around the Portal Station's barriers. Tak and Muey had waved them away from clogging up the queue. They had requested the Council to allocate them guides, so they could search for the advanced cities in other worlds at once.

Tak ushered a line of people through to Taste while checking safety certifications. He'd removed the bandage from his head.

"How long will you be gone again?" Tener pulled on Saida's arm, then reached for Naya so they could hold her hand, too. Naya hadn't worn a hood to cover her distinctive foxan muzzle. Her eyes flicked around every so often, watching the crowd.

"The trip will take a few days, at least." Marik dipped his head at the young foxan, his long hair sweeping back and forth like a tail. Unlike Saida and Naya, who wore the close-fitting silver buoy suits to guard against the overstimulation of Touch, he wore the same clothing made of woven plant fibers as when he'd shown up with the other Lunnites, which covered his arms and legs and hair-tail.

"Won't that be scratchy on Touch?" she asked Marik.

He shook his head. "We oil the fibers to keep them soft and supple, and so that they last longer."

"Huh."

Tener tugged on her arm again.

"You heard him! I won't be gone long." Saida gave a mock groan. "You're going to portal my arm out of its socket."

Naya tickled Tener under their arms and they giggled and squirmed. She set them down. "Now, listen here. I have something very important for you to do while we're gone."

Tener perked up, dark brown eyes wide, their black hair curling behind their ears. They grabbed the excess of their loose fur-pants as if standing at attention. They tended to produce their foxan clothing with lots of extra space around their body.

"I need you to take care of Darrow and Falrie for me, okay?" Naya chucked them under the chin. "They think they know everything, 'cause they're so old, but they need help crossing the worlds sometimes. Can you handle this job?"

Tener straightened and lifted their chin. "Yes, Ma'am!'"

Thank the Senses Naya had agreed to come along. She had such a soothing, competent presence. Saida stood a little straighter at her words, too. She wouldn't be alone on this journey.

"Alright, you're good to go." Alesio surveyed the packs, then pointed out one that had all its contents out to Saida. "Has all the essentials, but not too much that it'll weigh you down. Soothing balm, Liranel water, so it should last you longer, extra buoy suit—"

She kissed him and stuffed everything into the various fur pockets she grew around her waist. "It's perfect. Thank you."

"Stay safe." His voice stayed level, but his stance shifted lower to the ground like a fighter, as if he could do battle against the fact of her leaving.

She rose up and nestled her head against his neck, breathing in his petrichor scent, loving how it grounded her like she was the rain and he was the soil. "I'll be fine."

The hole in the sky loomed closer, today. As each day waned in Anthem, the world revolved the city away from the Hunger, but every morning, that Hunger remained. That little bit sticking out had grown, stretching and curling around the hole like a claw or arm, and another island in the sphere of obscurity had rotated into view; the largest one in the center, like the pupil of an eye. Vision remained its jagged, lavender self, joined now by the sapphire and emerald Scent. Neither of them seemed different, but she had no way of knowing how long any of the worlds had before the Hunger reached for them —or what would happen when they did.

The Epitaphs might know what to do. She for sure did not. And since her parents' memories remained spotty fragments, she had nowhere else to turn for knowledge.

She'd cared for the Sensory Plane her whole life. This mission extended beyond her personal desire to find the Epitaphs just to try and hear them speak. She needed to do her job and keep the worlds healthy and growing. That included pest control—even of the cosmic variety.

"We've stopped a monster before, Alesio. We can do this."

He jerked his head in a nod, his jaw tightening.

She and Naya stepped forward with Marik, through the portal.

The volume in her ears decreased and her skin tingled. The air warmed from the temperature of winter to late fall, and the sky darkened. The middle of the night tiptoed here instead of early morning, the stars and moon and the world of Taste's light brown light shining down. Scent should show, too, but the Hunger had eclipsed it.

The insides of her shoes felt stiff here. She missed going barefoot. Wind whipped all around, and the Glass Sea dimpled into wavelets like it shivered from the cold.

The Summit Wave.

She wheeled around, and there it roared, moving away from them, moonlight and Taste's russet glow reflecting off its crest at least a half mile off. *Okay. Good. We just missed it.*

"That's good, it's not too far away," Marik said.

Naya chuffed through her muzzle. "For what, spitting in it?"

"Here's the tricky part." Marik's foxan ears angled in the Summit's direction like weathervanes. "I've never tried portaling to it before. But I trust you, Envoy. You can do it."

"What?" Saida gawked at the Lunnite. "Why would we portal *to* it?"

He grinned at her, his bright green eyes reflecting the celestial lights like a tiny world. "We surf the Summit Wave."

"*What?*"

"We surf the Summit Wave! But we should portal now. From what I understand about your teleporting powers, you have more accuracy if you can see where you're teleporting, right?"

"R-right, but—"

"I promise, it's how we travel! You can do it, Envoy!"

"Um, Naya?"

Naya jutted out her chin at the Lunnite, her voice clipped. "Marik. How do we stay on top of the Summit Wave once we're up there?"

"I'll use Touch magic to keep us up there."

"I thought fox-people—I mean, Lunnites—couldn't use magic," Saida said.

"How many Lunnites have you met?"

Saida's mouth hung open. She snapped it shut. "I guess, just a few. But why keep this all a secret?"

Marik shrugged. "We don't want to let humans know that some of us have magic or tell them how to traverse the world. It's dangerous enough here. If humans knew how to surf the Summit, then they'd just hunt us for another reason." He paused, eyeing the Wave. "We should do it now, or it'll flow too far away. Then we'd have to wait till next week."

"Hang on. One more thing." Naya perched her hands on her hips like irritated birds. "How will we get down once we're up there? Saida can only teleport once a day." She paused. "Don't tell me we'll be up there all day and night."

Saida hadn't thought of that. She slanted her ears backwards as she glanced at Marik.

"Oh, of course not!" Marik said. "Getting down is much easier than up. The Wave will shrink and . . . well, you'll see." He raised his eyebrows at Saida. "Are you ready?"

She rubbed her hands together and swallowed. "Oh . . . kay." She summoned a portal and told it where she wanted it to create a way. It zipped up through the ground, then up the Summit Wave, a tiny glimmering speck to her. It opened in front of her, showing a cacophony of spray below, surrounded by darkness.

"Ready!" She screamed.

Marik used Touch magic. A large water sled formed under their feet. Unmoving water, like Muey's water sleds. The board widened where she and Naya stood but remained slim under Marik's feet. It carried them all through the portal.

FOR ALL ALESIO'S COMPLAINTS, he didn't *hate* the Council. He just hated attending the meetings. Cobbling together a government with representatives from each world had had its challenges, and he, Saida, and Saida's parents had done their best over the past year. But Sounddamn, everything took so much longer now. He'd declined becoming the Sound delegate because he was a performer, not a leader.

The Council met once a week to vote on certain issues and update everyone on events. Alesio didn't attend except to inform the Council of salient details, like after he and Saida explored new parts of a world. Even so, he hadn't had time to follow up with his contact on Scent yet and had nothing of note to report. He would have skipped this one, except that he wanted to scrutinize Hestafon's speech and actions, now that his suspicions about the wealthy Soundian delegate had flared up.

He regretted that decision. He could probably have unearthed the proof he needed if he'd just shadowed Hestafon in his day-to-day activities; here, he had trouble focusing after the Council had quibbled for a scintillating hour and a half about rice.

The Council had gone over reparations from Sound to Taste, of which Balt had insisted on a certain amount of grain and rice, and a large sum of notes to pay off the produce they couldn't replace. Touch kept their crops inside their shelters or caverns, and Lavoa had already harvested most of their crops as their world had reached late fall. The Cloves received at least some crops from Liranel, the grassland village outside the salt-flats. Now the Council had moved on to Tremain, the small Scentian village where the crowds had trampled almost all the crops.

The foxans had worked hard, too. Darrow had checked on Flock, while Tener had visited Suln and Liranel, the two tiny villages on Scent and Taste.

Alesio sought Darrow out before the meeting to ask him how his trip had gone, but Saida's father had shaken his head. "I'm sorry, Alesio. I didn't find any sign of Clef. I was only there for a few hours, though, checking with the leader there, so I might have missed something."

Apparently, Flock had suffered no deaths. That had surprised Alesio, considering the shrikers could have committed any number of horrible things and blamed it on the chaos, not to mention it had the largest population on all the worlds outside of Anthem. The smaller communities of Suln and Liranel had fared better, much like Tremain.

As always, Alesio had sat on the log, the spot for non-Council delegates placed behind the semicircle of stumps. This stopped him from reading anyone's lips. He had trouble hearing Xen, the Touch delegate, on the far left.

Hestafon cleared his throat, garnering Alesio's attention. He'd eaten one of those hard candies he always had on hand. "A certain number of Soundians have offered reparations for the crops they trampled on Tremain. Twenty-three have volunteered to help with fieldwork for a few weeks. Verrity, would this offer be agreeable?"

I wonder how many of those 'volunteers' were straiters coerced by Linia or Hestafon.

Verrity, the delegate for Scent, stood. Her homespun dress hung on wide shoulders, and she spoke in a low pitch, but she folded her hands in front of her with a feminine air. "I am not sure if Tremain will accept help. Many of the villagers are upset about what happened." She paused. "However, without aid to plant more crops, our harvest will be very weak this fall. If Soundians enter our world with clean clothing and agree to follow our rules, I can probably convince them."

"So be it." Yashalis pointed with her cane. "Hestafon, if you will inform the group of volunteers, and on Verrity's final approval, they may go to Scent."

Hestafon bowed, the dark purple bows on his jacket fluttering with the aplomb of a particularly garish ghost.

"Let's move on to solutions," Yashalis said. "Most of the Lunnites have asked to disperse amongst the worlds, searching for more of these 'advanced cities,' as they term them. They will need guides. I know you all are stretched thin, but if you could each spare one guide, it might help Saida's efforts as well, to find somehow an ancient text or some old, advanced magic that might have a way to deal with the Hunger."

The Council dickered over who to send on each world and Alesio's eyes glazed over. His report regarding his search for Clef would evidently wait towards the end of the meeting. He practiced holding his breath. He could reach thirteen minutes now in normal situations, and six minutes while fighting or exercising.

Where is Saida right now? Is she safe? That Lunnite had gazed at her like she was the sun, and he just wanted to revolve around her. And she had sounded so excited, and her expression had animated with such a brightness.

He knew that the Lunnite's words had interested her, not his attention. He *knew* that. But his knowledge and his feelings had broken from their respective orbits, no longer aligning as they should, no longer traveling in predictable or suitable patterns.

Xen, the delegate for Touch, said something. Alesio blinked back to the present. "I just don't like that these . . . Lunnites appeared out of nowhere. Why now? Why not a year ago?"

"Who knows what they want," Balt said. "And one of our most powerful assets leaving without so much as a please and thank you."

"Order! Stop speaking out of turn, for the Senses' sake. The Lunnites gave multiple reasons they didn't show themselves before now. We should not allow fear of new people stop us from pursuing possible solutions." Yashalis pointed at the sky. "*That* is what we should fear."

The Hunger had grown a bit bigger, looming behind the five planets gleaming overhead in a star pattern, almost as large as Vision. Thin, spiraling streams had begun to eat into the space around the Hunger, like rays of anti-sunlight.

"Speaking of solutions, report. Verrity and Falrie, how goes the interrogation?"

Falrie and Verrity stood. "It responded," Falrie said. Everyone's heads swung towards the older foxan woman. "We told it we worshipped it. It laughed, and said, 'Do not think you can build a cage to trap me with words. You are all doomed. You will all become Consumed, in the end.' Then it returned to its standard chanting."

Cold dread finger-picked a terse arpeggio up and down Alesio's spine.

"This is ridiculous." Hestafon dipped his hand in his jacket, where he'd already grabbed two hard candies from, then drew it back out empty and held a hand to his heart. "We should not antagonize it further. What if it escapes from the tree? It could attack someone!"

Is he trying to protect it?

"We could ask it harsher questions," Xen said.

Yashalis rapped her cane on her stump. "Falrie and Verrity, continue trying to trick it into revealing something. Alesio, how goes your search for Clef?"

Finally. He stood. "I'm working on a lead. I haven't had time to follow up on them yet. Other things kept demanding my time, like endless Council meetings." He didn't want to reveal the details of that lead, like his contact in Scent, in case Hestafon worked for Clef and the Hunger.

"Fair point," Yashalis said dryly.

Hestafon shifted on his stump, like a lying liar would.

"Perhaps we could draw him out with some cage matches," Balt said.

Alesio's breath sharpened in his chest.

"That could work." Hestafon tapped his finger against his chin.

"Don't they earn a bit of coin—notes, I mean?" Balt said. "And then we could put the Palates that we captured to good use."

He referred to the few un-melted cannibals. Watthe had ironically Consumed most of the Palates, changing them into those gray, dead beings. In the end, the twisted and magic-crazed foxan had melted all the Consumed into sludge and merged them into his own body, fashioning a giant version of himself. A few of the cannibals had either refused to become Watthe's servants or had escaped the Consuming process, and Alesio had helped the Tastians capture and imprison them a few months back.

"No." Alesio clasped his hands in front of him to keep them from shaking. "We've worked hard to shut down all cage fights in Anthem. It would be unconscionable for them to spread to other worlds."

"They are *Palates*." Balt spread his hands. "They've rotted in our jails without any purpose, eating our food when they have stated they would like to eat us. We would have income from the spectacle, and you would have a trap to lure your strait's leader out. A win-win."

"No." Alesio crossed his arms, his teeth clenched. Thank the Sound he'd ended up attending this meeting, if anything, to snip this ghastly idea in the bud. "I have other plans in place."

"Alesio." Hestafon struggled for breath for some reason. "Just consider it. If you, as Requiem, made an appearance—"

"Like hell!"

"I only meant it as a way to help—"

"Help who? Help you secure your role as Clef's puppet?"

"Alesio," Yashalis said, her voice a low warning note.

Hestafon blinked, then raised his hand to his mouth, as if to clench his jaw manually. "Well, I never!"

"Never what?" Alesio's words kept pouring out of his mouth faster and faster, like how an audience that took over a song from a performer would increase the tempo. He stepped over the log and strode-floated towards the piper. "Never had an original thought? Just go along with whatever a shadow leader of the straits would want you to do?"

Hestafon had fallen to his knees, as if struck by Alesio's words. His face had paled as he pressed his hand over his heart.

"Quite a performance," Alesio said, crossing his arms. "Have you forgotten this isn't a stage?"

"*Alesio!*"

A giant hand seemed to grip the back of his neck like he was a kitten. Then something yanked him backwards, and vertigo flashed through him. His body fell back to the log. He blinked a few times and rubbed the back of his neck.

Yashalis had used her Vision magic to shift his gravitational direction for a moment, so he'd fallen backwards. He'd seen her use her power just one other time.

"This is a serious accusation," Yashalis said. "Do you have proof of this?"

His neck throbbed. He glowered at the ground, feeling like a reprimanded child.

"I expect and demand better of you," Yashalis continued. We are all trying to save our worlds and you are focused on a personal grudge. You will be escorted out, and I do hope you'll have more to report on your search beyond leaping at a delegate next time we meet."

THE WIND WHIPPED around like a scythe. Marik crafted a Touch water shield around them to keep the worst of it from slamming them off the water boards and slicing into them. Wearing the Touchian buoy suits wouldn't save them from the intensity of such a force. Marik tucked his reed shoes under handles he had crafted on the board and stood, his toes gripping the edges of hardened water. Saida and Naya both crouched on the board and clenched the handles with both hands.

Marik controlled their board on the edge of the Summit Wave, so they remained stationary, and yet they seemed always about to fall off the edge. The water rushed under them and disappeared over—down into the blackness below—!

"Don't look down too much," Marik shouted over the cacophony of wind.

Saida stopped herself from shifting to foxan to preserve the dexterity of fingers, locking her hands on the board handle. She peeked at Naya. The fox-person had a death grip on her handles and pressed her face against the board.

"How long do we ride the Wave?" Saida shouted.

"Through the rest of the night," Marik said. "Six hours or so."

"How fast does it travel?"

"About as fast as an arrow."

So, if they traveled for six hours, that meant . . . a lot. A lot of miles. She calculated it in her head to distract herself. She'd improved at numbers ever since Alesio had taught her how to read and write, but those numbers soared much higher than her understanding. Regardless, it was farther than she'd traveled on any one world. She could direct her portals anywhere she'd already visited, which meant expeditions ranged around twenty to thirty miles, at most. Before that, when she'd wandered the worlds without a plan or much of a memory, she'd probably covered even less ground.

No wonder no one had found the Lunnites or their city before.

She recalled Linia standing stock still, pointing upwards: *"There's someone up there!"*

So, the Soundian hadn't lied or hallucinated in her fear. She'd glimpsed a Lunnite riding the Wave.

Saida concentrated on gripping the handles, but the cold sank its potent fangs into her hands and numbed them. She loosened her grasp and balanced on the board in a crouch. With Marik keeping the Touch shield, the high winds and bitter chill of the high altitude did not affect them as much, but she still had to warm her hands with her breath. Naya refused to open her eyes or move, but she did breathe on her hands as well, from time to time.

Saida eyed Marik. To keep up a Touch shield while maintaining the magic of the board must at least tax him. Alesio had tried to strengthen his magical endurance, but even with Sound magic, he could have managed maybe two hours of maintaining both magical effects at the same time. Marik must have practiced and trained to do this for years.

A couple hours had passed, and far, far ahead, a line of the sunrise had appeared on the curve of the world.

The light strengthened, illuminating the thin clouds below them, windswept and torn like rags. The russet and cobalt celestial body of Taste had long since dipped below the horizon, but the planet of Sound showed up, now, rising with the sun like an eager kid holding their parent's hand. Fifteen minutes later, when she squinted, tiny blue-black specks appeared on the ground. The depths, she guessed. A few times they passed larger, dark gray specks, which were probably caves.

A bird startled from below, flying away from the Summit Wave. It reminded her of an ant on a huge tree trunk. The reminder of the size comparison made her limbs seize up again and she closed her eyes again for a time. For all its power and magnitude, though, the Summit had never needed trimming, back when she could still sense overgrowths. It likely used up most of its magic in its never-ending travels.

As the hours passed, something nagged at the back of her mind. Something about the timing around when the Lunnites had arrived.

"Marik," she said. "Did your group surf the Wave to reach the Portal Station, before you arrived on Sound?"

"We . . . um, not exactly."

She waited. Naya turned her head to stare at him as well. As the seconds ticked on, her theory gained solidity, like one of Alesio's Touchian creations as he Shaped them.

"One of us can also teleport," Marik said. "It's as well you know. I'm sorry we did not tell you straight away, honored Envoy. But we did not want to reveal them in the presence of anyone . . . else."

She studied the Lunnite. He wanted her to keep this from Alesio. She saw no harm in holding the information to herself. It wasn't her secret to tell, anyway.

"I understand," she said. "I won't tell anyone."

Some of the tension smoothed in Marik's brow.

After another five hours or so had passed, the Lunnite's shoulders had hunched more and his stance had lowered into a crouch, as if his knees wanted to become best friends with the Wave. She shouted to him, "Are you alright to use magic for so long? We've saved days of travel. We could hop off and walk the rest!"

He shouted back, "I do this all the time! Don't worry, we'll be there soon."

Over the next hour, his hands trembled, then shook. Saida almost shouted to him again but then the Wave dropped a few feet.

Both Naya and Saida shrieked. The Wave lost a little of its steepness, and more of the actual drop hove into view, like a massive sharp slide instead of a cliff. Saida almost screamed a question at Marik but stopped. Sweat ran down his forehead into the fur on his cheeks and his legs shook. His ears had flattened on top of his head. Naya squinted once at their escort and flattened against her board even more.

The Wave smoothed out more over the next ten minutes, and the top where they had traveled slanted into a slight decline. The board nosed downwards, then picked up speed as they hit the steeper slope.

"Everyone hold on!" Marik shouted, and Saida and Naya both screamed. The crashing of the Wave thundered in their ears, and a little bit of wind and spray leaked through Marik's shield, slicing Saida's cheek like a knife. She'd kept her ears flat against her head, but some cold droplets still seeped in. Her stomach seemed to fall faster than she did, and her head lightened, and her ears popped, and her teeth rattled, and they plummeted down the slide of the shrinking Summit Wave like a portal falling between the worlds. The ground rushed at them, too close, too fast, and Marik shouted something again, but the roar drowned out his words, and the force felt like it yanked her arms out of their sockets, but she managed to hold on. The Wave evened out, then, flowing along the ground, and the water churned to white surf, and they rode it along for what seemed like forever, maybe for a few minutes, until it slowed, and slowed, and they slowed to a halt on the Glass Sea.

10

THE BABY HUNGER

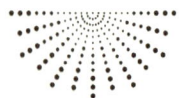

Verrity pulled Paras and Irisha aside in the morning, explaining the proposal from the group of Soundian volunteers. "I know the villagers won't like this, but we have just a few days before mid-spring. We can't plant everything in time otherwise."

The morning team flowed past them to the fields outside the village, leading the horses and dogs out on leashes and harnesses. A few stayed behind to rake the streets after the rush, keeping them clean of manure from the animals. Irisha's daughter, Miera, followed in their wake and scattered nonflower petals, her favorite chore.

"They'll come around." Irisha kept her expression neutral except for her pressed, thin lips, which spoke loud enough without words. Her daughter had dashed out in all the commotion, and Irisha hadn't found her for several agonizing minutes. "If we emphasize that they owe us a great debt."

Verrity tucked her hair behind her ears. "I thought I'd have to convince you, too."

"I see the benefits." Irisha watched Miera playing in the street, spinning in circles while scattering nonflower petals.

Like the other children in the village, Miera had stopped growing taller since last year. The foxans had explained the delayed aging effect of the Reconnection. How would parents like Ishira handle their children growing an inch in several years instead of six months? Four mothers had delivered babies so far this year in Tremain. None of them had aged past where the bones at the top of their skulls filled in, and their mothers would have to breastfeed for much longer. Years. Such a gift of time, and yet . . . the adjustment period for such a thing would pose new difficulties.

"What's important is the future, right? Not the past." Ishira paused and lowered her voice, glancing at a quiet Paras beside them. "Perhaps she or I should announce it, though?"

No one knows what the right thing is, but someone must make decisions. What should she decide? What would help Tremain the most? "That would likely be best. I'm trying to do what's best for the village." *Am I, though? Or am I just trying to cling to power to protect my own ego?*

Paras hugged her, her blonde hair tickling Verrity's cheek. How could they share a hair color, yet hers laid flat and lifeless against her scalp, while Paras's flowed around her face in soft waves?

Stop it. Stop being jealous.

"We'll convince them," Paras said. "Maybe . . . maybe this'll help you, too, you know? You talk about respectful and helpful otherworlders, but they just haven't met many. If these volunteers are nice, then maybe they'll start to believe you."

"I hope so." Verrity smiled. "Well, *you* won't. I have another job for you."

Paras bobbed with excitement. People who didn't know her tended to think of her as a fragile flower because of her slight stature and delicate facial features, but she had more of the spirit of a hummingbird—wound tight, always moving, and hungry to try out new places. In that way, she reminded Verrity of Saida.

"There's a group of reclusive, um, fox-people, that have appeared, and they need local guides in each world. They want to find information on the Hunger. I know you'd prefer to leave Scent, but—"

"Yes," Paras said, laughing, and kissed Verrity on the cheek. "Thank you, Verrity. Thank you!"

After giving Paras the information she needed, Verrity followed the path to the Portal Station with a lighter heart than the day before. Ishira would handle Tremain while she helped with the threat of the Hunger.

She'd left a little early to stop by that dress store. She lingered outside the shop, ogling the rose-pink dress with blue and pearl-gray flowers. It might fit her wide shoulders.

A few early risers passed her and then glanced back, whispering. Their voices carried in the cold, in the loudness of Anthem.

"—maybe he's looking at it for his wife."

"Well, it's just weird."

They had to know she could hear them, right?

She shook it off. She'd learned she had to, to keep going. Still, if she wore a dress like that, she couldn't help but imagine that the whispers would cease. Scents! A dress like that might just whisper to her how to truly represent her people both in how they wanted, and how she wanted. It might give her that straight-backed self-assuredness that Falrie had, even in front of sneering people like Balt.

"See something you like?" Falrie's voice startled her. She spun. The older foxan woman waited for her in her human form, the long silver streaks in her hair giving her a distinguished presence. Verrity wished, once again, that she could just change her outward appearance like the foxans could.

"Just looking." Verrity smiled, trying not to fake it. She pulled her overcoat close against her, having remembered about the cold this time.

The young foxan, Tener, skidded out from behind Falrie as if playing tag, wheeled, and peered in the window.

Verrity blinked. They must have gone through a massive foxan growth spurt, because instead of reaching her waist, they'd shot up the level of her shoulder. Their foxan ears reached to the top of her head!

Tener pointed at her. "That dress! It looks like you!"

"What?" Verrity tried not to stare at the young foxan. One learned in Scentian culture not to stare at obvious physical changes. The scents embarrassed someone enough, and no one needed extra fodder for mortification in the transition from child to adult. Their strange comment registered, then, and she shook her head. "How—how could a dress look like someone?"

"Well, it's pink. Like your human face. And flowery. You should buy it."

Verrity tried to process that. Her mouth hung open and her cheeks heated.

"Tener." Falrie raised an eyebrow at the young foxan. "What happened to trimming overgrowths on Sound with Darrow?"

Tener folded their hands in front of them and puffed out their lips. "Darrow said he didn't need me today, that I could go with you."

Falrie's nose shifted into a foxan muzzle, and she pinched the space between her eyes, scrunching the faint reddish stripes on the bare skin of her cheeks. "Did he now?"

"I won't get in the way! You won't even know I'm there. Please? I want to see the Baby Hunger."

"Absolutely not—"

"Please? Please? If I don't practice and try to understand them, the Big Hunger could do something I don't know how to handle! Like, I could practice how to run away better."

"Tener—"

"*Please?*"

"Senses help me." Falrie sighed. "Alright but stay behind me. And don't say *anything.*"

Tener pumped their fist in the air, bouncing up on foxan hind legs. Verrity smiled. She could see a bit of Paras in Tener in their tenacity and dynamism.

Falrie summoned a portal to the Primal Plane, and they strode through into that familiar resistance. They trekked up and over to the tree that Watthe had transplanted into, and the hole that lay at its roots.

It had grown.

Not that much, but more than enough for Verrity. From its center, two arms of emptiness stretched halfway up the trunk and a little on the ground like lunging snakes, twisting the trunk and parts of the ground back towards the center of the void. The pulling sensation had increased as well, and they had to keep stepping backwards to avoid falling into it.

Baby Hunger, indeed. It mirrored the Hunger above, just on a tiny scale, though it lacked the bits of substance that its larger counterpart seemed to possess. Tener stared at it in equal parts wonder and horror with the morbid curiosity of youth.

"The box I sent is just a single brick from the world of my body!"

The older foxan woman stayed farther back this time, keeping Tener farther away.

Taking the lead, Verrity allowed the entity to draw her a little closer. She and Falrie had agreed that flattery hadn't worked and had planned a different approach.

"What are you made of, sad little box?" Verrity asked. "Are you so worthless you only feel complete feeding on others' essences?"

Behind her, Falrie sucked in a breath. Maybe she hadn't expected such a hostile take from Verrity.

The snake-like arms hissed and rose up in front of them, lifting off the ground. "I am everything! I will consume everything!"

Tener appeared next to Verrity, having stopped moving backwards, staring at it with their big, dark eyes.

"Back!" Falrie barked. Tener scrambled backwards on foxan toes, their ears shifting to the pointed, tall ones on top of their head.

"But why? What made you so hungry?" Verrity continued. "Surely you haven't always been a soul-sucking leech."

The snake-arms opened at the ends, hissing, displaying throats and fangs. One of them opened to an *eye*. All three of them backed up again.

Falrie muttered, "What in all the Senses . . ."

"Hey," Tener shouted. "If you're so hungry, why haven't you eaten all of us yet?"

The Hunger in the sky rumbled and spoke like a giant wind tunnel. "I WILL FIND OUT WHAT BINDS ME, AND I WILL DISSEMBLE YOU MAGIC BY MAGIC, AND YOU WILL BE GLAD FOR IT IN THE END! GLAD!"

The snake-arms whipped forward past Verrity and caught Falrie by the arm. She screamed, but Tener opened a portal underneath the group, and everyone fell through in a tumbling morass of arms and legs, and Verrity couldn't see very well, except that the portal cut that dark snake-like nothing from Falrie's arm.

They landed in the dirty snow-sludge back on Sound, near the Portal Station, and Tener's portal closed above them.

The few Soundians in line at the Portal Station had hunkered down, holding their hands over their ears. An infant squalled. In the homes nearby, shutters slammed shut and voices called children in from playing outside. It seemed everyone held their breath.

The Hunger did not repeat its message.

Tener had shifted to full foxan, trembling against Falrie's human hips. Falrie's face and legs flickered back and forth from human to foxan, foxan back to human, so that they shrank, then grew, shrank, then grew. Her arm had a dark mark on it, like a bruise, and it hung limp from her shoulder. The nothing-snake had dissipated after the portal had cut it off.

We made it speak again!

After about thirty seconds or so, Tak turned the Soundians away from the Sound-Taste portal and jogged up to Verrity, Tener, and Falrie. He held a harmonica in his hands loosely, as if he'd forgotten about it. "Did you hear that? Was that the Hunger?"

Verrity braced herself with a breath. She could do this. Confidence flowed through her. The adrenaline from angering the Hunger as a strategy, perhaps? "What did you hear?" She asked Tak.

"It was so loud, I had to cover my ears. It didn't repeat, like that one horrible day, thank the Sound. I caught the word 'glad' towards the end."

"Stay on alert the next few hours," Verrity said. "Let them through the portals so they don't feel confined or that things have worsened."

Tak hesitated, like he wanted to ask if things *had* worsened, but shrugged and jogged back to the Portal Station, tucking the harmonica into his pocket. More people gathered in the surrounding marketplace, huddling next to the energizing power of the Portal Station.

Verrity surveyed the two foxans. Falrie held Tener's foxan form close against her. Her paw trembled, though the injured one still hung limp. Her legs stabilized as foxan hind legs, shrinking her.

"I told you not to speak to it," Falrie said to Tener.

"I—I just wanted to help."

"You could have been killed!" The foxan woman cradled her injured arm.

"Falrie," Verrity said. "They did help us escape."

The foxan woman's eyes flashed. She shifted her muzzle back into a human nose and mouth, compressing them, then stopped, seeming to notice how Tener had hunched away from her, ears flattening, a whine escaping their lips.

"You . . . you did help, little one." Falrie winced. "The idea of this happening to you, though, it frightened me." She held out her arm. "It feels wrong. It feels *disconnected*. Like it was pulled apart." She shivered.

Tener stared at their mother's arm, cocking their head.

"I shouldn't have let you come in the first place. This was my fault, not yours."

Above them, the Hunger's tendrils of nothingness looked like they had opened thin chasms overhead, further twisting their sky. The tendrils had lengthened, like long, coiling snakes.

"It said something about being bound, though," Tener said. "Isn't that a good thing for us?"

"A very good thing," Verrity said.

"Perhaps something blocks it from getting closer," Falrie said. "I wish we knew how to keep it that way, but if we question it further, it could learn how to free itself." Her voice quavered. "I will report this to Yashalis. No more visits to that thing. It's growing, and it's too dangerous."

"Wait, what?" Verrity shook her head. "We can still get information out of it. Once it figures out how to free itself, then it'll eat our worlds. It might do that anyway if it keeps expanding in the Primal Plane!"

"That thing caused the Severing." Falrie jutted out her chin, shifting to her human form, growing taller, but that acrid scent of fear strengthened as well. "It almost sliced my arm off. It's too volatile and dangerous for anyone to go near."

"We need more information—"

"I forbid it!"

Verrity stepped back.

Falrie narrowed her eyes to mere slivers. "We have our answer for the Council. Something already holds it back. We don't want to accidentally let it loose." She lowered her voice. "Good luck getting there without a foxan to help you."

Verrity bowed her head. "I—I wouldn't—" she swallowed. "I'm sure you know best."

PARAS PRACTICALLY MELTED once Verrity left. She and Ishira had already informed the villagers about the Soundian volunteers to accustom them to the idea, and she hadn't wanted any of them to let it slip that they already knew. So, she had her freedom.

Well, almost. She needed to supply Clef's men.

She tied a cloth over her mouth and nose and threw together a large basket full of potatoes, corn, and apples. She slid her arms through the straps and carried it on her back north of town. Miera had stopped dancing as she spread the nonflowers, watching Paras.

Paras lugged the basket along the small path and reached the Garden, surveying it with narrowed eyes.

The maze teleported a person based on scents from the different flora it grew. The magical area boasted a level of capriciousness that used to pluck at Paras's nerves, but she'd done this so many times she solved the puzzle within moments. It had patterns, if one knew what to look for. The thin band of flowers stretched for a few miles and surrounded a field. Within a few minutes she reached that field with the house in the middle, and the putrefying, fecal stench from the outhouse that should never have existed which the otherworlders had dug.

Scentians didn't use outhouses because the odor permeated through wood and radiated farther and stronger than on other worlds. She held her breath, because even through the cloth covering her mouth and nose, the stink itched at her eyes, so they watered.

She puffed her way to the front door, knocked, then dashed away, almost passing out from trying not to breathe. She sprinted back to the Garden before anyone opened the door, and so she didn't have to play at placating smiles and words exchanged through gritted teeth.

She grabbed her pack full of adventuring gear, which she'd rechecked the night before, and trekked to the Portal Station. Once on the other side, she showed the guard with the salt and pepper mustache her safety certificate.

"You the guide for Scent, then? Paras, right?"

She nodded. How did he remember her name? So many people funneled through each day.

"Well, alright then. There's the group of Lunnites, at the Sound-Vision portal." He opened a gate to a different line. The fox-human hybrids had crammed two at a time in front of the portal where lavender light streamed from.

"There's twenty of them," the guard said. "Now, I see you don't have your Vision certificate yet, so stay in the Portal Station on Vision and lead them straight through to Scent. Don't wander, and don't let them wander."

"Yes, sir!"

She'd made her peace with the fact that she would explore Scent and not a different world. She would leave Tremain and protect it at the same time. With light feet, she shouldered her way through the line and stood in front of the strange group.

She swallowed hard to stop the jitters. Verrity seemed to flounce around in other worlds like a butterfly in a field, free to roam wherever she wished, but she also went to those Council meetings in front of the other world leaders. Did her sister feel this anxiety in front of them?

"Alright," Paras said.

The fox-peoples' heads all swung towards her, their breath fogging in the cold air. Some had muzzles instead of noses, or fur instead of skin, and for a moment, she wondered if they would smell her deceit, her lies to her sister, how she had hidden the otherworlders who may have killed someone or at least kidnapped them and held them captive. Lies and betrayal didn't give off a scent, but animals could smell better than humans. Perhaps they could, on Scent. Were they animals? Some even stood on four legs instead of two.

The thieves, the takers of magic, her mother used to say of fox-people—well, her mother had used a different moniker back then.

They didn't leap at her or accuse her of anything. They hadn't stolen anything from Paras. In fact, they'd given her something: her freedom.

Paras straightened and projected her voice. "I am Paras, your Scentian guide. Stay close to me. We are heading through to Vision, but we are not visiting Vision, we'll go straight through to Scent."

They watched her with narrowed, slitted eyes and bunched together, but they did not raise a ruckus. Those with fur didn't give off smells like the dogs or horses when not brushed with nonflower petals, which surprised her. Maybe that would change in Scent.

"Have you all followed the requirements? You washed yourselves this morning, along with the clothes you are taking?"

Nodding all around. This was a quiet bunch.

"Alright then. A few ground rules before we go. We will not pass through Tremain. My village is somewhat leery of outsiders, and anyway, there's no need, as I understand you want to head towards a specific remote location. However, you should know that Scentians overall, me included, prioritize cleanliness above all. Therefore, I will lead you through a grove of nonflower trees, as is tradition, to cleanse any remaining otherworld scents from you. Other than that, when taking care of your business, please dig first, cover after. Any questions?"

They shifted but did not speak. Could they speak? Well, they must, or Verrity and the Council wouldn't have known they wanted to find those city ruins. "Do you have someone to speak for you?"

An older male Lunnite stepped forward. He had a normal enough face, with a beard, and he kept his hands inside the large sleeves of his cloak. Underneath the cloak, he wore simple clothing crafted of plant fibers. "I speak for the others." He spoke in a slow, hesitating voice. "We are happy you lead us."

They didn't *look* happy. Their eyes followed her every movement, as if afraid she would leap at them. What had Verrity said about them, that they lived in an abandoned city? Well, it didn't matter now. She'd travel with anyone at this point, if they were *going* somewhere.

"Alright, then." She led the way through the portal.

11

SEDELLA

Alesio twirled in the scent of the nonflowers like Saida had taught him by the trees outside of Tremain. Nonflowers smelled like nothing, smoothing the scent of the person who wore it.

Tak had warned him that Scent remained off-limits to visitors, but he had important business here, one thing he needed to try before portaling to Flock. He'd try to keep a low profile.

After his outburst at the Council meeting earlier, he preferred it that way, anyway. He still vibrated with rage at Hestafon, but a bit of embarrassment had crept in as well. At least Saida hadn't witnessed the Council leader yank him aside like a naughty puppy.

Back in Anthem, the sun had tipped past midday. The Council had met later in the day Anthem time, which they had agreed to use as a default since it existed more in the middle of the other time zones. Here in Scent, though, birds trilled in the sweet, gentle light of morning.

The townsfolk working the fields stopped and followed his passing with narrowed eyes. Many shook their heads and returned to pressing seeds in the ground for the second time that spring.

Alesio preferred their indifference. He didn't want news of his visit to spread.

He wove through the raked dirt streets, clear of any trash or refuse. He'd grown up in the dirt straits of Anthem, but here, the dirt wasn't . . . *dirty*. Even after the Hunger had materialized in their sky, the villagers of Tremain completed their individual tasks with a single-minded thoroughness he admired.

"Voice?" A young girl, maybe ten years old, darted over to him in the street and peered up at him with wide eyes and a clean face. She wore a washed-out blue dress, and a braid circled her head like a crown. "Voice of Reconnection?"

He smiled down at her. *Sounddamn it. There's my cover blown.* "You can call me Alesio."

"Alesho?"

"That's right."

"Alesho," she whispered, "Can you stop otherworlders from coming here? My mother doesn't like it."

"Miera! Get back in the house!" A middle-aged woman with the same blonde-ish brown hair, braided with the same crown, crooked her finger at the little girl. Miera scampered over to her.

Alesio sighed and edged closer to buildings, out of the openness of the main street. Within a few minutes, he reached the house of the person he had hired. He raised his hand to knock but the Scentian opened the door first. Alesio slipped inside.

The frizzy-haired man might have been a rainstorm in another life. His angled, jagged eyebrows clouded his brow.

"Thank you for coming," Raos said. "I did not want to leave Tremain again."

"I understand," Alesio said, though he didn't. "Did you find him?"

The Scentian hesitated. "I am sorry. I could not sense him on any world." He jerked his chin toward a bag in the corner, the bag of money that Clef had tossed to Alesio a year ago, now empty. Alesio had left the bag with Raos before leaving for the expedition to Touch. "It does not have a scent."

Alesio wilted in disappointment, then sighed. "It was a long shot. He only touched it for a few seconds."

Raos shook his head. "I have trained in trailing animal scents my whole life. But even outside of Scent, otherworlder scent is strong to me. The outside of the bag smells of you, but his scent coats the inside of the bag from the money he placed inside, which he must have handled often. Yet the owner of this bag's scent goes nowhere." He raised an eyebrow. "As in, *non*."

Alesio frowned. "He's cloaking himself in nonflower?"

"That is the logic upstream from what I smell." Raos handed him the bag.

"Does that mean he's on Scent?" A thrill rushed through him.

Raos held his hand open, jiggling his striking eyebrows up and down.

"Oh. Right." Alesio rummaged in his pocket and brought out the bag of salt he'd purchased on Taste. Scentians, unlike the other worlds, hadn't adopted the Soundians' notes as the overall currency and seemed to prefer goods from Taste. Raos snatched the little bag, sniffed it, then smiled. "Possibly. Though nonflower works on other worlds as well, now."

"But not as well, right? It's not as powerful outside its source world."

Raos scuttled across the room. He placed the bag of salt in a drawer lined with dried nonflower blossoms. He'd turned away so Alesio couldn't hear the first word he said. "— grows everywhere here, someone could harvest many at a great rate to increase the potency."

"Clever bastard." He sighed. "So, I'm back where I started."

"I'm sorry I couldn't help more."

Alesio bowed and left.

He'd tried locating Clef several ways. He'd tracked down the report of the cage fights on Touch to find a few brawlers in a cave demanding notes from the audience. This latest and least likely idea had also failed.

He'd have to search Flock. He clenched his fists. It was 'the logic upstream,' as a Scentian would have said. He didn't have any other leads to chase and considering his suspicions that Hestafon worked with Clef, he needed to go there as soon as possible, just in case the Soundian delegate had warned the strait's leader to change locations. He could almost hear that weasel's voice now . . .

". . . anything for confused magic?"

Wait. That *was* Hestafon's voice, coming from around the corner.

"Confused magic, you say?" The villager gave an audible sniff. "— describe the ailment further, otherworlder?"

The middle-aged woman that Alesio had encountered earlier strode across the street. "Teagen, you do be encouraging them. What did I tell you about trading your herbs to otherworlders?"

"— just asking for some meat, Ishira."

"Just ask Bekker or Raos, like the rest of us."

"Please, my Lady." Hestafon again. "I'm . . . I don't feel well. I need help from someone here, on Scent."

"You don't smell sick to me. Tremain is closed to otherworlder visits. Be off with you!"

"Please—"

"Get on with you! And you, skulking behind the house, the same to you!"

Sounddamn it. Alesio trailed out, holding his hands up. Hestafon stood there in his iconic silken pants and shirt with the purple bows on his lapels, ridiculous next to the woman in her simple homespun dress. His gaze landed on Alesio, and he jumped.

"Alright, we're going, we're going," Alesio said. "C'mon, Hestafon." He jerked his chin towards the road.

Hestafon hesitated, his gaze darting from Alesio to the stern glare of Miera's mother.

Alesio grabbed the piper's shoulders like the rudder of a ship and propelled him forward till they reached the path that led to the Portal Station, out of sight of the fields.

"What. Are. You. Doing here?" Alesio yanked the piper's arm, so they faced each other. "Like she said, Tremain's closed to visitors. Except for the volunteers."

"Then why are you here?" Hestafon's pale skin had paled further, and he clutched at his chest, almost crushing one of his ludicrous bows.

Alesio folded his arms. "To carry out my task for the Council. But it looks real suspicious, *you* sneaking around like this. Does the Council know you're here?"

Hestafon's mouth gaped in an accurate impersonation of a fish. He swayed on his feet.

Alesio rolled his eyes. "That's not gonna work on me."

The piper wheezed and grasped for Alesio. Alesio jerked back, and Hestafon fell forward, strands from his slicked-back blonde bun falling around his face.

"What the *hell!*" Alesio caught him just before he fell flat on his face. The piper's pulse hammered like a tiny woodpecker in his wrist.

Saida had had this happen often enough that Alesio could no longer reason against it.

Panic attack.

"Breathe, sounddamn it." Alesio forced the harshness from his voice almost like he Shaped it. "I mean, uh, breathe. One, two, three, one, two, three. There. That's it. C'mon." He levered the man to a sitting position and held up three fingers. "How many?"

"Th-three."

"Good. I'm gonna need you to count to ten with me, okay?"

Hestafon puffed in shallow gasps, seeping tears and snot and decidedly unpiper-like blubbering. Over the next ten minutes, Alesio talked him down from the precipice, the terror fading in his eyes.

"Now," Alesio said. "You're gonna give me some answers, okay? I just want to know what you were doing here, and why you just had a panic attack." He frowned. The man had clutched at his chest during the Council meetings. "Why you've *been* having panic attacks." He paused. "Is it Clef? Does he have some dirt on you? Wants you to do something you don't wanna do?"

Hestafon's eyes darted to Alesio, then away. "I'm sorry, but no. I know you want me to know things about Clef, but it's not that. Not at all."

Alesio studied the piper's white face, streaked with dirt from tears and the humble path they'd sat beside.

"Convince me. What is it, then?"

"It's—it's—oh, how can I explain this?"

"Just say it," Alesio said through his teeth.

Hestafon breathed in a deep breath. "It's like this." He pointed at his temple. "My magic has changed."

"What."

"My magic. It's . . . it's confused. It's crossed with another kind of magic. It's both Sound and Scent, now. And it's overwhelming!"

"I don't understand," Alesio said. "Do you have both? Like I have both Touch and Sound magic?"

"Not both." Hestafon curled his hands into fists. "It's like—I can smell sound, now. The birds in that bush? Their trills smell like citrus." He gestured upward as a breeze ruffled the trees above. "That smells colder and sharper the stronger it blows."

"How do you know you're not just smelling the breeze?"

"It's different. I can smell things that wouldn't normally have a smell. You bathed in nonflowers before coming here, right?"

Alesio nodded.

"Well, I can still smell the rustle of your clothing, it smells like soil after a rain. It leaves a trail I can smell for hours after, sometimes longer, depending on how intense the sound is. Ugh! I can tell you don't believe me, but I swear!"

"So . . . could you smell nonflowers? Or past them?"

"Well, in a way, I suppose. I told you; I can smell the *sound* something makes. It's different."

"I don't quite understand that bit." Alesio hauled off the bag from his shoulder and opened it. He tried to keep the excitement out of his voice. "What about this? Can you smell or hear or whatever the inside of this bag? I'm talking about old scents, from like, a year ago, not from me right now."

Hestafon frowned, but leaned closer to the bag, more strands from his bun falling around his face. He brushed them back. "A year ago? That makes it much harder, but . . . yes. This bag was kept closed, so the echoes of sounds have stayed in the folds of the cloth. There are vibrations of movements . . . old coins and the rustle of notes . . . a harsh voice that smells like . . ." His forehead wrinkled. "The tang of metal. Like blood. Rusted iron."

"That's Clef alright. Now, can you sense that same voice, that same rusted smell, somewhere else? Anywhere but the bag?"

"Clef? I don't know—"

"Can you just try it?"

Hestafon stared at him, then the bag. He rose, then closed his eyes, sniffing like a hound catching the wind. He kept his eyes closed for a long, long minute.

"Yes. But it's . . . faint. I think on another world."

Alesio's thoughts yanked on the reins of his good sense. He hauled them back with a firm grip.

Gather supplies first in case it's an extended hunt. I will not try to find him and forget to bring food and water and a real knife.

"You say you're not a puppet for Clef." Alesio poked the piper's crushed silken bow on his lapel. "Prove it. Help me track him down."

MARIK HOPPED off the water board, unslung his pack, and dug around in it, producing a soft bandage strip. He proffered it to Saida, bowing low, his ears folded over. Touch rashes reddened his face and neck. "Your cheek is bleeding. I apologize for my incompetence, Envoy. Are you otherwise injured?"

Saida took the cloth and dabbed at her cheek. "I'm fine. Naya?"

Naya still huddled on the water board. "I'm having some issues with my bladder. You both should stand over there."

"Ah. Right." Saida wobbled over a few steps to afford Naya some privacy, pointing with her eyes for Marik to do the same. The Lunnite lowered his head and waded over to stand next to Saida, his hands clasped in front of him. Beads of sweat ran down his neck and his fur there spiked.

Saida patted her cheek. She kept herself human, so she didn't scratch herself with a claw, though part of her wanted to cram herself in a hole for a week after the roaring of the Wave for so many hours. "So . . . do you all travel like that? It seemed kinda dangerous towards the end."

Marik's throat bobbed and he straightened to a ramrod posture. "I have ridden the Summit many times, but I may have overestimated my endurance with other passengers. I should not have risked your safety."

She studied him. The reddish-brown fur on his cheeks lent him more age than he perhaps had experienced, but the freckles under his eyes tempered the effect, tattling on his sideburns. His ears drooped, and his hair-tail hung limp in its wrapping.

"I'm just glad we got here in one piece." She surveyed the land around them. A strange forest spread out in front of them, the roots of the trees knuckling above the shallow water, and it breathed a languid humidity, warming the late fall air. "Speaking of . . . where are we?"

Marik raised his head, staring at her face instead of her feet. "I will show you the way. The Summit ends where our home begins. Our city lies inside the jungle, far away from prying eyes."

Naya joined them and squinted at the trees, wrinkling her striped muzzle. "A jungle? What is that? How are there trees here?"

Excitement surged through Saida. Riding the Wave had terrified her but it had also exhilarated her. She hadn't found something so fresh and unique as a separate ecosystem on the worlds in a long time.

Marik led them under the shade of the trees, and the Epitaph's signal strengthened further into a quiet pulsing all around her. "It is a kind of forest. The Wave always ends before it reaches the trees. The water is always warmer here as it moves slower, allowing this jungle to grow." He gestured at a little creature that leapt off one of the tree trunks, startled at their approach. "Small creatures like these trunk-frogs can live on the surface as well."

Saida peered at where the long-legged animal had jumped. "Trunk-frogs. Huh! That's amazing!"

The trees thickened farther in, until the dawn sunlight filtered through the foliage as dim moss-colored light. The magic pulsed along with the air and sweat trickled down Saida's back. After a few minutes, she had to wipe her forehead to keep the perspiration from running down her face and onto her slashed cheek. She opened her mouth to ask how much farther they had to travel, but the trees opened just then in front of them.

An elevated stone path rose a foot or so above the shallow water of the Glass Sea and led to an ancient stone city. The ruins interspersed with the foliage and trees of the jungle so that it seemed like trees grew out of the stone in some places, and some stone towers scaled all the way to the forested ceiling. Much of the stone had corroded, and some of the streets had crumbled, giving way to the Glass Sea underneath.

The Epitaph's magic pulled at Saida, like wind, or the gravity shifts on Vision. She wondered if it tried to speak to her.

"Welcome to Sedella," Marik said.

He gestured them forward and they followed the path under several stone arches draped in vines, though the first four had crumbled, leaving jagged edges. They found themselves between two pillars at least a house and a half tall, one of which had fallen inward. Past that, a wide-open courtyard of several large stone slabs branched to other, smaller streets, pockmarked with holes. The water of the Glass Sea winked in various little pools; its surface somehow dimpled even without a wind to stir it. Several wheels the size of houses rose out of the water at various intervals, dark green algae covering them with spots of rotting tawny brown like hundreds of eyes staring at them.

"There's no one else here right now," Marik said. "They've all gone off to search for Lunnite cities on the other worlds. But before I show you around, we can eat and rest, if you like."

As much as Saida wanted to explore this place, she glanced at Naya first. Touch rashes covered her bare hands and cheeks, almost matching the pumpkin orange stripes on her foxan nose, with more of a reddish tint. "That's a good idea."

Naya gifted Saida a quick smile. Marik led them a bit further into the city, around various holes in the street. The trees and jungle greenery pushed through them, so that it appeared from afar like the trees grew out of the stone.

She dropped back with Naya, speaking in a low voice. "Hey, Naya, I've been meaning to ask you something."

Naya waggled her eyebrows. "You think he's trying to kill us?"

"What?"

"Believe me, I had my doubts too, at first. But I don't think so anymore. He could've let us fall into the Summit at any point in the last six hours."

"Oh. I wasn't thinking about that. Though maybe I should have. Alesio would have."

Naya cackled. "Your lovestruck, *ex-cage fighter,* magic-singing lover would have told him to scoff sand in Taste the second he told us to portal to the Summit Wave." She brushed a sweat drop beading on her chin. "So, what did you want to ask me?"

"Well . . . do you want me to call you a Lunnite?"

"Huh." Naya shifted her pack on her back and tapped her chin with her fingers. "I still prefer fox-person. That's what I know. And Lunnite also seems to mean more than just descending from a foxan, I think it's kind of an homage to their goddess."

"Makes sense to me," Saida said.

They followed the Lunnite into a side street, then into an almost hole-free stone house with a large foyer. A table rested in the middle, carved out of the one of the tree trunks cut at the base, with a few wooden chairs around it. A cabinet set into the wall had a door that opened downward, and several knobs and little trays inside it. A fine layer of dirt covered everything, and bellbugs as large as her palm scuttled in the corners.

Marik swept dust and leaves from the table with his arm. "Sorry for the mess. No one lives out on the edges. I asked for resting accommodations at this spot, though, in case you did visit."

"The bugs here are huge!" Saida bounded over to the corner and inspected the line of bellbugs. One crawled up the wall.

"I would counter that the bugs on other worlds are quite small. One can hardly see the ants."

Saida pulled open the strange door and ducked to peer inside. "What is this? Some kind of place for food?"

Marik shrugged. "That one? We don't know. We think we know what a few of the ancient devices are supposed to do, like the giant wheels near the entrance of the city used to be watermills that probably harnessed the water of the Summit Wave as it dissipated through Sedella."

Saida brushed her hand down the door, then fiddled with the knobs. Nothing happened. "Maybe they need some kind of magic to activate them."

"That could be, though I have tried using Touch magic, and the handful of other Lunnites who have the ability to use it have as well, with no results." Marik produced four rectangular biscuits infused with honey on the table.

Saida snapped up one of them, her hunger flaring. She shifted to foxan and wriggled out of her loose and sweaty buoy suit wrapped around her chest and torso. She opened the fur pocket where she'd stored her water flask and sipped. Coolness soothed her dry throat, satiating her thirst in seconds. She mentally thanked Alesio for packing her Liranel water. A bottle of it bought in the Cloves cost almost a whole note, but her flask would last her the entire trip and then some. She closed the flask and tucked it back in her pocket, then shifted her fur back over it.

Marik stared at her in open awe. A shiver passed through her, a ghost of Carn's sickly admiration flashing behind her eyes. At her glance, he tipped his water flask up to drink, hiding his face.

"Saida?" Naya touched her arm.

She'd curled in on herself, full foxan on the chair.

Relief filtered through after a few moments. She was safe. She didn't fear such things anymore, not when she knew she wouldn't fall for false love like worship or admiration or unwanted advances. She could portal away at any time, whenever she wanted, and nothing could stop her from doing so. Not even herself.

She inhaled and straightened, shifting back to human and leaving her fur on out of politeness for the others, flicking her braid over her shoulder. "Sorry. Foxan cramps."

Marik coughed and choked on his water, his cheeks reddening even more under his reddish-brown fur.

Saida swallowed and rose. "Can we reach the Epitaph today?"

"If we hurry," Marik said. "But if you'd like to rest—"

"Let's go."

After a quick application of soothing balm on the Touch rashes they had developed, they traveled deeper into Sedella, maneuvering the crumbling streets. Marik had refused their offer of the balm, explaining that the foliage provided something similar. Some of the thinner trees had fern-like leaves the size of their heads and Marik reached for a few low-hanging branches, breaking off one of the leaves. He tore it down the middle and some sap seeped out, which he dabbed onto an irritated patch of scarlet on his cheeks showing through his brown fur.

A few times they had to weave around some streets, avoiding the stones of a fallen house Marik explained would block their way. The dim mossy light from the canopy strengthened to an emerald green, and they quickened their pace as the holes in the streets decreased. Layers of stone ringed the holes at regular intervals.

The Epitaph pulsed stronger, like the beat in a song, and Saida wondered if Alesio could have sung it. A longing pooled in Saida's stomach. She wished—oh how she wished—that she could sense the magic's words!

"Is the magic pulling at the water?" Naya halted in front of one of the pools.

Saida stepped beside her, watching as well. The water dimpled inside the pool, as if pulled by an unseen breeze, though the air here languished without any motion. As they watched, the water climbed onto the stone edges, then evaporated. Some of the cracks and jagged edges of the stone smoothed out.

She whirled to Marik, mouth open, foxan ears pricked forward.

He smiled. "The magic self-maintains the city, so the water does not weather the stone. Elsewhere, weather or age has broken down the magic, but it's strongest here." He hesitated. "The signal wasn't always this strong, of course. It started to pulse like this just last week." He pointed down the street. "Regardless, it's always maintained itself. And because of that, we can read the Directive."

A few hundred yards ahead, a bridge arched over a passage of water, and past that, one of the large, squat trees rose from the ground, though this one was made from stone. Or maybe someone had carved a life size sculpture of a tree. The Epitaph's power pulsed from it, and engravings of large, interlocking circles surrounded it.

Saida rushed on ahead. Someone had engraved a message in the stone of the tree in an unfamiliar language, different from the hand gesture language they'd discovered on the Touch expedition that Muey had translated. The letters, or words, looped in overlapping circles around other shapes, some of them stars or hexagons or pentagrams, or more circles. She recognized it as the same script as the rubbing that the Lunnite Tosn had showed them in the Cadenza.

"What does it say?" They hadn't caught up with her yet. She bounced on her toes. "Marik?"

The Lunnite quickened his pace to a trot, smiling at her. "We call it the Directive. This is the origin of what we showed you in Anthem, the rubbing that we brought." He pointed at the carving and translated:

"DIRECTIVE OF THE LUNNITES: we will find the Goddess Lunne, or the foxan Envoys will have to guide us to the afterlife. We must stop the decay of the Bridges."

"THIS MUST BE CENTURIES OLD," Saida said.

"We don't know this one's age for sure." Marik tapped the carving. "But we have another inscription detailing that the Severing had just occurred, dating it as the year of Lunne, 1410. From detailed writings passed down through Lunnite generations, we know the Severing happened around 830 years ago. So, yes. Centuries old, at least. This carving might be even older."

Naya counted on her fingers and her eyes unfocussed, probably calculating more numbers in her head. "That would place us in Year of Lunne . . . 2240 something?"

Marik smiled at her. "Correct!"

Saida brushed the stone tree with her fingertips, hoping against hope it would speak to her.

Nothing happened.

She inhaled sharply, her hands trembling.

"What about the large circles on the ground around it?" Naya squatted and traced the circles mentioned. "It looks like the same language as what's on the trunk, but on a huge scale."

Marik pointed. "Those large letters mean 'store.' Our archivist, Higa, thinks it means that the tree, the Directive, stores magic, and that's how it maintains the stone after all these centuries."

The Lunnite tilted his tall, foxan ears towards Saida. "Do you see why we worship Lunne, now? Do you see your importance? You are an Envoy of Lunne. You and the other foxans could perhaps chase this Hunger away or implore the Goddess Lunne to save us. If that fails and the Hunger consumes us, you can guide us to her in the afterlife. We have lived in Sedella for several generations and have protected this ancient knowledge."

Saida drooped, kneeling on the ground, her hands shifting to paws, her braid hanging over her shoulder morphing into her puffy foxan tail.

Is this true? Is this the only way I can help the worlds—figuring out how to find this deity that may or may not exist, or just oversee a ceremony when people die? Hot tears pricked at her eyes.

She just wanted Alesio's arms around her. Holding her the way she liked, cupping the back of her head just so. Enveloping her in his warmth, his silvery magic whispering in her ear, a promise, a prophecy she wanted to fulfill.

Marik perched a hand on her shoulder and smiled at her, his green eyes bright and reflective in the relative dimness of the jungle. "We have not given up all hope on this life. It is why we searched for you in such desperation; in the hope we can still find the Goddess before death." He pulled her to her feet. "But you are tired. You must rest."

She wished she had her teleport back.

12
THE WAREHOUSE

Alesio waited at the Portal Station on Sound, scowling at the sun that already sloped towards the horizon, lapping the smaller, purple planet of Touch. Saida had left this morning, but it felt like three days had passed. He wished he could talk to her about this bizarre plan he'd cooked up, involving—of all people—Hestafon.

Speaking of . . . Alesio frowned. The piper was ten minutes late.

He hadn't liked letting Hestafon out of his sight, fearing that the piper would somehow alert Clef of the search, but Alesio had no other choice. He had no idea how far the trail would lead, and failing to bring a pack of food and water when going into the wilds on any world was a sure way to die. Hestafon had apparently needed to follow up on some Anthem business before he left, so they had both gone their separate ways, agreeing to meet in the late afternoon at the Portal Station.

And now the piper was nowhere to be found.

Of course he's not coming, Alesio thought. *Even if he's not working for Clef, I almost assaulted him at the Council meeting.*

Regret and full embarrassment soured in Alesio's gut at the memory. Even as suspicious as he'd found Hestafon, verbally attacking him hadn't accomplished anything but lowering the Council's opinion of Alesio himself. It had also been a stupid way to show his hand.

Tak welcomed a group of three Tastians through and directed them where to find the now-infamous St. Rina's cathedral, opening the gates to the quick exit out of the maze of high walls now encompassing the Portal Station dais. In the evening hour, the marketplace surrounding the Portal Station's barriers had people massing like hotrats in a garbage can.

Several corner singers warbled at top volume, and two performers, a celloist and violinist, had set up a makeshift stage on either side. These two competed for the biggest crowd using the most sophisticated and professional techniques such as playing louder and faster with every piece and shouting insults about the other performer in between their sets.

Tak closed the gates again and elbowed him, passing him an extra bowl of sticky rice, covered with a lid. "Eat up, boy, or you'll waste away, bouncing up and down like that."

"Did you bring two portions for your dinner?" Alesio snatched the bowl, uncovering and sniffing it. It smelled like lemon and had the glisten of butter. The light from Vision's arrival portal glazed everything in more vivid hues, and as always, the mixture of magics made him feel like he could jump a little higher and breathe a little deeper. "Mmm. That's good."

"I'll have you know that I am a growing man."

Alesio poked him in the gut, which had rounded a bit in the last year. "I see that."

Tak lowered his voice, and Alesio aided his hearing by reading the piper's lips. "That's my child. Magic has changed things, men can conceive now, don't you know?"

Alesio blinked. With what Hestafon had told him earlier that day, he couldn't rule out such things.

Tak guffawed and clapped him on the back. "Hahaha! You should see your face!" He patted his belly. "This here's a child made of rice. Though Estro and I would love to adopt someday soon."

"You know, I could see that. You both would make great parents." Alesio tapped the bowl three times then spooned rice into his mouth. The tartness of the lemon and the richness of the butter told him they'd originated from Taste.

In the marketplace, the celloist had finished another song and hollered something about the violinist utilizing his instrument's bow for a distinct kind of gratification separate from music, which elicited raucous laughter from the audience.

"How's the practicing coming?" Alesio asked.

Tak pulled out his harmonica. His old friend had more time to devote to his hobby now, not having to keep quiet on the job like he'd had to at St. Rina's. He didn't have the ability to Shape magic, but he still enjoyed playing music. "I might steal your job soon at the Drinks De Capo."

"Hah! You and Saida both. She knows about key changes now."

"It doesn't take much to know more than you." Tak waggled his handlebar mustache.

Alesio gave him a playful shove with his free arm. "I know you're about to get some hot rice in your lap."

The *rasp-rasp* of cotton alerted him to someone approaching behind them. Alesio turned on his heel and blinked at Hestafon.

"What took you so long?" Alesio handed the rice bowl back to Tak. The wind gusted, foiled by the high partitions around them. Still, his breath fogged in front of his face, and he rubbed his hands together to warm them. He should've brought gloves. In the background, the violinist rejoined the celloist's gibe with the observation that the celloist was obviously new to both activities as he couldn't seem to employ his bow for either.

"As I already told you, I had some affairs to handle for the city." Hestafon sighed. He had on a cotton shirt and pants instead of his traditional silk and bows ensemble, though his blonde hair remained in the slicked back bun. "The volunteers for Tremain needed more instruction, and we spoke with Touchians to help Shape barriers at the other Portal Stations."

Tak placed a hand on the high walls. "I was surprised this

happened at all. I thought you said you'd do it but end up forgetting about it. Like what happened with the new houses in the straits."

Hestafon winced and held a sound cloth to his nose. "— things take time. And . . . would you mind not speaking at such a loud volume?"

Tak clicked his tongue. "Same old Testy Hesty, eh?"

"Delegate to the Council," Hestafon said.

Tak gestured through the opened gate leading to the portal. "You're free to go through, *Delegate*."

Alesio found himself wishing he could hear the next set of insults from the celloist, but he couldn't wait and waste more time.

The moment they passed through, Anthem's sunlight modulated from the high, crystalline coldness of a winter evening, casting long, purple shadows, to the lazy golden warmth of the Cloves' late spring afternoon. They both stopped shivering. Alesio bowed his head to the Tastian guard and gripped Hestafon's elbow with his fingers, propelling him outside the Portal Station and onto an empty side street. Alesio released him and pointed at Hestafon's bell case. "Prove that you can change sound into smell."

The piper raised an eyebrow and sighed, but he leaned over, unclasped his case, and plucked one of his smallest bells from its snug velvet inset. He closed his eyes and rang it.

Instead of a sound, the scent of maple sweetened the air around them.

Hestafon opened his eyes and peered at Alesio. "Proof enough for you?"

"Hmph. Neat trick."

"Trick, he says." Hestafon settled the bell back in his inset and snapped the case closed, shaking his head.

"Did you make it smell sweet because you love candy so much?"

"I didn't make it do anything. I chose the hand bell to create the least amount of noise, and that's what the magic decided to do."

Just because the piper could do what he said he could do, that didn't prove his loyalty. "Stay close. And don't even think about trying to give me the slip. I could catch you in three seconds. Walk next to me. No, on my right."

He gripped Hestafon's elbow again and prodded him through the main streets, keeping to the shadows, then ducked down another empty side alley.

"This isn't the way to the marketplace," Hestafon said.

"I changed my mind where we'd start." Alesio stopped. He'd tried to disrupt any route Hestafon might have planned in case he had sent a message to Clef somehow. "We can start from here."

Hestafon paused, staring at Alesio, then bent his ear towards the bag. He jerked his head up like a hunting dog. "That way." He stared in the direction Alesio had herded them, through the side alley and towards one of the smaller Cloves. Alesio couldn't decide if that was more or less suspicious.

Considering he said Clef's strongest sound-scent-whatever radiated from the Cloves, not Flock, everything about this is suspect.

Still, it was something. And he couldn't help that his stress had ebbed like a receding tide when Hestafon had said they needed to go to Taste.

Alesio gestured. "After you."

Hestafon swallowed and hurried on. He paused at the end of the alley, then, inclining his head as if to listen better, turned right.

The taste of early evening coated Alesio's tongue, a dust in the air from the people trudging through the streets, spiced with the ever-present salt-flats outside of town and coffee and honey from a nearby street vendor. To Alesio, it tasted like desperate hope. He might find Clef today.

The piper led him along a small, yet merry street, full of stone houses and thatched roofs. The Cloves had many people, though not quite as many as Anthem. Their city sprawled out over more area, since it had started out as several individual towns, and had, over the years, grown enough that they had built a massive wall around the entire spread. In this Clove, the people raised small gardens in their yards and weeded them without shoes, tasting berries, melons, and fruit trees, and of course, dirt on their skin without eating anything at all. Children raced along the rows of fruit, grinning with their mouths open as if catching flies.

Each Clove grew a focus crop, which they switched each year to keep the land fertile. Alesio didn't quite understand why but considering that transplants created variety and infused strength through mixed magics, the method made sense to him.

Some people had little stands on the sides of the road, and one young woman had a basket full of kandri peppers.

"Fancy a challenge, stranger?" The vendor sauntered over to Alesio, propping her prodigious breasts up with the basket. "When they're opened, the heat'll crips your tongue right up. Most men can't handle more than a single taste."

Alesio reddened and looked at the ground. "No thanks," he muttered.

"Sure about that?" She sidled over to him, her eyes roving over his shoulders and chest. Hestafon shuffled to the side as she crowded between them, picked out a pepper, and held it up. The scent of it so close gave Alesio the idea of what a fire might be like reincarnated as a fruit. "Why don't you just . . . try one? You might like—"

"I'm good on peppers today, thank you!" He dislodged himself from her, his face as red as the kandris, and dragged Hestafon along behind him.

He and Hestafon strode through the streets of the fruit Clove and reached the grain Clove, where short, still-green stalks of wheat and barley sprouted between each house like strips of a sea, waving in the breeze. Alesio trod on a particular spot where the people hadn't dug up the salt-flat ground, and he puckered his lips at the punch to his tastebuds. The people of the Cloves had dug up the salt where they wanted gardens, some of it five feet thick or more, and had piled it outside of town, but they hadn't rooted out every bit of salt from the city streets. They had also had to import water from outside the salt-flats on a regular basis, from the grassland steppes of Liranel. Balt had given everyone a history lesson in the Council meetings about how much labor his town had gone through to create the oasis of the Cloves.

Of course, the mention of anything outside the salt-flats had intrigued Saida, and on one of their expeditions they had followed a salt merchant for over two weeks—one of the longest explorations they'd ever done—traipsing through a mountain pass and ending up on the other side where the hills rolled like puppies and a stream from higher up the mountain flowed through them. They'd reached Liranel, a village of about three hundred and fifty or so, and the salt merchant traded their salt blocks for heavy jugs full of the vibrant stream water. The trade between the Cloves and the hill village had existed for well over a century, allowing the absurdity of an oasis in the middle of the salt-flats to exist.

Alesio smacked his lips. The first time he had drunk water that had originated *from* Taste had satiated him as much as drinking ten bottles of water at once. One swallow of Liranel's water could quench someone's thirst for a day and keep them alive for several. They should start a Portal Station out there soon. Maybe after they figured out how to stop the Hunger. Of course, they'd build one on Flock first, as the next largest city after the Cloves.

He sipped the water he'd brought from Sound. He'd purchased some Liranel water for Saida. She'd love it—maybe she'd do that little bobbing motion she did when she was excited, and her braid would flip back and forth over her shoulder.

Hestafon glanced back at him, then tipped his own water canteen up, gulping it. The piper's eyes widened, and he gasped, spluttering. Some of his hair fell out of its slicked back bun, fanning around his face.

"Haven't been out of Anthem much, have you?" Alesio hooked his water canteen back on his hip.

"It's not like the ground shouts at you in Sound."

Alesio huffed a laugh. "I'm sure anyone that visits Sound would say differently."

They reached the end of the grains area and reached another Clove full of warehouses, where people stored their produce to either sell to their neighbors or to the higher-up chefs. Hestafon marched for one of the warehouses, and Alesio held him back before they neared the main entrance. "Wait. We don't want to scare him off if he's in there."

Hestafon brushed at his forehead, grimacing at the taste of his own sweat on his hands. "Wonderful. I could use a moment."

They leaned against the outside of the stone warehouse. Alesio could taste the mixed bits of dirt, rock, and sand with his hands. "You sure this is the one?"

"I-I think so. And, you should know, there's a strong new sound-smell in there. I don't know it, it's musky but somehow sweet. It's giving me a headache."

"I'm sorry you have to suffer so much for my sake."

Hestafon stared at him.

"I'm stressed. Sorry."

"So, do we just run in, fists swinging like maniacs?"

"No and no. I'm going in, and you stay here. I don't see a piper having much fighting experience."

"True enough. Maybe we should return with reinforcements?"

"We could lose him if we leave. I've searched for him for months, and with that thing in the sky we have weeks left before something terrible happens. Maybe less."

Alesio led them around the large building until they found a side door. He pressed his ear against it and focused on the Sound room inside himself.

Sheet music lined the walls, much of it blank. Less of its magic filtered through on Taste, but some melodic lines showed here and there. He stepped forward and Shaped a string of rests on the wall, a long line of active silence. He opened his mouth and let the rests flow out from him, searching for any noise to continue their melody.

The Sound seeker was invisible to everyone, even him, but he sensed its results. It wove around the edge of the warehouse and streamed inside. Nothing tacked onto the rests' line of silence for several moments, until they relayed to him a clanging of scattered stones on a wooden table.

A man's voice said, "Six."

Another male voice, a sharper accent. Flockian. "Hah. Five."

They played Clinks, a common gambling game in Anthem where

the first person dropped anywhere from two to seven polished stones and the opponent tried to guess how many based on sound alone.

Alesio listened again, letting his line of rests wander a bit further. A quill scratched from a silent third person away from the other two. He could handle three people with the element of surprise. Beside him, Hestafon's hands shook, and his breathing labored with the telltale signs of someone new to fighting. Or maybe he suffered another panic attack. Alesio locked eyes with him and mouthed, "Ready?"

Hestafon, like most Soundians, could read lips. He nodded.

Alesio steadied himself with three slow, deep breaths. He tested the doorknob.

Locked.

He closed his eyes and entered his Touch magic room. He skimmed his hands over the walls until he found the cold metal of the doorknob and its adjoining lock, and he towed it through into his room and Shaped the whole thing into a metal spear tip, which he held in his hand.

He took his time. Shaping and physical exertion had much in common; he could travel across a field by strolling which consumed a little energy, or he could sprint across. Sprinting would travel the distance multitudes quicker but be proportionately taxing.

Over a minute passed in real time; metal required longer to Shape than almost anything else, especially on any other world than Touch. Alesio inhaled one more time, pulling in as much extra air as he could, and shoved the door open.

One of the men playing Clinks, a blonde man with curly hair, hopped off the box he sat on. Alesio hurled the metal spear tip at him. It dipped in the air but managed to embed itself in the man's thigh, who cursed and staggered, listing to one side. Alesio whistled, shooting two Sound knives straight from his lips at the smaller, wiry man sitting across the table from the first. One hit him in the shoulder, and he dove behind the table.

Alesio searched for the third man as his eyes still adjusted to the darker interior of the building. Motion to the left clued Alesio in. The man had snatched a mallet off the floor.

A whistle in the air from above. Burning pain flashed across the right side of Alesio's forehead and an arrow hit and skidded across the ground.

"Sounddamn it!" Alesio dashed towards the man with the mallet, distancing himself from the unseen archer. He hadn't heard any movement from them earlier, nor a snap of the bow string as they shot.

That's a sound bubble to keep me from hearing them. They were waiting for me!

He'd run right into an ambush. One picked to beat him.

Sounddamn you, Hestafon.

Sweat broke across his forehead, mixing and burning in his shallow cut.

Alesio had hoped to just detain people, but he had lost that luxury. The third man on the floor charged Alesio with the mallet. Alesio whistled three Sound knives that zipped into the man, all three burying into his chest. The man's body hit the ground and slid past Alesio, who dashed behind the cover of a stack of boxes, his heartbeat thudding in his chest.

He hated how easily he had shot those killing knives. Memories of cage matches flashed through his mind, and he fought them down.

"Nice shot!" A new voice, younger, sounded above him, from deeper in the warehouse. "It's impressive how you could miss a target that didn't know you were there!"

"Aw, silence yourself!" Another yell from above, this time from the direction of the arrow.

Alesio shot a pair of Sound knives that way, just catching a glimpse of a man up top.

The archer hummed up a sound shield before the knives reached. They dissipated to nothing. The archer backed out of view in silence.

He's producing a sound shield and bubble at the same time. That required a level of skill Alesio had not attained.

Alesio tucked himself behind the boxes. Factory equipment nestled in the corner, a clay furnace and crank turner. He recognized them from his short time working in the factory, before Clef had found him. One person would work the bellows to heat the cauldron of glass, and another would use various levers and cranks to pour the liquid glass into various instrument molds. The cooling instrument would roll out on the assembly belt, and more workers would test it for cracks, and string it. These seemed a bit forlorn and out of place amidst all the crates, like someone had shoved them there at random.

"What's wrong, Requiem?" The younger voice rang out loud and clear. "Did you forget the lyrics to our death songs?"

"Knock it off!" Another man yelled, one of the two he'd injured in the first few seconds.

It was helpful that they were all yelling. He didn't have to turn his head to hear all their words.

"You could just surrender," Alesio shouted. "Tell me. Where is Clef?"

"Oh sure, we surrender," another said quieter, someone closer to him from behind the boxes. A little hard to hear. A sharper accent. The Flockian. "How about ya step into the open so – can all talk?"

Alesio snorted. *Keep them talking.* "Sorry if I don't believe you, but even from here I can smell you're full of shit." He Shaped a Sound shield with the rest of his held breath just in case the Flockian could use Sound magic.

"Ha! I kind of like you—"

The smaller, wiry man Alesio had caught in the shoulder with a Sound knife stepped out from behind the corner of the boxes, swinging a club at head height. Alesio had pinpointed the man's approach and positioned himself on the wiry man's injured side so the Flockian couldn't attack with full force. Alesio ducked the swing and uppercut him in the jaw. A few teeth cracked and the man teetered backwards.

Guilt tapped on his heart, but these men would kill him in a moment if he faltered. Alesio kicked the man's knee backwards. The man collapsed like a sack of purpatoes.

Alesio pressed himself back against the boxes. He felt out of practice. His body couldn't keep pace with his racing thoughts.

"I present to you," The young man's voice rang out. "The Mighty Voice of Reconnection! Hey, Voice! Aren't you supposed to speak for peace?"

Alesio inhaled so he could shield against an attack. The air tasted off, like an earthy cinnamon. His mind sharpened, quickened, while his senses grew sluggish. His vision left streaks of afterimages. Cinnamon taste. Slowing.

Ixor.

Shit.

Either Clef had employed some Palates, or some of his non-cannibalistic minions had somehow acquired the slowing spice. He hadn't seen anyone throw a bag of it, but boxes and crates everywhere blocked his view.

Alesio doubted it was Palates. Watthe had turned most of the salt-wild cannibals into Consumed the year before, draining them and controlling their dead bodies. Alesio had found a sickening amount of ash-gray sludge on one of the expeditions on Taste; their bodies melted once Saida had transplanted Watthe.

Whoever had thrown the ixor hadn't hit his body or the potency would have clued him in right away.

Breathing would saturate him with ixor and using any more Sound magic would deplete the air he already had. He hadn't inhaled that much, and he could hold his breath for up to six minutes now in a fight. He peeked around the corner of the boxes, and an arrow planted itself inches from his eye. On the other side of the boxes more ixor drifted towards him.

"Come on out, Voice. There's no way the high and mighty Requiem fears a couple of cheap thugs!"

Alesio pressed his hand against the sides of the wooden boxes. He could Shape their softer material much easier than the small metal lock, so it took him about ten seconds to Shape one box into a spear and another into a shield. For some reason, his magic room had expanded, as large as two or even three rooms, perhaps fifty feet wide, and he had to sprint along the walls to find the right texture.

Back outside in the real world, sand poured from the first box, and small chunks of hardened clay fell out the other. The clay chunks held imprints of several tiny boxes, each a little larger than a tooth, and with little fastenings on each side.

Those molds looked like amplifiers.

"Alesio! Look out!" Hestafon yelled.

Alesio rolled to the side. Another arrow buried in the ground next to him. The archer had circled around the upper walkways for a better angle on Alesio.

Alesio darted underneath the walkway to escape the enemy's line of sight. Someone stabbed at him from around a corner, the blonde, curly-haired man he'd shot in the leg with the Shaped metal, using a spear of his own. Alesio blocked the spear, which embedded into his shield. The man pulled at the spear, tugging Alesio with his shield. Alesio struggled to keep his feet under him. *Damn ixor.*

He could craft an air shield with Touch magic to protect himself against more ixor, but he needed to save his magical energy, and he didn't need to inhale for another six minutes. He guessed he had about one more large use of Touch magic, or two smaller ones, based on how much of his inner room had had texture left on its walls. Anymore and he could drain himself, using too much of his remaining magic. *If only I could Receive better.*

The blonde man, who now wore a mask with a clear glass front and a filter to clean the air he breathed, swung a wide haymaker at him. Alesio blocked with his spear arm while he dropped the shield and slugged the guy. His punches had slowed like he swam through water, which left him open for attack. The man returned the blow to his side and Alesio released a small grunt, trying to hold his air in. He grabbed the blonde man's arm and countered with an elbow hard into his opponent's sternum while stepping his foot behind the man's non-injured leg. Alesio pushed through the attack, so the man tripped backwards, Alesio fell into the man's chest with his elbow.

Alesio swore he even *fell* slower—or the ixor had distorted his mind more than he'd realized. Either way, by the sound of it, the man had at least a couple cracked ribs. Alesio ripped the glass mask off the man's face and shoved it over his own. He sucked in a deep breath and tasted clean air through the filter.

By the Sound, his side throbbed. Even his elbow ached like he'd slammed it against rock instead of the man's chest. Ixor exaggerated all physical sensations.

His opponent lay on the ground, his mouth open, gasping for air—air that became cloudier every moment from the fine brown ixor powder. How much of that stuff did they have?

Had Clef bolted out a back door? Or had this all been a setup, and he'd never been here in the first place?

Hestafon cowered next to him, covering his ears, then his mouth, making it hard to hear all his words. "I swear, – didn't know!"

"You were supposed to stay outside."

"You were about to – shot!"

Alesio searched in the dim light for the archer above him. A young black man in his late teens or early twenties met Alesio's eyes on the upper walkways. His textured hair pushed his hood higher, showing a bit of his face.

"You took out another one." A hazy cloud spilled from the young man's mouth, and Alesio narrowed his eyes at it. "Guess you really are the best. Or were."

Ixor. This young man exhaled ixor.

How did such a power work without slowing the fighter down?

He caught fuzzy movement out of the corner of his eye; the archer drawing his bow. This Soundian was good.

The archer released another silent snap of his bow. Too fast.

Alesio ducked.

If he died here . . .

He pictured a morning he'd shared with Saida. The morning sun through the window. The warmth of her body next to his, her skin touching his, her heartbeat mixing with his, the smell of her hair, the sound of her breathing.

The arrow whistled above Alesio's head, brushing his hair.

I'm alive!

He snapped back into the here and now. Still holding his breath to conserve the air for Shaping Sound magic, he dashed through the edges of the descending cloud of ixor, surprising the archer before he could nock another arrow.

Alesio grabbed the wooden support holding up the walkway. In his Touch magic room—enlarged to the size of a small house, now—he found the wooden texture on the walls that represented it, pulled the magic through, and Shaped it. He hollowed it out and used the extra material from the inside of it to create protrusions like branches, the first thing he thought of. He poured as much magic as he could into it, accelerating the change and using almost everything he had. The time distortion rippled as it tended to when he pushed himself to his limits, and the walls of the room shuddered.

Switching in and out of the magic rooms didn't give him any real extra time, as he understood it. He'd tried to use the rooms' time distortion before to catch his breath or to plan something complicated in an urgent situation, but if he didn't actively Receive or Shape, both rooms forced him to leave. While inside them, everything seemed dreamlike, and time *felt* different, like it meandered to the side or at an angle instead of marching straight. The sensation reminded him of Vision's gravity shifts.

He returned from his magic room to the wooden beam snapping and crashing to the floor. Alesio staggered. His Shaping had almost drained him, smoothing the textured walls of his Touch magic room, though it remained oddly large. Touch magic was so *touchy*—he never knew how much Received magic he needed to complete a Shape.

It worked, though. The walkway bent with a groan and the archer fell. A big cloud of dirt and dust billowed up, but not enough to obscure the archer landing on the "branches" Alesio had Shaped. The man hung in the air, three different thin wooden sticks piercing his body.

The archer had held his Sound shield as he fell, which had silenced his scream.

Bleak despair tore through him as he fought off the old whispers.

He'd fought this battle before and won. He didn't kill in senseless cage matches, only when he had to. He used his voice for better things. He breathed in, raspy in the mask.

"By the Senses." The young man's voice rang out in the sudden quiet. He emerged from the dust about halfway to the ground, balancing where the walkway now rested at an angle. "You're way worse than he said you'd be. And by that, I mean you're awesome."

The impact had blown the ixor around the room, diluting it but also making it more difficult to avoid. Hestafon covered his face with his hands near the boxes, trembling.

Alesio adjusted the mask to fit it tighter. "Where's Clef?" he shouted upwards at the young man.

"What makes you think I'd tell you if I knew?"

"He's helping the Hunger! He's trying to destroy the worlds! Why are you working with him?"

"Why do you think, bug-ass?"

"He has something on you, then." Alesio's words sounded faster in his own ears. "Help me take him down. He's using you."

"Ha! He said you'd say that." His voice hardened, at the same time, gaining pace. "But you're the one who's stolen everything from me."

He strolled down the tilted walkway, leaving afterimages. Alesio's eyes hurt. *What does he mean by that?*

"What's wrong? Having a – trouble keeping up?" With each sentence, more ixor spouted from his mouth.

Alesio tried to lift his arms to a fighting stance. Almost three seconds passed before one obeyed, the other trailed even behind more, and the streaky afterimages of his own moving limbs almost caused him to lose his balance and his breakfast. He squinted down at himself. Ixor coated the left side of his body, probably from when the walkway had crashed into the ground and kicked up a cloud of dust.

I didn't breathe that much in. It shouldn't affect me just by touching it, even on Taste.

The young man ambled towards Alesio, though to Alesio he seemed to streak in a long blur, his mind and eyes so de-synced that he struggled to process. The ixor-user pulled a long, thin knife from a sheath on his belt like a smear of ash.

Hestafon rushed the young man, gripping the spear, hollering the whole time. The ixor user sidestepped the assault, and the next thing Alesio knew, Hestafon sprawled on the ground and the young man leaned over him. He breathed a cloud of ixor into Hestafon's face, who coughed and thrashed in a paroxysm of distortion.

Another blink, and the young man appeared less than a foot from Alesio's face.

"Surprised?" The young man's grin smudged his cheeks. "Thought you'd be safe if you minimized – breathing?" He grabbed Alesio's forearm and swiped it with a finger.

Pain seared him like a hot iron.

The ixor-user held up his finger covered in the ruddy brown spice. His voice and his face had begun to blur as Alesio's senses slowed. "My ixor works just – touching your skin. It sinks into your muscles and blood. So, you can – on holding your breath, but it won't matter. Your heart will beat – and slower, until your blood won't reach your brain." He flicked the spice from his fingertip into Alesio's face.

Alesio struggled to understand the too-fast words. He couldn't lip read anymore. He could almost feel his internal organs slowing. His chest began to hurt. Everything had smeared around him, the warehouse itself, the crates, his own hands, and yet his thoughts zipped like frenzied birds. If he could just grab the spear that Hestafon had dropped. It had fallen not two feet from him. Yet the mental command he gave his legs to bend and dive for the weapon took time to travel to those limbs, precious time. Five seconds seemed to pass before his legs braced for the dive, and by then, the young man had scoffed and kicked the spear out of reach, creating a blurred spear that seemed to stretch ten feet away.

"Your brain will race, and –, and race, till it shuts off, and you black out," the ixor user went on. "Like blowing out a candle. You'll suffocate with – lungs full of air."

He pushed Alesio with one hand, but though Alesio sent the mental command to dodge, once again, his body didn't respond in time. He fell backwards and hit the ground. It felt like he'd fallen off a three-story building, shunting his breath out of him.

"– guess – answer – before you die. – He's not –. – was, – minutes ago. Just missed –."

Is he talking about Clef? Alesio's partial deafness, combined with the ixor, made it almost impossible to understand the young man's words.

In another blink, the ixor-user had left the building. From far, far away, the young man's voice shouted, "Help! –! – – hurt men –!"

Why would he call for help? Did I imagine that?

His back screamed at him from the fall. His heart ached, straining and failing to beat at its normal rhythm. The ixor coated his body, every particle an ember. He almost blacked out from the pain.

What could he do?

The line of cleaner skin on his forearm sharpened into focus, where the young man had swiped his finger. The ixor coated him like flour.

A thought popped up, one of the dozens that whirred through his mind in that second, and he seized it. He entered his Touch magic room. It had increased to the size of a large house. Did it have something to do with the ixor?

He couldn't think straight, not with the ixor, not in the dreamlike effect of his magic room. He had a tiny bit of Received magic left. The walls' texture had a slight bump to them.

He called to mind the sensation of trying to Shape sand; how it could exist as so many particles, or a clump altogether. When he touched and imagined the endless expanse of the desert sand, it would bury him under its vastness. But he could form thousands upon thousands of grains of sand into a staff, a cube, or a shield, and hold its Shape with a stream of Touch magic.

Inside his Touch magic room, he dashed around, skating his hands on the walls, trying to find—there!

The fine, gritty particles of ixor, a patch low to the ground. This represented the particles touching him; they pulsed with a brighter energy level. Once he knew what to feel for, he could sense all the ixor in contact with him, including the bits that had seeped inside his body.

He focused on them all and pulled them through the wall.

Ixor ran across his skin like rain drops rolling down a window. It flowed through his body, seeped out of his mouth, his nose, the cuts he'd received during the fight, even the corners of his eyes. The particles scattered at his feet in his Touch room, though in reality, the ixor remained inside him. He hadn't Shaped them into anything yet; the particles would stay in him until he did so.

The magic room's enlarged size made it difficult to scoop it all up and press it into a ball. Hours seemed to pass in the time distortion as he trudged back and forth, and sometimes he swore that the ball would shrink or expand depending on where he lumbered. *I'm hallucinating now. Not good.*

He'd Shaped the ixor into a condensed ball. He left the magic room and tossed it as far as he could away from himself.

He could move his arms again. He could hear. His vision didn't smear and leave afterimages. Fatigue swept through him from the aftereffects, but at least semi-functionality had returned to him.

He needed to escape. Now.

Ixor still filled the air inside the warehouse. The second he twitched a muscle more particles would latch onto him. He spun and there lay Hestafon convulsing. Without a mask.

Alesio grimaced but grabbed the piper and slung him over his shoulder, dashing out, his muscles slowing once again. He reached the outside, lowered Hestafon's limp body to the ground, and threw up.

As he wiped his mouth, he realized Hestafon's breathing had shallowed out and slowed to a lethargic tempo.

Alesio tried brushing the ixor off the piper's pale skin, but the spice just smeared, and if his heartbeat had slowed, that meant it had slowed his organs like it had done to Alesio.

He kept his hand on Hestafon and entered his Touch magic room, searching for the ixor as he had before. More time passed than before, as he had to trace the particles through touching Hestafon's skin, which pulsed with less energy, but he discovered a small area high up on the wall with ixor's powdery texture. He tugged, Receiving the magic. Not as much sieved through as the first time, enough to cover him up to his waist, and he scraped the particles together with broad sweeps.

The piper's breath had slowed even further, and Alesio Shaped the particles with reckless urgency. He scooped the ixor up, packed the particles into several hasty balls, then returned to the physical world and tossed them away. The balls broke apart into a dusty cloud away from them.

The piper lay there, his chest rising and falling in short, shallow breaths, his hair all undone around his face.

Sweat covered Alesio like a blanket. He fell to his knees. If the fighter hadn't stuck around to kill Alesio, he must have disappeared. His vision had blurred again. His head ached, and his mouth had dried out like he'd camped a week in the salt-wilds. He groaned.

"Are you alright, sir?" Someone said. Their arms seemed too long, and their features ran off their face. He closed his eyes and groaned more.

"– ixor. – help! – might – Palates nearby!"

His head pulsed even stronger. "W-water," he managed to say, and then darkness overcame him.

13

THE GODDESS HEAD

Saida, Naya, and Marik slept from late afternoon until the
infant hours of the next day. They had to wait several hours
after that for the morning sun to filter through the firmament
of the trees before they could begin their explorations. A glowing,
neon moss grew over most of the squat trees, but the moss's light
didn't extend far, and pitch darkness waited outside it because the
jungle canopy covered the stars, the moon, and the light from the four
other Sensory planets.

"Almost all the streets have holes," Marik had said. "I know my way
around, but you both could fall or trip over a crumbling wall or
something."

So, they had all waited inside the house. Saida had tried to study
the Lunnites' language but had ended up pacing instead until the first
bits of dawn peeked through the tree covering like birds searching
where to build their nests.

The fuming heat had calmed down overnight, but the humidity
had already begun strangling the air. They set out under the dark
green canopy, sweat beading on their necks and pooling above the
collar of Naya's buoy suit. Saida left hers off and kept her fur on. A bit
of greenish-yellow marred Naya's cheek, and tender spots had

bloomed on Saida's knees from when she'd slammed into the water board at the end.

Another giant wheel moldered in a huge pond area, surrounded by stagnating algae and covered in the creeping vines. Saida stared at it. "Have there been overgrowths here? I know that some fox-people—I mean, Lunnites—can sense magic."

Marik helped Naya over a part of the street that had collapsed into the water. He had unwound the sleeves of his plant fiber shirt and the wrappings around his hair-tail much like one might unwrap long scarves, which dangled from his waist. The wind's teeth could not chew through the jungle trees, decreasing the need for skin protection and, in fact, discouraging it because of the heat and humidity. The Lunnites could unwind or wind the plant fibers around themselves depending on their need.

Other things had become clear as well. Marik did not possess the bulky legs of the Touchians who waded every day through the Glass Sea, but ropy, lean muscles flexed on his shoulders and arms from surfing the Summit Wave and Shaping the water with a steady, unrelenting, uplifting of his arms.

"We have maintained this city for generations," Marik said, as Naya crossed the street. "Though most Lunnites cannot trim magic as foxans can—" he smiled at Saida's open mouth— "Yes, over the 3,000 or so years we cared for this place, a few could trim overgrowths. But we rely on preventative measures. Most of us can sense when magic becomes restless, when it might need trimming in the future. So, we move whatever we can to a new area in the city, or even elsewhere on Touch. You see that bit of blueish ivy on the tower? My friend Trasi clipped it from the side of a house because she sensed it would want to emulate the sky. That's when it turned blue instead of green."

"So, you've done miniature transplants." Saida shifted to more of a foxan and leapt up without Marik's aid. Marik followed her smooth change, his bright green eyes the same shade as the neon tree moss of the jungle night. He looked away when she reached the top.

She tried to imagine herself from his perspective. He must have grown up on stories about foxans but hearing about something and seeing it had different effects on a person. Her shifting that ranged from one end of the foxan-human spectrum to the other, blending the barrier between, while he and the other Lunnites endured with the same form from birth, must have fascinated them, and maybe even maddened them, to watch. When she shifted in front of fox people like Naya, which had happened a few times over the past year as the small communities had crept out of hiding in the cities, many had reacted with wide-eyed jealousy, not this hero worship and undisguised devotion.

"It doesn't always work as well as we hope." Marik led them through a building with holes in the walls, swishing his long hair away from snagging on a rusted copper wire strung through the house. More of those wires had hung in other places around the city, tangled around vines or trailing off the houses.

Naya pointed at it. "I'm guessing you don't know what those wires did, either?"

"We have theories, of course, but it could be any number of things. Lunnites for generations have sensed that most of these devices are unhappy, but they never want to be moved. It's more like they're not doing what they want with their magic."

Saida brushed the rusted metal with her fingers. Maybe physical contact would give her an echo of a voice?

Nothing happened. She stepped away with a too-familiar ache. "Has anyone tried transplanting something here instead?"

Marik sighed. "We can bring magical things here but none of them have taken." He jerked his chin. "The Goddess Head lies ahead of us."

About fifty yards away, five stone pillars ringed a large carving of a woman's head that reached Saida's waist.

A few orbiting lines in the stone surrounded the site, like the ones around the stone tree Epitaph, except most of the lines had weathered into obscurity or cracked. Two of the stone pillars had fallen and crumbled in the street.

Faded and broken Lunnite script, those symbols composed of interlocking spheres, coated the inside of the larger circles and covered the Goddess Head like impressions of hair on its silvery surface. No weeds or vines climbed over it, and someone had wedged candles in the circular groove encircling the huge carved head like a constant vigil. An overhang of a nearby tower shielded the statue from rain and what little wind might have wandered into the area. No magic emanated from it that Saida could tell.

Marik strode over to it, and Saida and Naya followed, avoiding the many potholes in the street around it. He lifted one of the candles and held it over his head. "We honor you, Goddess. Guide us to your will, so may we better serve you."

Saida and Naya side-eyed each other, then bowed their heads too.

Marik motioned them over. "We care for it as best we can. But it's too far from the Directive, what you call the Epitaph, so weather and time has long since worn the carvings away. Just a small part remains, which has guided us since before the Severing, and beyond:

"WE HEAR that the cities on the other worlds are also thriving. We . . . have divined . . . close to a breakthrough. With all of us, we will locate Lunne, and . . . she will . . ."

"DO YOU SEE?" Marik's bright gaze bored into Saida's. "We must find the other cities. We already have an idea of where they are. And that's not even the best part." He pointed at one of the pillars. A small groove circled it, and somehow part of it had shading etched into it. It reminded Saida of the phase of a moon, and it had an 'x' on it on the lower right. She bent to examine the next pillar, one of the broken ones, and found the same thing, except for different shading. If Saida squinted, the circle at the top had squiggles that could have symbolized water, and that same circle had trees farther on, where an 'x' showed in its middle. Saida ran to the next one, a realization forming.

"This is a map of the five worlds," Naya said.

"Yes!" Marik pointed at the one with water and tree symbols. "That's Sedella. We think each of these 'xs' indicate another ancient city like ours. That circle has wavy symbols, that's Sound. They might have something underneath that have words, but they're too faded to make out what it said." He showed them the next one. "This one, well, it's a little hard to tell at all, but underneath it says 'Sen' and we think that one's Scent. That one's picture is too indefinite. And this one has a sun depicted on it and its matching word is faded again. We don't know about that one—"

"That's probably Taste," Saida said. "The salt-flats reflect the sunlight, so everything is brighter there."

Marik stared at her, his long hair swishing back and forth as a tail. "By Lunne. This. This is why you needed to see this. The others wanted you to start searching for the other cities right away, but you know more about the worlds than anyone, which will narrow down our search!"

Saida studied the map on the ground, hunting for more xs. "So, you think your ancestors figured it out? How to find Lunne?" She squinted at a symbol inside the groove. Something about it seemed familiar to her. "What does this mean?"

"That? That's the word for 'shape.' And yes, we believe they did. Or, perhaps, they got very close."

Saida pointed out the x on the one with the wavy line that he'd said could be Sound. "Is there a theory for why that x shimmers like that?"

"What?" Marik squinted at it. "What do you mean?"

"It's glittering, like a light shines underneath it."

Marik cocked his head, bending closer. Naya joined them. "I don't see it."

"Huh. Maybe it's just a trick of the light."

"I have a question, too." Naya waved for them to join her. "Is that the sun?" She pointed out five straight lines above the five-circle pattern.

"Our scholars believe it to be so."

"If that's the sun, then we could figure out where each of the xs would be." Naya tapped her chin. "That'd narrow down the search."

"Correct." Marik pointed at Touch's circle, which had shading etched about a fourth of the way across its face. "The illustration shows Touch at midmorning. So, during midmorning here, we hope to find the ruins on Sound here." He pointed at the x at the top of the circle with wavy lines, on the lighter side. "Do you see that it has shading to three-fourths of the world?"

"Evening," Saida said.

"Yes. So, we know that at evening on Sound, the x shows near the top of the world, roughly two to three hours past sunset based on this engraving. We didn't know for sure which world in the sky was which, but now that you opened the portals between them, we can see for ourselves and lead you there." He paused. "When the magic you call the 'Epitaphs' began transmitting energy across the worlds, many of them corresponded in direction to our rough estimates of the marked x's. They shine like beacons, guiding us to the other ancient cities, and we hope will lead to more information like what we have here in Sedella."

Saida drew in a breath. "Not all of them, though. We found an Epitaph already on Touch, inside a cave. It didn't have this circle writing."

"Correct. We sensed thirteen strong magics across the worlds, while the pillars display just five xs."

Saida paused, contemplating. What might the ancient foxans have meant for them to discover? Did a Goddess really exist that could fix things?

If I could just hear what they were saying!

Their absence still ached, real or not. She stared at the Goddess Head, at the mouth, and strained with her ears.

Nothing.

Naya studied the pillars. The fox-person had the mind of a scholar and a careful and studious manner. Years of hiding from humans in the Cloves must have polished her ability to analyze information.

"I need some time to process all this." Saida rubbed at her temples with her human fingers, stopping herself from picking at her braid. The end of it had thinned from her bad habit. "I think we should go back to Anthem and tell the others what we've found."

Marik's hair-tail twitched, his face impassive. "Yes. Of course. Of course." He paused. "You might want to see one more thing before you teleport back. It's . . . it might be frightening for you, though."

"What could be worse than the Hunger?" She snorted. "A year ago, I worked so hard to keep the worlds together, to stop them from drifting apart. And now, it seems it was all for nothing. It's happening again, all at once, and—"

Naya glanced up from her perusal of the pillars and Marik's hair-tail twisted in a knot.

Saida bit her tongue. "I'm sorry. I'm sorry, I don't mean to worry you."

She couldn't just voice her fears like that anymore. She needed to convey confidence. She didn't work alone any longer. She had her parents and Tener to help with shoring up the magic of the worlds, and Alesio . . .

"C'mon." Naya grasped Saida's hand. To Marik she said, "Alright. One last thing. Then we go back to Anthem."

ALESIO WOKE UP IN A SMALL, white room on Taste. He knew it was Taste because the musk of ixor lingered in his mouth like a weight, contrasted by an astringent, soapy flavor. He jolted up in the bed, confused, his thoughts churning.

"You're awake. Thank the Sound." Hestafon leaned forward in a chair on his right side, his blonde hair clean and straight, hanging down to his chin. He wore a simple wool tunic.

The encounter at the warehouse. The factory equipment. The young fighter who could breathe ixor.

"Water," he croaked.

Hestafon handed him a glass from a bedside table.

"How—how long was I out?"

The piper pulled the white walls aside, and they rippled like a blanket. Had Hestafon used magic? Alesio blinked; his vision clearing —those were curtains hung around his bed, and beyond them existed a larger room around him with more beds and people laying on them.

The piper sighed. "Twenty-two hours. I woke up not too long before you."

"*Twenty-two hours!* Why didn't you leave?" Alesio scrubbed at the sleep crusted in the corners of his eyes.

"Leave?" Hestafon leaned back, his forehead creasing. "While you were unconscious?"

Alesio blinked at him. "You're a Council delegate, and Anthem's leader. A full day and night have passed."

Hestafon fiddled with the clasps on his bell case on his lap. "Well, my station calls for me to do this, as well. Seeing to the safety of Sound by apprehending Clef. Something that only I can help with, as you pointed out. And you explained quite thoroughly this might take several days, so I was prepared for a longer time away."

He seems awfully dedicated to helping me.

Hestafon had saved him from that arrow. Why would he have done that, if Clef owned his loyalty?

Ugh. His head pounded, like someone trying to batter the door of his brain open with their fist.

Regardless, he needed Hestafon for something other than just tracking Clef down, now. He had to face that fact.

"Anyway," Hestafon said. "The physician here said that the worst of the effects should wear off after a normal night of rest. We had a hideous case of it, so we slept a lot longer."

A tall shadow appeared on the other side of the curtain. "Knock knock."

"Come in," Alesio said.

A tall black woman swept the curtain aside. Alesio angled his good ear towards her.

"My name is Christa," she said. "Good to see you're both awake. Ixor-poisoning is not something to brush off. May I check you over now?"

"Yes, of course."

The doctor checked his eyes and used some sort of device to listen to his heart. Alesio asked her, "Do you know of anyone who can breathe ixor? As part of their magical ability?"

Christa frowned and tucked her listening device away in a pocket. "I don't, but then again, I'm from the Cloves. Ixor comes from the dried and ground plant from Liranel. Someone with such a unique ability would likely come from there." She tapped him on the arm. "Does this hurt?"

"Just a little more sensitive. My head hurts, though."

"That should recede over the next few hours." She paused. "So. You are saying that a person with such an ability poisoned you?"

Alesio nodded. He stopped when the motion made him a little queasy.

"They must have an uncommon grip on their magic. By the time someone would ingest enough to slow their heart, they should have already stopped breathing, as the ixor floods the lungs first through their breath."

"We didn't inhale it," Alesio said. "Its effects worked just by settling on our bare skin. He coated us in it."

Christa's eyes widened and a few caretakers at other beds paused and glanced over.

"That would explain it," Christa said. "Such a power would devastate your heart in moments. It's a miracle you survived." She tilted her head. "Most people couldn't live through that."

Alesio reached in his pocket and fingered the casing he'd picked up in the warehouse.

Clef could manufacture amplifiers.

The hood had shadowed the fighter's mouth, but Alesio bet he might've seen a flash of silver on his teeth. Or maybe the young man had Hestafon's condition, a mixture of magic where one transformed into the other. Either reason could explain how the ixor user's Taste magic affected people through their skin.

Regardless, Alesio couldn't hope to win against such an ability. The young man had strung him along in the warehouse, played with him. He could have won without help from the other fighters.

"I gathered the ixor with my Touch magic," Alesio said.

"Otherwise, I'm sure we'd both lie in a different room with sheets over our bodies."

Christa's lips thinned like a musician's sound quality when they tried to sing outside their range. "I figured some sort of magic had saved your lives, because the amount of ixor in that warehouse could kill half of a Clove." She paused. "You must understand that this is a difficult story to believe."

Alesio tried to say something, but she collected her suspicion and penned it in with a strong breath. "You are both free to leave, as you exhibit no signs of ixor withdrawal or addiction such as skin breakdown or tearing. This leads me to believe you are telling the truth, and you are truly victims of an attack. But I would *strongly* advise you to stay another night so I can confirm you will not have adverse effects."

"I promise to take it slow," Alesio said, glancing at Hestafon. "But we have to get going."

She sighed. "No exertion such as running or climbing anything. I'm looking at you, Voice of Reconnection. You weathered the worst dose."

He smiled. "Thanks for the advice." He swung his legs off the bed, waiting for the pounding in his head to calm down. It did after a few moments, and he raised his eyebrows at Hestafon. "Ready?"

They left the healing house under several caretakers' glances and whispers, emerging into the waning sunlight of a busy street in the Cloves.

"Alright," Alesio said. "If you're sticking with me for now . . ."

Hestafon flicked his gaze over to him, then back away. He swiped his hands down his wool tunic, as if trying to reach into a pocket, then stopped himself. "Yes?"

Alesio struggled with the words in his mind, then spit them out. "I need your help."

14

O'ER TIME AND DELL

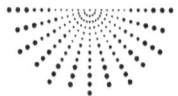

"This way." Marik guided them through more of the ruins, and they threaded around several piles of rubble as the streets and houses all but disappeared into the Glass Sea, here, covered in green and dark brown algae. After about an hour, the trees thinned, and the sun shone overhead once again. Or, it would have, had the Hunger not eclipsed its light. Marik rewound the strips of plant fibers swaying from his waist around himself like long, wide scarves. He also produced more fibers from his pack and re-wrapped his hair-tail.

They had reached the other side of the jungle. The water deepened to the dark blue, almost black of a depth, yet it stretched far and wide, so it seemed like they teetered on the edge of a cliff or peered down into a sky without stars. A magic welled from it like a slow, released breath, reminding Saida of a massive hibernating swanseize.

Things floated on top of and inside this depth. Trees, algae, and driftwood. The water from either end of the jungle flowed towards this area as if magnetized.

"One day after the Summit flows to an end, it begins here." Marik squinted at the sun. "It's time."

The ground rumbled.

"Hold onto this." Marik pointed at a bigger stone piece poking above the others. They gripped weathered handholds.

The sound increased, and the smaller stones danced on the ground around them in a frenetic jig. Something garnet appeared underwater, and it widened, and widened, and rocks appeared, jutting above the surface.

Rocks? Saida blinked. No. Teeth. A mouth as large as the gigantic depth had opened beneath the surface, like the jaws of the planet.

Then it snapped shut with the sound almost as loud as the Hunger's voice, but closer, like how she imagined experiencing an avalanche on Sound. The water of the depth rose, and rose, and rose, into a sheer cliff of a wave, and the jaw sank back down into the depths of the sea. The Summit Wave roared away from them, growing as it picked up speed and water from the rest of the Glass Sea.

They had to wait until the sound of it had dissipated before anyone could hear each other. Even so, Saida and Naya stared at it as it receded into the distance.

"And that's how we travel," Marik said. "The Lunnites that can use Touch magic jump on the Summit as it forms. There's not too many of us. Nine in our whole city right now. But I'm proud to say that I mastered it at a young age."

"What *is* that thing?" Naya shivered, the red fur peeking out from her Touchian suit-sleeves spiked from the water. "Does it ever rise farther than that?"

"We call it the Wavemaker. And no. It's as regular as the sun. Throughout the week, bits of flotsam and wreckage from the Summit trickle down from either side of the jungle, and that's what it eats. And every week, at this time, it closes its mouth and swallows all the debris."

Saida stared at where the mouth had gone. Her next words slipped out before she could stop them. "That's what it'll look like if the Hunger eats our worlds."

They jerked their heads over at her, startled. Naya followed Saida's gaze upward and paled. They regarded the void, high overhead where the Hunger had eclipsed the sun, showing their spots of land in stark contrast to the rest of their emptiness, especially the mass in the middle, and the corona of twisting clouds and skies surrounding them. Vision had just risen, casting a pale, purple reflection on the Glass Sea, creating the effect of twilight in midday.

The importance and urgency of her mission pressed on her, heavy and unshakable.

She had to fix this. Or, at least, find an ancient knowledge to tell her how to fix this, because she didn't know what to do.

"Let's go back," Saida said. "I want to try and find the next Epitaph on Sound, where it glowed to me."

Marik's face lit up. "I am honored to guide you, Envoy. I hope that, as we journey and read the ancients' words, we will travel closer to the Goddess's heart and find her soon. Before it is too late."

Saida shivered. "Before it is too late," she murmured.

Saida, Naya, and Marik just stared at the Glass Sea for a few moments, at the ripples and the receding cliff of the new Summit Wave. The sun peeked out once more from behind the Hunger, bringing the afternoon back.

When and where was Alesio right now? Did he walk somewhere in the evening, or under a night sky? His absence hit her like a sudden, knotted muscle. She missed his face, his voice, the way he kissed her . .
.

"Youbothready?" She asked Naya and Marik, her words running together.

Naya raised her eyebrows and smiled at her.

Marik's eyes widened and his hair-tail flicked behind him. "Whenever you would like. The sooner the better!"

Saida summoned a portal.

Her bond with Alesio quivered, that thread between them that Tener could see, she could suddenly *feel*.

Could she . . .

She tugged on the bond, entranced, and wound up the distance between them like yarn. She wound and wound, and there Alesio strode towards her, talking with someone. He stumbled at the sight of the portal, his dark-brown eyes widening and his mouth dropping open.

She ran to him, that thread shuddering like a plucked mandolin string.

He folded her in his arms and stroked her hair, and hummed in his magical silver tenor, and she melted. She settled like a bird on a branch after a long, long flight.

She'd teleported straight to Alesio. Not to a place, but to *him*. How had she done that?

"Saida." Alesio nuzzled his chin between her foxan ears, then kissed the top of her head. "How did you—is something wrong? Are you hurt?"

"You're my favorite place."

He squeezed her tighter. "I was worried about you."

His shirt possessed a faint, musky odor and his dark brown skin had a pale cast. "Why do you . . . your shirt smells like ixor." She gasped. "Did the Palates attack you?"

"Not exactly."

"Then why . . .?"

Someone cleared their throat behind her. Naya had stepped through Saida's portal along with Marik. Naya gripped both Marik and Hestafon's—*Hestafon?*—shoulder. Naya cleared her throat again and pushed the two head ahead of her. She glanced back and winked at Saida, her slitted foxan pupils reflecting the moonlight.

Saida had teleported to the Cloves. Nighttime reigned here, and the air had a brighter, brisker tinge than the languid moistness of Sedella. She drew it in her lungs, invigorated.

"Saida, I have so much to tell you." Alesio held her hand. "Do you . . . want to go to my house tonight and talk?"

She shouldn't want to. She shouldn't. But she wanted to stay with him as long as possible, as long as her nature allowed her. In case her fickle and forgetful heart shifted at a moment's notice. In case the Hunger consumed their world today.

Selfish, selfish. He deserves someone who knows they will stay.

She couldn't tell, but that voice sounded like Tricksy Stone. Or, at least, the part that had merged back with her when she'd transplanted Tricksy Stone into the Cadenza. The harsh, unrelenting part of herself that forced her to remember what she'd rather forget.

"Yes," she said, and hated herself for it.

". . . as big as the Summit Wave but submerged. It was like the world yawned and showed its teeth!"

"Something that large could be an overgrowth, right?" Alesio laid beside her and toyed with the tendrils of hair that had escaped her braid.

"Well, it flows, though. Overgrowths are stagnant magic. That thing sucks in debris then pushes a new Wave out every week. Keeps the Glass Sea clean." She paused, considering. "But I should send my parents or Tener out there. Just to check."

"Hmm." He wrapped a piece of her hair around his finger, rolling it so that his hand brushed her scalp. She shivered at the contact.

"Alesio. Are you listening to me?"

"I'm listening to that little gasp you just did."

She licked her lips. His closeness muddled her thoughts. Her breath hovered in her throat as if it had a different gravity. He strolled his fingers down the column of her throat, then back up to her cheek. He framed her face with his hands, searching her eyes like someone might search shards of the sky. "I missed you." His silver tenor cracked on the last word.

"I missed you too." The depth of his emotions both entranced and worried her, even though she felt the same. "Are you sure you're alright?" She touched his cheek, frowning at the unnatural pallor of his skin.

"My head still aches some, but it's gotten better than when I woke up. That was intense." Her hand stiffened on his cheek, and he inclined his head and pressed his mouth to her palm. "I promise to take it easy for a few days."

"Well . . . doesn't ixor increase both pain and pleasure?" She wiggled her eyebrows.

He laughed. "Sadly, that symptom's gone." His smile faded. "I don't like that Clef has someone like that in his employ. That he could somehow affect us even when we didn't breathe it . . . that's a powerful ability."

Disappointment stung her at his change of subject, but she quashed it. He hadn't rebuffed her; she knew more than anyone how fear could stifle most anything. Hadn't he helped her out of those moments, when she couldn't seem to free herself from Carn's words in her mind?

She laced her fingers through the dark curls of hair behind his ear and struggled to arrange her thoughts into words with the effect of gentleness as well as the intention of it. "I wish he was locked up. I worry about how he haunts you."

He stilled and glanced away, his shoulders hunching.

She drew his chin back. "Did I upset you?"

"No. That's . . . an apt description. Haunting." He dragged in a breath. "He'll target you, Saida. He knows I care for you. I have to . . . I have to find him. I have to stop him before he—" He covered his face with his hands.

"Hey. Hey, it's okay. I'm safe." She hugged him, murmuring soothing sounds on his right side, and he breathed in jagged gasps against her chest, as if Sound knives had torn him up on the inside.

She kept talking, rambling, not knowing what else to do. "You'll find him. He's not all-powerful, you know. I'm sure the grand and magnificent Lunne will stop him."

He chortled maniacally into her shirt. She giggled, and then they guffawed together.

"Don't let the Lunnites hear you say that." Alesio wiped his tears with a kerchief and blew his nose. He paused. "Marik's being a gentle . . . uh, Lunnite, with you, right?"

"He is. He seems a little stuck on me even more than my parents or Tener, but I think that's just because of the Reconnection. Or maybe it's just because I'm the foxan he's traveling with."

"I could come with you tomorrow, to hunt for the next city."

"Didn't you want to keep tracking Clef?"

He stayed quiet a moment.

Had she responded too fast? Hadn't they both agreed to follow their separate goals? Her throat tightened. She'd kept her distance for a grand total of two days. How could she both want and not want something at the same time?

"You're right." His voice didn't sound of magic and sweet silver.

She swallowed, trying to ease the lump in her throat. An invisible rope seemed to stretch between them, and both kept trying to pull the other close at different times, and the other pulling away. She wanted to try and right her left turn, to pull him close again. She shifted into a foxan and burrowed against his side, curling under his arm.

"I'm sorry," she said. "I want you to know that I don't like it, that we're apart. I didn't mean that I *want* you to stay away."

He paused, then he rested his hand on her flank, and buried his face in her soft belly. She purred, trying to help soothe him. He seemed to relax next to her.

"C'mon. I want to show you something." He stood, holding out his hand, and she clasped it. He pulled her up, and she shifted to her lighter foxan form, vaulted upwards, and hooked her legs and arms around his torso. He staggered. "Oh, dear, I seem to have acquired a backpack on my front. This is unnatural, quite unnatural!"

She giggled. He spun around, and she shrieked and clamped her legs tighter to keep from flying off.

"Hmm. Guess it's just a part of me now." He shrugged. "I'll just head to the bathroom." He waddled through the bedroom door towards the bathroom. She grew longer, human legs and braced her feet on the doorframe, giggling harder. He started laughing, too, and bent and lifted her legs in his arms, like she sat on a chair. "Where shall we go now, Oh Important One?"

She pointed. "To what you wanted to show me!"

He carried her down the hallway and stopped at the closed door on the right. Freeing one of his hands, he inhaled deeply and opened the door. "I present to you: your new den!"

ALESIO HAD AGONIZED over showing her this. But she had teleported to him, somehow, and she'd said, *you're my favorite place,* and he wanted to show her. He wanted to let her know how much she mattered to him.

He'd lined the room with shelves. Shelves upon shelves, and a ladder to reach up to the high ones. He'd brought in large transparent jars, paper, shells, and little vials to hold her various types of magic. He'd used Touch magic to create the special shelves with pockets for the vials. Darrow had helped portal some of the things in, and he and the other foxans had contributed a couple trimmings to fill out the room. It had still felt empty, so Alesio had decorated with some herbs from Taste hanging from the ceiling, and a chair with a soft blanket he'd Shaped with Touch magic—difficult to do, as he'd never done fabrics before, and it had several holes— hanging off the back.

Saida hopped off his arm. She spun in a slow circle on human legs, while shifting her torso and head to foxan, her bright red braid transforming down her back into her puffy, furred tail, which curled around her calves. She leaned towards the shelves as if trying to listen to a distant voice.

"I—I know you miss your magic friends." *Damn it, stop stammering.* "I'm sure you'll sense them again. I know you will. And when that happens, this'll be here, ready to fill up with new friends."

She reached with her foxan paw and touched one of the jars with a revolving image of a lavender sunset.

"That's—Falrie brought that one. Not big enough to transplant, she said. And the one over there, with the sticky—yes, that one—Tener brought it from Taste, it's a rubbing of a cinnamon olo. They said it just wasn't ready to find a home. If you don't want them, because you didn't find them, I understand. I just thought, you know, it'd help you feel at home a little bit here. Even if . . . even if I do age a lot faster than you, and, you know, pass on. You would have a place to come back to. Just in case."

Tears glimmered in her blue-black eyes, like a depth that he could drown in.

Darrow had warned him that she might not use it, but she'd missed her friends so much. And he'd wanted to give her a place to feel safe. A place she would fly back to if she lost herself. She'd seemed to miss him so much, and that had made him so happy that he couldn't wait to show her any longer.

"Saida?" He swallowed. "Can you say something?"

Tears trailed down her cheeks. "It's wonderful."

WHEN HE'D ASKED her to live with him, he'd meant this.

She'd agreed to "move in," except she still hadn't stayed the night at his house any more often than normal because of her search for the Epitaphs. Their relationship hadn't changed much because of that, and this overture of his showed her the extent to which he wanted to change things.

He wanted her to make a den here.

She *wanted* to. As soon as he showed her the room, a powerful desire to curl up on the chair next to the trimmings had overwhelmed her. She hadn't thought about her den much since Watthe had destroyed it in Between. She'd carried Tricksy Stone and Goosefeather everywhere. But there was something about having a default place with all her favorite voices, a place where the trimmings not large enough to transplant nestled and chattered to each other. An anchored place, a bond to an area, that she'd missed without realizing it. A home.

A home with him.

"You're thinking way ahead of me," Saida said, stopping herself from touching each one, trying not to hope for voices.

"When you left with Marik, I found myself at a bit of a loss," he said. Did the natural silver stream of his voice tremble in the air? How much of his magic had she missed these past few weeks when she couldn't sense it? "I was—" he clamped his lips shut for a moment, then continued. "I just wish I could protect you in every way. I know I can't, but I can try to provide you with a place to build for yourself. A place to feel safe."

"I left for just two days." He must have planned it for several weeks, if not months. He'd added the types of containers she kept her trimmed magic in. He'd coordinated with her parents and Tener to add in magic trimmings. The conversation she'd had with Falrie surfaced in her mind, when her mother had mentioned that Darrow had helped Alesio by portaling in shelves and furniture. They'd all worked so hard to design a welcoming environment for her. It showed her with a burst of clarity how much he'd invested in their relationship. How much he'd invested in her staying with him.

How can I promise I'll be the same person who wants this in five years, or ten years from now? What if I'm forced to travel throughout the five worlds and leave him alone for longer and longer? Doesn't he deserve better? Someone who can promise not to change? What if a future version of myself decided to break it off with him, or maybe I found out I didn't like him, like what happened with Carn? How much would I hurt him?

Why would she think that? Alesio had done all of this for her, and she thought about leaving? How could she compare him with Carn?! What was *wrong* with her? Carn lived in her past. He'd done something unforgivable. She'd killed him. She didn't have to think about him anymore.

But she used to believe that he loved her, and then, her view of love had changed. She had shifted what she believed, how she felt. Could she trust that wouldn't happen again? For all her transforming of form, she'd stayed the same on the inside for centuries before she'd met Alesio. And then everything had changed in a year.

Alesio gave a nervous laugh. "I might have planned the room for a while. You leaving just helped me put the finishing touches on it." He paused. "Do you really like it?"

"I really *love* it."

Did she dare tempt her own nature?

Strangling the fear shouting at her, she shifted to human with her foxan fur on, crossed to him, and kissed him, craving his touch despite that part of her mind that screamed *Selfish! You're being selfish! How can you enjoy any time together when you can't promise forever?*

He brushed her wet cheeks and kissed her back. "Salty."

She chuckled, and he slid his tongue into her mouth. That sensation! She'd never tire of it. *Selfish.* No, she liked this too much. He pulled her closer, and she melted against him like butter on toast.

He lifted her like his mandolin, carefully, but with ease, carrying her through her den's doorway (Senses, already she thought of it as hers!) and down the hall, still kissing her. Did he use Sound or Touch magic to navigate? Her insides warmed. She slipped her fur shirt off her shoulder, so her sleeves rested on her upper arms. Even all her tail had transformed into hair, and her braid unwound into waves rippling around her, and her ears had become like little shells on the side of her head. She'd never shifted all the way before, and she'd never felt like this, never, ever, and he'd laid her on the bed. He hovered over her with more space between them so she didn't feel caged, or trapped, and that knowledge heated her insides even more, in a way that she'd never felt with Carn, and she *murred* deep in her throat, that husky sound deeper than a purr she couldn't control, and allowed more of her fur to recede over her breasts like a tide, like he was the moon and she was a sea pulled by the gravity of his gaze, and he growled low like a foxan himself. He bent down and licked his way from the top of the swell of her breasts down to where she'd revealed herself. *Selfish.* She arched and he caught her back with his large hands, holding her in that position. She bucked her hips upwards, and he settled his hands there, then slipped them up her back again, dragging himself up while his tongue flicked to her neck. She groaned and her hands quivered in his hair, and he bent his head to hover over her breasts, and she wanted, she wanted, she wanted to stay!

Selfish, selfish, you'll just hurt him!

"Saida?"

"Mmmh?"

"Saida, what's wrong?"

He had stilled, and his eyes searched hers frantically. He confined his breath. She used to know when he did that when his Sound magic paused, the natural trickle slowing to a stop. Now, she noticed because the slight air from his lips had ceased puffing against her.

The heat in her core refused to leave, and her body wanted to arch, to squirm in delight. But his hand brushed her cheek, wiping away tears she hadn't known were there.

He rolled off her. "Did I hurt you?"

"No. No . . ."

"Did I frighten you?"

She shook her head. Without lust to keep it away, guilt slammed into her full force.

You were going to do it. Even when you didn't know if you led him on.

Was that Tricksy Stone's voice? Would they say that to her, if she could hear them in the Cadenza?

Shame curled her insides like withering leaves. She couldn't meet his desire-darkened eyes.

"Did you . . . lose something?"

She had forgotten herself in the haze of lust, forgotten who she always would be, her one consistency. Change. Always changing. Unreliable.

She licked her lips. "I—I don't know."

His arms tensed. She'd hurt him, with her vagueness. She needed to fix it, at least for now, until she figured out what to do. "Can we just hold each other tonight? Nothing—nothing else?"

She didn't shift back to foxan in the backdraft of lust and shame. Her foxan form always shouldered the difficult things that her human side couldn't handle, as if in the transformation, it locked away some of the hurt and emotion into a separate place, a more distant place. Sometimes she shifted when her human side weighed too much, when the complexity of multiple feelings confused or frightened her, and she needed to bleed some of them off, and sometimes she shifted to do so without realizing it. Did Alesio refer to that when he said he feared that she'd lose herself? This time, though, her body hadn't shifted on its own, she'd done it, she had wanted it. She hadn't wanted to lose any of this tortuous, glorious feeling.

"Can you tell me anything else about what just happened? If I did anything to cause it, I need to know."

"I just missed you today. I just want to stay with you without—without that."

Liar, her body said, her breasts aching with the need for more touch. She'd gone cold, but they hadn't received the memo.

Liar, her mind said, or the part of her that used to be Tricksy Stone, said.

Liar, her heart said, and out of the three she worried the beat of it would tell on her, its rhythm a type of emotional code that he could read. But she couldn't bear to lie to him with her body about the future.

"Of course, Starlight."

Somehow, as he nestled her against him, with his facial hair tickling the back of her neck, she couldn't help but worry that she lied to him, being with him at all.

OPENING WINDOWS

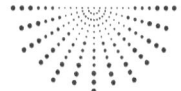

A lesio and Hestafon shuffled along a convoluted gravity path about thirty minutes travel from Lavoa, Vision's lone village. Saida had left with Marik and Naya that morning to hunt the next Epitaph.

Towards the end of the fight in the warehouse, the ixor Shaper had said something about Clef, that they had 'just missed' him. If the fighter spoke the truth—a dubious prospective, at best—then Hestafon's strange tracking ability had worked. Maybe Clef had seen them arrive had ducked out the back. Hestafon had sensed Clef's new direction on Vision and had sought Alesio out at his house, and they had used the Portal Station to travel to Lavoa.

Though they hopped worlds, they couldn't escape the winter, which gripped this area of Vision the same as it did on Sound. Snow fell in swirling gravity paths around them. Saida had reminded Alesio to bring gloves.

"You're leading even faster than you were on Taste," Alesio said. "Have you figured something new out about your mixed magics?"

Unless he's leading me into a trap—

Alesio shook his head. If Hestafon had pledged loyalty to Clef, why would he rush in with a spear to try and save Alesio's life? Or stay at Alesio's bedside when he had ixor poisoning?

Unless Clef had arranged it all as a ploy to distract him. They still weren't heading for Flock.

Hestafon glanced back at him and held his bell case up. "Even before all this, I created magic a bit differently from you, I'm sure you know. You use your voice, and I use bells. But it still starts the same, with Receiving. When I want to Shape magic, I listen first, and I hear the bell before I ring it. It's like imagining what a sheet of music sounds like in your head. It's like—it's like I'm listening to what it wants to sound like."

"I've tried something like that," Alesio said. "Well, I've tried waiting for the magic to say something. But all I get is silence. Wait!" He reached for the piper's elbow, yanking him backwards. "Slow down. See that glimmer, and how the snow bends in direction? That's a gravity shift. You would've fallen to the right."

"It looks like something a child might draw." Hestafon rubbed at his eyes.

Alesio had to agree. To their right, the dirt piled into a small mound and the snow flurries dropped that way, too, leaving a thin, dusty layer of white on top. A few feet above that, another short gravity shift ended, where more dirt had piled, like on the ceiling of a little room. About ten yards above *that* and on a slant, enough soil had settled for a tree to grow. It grew down, at least from their viewpoint.

He imagined dirt and seeds and rain swirling through these shifts throughout the ages. It hurt Alesio's head to try and view it from a "normal" perspective, whatever that meant in Vision. The flurrying snow gave some indication as to the shifts' path, but the wind gusted at times and carried the flakes regardless of gravity. Thankfully, the snow remained as a powder, instead of forming ice on the shifts. The little boy he he'd failed to save flashed through his mind.

"I'll check for gravity shifts," Alesio said. "You tell me if I veer off course."

They traveled for an hour or so, quiet, navigating through a patch of glimmering shifts that ushered them upwards, then backwards at a slant, then to the left, then back down to the ground. Hestafon redirected them a bit to the left. The residue of sluggishness from the ixor-poisoning had dissipated as they traveled, which relieved Alesio. He needed himself in top fighting condition if they found Clef and his ixor user, not to mention other possible ex cage fighters.

"So, what do you call your ability, anyway?" Alesio asked. "Smearing? Helling?"

Hestafon chuckled. This time, the piper wore a down feather vest over his cotton shirt and pants, and he'd tied his hair back in a ponytail instead of in a bun. At least he'd had the sense not to show up in silk robes. "Helling seems like an apt name. It feels like hell. Well, maybe not as bad as it was, but it's still overwhelming at times." He glanced at Alesio and hesitated, as if leaving the door open for further conversation, and Alesio recognized the tactic as what he often did with Saida. Not pushing. Waiting for the other person to move first to give them a sense of control.

Alesio had pocketed a few small twigs when they'd started out. He grabbed one and released it. It zipped up much too high in the sky for comfort before landing almost thirty feet above. He pointed Hestafon around the shift and found a different path with a gradual slope upwards. They trekked up for quite a while into the sky, finding a switchback that let them hop onto another easy, horizontal route at least seventy feet in the air. The clear winter air invigorated Alesio while he moved, keeping warm, and something about the vast wilderness laid around and below them, so different than the urban environment he associated Hestafon with, created an easier environment for him to start his questions, and start through the door of conversation the piper had left open for him.

"As for me," he began, haltingly, "I can tell I should be able to access more magic than do. I imagine my magic as a place inside myself, a room, and the magic waits behind the walls. When I Receive, I pull the magic through to Shape it." He paused, balancing as the gravity shift narrowed, then widened once more a few feet later. "Back when I fought Watthe, I guess I pulled more through on instinct, because I've never done anything at that level since. I've even tried on the Primal

Plane. I just don't know how to access it." *And that ixor fighter will shred me if I can't.*

They reached the end of the horizontal path, just wide enough for them both. They crouched on the edge of a precipice, where a broad gravity shift had produced a wall of dirt seventy feet high, coated in a thin layer of snow. Ahead and upside down to usual gravity, a large tree had started growing downwards, but several small shifts had twisted its branches so that they grew every which way. Over the ages, dirt must have caught in the branches, creating a massive hill in the sky that glimmered with the first few flakes of snow.

Above this strange hill, the planet of Sound contrasted emerald and sapphire in Vision's lavender sky. The Hunger revolved behind them like a silhouette of someone peering through a window.

Alesio had always taken the other worlds in the sky for granted, like big round, orbiting clouds. Now, he found himself appreciating them more that he knew people on those worlds, and that the Hunger threatened them all.

He tested the shift with one his twigs, and the gravity sucked it down at first, then sideways, so that it fell to the dirt and stayed there. He took a deep breath and hopped off the precipice, and the gravity yanked him down and then sideways, reorienting him so that his new down became the cliff wall, and his new sideways the ground far below.

After some hesitation, Hestafon followed. He spoke behind Alesio. "You know when my magic mixing happened?"

Alesio shook his head.

"When the foxans created the Portal Station on Sound. So much new magic poured into our world that it twisted mine. And at first, it angered me, because I couldn't perform the same way I used to. And I thought . . . well, I was also quite angry at you and Saida. I didn't like the other worlds' magic mixing with mine, because it terrified me."

Alesio stopped and looked back at him.

Hestafon's lips tipped in a sad little smile. "You can stop glaring, I've learned what a statement like that means now."

"It wasn't hard to guess that you disliked Saida or me. You made that clear all the way back at St. Rina's."

"Yes, well . . . after a time, the openness of the worlds and the new magic forced me to sense things differently. Receive things differently. And it changed the way that I saw other things." Hestafon's hands spasmed, then he unwrapped a candy and popped it in his mouth. He spoke around the hard piece of caramel. "Such as how I treated others. How I treated you, and the straiters, and then of course your foxan friend." He lifted his chin and met Alesio's eyes. "The way I sounded when I spoke to you, it smelled wrong to me, like something rotten. It forced me to hear how I must sound to others. I only understood this in the past month, and the contrast to how I thought I sounded, compared to what I sensed, well, it created quite a panic for me."

Alesio stared, taken aback by the bluntness of this admission. The wind gusted then, sending heavier, denser flakes of snow through the shifts around them like rivers of white. The memory of Hestafon collapsing in the Council meeting flashed through his mind. He didn't know what to say, so he tried to change the subject. "Why do you eat those, anyway?"

"They help remind me to act better."

"Candy . . . helps you act better."

"Well, it didn't start out that way. I just liked candy, growing up. Always had a sweet tooth. But then, when this started," he pointed at his ear and nose, "It helped to, um, just remind myself to—well, sweeten my voice. I have to struggle to keep my words understandable with a candy in my mouth and having to do that reminds me to work harder to keep my words from hurting people." He paused. "Anyway, even though the openness of the worlds confused and angered me at first, it also helped me understand . . . those other things. The same thing could be said for your magic. You said you know there's more magic 'behind the walls.' The problem might be that you think of your magic as behind a wall in the first place. Why don't you open a window?"

A window? Ridiculous. It was too simple.

Except . . . he *had* imagined his magic as a room, a simple thing.

He descended into the room with textured walls. He passed the coldness of the snow, searching for . . . there! A large patch of dirt crumbled at his fingertips. His physical body didn't brush against much other than dirt or stone, so it didn't take long to find. With more than a little skepticism, he imagined a window there instead of the wall; a large window that stretched almost to the floor.

Dirt poured into the room like a small cave-in, burying him up to his knees. He staggered under the weight of it. His magic room expanded to three times as large as normal, the size of a small house, like when he had fought the ixor-user.

"I am here; I am here! Can I be lots and lots of flowers?"

The dirt . . . had a voice?

He knew how much soil he had access to. He knew it like he knew how to pitch a note to harmonize with a song. A literal ton and a half of dirt waited for him to Shape—a shallow yet wide volume stretching along the cliff wall he trod along like the ground.

It was too much. Far too much. The magic room's newly expanded walls bowed, still shuddering.

He was going to flood.

Even though he'd never flooded before, he could sense it happening even as he realized it. That first expansion had felt like he'd finally Received up to his full capacity.

But he'd still Received *way* too much. He felt bloated, magically, like he'd eaten too much rice too fast, and it had expanded in his stomach beyond what he expected.

"Can I be flowers?" the dirt asked again. "Lots of flowers? At least five!"

"Could I just use some of you? I can't Shape so much."

"Why did you ask for *me*, then? Why didn't you ask the smaller dirt in front of you?"

He was talking to magic. Like what Saida said she did. No, like what Saida *did* do.

His body convulsed, full of magical energy he could not use. He fell, his limbs unresponsive to his commands, yet shuddering with the excess of energy, locking him in a perpetual spasm.

Hestafon's voice came from far off. "– got you! I've – you."

As he could not Shape such a large amount of magic, and it refused to divide itself for him into pieces small enough for him to use, his magic space kicked his consciousness back into reality, and that consciousness faded within moments.

What seemed moments later, he blinked awake. Hestafon had laid him down in some sort of . . . cave and covered him with pine needles to shield him from the cold. Outside, the light had waned, the sun shining off about an inch of new snow. The Hunger had vanished from this side of Vision's sky.

"You're awake!" Hestafon hovered over him. "Are you cold? Do you need more pine needles?"

"What—what time is it?"

"Early evening."

That's the second time he's stuck around while I was unconscious. Alesio cleared his dry throat and reached for his water flask. "By the Senses. We lost an entire day."

"I have experienced flooding. It is not pleasant."

"No. No it's not."

"However, you did gain access to more magic than before, correct? You mentioned in a Council meeting that you have never flooded."

Alesio groaned and set the water down. "Yeah, your little trick worked."

And I could hear the magic speak. I need to tell Saida she was right.

Hestafon beamed and Alesio slipped back into sleep.

The next morning, they woke to a clear day and a bright, pink-purple sunrise. Hestafon led them up a gravity shift as broad as a city street. It thinned out the higher they climbed, until they had to find a way across to another wide enough to step. It seemed like it just kept going, higher and higher, perhaps into the spaces between worlds. The Hunger loomed like the bottom of a well as Mona had described, draining the sky towards it, and Alesio found himself hoping that the gravity shift would lead downward, so they wouldn't have to stare into that maddening spiral.

As they traveled, Alesio practiced trying to open the tiniest windows he could in his magic spaces—which seemed to have stayed expanded to the size of a small house—Receiving the dirt or snow that had piled on some of the ends of the gravity shifts and asking it to Shape into various small items like spoons or guitar picks. They often named themselves based on their origins, and many had ideas of what they wanted to become. It fascinated him that they gave themselves different names, even though they derived from the same area of dirt or snow.

As they continued, the snow melted on the smaller, thinner shifts, leaving them muddy and slippery.

"We're close," Hestafon said, and Alesio jerked out of his magic space like a fish caught on a hook.

The piper pointed upwards at something resembling, at first glance, a sphere of dirt hanging in the sky as large as a building. "There. The smell is stronger here on. Like Clef uses this path often." He rubbed at his nose. "Shouting, apparently."

Alesio studied the area, trying to quiet his pounding heart. A small stream gurgled nearby, rising off the ground in a series of looping gravity shifts, creating the effect of arches of flowing water. These evened out into an upside-down creek, like a mirror image of the one on the ground, except smaller. The gravity shift of this area spanned as wide as a brick piper road, and much dirt and melting snow had piled around the creek, out of which grew an upside-down tree.

The tree's branches had caught dirt falling upwards, as if its orientation had confused the branches into becoming roots. Snow had then piled on top of the dirt, though it had begun to melt. This had created a strange second hill and the effect of a sphere of white.

The gravity shift they walked bent ahead of them like an elbow, then straightened like a giant's long forearm into a path parallel to the normal ground, ending in front of the sphere.

Alesio whispered to Hestafon. "We don't know how many fighters are in there. Looks like it could hold at least ten people. So, we need to sneak up to immobilize them with Touch magic. Ready to sneak in there?"

A shout pierced the quiet, cold air like a shrike call. Clef's voice. "You wanna ask that again?"

Alesio froze. They had nothing to hide behind, and the ground waited at least fifty feet below them.

He burst into motion. He careened around the bend as fast as he dared and sprinted towards the hill.

"Get out of here. Out! Fetch some water or something! I'm parched as a Palate without their morning's blood tea."

A small figure emerged from the spherical hill, stalking out onto the thin horizontal shift, straight towards them. The figure paused.

It was the young ixor Shaper from the warehouse.

"THIS WAY," Saida pointed. "The Epitaph calls from that direction."

The sun sank into the horizon, forming deep, charcoal-gray shadows in the valleys of the mountains ahead. The planet of Vision rose on the other side like a larger, dusky mirror, lending the shadows and the snow a grayish-purple hue. Snow drifts lay heavy on the ground; the fluctuating of the season quickened in the higher altitude.

Saida shivered and stuck her hands back into her coat pockets, a human coat she wore over her foxan one. She'd learned much of singing and music this past year, and the wind's haunting moans that sharpened into shrieks when it gusted reminded her of a melody line that had lost its way into the minor key. Alesio might have composed a song out of it.

"Let's try and find a place to camp for the night." Marik tramped forward, sinking into the snow up to his calf. He'd wrapped his long brown hair-tail around his head like a turban in his plant fiber strips, keeping it out of the snow, and wore thick pants and a long wool coat, purchased in Anthem. Well, Naya had purchased it for him, considering he hadn't had any notes to speak of. "The temperature will plummet when the sun sets."

Saida pointed. "There's a pocket in the cliffside ahead. It should help keep the wind off."

They slogged along the mountain pass. Though the heavier Marik sunk deeper than Saida and Naya, the snow took advantage of their shorter stature and ascended to their knees. They'd started the day with Saida portaling them as close to Sound's Epitaph signal as she could, a mountain that she and Alesio had trekked six months prior, about two days straight travel from Anthem and the opposite direction of Flock. The cold and the snow had slowed their pace as everyone tested each step for solid ground. If Saida had shed her heavy human coat and shifted to full foxan, she could have scampered on top of the crust, but she could also break through to a fissure in the mountain, or to where the drifts built up and stretched like false ground over hidden, treacherous edges.

They reached the pocket in the cliff where it seemed a giant had scooped out part of the mountain. Not quite a cave, but enough room for them all to huddle inside and not fear falling off in their sleep. Saida nestled against the snow-covered rock. She welcomed the cold, for it had stopped her from thinking about how much she missed Alesio's voice.

She could imagine how Tricksy Stone would've responded to that. *"Still trying to avoid what you're afraid of, I see!"*

What would worrying do? She retorted.

Of course, they didn't respond. Even her imagination of their memory had faded.

Naya brought out some cheese studded with almonds from Taste that she cut into thirds, handing them each a triangle, and the tartness and sweetness of it mixed filled her mouth with flavor. Then the fox-person gave each of them a sip from her flask of aliberry wine, which trailed fire down Saida's throat and pooled in her stomach like a bath on the inside. She sighed and settled further against the rock as a balled up foxan, covering herself with her human coat, her eyelids fluttering shut. Sometimes it was nice not to think of things, just to eat good food and drink good drinks, and allow sleep to rock the niggling fears and doubts into oblivion.

They woke with the dawn, as the sun peeked over the horizon of one of the valleys, piercing them with the sudden glare. The planet of Vision had long since set, but Taste had risen, reflecting a russet light from its desert side. They ate a small breakfast of purpato bread from their packs and set out, crunching through the hard crust of the top layer of snow.

"Footprints!" Marik crouched next to a dip in the snow. The chapped skin around his lips and eyes had turned puce, the freckles stark against his paled skin. "Someone has traveled ahead of us. One of my people, perhaps."

"I wonder how far ahead," Naya said. She wore a thick human coat as well and a hood pulled over her face.

"Not far, since snowfall hasn't covered these," Marik said. "Maybe we'll catch up with her."

"Didn't most of the Lunnites go to Scent?"

"It's probably Etha. She likes to strike out on her own, and she gets impatient."

They trekked on with renewed urgency, following the Epitaph's call, which matched the footprints leading onward. To Saida, the Epitaphs had almost identical strength levels across the worlds, except for this one. This one sounded a *bit* louder, and she wondered if that's what the glittering had meant on the map of the worlds on Sedella. It sounded like a violin, a drag across the strings hovering on a high note, then back and forth in a frenzy a few times pitched a little lower. It sounded panicked.

I'm coming, she wanted to tell it. *I'm coming! Hold on!*

A few minutes later, however, a shrike's keening call pierced the air. Naya and Saida flattened themselves against the cliffside, Saida shifting her legs to foxan to shorten herself, but keeping her torso and arms human to create as small a profile as she could against the rock.

Marik froze, his eyes wide, his ears angling this way and that like a weathervane.

Saida pulled at his arm, hissing, "Back!"

The shrike wheeled around the mountain, swooping by them. "Zeek! Zeekeekeekeek!"

The sound punctured the crust of the snow like darts. The large, carnivorous bird sailed downward into the valley ahead, then disappeared into the forest below, its cries still reverberating back to them in the cold air.

"What . . . what was that?" Marik said.

"Shh," Saida said.

They all waited, searching the forest below, until the bird reappeared as a far-off dot on the other side of the valley, flying to the next mountain over and vanishing again in its shadow. The sound of the Epitaph frenzied, then resumed its long high note, like it waited along with them.

Saida sagged. "That was a shrike. They're predatory, and vicious besides. They can use Sound magic to kill their prey." She peered around at the rock face of the mountain, pricking her foxan ears for the sound of any other possible shrikes. "It might have a nest nearby. In any case, we should keep as quiet as possible. Noise travels further in the cold, and on Sound."

The far-off call of the shrike sounded, as if to emphasize her point. They all shivered.

"I've heard of them," Naya whispered. Snow had settled on the edge of her muzzle, and she wiped it off. "I didn't know they were so big. Almost as big as a child."

"I hope your friend ahead of us is alright," Saida said to Marik, eyeing the footprints they still followed.

The Lunnite sucked in a shallow breath. His chapped lips had cracked, and his foxan ears had bits of snow on the tufts. "Me too," he whispered. "As an elder, she should not have ventured alone. Leaving our city was difficult enough for them. Now they push themselves."

"It's the same with my parents," Saida said. "Change is difficult for them. For all of us, I guess."

Marik considered that with a frown, as she'd committed some kind of sacrilege by comparing Lunnites and foxans, but since she'd said it, he couldn't discount it. The cognitive dissonance designed an interesting wrinkle on his forehead.

They continued in somber silence for a time, until they neared where trees began to grow on the mountain slope. Their boots crunching through the crust echoed in Saida's ears. The ground leveled out and they traversed into the valley proper, the forest overhead.

Saida forced herself to glance at the Hunger, and the hugeness of them in the sky captured her breath and attention. "Is that a second tendril?"

The others jerked their gazes upward.

"Damn it," Naya said.

"I bet it's trying to sever the Planes again," Marik said after a few more moments.

Saida frowned. Something didn't make sense to her about that. In the crisp mountain air, the smaller spots and the large mass of not-nothing in the middle stood out in contrast, and the second arm made the whole entity resemble a giant rotating crab. The corona of twisted skies around the Hunger had thickened to almost twice their base size, wrenching the clouds and firmament into threads of spiraling color.

This is just a brick of my body! I will come soon!

"They caused the Severing all those years ago with just one small part of them." She spoke in a soft tone. "The rest of them reached us. They're the size of a world. No, bigger, now. So why *haven't* they severed our magic yet?"

The other two stared at her.

"Marik!"

They all jolted. Through the hush of the snow-burdened pines, someone waved, their finger to their lips, and the redness on their hand against the white of the snow called them like a tolling bell. It was Etha, the Lunnite elder with the foxan snout. They hurried over to her. She'd wrapped plant fiber strips of her traveling cloak on a puncture wound, but blood still soaked through.

"Etha!" Marik knelt next to her. "When did this happen?"

"Half hour ago, or so." Etha grimaced, her snout wrinkling, her thin voice straining. "It's not deep, but it's still bleeding."

"Hand wounds do that." Naya slipped forward and dug some

bandages from her pack, which Saida recognized as Sound cloths, and a vial of something creamy white. The fox-person unwrapped the soaked strips from the Lunnite's hand, which still trickled red. "Brace yourself. This should be cleaned."

She emptied her water flask over it. Etha scrunched her eyes shut, shuddering from the shock of the icy liquid, but did not cry out. The water ran red, and Naya dabbed some cream on it from the vial. Then she used the bandages to rewrap Etha's hand much tighter with efficient motions.

"Thank you," Etha said. "You're very practiced at this."

Naya shrugged and shouldered her pack once again. "I live in a world where cannibals could attack. You learn what you need to."

"Cannibals?" Etha shuddered, the burnt orange fur on her forehead puffing up. "I didn't think something could scare me more than that shrike, but that might do it." She turned to Saida. "Envoy, the strong magic you call the Epitaph lies about a mile ahead. Those horrible birds chased me out of the ruins. I didn't know they could use Sound magic!"

"Shrikes?" Saida asked. "How many?"

The Lunnite shook her head. "The whole place is infested with them."

Saida set her mouth into a grim line. She'd run across a colony of shrikes once, many years ago, near the town of Flock. She'd teleported away at once.

The branch of a pine tree nearby snapped, releasing its weight of snow. The sound echoed through the area like a thunderbolt, and they jumped.

"We should teleport back to Sound," Saida said. "This is too dangerous for you all. I can come back tomorrow."

"You could teleport us if we're cornered," Marik said. "We need to reach the Epitaph as soon as possible, right?"

Saida clenched her hands. She'd shifted into a foxan without realizing. She shifted back just in time to stop her claws from piercing into her paw pads.

The Hunger could sever the worlds' magic at any time. Or perhaps worse. No one knew what they could do. But judging by their name, they could consume the entire Plane—people, cities, nature, and all.

"We'll wait until night," she said.

PARAS HAD LED the group of Lunnites west, where Tosn, the older Lunnite male with the beard, had requested. Paras hadn't explored beyond a few days travel in that direction.

The weather had warmed up the last two days, and the wind had gentled with whispers of a spring rain. She directed them to shelter under a rala tree, those large, arching branches covering them from the flash downpour. The warm sky mixing and splashing in the dirt always roused nostalgia in Paras, as if she had been a plant in another life. She breathed in the heady scent and shivered as the temperature cooled off all around.

The Lunnites huddled under the rala tree as the quick, yet heavy rain pushed rivulets of mud and sticks around the rala tree, rousing smells of decayed leaves and other dead things. One larger stick created a tiny makeshift dam, and soon a pool of muddy water formed there.

After three minutes, the rain lessened, then stopped, and then almost without warning the sun rushed back out as if afraid it had missed something. Paras motioned them all back out. "Watch out for slippery places."

They followed her without much chatter. She preferred it that way. She could imagine she traveled alone, with no responsibilities, just her and the long grass of the field she strode through, and the yellow flowers with the orange centers that peeped out above them like children playing peekaboo. The scent of the flowers filled her nose, transporting her back in a memory to a time when she ventured out by herself the first time and had passed a field like this one, with the same flowers. She'd daydreamed about living as one of the rabbits munching on the flowers. Then one of the Lunnites treaded on a stick or splash in a puddle and it shattered the fantasy.

"I didn't know so many smells existed in all the worlds, let alone one." Tosn huffed beside her, and she slowed down. Most of the Lunnites had a similar height to hers, but she had a consistent, fast pace, and the older ones couldn't match it.

She smiled at him. The petrichor, so earthy and strong, welled up from the ground like an adventurous perfume. If magic ever awakened in her as it had for Mother Rean and Raos, the village's animal tracker, perhaps she could have Shaped something from it. Water beads shone like reflective eyes in the field ahead, weighting the tips of the long grass and bowing their stems.

"Rain stirs up the ground like a ladle in a pot. It makes all the settled scents rise to the surface. Do any of you wish for more face cloths?" She said the last part a little louder.

The Lunnites still acted somewhat wary around her, but instead of pulling away from her voice, sometimes they huddled closer to it. One raised their hand, and she pulled out another cloth from her bag and handed it to them. They grasped it with a delicate grace and bowed to her, and the gesture differed so much from the thieving, greedy, snarling fox-people the old stories portrayed that a sudden shame clouded over her like stormy spring skies. She swiveled and led the silent group on, pausing when she needed Tosn to tell her their heading.

He, and as she understood it, most of them, could sense the Epitaph. He had explained that the group had vague guesses as to how long before they'd reach the powerful magic, somewhere between three days and three weeks. He'd spoken of confusing calculations based on ancient maps on their world and bowed, his head down. They seemed to do that a lot. "I apologize for the ambiguity. It is difficult to parse the time it takes to travel when we do not know the world."

She'd shrugged. She hoped the journey lasted longer, anyway. Her skin had a healthy tan from the excursion on Touch instead of her normal pasty white, staying close to the village under the shade of the trees.

After another day full of sun and another sudden spring shower, she guided them to camp by a lake, on the leeward side of a hill. She hadn't explored much past this way, and excitement built inside her like a petal about to unfurl. *New terrain coming soon!*

Algae floated on the lake, producing a strong smell of decaying plants wafting downwind to them, even as they peered from the hilltop.

A distant honking echoed in the sky. They craned their necks up. The wind rushed and the honking grew louder, and then so did the sound of large beating wings.

Oh. Oh no. It is that time of year, isn't it?

"Everyone, lie down!"

The Lunnites obeyed her order, pressing their faces into the hillside, following Paras's lead. The honking and the beating wings grew louder.

The sky whitened, and even Paras, who had experienced the migration once before, cringed at the thundering power of the huge wings overhead.

The flock of swanseizes flew down to the lake and settled on the water like giant roosting clouds—if clouds had long, snakelike necks, black flecks for eyes the size of fists, bright pink ribbed throats, and beaks with serrated maws that could saw through a man's bone in seconds. Not that they used it for that purpose. Thankfully, they used their jagged jaws to shred through ice and dig into the scree to reach the deep roots of herbs on the mountains they hibernated in.

"Tosn, tell everyone to stay down and keep quiet," Paras murmured. "The wind is blowing towards us, so they can't scent us. But if anyone stands up, they will see."

"Would they try and eat us?" Tosn watched the flock with a terrified fascination. Some of them snapped at each other and flapped their huge wings when another invaded their space. The lake rippled at their movements, and the algae juddered apart and reformed, sending up more rotten-egg smell.

"They don't eat meat," Paras said. "But they're territorial and aggressive. They mate here. So, if they feel threatened . . . well, we should stay downwind."

The Lunnites crawled back down the hill and the sun slowly fainted in the sky. They pressed close to her, now, instead of away. Tosn tasked a younger Lunnite woman with keeping first watch, and she smiled shyly at Paras. Like the other Lunnites, she wore a cloak and clothing fashioned out of plant fibers that smelled of many layers of oil, both of which she could unwrap to various degrees. She'd stowed her cloak in her pack and unwound her pants into shorts and her long sleeves into a sleeveless top. She had black, glossy fur on her head instead of hair, and this fur covered her arms and legs as well. Though she had foxan irises with slits for pupils, she had a human mouth, ears, and nose instead of a muzzle like some of the other Lunnites. Her chartreuse eyes shone bright as she gestured up the hill and flapped her arms like a swanseize. Paras grinned back.

The light dimmed, and the stars and moon and worlds of Taste and Touch shone with a winter brightness. Overhead, the Hunger had just begun to sip at the organic blackness of space, cresting the horizon and pulling at the sky like a second, deeper nightfall. A strand stretched out of the mushrooming ridge, tugging and twisting further areas that the center mass could not yet reach.

For the first time, Paras was glad that she couldn't Receive magic well enough to Shape it, that she couldn't sense it beyond her own increased sensitivity.

"Tosn," she whispered in the darkness, after a few minutes.

"What is it, Miss Paras?"

She wrestled with her words. She was the mover, not the talker like Verrity. "Do you . . . can you Lunnites sense magic, like the foxans do?"

Tosn remained still on his cloak, which he had used as a blanket roll for his head. "Many of us can sense it," he said after a few moments. "On Touch, it is a texture, or a temperature. The smoothness of a rock might hold magic where the constant lapping water has sanded it down to a sleek perfection. Or, quite often, the depths hold water that wish to ride the heights of the Summit Wave. Here, it is different. It is a fog I can see with my nose. Patches of it floating almost everywhere. The rain created great fog banks of it, rolling like a sea in the air."

"But you can't Shape it, like lots of humans can?"

A beat of silence. "I cannot."

Interesting. Does that mean that some Lunnites can? "Isn't that frustrating?" She swallowed. "I mean, I can't even sense it the way you do. I can't Shape magic, either. Not many in Tremain can. And sometimes—well, I wonder, if I travel enough, if I move enough, it'll trigger something inside me, and I'll be able to."

She clamped her lips closed. *Shut up!* She'd never even told Verrity that, so why was she spilling her senses to this—this Lunnite?

But they reminded her of the villagers. The way they crept with wariness in their eyes, ready to leap back at any moment. After she'd steered them closer to their goal of this Epitaph, guiding them through her world, they'd begun to welcome her.

Tosn did not speak for some time. "We are who we are. Sometimes that means we can't do what others do. But it also means we can do things that others cannot."

Paras licked her lips. *He seems so content.* She couldn't understand. She wanted so many things, things that others didn't think about when they had them. She wanted to Shape Scent magic. She would treasure meeting with Falrie and adventuring outside of Scent.

She rolled over to her side to avoid the Hunger in the sky, and the stars, winking at her like treasure that she could not have.

The next morning, as the dawn crept closer on bluish gray feet, a rush of wings woke them all up. The swanseizes rose over the lake. They twirled around each other, rising higher and higher like a pillar of white. They swept, dove, then mounted air currents above the lake in ever-changing, hypnotic formations. After many minutes of this, the shifting drifts of white began to pair off, twining their necks around each other, flapping their outer wings to keep aloft, and the formations broke into a scattering that fluttered back down onto the lake like huge snowflakes.

Everyone had crawled up the hill to watch the breathless display, but now Paras turned to Tosn. "We should leave. Once they mate, they'll want to build nests around the lake. We don't want to be here when they do. They are *very* territorial."

They hurried away in quiet, but a new kind of quiet than when they had started, built more from hushed awe than fear.

16

THE LIES WE TELL OURSELVES

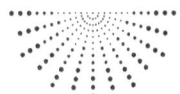

"They're here!" The young man's shout streamed ixor towards Alesio, like a lance of slowness that the wind conveyed on its shoulders along the horizontal gravity shift. A few of the particles blew out of formation and a dissenting shift seized them. Those particles fell in a zigzag up, then left, then up again.

Shit. The young man's shout would've alerted all of Clef's men. How many would Alesio have to fight?

Alesio set his teeth and kept dashing forward, towards that bolt of ixor, which traveled much slower than Sound magic, maybe about the speed of small blowing leaves, but it would still reach him in another five or so seconds. Still, Alesio couldn't dodge it, not on such a thin gravity shift.

"Hold your breath!" Alesio shouted to Hestafon behind him, not daring to turn his head. He had to keep his balance on the thin gravity shift. Then he sucked in a deep lungful of air, keeping it in reserve, and focused on the ixor problem.

Sound magic wouldn't blow it away, but if he had access to some dirt, he could Shape a wall of Touch magic. Unfortunately, the thin gravity shift had almost no soil or even snow built up on it.

He could form a Touch shield of air to block the particles from reaching them, but he couldn't hold it for longer than a few seconds.

The ixor-bolt had almost reached him. Parts of the powdery substance had drifted on the wind to his right, but most of it surrounded them intact, like a visible belch.

Hestafon shouted, "Save your magic! Stop!"

The piper had dashed as well, staying closer than Alesio had realized, just a few feet away.

Alesio halted with the grace of a bull in mid-rush, barely keeping his balance.

The ixor lance blew closer on the wind. What could Hestafon do?

A sweet, thick aroma filled the air and the particles of brown ixor stuck to it, creating a clear space about three feet in front of them.

Hestafon huffed, blundering to a stop behind Alesio. "Ah! It worked!"

"Wait, what do you mean, 'ah, it worked'? You didn't know if that would work?"

Did he Shape a Scent shield around this spot? How does that work against Taste magic?

Well, sometimes Alesio could taste a strong smell, or vice versa. Maybe the two influenced each other.

"Didn't think I'd see you two again." The young ixor Shaper stopped a few yards away from them, shrugged off his cloak, and left it on the air at his feet. He had black skin like many Tastians, and his textured hair rose a few inches above his head in a full shape. Stubble dotted his chin and . . . his mouth showed a silver sheen when he spoke.

So, Clef had learned how to manufacture amplifiers, and he'd installed one in this young man's mouth. That allowed the Tastian to affect people with his magic even if they didn't taste it.

An amplifier on someone who breathed ixor. Did that mean the young fighter experienced everything amplified, too?

He didn't have time to think about that right now. He couldn't let Clef slip away again. The ixor Shaper must have alerted Clef inside the sphere, but the old strait's leader hadn't appeared.

Reaching inside himself, he Shaped a sound-spear and hurled it past the ixor Shaper. The spear pierced the grassy mound, then dissipated. "Come out, you coward!"

The young man's eyes widened, and he jerked his head to glance up and over his shoulder.

This wasn't unfolding how Alesio had envisioned. Instead of a long chase through several worlds, never catching up to Clef, like in a dream, they'd found him after a relatively short time. Instead of hunting him through the twisting, unknown streets of Flock while fending off ten shrikers at once, the old strait's leader had hidden inside a ball of dirt in the sky, guarded by one, albeit dangerous, young man.

Alesio didn't know how Clef would react anymore. So, when the familiar figure with the wiry frame, dark brown hair, and the most punch-able facial features stepped out of the hill on a higher gravity shift closer to the roots of the tree, Alesio's blended feelings of relief, confusion, and fresh worry mixed inside his body like a dissonant chord.

He'd found Clef. Finally. Well, Hestafon had done the finding part.

When would the cage fighters burst out of hiding? Or had Clef really cloistered himself in the wilds of Vision with one guard? Did he believe the ixor Shaper could protect him by himself?

Clef gestured with a "go on" flicking motion of his fingers to the ixor Shaper.

Alesio's hands trembled. Clef had used that motion during his childhood as a gesture to start a cage match.

Alesio fashioned a Touch air shield and dashed to the right through the ixor surrounding them, ignoring Hestafon's gasp. He did not try and feed the shield more magic to repair it, so the shield dissipated once the particles hit it. A few of the particles clung to him, but not many. Not enough to slow him perceptibly.

He'd observed from the errant particles his best path forward, and leapt in a zigzag up, then left, then a long jump up. His efforts awarded him with a ledge of air above the ixor fighter, the ledge where Clef had emerged on. He barreled onwards toward the old strait's leader.

"Hey!" The young man jumped up after him, catching the ledge only visible by a glimmer. His ixor-fueled shout, like an arrow of the slowing spice, just missed Alesio. "Stop!"

His second shout caught Alesio's foot, and he tripped and slammed down on the ledge, the rest of his body still trying to match his momentum. Tears sprang to his eyes from the impact, but he heaved himself back up, dragging his foot, which now lagged a few seconds behind. He faced the fighter, because trying to run away from him on a straight path would mean certain death.

On the cliffside, Hestafon clutched at his bell case, his eyes squeezed shut. Alesio couldn't tell if the piper concentrated on magic or that fear had overtaken him. Or . . . maybe he didn't want to face the consequences of his betrayal?

No. Alesio didn't believe that anymore.

"You're being used!" Alesio held his hands up. "Clef won't just give you power! He'll trap you with it."

"Wow! Never! Thought! Of! That!" With each word, the fighter released a spurt of ixor. They streamed towards him. Not as fast as Sound knives, but Alesio couldn't dodge them all, not on this narrow ledge. They would reach him in a couple seconds.

He closed his eyes.

Clef's appearance had frazzled him enough that he hadn't thought to use his new knowledge, he'd just reacted. But he could do better. He had to do better, or the ixor Shaper would destroy him.

Inside his house-sized space of Touch magic, the dirt had disappeared, as he no longer touched it. He just had access to air.

Now that he had learned from what had happened on the cliffside, he imagined opening a much smaller window, more of a peephole right in front of him, just the air that touched his hands.

"Nice to meet you! My name's Alashalah! I would love to be something else for a little while! Anything else! What about hands? I could be a pair of hands. Oh! Or a feather! I've felt those in the sky, on the birds! What about a bird? Could you Shape me into a bird?"

Alashalah kept changing inside the room, shifting around and half forming into the things they suggested even without Alesio's guidance. Their words overlapped, almost like it became bored with the sentences halfway through.

"How does a shield sound?" he asked them.

"You mean, how does a shield *touch*? Hehehehe!"

They formed as they spoke. Even as they did, however, they tried to form into something else, and he had to reShape them. He understood, now, at a more intrinsic level, why wrangling air required constant focus—it was because the Shaped air got bored or distracted. Its nature was formless, meant to circulate, to diffuse, to change. It was like trying to herd cats.

He opened his eyes, his attention divided as he tried to maintain control of the magic while fighting. A wavy shield of air had appeared in front of each of his hands, just the section that he had opened a window to.

As soon as the ixor touched the magic, either he would have to release the shield or feed an even stronger stream of magic into it, which he couldn't afford to do. He had to make it count.

The first ixor cloud flew at him chest height, and he ducked under it. The second, right after it, would have hit his left thigh, but he struck it with one of his fists, covered in Touch magic. The ixor sprayed away.

The shield of air around him popped, and he reShaped the remnants around him, which cost more magic than the first time, since Alashalah, or what remained of them, didn't seem as enthused to reappear. Alesio would drain himself if he had to keep doing that. The third cloud puffed at his feet again, trying to trip him, and he leapt over, keeping his slowed foot higher up. The fourth would have hit his neck, but as he jumped, it glided at his chest, and he brought his fist up just in time to smash it away. The fifth and final cloud of ixor flew under him, as the young man had aimed it at his shins.

He landed, dashed down the path as fast as he could on his slowed foot, then leapt sideways off the ledge and onto the gravity shift that angled up and twisted like a ribbon, and climbed it like a spiral ramp, the gravity aiding him, pushing him upwards. He had to slow down so as not to slide off the curves of the ramp, where different gravity shifts would yank him in different directions.

He needed a moment for his magic to replenish, or he'd drain himself in the next few seconds. Besides, he didn't want to hurt the young man if he didn't have to. Memories of his fight in the warehouse flashed through his head, of that bowman impaled on the tree he had Shaped. He wanted to do things differently this time.

The young fighter had followed him up the twisting ramp, as he had hoped. Clef remained on the air ledge below, watching the fight unfold like always.

Alesio reached the top, his feet sinking into a pile of snow, unmelted in the shade of the hill. It was upside down compared to the real ground far, far below. Using the last of his magic, he opened a tiny window to the loose soil growing under the snow.

"Nice to meetcha," the dirt said. "The name's . . . uh . . . hold on here, let me think, didn't expect to be called through, you know? Not that I'm complaining. Been waiting here for too long. Jumped at the chance, really. Hrmm . . . let's see . . . I've got it! The name's Sig. Not sure why, that's just what it is."

"What would you like to be, Sig? Just for a moment, I don't have the strength to form you permanently." Dirt didn't have the durability of wood or stone. It would crumble if no magic maintained it, but it lasted longer and more efficiently than trying to Shape air.

"Hrmm . . ." Sig said. "Just for a moment, you say? Well. I would like to look at the sky for a bit, I would. The one with the sun in it. Been staring down at the same place for too long."

"I can do that," Alesio said. He Shaped the plot of dirt under the snow into a long, long pole, almost two yards long, jutting to the side off the ramp.

Alesio gulped in a breath and jumped to the pole, catching hold of them. The gravity shifted and tugged Alesio upwards, into the sky.

Sig yelled, "Now that's more like it! What a view! There it is, that beautiful sun!"

Sig kept lasting, and Alesio had the sense that their endurance persisted because he'd asked the magic what *they* wanted. The logic upstream, as a Scentian might say, indicated that magic would stay longer as something they wished for themselves, yet their impermanent Shape still used far less magic than he'd expected.

Alesio edged out to Sig's end, hand over hand, watching Clef's fighter leap up the spiraling, twisting gravity shift below him. As he did, Alesio retraced the path of gravity with his eyes that he'd seen earlier, when he'd set up this plan.

Just before his magic ran out and Sig regressed to loose dirt, Alesio let himself fall upwards. But he'd edged out far enough to catch another twisting knot of gravity, which he hauled himself onto. The gravity shift coiled downwards, and he followed it, sliding on a muddy part where the snow had melted and just catching himself from falling. From there, he hopped down a few feet to another gravity shift, a downwards angle that ended near the ledge with Clef.

He'd trapped the young fighter on the gravity shift, high in the sky, unable to jump the distance to the gravity knot that Alesio had using Sig.

A whistling clued him in, and Alesio twisted on reflex. He caught a bit of the real knife on his left ear that Clef had thrown at him from behind just over twenty feet away. Alesio angled his right side towards the strait's leader to hear him better, as Clef couldn't use Sound magic.

"Getting sloppy," Clef said. "What's wrong, Requiem? Can't even sing the death song of a teenage boy?"

"You're sick."

Clef had a narrow, pinched face and polished, glittery gray pupils. His dark brown hair had thinned, and his cheekbones jutted out as if his bones had sharpened.

"Baylor!" Clef said. "Get down here. Or you know what happens to your poor old dad." His words had longer rests between them than usual.

Alesio's fingernails dug into his palms so hard he might have drawn blood. *He's using the fighter's father as a hostage? Just like he did to me?*

Clef grinned.

Alesio charged him, snapping out his real knife from its sheath and feinting to the right. Clef dodged to the right, as if anticipating the feint, and tried to headbutt him in the chest, but he moved too slow, too obvious, and Alesio danced to the side.

He's faster than that. What game is he playing?

He kept doing things Alesio couldn't expect. Hiding out in a world he didn't expect.

Alesio clenched his hands and jabbed with the knife up to Clef's sternum. Clef just barely dodged, and Alesio used that time to hold the knife to the older man's neck. "Don't. Move."

Clef chuckled. "You won't do it."

"You don't know that." Alesio's hand trembled. The memory of that bowman, impaled, flashed through his mind.

"Oh, but I do. I know everything about you, Alesio."

No! He had Clef at knifepoint, right here! He could end the constant worry for Saida's safety.

Was he . . . too weak? Too incompetent?

"If I don't contact my men by tomorrow, they have orders to kill your precious fur-mix," Clef said. "I wonder what's faster? A portal or a Sound knife? Do you want to find out?"

Alesio clenched his teeth, locking his Sound magic behind his lips like a cage. That sounded like an empty threat. Clef's men would have no way of tracking Saida with her ability to portal wherever she wanted. If he just killed Clef here and now, he could ensure Saida's safety. Though, he also needed to interrogate the ex strait's leader for information on the Hunger. *Sounddamn.* He'd almost forgotten about that.

Clef snorted. "You may have tried to modify your key, but you sing the same old song." The old strait's leader cocked his head, so Alesio's knife scratched his neck, leaving a thin red line. "The old you would do it. The better version I trained you to be. Requiem. *He* would save her. He would do what he had to."

Why did Clef antagonize him, as if he wanted Alesio to kill him?

Wait. How did Clef know his unconscious thoughts?

The strait's leader had always possessed an uncanny ability to know when someone lied. But this . . . this was like Clef had plucked a string of feelings from his mind and said them aloud.

Because a part of him didn't want to slice Clef's throat. Despite everything. Maybe because of everything.

The child inside him had clawed and bit in the cage matches, pitted against older kids, against heavier and more experienced fighters. He'd fought for the crowd's adoration, for the roof over his and his father's heads, for food to eat. But he'd also fought for Clef's attention, even when—especially when—Clef had cuffed him over the head for losing a match or beaten him senseless for not throwing a match. Because sometimes, Clef wouldn't beat him, or smack him around, but patted him on the head and told him, "Good job, kid. You earned me lots of notes today," and part of him yearned to hear those words again, and this, *this* was the reason avoided Flock, the obvious place to search, because he'd feared this part of himself, this need for validation that he was good enough, that he wasn't a sounddamned screw-up whose sole talent came from something he couldn't even control—his bad ear—and his fear of that part of him that searched for Clef just to hear those words again from that sounddamned oil-slick voice.

I know everything about you, Alesio.

That didn't hold true anymore, though. Clef didn't know how he'd changed in the past year. How much he'd shifted to believing in himself, in his abilities as a performer, instead of working as a brute fighter. Clef had never understood his dream, so of course he wouldn't understand that Alesio had Shaped it into reality.

Whispers sounded from behind him. Something hit the middle of his back, and the slowing happened in his core.

He gritted his teeth. "Found a way out of my trap, did you?"

He circled around Clef, still holding the knife to the strait's leader's throat. The world already smeared around Alesio as he faced the young fighter.

Baylor grinned, showing that silver sheen in his mouth. With each word, ixor puffed out. "Wasn't that hard. Infused your dirt pole with ixor so the magic stayed in place longer."

"Clev . . . er," Alesio said, and Baylor's eyes widened.

Did the young man crave that same attention, that validation, as Alesio did?

"Stop wasting your breath," Clef said. "Hit him with a shout, idiot!"

The cloying musk of ixor seeped all around him. Alesio's heart slowed. He could barely keep hold of his knife against Clef's neck. Time warped. Each breath depleted ten seconds.

His arm dropped.

Clef glided out from Alesio's grasp and pivoted. The strait's leader slid the knife from Alesio's senseless fingers and slashed his cheek.

Twice on the left. Twice on the right.

The flashing, searing sensation almost crumpled Alesio to his knees. The ixor compounded the pain, flaring it like oil on a fire. Blood dripped down his face.

"There," Clef said, panting, his form blurring. "Now you match your fur-mix." He cackled that new, horrible laugh. "You've always been such a softhearted fool, Alesio. I told you, you should've killed me. How would I know anything about the Hunger? Now, I'll just slip out of your reach again." He winked, but it was like a slow blink to Alesio. "Never worry. I'll keep in touch."

I never said anything about the Hunger. How did he . . .

The smell of something different drifted on the breeze.

Hestafon had snuck up behind Baylor. He rang two bells with an urgent flicking of his wrists. They didn't produce any sound, but both Clef and Baylor began to cough, their eyes reddening even more. Clef blinked, and Baylor pressed the heels of his hands to his eyes.

The piper had created the smell of a kandri pepper. That one the flirtatious Tastian merchant had tried to sell him. Except this possessed a much more intense smell than the uncut fruit, like Hestafon had sliced the kandri open.

Alesio needed to use this moment of reprieve. He closed his eyes and found the particles that had settled on himself in the Touch magic space as he had done before.

He had to Receive first. He didn't have much magic left, but when he listened to what the magic wanted, Shaping them cost less effort. He opened a tiny window to them.

They poured out, screeching, their words warped from slowness. "I aam Zziiaar. II woould liike tooo bee ground. I aam tired of driftiing."

"I could do that for you," Alesio said to them.

He Shaped Ziar, and because he hadn't tried to convince them of anything, they next to no energy. They condensed into a flat square that he called "ground", and they seemed happy with that. He opened his eyes, one hand holding Ziar.

Clef's eyes widened. He started to whirl to run, but Alesio shot out his free arm and punched him in the throat.

Clef clutched at his throat and would have fallen if Alesio hadn't grabbed him and slammed him on the invisible ledge. He reacted with more lag than Alesio did, even in Alesio's slowed state.

This close, the veins of his eyes bulged red. *He must've used ixor. On purpose?*

Blood dripped down Alesio's chin. He shook Clef. "Where's Baylor's father? Where is he?"

The young fighter watched from a few feet away behind Clef. He closed his mouth, tightening the seam of his lips into a line. His shoulders curved in as he hunched, which lifted years from his taller, gangly frame, and his gaze darted between the two of them.

Clef chuckled. "I'm not worthy of her."

Alesio froze. "What did you say?"

The old strait's leader's eyes glittered with glee. He swung his head from side to side and sang in an eerie tone, "I'm not enough to keep her grounded. She's going to drift away."

"Don't listen to him."

Alesio tensed at Baylor's voice, expecting more ixor. Then he processed what the young man had said.

"Shut up! Shut up shut up!" Clef thrashed in a sudden mania, spittle flying from his mouth.

Alesio jolted his head back. The Clef he knew didn't lose himself like that. Senses, the Clef he knew hadn't used ixor, either, had preferred to stay sharp and quick.

Baylor hunched his shoulders even further, avoiding Clef's manic gaze. "He can't Shape Sound magic, but he can hear real well—"

"Baylor," Clef said. "This man will kill your dad before the day is done. Haven't I told you, Requiem will seek vengeance? He impaled my archer in cold blood!"

"That's not true!" Alesio tightened his grip on Clef's throat. "Well, I mean, yes. I did do that." He wasn't sure why Baylor had switched sides, but he had to make the most of it. "But believe me, he's blackmailed me my whole life, too. He's threatened my dad. I know what he's doing to you. I will *not* hurt your father."

Baylor's eyes shot back and forth between Alesio and Clef, erratic and wide.

Clef thrashed. "I will! I will have your father killed! You won't find him in time!"

Alesio tightened his grip on Clef's throat. "Not if *you* want to live."

"You're keeping me alive?" The straiter leader's voice smoothed again. "Alesio, I'm touched."

"He can hear the lies in your voice, the lies you tell yourself. He uses them."

"Betray me, will you?" The skin under Alesio's thumb rippled when Clef laughed. "Too late. I already told them to give your dear dad a long, slow death. You'll never find him in time."

Alesio stared at Clef, at those glittering gray eyes, at the crimson veining around them. Clef had always had the uncanny ability to know when someone lied, but Clef couldn't have known his darkest fears about Saida unless his ability had strengthened somehow, as Baylor said.

A plan flashed through Alesio's mind.

"– think he's keeping my father on Scent," Baylor murmured, and Alesio chanced a side glance, meeting his eyes. The young man's lips peeled back in a snarl and his nostrils flared, his breath shortening into pants. Baylor closed his eyes, and his face smoothed again.

Alesio turned back to Clef. "You bet I'm keeping you alive. I need you to talk to a magic box."

He punched Clef in the side of the head, knocking him unconscious.

WHEN THE SUN had dipped below the horizon and just the dark purple, reflected light of the planet of Vision showed, Saida and the others crept through the forest.

The Epitaph called to them in several pulses of quick succession. The group followed in Saida's footprints, where, as a foxan, she'd found the softest and lowest area of fresh snow, to avoid crunching through the frozen crust, slinking forward on her toes. She wore her human coat over her foxan one to keep the wind off, which Alesio had had tailored so when she shifted, the coat would not fall off her but cinched at her wrists and stomach.

The wind had quieted as they traveled down the mountain, but in the clearing, it howled with renewed ferocity. Broken stone houses started showing up, and the air warmed, somehow, to a more bearable temperature. From a nearby bluff, some kind of stone tube descended, propped up by pillars. Sections of it had fallen, but Saida could tell the tube used to extend to many of the houses. Icicles hung off the section closest to the cliff. She hazarded a guess that the tube connected to a stream up on the bluff and had once conveyed water to the various homes.

Ingenious, she thought. The people in Anthem kept water in giant jugs in their kitchens, but they had to lug that water from a well every day. Some of these contraptions didn't seem to require magic to work —they just worked because of the laws of nature. Well, she imagined that they would work without magic. She didn't know that for sure.

Naya gasped, the sound muffled by the rags they'd stuffed in their ears to dull the sharpness of a shrike's shriek. They all spun, and there in a crumbled house lay a shrike nest. Its owner had arranged sharpened sticks pointing in all directions in a large, crude circle.

Dried blood covered their ends, and small bones hung on them like the worst kind of decoration.

Saida gestured them on. More abandoned shrike nests appeared. The group hid behind the ruins and peered around the sides of half-buildings. Saida found another of those strange cabinets that she'd seen on Sedella, crumbled on one side. It reminded her of a hearth where people baked bread.

Etha pointed out a nest with eggs in it and no parents and then indicated her injured hand. The parents must not have trailed her past the town so they could protect their nest. Where they had they flown off to? Hunting, probably.

Saida's heart thudded so hard in her chest she feared it would create Sound magic and give them away. The moment a shrike spotted them it would alert the whole colony. The wind howled, masking the sound of their footsteps. They started forward.

Something moved out of the corner of her eye. A shrike with dull white and brown colors nested on the roof of an unbroken house ahead, like some kind of irate mashed potatoes with eyes. The ridiculous image caused manic laughter to bubble in Saida's throat, which she suppressed with a painful swallow. The stress must be getting to her.

She stopped them and gestured for the group to circle to the other side out of the shrike's view. She shivered a little in the wind, but the air had warmed the farther they infiltrated the infested city. The ruins must have curbed the wind's effects.

She couldn't help but recall the song that Alesio had sung on the Touch expedition:

A SHRIKE HUNT! A shrike hunt!
   Keep your knives at home!
   Strike first! Strike first!
   Or you'll become its home!

. . .

THE GROUP SLIPPED around the next house, Saida leading the way as she followed the Epitaph's call. They stopped short in front of a ring of five stone pillars. One of them had broken off, leaving a short, jagged section like a rotting tooth of the earth.

Just like on Sedella, the grooves of several large circles showed on the stone ground, and the engravings of ancient Lunnite script covered the pillars, the circles, and the silver Goddess Head. And there, right in front of them, a shrike nested on top of the Goddess Head.

I wonder if the heads produce magic somehow, but I can't sense it. It seemed important enough, just like the one on Sedella, that it should produce magic. But nothing emanated from it that she could tell, and no voice spoke from its lips.

Something else sounded, though. Soft calls of the shrikes in their nests echoed from all around. "Zeee . . . zeeee . . ."

Etha lifted her hands in a *what do we do?* gesture.

Naya grabbed a pebble from the ground and pantomimed throwing it, then hiding against the wall's shadow as she counted down on her hand from five. Then she pretended to run.

No one else presented a different plan, and the longer they stayed there, the more dangerous it would become. Naya hefted it in her hand, the rest of them huddling against the wall, then hurled it over the shrike and the Goddess Head. It clattered to the ground on the other side of pillars. Naya splayed herself against the wall next to the others. She held her hand up, counting down from five.

The shrike on top of the Goddess Head popped up. "Zeek?" It launched itself towards where Naya had thrown the pebble.

Questioning calls echoed all around them. "Zeek? Zeeeeek zee zeek?"

A flutter of many, many wings overhead.

Naya counted down, and they all waited for the beating of wings to stop. Five seconds passed. Fifteen. The hundreds of cries of "Zee zeek zeeek zeeeek!" pierced her sound cloths, hurting her ears.

Then the group scuttled past the pillars into the ruins of another broken house. Something huge loomed out of the night, and Saida almost ran into it. Marik yanked her back into a hidden alcove with the rest of them. He released her and mouthed close to her face, "Apologies, Envoy!"

Rib bones the breadth of a swanseize's wingspan curved around the nest like a huge cage. The spine of the dead thing curved past the shrike nest, the breadth of it decreasing like a fish tail that ended outside the ruins of the house.

An enterprising shrike had somehow managed to spike the large animal onto the fallen pillar's jagged end. Then it had hollowed the animal out and added normal sticks inside the ribcage to complete its nest, hidden well. The unlucky animal had the broad, flat skull of a centiel. Though she'd never encountered one, that fish-like body and broad face matched stories the people of Anthem told, stories of giant eels skittering up from the sea caves of the sound-wilds on hundreds of small legs.

Saida had almost stumbled right into the ribcage encircling the nest. She swallowed bile that rose in her throat.

The shrike lurking inside the centiel's bones had reared its head up, studying the ring of pillars. If the strident calls of hundreds of its fellows hadn't drowned out the sound of the group's movements, it would have heard them.

The group waited for quite some time before the bird nestled back down on its luxury accommodations. They tiptoed in the shadow of a taller building nearby and caught their collective prodigal breaths behind the next hollowed out house, and they went on.

The Epitaph's frenzied notes grew in urgency, calling faster, faster. The air warmed even more until it seemed spring had arrived, even though the wind howled as strong as ever and should have jabbed like icicles at their faces. They maneuvered around four more houses before they found it.

Another stone tree awaited them, taller and thinner than Sedella's, with a hole in its center crossed by thin bars like the strings of an instrument. The Epitaph's magic strummed the wind across the bars, commandeering the force like elemental fingers, a chord followed by the quick, finger-plucking notes of urgency. Heat flowed outward from the tree.

Saida stared at it for a long ten seconds before she understood.

The Epitaph's magic on this world changed the sound of the wind into heat. The shrikes had claimed these ruins because the Epitaph heated them in the middle of winter!

Marik and Naya stared at the tree with open mouths. They drew closer, holding their hands out to the warmth. The heated air shimmered in front of the tree. The same large, circular script displayed on its bark as the Epitaph in their home of Sedella, also weathered and worn.

Saida stayed back in her foxan form, her thoughts racing. A shrike could spot them at any moment. She wanted to figure something out before she had to teleport them out of there. They needed to use this opportunity, this moment, the best they could.

Alesio would know what to do with this Sound magic. Maybe *he* could've heard this Epitaph. The sharpness of his absence struck her like a shrike call, and she blinked, trying to keep back tears. She wanted to teleport to him, but she stopped herself.

Then something in the Epitaph's long, high note *did* say something to her. The note hovered in the air, like someone perched on a cliff, like it had responded to her cry. It responded in a way that the one on Touch had not, like it reached out to her and wanted to hold her hand.

Sing

Sing? It wanted her to sing?

Yes, it did. The surety flowed through her. It had called her here because Sound magic had called to her through Alesio, had always called to her through the magic voices, and she *longed* for them, for the sound of friends in the past, for a silver tenor in the present, and for hopes against a silent future.

Sing, it said. *Sing.*

Tears pricked her eyes. *Tell me more. Please, don't stop! Keep talking!*

The scream of a shrike pierced the ground next to them, and they all jumped. One of the murder birds soared over them.

"Zeeeeek! Zeeeeek! Zeeeek!" Hundreds of screams echoed it, and all of them slapped their hands over their ears, pushing the rags further in. One dove towards them.

Sing!

I'm not a singer. I don't have the song you want. I just like the sound of someone's voice!

Marik Shaped some dirt into a small overhead shield, forming it just as the bird crashed into it, trying to pierce Naya with its beak. The dirt crumbled overhead, but before the bird could flop away, Marik reShaped a larger portion of dirt, covering everyone in a kind of dome.

"Portal us!" Naya screamed.

Sing!

The rest of the notes translated to words in her head.

Sing we are one, we are one, we are one

They pushed into her mind several images one after another: the squat stone tree on Sedella. Then another, tree, unfamiliar, a stone apple tree with an orchard around it. Then several rala nut trees, also stone, forming a stone arch. Then a stone tree with many small leaves, and lastly, themselves, a stone tree shaped like a giant instrument with stone strings. The images flashed several times in quick succession, overlapping on each other, blending, all with the same roots.

We are one we are one we are one

The meaning of it crashed into her, the intention behind the phrase like a sky clearing up after a storm. The five Epitaphs in these Lunnite cities all had the same roots; they'd just branched out into different worlds, and they wanted her to sing that phrase.

More birds snicked into the dome's outside like deadly rain, and others sent just their shrieks. Marik grunted, keeping the shield Shaped with a steady stream of magic. "Envoy, if it is not too much trouble—"

"Portal!" Naya shouted again.

Saida pointed towards the tree in the sudden darkness of the dirt dome. She didn't have time to explain. "That way! Follow me!"

Marik let that portion of the dome collapse, and Saida tore out of it. The others dashed behind her, and she keened at the tree in a foxan howl that would've made any audience in Anthem wince, "We are one!"

The Epitaph shimmered as it rendered her words into heat. Then the tree glimmered into transparency and divided into four sections, like tall doors. Each showed a different place. One of them displayed the squat jungle trees of Sedella.

The shrikes had swarmed like a thundercloud. Their cries ventilated the ground a few hundred feet away: "Zeek zeek zeek zeek!"

"Get in!"

They hesitated, confusion in their faces. She rose on her hind legs and headbutted Naya in, then jerked her head sideways at the Lunnites.

They dashed in. She followed.

They tumbled out of the stone-tree Epitaph inside of Sedella. The shrikes' calls pierced through the portal and one hit Saida in the back against her human coat and two struck the back of her neck.

Her sound cloths saved her. Instead of the Sound magic hitting her with the sharp lethality of arrows, they thudded against her like hurled rocks. They hurt more than they would otherwise have, though, because of the intensified magic of Touch. She cried out in pain.

The dark cloud of birds hovered outside the portal, and she sang the song again, understanding, now, how the magic of it worked. The stone-tree Epitaph changed to solid stone again.

The back of her neck throbbed. She shifted and pushed her human hands past her thick human coat and dabbed at where it hurt. She winced and her hands came away bloody.

Marik and Naya sprawled on the street nearby. Etha had managed to keep her footing, but she hunched over, her hands covering her face. Saida had shouldered the brunt of the hits, as she'd had to push the others inside. Their thick human coats had protected their backs.

"Where—how—" Naya blinked and tried to stand, but her ankle twisted under her, and she fell back to her knees. "Where are we?"

Marik sat up, then scooted around to stare back at the Epitaph. His hair had unwound from its turban and fell in crimped waves around him. "We're in Sedella. Etha, it's alright, we're in Sedella!"

A wave of exhaustion passed over Saida. She swallowed and plopped down next to Marik, shrugging out of her human coat. Beads of sweat had already slicked her lower back from the ancient city's humid air. His luminous green eyes flashed to the back of Saida's neck. "You're hurt!"

"We're all hurt, genius." Naya grimaced as she straightened her leg in front of her. "I'm pretty sure I just twisted my ankle."

Marik unshouldered his pack and dug out extra plant fibers that he used for his clothing. He reached for Saida's neck, and she arched away from him on reflex.

He paused. "You are bleeding. I cannot let you stay in this condition."

"I'll take care of it," Saida said through gritted teeth. She didn't have a real reason to refuse his help, but something in the assumed manner he had reached for her had set her off. Touch magic heightened the burning pain in her neck and back and she breathed through it as she pulled out some more sound cloths from her pack, holding it over her injury.

Marik paused, his hand still outstretched. She jutted out her chin and glared at him, and he bowed his head. "We thank you for saving us, Envoy, and for thinking to teleport us to our home."

"I didn't portal us," Saida said. "I unlocked the Epitaph."

They all looked at her.

"What?" The dark orange fur on Etha's forehead had fluffed up. "Say that again, if you would. I must have misunderstood."

"They're an ancient Portal Station." Saida hovered her hand over the stone tree Epitaph. She knew, now, how to activate it, not just the one on Sound.

"Huh?" Naya asked.

"What do you mean?" Etha plodded over to the Epitaph and brushed her fingers over its surface. It remained stone. "Unlock it? It was locked?"

"I . . ." Saida licked her lips. "Sound's Epitaph. They said, '*we are one.'* It's a passcode, somehow, I just knew it would unlock the Portal Station. Because that's what the five Epitaphs are, in the ancient Lunnite cites you're all searching for. They're one big Epitaph. Five trees with one root system, all linking to each other."

Etha covered her snout. "But that means—that means—"

"We can portal straight to the other Epitaphs," Naya said.

THE ROCK CONSTELLATIONS

Saida stretched, disengaging from the massive fur ball comprised of her parents and Tener. She hadn't gone back to Alesio's house the night before, but had stayed in the Primal Plane, curling up with her family after she'd told them everything her group had discovered.

Falrie muttered something unintelligible and buried deeper into the fur pile, away from the sudden lack of warmth. Saida yawned and her tongue curled as she dug her claws into the raw magic of the Primal Plane's "ground." It had the texture of cold sand, malleable and dense, pleasurable to stretch her claws in.

A few feet away, Marik stared at her, then, when she blinked at him and stared back, he jerked his gaze away. Saida shifted to a human face, rubbing at the sleep in her eyes and licking her dry lips.

Marik's ears folded in at the tips and his cheeks reddened under his reddish-brown fur. "Um. Good morning."

Saida yawned and nodded as she shifted all the way to human, growing her clothes at the same time. Marik averted his gaze, but he blushed even more. He'd done the same whenever she'd shifted while traveling with him on Sound through the mountains. Maybe Lunnites thought of a foxan shifting as something mystical, something they shouldn't see.

She shook her head. She didn't have time to wonder about whatever Marik thought. After the group had tumbled through to Sedella the night before, she'd portaled everyone back to the Primal Plane's Council meeting area. From there Etha and Naya had gone through the permanent portal to Anthem, while Marik had elected to stay in the Primal Plane. She instructed the two of them to inform the Council members about what they had discovered—that five of the Epitaphs linked to each other, an ancient Portal Station extending to the five worlds.

They connected in a more efficient manner than the Portal Station that Saida and the other foxans had built. Each tree acted as both an arrival and departure portal to all the other trees. Had the Epitaph— the foxan who had transplanted—merged with another magic to create such a far-reaching power? Or did the ancient Lunnite runes power them somehow?

More and more, she'd focused on trying to stop the Hunger rather than spending time missing Goosefeather and Tricksy Stone. It felt like a betrayal, even though it was a necessary thing. Concentrating on her actual mission.

Could she hear Tricksy Stone if she returned to the Cadenza now?

She didn't have time to go and check. A part of her feared to try. Because . . . what if it still didn't work?

Falrie shifted part of her leg to human in her sleep. Saida wanted to leave before the pile woke up. Tener might ask why she hadn't stayed the night at Alesio's like she'd said she would. Would the young foxan see anything different in her and Alesio's bond? Had it frayed because of her decision to distance herself from him?

She'd hoped that the revelations her group had discovered would help clear some of her parents' distant and faded memories. It had seemed to almost work. Darrow had said that heated air with Sound magic did sound familiar. Falrie had nodded along when Saida had told them about the Epitaph tree. After all, they had remembered how to create Portal Stations before this, though not the kind that worked both ways like the Epitaph tree did.

Other than that, though, neither of them had any moments of clarity. The Severing had happened in their youth, and they had fled to Between and suppressed the memories of the time before out of fear. Saida had had trouble remembering a traumatic event after repressing it for just a hundred years or so. They had stifled their memories for around 800 years.

Tener snored a tiny snore from somewhere in the pile. Saida tapped Marik's arm. "Ready to go?"

The Lunnite blinked at her, then stared at where she touched him. She dropped her hand and summoned a portal to Sedella. They strode through without any lag time. She used to have to wait at least a few seconds for the portal to deposit her, before she and Alesio had reconnected the Sensory and Primal Planes. The other side showed clear to her now, and she could just step from one side to the other like passing through a doorway. The Epitaph's squat, stone tree waited for them.

She waited for Marik to leave to gather some extra tools from his house in Sedella. He explained to her that he needed a better trowel and brush to clean dirt from stone and some more paper to produce rubbings.

She hesitantly placed her hand on the Epitaph tree's trunk. The stone felt grittier, more abrasive, on Touch.

Nothing.

Disappointment threatened to crush her. The intensity of it weighed heavier after hoping again. Hope, after all, fell farther the higher it climbed.

How had she heard the voice of the Epitaph tree on Sound, then? Did she hold a loose connection with Sound magic, through Alesio?

Good thing I didn't try to go back to the Cadenza. She had stopped her hope from climbing high enough that it would've shattered when it fell.

Had she done that with Alesio? Let her hope climb too high? Taste something too sweet? Hear something too beautiful?

What would she do when it all crashed down? When she had to gather pieces of herself back into a semblance of function again?

Marik returned fifteen minutes later, his pack bulging with supplies. Saida touched the squat stone tree and spoke the passphrase. She knew, somehow, that to unlock the portals on Touch, she didn't have to sing the passphrase but had to speak it while touching the tree. "We are one."

The stone tree turned transparent, and through it, four paths branched out to four different silhouetted trees. One of them they already knew, the tall and thin tree in the shrike-infested ruins on Sound. Another had many small leaves, and another seemed like a fruit tree of some kind. The fourth linked with more than one tree, forming an arch.

She and Marik chose the path that led toward the tree with small leaves. They blinked, their eyes adjusting from the softer light filtering through Sedella's canopy to Vision's bright afternoon lavender sun. The sun beat down summer hot, telling Saida that they had discovered a new area of the world of Vision, since the area around Lavoa languished in winter. That, and the new view of Taste, low in the sky and rotated to an unfamiliar side, with the bronzed, salt-flat area showing a little, but most of it dark blue.

They emerged from the Epitaph tree into a tilted world, which confused Saida for a moment. They'd portaled onto a slanted gravity shift about twenty feet above the ground. Many of the Epitaph tree's small leaves flickered, shifting color every few moments, but towards the top, the branches had snared an inexplicable section of night sky in the middle of the afternoon.

The hundreds of leaves together in that part of the tree created a picture, like some giant had painstakingly arranged all the leaves with the different shadings to create a display of the stars and the top of a tower, on which rested a silver sundial. She guessed that the rest of the leaves should show the rest of the image.

The leaves' color flipped through many different colors every few seconds. The flickering effect strained her eyes, and she had to look away. *Is it showing a real place? Or an illusion?*

The Epitaph trees on Touch and Sound had each incorporated that world's magic somehow, through the Lunnites' runes. The Epitaph trees didn't just act as Portal Stations; they also functioned as some kind of magical center in each city, absorbing magic, changing it, and then distributing it back out into the area around them. Here on Vision, the sundial in the tree's picture had the same silver as the Goddess Heads. Maybe the tree leaves presented another city that the ancient Lunnites had built.

Marik had changed back into his plant-fiber clothing. He'd gone without sleeves this time, and had not re-wrapped his hair around his head, leaving it to swing free as he seemed to prefer. His tall foxan ears flicked back and forth along with his eyes. He gazed at the Epitaph tree's image, but also all around them, at the entrancing and convoluted area of Vision.

The familiar grooved circle surrounded Vision's Epitaph tree, but in a different way from the others. All around them, large rock formations twisted and revolved, some emerging from depressions in the ground, some beginning in the air, like partners in an elaborate dance, some of them ending back where they started in a strange, mind-boggling pattern. Various levers, pulleys, and gears, like what Lavoa and many other ruins in Vision had, seemed to direct much of the rock clusters' movement, small and large wheels turning everything in a pre-set manner. The grooved inset surrounding the tree displayed like a circle when viewed at a specific angle at a specific time. The eye trying to follow the stones' movement would end up tangled in a knot.

Tricksy Stone might have originated from a rock field like this.

"What is it, Envoy?" Marik asked. "Is something wrong?"

Tears trickled down her human cheeks. She wanted to shift and cram the emotions into her foxan form, but she resisted. She used to do it a lot before she'd met Alesio, and she'd lost time, that way, and focus. When she shoved all her feelings into her animal side, she tended to dissociate and forget things. She didn't want to get into the habit again and give him even more reason to worry. She still did it without realizing it from time to time, and she hadn't grasped how often.

It forced her to feel a lot more all at once, instead of repressing and ignoring it over a long period of time. The grief manifested like a physical pain inside her, like a gray-blue chunk of stone in her chest. Or the absence of one.

She brushed the tears away and swallowed, arranging her features into a placid expression. "It's nothing. Foxan allergies."

Marik stared at her, but then his gaze snagged on something past her. "Oh, there's the Goddess Head!" He ran forward, and she held out her hand to stop him, but he'd already stepped too far, and the gravity jerked his feet upwards on the slant. He yelped.

"The gravity changes here. Shuffle forward with a few steps at a time. The gravity shifts will show by the wavering in front of you."

Marik nodded and inched past her. He followed the curve of gravity upwards, then sideways and around a grouping of rocks. She raised herself on her tiptoes and squinted where he'd gone. The silvery Goddess Head showed through the rock fissures.

Saida shuffled forward with her feet to test the gravity, following the groove around the Epitaph tree, passing a few rotating pulleys and smaller gears. As usual, movement helped her collect herself again.

This machinery must have begun working after the Reconnection last year had jumpstarted all the Epitaphs—she couldn't imagine that the metal and stone and wire of this contraption would have worked without ceasing for 800 some years.

"Marik," she said, aiming her words through the tangle of rocks, "Why does the Epitaph's magic work differently here?"

He jerked up from his study of the Goddess Head, already deep in concentration though they'd arrived fifteen minutes or so ago. "What? What was that?"

Saida frowned. "On Sedella, the Epitaph tree repaired its own stone and the stone around it. In the ruins on Sound, it warmed the air around it. But here, the Epitaph tree's magic, with that flickering picture in its leaves, seems less powerful than the magic of these revolving rocks, which are farther away."

"Oh. Huh, you're right." Marik's voice echoed through the spinning clusters, sounding more distant as he shuffled around. "There's a line of broken script around the tree here, but the one that leads from the tree to the area with the rocks is intact. Perhaps the Epitaph's power that otherwise would have gone towards creating that picture moves the rock formations." He hummed. "Fascinating. That implies that the ancient Lunnites could power different things in their cities through the Epitaph." His voice trailed off.

Saida squinted at the weathered circle symbols carved in the groove under her feet. One of the symbols rearranged itself as she peered at it upside down, as if the world of Vision had allowed her to translate some of it herself, and she recognized it as the word that Marik had explained on Sedella: *Shape*. The letters twisted and untwisted just like the rocks. *Receive. Shape. Receive. Shape. Conversation.*

The last word didn't have a symbol, but resolved in her mind as the meaning of the two other words braided together.

Why couldn't she hear the Epitaph's voice here? She'd thought, back in the infested shrike city on Sound, that her ability had returned. But, once again, the power of the Epitaph pulsing through the rock formation did not translate into words.

Marik exclaimed something.

"What was that?" she called through the fissures.

Marik's words whipped through the tunnel at various volume levels, and she had to crane her neck to hear the words. "Part of the text on the Goddess Head isn't as faded as the one on Sedella. Actually, there's a lot protected because of the overhangs of the rock formations. Higa, would be so jealous of me right now. She's studied the ancient script more than anyone in Sedella. It's the most difficult to find preserved, because the circles are thinner and weather easier, but another thing is that it's easier to see here on Vision. Everything is so much crisper, here. Anyway, I can make out two new parts. 'We who combined our magics and' . . . um . . . I think the word here is absorb . . . 'absorbed the ore to become.' The rest of that one's too worn down to translate. And then, this other section. 'When increased,' uh, I'm really not sure about this word, but maybe it means space? Uh, 'the space magic will power the ship.'"

"Space magic, huh? Nothing I've ever heard of before. You?"

"What? Oh, no, I haven't."

"Maybe it's a mixture of Vision magic and how it changes gravity." Saida squinted upwards at the rocks. "And it sounds like they had some kind of special ore. That could be the space magic, some kind of thing like these rocks that moved around. Maybe that's what powered their ship?" She paused. "Did the ancient Lunnites build a ship to search for Lunne?"

"Seems so. There's something else about the translation I'm not understanding." He resumed his mumbling, and this far up, the wind pocketed his words.

The lever next to it had a symbol with a curve. She pulled it, and the gravity shifted to a gentle slope. The rock clusters nearby shifted, rearranging to avoid colliding, obeying the new rule she had just imposed. A rock at the perfect height for her to step on revolved close by, and she did so, letting it carry her upwards on the gravity shift. She hopped off on one of the still rock formations as the gravity shift ended. The rock glided at an easy pace for this, not fast at all.

Here, another lever waited, along with a sequence of arrows at her feet: left, up-right, and forward. She could tug the lever several ways rather than just two like the others.

"Marik," She shouted down. "Watch out, the rocks will change positions, okay?"

His distant voice floated up to her. "What? Uh, okay?"

She pulled the lever left. A formerly still formation of rocks joined the dance, and those around it accommodated it by shifting their pattern once more. She pushed the lever up and to the right, and another stable cluster moved, creating an even more complicated configuration. The rocks themselves almost seemed sentient, but still following a slow, pre-set pattern. She pushed the lever forward, and her rock lifted straight up through what felt like the eye of a thunderstorm, except the storm clouds were rocks.

The rock raised above them all. She peered down.

Nothing jumped out to her as a pattern or a picture. She let her eyes drift half-closed. The ancient Epitaph tree's leaves flickered every so often just below her. Did this rock function as a viewing station for the tree's picture?

The tree's picture did not change, but below her, the stones seemed to. Their shapes had created a depiction of five interconnected spheres arranged above a flat circle.

A small blue circle. A large lavender circle. Two blue-green circles, one of them a little bigger than the other. And a bronze and green circle.

Her mouth dropped open. These rocks represented the Sensory worlds.

Another cluster of circles displayed below and to her left, and her right, and several more beyond, as far as the outcroppings of floating rocks extended. She gasped, kept her head still to keep the view, and counted.

Twenty-four. Even more might show beyond her sight. Twenty-four clusters. Not all of them had five circles. Some of them had as few as three, or as many as seven. They sported vibrant colors such as deep reds and blues, or yellows and whites. Obvious gaps showed in some places, however, almost like a giant hand had ripped out some of the clusters—Planes, she realized.

"Marik," she whispered. The wind whistled up here, and her throat had tightened. He hadn't heard her, of course. "Marik!"

He still couldn't hear her. She had to undo all her work and trek back down, huffing with excitement as she shuffled her feet. He had retreated to the other side of the Epitaph to avoid the soaring rocks. "Marik! Follow me! You have to see this!"

She repeated her actions, guiding him to the top viewing rock. Ignoring his repeated questions, she pointed down. "Look. Keep looking. You'll see it."

He obeyed, staring outwards for several minutes. His hair drifted in the wind, almost tangling with her long braid's straggly ends.

"Oh," he said. Then, "Oh!"

"It's a map," Saida said.

Marik lifted a hand to cover his mouth, then fell to his knees. He tipped a little too close to the edge and a gravity shift tossed him forward, then down, then propelled him in a backwards arc.

"Marik!"

One of the moving rocks caught him before he gained too much momentum, and he landed on his back, not too far down, about a third of the way.

Saida levered the viewing rock down. She eyed the gravity shifts and chose one that led up and to the right, away from him at first, but ready to meet him once the rock glided into her gravity shift. She jumped over to him. "Are you hurt? You fell at least ten feet!"

The Lunnite groaned. "Nothing's hurt except my pride."

Saida smiled at him, gripping his arm and helping him up. "It's okay. Everyone falls the first time in Vision." She circled him, checking for broken bones.

His neon green eyes had dilated, and he hugged his arms around himself. The wind riffled through their hair braids as the rock conveyed them in its pattern. "Is . . . is that so?"

"Why are you looking at me like that?"

"Like what?"

"Like I'm a shrike or something that might eat you."

He coughed, and his cheeks reddened. "Head . . . rush. From the fall."

She peered back up at the constellation of rocks, rotating above them. "Do you know what this means?"

"My head is fuzzy. Feel free to explain."

"That other Planes exist out there. Dozens of them. Maybe more."

His eyes widened, and they both sat there processing the information.

"It makes sense." She pointed upwards at the Hunger. "*They* came from somewhere else. I just . . . I didn't think about . . . there being other Planes. Other people."

"Other magics." Marik's eyes had glazed over. His ears had flicked back. The rock flew underneath a set of others, grazing the tops of their heads so they had to duck. They found a way down to the ground to avoid any unfortunate collisions. Though the rocks seemed to avoid each other, she didn't know if their awareness extended to living things.

They sat there for a few minutes, staring upwards.

"I can't even imagine something like that," Marik said. "The worlds we know are already so vast. I . . ." he shook his head.

"There had to be more, though," Saida said. "More people. More planets. All those stars in the sky. They're places!"

Marik rubbed his eyes. "I can't . . . that's too much for me think about right now. I must focus on what I understand, or my head feels like it will explode. I translated another section where the rocks protected the script from the weather. It said, 'We divine . . . potential of the ore along with . . . could transmute.' That's all I could figure out, though."

"Divine? Wasn't that a word on the Goddess Head in Sedella?"

"Correct."

"Maybe your ancestors could predict the future somehow. Maybe they voyaged from one of these other Planes, and they could do magics we don't even know about."

The light had dimmed, and darkness crouched in the corners of the stone formations. A verdant forest growing sideways out of a hill in the sky had obscured the sun, which had delved lower in the sky than she'd realized. "How is it so late? I thought we'd been here for a couple hours or so."

Marik groaned. "I was so focused on translating the text I didn't notice."

Saida swallowed. "Same, I guess."

Hadn't it? The ancient Lunnite script had kept her attention so long. Did Vision's Epitaph tree have some kind of hypnotizing ability in those flickering leaves? Did they want her to stay for some reason?

Not understanding them made her suspicious. She'd never felt that way around magic before, not even with overgrowths. She'd always understood why they did what they did and wanted what they wanted. It startled her, her sudden fear of what she didn't know. It reminded her of how human crowds still unsettled her at times.

Or, maybe, she'd had an episode where she'd drifted for a while and forgotten herself. That explanation terrified her just as much. Well, it would have terrified Alesio more. He would have noticed right away, knelt in front of her and held her hand, grounding her back into normal time. She missed him so much, like she missed Tricksy Stone and Goosefeather. More, even.

But knowing what she knew about herself, if she loved him, shouldn't she end the relationship? The distance she'd constructed between them these past two days had sharpened her uncertainty further, and it cut her open like a Sound knife.

Closeness, both physical and emotional, no longer left her trembling or filled with dread, as if someone had shoved her into a cage—indeed, his hands and his heart excited her.

But she could change. She might not want the same thing in five years, and she could abandon Alesio, leaving him alone. That terrified her. Made her hate herself for not being able or willing to stop changing for him.

But if she couldn't change, she wouldn't be free. She wouldn't be herself.

Love, real love, is about helping someone because you want to. Because you care about them, and that's all that matters. He'd said that to her a year ago, after she'd refused to use her magic items to teleport them out of danger.

Could she love him enough to stop from hurting him, or would she stay the same selfish person who refused to do the right thing?

Her breath shortened and shallowed. She sipped in small breaths, her hands trembling, her paws trembling, her muzzle shortening, then lengthening, her vision tunneling. She couldn't even control her own shifting, why did she think she could control her future self? Out of the corner of her eye, Marik reached for her with a hesitant hand.

She couldn't think about this. She couldn't.

"We can't stop here." She strode up towards the flickering tree.

Marik followed without a word.

18

FEAR IS A STRANGE THING

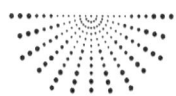

After Alesio had knocked Clef unconscious, he fashioned Touch handcuffs of wood around him then found some rope, and bound him with those, too. And gagged him. Just to be safe.

Unfortunately, such precautions meant Alesio had to drag the unconscious Clef in a litter he'd Shaped from wood behind himself.

Baylor, the young ixor Shaper, followed Alesio like a shadow. Hestafon took up the rear, as Alesio didn't trust that the young man wouldn't flip back to Clef's side at a moment's notice. He'd pared his edgy, flippant responses down, leaving just an outline of his former self, his remaining density a dogged determination to find and save his father.

Alesio knew that mindset all too well. The parallels did not lose him, and he had a twisting sensation that Clef had manipulated the young man's situation to resemble Alesio's to mess with his mind.

"I promise that we'll find your dad," Alesio said, and Baylor flinched and jerked his head towards him.

This sudden submissive version of Baylor did not sit well with Alesio. He missed the young man's saucy quips and devil-may-care attitude, but more than that, it confirmed his suspicions that Clef had abused Baylor after fights, especially if he had lost. He knew, because he'd lived through it. Every twitch, every flinch, every part of that hunched posture echoed Alesio's young life.

Baylor may have switched allegiances, but he didn't expect to switch experiences. His body braced for a beating.

That tore Alesio up inside. He wanted to reassure the young man that he would never abuse him as Clef had, that he wanted to support and encourage Baylor in the same way that Alesio wished someone would have for him.

But if the young man's experience mirrored Alesio's as closely as he thought, any comforting words would mean nothing to Baylor. Only actions would translate to anything. Not just that, but something in how the young man's gaze darted back and forth and slid away from any eye contact told him that Baylor could morph back any moment into fighting as a response instead of subjugated obedience.

Alesio snuck a few glances at the silver in Baylor's mouth, clamped over his teeth.

Should I try to pry that thing out so I could handle him, if he does snap?

The young man could have an addiction to the ixor he produced, though. Had that physician on Taste described the symptoms of ixor addiction? He couldn't quite remember, but Baylor's lips did seem chapped and had even bled a little. The ixor could have caused that, or the amplifier itself, perhaps. Something in the young man's thousand-mile stare told Alesio that the spice affected him at least mentally, if not physically. Hours could seem like days to him, or weeks when paired with the amplifier.

Alesio didn't dare try to convince Baylor to give up the amplifier. The young man seemed unstable and asking him to give up such a powerful edge could loosen his grip on the remaining sane thought he seemed to cling to.

And Alesio had even more qualms about forcing the matter. Unless Hestafon could repeat his stunt with the kandri pepper scent, Baylor could kill them both before Alesio could pry the device out.

At some point, Baylor motioned to a nearby bush, indicating he needed to answer nature's call.

"Yeah, yeah, go on." Alesio set the sled handles down and stretched the stiffness from his arms and back. He waited for the young man to leave their earshot, then spoke to Hestafon in a whisper. "So. Tell me. How did you do it? The . . . pepper thing?"

Hestafon shook his head. He also kept his voice low. "I had an epiphany, I realized I had never considered the magic's desires before; I just imposed my will on it, ordering it around just like I used to do to people." He paused. "So, I . . . instead of Receiving and then Shaping magic into what *I* wanted, I rang a discordant chord with the intention to attract magic from the Primal Plane that wanted to become spicy." Hestafon grinned in the old way that Alesio would have considered arrogant—now it just looked self-satisfied. "The magic did work better that way, didn't it?"

"You're fishing for compliments. But yes. Yes, it worked well."

Baylor reappeared on the trail behind them, giving them a reason to stop talking, though Alesio pondered how he could practice what the piper had explained. By filtering how he Received so the magic's goals aligned with his own, Hestafon could do more with his magic than before.

After a few hours, Clef woke. He tried to say something, but the gag blessedly muffled his words. After that, in unspoken agreement, they did not talk among themselves. None of them wanted Clef to hear the inner lies they might tell themselves while they spoke about the weather.

Clef watched them all with a manic gleam in his eyes, and Alesio shivered, wondering how strong the old strait's leader had become. Did the sound of Alesio's footsteps gossip about his inner thoughts? He wished he could ask Baylor for the particulars of how Clef's ability worked, but he'd have to wait until Baylor seemed less likely to stab him.

That night, Hestafon located the cave he had found before, and they camped there again to stay out of the cold winter night, building a fire on the cave floor. Alesio took first watch guarding Clef—and, furtively, Baylor—then woke Hestafon up for second watch. The piper might not have a chance in a hand-to-hand fight, but he could sound the alarm. And Alesio *had* to sleep at some point.

Hestafon yawned and stretched, his gaze darting to Clef, tied up and sleeping against the cave wall. Clef didn't have the grayed skin or a hole in his chest like the other Consumed had had. His polished gray eyes, however, had changed from brown. Maybe he hadn't melted into sludge like the rest of the Consumed because Watthe hadn't Consumed him all the way.

Alesio hadn't told Hestafon why he'd kept Clef alive. Alesio trusted him now, but he had the sense that saying his plan aloud would make it sound irrational. Ridiculous.

Well, Hestafon's ridiculous theory about windows for Alesio's magic had proven right earlier. Maybe this would work, too.

"Hestafon," Alesio said. "Do you think you could smell if Clef lied?"

Hestafon sat up and rubbed the sleep from his eyes. "Hmm. What did you say? Are you speaking of his strange ability to hear lies? I'm confused."

"Sort of," Alesio said. "He does seem able to, uh, hear lies. Not just if something's true or not, but the actual words of a lie, someone's full thoughts around their lies. I want to use his ability to listen to that small Hunger in the Primal Plane, to listen to what they're hiding."

"Oh!" Hestafon said. "Oh! That's ingenious!"

A little glow of pride warmed Alesio at the piper's praise, which surprised him. When had he started caring what Hestafon thought of him? He shook off the emotion and continued explaining. "But the trouble is, I can't trust *Clef.* I need to know if what he's telling me is true or not."

"I understand, now." Hestafon tapped his chin, staring at the sleeping Clef. "To answer your earlier question, I believe so. Some of his words have a rotting odor. Almost like he uses outdated or decayed truths on purpose, instead of the current facts. Different from that sharp metallic smell of knives and blood."

Alesio let out a relieved breath. "Okay. Good. Then we might be able to help Saida and the others." He picked up a stick and threw it on the fire, and glowing embers flared, illuminating Baylor for a moment. He lay outside of a cave, huddled in a pile of leaves.

"I really thought he would be in Flock," Alesio said.

"Well, yes. I assumed the trail would lead there as well, at first. But, in the end, I suppose he wouldn't hide somewhere we searched. I sent at least ten search parties to Flock over the past five months."

Alesio was suddenly conscious of trying not to breathe too loudly, in case the piper might smell the sound of shame from him.

"Of course . . . if you believed I was a traitor . . ." Hestafon flexed his hands. "I will go and find more wood for the fire."

"Hestafon. Wait."

The piper paused.

"I'm—I'm sorry. For not trusting you."

"You had good reason. That was before our little escapades began, after all." Hestafon's voice was strained. "And I forbid you to go. I'm sure that didn't help your misgivings. It's hard to know if someone has changed or just wants to give the appearance of change to others."

Alesio licked dry lips. He took a swig from his water flask. "I made excuses in my own head not to go there, anyway. I could have just gone."

"Why . . . why didn't you?"

Alesio studied the unconscious Clef. He'd hit the old strait's leader hard earlier to keep him knocked him out. He did *not* want Clef to peer inside his thoughts and speak them out loud again anytime soon.

"I don't know Flock like I do Anthem. And the shrikers—"

"Flock isn't as dangerous as you might think. The search parties found hardly any of that violent group."

Alesio raised an eyebrow at Hestafon's interruption. "Well, then, they need their eyes checked. I *saw* two shrikers extorting someone the one time I went there with Saida."

"Did they have the shrike tattoo on their necks? Or their forearms?"

"What? Why should that matter?"

Hestafon watched the new log burn down for several moments. "Did you know that Mona helped with the last search?"

Alesio started. "Mona, as in . . . currently dating my father, Mona?"

"She was quite insistent you not know. She said you'd be overprotective and such. But she was very intent on, and these are her words, 'finding that gray corpse bastard that tortured the only two men that matter in my life.'"

Alesio cleared his throat. "That does, uh, sound like something she'd say."

"She reported the same thing that the other searchers had. They found a few melted piles of sludge in a basement. Like the Palates on Taste, remnants of the Consumed. But no massive gang network shaking down citizens for thirty-second notes."

Alesio felt a sense of déjà vu. He'd had a version of this conversation before with . . . with Mona.

Don't just look in Flock. Also, the city isn't as dangerous as you all seem to think.

"They must've missed something." Alesio clenched his jaw. "You've said differing things at the Council meetings. You've acted afraid of Flock, but now you're saying the city's harmless?"

"One of the search parties . . ." Hestafon's hands trembled, and he breathed in a deep breath. "Another search party did find something else. I have hesitated to tell the Council. But I should have."

Alesio's hand twitched to hover above his knife handle. He regretted the motion as soon as he did and forced himself to drop his hand to his side. Hestafon tracked the aborted movement, then stared into the fire.

The log crackled, splitting in the flames.

"They found out," Hestafon continued after several seconds, "That the reason the famed shrikers disappeared is because Flockian citizens hunted them down, if they weren't already melted into that strange sludge."

"*What?*"

"Citizens have also hijacked the sign of the shrike to confuse their oppressors, to disarm them. If they tattooed the bird on their arm, they are the new shrikers, the ones trying to win back their city. They have done this all on their own, without aid from Anthem, because I was too much of a coward to bring it forth. Because I *did* fear Flock and its army of cage match fighters I'd heard so much about. Because I was not acting as Sound's overall delegate, but just Anthem's. The citizens of Flock have had to face Clef's ilk alone. I began to understand how much I had failed them, and then I began to fear them in a whole new way. They were upset. They were angry, rightfully so, at my neglect and discrimination of them. They hated me." Hestafon passed a hand over his face, his forehead lined like Tremain's raked fields. "And then, everything happened with the Hunger, and I hesitated again in sending them immediate aid."

"Why?" Alesio whispered, though he thought he knew.

"I feared that they would rise up in rage, that I would dare send aid after ignoring them for so long. That they would cast aside any from Anthem who tried to help. Fear is a strange thing, is it not? It crops up even after the threat has passed, like echoes in a cavern. Darrow returned with that report, about how they'd done so well alone, and all I have been able to think about for the past few days is wonder how they're faring without Portal Stations, while every other city and village believe they are monsters. And still, I am afraid. I wanted to help you, and come with you on your journey, but really, I just wanted to—to avoid the decision on the Council." Hestafon covered his face with his hands. "I've tried to be better. I've tried, Alesio. But I'm the same. You were right to not trust me."

The log snapped, and the two halves buckled onto the embers. Light and heat flared. Outside the cave, Baylor's eyes glinted in the firelight. How long had the young man been awake?

Mona knew all this. Why didn't she come out and say it?

She had, though. She'd spoken of the Flockians who had visited the De Capo and he'd brushed her reasoning off. He liked to think that he would have believed her account of going to Flock, but now . . . he was starting to see how blind the fear of Clef had made him. How it had made him see things that didn't exist.

Every other city and village believe they are monsters, Hestafon had said.

Alesio couldn't point fingers at the piper for his faults. Not when

Alesio himself had misjudged Flock based on his own fear and ignorance.

"You're right," Alesio said. "Fear blinds us. Controls us, if we let it. I never would've believed you about Flock except that I think Mona tried to tell me." He swallowed. "And I, for one, feel like an absolute hotrat. Deep fried in shame and battered in regret."

Hestafon choked out a laugh.

"But you were wrong about not changing," Alesio continued. "The old Hestafon would never have admitted what you did. Or that it was wrong."

The piper took in a deep breath. "I will call a Council meeting to send a team out there the moment we get back. And . . . I want to be on it. To apologize directly."

Alesio nodded, trying to process everything he had just learned. He rose and paced a few times, and caught sight of Clef's pinched, thin face, slack in sleep. Without any grimace or manic grin to stretch it, the loose skin folded close to his ears. Alesio couldn't imagine that Clef would have planned for mere citizens to overpower his trained and battle-hardened followers.

Even as Alesio wrestled with his own arrogance and bias, he gathered some solace in that. Because, for the first time in his life, he'd found clear evidence that Clef's puppeteering strings could not stretch across the entire Sensory Plane.

Alesio settled on the ground and fought to sleep. The next morning, they allowed Clef time to use the facilities of the woods and ungagged him for water, which he used as an occasion to scream for ixor. They shoved some water down his throat and Baylor hit him with a dose of ixor to keep him quiet, then Alesio re-gagged him.

They arrived at Lavoa's Portal Station at dusk, and Baylor followed, still silent.

⸻

"I STILL NEED a Scentian to gather nonflowers up north today, by the Garden." Verrity swept her gaze over Tremain's field teams. The fifteen Soundian volunteers that had arrived that day glanced among themselves, their brows furrowing at the strange term. She'd directed them to help with the planting, so they could remain near the village and not get lost.

No Scentian villagers raised their hands in response to her query. Her people tended to avoid the Garden, a magical maze a mile or so north of Tremain, because navigating through it cost mental effort and circumnavigating it cost time.

Verrity shrugged. "Alright then, I can—"

"I'll do it, Mother!" Ishira bolted up, brushing dirt from her dress. A few leaves from the nearby trees had blown into her braided hair.

"Thank you, Ishira, but you're supposed to have the afternoon off. You just finished your morning planting shift," Verrity said. "I can do it. My meetings with the foxan have ended for now."

"I'd like to, though," Ishira said. "It's quieter up that way. The Garden doesn't bother me. I'll eat my lunch there." A sour scent of fear emanated from her, which she suppressed with an embarrassed look.

Lust and fear. Scentians could smell the two emotions, as bodily reactions created them both and produced a discernible odor. They also happened to be, at least in Verrity's opinion, the two most awkward emotions.

Verrity had often wished her people could smell hope, or irritation, or trust instead. Even anger would be better than fear, because fear so often sidestepped logical reasoning in its origins and how it manifested. When people smelled fear, it often created confusion as to why.

Is Ishira afraid of me? Or the Soundian volunteers?

Integrating the otherworlders' assistance with the planting had gone about as well as Verrity could have hoped for. Awkward moments had transpired like the previous day when a Soundian had ignored the all-important rule of cleanliness and arrived in attire so grimy and sweat-soaked they'd had to lend him a set of clothes, then bathe in the stream, then perform the ritual nonflower cleansing. This blatant violation had exasperated a few of the villagers, however, the man had explained that he didn't have another set of clothes. This had oscillated the Scentians' frustration into that of confusion and then compassion, and Verrity had ordered him given two sets of clothing: one to work and one to take home for himself.

A moment like that had highlighted the difference in wealth between the Scentians and the otherworlders. For though the Scentians lived in a dirt village, they lived happy, quiet lives, and ate good, clean food. These Soundians might have lived in a huge city, but many did not experience pleasure in ways that mattered to the people of Tremain. The Scentians had begun to realize that dichotomy, and it showed in how they worked together with the otherworlders easier, and did not shy away from them, or emanate the scent of fear as much.

The Scentians' shifting attitudes had informed Verrity of an important detail she'd missed before about her people: that they'd felt humiliated by the otherworlders at first, with their fancy cities and concert halls, their large buildings and sprawling streets, their cobblestone roads and their loudness. Not just in Anthem, but in the Cloves, too, because all cities were loud to someone living in a village. The incident with the grimy Soundian had helped the people of Tremain take pride in their quality of life.

The other volunteers had respected the rules and tried to help. Nothing like the panicked groups that had dashed through the Portal Station a few days ago.

While the people of Tremain might have begun to relax around the otherworlders, they had tensed up more around *her*. Emanate fear around *her*. Like what she guessed Ishira had just done.

"If you really want to." Verrity clapped her hands, not wanting to pause and call attention to Ishira's faux pas of emanating an uncouth scent, though everyone in a ten-foot radius would have noticed. "Alright, back to it, everyone."

Verrity crouched with the team of mixed groups to plant beans next to elder woman Nirin, loved by everyone for her warmth, inability to keep her mouth shut, and ginger tea that she brewed from her personal herbs. "A good day for planting, eh Nirin?"

The elder bobbed their head, not looking at Verrity, just pressing her seeds in the ground.

Verrity fell silent.

The distance between her and the people of Tremain manifested in the small things, like the wrinkles accumulating around someone's lips when she passed, or how Ishira had noted that herself or Paras should tell the villagers about the Soundian volunteers. It showed in the way elder Nirin inched further down the planting line without speaking to Verrity.

It was also in the big things, like when Ishira herself produced scents of fear around her, and Verrity was left wondering: how much longer could she remain their Mother if they didn't trust her anymore?

What if they want me to step down as Delegate, too? What will I become, when I'm not leading any longer?

A year ago, even the contemplation of such things would have silenced her for days. Now, she could study the reactions of her fellow villagers without wanting to hide in a corner, even if it still shook her assurance. Scents, she could do things like meet with the Council without cringing!

The last few days, though incredibly stressful, had bloomed her confidence from a green bud to an open flower, watered by stepping out of her comfort zone and interrogating the small Hunger. Her time with Falrie and Tener lingered in her mind like a scent in a closed room.

Taking direct action for her world's best interests had felt good. Not just good, but *right*, like she had done her part in protecting Scent in her role as a delegate. It had filled her with a stronger poise and surety than ever before.

Of course, Falrie herself had punctured that developing confidence with her outburst. However, much like how Shapers described how their magic refilled in their bodies, that confidence had trickled back to Verrity over the past day.

She hadn't lost it. Not yet at least.

But that involvement with the foxans and the interrogation of the

Hunger had driven the wedge of distance further between her and Tremain. How could confidence find her while she spent time with the foxans, but not with her people? They slipped away from her, whispering among themselves, working without her direction or guidance. Did they even need her anymore as their Mother? Could she afford to lose that role when they might also revoke her status as their delegate?

If I lose one or both positions, will I lose this confidence? This new self I love who stands tall in front of world leaders, and challenges evil magic with a strong voice, and who is working up the courage to buy that dress and the river take what other people say?

A blurred ball of fur dashed towards her, bounding over the planted rows. "Verrity! Verrity!"

"Tener? What are you doing here?"

The young foxan panted, their pink tongue dangling out of their muzzle, then shifted to stand on human legs, retaining their foxan form for their upper half. "I know how to talk to the Hunger!"

Some of the volunteers jerked their heads up and stared at the blatant display of shifting, or Tener's alarming words, or both. Verrity blinked in surprise, then shepherded the young foxan out of the field. "Let's talk over here."

"But we have to go now!"

"Tener, can you lower your voice for me, please?" She waited till they bobbed their head. "Don't you remember what your mother said? We could make things worse."

The scent of fear Falrie had emanated, however, coupled with how the elder foxan had lashed out at them both, gave Verrity pause.

It made sense that Falrie was afraid. It would be insane not to fear the Hunger and what it could do. But they'd made progress! They'd gotten it to speak and reveal something about itself! Avoiding the Hunger to avoid making things worse didn't make sense when things would worsen anyway. Falrie had allowed fear to paralyze her.

Tener spoke in a strained whisper. "But I know what to do. We need to talk to the part that's *not* the Hunger."

"Tener . . . that doesn't make sense."

"I figured it out when I trimmed magic with my Dad yesterday for the next portal. I heard the magic speak for the first time, like Saida used to! They're made up of different voices, depending on who you want to talk to. There was a shadow on Vision from a cloud that we had to trim. They grew too strong and dark. We coaxed a portion of the shadow onto a nice bright white sheet they could nuzzle into. We didn't want to take the whole shadow, just a slice of it, so we asked, like we always do, like Saida says to. And they said yes! We could hear them! I think Dad could hear them, too, but he seemed confused. Anyway, the magic that spoke was still part of the whole shadow but also a piece of magic by themself. So, what if we try to talk to part of the mini hunger fused with the tree? The tree was formed from Watthe, who was Sensory magic. There could be a piece of them that will talk to us!"

"You're talking to the wrong person right now," Verrity said. "This seems to warrant the foxans' expertise. Not a human."

Tener reached up as if to pull on Verrity's arm but stopped and morphed to their full human form, growing a loose fur shirt and baggy fur pants. Their ears brushed Verrity's cheek instead of her shoulders; they'd grown taller again. Their triangular face had sharpened into adolescence, and the black freckles on their cheeks and around their eyes had faded.

"Please." Something in the way they spoke gave Verrity pause, like it held more gravity. "I feel like the small Hunger knows something we *need* to know, to survive."

She bit her lip. "Falrie will be upset with you." *And me, for letting you.*

The older foxan woman had given Verrity a lot of her newfound confidence, after all. Verrity didn't want to reward that gift with cause for anger. But she had already decided, hadn't she? The second the young foxan had barreled into the field, she'd known, and her heart had leapt at the chance to act as Scent's delegate, to try and protect them in the best way she could.

Tener smiled in a gentle way that told her they already knew her decision. "Falrie's always upset with me."

Just as Tener raised their hands to open the portal, Darrow appeared on the path leading from the Portal Station and loped towards them in his foxan form. "Tener! Wait!"

Tener's hands twitched, but they didn't open a portal.

He reached them in moments, his human legs pumping, panting from his foxan muzzle.

"Dad, please, I need to go to the Primal Plane!" Tener reiterated what they had said to Verrity with the speed and vigor of an ice-melt stream.

Darrow processed the flood of information as he caught his breath. He shook his grizzled gray head. "I know, I'm coming with you."

Tener had their mouth open, about to continue, then snapped it shut. They glanced at Verrity, then back again. "You're—you're not upset? Even though Mom wouldn't want me to?"

Verrity clasped and unclasped her hands in front of her. She didn't quite understand their relationship with the two elder foxans, since Tener wasn't their child. And yet, Mother Rean had mothered the whole village before she'd died. Now that she'd had a moment to think, she didn't want to wedge herself in the complicated muddle of a family's disagreement . . . and yet, if they could do anything to stop the Hunger, they had to try.

"I had the same idea as you," Darrow said. "From the shadow of the cloud we trimmed yesterday. I tried to tell Falrie, but the moment I mentioned the small Hunger she wouldn't hear any more, like she'd gone deaf to my reasoning." He shook his head. "Her arm still hurts, where the Hunger touched her. I think her fear of it has clouded her logic."

Tener paused, as if not knowing how to respond to their parents' dispute. They opted to focus on the first part of Darrow's explanation. "You mean, you can hear the magic now, too? Like Saida used to?" Tener reached and gripped Darrow's hands in theirs.

"A little, and just in the past few days. I can sense some words, sometimes." Darrow swallowed, then smiled at Tener and nuzzled their cheek with the side of his face. "Leave the explaining to me. Right now, let's try and find some answers."

Tener looked to Verrity. "Are you still coming?"

In that moment, Verrity solidified her decision. Gave it proper support. *Believed* in it, instead of just reacting to the opportunity in front of her.

Whether her people wanted Verrity to remain as their delegate or not in the future, didn't mean she couldn't be their delegate now.

The villagers had elected her to represent them and speak for their best interests, regardless of how she'd felt about her appearance. While they might not trust her for much longer, she had done her best to better their lives, to nudge them towards open-mindedness and to focus less on their fears.

Meanwhile, she had a duty to make decisions. She couldn't freeze in fear of what otherworlders assumed from her appearance, or what would happen if Tremain told her to step down as their Mother, or how Falrie would be upset with her.

The foxan woman's own words echoed in Verrity's mind: *No one knows what the right thing is, but someone must make decisions. We're just the ones who must make them.*

She straightened her shoulders. "I'm the delegate for Scent," she said, and for the first time, she allowed herself to believe she belonged in that role. "That means I have to consider what's best for my planet." She swallowed. "If we don't do everything in our power to try and stop the Hunger, it'll just keep growing and growing fast. We might somehow make things worse, like Falrie said. But us avoiding danger now just allows that danger to come for all of us sooner."

THE SUN HUNG low on Taste, but at least it remained in the sky. Saida thanked the Senses they still had light to work by here. She could almost catch the tang of her and Marik's desperation on the wind. They teetered on the verge of understanding something, maybe something even bigger than what they had discovered on Vision.

A map of other planetary systems. Other Planes. She still couldn't quite wrap her head around that. Had the humans felt this way when she'd opened paths for them to the other Sensory worlds? Overwhelmed? Not quite fear, but a tripping of the heart all the same, because her scope of understanding had shrunk to a much smaller size?

The Epitaph tree here manifested as a stone apple tree, posing in a real orchard without any apples growing on them. The taste of the crisp fruit from the other trees on the wind glazed her tongue each time she breathed, like she experienced sugar for the first time.

The Epitaph apple tree and the now-familiar five pillars surrounding the silver Goddess Head rested within about fifty yards of each other, much closer than on Sedella or even the revolving stone formations on Vision. This Goddess Head had cracked almost all the way down the middle, but the two halves remained connected at the bottom, giving the impression that someone had cleaved the head with a giant axe.

The two stone grooves circling the two ancient landmarks overlapped, and while Marik had gravitated to study the script on the Goddess Head, she'd traced the path around the Epitaph tree, then the Goddess Head, then the inner circle of their overlapping intersection. Movement always helped her concentrate, and she liked following the little groove as she searched for the Lunnite symbols she'd learned on Vision: *Receive. Shape,* and how they had coalesced into meaning *Conversation.* It reminded her of learning how to read; how individual letters merged to make a word. These old runes and magical symbols were another kind of language.

"Divination, consumption and . . . transmutation." Marik had crouched next to the broken Goddess Head, scratching away ancient dirt from the circle script that created the impression of its curly hair.

"What was that?"

"Those three words repeat around the Goddess's forehead," Marik said. "See, past where it's fractured? That, and the fact that the words are repeated makes me think they're important. And then there's the other mentions of divining things on Vision and Sedella. I wonder if .

. ." his voice trailed off and he resumed picking at the packed grit and grime in the script with his tiny spade-like digging tool.

Every so often Saida peered up at her surroundings and the Epitaph tree. Had the ancient Lunnites planted this orchard in their city around the Epitaph, or had it sprung up in the wilds after the Severing, the Epitaph's magic summoning it somehow?

The foundations of a few stone buildings showed among the trees, but the roots of the apple trees had broken them. Long tubes of stone, long since cracked and lying in halves or multiple pieces, crisscrossed through the trees. Tiny holes spaced the tubes at regular intervals. The holes would've allowed water to spray out into the orchard, watering the area at even and efficient intervals, powered, perhaps, by the Epitaph itself. How much knowledge of manufacturing and other lifestyle benefits had stemmed from the Lunnites, passed down the generations and spread to other worlds? To other *Planes?*

The ancient Lunnites must have created the other strange structures and contraptions to ease the peoples' lives in some way. Perhaps the rusted copper wires hanging in Sedella's houses used to create beautiful music, like the strings of some kind of giant musical instrument. Or maybe the strange cabinets on Sedella and the shrike-infested city, perhaps they had baked bread in a kind of hearth. Anthem's instrument factories had always seemed so advanced compared to what the other cities could do, but an Epitaph didn't power them, nor ancient, strange Lunnite magic. Perhaps, however, that knowledge originated *from* these ancient peoples and all their innovations.

On one of her trips around the apple tree groove, she discovered those two symbols again, and what they had translated to: *Receive. Shape. Conversation.* She plopped down and brushed the script with her fingers, absence aching where the voices used to sound in her mind. She had the urge to return to the Epitaph on Sound regardless of the shrikes, just to listen to their voice again.

"Interesting." Marik's voice was louder than she'd thought it'd be. She'd wandered around the groove closer to his side of things, and he'd wandered away from the Goddess Head.

She trotted over to him. "What? What does it say?"

Marik startled at her proximity, then pointed. "There are symbols of the different planets, and underneath them are images of their respective magics, I believe, see here—a hand, ears, eyes, and under these other two I think used to be a mouth and a nose. And there, an arrow points from each planet and its magic symbol towards the Epitaph. I think . . . I think this means each Epitaph tree pulls the other worlds' magics through their respective Portal Stations and pools there, and that's how they have all this power to do things like repair stone, or heat the air, or fly rocks around."

"A store," Saida said. "Isn't that what you said in Sedella? That the Epitaph is a store?"

"So we think. I want to check something on the Goddess Head again." He jogged back over and resumed his muttering and tracing, and she returned to following the grooved line around the Epitaph a few times, following the letters.

"I had a mistranslation!" Marik said, seemingly a few moments later."

Saida jerked, annoyed at having to surface from her daydream again so soon. "What?"

She'd shifted into a foxan to better shove her nose into the groove, to taste the shape of the words on her muzzle, hoping that would trigger some new understanding and a voice would resonate from it, like on Sound. It hadn't, though the trace taste of apples on stone and in dirt had distracted her; she'd contemplated how bits of the apples had nourished and intertwined with the soil, remaining long after those apples had decayed.

"I've found the same phrase as the one on Vision. You know, the one that said, 'When increased, the magic will power the ship'? Most of the text is faded, but I can read a word that I mistranslated before, because that circle is clearer here. 'When amplified . . . magic . . . the ship.' Ugh, Higa would've figured that out hours ago."

"Amplified magic?" Saida paused. "Wait a minute . . . could the ancient Lunnites have used *amplifiers*?"

Marik's ears angled towards her, curious. "What are amplifiers?"

"They're a rare metal. They strengthen human magic somehow. They're silver." She stared at the split halves of the Goddess Head. "Silver like that."

Marik spun and studied the Goddess Head, then knelt before it, his hair draped around him like a cape and resumed mumbling to himself.

DARROW CLOSED HIS EYES, then a portal appeared to the Primal Plane. They followed him through it, Tener with alacrity, Verrity hesitating yet determined. She might have more confidence now, but that didn't mean she preferred jumping into a portal where an all-consuming entity waited for them.

The small Hunger had gorged on much of the area, its ropy arms swelling into swaths of the Primal Plane's landscape. They had to avoid the three broad bands of it, reaching and curling around, walling off escape not just in front of them, but above and below. Next to the swirling raw magic of the Primal Plane, it pulled Verrity towards it, like she wavered on a high cliff, and she had the urge to jump off. The litany it repeated reverberated from those areas.

"Can you ask your questions here?" Verrity floated between two of the large arms and she felt like two chasms yawned on either side, an endless expanse of nothing. *What would happen if we fell in there??* She swallowed and pulled her dress close around her. "I'm not sure if we can reach the tree."

Tener and Darrow looked at each other, then shook their heads at the same time.

"Oh. Well. Alright. Let's just take our time, then..." She wobbled, and almost fell towards the small Hunger, but righted herself.

They all sidled, one at a time, with careful precision. The foxans seemed to maneuver easier than humans could in the Primal Plane, which she supposed made sense, considering this place birthed them.

At one point, one of the chasm arms lashed sideways, cutting off their path, and they had to double back and go a different way.

They reached the tree—or as close as they could manage. A sphere of the now not-so-small Hunger surrounding it about the size of a small house. Just that tree remained in the middle, as if clinging to an invisible cliffside.

"How can we get over there?" Tener asked.

The two foxans had reverted to their smallest forms to better sidle past the bands of the Hunger, and grip with their claws into the Primal Plane's magic. Verrity had none of these advantages, and she stayed in a half crouch to keep her body lower to the "ground" and ready to launch herself in a different direction.

The center mass elongated, part of it vacillating towards them like a snake scenting for its prey. The three of them sidestepped the tendril, and Verrity studied the main body. Then she had an idea.

"We have to distract it," Verrity said, pointing. "Look. The center shrank when it made that longer bit. We'll need to force it to make enough . . . uh, snakes? So that the main part of it diminishes. Then you can get closer."

The tendril slithered back towards them, as if drawn to sound.

"Let's split up," Darrow said. "So we can split *it* up."

They did so. Verrity and Tener headed one way around the center mass, Darrow the other. The tendril followed Darrow, while the small Hunger formed another to slink after Verrity and Tener.

"It's working!" Tener leapt around a bracing wall of nothing on one side. "Look!"

Verrity didn't dare look. She couldn't stop herself with claws like they could, and the Primal Plane's thick air slowed down her movements. She worked her way around the nothing wall. "Is it small enough yet?"

"Maybe?"

"Let's be sure. I'll run farther away to draw more of it out. You stay and wait for an opening."

"But—"

"Hey! Over here!" She waved her arms, then pounded on the soft, malleable "ground" of the Primal Plane.

The tendril snaked towards her and Tener again, faster. Tener watched her, their eyes wide, and she jerked her chin for them to step away quietly.

Then she swam away from the small Hunger's center mass. A broad swath of consumed area blocked her right side, so she veered left to stay away from it.

"Look out!" Tener shouted behind her.

By instinct she launched herself farther left. The tendril that chased her had risen high above and tried to dive down in a sneak attack. It hit beside her with a *whump* sound, as large as a fallen tree trunk. She screamed, but swam with her arms faster, trying to keep her trajectory away from the Hunger's main body, to force it to use more of itself to reach her. She rose higher from the ground and swam back down so she could launch herself again. It was the only way she had any kind of speed here.

"Now!" Darrow shouted.

Verrity chanced a look backwards. The Hunger had unraveled itself like a ball of yarn from both ends, trying to catch both her and Darrow on opposite sides. Tener waited in the crux of it, keeping themself floating above the ground, their tall ears flattened. At their father's shout, they swam closer to the tree in the center of the mass, now just a few yards across.

They bent down and touched the base of the tree with a paw, just underneath the void that flowed outward from it.

"How can we stop the Hunger?"

Verrity blinked. How could such a blunt question do anything?

She kept swim-dashing, trying to keep the small Hunger occupied. Another consumed area ahead of her stopped her forward motion, and she jerked to the right this time. Zigzagging would force it to use more of the chasing tendril's mass.

"YOU CANNOT STOP ME, I AM INEVITA—"

"Find . . . city of Kolsuv Mor . . ." A thin, almost skeletal voice broke into the Hunger's louder voice, rasping from the base of the tree. Verrity almost couldn't hear it, since she'd gone a fair distance, at least twenty yards away.

"NO! I RULE, NOT YOU—"

". . . where it began . . ."

Verrity shot a quick glance to the side. The tendril chasing her had paused, the end of it tilted like some kind of eldritch head without a face.

"SILENCE!"

"Break the circle . . . destroy the tree in my . . . twisted homeland . . ."

The tendril bunched back towards its center body like hair brushed the wrong way, creating a mass of snarled and twisting absence.

"Tener!" Verrity shouted. "Run!"

Tener bounded back towards them as a foxan, leaping through the air away from the tree and the spherical mass. On the other side, Darrow raced around the edge back towards them.

The small Hunger's center shook as a distortion of reality. "YOU TRICKED ME! YOU TRICKED ME!"

Tener squeezed out just in time before the two tendrils reassembled into the small Hunger, as large as a house again and much angrier than any other house Saida had met.

"Time to go, time to go!" Darrow shouted.

The sphere boiled, as if about to erupt, and they dashed towards the permanent portal that led back to Sound.

RECEIVE. *Shape. Conversation.*

Saida traced the stone imprint with her fingers—human fingers, as she shifted back on purpose—and the musk of dirt sprang to her tongue, and the sweetness of apples that had fallen and decomposed year after year. And disuse. She wondered what the Epitaph tree here could do. The other ancient portal trees had each facilitated a unique and interesting magic, though on Vision's she hadn't figured out what the image on the leaves depicted.

A fat squirrel scampered down a different apple tree, grabbed a pebble, and crammed it into its mouth. Saida frowned as he watched, hoping the stupid creature didn't try and swallow it.

The squirrel scurried over to the Epitaph apple tree, then pulled the pebble out and pressed it into the base of the tree.

The tree swallowed the pebble like quicksand.

Saida blinked, her mouth falling open. A few moments later, an apple grew on its bare branches, and the squirrel skittered up and grabbed it.

Taste magic? She'd never found such a thing before on Taste. Of course, the worlds were vast, and the other Epitaph trees had all exhibited something new to her. Still, something about it didn't seem to fit.

She felt like she had almost climbed to the top of a cliff, and her hand kept missing the last ledge.

"Saida?"

She blinked, turning on her heel, and tasted cheese on the breeze. Marik held some out to her, his outline more of a shadow in the darkness. "It's been several hours. Are you hungry?"

His outline blurred, and her brain transposed Alesio's face over his. She swallowed and reached for the cheese, and he deposited it in her upturned paws. She'd shifted to foxan again without realizing it. She tried to shift back, but she kept blurring back and forth, back and forth, never settling on one form. It disoriented her.

Marik tapped her shoulder. "Saida. You should sit down. Are you feeling sick?"

She crouched, then lowered her knees to the ground. She grabbed her tail and picked at it, the ends dirty and ragged, almost showing a bit of the tailbone. She needed to brush it out. She needed to stop picking at it. How did humans deal with their emotions all the time without a safe place they could retreat to and avoid the unrelenting drizzle of grief, the misty, eerie fog of uncertainty?

"Saida?"

His voice sounded far away, like the portals last year when the worlds drifted. She drifted.

"Saida, are you alright?"

"What? What do you mean?"

"You seem unwell. Discontent. Is something troubling you?"

"It's—it's Alesio!"

Oh, Senses. Had she just blurted her internal thoughts out to someone she'd met a few days ago? She considered him a friend at this point, but still.

Marik paused, perhaps weighing the incongruities between how a deity's ambassador should act—calm, collected, competent—and how she'd personified the opposite of such traits. "Are you unhappy with him?"

Sensation returned to her. Her paws pressed on the ground, and she could taste the apples on the breeze, the cheese that Marik had given her, and the tears on her own skin. She could even taste a bit of the oil rubbed into the plant fibers of the Lunnite's clothing.

She nibbled on the cheese, and the flavor burst on her tongue. Nuttiness. Sweetness. She sucked in a breath and gave the cheese back. "If anything, I'm a too happy sometimes. I miss him too much."

"What do you mean, too much?"

"I mean . . ." She waved her arms wide. "Too much. Loving someone means you care about them. What happens if that changes? What happens if that love shifts?"

"Has it shifted for you?"

She shifted to full foxan. She curled up on the ground, tucking her snout over her tail. "It's already shifted in that I miss him more than I used to."

The Lunnite's forehead wrinkled. He opened his mouth, then closed it again.

"I'm always thinking about him. I wonder what he's doing, and what world he's on. I wonder what I can do so he stops worrying about me, how to soothe his anxiety. I wonder what his kiss would taste like here, under these apple trees. I can't stop thinking about him, and I hope he's thinking about me. And I don't know if it's fair to him. Because what if I'm not always like that? What if I shift on the inside? What if I change into someone who doesn't think about him? At the start of this expedition with you, I missed my old magic items so much that I left with you because I thought I'd find a way to speak with them again. But now, I've changed. I hadn't thought about my old magic friends until this morning, and what if that happens to how I feel about *him?*" Her voice cracked on the last word. She had morphed back to mostly human.

Marik paused for a moment. "I'm happy to taste the apples with you."

She blinked.

"I'm happy to be here with you, even when you're talking about loving someone else."

She sat up, scooting away from the Lunnite.

"Saida—"

"I think you've misinter—"

"Saida, I know we've traveled together for almost a week. And I know this is presumptuous of me. You're an Envoy, I'm just a Lunnite." His hair-tail twitched back and forth. "But I already know that I would love to care for you. If love means you care about someone, and wanting what's best for them, then I want what's best for you. What do *you* want? Do you think you'll change in the future? I'm just saying, if you wanted to love more than one person, I . . . I would be here."

"Oh. Oh, um . . ."

"I would never presume to come between you and your human." His ears folded over, but he leaned closer to her. He twisted his long hair together, and the ends twined around the ends of her braid. "I just wanted you to know you have options. I wouldn't mind that you have another partner. You're the Envoy of Lunne, you deserve many lovers. I would be honored to be just one of them."

She leaned away from him, even as she kept shifting, scooting away with her hands, her paws, on her head. "No, no, no."

She couldn't begin to imagine a relationship with Marik, this person she'd met so recently, but she hadn't planned to fall in love with Alesio, either. Everything about her changed all the time. Her physical form, her feelings about love, her magical items . . . she wished she didn't shift. She wished she would stay the same! She didn't want her feelings to change! She hated her possible future self with a sudden intensity, that concept that she might someday want to forge a bond, a golden thread of connection, with someone else.

She didn't want to tell Alesio her fears. If he found out she thought she might not love him in the future, it would hurt him so badly. Nausea roiled in her gut, imagining that. Would he think she didn't love him now? But if she waited, she would just hurt him more later, if those fears did come true. If she waited for five years, or ten years, and their love grew wide and solid roots that reached deep into their hearts and *then* she changed, shifted into another kind of Saida, a Saida that didn't love him anymore, that somehow had changed like she'd changed her feelings about Carn, it would hurt him even more than ripping out the love that had grown between them now. Her heart drummed fast, so fast. Her human side sweated, and the sweat remained when she shifted to foxan, so hot, slicking her fur. She couldn't know the future. How could anyone promise anything when they couldn't know the future? Her heart tried to escape the prison of her chest, pounding on the walls, fast, so fast.

She thumped to the ground on her forelegs, then her human palms, slipping on her own sweat. She'd shifted to foxan again. She should stay away from Alesio.

No! She wanted to teleport to Alesio! She wanted to stay with him! *Selfish, selfish* . . . Was that Tricksy Stone's voice in her head? What was that ringing in her ears?

Receive—

She flicked her foxan ears down. Yanked her braid away from his long hair. "I can't! I can't!"

Marik had his hand out, as if he'd been about to place a hand on her shoulder. He paused midair, then his ears folded down. "I . . . I understand. I didn't mean to upset you. Please forgive my impertinent—"

"I wasn't talking to you!"

Marik's bright green eyes widened. "What do you mean?" His ears perked back up. "Who *were* you talking to?"

Saida heaved in a breath. Her limbs tingled from adrenaline, and the musk of the dirt on her paws weighed heavy on her tongue, mixing with the sweet tartness of the apples all around. "What?"

"Who were you talking to?"

She traced the words again with the sensitive pads on her paws. "The same thing I heard . . . on Vision." When had she began hearing a voice, instead of just saying the words in her head? Why did her ears ring like that, like a bell?

Receive.

"I'm listening." She pressed her hands on the dirt, squinting at the imprint of the circle in the dark. That didn't help. She frowned and crawled to a different area with the same result. "I'm listening. Where are you?"

Shape.

"I can't Shape magic. I don't use it that way."

"Saida," Marik said. "You *do* Shape. You just have different magic than humans." He hesitated. "Like your shifting, or when you create transplants."

Someone had tried to talk to her. No, she had tried to talk to herself. The part of her that had once merged with Tricksy Stone, and a part of her that had once merged with Goosefeather. She hesitated, then reached up and touched her own ears, those ringing ears.

Conversation.

If she could Receive magic the same way as humans, maybe she could do it the way humans did. How Alesio did. She imagined a room inside herself, inside her ears, because she needed to hear the magic better, and the bells resounding in her head seemed to emanate from there. She imagined the room like the one she'd had in her cave in Between. No . . . like the den Alesio had built for her in his house. She could see it, though no transplant nestled on the shelves and the spaces where Jar of Sky, and Leaf Pile had once rested. Her chest ached.

But she could sense someone else, there, now, something distinct and separate, but also part of herself.

Who is speaking to me?

The structure seemed to allow her to hold those voices up, to hold the belief that she could hear them. The shelves stretched all the way up in her imagined room and wrapped all around.

"Hello," the structure said, with the ringing of the bells behind the voice fading away. "Can you hear me now?"

"Yes! Please don't leave! Who are you? Please keep talking!"

"I'm the part of you that hears magic, like a magical ear."

"Why wouldn't you talk to me until now?"

"I've been talking this whole time. You stopped Receiving magic voices because you stopped wanting to."

"Why would I—I've tried to hear magic this whole time!"

"Yes and no. I'm a magic ear. I've listened to your thoughts and your heart, even the parts you shut out. You fear losing parts of yourself again. You used to converse with Goosefeather and Tricksy Stone because you feared bonds with humans, but now, you fear conversation with magic, because losing your magic items hurt you so much. You wanted to avoid losing another friend." They paused. "Your strongest bond with a person is fraying. You will not last long, this way, losing all your connections and communication."

Her heart squeezed. "Already? I'm shifting already?"

"It is not your shifting nature that is the cause, but your fear. For you, it has always been fear."

Because of her fear?

No. No, she couldn't focus on that right now. She had had a breakthrough in hearing magic again, and she needed to use it to listen to the Epitaph tree. She might learn something that could stop the Hunger. "I want to Receive the magic around me. Can you help me hear it?"

"I already have. You just need to let it through."

Something opened in her ear, as if she'd shaken it free of water, and the room of her Magic Ear displayed something new. Five trees: Taste's apple tree, Touch's squat stone tree, Vision's slanted and flickering tree, Sound's instrument tree, and what must be the tree on Scent, a rala tree.

They all spoke at the same time, their voices overlapping yet faint, like echoes of something said long ago. *"Danger!"*

She repeated the words aloud. Dimly, she heard Marik rush towards her, and the scratch of his pen as he copied her words down.

"My final thoughts," The Epitaph trees continued. *"It is too dangerous! The formulae are faulty! You must listen. The magics from the colonies might not handle the amplification! We must find a different way."*

"The . . . colonies?" Marik repeated. His voice sounded echoey while she listened from inside an imagined representation of her own ear.

Roots appeared underneath the five trees, knuckling up out of the floor and connecting them. The roots had a different ambiance, a different feeling than any magic she'd ever known.

It felt like water transforming into stone.

It felt like wind changing into heat.

It felt like despair lifting into hope.

It felt like leaves flickering to display a picture.

It felt like a stone becoming an apple.

Magic that changed one substance into another kind altogether.

A magic not from the Sensory worlds.

How had she not realized it until now? None of the Epitaph trees' magic were just Sensory based. They *changed* the Sensory magic into something else.

The five Epitaph trees connected into one. Epitaphs formed when a foxan died and transplanted into a world of their choice, merging with the magic of that world. This Epitaph exhibited a new type of magic, from another Plane, from one of the other sets of worlds displayed with the rocks on Vision. That meant that another Plane's foxan must have transplanted here, becoming the Epitaph trees. They had intertwined the magic from their Plane—changing magic, magic that changed a substance into another substance—with the Sensory magics.

A maelstrom of sound echoed towards her from the Epitaph. Then two beings' voices emerged: the roots and the trees.

"My final thoughts," The roots intoned. *"I am worried about the formulae and the remaining variables. But the longer we delay the more*

arduous the task becomes. The Bridges will decay in a decade, two at the most. We must find Lunne before that happens!"

"My final thoughts," the trees said. *"It's too dangerous! The formulae are faulty! You must listen. The magics from the colonies might not handle the amplification! We must find a different way."*

This . . . was a recording, somehow. A log of the foreign foxan's final thoughts as they had transplanted into the Sensory worlds. She could sense that they had merged with a tree on each Sensory world and joined them together with magic. Parts of them had bubbled back to the surface from this merging, however, perhaps based on the original magics and people, or somehow a mixture of them all, and these identities had engraved their last thoughts into a never-ending message.

Regardless, they were dead. The foxan transplant from Transmutation, now the combined Epitaph trees, was dead. They could not speak with her in a true conversation.

Did that mean that Tricksy Stone was dead, too? Even if she could've heard them, would their words be restricted to an echoing elegy like this?

The Epitaph trees repeated their final thoughts with an urgency she could not help but imagine crossed the boundaries of time and death, as if they had awakened with a singular, all-encompassing purpose. The cadence, the timbre, the resonance of the five trees' voices all pitched together to scream one meaning, even if Saida couldn't ask them anything.

Danger.

Then, next to the five Epitaph trees, the fractured Goddess Head statue flickered into existence inside her imagined Magic Ear. She barely had time to catch her breath.

This was all too much. She couldn't process all this information at once.

But she had to try.

The Goddess Head spoke in fragments, which made it hard to understand. She repeated their faint words aloud and paused where it seemed more natural. Doing this helped her understand the message easier.

Change's three worlds of Transmutation, Divination, and Consumption will work together to keep the Planes connected. Combining Divination's silver ore with Consumption's ingesting magic, then Transmutation magic, many of us have Shaped ourselves into Amplifiers. We will do everything we can to power our ship to find Lunne and force her to reconnect what she has neglected. We need to siphon unique magics from each world, purify them all to raw Spatial magic, then teleport it back to the world of Transmutation to power our ship. The combined drain to the Planes will refill after Lunne reconnects the Bridges. All that matters is finding Lunne."

The magic from the Epitaph trees, the adjoining roots, and the Goddess Head shuddered and cried out.

Confused, Saida left her imagined room where she'd found Magic Ear. She squinted in the growing dark, panting, with a human face and arms, and foxan legs, foxan paws.

The Hunger rotated above them, as distinct from the normal darkness of the night as a depth in the Glass Sea, the flecks of land like algae spotting their surface. The Hunger had five tendrils now, all swirling and twisting, as if someone up there wrung out the towel of the sky, and one of them had snaked close to Saida and Marik's side of Taste.

She blinked. Were those *teeth* in the tendril?

The Epitaph, no longer divided, spoke in her mind as a whole, without her having to visualize them in her Magic Ear. Something seemed to click, as if the Epitaph became even more aware of her presence, and a new message began, a new recording. It had the energy of someone grabbing her face and screaming. But the message wasn't meant for her; it was directed at the Goddess Head behind her.

"You must listen. This is my final thought. The mixed magics siphoned from various Planes and stored in Lunnite colonies might not purify! You Amplifiers may not have merged with the Sensory Plane, but we have! We do not want anything to happen to it! Even if more Lunnites succeed and become Amplifiers, the amount required to purify the magic back to Spatial is too vast. It might backfire. It could create a void on Transmutation!"

"A void?" Saida formed the words with almost no breath, no sound.

"You must listen! We must not go through with the ritual!"

A void.

A void like that horrifying, rotating absence above them?

"THERE YOU ARE, TRAITOR. YOU SHOULD HAVE STAYED SILENT." The Hunger writhed and uncurled their tendril-arms. "I KNEW THERE WAS SOMETHING HOLDING ME BACK. I SHOULD'VE KNOWN IT WAS THE *ONE* ANNOYING DISSENTER IN MY HEAD."

The Hunger's tendril stretched closer, closer, until it loomed as large as the entire ruins, spanning a mile or more, blocking out the sun and the sky overhead, centered straight above Taste's Epitaph tree.

The tendril opened a *mouth* on the end, a ridged mouth with those teeth bared and flashing and rotating inside. Saida remembered, in a surreal moment, how the box in the Primal Plane had displayed worm-like tendrils and fangs. A giant throat the size of a city hovered over them, an abyss leading into the heavens.

A smaller tendril whipped out like a tongue and wrapped around the Epitaph tree.

The Epitaph tree screamed in Saida's mind. The Hunger's tendril ripped them out by the roots and swallowed. The apple tree disappeared up into the emptiness of the colossal snake's throat. The tendril-tongue kept pulling, dragging the other four trees out through their connected roots. The Hunger swallowed them all, and their voices silenced.

Marik Shaped a dome over their heads, pulling Saida to the ground, his hands shaking.

But then, the dome disappeared, crumbling upwards into that horrible, ridged throat-canopy, and the pull of the Hunger yanked Marik's magic out of him, as well. It streamed up into the tendril's gaping maw with the sense of a passing touch on Saida's shoulder.

Marik screamed and collapsed to the ground, gasping, holding his chest as if he had a gaping hole there.

They both trembled for seconds, or hours, or days, under the snake's open throat. Saida had shifted to her smallest foxan form, flattening herself on the ground.

"AHHH," the Hunger said. "*NOW* I CAN EAT!"

The tendril-snake pulled away from them, lifting into the sky. It reared backwards, the head of it still in front of the planet of Taste.

Then the Hunger's other tendrils burst outward, five of them, towards the different Sensory planets. The one that had hovered over Taste didn't return to Saida and Marik's area. No, all the snake-arm-tendrils had specific areas they favored. She had a feeling that she knew.

The cities. The places with the most people.

The Hunger tendrils breathed in, sucking Sensory magic from across the five worlds into its five colossal snake mouths.

Millions of different voices streamed upwards, screaming and crying both as one and as parts of each other. From the sheer density of their agony, Saida could tell that they cried out from the most populated areas—the human cities.

"Don't let them take me/us!"

"I/we waited so long to be Received!"

"I/we want to be Shaped, to keep my/our names!"

"Don't let them take me/us! Don't let them, don't let them!!!"

"LUNNE IS GONE," the Hunger said, from the center. "HOPE IS GONE. ALL THAT IS LEFT IS TO CONSUME, AND CONSUME, UNTIL THERE IS NOTHING ANYWHERE."

Saida felt like a mouse frozen in the gaze of a shrike. Marik, beside her, screamed something at the sky and shook his fist, his ears flat against his head.

In that moment, like a mouse darting to safety once the shadow of a shrike had flown over it, Saida decided.

Find Alesio.

The portal opened underneath them, and they fell.

THE DRAINING

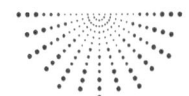

Many months ago, Alesio had secured a stone cellar in Anthem to hold the old straiter leader in. Alesio had asked Darrow to help him portal a fighting cage inside, the same one that Clef had once forced him and many other straiters to fight in. It hadn't been necessary, but it *was* cathartic to shove him inside, his hands still bound by the magical Touch cuffs Alesio had Shaped out of a tree branch.

Clef sprawled to the stone ground on his knees inside the cage, unable to catch his balance from Alesio's push. Alesio swung the cage door closed and locked it.

The old strait's leader grunted and rolled to his side on the other end of the cage, near the back wall of the cellar, eyes gray and glittering.

Baylor and Hestafon flanked Alesio on either side, staring in at their prisoner. None of them spoke, because none of them wanted Clef to reveal their innermost struggles.

Clef studied them, head cocked, as if daring one of them to break the silence. He seemed to listen to the way they breathed, to the sounds of their footfalls against the stone, his mouth curling at each of them.

The twist that Hestafon had revealed the night before about Flockians revolting against the shrikers kept running through Alesio's mind. Even though it had forced him to face a part of himself he didn't like, it had also given him hope. The outcome in Flock had not gone Clef's way, which meant Alesio could thwart him, outthink him.

Alesio just needed to find Saida, tell her his plan—

"THERE YOU ARE, TRAITOR. YOU SHOULD HAVE STAYED SILENT." The Hunger's booming voice echoed down to the stone cellar like a shockwave. "I KNEW THERE WAS SOMETHING HOLDING ME BACK. I SHOULD'VE KNOWN IT WAS THE *ONE* ANNOYING DISSENTER IN MY HEAD."

Alesio had pressed his hands over his ears. The voice reverberated in Sound so loudly it hurt. He inhaled, about to Shape a Sound shield around them.

"AHHH," the Hunger said. "NOW I CAN EAT!"

Pain.

His skin, oh the Senses it had lit on fire, and his throat! It burned! It burned!

He screamed, and magic streamed out of him, leaving him, *leaving him*, flowing up into the ceiling!

"I don't want to go! I don't want to—"

The voice of the magic, his magic, screamed along with him. He'd collapsed to his knees. Blood dripped from his hands, from clenching his fingernails into his palms.

Baylor and Hestafon knelt beside him, their mouths open, their hands over their ears, but no sound emitted from them. Or, rather, he couldn't hear their screams. He couldn't hear his own, he only knew he screamed because of the breath leaving his throat.

"LUNNE IS GONE," the Hunger said. "HOPE IS GONE. ALL THAT IS LEFT IS TO CONSUME, AND CONSUME, UNTIL THERE IS NOTHING ANYWHERE."

This resembled draining. But it was worse. It was more of a ripping sensation, sharper and more jagged of a pain, leaving an absence in himself. He felt like he couldn't breathe. He thrashed, trying to claw a modicum of magic back—

A portal opened in front of him, and Saida stumbled into his arms.

She twined her foxan self around his chest. He tightened his arms around her, but he couldn't feel her fur, or how she pressed herself against him. He just saw it. His hands slipped over her, and he realized his hands had slicked with his own sweat, though he couldn't feel it. It was like he held a ghost. Her ears lay flat against her head, and her galaxy eyes had shrunk to pinpricks of space in her white, darting gaze.

"What's happening?" He still couldn't hear his own words. His throat felt like a razor had scraped it and tears sprang to his eyes.

A moment passed, or perhaps several minutes. Pain surrounded him, lived inside him like a fire. Then he coughed, and air returned to his lungs, and the voices from his magics ceased screaming.

Saida said something, but he couldn't hear her either, even on his right side. He turned to read her lips.

"Alesio. Alesio, I'm sorry—we found a magic holding the Hunger back, but then the Hunger found us and ate the magic that we found—"

A shadow moved in the corner of his eye, and Alesio pivoted on his heel, grabbed Clef's cuffed hands through the cage bars, and bent them backwards. He had to trust his vision, because he still couldn't feel anything.

"You bitch!" Clef screamed, Alesio reading his lips. "We're all going to die because of you!" He strained for Saida against the bars, spittle forming in the corners of his mouth, and Alesio braced himself and pushed harder.

Saida scuttled backwards, ending up next to Baylor and Marik. The Lunnite must have teleported along with Saida. Marik interposed himself between Saida and Clef, spreading his arms.

"I hate you! I HATE you! I HATE YOU!"

Alesio kept hold of the strait's leader but centered his gravity a little lower to the ground, ready to spring in case this triggered Baylor somehow, ready for the young man to switch sides again.

"Hestafon!" Alesio said. "Be ready."

The Council delegate wrung his hands, and his sage green eyes rolled up in his head. His pale skin had grayed around his nose and his ears to the shade of smoke. "My magic is gone . . ."

A restless need to move, to find what he'd lost, surged inside Alesio. The effects of draining. He recalled the last time it had happened, and how his magic had refilled. This memory helped him control the restlessness with a monumental effort. His hands had paled to a sallow brown with a yellow undertone, and he guessed that the same yellowish undertone, much like Hestafon's, had applied itself to his ears. *That* had not happened before.

Would he become a shallow husk of himself? Would he melt down, like those who Watthe had Consumed last year?

What had just happened?

Marik had fallen to his knees beside Hestafon, his breathing shallow and his foxan ears flat. His mouth hung open like a broken trapdoor, and the black parts of his eyes had swelled to almost a full eclipse like Hestafon's and Clef's. The bare, reddish-brown skin around his eyes and lips hadn't changed color, but his hands had. That made sense, since he could use Touch magic.

Clef pressed the side of his face against the bars and his eyes rolled at Saida. "All your fault!" Gray had splotched his ears, matching the polished gray of his eyes, highlighting his thin, pinched face so it evoked the look of a skull. "You called the Hunger when you found the box!"

Vibrations above them shook the small lantern hanging from the ceiling, which threw frenetic shadows around the cellar.

Alesio cursed. Had the Hunger drained the whole city of Anthem? Or everyone, across all the worlds? Or, perhaps, had it—they, he corrected himself, Saida had always referred to them that way and now he understood more than ever why, after the magics had spoken to him—had they Severed the Planes again? Mass panic would follow; much worse than the first time the Hunger had just appeared . . .

He wrenched Clef's arms down and back through the bars, then shoved him backwards, sending him sprawling.

Saida had just teleported here, so she didn't have a way to portal them out. Otherwise, she could have portaled him and Clef to the small Hunger in the Primal Plane, as part of his plan to help her. *Oh, shit. Clef can't use his powers either, now.*

They had more pressing things to worry about. Clef had returned to screaming along with Marik and Hestafon. Alesio could tell because they all had their mouths open.

Baylor seemed unaffected, probably because the amplifier he wore in his mouth had prevented the Hunger from draining him in the first place. Saida also seemed unscathed, and had teleported, even while terrified out of her mind. Perhaps the Hunger hadn't targeted foxan magic, but humans. But then, why had it affected Marik?

Oh. Right. Saida said he can Shape like humans.

Alesio's left ear, his bad ear, radiated a calm coolness, almost like it helped calm the panic from the deafness in his right ear and the numbness in his skin. The same thing had happened the first time he'd experienced draining. He sighed in relief. At least that was the same.

"Let's go, Saida!" He shouted, not knowing the volume he needed so she could hear him with everyone else screaming. "We have to stop the citizens from stampeding! They'll panic worse this time!"

He wanted to tell her so many things. But he couldn't explain them in the small moments here, not when everyone in the worlds had lost their minds.

Clef rose, holding his cuffed hands in front of him. Alesio read his lips.

"Baylor," Clef said. "Open this cage."

Baylor hunched his shoulders and shook his head.

Alesio glared at Clef. "Shut up." The strait's leader could also read lips. Most Soundians could, those who wanted to keep a sound cloth in the ears for protection against Sound knives. "He isn't your puppet anymore."

"Oh, isn't he?" Clef wiped some of the spittle from the corner of his mouth. Red surrounded the gleaming gray of his pupils and irises like a ring of scarlet fire. "Baylor. *Breathe.*"

The young man jerked, and his hands began to shake. Sweat beaded his upper lip. Then he sprang at Alesio, ixor leaking from his open mouth.

Saida yanked Baylor backwards with human arms, pulling the young man to the ground. He breathed on her hands, slowing them, so she slammed into him even as she yanked him back. They tumbled to the ground near Hestafon and Marik.

Hestafon had stumbled to his feet, and he'd closed his mouth. Maybe something with his mixed-up magic helped him function at least on a basic level, somewhat like Alesio.

"C'mon, Baylor," Clef said. "Did you forget I have your father? Did you think I wouldn't torture him?"

Hestafon faltered forward, his green eyes flicking between Baylor and Clef, focusing on their lips. "Leave the poor boy alone!"

Clef laughed. "Why? Because he's a poor boy? Trying to prove you're not some rich clown who somehow still thinks he's in charge of Anthem? Look outside, you foppish buffoon!"

Hestafon bowed his head, a few wisps of blonde hair fanning around his face, and Alesio wished he had magic for just two seconds so he could Shape a permanent bubble around Clef's lips. No, he just wished he could kill Clef.

But Alesio still needed the man's ability so he could find out the Hunger's weakness. Although . . . at least for now, besides Baylor, none of them could even use magic. Alesio clenched his fists and crouched, waiting.

He can't control me anymore. He's not unbeatable. He had to believe that.

Baylor heaved himself up out of Saida's slowed grasp. He shook even more, and blood leaked from his mouth along with the ixor, which had slowed. His pupils had dilated so far, they had almost eclipsed the brown rim.

"What did you do to him?" Alesio growled at Clef.

"I didn't much like when you stopped listening to me," Clef said. "So, I invested more serious measures in my next project." He threw his head back and cackled in a high-pitched voice.

Is he pretending *to be crazy?* That would be like him.

Clef jerked his head back down. "Baylor! *Breathe!*"

The young man jerked again. Sweat had trickled down from his textured hair in several different trails. A tiny cloud of ixor dribbled from his mouth, along with blood, mixing in front of him.

"Hey." Alesio faced Baylor. "Remember what I said? I'm gonna save your father. I meant that. We're gonna find him, together, okay?"

"Baylor! I said, *breathe.* And kill that fur-mix. She's to blame for everything!"

Baylor jerked at the third command but didn't puff out any more ixor. His dilated eyes fixed on Alesio.

"Do you. Promise? We can. Go now?"

"Breathe, you miserable excuse for a drug container!"

Alesio controlled his dismayed reaction. The mob outside would obstruct them from going anywhere fast. But Baylor teetered on the edge of sanity and if *he* fell off, he could kill everyone in the room and far more besides.

Alesio wouldn't risk it, not with Saida there. He needed Baylor away from Clef's brainwashing. "I promise. Now."

Baylor pressed his eyes shut and clapped his hands over his ears.

"Breathe! Breathe! Sounddamn it! I need it!"

Alesio frowned at that last part. Clef, admitting he needed something?

Yup. Clef's addicted to ixor.

Baylor sucked in a deep breath, and with it, he absorbed the ixor that he had breathed out into the room back into his mouth. Blood still covered his mouth.

"Let's go," Alesio said. "We'll head to the Portal Station. Let's find your father."

He helped Saida and Marik up. Ixor still slowed Saida's hands, and Marik couldn't manage much beyond stumbling and screaming. The faintest echo sounded from his open mouth.

They stumbled out of the cellar with Baylor leading the way, dripping blood onto the floor.

Should I have Hestafon stay and guard Clef?

Without any magic, though, the piper had no chance of stopping a mob from opening the cage. And, if Alesio tried to bring Clef along with them, the strait's leader could easily escape in the mass panic.

Hundreds of people thronged the streets, pushing, shoving, heading towards the Portal Station, towards that source of energy, of vitality. Saida had said the Portal Stations had restorative energy for humans, and he'd sort of felt it, before, but now, it drew him like a moth to flame. Or it could open the way to other places where he could search for what he had lost.

Everyone's limbs jerked and dilation had eclipsed their eyes, as if trying to recapture their magic by saturating their eyes with sunlight. Dull, stone-gray blotched the skin around everyone's temples and ears like a viral rash. Most of them didn't have cloaks or gloves or winter outerwear on.

They all had their mouths open, screaming, and no one could hear each other.

Is all of Anthem out here?

A few people huddled in alcoves in their doorways, their hands over their heads, those few that handled their loss of Sound magic better than others. Most everyone running also had their necks craned up to the dark sky, at that darker void that had uncoiled its arms, at the pupil in the center of it glaring down at the arm that loomed so close it resembled a giant tunnel above them, teeth flashing. They ran, and ran, their necks craned up and trampled anyone underfoot who fell. As he watched, someone tripped over another, but they continued to scream at the sky even as they crawled over each other. Their behavior would appear deranged to anyone who had not experienced draining; but Alesio knew that manic sense of loss, of panic, that raw, torn open place inside like a set of empty lungs, the *need* to fill it back up, to breathe. He had to fight against letting himself join the raving throng and rage at the heavens. Their lips formed many of the same words:

"Give us back our magic!"

"We will worship you! Just don't consume us!"

"Give it back! Now!"

The dull roar of it sounded far off to Alesio as if he'd sunk underwater. His feet seemed to hover in his shoes, the ghost of pressure against them. Both of his magics had never drained at the same time for him before, but their two strands seemed to anchor him to his sanity, even while drained, better than most everyone else. Like how more transplants helped connect the worlds, the more magics a human could Shape connected them better to their magic.

That also explained how he could focus better than the masses of Soundians around him, their arms reaching out in front of them and towards the sky, weeping with senseless abandon. He had that urge, too, but he could control it. Hestafon, also, had closed his mouth and his eyes had lost their glassy look.

Alesio grimaced. "Everyone, hold onto each other!" He motioned for everyone to link arms and did so with Baylor, angling through the crowd.

Saida linked his arm with hers. She stayed human instead of shifting to foxan like her instincts must have screamed at her to. She must have realized that the panicking people would zero in on her as someone who could portal them somewhere. Marik linked with Saida's arm, and Hestafon linked with Marik.

Alesio leaned towards Baylor. "We're going to Scent, right?"

The young man squeezed his lips closed and nodded. Bits of skin had peeled off around his mouth, creating open sores. Someone clipped his shoulder, and he flinched.

They needed to find Baylor's father fast. If Clef's men killed him before they could locate him, it could shred the rest of Baylor's control. He dared not trifle with the young man's amplified power—not when none of them had magic to fight back.

When Clef had forced Alesio to fight his last cage match, his opponent, Brezeek, had worn an amplifier. It had allowed Brezeek's Sound knives and other Sound magic to retain their Shape even after they'd hit. But Baylor's amplifier seemed even stronger. Had he unlocked more power from it, somehow? Or had Clef learned from manufacturing amplifiers how to utilize them better, and had instructed Baylor with that knowledge?

He shivered. An army of cage fighters at Baylor's level would overpower everyone.

But Clef seemed . . . upset about the Hunger. He'd roiled with rage at Saida, blaming her for bringing the Hunger to their Plane. Maybe he didn't serve the entity in the skies after all?

Alesio shook his head. Clef loved to make Alesio second-guess himself. He wished he could ask Baylor, but in all the mayhem, he doubted the young man could hear him.

They had almost reached the Portal Station. Had the barriers the Touchians Shaped held up?

People shoved him from behind. On their left, someone slipped in the slurry of snow that had fallen a few days ago, and then another, and another, creating a morass of flailing limbs. Hestafon grabbed a little girl up from the ground, yanking her out of the heap. Doing this slowed the piper, however, and the press of humanity almost ripped his hand out of Saida's. The piper linked his arm with hers again.

Marik had trouble keeping up because of the draining and Alesio had to pull harder than he would have liked to keep the pace of the crowd. He missed his magic as much as he would have missed an arm or a leg. He kept trying to reach for it just to find that distressing absence in his rooms of magic. No texture dimpled the walls in his Touch magic room, and no magical notes scrolled across the walls or the ceiling in his Sound magic room. The magic of the Portal Station itself did nothing but add fuel and verve to the vacuum within, lending him vitality but not the connection he needed to his own magic.

Someone yanked on his arm. It felt like the barest tickle, like a butterfly landing on him. Alesio whipped his head around. A group of Soundians pointed at him. He tried to angle his right side that way on muscle memory, and of course he heard almost nothing. He read their lips, and the muted clangor of their voices sounded like a distant whisper.

"It's the Voice! The Voice of Reconnection!"

"Hey! Reconnect our magic!"

He shook his head, trying to motion that he had to leave. No one understood anything or cared in the panic. More grabbed hold of him. He shoved them, not knowing how much force he needed. Most of them fell off, but others seized Saida, pulling her away from him.

At that, he released Baylor's arm and charged the three that had hold of her, twisting their wrists away from her, kneeing someone else in the gut. They didn't fight back so much as grasp at him like clinging vines, and he ripped them away. Saida had stumbled to the ground, and he held out his hand to her. She leapt and grabbed it, and he felt the slight tickle like a bellbug on his fingers. He hoped he didn't grip her hand too tight.

The crowd had pushed the others to the other side of the dais, almost inside the portal to Vision. None of Anthem's departure portals flowed straight to Scent, so that one worked as well as any.

Much of the mass pushed them into the Portal Station, trying to pack as close as they could to the rejuvenating magic still radiating from it. In here, everyone stuffed through the three different departure portals, some people climbing on others' shoulders. The high wooden walls Shaped with Touch magic had stayed up, but the gates between, meant to open and close to allow for shorter or longer lines, had not. Too many people forced their way through, even with the constriction of the barriers.

"Hold on!" Alesio roared to Saida, checking he still had her hand in his. People pressed too tight against them to try and link arms again. Her foxan ears, which she always had trouble shifting to human, pressed flat against her head.

Someone hopped over the others and reached for his face. "Sing us back our magic!"

He didn't see Tak or Muey anywhere. The distant sounds and gentle pressures created a surreal sensation, as if he had become a ghost.

A bit of pressure jostled him forward. The masses behind him had shoved him and the others through the portal to Vision.

His sight darkened and blurred to vague shapes and shades of gray from charcoal to pewter, to smoke, to fog.

What is happening?!

Everyone's shapes blurred, their features hazy. He couldn't read lips; he couldn't see anyone beyond obscure outlines. Silence and numbness gave him no suggestion of the ground under his feet, or the crowd pushing him. He could still smell the mud of the churned-up ground under him, and he could taste blood from a cut on his lip.

Why would he have lost his vision just now? He didn't have Vision magic!

A light tap from behind. Someone must have shoved him or something equivalent for him to feel it. The smoke-gray shape next to him, Saida, had drifted away from him, as did the other fuzzy outlines of the rest of the group. He must have lost his grip on her hand. But why did that larger, darker area withdraw as well? Was that the ground? Why was it revolving away, as if . . .

His stomach dropped.

He had lost his ability to see, so he had also lost his gravity. He was falling up.

Why? How?

In the absence of most of his senses, his mind worked on the problem with crystal clarity, and the answer presented itself to him.

The Hunger must have drained everyone's magic so far that the entity had affected their ability to Receive the base sensory magic on *any* world.

He hadn't known that could happen.

A throbbing ache began behind his eyes. He feared to even consider what such a thing could mean. Had the Hunger not just drained them, but severed their ability to sense their origin world's magic?

He couldn't think about that. Not right now. He still fell. A second or two had passed. His thoughts rampaged through his mind at a mile a minute. Why hadn't the other people falling with him? Hadn't they lost their gravity, too?

Wait. No, if my gravity is gone, I'm not falling. I should be floating in place.

But someone had shoved him from behind. That must have

changed his trajectory, sending him away from the others, probably spinning.

By the Senses. Vision? It had to be Vision?!

He could have handled a lack of taste or smell without too much difficulty. But this? Without gravity, how far would he fall? If he hit a gravity shift, would he blast through it, or slow down because he had retained a small ability to Receive? He'd never considered it as Receiving gravity before.

Wait. Why in the Senses is gravity a part of the magic on Vison? Suddenly that seemed an unfair add on. Sound didn't also have fire magic, after all.

The lack of yet another sense renewed his own panic and dread. He flailed in slow motion. He just wanted to move, to reconnect to what he'd lost!

That cooling sensation from his ear helped calm him yet again. He breathed in and out, feeling his lungs inflate on the inside. It happened in what felt like forever, but he counted just a few seconds in his head.

Would the people of Lavoa themselves have stayed indoors? Or would the restlessness from the draining have driven them to temporary insanity as well?

A large area of lighter gray had rotated into the paltry sight he had. That had to be the sky, because in the middle of it loomed the mass of mostly nothing except for its core, an absence of even darkness. The Hunger.

Oh, shit. Shit-sounddamn-it-shit-shit-shit!!

He'd counted to five. Five seconds of floating.

This seemed like the end—

A musky cinnamon scent puffed around him.

Ixor.

SAIDA WATCHED Alesio spin upwards for a half second of forever before she had breath to scream.

Everyone around her had begun floating a little off the ground as soon as they emerged in Lavoa. Alesio hadn't grasped her hands tight, so she'd had to hold on to him. He didn't seem to have most of his sensation of touch, and so probably didn't want to hurt her by accident. The ixor still slowed her hands from trying to stop Baylor earlier in the cellar, and everything she touched with them was intensified, but she didn't want to lose her grip.

Then someone had shoved him from behind as more people rammed through the Portal Station, and their hands had slipped—!

"Baylor!" She shouted and pointed at Alesio. "Hit him with an ixor bolt!"

Baylor stared at her. The amplifier in his mouth had protected him from draining. She gestured again, more urgently, and he squinted at Alesio, pursed his lips, and shot an arrow of ixor.

It hit, slowing Alesio's spin and momentum. He seemed to stop at first but then kept rotating at a leisurely pace.

More people overflowed into Lavoa's Portal Station, some jumping through from the other side. Those with any momentum continued their trajectory and motion. Some floated, and others flew forward a little higher off the ground because they'd jumped through the portal.

Saida paused, trying to understand. Why had people lost their gravity here? Had the Hunger consumed the gravity shifts here? But no, that didn't make sense, because both she and Baylor stayed on the ground without any trouble, and shimmering lines of gravity shifts still threaded through the sky, with little hills and areas of dirt and rocks and snow.

Marik had paused as he'd come through and others had shoved him forward and downward off the dais, so he remained on the ground. A thin layer of snow covered the ground here, already muddied from foot traffic. The Lunnite had found one of the signs Lavoa had posted in the ground depicting an arrow, showing normal safe paths through the town. He gripped the sign with the same level of dedication as when they'd watched the Wavemaker create the Summit Wave.

He was sobbing. "Can't see. Can't see!"

So, those the Hunger had drained had lost their gravity and their vision when they'd stepped through to Vision? She couldn't understand why. Everything happened too fast.

First, they needed to bring Alesio back down, so the group could continue through to Scent and find Baylor's father.

But . . . they couldn't just ignore these people. The Hunger had likely drained most everyone on every world. But on Vision, even the slightest motion upward would lift a person into the sky.

Some Lavoans had exited their houses, shuffling around without direction, screaming in sightlessness at the ground, the sky, or each other. Their muscle memory served them, however, as they did not run or move their limbs too fast, and so avoided accidental flight. A few of them did throng the Portal Station, seeking that connection to magic, and the Soundians swarming out from there jostled and pushed at them.

For their part, many Soundians had already begun their unintentional journeys floating into the sky, most of them not as fast as Alesio. Someone had hit him upwards, which had lent him more momentum.

Some people who had already teleported through when this first began, perhaps twenty minutes before, had fallen upwards very, very far, specks of spinning Soundians, falling upwards towards the Hunger. Others flecked the landscape of Lavoa's skies like frozen birds with various trajectories. Well, frozen in their forward motion, and flailing in panic.

Nearby, Hestafon had risen three feet off the ground. Saida loped over to him and tugged him back down like an errant kite. Without gravity, his body had lightened to that of nothing at all. She pushed him towards Marik and the sign.

"Hold onto that!" she said. Then she realized the piper could not hear her *or* see her, and so she pressed his hand to the sign and hoped the forceful pressure would convey her message. He clutched at it with the same fervor as Marik, so maybe they didn't need her urging.

She couldn't imagine the terror from losing so many senses. To not know what happened around her. And yet, their clawing hands and sobbing screams told her that wasn't the worst part. It was that they had lost their magic. She could sense the holes inside each of them, a place where the Hunger had ripped away the magic lining them on the inside.

Alesio had lost his sense of Touch, along with Vision *and* Sound. Though slowed, he still floated away from her. She squinted, picking him out in the sky. Maybe about ten seconds had passed since they'd arrived in Lavoa.

Some of the ascending people had managed to grab hold of a ledge of dirt to pause their motion. They passed through gravity shifts that didn't have material substance, and those with snow slowed them, but many shifts boasted soil, rocks, and trees that caught the humans like flies in a web. Alesio had somehow managed to avoid such helpful obstacles and still spun upwards, about twenty or thirty feet up.

"Baylor," she said. "I'm going to bring Alesio down. But we need to stop the people from portaling here, or they'll probably die."

The young man's expression itself seemed slowed. He clenched his jaw in anguish, as if she had come up with a particularly persuasive reason to saw off his arm. She didn't know much about the young man, except that Clef had used and manipulated him, and that he wanted to save his father, so he had defied the old shadow leader's wishes back in the cellar. He probably just wanted to get to Scent as soon as possible and ignore everyone else. She could relate to that myopic goal, considering how she used to avoid humans at all costs when she trimmed magic, but Alesio had taught her that all humans weren't so bad.

Individually, at least. In crowds, they tended to sour.

"Baylor, please. Think of it like this. All these people are fathers or sisters or mothers to *someone*. They matter to someone else, just like your father matters to you."

More people bubbled through the Portal Station. A few jumped through, flying straight at them. Saida grabbed them and pressed them to the ground.

Baylor finally nodded.

"Slow them all, okay? Can you Shape a net or something to slow everyone portaling through?"

"I. can." His chapped, bleeding lips puffed ixor out as he used the words to dart a few falling upwards nearby.

"Good. You do that."

She pushed herself onto an angled shift upwards, her front paws still slowed and crunching into a cold, packed layer of snow an inch or so thick. The snow hadn't been trod on too much here to muddy it. The coldness of it stung her ixor-slowed hands and she winced.

She knew the area around Lavoa well, including the gears, cranks and levers that rotated or altered the direction of some of the gravity shifts. Most of the shifts nearby had polite slopes that wouldn't just throw someone straight upwards.

Alesio had rotated another five feet or so. She braced herself for the pain and pulled a lever on someone's roof, lifting the shift a few degrees. She slid on her belly in the snow, gaining momentum, until she reached the end. The shift deposited her at an angle facing the sky, giving her an eyeful of the Hunger, closer than ever, the fangs in their bulging tendrils like bloated corpses, the circling gray absence like a Plane's mausoleum.

Alesio had floated a bit higher up and to the left. She eyed the nearby shift that arched like a rainbow and leapt to it, landing on her back legs, balancing so she did not have use her front paws. The shift buoyed her upwards like a cork in water, and at its peak, she jumped to another nearby that flipped her upside down to the ground but ended right next to Alesio.

She tumbled onto it, catching the shift's side with her back claws so she didn't slide off. She righted herself, shifted to human to gain a few feet of length, and stretched her slowed hands out to him.

Some of the ixor had worn off by now for her. She tried to catch at Alesio's boots, but they spun just as her hands closed. She inched out a bit further on the shift, on the very edge. *Careful. Careful.* The shift that had hold of Alesio could catch her center of gravity and pull at her as well.

She reached back with one hand and gripped a small tree growing out of the soil on the upside-down shift. Then she leaned forward, letting the gravity that pushed at Alesio yank her. That gave her the few inches she needed to reach him, and she slowly closed her fingers around his shirt front as she held onto the tree with her other hand. The two gravities buffeted her like strong winds, each trying to claim her.

Shifting to foxan shortened her body, and therefore the distance between her and the tree, and she towed him towards the upside-down shift. His momentum shifted, as he had none of the gravity that she did, and she tossed him onto the upside-down ground, releasing him.

Then she pulled herself back towards him, using the tree as a ballast. Still slowed, he hadn't even reached the upside-down ground, even though she'd tossed him.

Breathing hard and sweating from her short time in her human form, she glanced down at the ground, checking on Baylor's progress. He'd shot many ixor arrows at the people in the sky, slowing all of them. They seemed to all float in a depth, now, instead of falling in various directions.

He'd also done as she'd asked and created a kind of ixor net around the Portal Station, thick enough to catch what seemed like a veritable hill of tangled humanity, pushing outwards like fish caught in a fishermen's net. She hoped they wouldn't suffocate or cause too many broken bones, but that seemed safer than letting them fall into the sky towards the Hunger.

Speaking of which . . . she should figure out how to bring down those people frozen in the sky. They would keep falling, even slowed, and they'd hurt themselves or die whenever they gained their gravity back and fell the long way to the ground, or some other gravity shift yanked them like puppets on strings.

Their gravity would return to them, right? And their senses?

She didn't know. She hoped so. She couldn't do anything about it. *Focus on what you can do to help those in front of you.*

"Alright, Alesio," she whispered to him, though she doubted he could hear her. "I'm gonna send you back down, now, okay?"

She aimed him like she threw a rock, finding a path where no dirt or rocks in Vision's layered landscape would block him, then pushed with all her strength at the middle of his back, so he wouldn't spin.

He fell downwards at a slow, slow pace. She wondered if she stepped on him like a platform, if he would fall faster, or not, but she didn't try. She needed to stay up here to save the others.

"Baylor! Hey, Baylor!"

About twenty seconds passed before he noticed her. He'd stayed close to the net of screaming, sobbing Soundians, and that probably made it hard for him to hear anything. She pointed at Alesio, and he trotted towards the angled gravity shift to catch him and tow him back to the safety of the ground.

ALESIO DRIFTED.

He had so much time. He understood that Baylor must have slowed him with ixor to stop him from falling too high. He had to trust that he and Saida had a plan. He tried not to panic.

It felt like an hour or so passed. The ixor arrow had puffed into a cloud and slowed all of him, but the cloud had had a lighter density than what had encompassed him in the fight at the warehouse. It didn't slow his internal organs.

Then a smoky gray blob with vague, blurry points on the top of their head rotated into view. Saida. She grasped his shirt front, and it felt like a curtain brushed against him. After what felt like fifteen minutes had passed, he bumped against a darker gray area—the ground? —which sent a jolt through him stronger than anything so far. Though not painful, it did break through his dulled sense of Touch, perhaps because of the ixor. The two effects didn't seem to cancel each other out, but intensified what little Receiving he did have, and his pain level. He might've grunted from the impact, but he didn't know. He still couldn't hear much.

Someone caught him. A pewter-gray face with a charcoal puff on their head. Baylor. Everything moved faster, then, almost like Alesio had passed out in between blinks, and his body had oriented in a different direction. Baylor must have pulled him along at a faster rate, like what Saida had done.

Baylor leaned close, and the planes of his face sharpened into more detail, so that Alesio could read his lips.

"Hold on."

Other vague shapes gained focus and a little color. Marik and Hestafon. They clung to something, and Baylor had guided Alesio's hands and clasped them to the same thing. A little way off, a mass of monochromatic shapes writhed like ghosts trying to escape the ground.

LAVOA DIDN'T HAVE levers and gears this high up. They had them in the town on their roofs and streets to keep the gravity shifts safe and controlled.

Saida contemplated how to reach the next ixor-slowed person, a middle-aged woman in a faded straiter dress. Tears seemed frozen on her cheeks, her mouth open in mindless fear. She pinwheeled slowly at a slight angle upwards away from Saida.

A few feet from her, a child hugging his knees plunged in slow motion in the same direction. They probably knew each other. And above the child, a thin gravity ledge waited that she otherwise couldn't reach. It glinted with ice.

Saida swallowed, and jumped onto the woman as a foxan, landing on her back legs, though without her claws. Then she launched herself off the older woman, sending her down to the ground, and leapt onto the child. The decreased surface area forced her to sink her back claws into the boy's shoulder, but she shoved away from him and jumped again before she lost her balance. He descended like the woman, and Saida tumbled onto the slender gravity shift in a somersault. Her front claws, still slowed, punctured the thin ice and the packed dirt underneath just in time to stop herself from falling off it, hanging off the edge. The ice *hurt*, as if it had torn her skin off. She scrabbled her whole body back up, trembling from the exertion.

She'd sent about twelve people back down to Baylor, who sprinted underneath her and caught those she sent. At this point, she'd rescued all those hanging just above Lavoa. She'd climbed into the middle part of the sky, before the air sharpened in the lungs, but the coldness of it still stung more than it did below.

At least it's not windy, she thought. Wind would push people around like chaff. It would've made rescuing them almost impossible. As things stood, she had to deal with ice. She eyed the scraped skin of her paw pads, grimacing.

As she ascended, she became less familiar with the gravity shifts. She had to pick them out and plan her path with more caution. Less soil and rock had made it all the way up here, making the shifts harder to spot, though ice glittered on many from melted snow that had quickly refrozen in the colder air. Most trees and hills grew on shifts closer to the ground, unless the shift had enough surface area to snag lots of soil the wind tossed its way. The people who'd risen this far were farther apart, too, as their trajectories had widened the further distance they'd flown.

Baylor had managed to hit just two people with ixor arrows at this range. Everyone else had soared beyond his reach, becoming mere specks like grains of sand on the beach of the sky. She couldn't save those people, but she could try to save the two he'd managed to slow.

One was close to her. She'd chosen this path earlier to save the woman and her probable child, but also to attain this ledge. Next to her, a horizontal looping shift had deposited an old man onto a tiny sideways cliff with about two feet of ice. He balanced there, slowed and stopped.

Saida drew in a deep breath and sprang at the looping shift. It spun her in a tube of air, spiraling until she reached the "bottom" with the ice. She landed on top of the slowed old man, keeping her claws retracted just in time. He would have slid on the ice from her impact, but she flattened herself on top of him, holding him there.

Her weight had to have hurt him, slowed as he was. Poor guy.

She climbed to her feet and studied the ground and how to pinpoint his path to it. That cost her about thirty seconds, since the distance had grown so far, but she found one and propelled the old man on his way.

A little vertigo assaulted her, and she had to look away from the city of Lavoa, which seemed like a square in a vast white quilt.

It's fine, she told herself. *The Summit Wave was way higher than this. Besides, if I fell, Baylor would catch me with an ixor arrow.*

She hoped.

Still, she didn't want to plummet for what felt like hours through the sky if she didn't have to.

One down. One to go.

She had to maneuver around and backtrack a few times to reach the last person, another child, which took longer than she would have liked. Baylor's patience wouldn't last forever. From the sun's position in the sky, about half an hour had passed since they'd arrived in Lavoa, if the Hunger hadn't hauled the sun towards them as well. Baylor's nets had worked well, stopping any other people from portaling into a world without gravity or sight. Saida's paws had shaken off most of the ixor effect by now. She hadn't taken a concentrated dose.

The child had floated far away from most gravity shifts. A few glinted like icy spiderwebs, but she had no idea which direction they'd send her in, and they seemed too thin for her to even sidle along.

She glanced down. She'd left Lavoa and had ventured into the wilds. Baylor waited below her the size of a bird. No gravity shifts glinted between them that she could see. The wilds often had broad stretches without gravity shifts.

Wait. Does he have someone with him? No, several someones?

Then the someone became bigger.

He had pushed someone up at her. Slowly, with probably a small amount of ixor on them, considering that they still moved faster than the others he'd hit with ixor arrows, but not at the rate of falling.

Then he sent another up, a little farther away, and in the direction of the child.

Oh, by the Senses. Is he insane?!

She had worried about his impatience. Well, it seemed that fear was realistic, because Baylor had sent her people as stairsteps. Her desperate tactic earlier must have inspired him.

Gritting her teeth, she prepared herself to jump on the first person-platform. She'd use this method because she didn't see another way, but she didn't have to like it.

She landed on the first person—a nice, broad man—and waited a fraction of a second, curious. Would he float down faster?

The answer was yes. She lost a few feet that way. Scrambling, she leapt on the second man, who had risen next to her. Baylor had sent her another large one. He must have selected them for their girth, which she appreciated. They didn't seem to appreciate Baylor's methods, though: they thrashed and yelled in slow motion.

Then the third, and the fourth—and by the fifth, she reached the child and sent them downward as well, waiting longer. She teetered on them until the ground neared a few feet away, and she jumped off. The child slowed once again, and Baylor grabbed them.

She eyed the young man, thinking to give him a piece of her mind, but discovered that part of her agreed with his method. She'd had no other way to reach the child, after all.

Fatigue weighed her down, and blood trickled from Baylor's lips. The Hunger might not have drained him, but it had to have removed some magic from him. And then he'd used a lot of magic, with emotions running high.

Baylor had created another ixor net, denser, to hold the people she'd sent down. He gestured at it. "What do we do with them?"

"Uh . . ." She peered at the city. "I think we should try to get them inside a building, so they won't float away."

They trudged, pulling the people. Saida had the idea to link all their arms together so they formed a chain, which they could just pull from the front. Their combined weight of fifteen people felt like pulling a kite. They hauled the string of Soundians back to Lavoa. They knocked on a door, and someone shouted in a sobbing voice, "Come in!"

Something Yashalis had said flashed through Saida's mind. *We do not run on our world; we train the behavior away at a young age.* Even while drained of their sight and gravity, the Lavoans had not stampeded—or she supposed, floated—in such debilitating fear that it had driven them into danger or into hurting others.

"Please," Saida told the first family, who floated blind on the ceiling of their home. "Please take these people in. They can't move; they've been slowed by ixor."

"Leave them here with us," the father said between bouts of tears, and she and Baylor maneuvered the chain of Soundians inside the small home. Not all of them fit, and they repeated the request at another house, whose occupants said much the same.

"Can we go now?" Baylor asked, and she didn't like how he asked the question with a cringe, as if she might hit him for asking again.

"Yes," she said. "Let's go. I'm sorry we had to do other things first."

He nodded, still ducking his head away from her. They jogged the short distance to the Portal Station and encountered chaos.

The net of ixor Baylor had cast over the Station had broken, and the people had burst out of it like a clump of silkseed blown by a wind and puffing everywhere. Some of them had toppled off the dais. Most of them still seemed at least somewhat slowed, but the net had lost its potency from how many people it had caught. Several people had swarmed Alesio.

***

ANOTHER LARGE GROUP of smoky blobs had boiled over from the pot of the Portal Station. They fell on him by accident, but they did recognize him up close. Just like him, they could details sharpened for them in closer proximities.

They shoved him, pressing on him. Their smoky limbs reached for him, grasping for him like heavy curtains. He couldn't lurch away from them or let go of the sign that Baylor had pressed his hands to. He was terrified of losing the ground, of being shoved into the sky again.

Something pushed him down, and faces materialized in front of him, inches from his face like ghosts, monochromatic and muted, and the sudden surrealness of it froze him with terror.

Maybe he'd died. That would explain his failing senses. Maybe this was what ghosts experienced in the living world.

He read the peoples' lips as they screamed in feathery whispers:

"Reconnect us, sounddamn it!"

"Give us back our magic!"

"That's not how it works!" He shouted back, knowing they couldn't hear him.

After Reconnecting the Planes last year, the magic from the Primal Plane had revitalized the fading remnants in the Sensory Plane. The Hunger, however, had not separated or consumed the magic from the worlds, but drained it from the humans. The ache of it, the void where most of Alesio's magic had lived in his body, quivered and shook inside him like a ragged piece of cloth left from a torn shirt. Even knowing that he could push himself up into the sky by accident, that need to *reach*, to *move*, plucked at him like a dissonant chord unable to resolve in a major key.

Someone shoved him again. On instinct, he tried to enter his magic room—now, house-sized, he'd forgotten—of Touch to create a Touch air shield around himself, but the magic remained behind the wall like a silhouette of a bird, flying repeatedly into a pane of glass.

"It's okay, it's okay," he said to the bird, to the magic. *"Don't hurt yourself. Stop! Don't hurt yourself!"*

He splayed his hands on the window, and he could *see* through to the other side, to where the magic lived in the Primal Plane. They wheeled and soared without a stable form, then broke into bits, then grouped again into larger globules, constantly changing, wishing to gain substance and semi-permanence in the Sensory Plane. He could not Receive them.

Back in the Sensory Plane, faces bobbed in and out of his blurry sight as the Soundians shoved at each other to reach him. He'd lost his grip on the sign. He floated upwards again. But many, many others had joined him this time, perhaps fifty or more gray shapes just in his view alone.

"Give it back! Give it back now!"

"We know you can do it! Why don't you do it?"

Someone towed him away, and he caught a glimpse of Baylor and Saida through the haze, a few inches away.

Pearl-gray tears streamed down Saida's face. "Let him go!" He read her lips.

20
THE FASTEST WAY

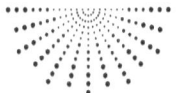

A quiet moment lapsed where everyone caught their breath for screaming.

Over a hundred Soundians had burst out of Baylor's net around the Portal Station, all of them falling upwards from the packed density of the area and the force from those behind them, shoving their way through from Anthem's side. They flew in every direction, left, right, upward.

She couldn't keep asking Baylor to slow everyone. Even with his amplifier he would run out of physical energy. They had no way of plugging the portals, though they'd slowed the flow for a good while. That had to be enough.

Saida used people as platforms, jumping off them now without any qualms to reach Alesio.

The mass of Soundians had scattered in every direction about twenty feet, and some of them cried out in physical pain, along with the pain from the loss of the magic. Alesio didn't cry out, but he would have lost his sense of touch, so maybe he couldn't feel if something hurt him. She wanted to check him for injuries, but she didn't have time. She had to portal *now* if she wanted to reach everyone, and she couldn't save them all if she just tried to leap from one to the other.

Saida had already teleported once today, but another portal pinged on her senses, when normally they wouldn't respond to her searching for them.

Alesio couldn't see well here—it seemed that the Hunger's draining affected those not just in their own worlds, but any that they traveled to, as well—but if she mouthed words inches from his face, he seemed able to read her lips.

"Portal! Where?" she asked.

"Scent!" Alesio shouted, and his voice cracked, and rasped. Like most of the other humans, his skin had grayed from the area of his body where the Hunger had drained him. His ears, his hands. "Take us to Scent!"

She Received.

She imagined a room where her Portal magic originated—not just inside her but linking to her. She imagined her body connected to the gravity shift, to the air around her. She felt all at once huge, as large as a flock of swanseizes, as if she'd connected to a bigger part of herself, as if she'd always been this large. She *was* the ground, the air, the spaces between, and the portal she Shaped, into a dome, to catch even those who'd fallen outward, or down to the ground—

The dome portal shimmered, and the group plummeted into it.

They landed right outside of Tremain, on the weeded fields, in a tangle of arms and legs.

Saida—as herself once again—landed on top of a human, retracting her claws just in time.

She blinked. The sun shone overhead, and the temperature had warmed. The drastic and quick shifts between times and seasons confused her senses for a moment.

I teleported twice in a day!

She'd had so many revelations in the past few hours that she could just focus on each newest one. Well, except for what the Epitaph on Taste had said. *The amplifiers used to be people! And—the Epitaph trees was a foxan, or multiple foxans, from a Plane with strange magic that became the Hunger! And—*

Priorities. One thing at a time.

She nosed through the tangle of humans as a foxan, cursing her slowed reaction speed, searching for Alesio and fearing the worst. The group hadn't fallen far once they regained their gravity on Scent, but they wouldn't have had a lot of time to brace themselves. Did ixor increase his pain even without a sense of Touch? She pushed past Marik and kept searching.

"Alesio!" She called out, forgetting again that he couldn't hear her well. She shoved a young man aside with her muzzle who sprawled over three others, revealing Alesio underneath. The mob had ripped his shirt in various places, and multiple scrapes and bruises marred his skin. She shifted to human, tugged him out of the pile with her arms, and set herself in front of him, close enough so he could read her lips. "Can you walk? Is anything broken?"

He coughed. "Can't feel much . . ." He spoke loudly, as he couldn't hear himself well, or perhaps at all.

She ran her arms over his legs and arms, checking for odd bends or bad bruising. She counted over seven bruises and five bleeding cuts, the worst one a large purple bruise on his ribs the size of her head. Of course, they wouldn't know for sure until he could feel again.

He clasped her against his chest, a veritable wall of muscle against her. "I'm okay. Are you? Saida?"

She nodded and opened her mouth, but she had no idea what to say. She just wanted to talk to him, to have a conversation instead of cutting him off or pushing him away. She wanted to tell him that she wanted to stay. She wanted to say that she would never leave him again.

Magic Ear had told her that their bond had faded because of her fear. She'd decided to strengthen it instead of letting that happen, to transplant another part of her heart into his, for he was her favorite place to be.

Selfish, selfish, you'll just leave him in the end and hurt him even more!

No, no! she thought back. *I've chosen to believe that I won't leave.*

You can't know *that.*

She shoved the voice away and helped him stand. That stone gray color still marred his ears and his hands, as if he'd gotten frostbite.

Maybe he had, considering that neither Vision nor Sound's winter would have affected him. "Be careful. You could have a broken ankle or something and not know it."

"I'm okay," Alesio said. "I think . . . I think I can still Receive a small bit. I could see shapes on Vision. I can hear and feel a little better now, too. If something was broken, I'd know it. I think."

The people around them began to groan and sit up. A few of them clutched at their wrists or ankles, and one woman's leg had twisted under her. Their eyes darted like bellbugs in lantern light.

Saida dared to glare at the sky. The Hunger's long arm-snakes had stopped revolving and towing the sky towards themself. The spots inside of them had grown larger, almost bloated. They hadn't pulled magic since those first few horrible minutes, when the magic across all the worlds had screamed as the Hunger had ripped them from their humans. Almost like they had a limit as to how much they could pull at a time.

How long did they have before the Hunger began pulling more magic away? Would they just eat magic, or try and consume their whole Plane, tree by tree, rock by rock, person by person?

Did the Hunger remember what they used to be? How could she use what she and Marik had discovered to stop them?

"Saida. Saida?"

She blinked, refocusing on Alesio's face.

"I have so much to tell you. But . . ." His dark-brown eyes flicked first to Baylor, who had bunched himself into a tight knot on the ground, then to the crowd still in shock from the fall around them, then to the otherworlders, the bulk of them Soundians, but some from the other worlds as well, sprinting at random in several groups of twos and threes. Some of them had cloths tied around their mouths and noses and had stone gray mottling near their ears. *The Soundian volunteers.*

A tattered line of beleaguered Scentians—she identified them via the gray blotching around their noses—guarded the field at specific points, rebuffing the Soundians who, in their erratic, mindless panic, tried rushing into the fields. Some of the Scentians had spun toward their group in surprise and terror. Hestafon untangled himself from the fallen group and limped towards them.

"We should help the villagers," Saida said. "If Soundians trample their fields again, they won't allow otherworlders here ever again." Some of the re-planted fields showed damage already, even though the chaos must have started an hour ago at the most. Their group had also managed to crush some plants in the fall. "And . . . more people could die in the chaos."

"You promised." Baylor's voice faltered. His pleading made him sound younger than had before, maybe sixteen or seventeen instead of early twenties, while the quality of his voice had become hoarse and rasping. He had risen to a crouch, and he stared at Alesio with what seemed a dark ixor-cloud in his eyes. "You promised. My father. My father!"

Hestafon stepped forward, clasping his hands in front of him. Blood ran down his leg from what seemed a large cut on his shin. "Young man. I might be able to help. Do you have anything from your father? Something that he carried?"

"Nothing, nothing." Baylor pitched forward on his hands, as if ready to leap at Alesio. The peeling on his lips and around his mouth had worsened from using as much ixor as he had on Vision, and blood spattered on the ground as he spoke. "You stole everything from me. Clef told me. You're the reason—" he smacked his own head with his hands, coughing. "No, stop it! He isn't like that! He promised!"

Saida swallowed. That segmented way of thinking . . . she could relate. She'd started fragmenting to help herself cope with what Carn had done to her, chaining her and keeping her to touch whenever he wanted. Baylor seemed to have done the same, letting himself splinter into different consciousnesses, even different personalities, to avoid thinking about how Clef had manipulated him and abducted his father.

"Baylor. Listen to me." His eyes darted to her, ixor wafting in a little cloud from his mouth. "We need to ask the Scentians about your dad, if they know where he might be. But they can't help us right now, not until we help them first. This is the fastest way to find him, alright?"

Baylor's jaw clenched and his breathing shallowed.

She hated to ask this of him. She'd already delayed him on Vision, and using so much ixor back there also seemed to have worsened his physical state.

But she spoke the truth. The suspicious people of Tremain would not help them find his father while otherworlders trampled their crops.

The Soundians that had fallen with them had begun to stumble upright, groaning, that fever still in their eyes, the panic of their absent magic still driving them. A few runners threaded through their group, and one bumped into the young man.

Baylor didn't even blink. His voice sounded like it had been skinned. "The fastest. Way?"

"The fastest way," Alesio said.

Slowly, Baylor nodded. She and Alesio both sagged with relief. Though, how they would accomplish handling the Soundians, she had no idea. Tremain didn't have a proper gate system like Anthem did, not for this many people.

Marik stood off to the side, his long brown hair twisted in his hands like a rope. Some of the villagers from Tremain left their line of defense around the fields and strode up to them. Many had tears stains and swollen eyes from crying, and dirt stained their faces and hands, and the gray marred the skin around their noses. Verrity led them, her dress stained with grass and mud. She'd gathered her hair in a low ponytail at the nape of her neck.

"What has happened?" she asked Saida. "Why are the otherworlders screaming at the sky?"

"Are you all not affected by the draining?" Alesio asked.

One of the people from Tremain stepped up beside Verrity, a blonde woman perhaps in her mid-twenties, a little older than Paras and Verrity. "The sky void stole our magic, yes. But why does that matter? We are not mindless animals, to scream like we are caught in a trap."

Saida bristled at the subtle jab. "They feel like they miss something vital, like air."

The blonde woman opened her mouth to speak again, but Verrity stopped her with a hand and a warning look. "Every day, we diminish the scents in our village with the nonflower," she said. "Maybe this is why the loss of our magic does not affect us as strongly."

Alesio sucked in a sharp breath. He scanned the group of Soundians that had fallen through Saida's portal, then the small groups dashing in random paths outside of Tremain's fields. Gray marred the area around some of their mouths instead of their ears, which meant that Tastians as well as Soundians had panicked. Since the Cloves and Anthem had the most people, it made sense that they made up most of the crowd.

"I have an idea that might help. Well, the Soundians at least." He darted to the front of their group, using his broad frame to bull his way through when he needed to. He waved his hands and spoke in a slow, dramatic manner, exaggerating his lip movements. "Everyone! I know you are all scared. I have a way to help!"

They gushed towards him like water loosed from a dam. "Reconnect us!"

"Voice, reconnect us!"

Saida braced herself with foxan hind legs, ready to jump in between to stop them from tearing at him again.

Alesio held his hands out in a performer's stance, not a fighter's: wide, spread arms, palms up, back straight. He planted himself into their attention as a true performer, his body the trunk and his voice the leaves. Even though he couldn't yet Shape magic again, the silhouette of it showed in how he carried himself, like a shadow where the magic wanted to connect and support him. "I can help you reconnect yourself. Everyone, stop! Read my lips, I will help you now!"

They stopped reaching for him and quieted, though still seething like a restless tide. Saida breathed a sigh of relief.

"I need you all to remember the last time you used a sound cloth."

The group of twenty or so Soundians shifted on their feet. Some furrowed their brows. They all leaned closer, squinting at Alesio's lips to read them easier. A few on the sides seemed to have trouble following past a few words, shaking their heads. Though most Soundians could read lips, that didn't mean they could do it for complex sentences.

Alesio continued, though. The middle of the group, about twelve or so, still watched him intently.

"Remember the sensation of feeling muted, or, if you jammed a sound cloth in, no sound at all? But you knew it was still *there?*"

Even as he spoke, those watching him smoothed their furrowed brows and relaxed their tense shoulders.

"That's what's happening right now," Alesio continued. "Sound is still there. You just have a sound cloth in right now, alright? I know the Hunger stole your magic. I felt it, too. The Hunger drained us so far that we lost the base senses of our origin world, *and* whatever world we are in. But do you see the villagers behind me?" He gestured at the people from Tremain. "They're keeping calm, because they are used to depriving themselves of their world's magic. So, for now, until your magic refills, focus on that, okay? Focus on that feeling when you stuffed a sound cloth in, not hearing anything, but *knowing* that your magic was still there. Think of how, when you read a person's lips, you can 'hear' their voice in your mind. Or, even if you have a sound cloth in, when you see bacon hitting a hot pan, you hear it sizzling. Or when you tap your bowl three times to honor the Goddess of Sound, you can hear the clinking sound. You can hear it, right? Your mind fills in the noise. Focus on that sound. Feel it. Feel the connection to your magic refill. Because it *is* coming back."

Some of them had closed their eyes, perhaps audibly picturing one of the sounds he had mentioned. Those who had done this had calmed their frenetic movements. Alesio bent close to someone with their eyes closed, an older man with a bleeding temple, and shouted in his ear. "Can you hear me?"

The man's eyes flew open. He clasped Alesio's arm with thin, frail hands. "You reconnected me!"

"I didn't do anything," Alesio said, still over-emphasizing so they all could read his lips. "Your magic reconnects as it slowly refills. I'm just here to point it out to you."

The Soundians in the middle who'd comprehended Alesio's words sucked in a collective breath and copied what the older man had done, gaining control over themselves and their fear. Seeing this, those on the sides who'd had trouble reading Alesio's lips surged closer to those in the middle.

"How did you do that?"

"Me! Help me!"

Alesio waved his hands, and the core group who had calmed down zeroed in on his face, on his lips. "Tell everyone what I told you. Help me Reconnect everyone here."

He's so good with people, Saida thought. *Even without his magic, he knows how to help them.*

With more people repeating Alesio's message, those on the sides gained their autonomy within moments. Alesio led the calmed ones out of the field like a shepherd, and more people ran up to them. "Do you have your magic back? How? How?"

The soothed group repeated Alesio's message, and the people of Tremain did, as well, in their line surrounding the field. The Soundians, most of who could read lips, calmed, and those from Taste and Touch could hear just fine. Alesio changed the message for them. For the Tastians, he spoke of when the tongue burned, that they knew their magic would return. For Touchians, he talked about the buoy suit, and how it sapped the sense of Touch for them.

The Touchians didn't need as long to calm themselves as the Soundians or the Tastians.

I wonder if it's connected to how often they deprive themselves of Receiving their magic? The buoy suit acted in a similar way to the nonflower, cutting away the sense almost completely, whereas sound cloths muffled sound but did not deafen a person. Soundians also didn't typically use sound cloths every day. Tastians trained themselves to eat and drink slowly, but for the most part, they did not attempt to lessen the potency of their food or drink.

The soothed crowd expanded to at least fifty soothed people. Still, though, more and more people streamed past like a snow melt river, chaotic and frenzied.

Verrity sidled through the press of calmed people back to Saida and Alesio's side, the hem of her dress and the whole front now stained with mud and grass stains. "We need to stop more from coming through, or this will not end!"

Alesio waved his arms. "Alright. Listen. Listen to me! We must stop the influx of new people to Scent. We need to stop them from hurting themselves and others. We need to help the people of Tremain! Now, listen to Mother Verrity." He bowed to the Scentian leader. "You must overemphasize your words, so they can read your lips."

Verrity stared at the crowd in front of her. "Right. We need to raise the fences." She straightened her posture. "Otherworlders! Are you with us?"

They shouted back. "Yes, Delegate!"

The Scentians worked with the crowd of otherworlders to handle the flow of panicked people, including those that had just arrived via Saida's teleport. Verrity, with Saida and Tener's help, directed them in teams to push the fences back up around the Portal Station and close off the gates leading to Tremain, funneling the Soundians straight back into Sound. While in this pathway, Alesio, Hestafon, Saida, and a growing group of soothed Soundians spoke to those who had at least stopped screaming.

"Do you feel that spark inside? It is there! I know you are afraid, but please return to Sound and shelter in your homes. We are working to stop the Hunger!"

A sprinkling of the crowds funneled from Taste or Touch through the two arrival portals. Saida and Tener helped ensure they left through the correct departure portal.

Baylor tried to help, but within a few minutes someone shoved him, and he careened at them, bleeding from his skinned lips, and Alesio grabbed his shoulder and pulled him away.

Saida swallowed hard. She had almost suggested that Baylor use his ixor to help slow the crowd, but his unstable behavior outweighed the benefits. The young man seemed at his limit emotionally and magically. What if he killed a whole group of people by stopping their hearts?

Some people tried to climb over the fence, but Marik, the Soundian volunteers, people from other worlds, and the Scentians forced them back down. Others tried to run or shove. Some froze, sobbing, or screaming at the sky.

After what felt like forever, but probably after thirty minutes, Saida recognized some of the people. Many had teleported back for their third or fourth time, and each time, they had calmed a bit more. By the fourth time through, most of them had calmed down, some of them even peering at another explaining Soundian's lips, as if they had returned to clarify something on purpose.

Interesting, Saida thought. *Maybe just a certain number of citizens have the instinct to seek out a different world when disconnected from their magic.*

The people stopped flooding from the arrival portals. Some still staggered through from time to time, but it had stopped for the most part. Of course, that didn't mean everyone would just stop rushing around and trampling each other on their own worlds.

Saida pulled Alesio aside, melting against him. They held each other close for the first time in what felt like years.

Tired. She was tired. She'd had a long day of wandering the ruins with Marik and discovering ancient truths, and though the sun had just started to set, time, for her, had raced past evening into the middle of the night.

"Saida," he murmured against her ear, "The magic does speak. I heard it! Well, I heard them. More than one!"

She stared at him, and then the words registered. Joy welled up and she hugged him tight around his chest. His warmth filled her with lightness, and she couldn't remember why she'd denied herself this.

"There's something else. There's so much, but I have a plan to learn how to stop the Hunger." Alesio lowered his voice, and it rumbled in her ears. "Clef can hear the lies people believe. That means he can figure out the truth of things. And not just in people, but in magic, too. He might hear the lies the smaller Hunger tells themselves."

Saida's eyes widened. "The lies? You mean, if they say they're invincible, but they have a weakness?"

"Maybe," Alesio said.

She tapped her chin. "It could work . . . even better than the small Hunger, we could try it on the Goddess Heads."

"You mean the big statues of Lunne? Why would they be better?"

She had so much to tell him. The words jumbled in her throat, but the reasoning smoothed out in her mind. The Goddess Head on Taste had ignored the Epitaph trees' ancient warning. *Pointedly* ignored it.

Whenever she ignored or avoided a certain topic, it almost always meant she didn't want to face whatever truth waited for her. "I—I just think we should start there." Then she frowned, considering what it meant. "I don't want to poke holes in your plan, but what's stopping Clef from just lying to *us* about whatever he hears?"

"That's why we need Hestafon. He can smell sounds. I know, it's weird, but he *can*, I've witnessed it. So, Clef listens to the magic's words, because he can hear the actual lies that someone believes. And Hestafon sniffs out whether Clef's words smell more rotten than usual."

Saida caught her braid in her hands, worrying at the frayed ends, remembering just in time to lift her face so he could read her lips. "It seems . . . a bit complicated. I've learned how translation can confuse meanings these past few weeks."

"I know. I know, but it's the only thing I can think of." His eyes flickered to Baylor. The young man had huddled next to the fence, holding his head and rocking back and forth. "But, before we try that, we need to find his father. I've put him off long enough. Clef's holding him hostage somewhere, he thinks here on Scent."

"Alesio, wasn't he the one you fought in that warehouse? The one who almost killed you and Hestafon?"

"The same. He's not all in his right mind. He almost lost control back in the cellar. He's way more powerful than Brezeek, that shriker with the amplifier that I fought last year in the cage match. Maybe because he's used an amplifier longer. And his ixor magic is dangerous, but it's *not* his fault."

Alesio's jaw tightened. He hadn't had time to shave the last few days, creating a disheveled yet sensual air, as if he had just woken up next to her.

Focus, Saida! Now is not *the time. Stop thinking about his lips. No. That doesn't mean you can start thinking about his* other *parts! What is wrong with you?*

"Clef brainwashed him to hate me." Alesio continued, unaware of her distraction. "Probably to torture me and then kill me. I had to promise him something that would distract him from that, or he might have killed everyone in that room. But more than that, I want to help him. I might have … I could have turned out like him."

"Oh, Alesio." Saida reached and cupped his cheek against her palm. He leaned into her hand, and she smiled. He'd picked up some of her foxan mannerisms. Why had she held herself apart these last few weeks? "You're not helpless against Clef anymore. He can't control you."

"I know. I know."

She leaned into Alesio's strong arms, and breathed in his scent— sweat, and dirt, mixed with fresh rain. She carried odors, too, stronger here, of wet fur and sweat and mud. He wouldn't smell her as well here on Scent, at least not for a while. And though his hearing and his ability to Receive her touch seemed to mend, those senses didn't seem all the way back yet. He traced a line along her jaw with that delicate control in his large hands that she adored, and she closed her eyes, aching for the sensation.

But they didn't have time for that. She sighed and hugged him close, then bent back so he could read her lips. "Alesio, I can hear magic again! And when I was at the Epitaph, they explained some things. The Hunger used to be three worlds, well, another Plane, really. One of their worlds, I *think* it was called Transmutation, planted colonies here, before they became the Hunger! One of the Epitaphs—well, five of them but they were all one Epitaph with five trees—tried to stop Transmutation from performing some magical experiment, but they didn't stop, and the magic backfired, and that's how the Hunger was created. And earlier, I teleported us again, even though I'd already used my portal for the day. I made a room like you do, and it worked! I learned so much, but now I just have more questions! I still don't know how to stop the Hunger, and now it's drained everyone's magic. But I wanted to tell you. I'm sorry I avoided you, I want to be with you, even though it's not fair to you—"

"Whoa. What's not fair is how fast you're talking. I can only catch every other word or so." He chucked her under the chin. "I wanted to tell you something, too. I knew you weren't ready to live with me, but I asked anyway. I'm sorry for that."

He was sorry? She let out a little laugh. She just wanted privacy with him, to tangle her hands in his hair, and kiss him—

"What did you say about the ancient cities?" Marik had held one of the fence posts in place while a Scentian shoved dirt around it to secure it better. He released the fence post and stalked over to them, his brow creased, his ears slanted back. "Please say what you said over again. I must have misheard."

Ah, that's right. Marik wouldn't have heard the magic explain about the colonies of ancient Lunnite cities. His hands shook, and the smudges of dirt and scrapes on his face couldn't hide his shocked expression, or the undercurrent of anger in his clenched jaw.

A large group of the Scentians, Soundians, and Tastians had finished with their work of fastening the fences and had gravitated to her, listening and reading her lips as she'd ranted about the Hunger. Some cried, and some clenched their hands into fists.

Alesio paused. "Can you explain what you learned about the Hunger a little slower?" Alesio raised his voice and spread his arms in his performer's stance. "Maybe to everyone? If there's one thing I've learned in the past few weeks, it's that open communication can help stop confusion and anger."

She'd shifted to foxan legs and paws as the humans had gathered. She swallowed and shifted back to full human to lend her height in front of the crowd, and so they would receive her words without prejudice. Most everyone from Tremain and the Soundian volunteers had gathered around. But Alesio held her hand in his, and it did not shift back and forth.

She looked at Marik. "I'm sorry. Brace yourself for the truth."

His jaw tightened, and his throat bobbed. She rallied her energy and spoke.

"We've discovered some things about the Hunger." She wondered if the entity would try and interrupt her, but no voice boomed down. Maybe they had gone into a sort of food coma. "The Hunger sent colony cities to each of our five worlds, centuries ago. Before they became *that*." She pointed at the sky.

She contemplated explaining about the amplifiers, too, and how the citizens had somehow transformed themselves into the Goddess Heads, but she could only explain so much without confusing everyone. "Those colonies are all in ruins today. A foxan from this other Plane transplanted to our worlds, merging with our worlds' magic, and connected their colonies on different worlds as an ancient Portal Station. I've been calling them an Epitaph."

They'd been more than that. The Epitaph trees had also used the Hunger's transmutation magic to perform unique and powerful magics on each world. But again, the crowd wouldn't understand such complex detail at this point.

Shocked silence. Marik shook his head, his hair swishing back and forth, twitching at the ends.

"This Epitaph spoke to me, the part of them that merged with the Sensory world when they transplanted. They were holding the Hunger back, protecting our worlds because they had become a part of us. But then the Hunger found and consumed the Epitaph and . . . well." She dragged in a deep breath. "I don't think anything holds them back, now. That's when the Hunger drained you all."

21
SECRETS

Alesio's mind reeled from what Saida had just revealed. Even as it did, however, he recognized two threats:

One, the crowd would spiral into further panic in a few moments if left unmanaged.

Two, Baylor watched Alesio with a hawklike, unnerving intensity. The young man would run out of patience soon. He could sense it, like a Sound knife twirling in someone's hand.

"Hey," Alesio turned to Saida. "Can you be my left ear right now? I need to hear everything they're saying."

She smiled at him and nodded.

He stepped in front of her, blocking the audience's view of her, and spoke with great enunciation and slowness. "We have a plan to find out the Hunger's weakness. But we need to work together and not panic."

He paused. Revealing more information was a risk. But the magic had taught him that more communication tended to work better than less. "The Hunger works with a human named Clef. Some of you may have heard me ask about him before. We caught him, but he doesn't work alone. I'm asking all of you, now: does anyone know of an underground movement that supports the Hunger?"

The villagers cupped their hands around their mouths and whispered among themselves. He found himself a little jealous the Hunger hadn't stolen their hearing, while sound remained spotty for him. Losing his sense of smell while on Scent didn't seem as debilitating or difficult to manage as losing sound or touch, but maybe that was because he hadn't lost it. Not really. If he left for a different world, his sense of smell would return. And losing a sense of smell didn't have the same impact for him as losing his vision . . . though, maybe the Scentians would disagree with him.

"Why would a human work with the void?" The woman with the braided crown said. Sound filtered through clearer and better to Alesio as time passed. Saida repeated the question closer to him, and on his right side.

"Because he's not just human anymore," Alesio said. "Watthe Consumed him a year ago."

"He . . ." Baylor's hands twitched, and everyone's gazes jerked towards him. "He. Wants. To take over." He bit his hoarse words off one by one, as if to slam his mouth closed and keep the ixor inside. Talking had to be so painful for him. "To offer everyone up. On the same world. Easier. To. Digest."

More hands cupped around ears. Whispers even Saida wouldn't catch.

Alesio spread his arms for the benefit of the crowd. "How? How does he plan to take over?"

"Ixor." Baylor clenched shaking hands. "Trained. Cage. Fighters at the portals . . ." He hunched his shoulders. Saida leaned closer and repeated his words in Alesio's ear. "But mostly . . . me . . ."

How many cage fighters does he have left? Hestafon had said that the Flockians had dealt with most of the cage fighters in their city.

A few Soundians in the crowd had read Baylor's lips. They began shouting. "You're working *with* them?"

"He's helping the Hunger!"

"Tie him up!"

Verrity held her hands up. She emphasized her words so the crowd could read her lips. Since she faced away from Alesio, Saida had to repeat her words in his ear. "Let's hear what the Voice of Reconnection has in mind."

Alesio inclined a grateful nod to the Scentian delegate. "Baylor, Clef holds your father hostage. How about we find him and bring him to safety? Would you try and stop Clef, then?"

Baylor's dilated, black eyes seemed to burn. "I will. Do everything. I can. To Stop that. Bug. *Ass.*"

"Wonderful!" Alesio swept his hands in a theatrical circle, drawing the crowd's fixation away from Baylor. Much of performing, like fighting, was just redirection. "This young man has done his part. He fought against Clef at great risk to himself, even though Clef holds his father hostage. Now, it's your turn. Has anyone suspicious come through here with a captive? Any sign of a struggle?"

Silence. The Scentians shuffled from foot to foot. Some clasped their hands in front of them. The Soundians had grouped together for the most part, though a few of the volunteers remained nearer the people of Tremain. The Tastians and Touchians seemed to have mostly returned to their respective worlds by this point.

Verrity sighed, turning to Alesio. "They could hide anywhere on Scent if they wanted to. But—"

A little hand waved, and the girl he'd met in Tremain ran towards him, the crown of her braid shining. "There's those men that came here—"

"Miriam!" The mother grabbed her and pulled her back.

Verrity frowned. "Ishira? What is she talking about?"

The mother, Ishira, bowed her mouth down in an anguished arc, and she wouldn't meet Verrity's eyes. "It was your sister's idea."

"What does Paras have to do with this?"

Raos, the tracker Alesio had hired to track Clef down in the first place, shouldered his way through the crowd. "A few men came here in the chaos of the Hunger appearing. They had someone with them, tied up. They demanded we hide them." He pointed. "They're up that way a couple miles, holed up in the Garden."

"Why did no one bring this up to the Council?" Hestafon glanced at Alesio, then at Verrity. The Scentian leader still stared at Ishira, her shoulders tensed.

Raos's zigzagging eyebrows scrunched like twin lightning bolts over his eyes. "Have you never feared for your loved ones' safety?"

Hestafon opened his mouth, then closed it.

"They told us they represented a large, powerful group of another world," Ishira said, "and that they would kill our families if we said anything." She jutted her chin at Verrity. "We kept it from you, as you would've tried to intervene with the Council, and this Clef would have had us all killed. Do you see now why we do not want otherworlders here?"

Alesio had written off the fear in these people's eyes—manifesting as cowering for some, and hostility in others—as simple opposition to the unknown.

He clenched his fists. *I was so blind.*

"This is how Clef controls people," Alesio said. Ishira's eyes skittered back to him. He continued, "He tells them that to oppose him means death, or worse, death to your loved ones. However, he is not all-powerful. He just likes other people to think he is. We have him locked up in Anthem. I promise you: I will stop him from doing Tremain harm."

The Scentians' eyes widened, and they whispered to each other.

"Hestafon." He gripped the piper's shoulder. He could detect a bit of the cotton texture of the man's clothing now. "Your magic is refilling too, now, right?"

Hestafon nodded.

"I need you to go to Sound and guard Clef. I'm counting on you."

Hestafon's mouth dropped open, then he breathed in through his nose. Tears glittered in his eyes, and he jerked his head up and down.

Saida seized Alesio's hands, curling her fingers over his and brushing her thumb over his knuckles. "I'm going with you. Don't you dare say I can't."

Alesio hired a deep breath loitering in the alley of his lungs. "There could be a fight. You're tired."

"We're *both* tired." She gripped his arm, her ears pricked forward. "I don't want to . . . I want to stay beside you."

Senses take him, but he didn't want her to leave his side either. And he needed to stop trying to protect her from everything—no, that wasn't quite it. He needed to trust her when she said she could handle something.

Alesio turned to Raos. "I need you to lead us to where Clef's men are hiding."

22

THE PEOPLE OF CHANGE

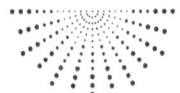

T ener had grown a lot over the past year, of course, but in the past few weeks everything had accelerated. Their body had shot upwards into all awkward legs and dangling arms, yet their mind had grown even more. They *stopped* before they said things, now.

They portaled back to Sound with Darrow after speaking to the baby Hunger—no, accuracy mattered: the tree that the small Hunger had merged and shared information with—and they returned to people screaming and running around, but even more so than the last time.

Tener bore a thought they did not share out loud. *Sounddamn.* They'd learned the word from Alesio, and their dad would grimace to hear it from their mouth.

Darrow crouched and turned foxan. They had teleported to an alleyway near the Drinks De Capo to avoid the crowds, but even in that small space, a few people ran in and out with their hands over their heads. As always, a minute or so passed before they adjusted to the increased intensity of magic on Sound, and with everyone screaming like that, it took the two of them a bit longer.

"Follow me," Darrow said. Tener thought of the older male foxan as their dad, even though the Primal Plane had sired and birthed Tener. They liked the idea of fathers and mothers, of attachments to people. Tener wanted to bond with as many people and magics as possible, to string as many of those golden threads as they could. It seemed what the magic wanted to do. After all, what were transplants but strings attaching one world to another, and what were people but worlds orbiting each other?

With Darrow leading, they both leapt up onto a garbage bin, scrabbled onto a horizontal pipe, then clambered to a balcony on the second floor of the building in the alley. They climbed a set of stairs fixed to the wall up to the roof; one of the many secret pathways that the fox-people had created to stay safe from the confusing hostility of the people of Anthem.

From there, they slunk along the roof and faced out towards a larger street. The chaos below reminded Tener of an anthill after someone had poked at it with a stick. Most people ran around in large groups. Here and there, a few knelt and screamed at the sky, their arms upraised.

"They're saying that their magic is gone," Tener said. "That they can't hear anything."

Darrow started, then listened as well, his grizzled foxan ears swiveling forward and back. "Can you . . . can you tell if their magic is gone or not? With your Bondsight?"

Tener cocked their head and squinted. Each person had several bonds connecting them to various other people, still glowing golden yellow, some of them brighter than others. But they also each had a bond connecting them to the ground, to their world. Those bonds had darkened, but the threads remained attached to the ground like gray ropes. It reminded Tener of Saida's bonds, both those that had dimmed, and those that had disconnected, swinging around her like the unraveling ends of a washed-out shirt.

They hadn't wanted to tell her about those. Just like they'd feared telling their parents about the bond tearing between the two of them.

What good would it do, to say anything? To point out that something they already felt, or that, in Saida's case, haunted her?

"Tener?" Darrow laid his paw on their shoulder. "What do you see?"

"I think . . . I think they're just drained," Tener said. "Worse than we've ever seen. Their bonds with their magic are gray but not cut. So, their magic should come back." They paused. "Did we do make this happen? Did the Hunger do this out of revenge for what we did?"

Their dad sighed and scratched his side with his back leg. "I don't know. What I do know is that we need to tell Saida what we found out."

"But we need to help the people, too." In the last panic, Falrie had relegated Tener to slinking through various secret pathways and speaking with the fox-people, pointing out where the people turned to violence, but just watching. Not intervening.

Tener paused, then added, "I don't want to watch more people die."

They shifted to foxan like they always did when something scared them, changing to a smaller physical form as if to hide from their thoughts, growing claws and sharp teeth as a last resort in case they Shaped their greatest fear into existence, like what the humans seemed able to do, and they had to fight it. "Is this what being older will be like all the time? Having to do everything all at once, all the time?"

Darrow's muzzle had grayed in the dim light; the four stripes faded red on his cheeks. He'd stayed most of his life in a small world, alone with Falrie and Saida, and now that everything had opened, he hesitated with certain things. Like his bond with Falrie. It strained, its light guttering at times. The wrinkles around his mouth and eyes sagged a bit more. "I'm sorry. I wish I could protect you from things like that. Let you grow up like normal." He glanced at Tener, then away.

"It's not the death that's making me grow," Tener said. "It's the magic, trying to make up lost time."

"Maybe it's both," Darrow said.

Tener recalled the jarring sensation of stretching tendons, twitching muscles, the sense of vertigo from their sudden height. It had happened the day after they had watched that human boy fall into the Hunger on Vision. He had screamed for so long, as far too many people had wrestled for access to the Portal Station on top of him. That day, Tener had willed themselves older, faster, taller, stronger, so they could save someone when they needed to. "Maybe."

"We should check the Portal Station either way. Maybe we can find Falrie and Saida there and help the guards keep the fences up. Do both."

THE EPITAPH'S MAGIC, according to the Lunnites, had disappeared from their senses the day before, but they found where it had emanated from anyway.

They'd traveled for three days altogether through Scent's western grasslands and reached an ancient city with a grove of rala nut trees. The trees wove together like tall people holding hands, surrounding the ruins of the city, which stretched about a mile across. Ancient towers showed above the tree line.

When they reached the entrance, they found a hole in the ground. But the trees next to the ripped-out earth, and the air, too, evoked a jaggedness, like the edges of a torn cloth. It was like a monstrous hand had wrenched something important from this place.

Paras didn't have to puzzle it out, not when the Lunnites huddled behind her like children watching someone wring a chicken's neck for the first time.

Higa, the black-furred Lunnite who had smiled at Paras the night of the swanseizes' appearance, stumbled forward first. The nearby trees seemed to hold their branches over the hole like people bending over a casket.

"It was here," Higa said, in tears. "Just yesterday, it was here." She glared up at the Hunger. "The void consumed it. We all sensed it yesterday. All those voices of magic, crying out . . ."

Tosn and the others joined her. They all huddled around the hole and keened in high pitched voices, some in foxan-like whines.

Paras shifted uncomfortably. The Hunger had moved in the sky yesterday, those tendrils reaching out like the arms of a god. The tendril snaking towards Scent hadn't approached their group, but it had come close, from the direction of Tremain, and Paras had feared the worst.

Guilt had slammed into her. She'd left her people for that thing to slaughter and perhaps eat them, all because she'd wanted to play adventurer.

She'd realized, then, that she hadn't even worried about the right thing. The thing in the sky had seemed so far away. Not like the raging mob of Soundians who had wrecked the fields.

But just because something was far away didn't mean it couldn't affect her.

She'd thought she had more time. Weeks, perhaps months, to find an amplifier so Linia could fix things. Well, Paras didn't know if Linia could scare off a Plane-sized maw.

When it had happened, the Lunnites had all gone stiff, their heads quivering. They'd whispered about magic voices crying out in pain and sorrow, and they'd keened in the same manner as they did now.

At that, Paras's fear had abated somewhat. If the Hunger stole some magic, at least it hadn't stolen *people.*

But the Lunnites had reacted as if the Hunger had done just that. Guilt curdled in her gut like sour milk, that she felt relief while they felt such obvious pain.

Paras wasn't a part of that world. She didn't have magic, so she didn't know when something happened to said magic. Yet, the mutilation in the soil in front of her did tell a tale of grief and terror, in the way that any scar disclosed a story about the harm that caused it.

She sidled around the hole and studied the trees next to it on one side. Gnarled knots in the wood created strange circular symbols. Some of them seemed pulled apart, the knots stretched.

"Um," she said. "I know it's not what you came for. But there's stuff here. Writing, I think."

Higa glanced at her, then sidled over. She brushed at the circles, then at the tears on her cheeks. "She speaks truth," she said to the group. "We can still study the other ancient Lunnite symbols here. And perhaps we can find another Goddess Head, here, if it is the same as Sedella."

"So, it's ancient Lunnite language?" Paras forced her gaze away from Higa. A line of circular symbols connected other, larger circles like the chain of a necklace in between gems. "It's beautiful."

After a while, the group drifted past the horrible hole into the ruins of the ancient city. A slight warmth spread through Paras's hands and feet. A sense of connectedness suffused her, like someone had just slipped their hand into hers.

This effect came from the rala nut. Verrity had used the nut's powder often growing up, around the time when she'd wanted to grow breasts but had instead grown facial hair and developed a deeper voice. Paras had always preferred movement for her medicine. She hadn't wanted to settle or "connect to the ground," as those who used it tended to describe it.

But breathing this in didn't lock her in the same place. Indeed, the ground and the air seemed to walk alongside her. Somehow, the sensation had affected her even though the rala nut buds still formed on the trees.

Had the magic that the Hunger had ripped away created this soothing calm? She could tell it faded on the breeze, even as she breathed it in. They breathed the remnants.

"What is this feeling?" Higa brushed her hand against the rala tree. "It is . . . like the sun has shone on a valley in my heart."

"The tree's scent is not supposed to be so potent." Paras brushed her hair out of her face, warmth spreading in her cheeks. "These are rala trees, and their nuts, when ground into powder, produce this effect. Some use it to feel happy when they are sad. We also believe that, when mixed with fertilizer, it can help our plants grow better and more solid."

Tosn, Higa, and the other Lunnites marveled at the rala trees and Paras basked in their warmth as well.

She wished she could've shown this place to Verrity. Even though her sister didn't use the rala nut as often anymore, she'd love it here. A bubble of laughter escaped her. She wanted to run and jump and play like a child. The Lunnites followed her, their grief commingling with ease and laughter like mixture of sour and sweet scents. They began to chatter amongst themselves more, gathering around the other trees and studying the remaining script.

"C'mon!" Paras gestured to them. "Didn't you want to travel this city?"

Tosn waved at her. "We will study the area of the Epitaph. We must try to find all we can before the magic fades. If you would so desire, feel free to explore."

Free to explore on her own! She grinned and pranced into the ruins, the effects of the rala nut bubbling in her veins. She'd found such a lovely new place! She'd found the ancient city that Linia had wanted her to!

Ah, right. Linia. She had a job to do, here. Once she found an amplifier, and maybe one for herself, she could protect Tremain, if not from the Hunger, at least from the reverberations of it ripping magic away from people. That would've caused panic and chaos even worse than the last time. Had the Soundians mobbed her village again? The Touch magic barriers that the Council had crafted around the Portal Stations should help with that. But her mission to protect her people might have even more importance, now.

Raos, the village tracker, could Shape Scent magic, so he could use an amplifier, if she found an extra one. She didn't quite know how they worked, of course, since she couldn't Shape magic herself, but if Linia wanted one to protect her estate and could stop the crowds on Anthem with one, then one should work well enough for Raos to protect Tremain from any other otherworlder mobs.

The reminder of her mission sobered her a bit. Or perhaps the effects of the rala nut had worn off.

She glanced up at the sky. The Hunger loomed much closer, those arms reaching and twisting the sapphire heavens around it like ropes, pulling more and more of it into that nothing, growing larger than the other three planets currently in the sky. It had stopped rotating, but those spots inside of it seemed to have grown like bloated ticks on a cow. Perhaps full of the magic it had consumed.

A pocket of rala nut scent wafted on the breeze, lifting her spirits a bit again. The sun shone bright, and she explored where no one had for probably hundreds of years. She couldn't remain melancholy while doing what she loved.

She wandered through the ancient city, slower now, keeping her eyes downward as she searched for those little silver things Linia wanted.

I wonder what Verrity's up to right now. The lie she'd given her sister tasted sour in her mouth, like the ruby-red stone fruit she'd bought from the Tastian merchant she had eaten before it ripened. Away from her home, away from the monotony of planting and weeding and harvesting, she wondered if she could have tried to secure the expedition without deceiving her sister. She could have tried gathering Soundians as volunteers instead of relying on Linia . . . well, except that she wouldn't have known about finding amplifiers, the thing that could protect her little town from the danger of the big cities.

The Lunnites huddled at the archway, pouring over each tiny mark of the trees, exclaiming from time to time. She'd had so many reservations about them just a few days ago. Meeting so many furred . . . people . . . at once had triggered an instant wariness. If guiding them hadn't freed her from Tremain, she might never have met Higa, or Tosn, and found she related to them more than she would have ever imagined. What if otherworlders weren't all bad, either?

She hadn't had much interaction with them, beyond the Soundians trampling their fields or the random merchant selling something in Tremain. But the Soundians had feared the thing in the sky. They hadn't set out to ruin Tremain's crops; they'd tried to escape. She knew a thing or two about running away from what scared her and trampling something precious in the process. Could she ensure Tremain's safety in a different way, instead of controlling the Soundians to stay in their homes?

"Over here! I found the Goddess Head!" Higa called out from a few abandoned buildings over.

The Lunnites all rushed in that direction, and Paras picked her way over as well, a bit slower as she kept her head down, searching for a gleam of silver in all the crumbling stone.

Higa had found the stone face of a giant woman, half of it sloughed off and lying in chunks on the ground like clumpy gravy out of a pan. A large, grooved stone circle with five pillars surrounded it, and circular inscriptions lined the circle, the pillars, and the giant woman. The face's other half lay in chunks on the ground. Dirt and grime covered much of the face, obscuring more of the inscriptions, which covered the entire span of the area. It had also hidden a silver shine.

Paras paused. Linia had described that an amplifier should have a circular script etched into the silver material, though she hadn't mentioned they came from these statues.

Maybe she didn't know, Paras thought, and that thrilled her, to have discovered something like that. That statue, if it was all amplifier silver, could probably channel some massive magic, if being shattered hadn't ruined its capabilities.

"What could have cut it like this?" Paras knelt and touched one of the shattered pieces.

Tosn peered at an inscription over the Goddess's eye. He brushed the stone with his paws, clearing away some of the dirt. "Perhaps a lightning strike . . ." He tsked his tongue and brought forth from his pack a set of brushes. "Higa! Kodz! We need to clean these to read them."

The Lunnites set to work brushing and cleaning the inscriptions with various brushes. Paras wandered further away, trying to keep tension out of her face and shoulders. Once out of their lines of sight, as they all faced the Goddess Head, she bent and gripped a small, shattered piece, about the size of her palm, hiding it in her fist. She moseyed away to pocket it in secret. She had a sense that if the Lunnites found out that she had snatched a piece of their hallowed statue it would upset them.

She hadn't expected to find one so fast. Disappointment coiled inside her gut, which confused her as to why.

She could grab one more piece, one for herself, for her to use to protect Tremain. Though, she'd have to wait before trying that again. Someone might see her. That would take longer.

She wandered further, and further, and then the Lunnites' excited chatter didn't reach her any longer. She flopped next to the stone foundation of a house, which had long since crumbled, and poked around in a crevice in the side of the foundation. Fungus grew there in the shadowed part, and it smelled savory, like rich broth. She tried to imagine who might have lived here, all those centuries ago. Whoever had constructed the houses had planned them close. Had they enjoyed such near quarters with their neighbors, or had they felt crowded, like they had nowhere to go?

She angled her face up to the sky, letting the sun warm it, keeping her eyes closed so she could pretend in clear skies. When had peace last reached her while she relaxed? She imagined people greeting each other in the marketplace, pointing out potent herbs and spices, praying towards the Goddess statue in the center district each evening. She imagined this town with no borders, no invisible lines between the city or country dweller, foxan or human. They even worked together with those from Other Planes; those strange people shaped like trees with many long, flexible branches for arms, who wrote those circles on their skin and who had arrived via the long, long portals between Planes called Bridges. These tree-people, the people of Change, promised they would help everyone find the Goddess, Lunne, and ask her to reconnect all the Planes via the crumbling Bridges, some of them not functioning any longer. Some of the tree-people ate a silver ore that grew on one of their worlds, and using Transmutation magic, Transmuted themselves into Goddess Heads, and others ate just a tiny amount and Transmuted small parts of them like fingers or toes to give out as samples, to prove to the worlds they colonized what they could do. But then, something had happened. A flash of light, bursting from the Goddess Heads across all the Planes, shooting upwards like hundreds of reverse lightning bolts!

All the people, foxans and humans alike, cried out, as everyone and everything in the cities had crumbled into pieces, cut like so much wheat at the stroke of a scythe.

She was crying. When had she fallen to the ground?

She hadn't just imagined that. Those tree people had been other— other*planars*, not just otherworlders! What had caused those blasts of light?

Magic. She'd Received magic. Something had triggered inside her, like she'd always wanted, but it hadn't happened while she moved. She'd laid next to the fungus, and from that vantage, it grew next to a silver box the size of the pad of her finger.

The same color as the Goddess Head.

She had Received the fungus's Scent magic, which had grown next to the amplifier. The amplifier, along with the other one in her pocket, had increased the fungus's Scent, which held the memories of this place in its delicate vines under the ground.

She could . . . she had the magic to smell memories. The two amplifiers had sent her far, far back, farther than she could've by herself or with just one, and they had shown her the ancient history of the place.

Had she done this before, and just not realized it? All those times where she had daydreamed, imagining herself in the past . . . had she Received magic?

She contemplated. Should she pull out the box? Did she understand this magic? What if the fungus had created the effect, not her?

But no . . . she could tell she'd done it. After the shock of the amplified version, she could sense something inside her that had hidden for a long time, as if behind a curtain.

She held her breath and reached for the silver box. The cool metal met her fingers, and she tugged it out. The vison had shown her that this amplifier had once perhaps been someone's finger or toe.

"Are you alright?"

Paras jerked around, hiding the smaller amplifier in her clenched hand. Higa stood there.

"Fine," Paras said.

Higa tilted her glossy head, her chartreuse eyes narrowing. "You have tear stains on your face."

Paras scrubbed at her cheeks with her free hand. "Just—just thinking about what this town might've been like."

"Oh." Higa surveyed the foundation around them. "It is quite sad, these ruins across all the worlds. It's strange that so many people lived before us, when none of them can tell us their stories. Except through those inscriptions."

Paras blinked. Afterimages flashed through her mind's eye from the amplified vision. "It seems that—something terrible happened to them."

"The Severing." Higa sighed. "That's what we Lunnites believe. As the Lunnites' archivist, I have studied it quite thoroughly."

Verrity had told her the story, and Paras had repeated it from the foxans. That something had arrived and somehow severed the Planes, strangling the flow of magic from the Primal to the Sensory. But then, had that light burst from the Goddess Head? Paras swallowed, gripping the amplifier.

Higa sat cross-legged in front of her, her hands in her lap. Her plant fiber clothing covered her legs but not her arms, gleaming with the layers of oil. "Anyway, um, I just wanted to tell you, those giant white birds—what did you call them?"

"Swanseizes."

"Their dance over the lake . . . did you know they would do that?"

Paras tightened her hold on the amplifier in her hand, hoping to hide the gleam of metal in her fist. The Lunnites worshipped that statue, after all.

I'm not doing anything wrong. They both wanted to fix their worlds, just in different ways.

"I've seen it once before." She paused. "None of my village has, though; they're all too afraid to travel that far. I didn't guide you that way on purpose. it's kind of dangerous. But since we were there, I'm glad you got to see it."

"It was like—I don't even know! I've never seen anything like that! I don't have anything to compare it to."

Something uncurled inside of Paras and loosened. "That's why I love to explore. To experience things I can't compare anything with."

"Well, I'm sure we can convince Tosn to take us back there, or here, if you like." Higa laid a hand on Paras's fist, giving a shy smile. "Together?"

Paras blinked. Higa gave off a trickle of pheromones. She had for a while, now that Paras focused on it.

Heat suffused in Paras's cheeks. "Oh. Um." She stared back. Higa's yellow-green irises reminded Paras of a forest in the summer, verdant and luxuriant in the loam of her sleek, glossy black fur. She smelled like it, too, mingled with the oil and plant fibers she wore. How would her carmine lips brush against Paras's? Soft and yielding, or hard and passionate?

She cleared her throat. "I'd like that."

Then another part of what the Lunnite had said registered. "Wait. What do you mean, Tosn can take us back?"

Higa grinned at her. "Seems like as good a time as any to tell you, since you would figure it out tonight. Tosn can teleport like a foxan. A few Lunnites can do things other than sense magic." She waved her hands. "He couldn't teleport us here, of course, since he hasn't been here before. But now that he has been here, he could portal us here again. We will portal back tonight to tell the Envoy, Saida, about our discovery. We believe she will guide us to find the Goddess."

It was perfect. Paras could deliver the small amplifier and the piece of the Goddess Head to Linia much sooner than she'd hoped.

But now, she couldn't help but ponder what her vision had showed her. A massive light bursting out of the Goddess Head, shooting up into the sky.

Paras gulped, then forced a smile at Higa. "Sounds wonderful."

23

DIFFICULT TRUTH

Saida cleaved to Alesio's side as they followed Raos, the scuttling, middle-aged Scentian with the thundercloud hair and the zigzagging eyebrows. Indeed, his eyebrows were so striking, he gave the impression that his own head had struck him with lightning. He scurried down a vague path leading away from Tremain. Long, itchy grass had overtaken it here and there, like the path wished to become a meadow.

Selfish! Selfish! Selfish!

Why couldn't she have stopped hearing *that* voice? They didn't sound like Tricksy Stone anymore. They had similarities to her old friend in that they tried to get her to face difficult places, emotions, or ideas. But this voice didn't have Tricksy Stone's wit and good-natured ribbing. They weren't merely sarcastic. They were afraid.

It's always been your fear, Magic Ear had said.

She blinked, fatigue weighing down her eyes like a gravity shift. For her, time had dragged into the wee hours of the next day. She'd stayed up all night before, but not like this. Not with ixor in her system, and not with such relentless terror driving her blindly forward like a mouse trying to escape a forest fire. She'd never been so tired. She used her human legs to stride farther but shifted her feet to foxan pads to grip the ground because she didn't trust her balance.

She caught a whiff of her underarms and grimaced. She needed a bath. She hoped Alesio hadn't noticed. He didn't smell like a garland of roses either, but wet fur and sweat produced a particularly pungent combination.

Her portal, or portals, now, hadn't recharged yet. The Epitaph's scream echoed in her mind. It reminded her of how the transplants had screamed when Watthe had eaten them.

Wait.

She groaned and scrubbed at her eyes. They burned, wanting to close. "I can't believe it. The answer was right in front of me, all along..."

Alesio's brow rumpled as if it wanted to fit in with the disheveled state of his beard. His stride slowed as he bent towards her. "What are you talking about?"

His Receiving must have returned to him, if he could hear her muttering to herself on his right side.

"The Epitaph—they were a transplant from one of the worlds the Hunger used to be. I could have tried to use them as an emergency portal to the Hunger!" She lengthened her fingertips into claws and scratched at an itch behind her ear. "If I'd just figured it out faster, I could have done it before the Hunger reabsorbed them."

Alesio's eyebrows rose. "Huh. You mean the way Watthe used your transplants to portal around?" He sucked on his lower lip in a way she wouldn't have minded him trying out on hers. "But, even if you had, there's no way of knowing if you'd even survive. It might've just consumed you."

"That could have been our one chance to stop the Hunger."

"We don't know that."

They slowed, and Marik and Baylor lingered behind them instead of passing by. Ahead of them, Raos glanced over his shoulder, shrugged, and folded his spindly legs to sit cross-legged on a part of the path that still considered itself a path instead of an overgrown field, waiting for them to catch up.

Saida turned Alesio's hands over. The gray had become less apparent, less stark, against his dark brown skin. He smiled at her, then stroked her fingers with his.

Senses take her, but relief flooded her. Relief she didn't have to leave him again, this time for a reason other than her own fear. She didn't have to decide to sacrifice both herself and their bond after she had just decided to stop fearing she would change their relationship.

"Envoy," Marik said from behind her. "Might I have a word?" The Lunnite had clamped his jaw shut so tightly she wondered how he could speak without it snapping.

Alesio moved into a subtle defensive posture, widening his stance and slightly bending his knees. It was like he shifted in a different way, changing his form into something he could battle with, since he didn't have claws or fangs. He glanced sidelong at Saida.

She mouthed, "It's alright." She didn't fear herself, or the decisions she might make, any longer. She didn't want him to, either.

Alesio released her hand, his invisible claws and fangs retracting as he straightened again. "Okay."

Saida loved him even more for that.

She nodded to Marik and resumed walking, while Alesio strode ahead, no longer accounting for her shortness. "What did you want to say?"

The Lunnite swallowed, his throat bobbing. "I—I just can't believe what you said. I can't. What the magic said . . . I know you've had trouble, hearing the magics—maybe you misheard?" His voice strained. "Please. I mean no disrespect. It's just—this might just *kill* Tosn."

Tosn who?

Oh. Marik referred to the older Lunnite who had spoken with her at the Cadenza, along with Marik and a Lunnite woman. The Lunnites had to be a tight-knit group, living in the ancient ruins of Sedella together, terrified of leaving.

She sucked in a breath, pondering his words. She *had* had trouble hearing the magics. Maybe she had imagined Magic Ear, the Epitaph, and the Goddess Head's voices.

No. She was finished doubting her ability.

"I'm sorry, Marik, but I know what I heard."

The Lunnite bowed his head, his eyes glinting with tears, and Saida wished she could help him. In the past few days, while pouring over ancient script together, skulking through the shrike infestation, and teaching him how to walk safely on Vision, he had become a friend. She wanted to hug him but also didn't want to give him the wrong idea. She settled for patting him on the shoulder as one might pat a dejected butterfly, with a great deal more hovering than patting.

His hair, which he'd twisted together, lashed back and forth at the ends like an agitated cat. "This would mean I descend from the people that created the Hunger."

"Maybe." Saida considered it. "Or you could descend from a foxan and human pairing here on the Sensory Plane. You said yourself that your ancestors settled in the ruins and began to believe in Lunne *after* reading the ancient scripts. There's no real way to determine which. And ... does it matter? You're still a Lunnite, right? You still believe in the Goddess. Just because this ancient civilization from a different Plane failed at finding her, doesn't mean you have to stop believing or searching for her."

He clasped trembling hands together, his lips thin. "I don't know what I believe anymore."

She stayed quiet, just plodding beside him for a few moments. "It must be difficult, finding out something so different from what you knew your whole life."

"I'm not so much angry as—well, that's not what I keep coming back to. Though maybe it should be." He sighed, and his hair-tail stopped twitching. "I'm more worried about the elders. They've believed for so much longer, this secret will devastate them. It might drive them mad."

Saida swallowed. "I know a little bit about elders losing themselves. My parents aren't the most lucid. They still haven't recovered most of their memories from before the Severing."

Marik's muzzle wrinkled in a grimace, and she had the distinct feeling that she trod on sacrilegious ground. He shuddered in a deep breath, then released it. "How do you help someone like that?"

She paused, trying to consider her words. "I used to think I needed to remind them of their past, so they didn't lose themselves. But I've learned that's not what's important. The important thing is to stay near them, to be around them. Even if they . . . lose who they were, that doesn't mean you have to lose *them*. People aren't one block. They're made of lots of different pieces, like magic. So, if you lose one side of them, you just need to learn how to love another."

He stared at her in a funny way, like she had sprouted wings. "Saida. You're so . . ." he blinked and cleared his throat. "I'm sorry I was angry with you. It's not like you meant this to happen." He frowned. "I disgraced myself, treating you in such a manner."

Saida shrugged. "Anger makes sense after what you've had to process. I'm just the one who had to tell you."

Speaking of anger . . .

Beside Marik, Baylor trudged behind Alesio. The young man's face contorted as he stared at Alesio's back, his eyes dilated, the peeling on his lips glistening red and clotting in places. An unsettling grinding sound emitted from his mouth, comparable to a very small rockslide, if that rockslide slid upwards from a throat instead of downwards from a cliff.

She didn't understand this young man's hostility towards Alesio, but she could guess at the reason for his overall aggression and mental instability. The amplifier in his mouth expanded his capacity for Receiving and Shaping magic in vast amounts, and she suspected, had provided enough to stop the Hunger from draining him. She could sense the magic pooling inside the amplifier, which also somehow remained separate from his body.

If the ancient Lunnites really had changed themselves into Goddess Heads by using a mixture of their own magics, she regarded the amplifiers with even more caution.

She tried listening to their voice.

"I am a sample of Lunnite technology to help people understand what the Goddess Heads in the cities can do. I am here to help the citizens of the Sensory Plane!"

Magic had voices. They *did*. The reassurance that she had not imagined it earlier in all the high emotion and blur of the Hunger's assault pricked her eyes with hot tears.

Thank you, Magic Ear, she thought.

They didn't respond, but they didn't have to, because the amplifier had spoken through them.

So, this amplifier hadn't broken off from one of the broken Goddess Heads. Someone had designed them this way. How did that work? She tried to listen to more, but the amplifier just repeated the same phrase, just like the Goddess Heads and the Epitaph had. The transformation from ancient Lunnite to amplifier seemed to have stripped their consciousness, so they existed in a kind of death, but they also enabled a perpetual overgrowth inside of Baylor. Whenever he would Receive, his expanded capacity would allow an equal amount of magic to flow through him without flooding or draining him.

Such a high level of magic use had to do something to a body, however, especially when it was ixor. Ixor slowed the body and so it seemed to quicken the mind. While Baylor didn't seem affected by physical slowness, that didn't mean he'd escaped the mental acceleration as well.

Did time exist differently for this young man, stretched out in vast measurements of agony, an hour distending like a snake's jaw into the size of a day, or a day into a week? She stopped herself from reaching to trim the overgrowth. Doing so wouldn't fix the problem, because the amplifier themselves didn't have much magic. They existed as a conduit that allowed the user to Receive and Shape more than they would otherwise, and the moment she trimmed the magic seeping from them, more would just flow through. He needed to remove the amplifier.

But . . . doing that could cause Baylor serious distress as well. His shaking hands and his bloodshot, dilated eyes indicated ixordependency. As if triggered by her gaze, he coughed, and blood spattered on some grass by the path. The Shaping of so much ixor while wearing an amplifier must have chewed him up on the inside. And she'd asked him to his magic so much on Vision.

All of that added up to several reasons for the young man's erratic violence and affinity for jumping at people.

It's a wonder he's lasted this long at all, Saida thought. *The hope of freeing his father must help keep him in check.* She shifted her fangs to human teeth before biting her lip. She hoped his father was alright for both his sake and theirs.

The Goddess Heads had almost no magic as well, from what little she'd sensed on Taste, but now she wondered if they could still work. Most of them had cracked, some of them into pieces on the ground, and the symbols covering them had weathered. Still, could she use them somehow to drive off the Hunger? Could Alesio pour magic into them and, for instance, Shape a planet-sized hand that slapped the entity far away from their worlds?

No, that wouldn't work. Any magic that touched or even neared the Hunger would just feed the monster.

Could she transplant something from the Sensory Plane *inside* the Hunger? Like what she had done to Watthe? Could that somehow rebuff their consuming ability? What if she disintegrated the moment she arrived there?

She stared at the young man for a couple seconds. Baylor had to have noticed such blatant scrutiny, but his gaze never wavered from Alesio's back. Meanwhile, beside her, Marik watched her watch Baylor, which she also tried to ignore.

She'd have to find a way to teleport to the Hunger to try the transplant idea, and she didn't know how she could accomplish that now.

"Don't you, though? After all this, you still avoid the truth."

Saida blinked. In her head, Tricksy Stone's dry tone was undeniable—or at least the part that she had first poured into Tricksy Stone to create the bond between them. The part that had merged back into herself after transplanting her old friend into the Cadenza's ceiling. It had such a different timbre from the voice that whispered *Selfish,* she couldn't believe she had mistaken them for the other before.

"My name is Difficult Truth. Nice to meet you, Saida."

She paused. *Nice—nice to meet you.* She swallowed. *What am I avoiding, then? Tell me.*

"You know how to reach the Hunger. You just don't want to leave Alesio."

She licked her lips. *I . . . I don't know for sure. I'll wait for Clef to confirm it.*

It had to do with the Goddess Heads. Her mind refused to go any further than that, though it stalked the mystery like she might hunt a large spider in her foxan form: wary of any sudden counter strikes.

Beside her, Marik's hands swung in rhythm with her steps. She couldn't miss, now, how he angled his body towards her, or how the ends of his hair twitched close to the end of her filthy, mud-encrusted braid. Though the information she'd given had angered and disheartened him, he still seemed interested in a relationship with her —at least, subconsciously.

But she didn't want to be with Marik at all. She wanted to stay with Alesio as long as her fickle personality allowed. She'd teleported to him in that crystal clear knowledge, even in all the terror of the Hunger, she had to hear *his* voice, hold *his* hand, feel the warmth of *his* body next to hers.

Selfish!

Was it selfish, though? Magic Ear had told her that her bond had faded with Alesio not because of her changing nature, but because of her *fear* of her changing nature. She'd created a self-fulfilling prophecy.

"Yes," Difficult Truth said. "I tried to tell you that for ages! I had to relay it through Magic Ear, because you weren't listening."

Did that mean that if she continued choosing Alesio, she would continue to stay with him, controlling her fickleness like she could control her shifting?

Difficult Truth?

"Theoretically," Difficult Truth said. "I can't promise anything for certain." At her internal sigh of exasperation, they seemed to wave their 'hands,' which had the unnerving effect of fluttering in her stomach. "Hey, I'm not a fortune teller. I'm just things you already know but don't want to admit to yourself."

She wanted to believe she could choose her future that way. She wanted to so, so badly.

Saida shaped Marik a smile of friendship she hoped he would receive as such, and nothing more, then quickened her step to walk next to Alesio again, linking her arm with his.

Raos had led them further along the path for several minutes, a hidden path leading north from Tremain. She and Alesio had spent a good amount of time exploring each world, but less time on Scent than the others, because of the locals' view of outsiders.

After a minute or so, Alesio leaned down and murmured in her ear, "I like what you said."

"Hmm? What did I say?"

He interlaced his fingers with hers, producing a pleasing harmony out of their hands. "The part about learning to love the new person. If they lose who they used to be."

She smiled at him, and her throat constricted with the conviction that she never, ever wanted to lose this music between them. "You did say you're good at finding me." She paused. "Wait, you could hear us? Is all your magic back?"

"I can't Shape. But I can fully Receive again. I can feel, and I can hear." With his other hand, he touched each finger to his thumb. Most of the mottled gray portions of his ears and his hands had returned to their normal, dark-brown color. The way he collected his breath, though, and held it caged inside his chest, indicated worry.

She knew the cause for his remaining concern. Had the Hunger cut off the humans' ability to Shape? Severed the connection? She gripped Alesio's hand and squeezed it, and he squeezed back.

Raos scuttled rounded a bend in the path and stopped. "We try to stay away from this area. We call it the Garden. It's a maze that stretches a few miles long, but just a few hundred yards wide. Most of us don't like dealing with the maze, so we go around it if we want to travel north."

The dirt path thinned further and looped through a wide area encompassing various trees, flowers, herbs, and vines. The last bit of light from the setting sun cast shadows of the foliage ahead, toward a clearing. About a hundred yards away, a house stood in the middle of the clearing where nothing grew except for grass.

"Who lives there?" Alesio asked.

"Normally a villager who prefers solitude. But the otherworlders forced him out so they could use the house."

Saida tilted her head and inclined her ears forward. A transplant covered the entire area, a merged magic of Scent and something else she couldn't quite place.

"Come play! Come play my game!"

Once again, relief flooded through her, that she could hear the magic. It was one thing to hear the amplifier's voice, or her own internal pieces of herself, once more. But hearing a transplant's voice, now, that was her proof. She blinked back more tears and swallowed what felt like an egg filled with delight in her throat.

"What is your game?" Alesio asked.

Oh, that's right. He could hear magic voices too, now. More evidence that she hadn't imagined the voices.

Could she hear Tricksy Stone's transplant now, if she had time to visit the Cadenza?

Raos nodded towards the Garden, scratching at his grayed, frizzy head energetically, as if he wanted to produce sparks from the friction. "The maze magic changes its scents day by day. And it . . . well, follow me inside, but hold your breath while I explain."

He stepped onto the path and the area rippled like a gravity shift. Raos disappeared.

They followed him through and found themselves on the same path, crowded next to the Scentian. He inhaled next to a flowering cherry blossom tree and vanished again but reappeared almost in the same instant about twenty yards to their left, next to a spread of purple flowers.

"Okay," Raos said. "The cherry blossoms lead here. We must find the plant or tree scent that portals us to the middle. There's always an underlying pattern of some kind." He grimaced. "The Garden will hide the pattern scent in different-looking plants or flowers, so you can't just try and look for lots of cherry blossoms, for instance. But that's how you find the pattern, because it doesn't match what it's supposed to be." He inhaled, and the Garden teleported him across to the other side next to a spray of daisies.

Alesio frowned. "Couldn't people just hold their breath and get through that way?"

"Once you're in the maze," Raos called, "it's like you're walking through a different place altogether. You can't see or hear anyone inside, and no one outside can see you or hear you, either. It won't let you through until you solve the puzzle in the path it intends."

The Garden giggled and sent whispers from all around. "Try this way! Or that way!"

Saida needed to breathe soon, she couldn't hold her breath as long as Alesio. She shifted to foxan for better balance and accuracy, calculated with her haunches, then took a running jump, landing past the cherry blossom tree and next to some long clumps of green grass. She sniffed.

The smell of lemon teleported her as if an invisible portal had sucked her inside, and she reappeared where the path forked to the right, next to a decadent vine covering a tree like a resplendent dress of small white flowers.

From these, she smelled something sweet and fruity with a musky undertone. She didn't know the name of that scent or the flowers. It teleported her to a rose bush far enough away she couldn't see the others next to a little stream. Instead of the scent of roses, she smelled something almost like licorice mixed with pepper.

She wrinkled her nose even as she teleported to a spray of lavender like a purple fog at her feet. The others had teleported to various areas already, as well, but she could see Baylor and Alesio nearby, on the other side of the white vine.

"There's a rosebush that doesn't smell like roses!" she said, waving, holding her breath so she stopped teleporting. "But I don't know what it was. You get to it by smelling the lemongrass, then the white flower vine!"

"Oooh," the Garden said. "But can you find the others?"

When the transplant spoke, it called to mind wide-open fields, a kind of wonder tinged with melancholy. Something was familiar about that voice.

Alesio appeared next to Saida, making it difficult to stay in the same space with his breadth of frame next to her. He rubbed at his nose. "I think the rosebush smelled like fennel."

Baylor stepped backwards from the white vine next to a plant with red peppers growing on it. The young man teleported to what looked like a tiny forest farther up the path on her other side. She squinted. Parsley.

Saida sniffed the lavender. It smelled like lavender, that calming, sweet scent, and it portaled her to another rosebush near the first rosebush and the stream. This one smelled like a normal rosebush, on another loop farther up a path that Marik had ended up on, next to a reddish-looking tree. Behind it, she spotted the purple flowers that Raos had first teleported to.

The rosebush portaled her to a line of golden curtsy flowers, which she held off on smelling, in case anyone else had figured out anything. She began to understand how this could get frustrating, if the villagers just wanted to get on with their day.

Alesio hadn't followed her to the curtsy flowers, and he teleported far back towards the beginning. Saida could tell because he cursed from that direction.

The Garden giggled. "Try again, try again!"

Marik smelled the red tree. His eyes widened, then he disappeared, and his voice came from farther up the bend. "That smelled strange. Like you said—sweet and peppery."

"Okay, that's two of them," Saida said, and inhaled as she spoke by accident. The curtsy flowers smelled like curtsy flowers, a sweet blend of honey and vanilla and something green. They portaled her next to the flower shrub on the other side of the tree, which had coarse green stalks growing from it. She knelt and spied white bulbs peeking from the ground. Garlic? She held off on smelling them. "Anyone else?"

"Over here," Raos said, from far to her left. "The aliberry bush I just left. It's fennel." He ran his gnarled hands though his thundercloud of hair. "They sure love their strong scents."

"I do, I do!" the Garden said.

Dusk had set in, creating shadows everywhere in unexpected places, like night had tottered out of hibernation and kept tripping over rocks.

"Okay," Alesio said, his voice echoing from somewhere to her left. "So, we need to try and only breathe the fennel ones, trying to move towards the end?"

"Usually there's four in the pattern," Raos said, his voice faint. "But yes, you have the right idea."

"I can get to the rosebush," Saida said, running out of air again. She smelled the white vine, which took her to the fennel rosebush and the stream. She pulled in a deep breath of the licorice pepper smell—tried not to cough from the sweetness of it—and held her breath again once she teleported to the lavender. "Where to next?" she called.

"Try the aliberry bush," Raos called. "I think it was close to where you are."

She followed the Scentian's directions, loping through the looping paths. She found the aliberry bush just as her breath whooshed out of her, and she dragged in another sweet pepper lungful. She coughed this time, losing her breath almost at once. The aliberry bush took her to the garlic she'd spied earlier, and she couldn't help but breathe it in. It smelled of garlic, and she portaled to the cherry blossom tree at the start.

"Sounddamn it," she muttered.

"Oh no! Whatever shall you do?" Once again, the Garden's voice echoed with a voice that sounded like an old friend.

It's space, Saida realized. *It's a transplant of both Scent and Space magic.* She didn't know if the word "space" matched what she sensed, because it didn't hold a Sensory sense at all, though somehow it remained familiar to her. Listening to it felt like staring up at the spaces between the stars or gazing down from the top of a mountain.

What other magic must have transplanted from other Planes that had escaped her notice before? How could she have missed them?

Perhaps it was like when she looked for something, she picked them out easier?

"Found the fourth one," Baylor said, his voice faint and small, from far away. "It was all the way in the top right corner. It's the sage."

"It has corners?" Marik asked.

"Okay," Alesio said on Saida's left. He touched his finger against his lips in a categorical sensual gesture, as if he wanted to distract her with ideas of other things he could touch. He had to be doing that on purpose, right? "And the aliberry bush is where?"

"I can see it," Saida said. "It's close to the start, almost straight ahead of me."

"The red tree is to the left of the start, past the purple flowers," Marik called.

"Okay. Everyone, take a deep breath, and try to get back to the start," Raos said. "Let's all try to do this together, or Scents know you'll all wander in here for hours."

They all managed to make it back to the cherry blossom tree. Saida breathed in once, which took her to the purple flowers, but she trotted back the twenty yards or so.

"Aliberry bush first," Raos said leading the way. They all inhaled the scent of fennel one after another, crowding onto the path next to the garlic. From there, he cut across the Garden, leaving the path, and strode past the aliberry bush they'd just smelled, then to the red tree on the other side. Saida barely made it but just managed to hold her breath long enough.

The red tree portaled them farther up the path on the other side of the stream in the top right corner. *Where does it come from?* Saida wondered. *If this is from another place, is there a world with part of the stream cut out?*

They all splashed across the burbling water over to the fennel rosebush, Saida pointing out the way. The fennel rosebush portaled them the lavender, and Baylor led them to the sage farther up the path in the top right corner of the Garden, and smelled it.

"Very good! Very good! Thank you for playing my game!"

The plants and the scents all shuffled, and the Garden deposited them next to the house in the middle. A kind of shimmer showed where the space magic had intertwined with scent behind them.

"Come play again! Don't forget!"

24
THE MESSAGE

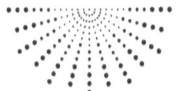

I f someone had told Hestafon a week before that he'd miss his new magic, he'd have laughed and told them if it happened, he'd dance in the streets.

Yet, in the short time since he'd acquired his mixed-up ability, it had become less overwhelming, and he'd even started to *rely* on it. Somewhat like having a visceral reaction when tilting a poisoned drink towards his lips, it had its benefits. If he suspected a person of ill intent, manipulation, or otherwise negative behavior towards him, he could process their ambiguous tone and Shape it into a smell. If he liked the smell, he carried on talking to the person. If it smelled rotten or putrid in any way, he bowed out of the conversation.

It had illuminated many meetings he'd had as a Council member with Balt, showing him with frustrating detail the Tastian delegate's sulfurous words. It had struck him as quite ironic that the leader of Taste had a voice that smelled like rotten eggs.

Now, with his magic stripped from him, he couldn't sort the difference any longer between the angry and the hurt or the angry and the vengeful. That frightened him the most: that he didn't know by scent who to trust. A least, in the manner he'd come to trust Alesio in the past few days. Or how he'd started to trust himself, as soon as he'd decided he would visit Flock.

Of course, it didn't much matter when he couldn't have 'bowed out' of the conversation of shoving, crying, and screaming people. Thankfully, Scent's arrival portal sat on the edge of Anthem's Portal Station dais. The masses pushed Hestafon through the trampled gates and out into the wreckage of the surrounding marketplace with all the mindless vigor of a river shunting a twig through a heinous labyrinth of boulder-infested rapids.

I need to get to that cellar.

The crowd pulled and pushed him along, and he flowed with it to lessen the chances of someone clawing or trampling him. He waited for the right moment.

There! A break in the stream. He speared his way through, stumbling into a side alley. The crowds had deposited him farther back in the straits, which he didn't know as well. Clef's prison was more towards the middle of the city, back near the Portal Station.

He pressed his back against the side of the alley, catching his breath with his hands on his knees. The texture of cotton against his skin still jarred him; he'd worn silk his entire life up to these last few days. But the *swishing* sound of it, which he and the other pipers had always found more pleasing than other fabrics, had smelled stale, like an abandoned mansion full of musty, unused furniture. Cotton's sound had smelled cleaner, healthier, especially when he'd had to run or sweat in it. Sweat dampened the cloth under his arms, now, even though he couldn't smell it, which he supposed he should be grateful for.

He kept trying to use his magic and bumping up against that horrifying, jagged hole inside himself, like a torn-off limb, except his mind conjured it back like a phantom. Or, dared he hope that it would return? A far-off murmur of voices whispered in his ears, but he still could not Shape it into scent. Did that mean that his Receiving had returned, but not his Shaping?

The winter wind had already chilled the sweat on his skin, and the cold air burned in his lungs. Where had he ended up? St. Rina's showed above the buildings to his north, far ahead. Farther than he had hoped. That meant he would need to head northwest but doing that would prove difficult in the straits. Strait streets were *not* straight, they wove and meandered, unlike the piper district's efficient, straight lines.

The light of the stars, Vision, and Scent overhead cast some illumination, but not as much as they should. The Hunger had grown larger than Vision, now, and eclipsed much of its light. He squinted closer at the structure he'd hidden behind in the darkness, some sort of low wall. Instead of straw, dirt, and wire holding the edifice together like most houses in the straits, or brickwork on the piper side, this wall had lines of small sediment laid on top of one another. Hestafon frowned. A Touch magic user had Shaped this. Hestafon had approved these new houses for people in the straits over six months ago and the builders should have finished them by now, but the sediment lines stopped at a few feet high. His difficulty with his own magic had distracted him from following up on the work.

His heart sank. He needed to do better. Not just for Anthem, but for Flock, too. For all of Sound.

Alright. Left here. He braced himself to dive into the swarming crowds. Most of them headed in the direction he needed, at least for now.

"Psst!"

Tener, the young foxan, motioned him from an opening in the ground, holding a door that opened upwards with a human face and an arm poking out a few inches. "In here!"

"I need to guard Clef. It's important," Hestafon said. "He's imprisoned near the station."

Tener cocked their head. Their face hovered somewhere between feminine and masculine. "Oh. Okay. We can get you there."

"We?"

"C'mon!"

Hestafon didn't have a better way, though he sorely wished he did.

He lowered himself down, trying not to let his disgust at the dirt overcome him, and followed the foxan in the dark through an enclosed, tight tunnel. Even in the semi-darkness above, he'd relied on the light from the planets, and nervousness rose in him, without that feedback of his senses.

The foxan loped ahead. The tunnel sloped up, and then the brighter darkness of the night sky ahead lit up where it opened into one of the half-built houses. Someone carried a half-hidden lantern.

Darrow, Tak, and a fox-person he didn't know had gathered here. Several injured people laid in rows, and Tak and Darrow tended to them, giving them water and propping their heads up with pillows or piles of straw.

The fox-person met Hestafon and Tener at the entrance holding a lantern. "Oh! The Council delegate! Are you hurt?"

"No, no," Hestafon said. "But I need to get somewhere, and quick." He paused. Did his words sound stuffy or smell sour? He couldn't hear himself well and he feared he spoke too loudly to compensate. He wished he had some of his candies left, but he'd used the last of them when he'd spoken to Alesio the day before. "I'm sorry. I don't know your name."

"It's Naya." The fox-person ushered him in. Tener had already bounded into the half-finished house. Far-off screams sounded from nearby streets like eerie ghosts calling to each other in a fog. Sounds trickled back, but they remained muffled until people got within five feet or so.

"Hestafon!" Tak waved at him across the room. A few lanterns rested on the ground, giving a low light to the area. "Glad you're alright." Someone had torn out the left side of his handlebar mustache. Spots of blood had dried on his upper lip.

"Looks like you might need to rest, yourself," Hestafon said.

"Ah, I'm alright." The older piper gentleman limped from one injured Soundian to the next. "Nothing a good rice bowl won't fix. Have you seen Alesio?" He spoke louder than the fox-person had, almost shouting, though he didn't seem aware of it. Perhaps Tak hadn't recovered as quickly as the fox-person. Had fox-people been drained? Or, had the Hunger just taken some magic from fox-people instead of all, since they had both human and foxan sides?

"He and Saida are safe on Scent," Hestafon explained. "He told me to guard Clef. It's important."

Darrow turned towards them. "Saida's with him?" The foxan shifted to his human form except for his muzzle. "Thank the Senses. We need to tell her and Alesio something. But we'll have to wait till everything calms down."

Many people lying on the ground had limbs bent in unnatural ways, like the branches of a tree growing in opposite directions on Vision, and some had gruesome, gory wounds. Hestafon swallowed, brushing back a few wisps of hair that had escaped his ponytail. *I need to do better by them. I need to protect them.*

"Did the Touch barriers at the Portal Station hold?" Tak asked. "I was lost, for a while. Screaming with the best of them."

"They held," Hestafon said. "Though, people still shoved the gates aside." He paused. "How did you escape the draining's hold on you?"

Tak shrugged. "I didn't, not really. The foxans found me and Estro and talked us down from the worst of it. Then I felt the magic start to refill." He shook his head. Up close, the older man's salt and pepper hair possessed more salt than pepper. "About the Portal Station. We need the whole thing to be Touch-magic, though I don't know how the gates would work."

"You'd need Touch magic users ready to shut the gates and close the portal access." The speaker appeared from a different, larger tunnel on the other side of the building, a tall woman with huge leg muscles. Hestafon recognized her as Muey, Touch's official guide. She assisted Falrie with carrying someone. The two of them laid the new injured Soundian down close to the tunnel entrance. They had almost run out of room.

"Falrie." Darrow trotted over to his partner on his toes instead of his whole foot, like foxans did. "Saida is safe. She is with Alesio on Scent."

"Thank the Senses." Falrie released a held breath. She grabbed a lantern from the ground and inspected the new injured person's wounded side. She shifted to her foxan form, her long hair disappearing, her speckled gray fur appearing with her orange stripes on her cheeks and across her back.

"I'm taking Hestafon to Clef," Tener announced.

"Good," Darrow said.

"What?" Falrie said at the same time. She jerked her head up.

"Alesio said to. It's important."

"Naya can take him," Falrie said.

The lantern light played off the foxans' faces, creating shadows where Darrow and Falrie avoided each other's eyes and Tener stared between them as if trying to stay in the middle, instead of siding with one or the other. Hestafon wished he had his magic so he could smell the tones he couldn't quite parse in their speech.

The young foxan had shifted to human and wore baggy fur clothing they'd grown themself as foxans tended to do, and their short hair curled around their ears.

"Alright," Tener said.

Naya, the fox-person, led Hestafon through the larger tunnel that Muey had come from. Some of the scratches on the walls looked fresher than others, indicating that someone had widened it, perhaps for recent human foot traffic. The path slanted up after a few minutes, and Naya lifted the cover a half inch and listened before she raised it all the way. With a swift movement, she flowed out of the tunnel, spun, and held out a hand to help Hestafon up. He took it.

She led him through a back alley, then up a crumbling staircase to the second story of a bar, then leapt across to the next building. She peered back at Hestafon, the starlight reflecting in her eyes as if she, too, were curious if he could follow.

Hestafon shivered in the cold, and his breath fogged in front of his face. He swallowed.

Alesio needs me to do this. I don't want to let him down.

He launched himself into the air and landed a little rough on the other side, scraping up his hands on the stone ground. Pain flared bright and sharp, but the lines of suffering people flashed through his mind, and he clenched his jaw and kept going.

Naya slunk along a rooftop past a line of large pots, which

concealed the path from the ground. Rumors abounded among pipers about the secret paths of the fox-people. Hestafon had feared that they would use them to creep up on him at night and steal his magic. Now, even contemplating such stories smelled rotten to him.

She escorted him through back alleys, fences, balconies, roofs, and tunnels. Most of the ways had been enlarged like the first.

They reached the building where they had imprisoned Clef, and Naya steered him to a back door that opened to the room above the cellar. A window permitted a little moonlight to shine through. It also showed the drained groups of Soundians dashing about outside, and one of them pressed a wide, glassy-eyed face against the glass—until someone else shoved them away.

Hestafon shivered, but not from the cold.

"Thank you," he told Naya. "I know it's a sign of trust, showing me this way."

The smell of trust, which he'd sensed from Alesio's words, had smelled like an apple ripening on a tree; sweet, crisp, and fresh. New. Vulnerable. Precious.

She seemed to deliberate about something, then she shone her foxan teeth to him in a smile. "Tener was right. You have changed." She hesitated. "If . . . after all this is over, and we're still here . . . could you do something about Balt? He fosters the old fears about my people, and Tastians tend to follow who's in charge."

"You live in the Cloves, then? How do you know the secret ways in Anthem as well as you do?"

Her muzzle wrinkled. "If you've had to search for safety your whole life, you tend to know how to find it no matter where you are."

That sounded like it would smell like something crushed into pulp, and acidic. Like a just-squeezed lemon.

"I'll bring it up to the next Council meeting — at least, the next one after dealing with the fallout from all of this."

She nodded once and disappeared back down the tunnel.

He made it, though not on his own. He'd made it because of those he used to despise.

With a new level of gratitude, he opened the door to the cellar. *Please let him still be here. Please let no one have let him out.*

Balt's face startled him. The Tastian delegate had a key in his hand, and he faced Clef's cage.

ALESIO, Saida, Marik, and Baylor crept closer to the house, built in a field of sparse grass. The sun had dipped below the trees, and everything had dimmed to dusk.

Within moments, they all smelled the outhouse.

In Tremain, the villagers managed their waste in a systematic, vigilant manner. They had designated troughs in their fields where they buried their waste, using it for fertilizer. They rotated workers in charge of raking clean dirt over the troughs and they scattered nonflower petals on top to neutralize any possible escaped odors.

The design of an outhouse—an open hole in the ground for waste, even one enclosed in a little shed—was an abomination on Scent. Clef's men, though, didn't have any notion for such meticulous hygienic standards. The area reeked of fecal matter and urine, and it burned in Alesio's nose. He clamped his hands over his nose, and the others followed suit. If only they'd gotten here before everyone's magic had begun to refill. Even with their reduced Receiving, Alesio had to focus so he wouldn't add vomit to the list of scents in the air.

Raos grimaced and waved his hands in front of his face. He pivoted and disappeared into the Garden, retracing the route backwards the group had solved. If the Scentian's Receiving had been normal, he probably wouldn't have guided them through the maze, knowing such an odor awaited them.

Saida, still a foxan, had flattened her ears and wrinkled her snout, glaring at the house and the smaller outbuilding beside it, where the offending scent leaked from. Marik ripped up grass and held it over his nose and mouth. Baylor clenched his shaking hands at his sides and violence vibrated in his gaze.

If Clef's men held the young man's father here, they had tortured him—and themselves, if they didn't have masks to filter out the stink.

Alesio motioned for their group to follow Marik's lead of grabbing grass and holding it over their mouths. He dug in his pocket and found a spare sound cloth that he passed to Saida. He could hold his breath for longer than everyone else, anyway, though the stench still burned in his nose and eyes.

The young blonde woman had warned them about the stench, and that three guards stayed there. Alesio could handle three with the element of surprise and Baylor on his side.

Saida's eyes had drifted closed more than once, only for her to shake herself back awake. He didn't want her anywhere near Clef's thugs, but if he didn't give her a job, she'd try anyway.

"Baylor and I will sneak around the back of the house," he whispered. "Saida, you and Marik go to the front door, and after about thirty seconds, start making noise. Pound on the door or something."

They nodded in agreement, eyes watering.

He and Baylor crept around the house towards a back door and a window. The back door appeared unlocked, but testing the handle without a Sound bubble could alert Clef's men. They peeked through the window.

Two men and a woman perched on chairs around a table. They all played a card game. A stone skillet simmered over a fireplace, which lit the room with a cozy yellow light, cooking some sort of vegetable and meat mixture. A closed door led to a second room without windows.

That's probably where they're keeping his father.

The guards all wore masks covering not just their noses, but their mouths as well, with glass over the main part and a filter that cleaned incoming air and allowed it to depart—the same kind that the thugs Alesio had fought in the warehouse had worn.

Huh, he thought. Such a device would benefit the Scentians. Tastians had engineered them to fight against the Palates' ixor use.

The man on the right sported nine tally marks on his arm,

marking him as a cage match fighter with nine kills. Alesio recognized him as Ivar—a Soundian he'd fought in a match several years back. *Weak knee.*

The man on the left had a greasy, drooping beard extending past his mask in the exact shape of a rat's tail. The woman sitting across from him possessed brass knuckles and the large, muscled calves of someone who lived on Touch and had waded through shallow water her entire life. She could also be a Touch magic user, but she wouldn't be able to Shape in this fight. Hopefully.

Sounddamn. Alesio had hoped that, with Baylor's amplified magic still working somewhat, they could knock out the opposition. Then he wouldn't have to worry about fighting and potentially having to kill anyone. But with masks, Baylor would have to produce enough ixor to affect them by just touching their skin instead of inhaling it. The Hunger had to have affected Baylor's magic some, even with an amplifier, and he might not have enough refilled yet. The young man had already used a lot of magic on Vision, slowing all those people. His lips had stopped bleeding during the reprieve in Tremain, and clots of blood had formed on his peeled lips.

Alesio mimed breathing out and touching his arm and then raised his eyebrows at Baylor. The young man shook his head.

Pounding sounded on the front door. The three guards sprang up, facing away from them.

Alesio kicked the back door. It slammed open, and before any of the people inside could whirl around, Alesio threw one of his knives at the woman, aiming to wound her in the shoulder so she couldn't punch. She blocked it with her forearm.

Ivar shot a quick, real knife back at Alesio, then ducked behind the table. The knife lodged in the door quivering next to Alesio's cheek.

Baylor charged through the door and Rat-beard hurled a pouch at him. A cloud of ixor puffed up, brown and thick, but Baylor, unfazed, decked Rat-beard in the face. The guard reeled, and Baylor pounced on him, ripping off his mask and breathing ixor into his face.

Alesio threw his second knife at the front window, shattering it. Ivar, hiding behind the table, jerked his head towards the noise, then back as Alesio leapt over the table and tackled him with a knee to the face. Alesio gripped his third and last knife and rapped the cage fighter on the head with the stone handle. Ivar dropped.

Alesio and Baylor flanked the woman, who had ripped the knife out of her forearm and crouched in a wide stance, her calves bulging.

The front door banged open, and Marik sprang through, eyes wide and frightened.

What is that idiot doing?! Can he fight?

The woman's eyes flicked to the Lunnite. She lunged for Marik and grabbed him by his hair. Alesio rushed forward, ready to stab with his knife at her shoulder. The woman yanked Marik into him, and Alesio had to drop his weapon to catch the Lunnite without stabbing him.

Baylor rushed in from the other side, but the woman spun to face him, and punched Baylor in the stomach with the brass knuckles, then threw a cross at his temple, knocking him to the ground. He moaned and curled on his side, protecting his head with his hands.

Alesio pushed Marik to the side and reached for his knife on the ground, but the woman barraged him with punches, angling him away from his weapon. Alesio backed up, dodging left and right, then snatched one of the chairs and blocked with it.

The woman kicked Ivar in the side. "Wake up!"

The cage fighter groaned and rolled over.

Saida launched herself as a foxan through the front door and landed on the woman's back, clinging with her claws. The Touchian screamed and tried to reach behind her back, but Saida scrabbled higher and bit deep into the woman's ear. The woman screamed.

Saida springboarded off her back and landed on all fours across the room. The Touchian woman dashed at Saida before she could react. Alesio grabbed the skillet and flung its boiling contents onto her back.

Her scream rose in pitch and volume. She arched her back and spun around. Alesio leapt over the waking Ivar and smashed the skillet against her head.

The woman dropped, slumping to the ground. Carrots, gravy, and beef lay strewn across the room. Alesio swung again and hit Ivar again right as the cage fighter tried to stand, laying him flat out.

Silence reigned, except for the sizzling of food on the floor. Alesio maneuvered out of any stray ixor particles and allowed himself to breathe. The smell of the food didn't drown out the horrible fecal smell or the strong, sharp scent of urine from the outhouse. Alesio gagged, and he had to stop breathing, or he'd throw up.

His Receiving really had returned at the most inconvenient time. Though, he'd still choose the worst smell in all the worlds over that horrible, ragged hole inside himself, that frenzy akin to drowning.

Baylor stumbled to his feet, bleeding from the brass knuckles to his temple. He tottered towards the door leading to the side room.

"Here, this should help." Saida held out a mask to Alesio. She had already tugged one of the masks on over her own mouth and nose. It was the mask the woman had worn, and his hit from the pan had cracked it on one side. It also didn't fit her, too big against the sharp angle of her jaw, even when she shifted to a human.

Still shoving down the vomit rising in his throat, he took the proffered mask and slipped it over his face. The smell dissipated, though the cloying taste in his mouth remained.

"My dad's not –," Baylor said from the one other room, the bedroom, in the single-story house. Then, louder: "My dad's not here!"

Alesio peered inside. The bedroom had one large straw mattress against the wall and two smaller dirty piles of straw. The other mask dangled loose in Baylor's hands. Fresh blood trickled from the sides of his mouth like drops of crimson rain coalescing down a pane of glass.

Baylor's father could be imprisoned in only one other place.

Dear God of Sound, please let me be wrong. He didn't know if he believed in any gods, still, but this . . . this, he would pray for. Hope against.

"Stay here," he said to Baylor.

The young man's eyes panned up to him, his pupils a portrait of pain. His jaw twitched, and he rushed Alesio, shoving him up against the wall, his hands clamped around his throat.

Saida gasped, and Marik shouted something.

Alesio croaked, "Don't hurt him!"

Baylor huffed in front of him, bits of ixor leaking out from clenched teeth, swirling in the air between them, against Alesio's mask. A sheen of old sores on his lips, healed over, shone in the yellow lamplight, contrasted with the new ones that glistened red as viscera. "You. Are. The one." He swallowed, and more ixor puffed out. "The one. Clef said. Would stop me. From finding him."

Alesio's vision blurred. He rasped, "Listen to me, Baylor. I will not stop you. Do you hear me?"

Baylor huffed, and his hands trembled around Alesio's throat. Stars burst in Alesio's eyes.

"Won't . . . stop . . ." he pushed the words out, then released Alesio.

Alesio coughed on his knees, dragging in polluted air. Saida's hands fluttered over him like frightened birds, checking his heart, his bruised neck. His vision blurred back, and Baylor covered his mouth with his hands and banged his head against the door.

"Shut up. Shut up! You're lying!"

Alesio scraped in a breath, shoving down his gag reflex from the fetid air. His throat hurt. "Baylor. All I ask is that you wear a mask while we check the outhouse, alright?"

Baylor stopped hitting his head and swiveled towards Alesio.

Saida threw herself between them, claws out, and growled at the young man in her full foxan form, her back arched, her tail-braid puffed up. The mask didn't fit over her muzzle and spun halfway around her face.

Baylor just stared at Alesio. "Why?"

The truth of his question reached Alesio. He Received it, the sound of it, the damage in it. He wasn't asking why Alesio wanted him to wear a mask. He was asking why Alesio cared when Baylor had just choked him.

Alesio drew in another breath and coughed. "You're not immune against . . . what we might find." His voice sounded muffled through the mask.

Saida stayed between them, but she stopped arching her back and the fur of her tail smoothed back down. She settled back on her haunches and shifted her paws to hands, fixing the mask back over her face.

Baylor Received Alesio's words, and he didn't seem to know how to hold the kindness in them, like someone had given him flowers, and he didn't know he was supposed to smell them.

Alesio pivoted to Marik, giving Baylor privacy to process. "And you. Why did you rush in like that, earlier? I told you to wait outside the house."

The normal reddish-brown skin around Marik's eyes had paled, his freckles a sharp contrast. He stared ahead with glazed, unseeing eyes.

Some people couldn't handle any form of combat or violence. Alesio sighed. "Get back to the Garden, okay? We'll take care of things here."

Marik drifted out of the house. Baylor shambled out of the Lunnite's way, then pulled the mask over his nose and mouth.

"Your mask doesn't fit," Alesio said to Saida. "You should go with Marik."

Her ears drooped, the tips folding over. "I just – to stay with you." The fog of her breath clouded her mask, so he couldn't read her lips well, and she spoke in a whisper.

His throat swelled up, and he almost couldn't speak. He said in a rush, "If it gets too bad, run out, okay?"

She nodded, ears picking up again. They left the house, tottering towards the small outbuilding. In the few minutes of intense fighting inside the house, the sky had purpled on the horizon, and higher up, varied to a dark blue.

Alesio stretched his hand to open the door, then glanced sideways at Baylor. The young man's hands shook.

Alesio released his held breath to say, "Hey, stay with me, okay?"

Baylor's eyes glittered, and his chin wobbled, and then, that horrible, horrible night when Clef had kidnapped him and he hadn't known if his father had died flashed through Alesio's mind. He remembered the rage, the fight building inside him, the way he wanted to rip apart anyone in his way. He wanted to reach out and hug Baylor, envelop him and tell him that it would all be okay.

But he didn't know if he could promise that.

Alesio gestured at the door and stepped aside. Baylor yanked it open.

They all dropped to their knees, gagging.

A man covered in waste sagged below them in the hole. Ropes around his wrists suspended him in the air, connected to a pulley system on the ceiling.

Saida ripped her mask off to throw up, then grimaced and slid it back on. Alesio's eyes watered and he almost gasped and breathed in, but he stopped himself.

Clef's men had dug a hole and left the prisoner inside it. They probably only let him up to eat and drink. Baylor's father wore stained, filthy rags and red, open sores covered his emaciated body. He knelt in the muck, his head bowed.

But he was alive. His breath wheezed.

Baylor shouldered in front of Alesio and heaved on the pulley ropes with a numbness, another variety of glazed eyes than Marik's. The shock of absolute horror.

Alesio grabbed the rope and helped Baylor pull, blinking against the irritation in his eyes from the sharp, acrid urine, and the overwhelming rotten smell of stagnating feces.

He had no words. He had no mercy in his mind. If those guards had appeared in front of him, he would have stabbed them in the heart.

Baylor called to his father as he hauled on the pulley. The ropes creaked. "Say something. Please. – anything."

The tortured man's head lolled as they pulled him upwards by his tied wrists. Alesio released the rope and towed the man out from over the hole.

This close, the fumes engulfed Alesio. He did not smell anything directly, but the odors thrashed at his skin and the air around them like distant wet smacks of fetid, rotting vines. Tears sprang to his eyes and flowed down his cheeks from the irritation, and he crimped his lips shut so it didn't assault his mouth.

"Baylor," he said. "Let go of the rope. We need the slack."

"Dad, please wake –."

What is the purpose of such extreme torture? Baylor did what Clef wanted until just a few hours ago!

Baylor released the rope, and they laid his father on the grass outside the outhouse, the pulley creaking. Alesio stripped his mask off and fit it over the man's face, then he fumbled his knife out and began sawing through the slick, stained knot that tied his wrists together. Baylor pulled out his own knife and hacked at the rope, somewhat unnecessarily, that attached his father to the pulley system.

Alesio let him. Senses knew he needed to hack something.

The ropes parted after a minute or so, Baylor managing to sever the other faster, acting with less care, then returning to his father's side, still murmuring in that hoarse, rasping voice. Alesio cleaned his knife on a patch of grass, then slid it back in its sheathe. He had to keep doing things, or the thoughts would materialize, and they would not be gentle or kind.

He should tie up the unconscious thugs inside the house. But if he did that, he would not just tie them up. He'd kill them.

Besides, they needed to get Baylor's father medical attention. Alesio didn't know how the man had survived down there as long as he had, but he seemed on the verge of death. Every minute could count.

Saida reached in one of her foxan pockets and drew out a small vial. Alesio watched dully as she swiped the container through the air in the outhouse and corked it, almost uncomprehending. The squalid odor around the outhouse decreased enough that he could breathe through the mask without it burning his nose. He wondered if the magic spoke to her privately and shuddered to imagine what their voice might sound like.

She paused and stared at something inside the outhouse, her depth-blue eyes reflecting the starlight and her hand clenching at her side. He shuddered in a breath away from the outhouse, away from

Baylor's father, and marched back over, peering inside the putrid torture chamber.

The last bit of the sunset illuminated a message inked on a semi-clean area: *Did you find him in time, Requiem?*

His mind blanked for a moment.

Clef had done all this to mess with him. Using and grooming a vulnerable young man like Baylor who had a dangerous and unique power. Just like he had done to Alesio. Forcing Baylor to work for him by using his father as a hostage. Just like he had done to Alesio. This though, this was beyond what Clef had ever done. With this, he said, *You will never be free. You are mine. Even when you think I'm gone, I will always pull the strings.*

The last bit of light faded above them. Exhaustion dragged at him like weights.

"Please, Dad. Please. Please. Please."

The litany of Baylor's desperate pleading created a melody line in Alesio's head. A song of terror, of stark, raw fear. He listened to it, the whispered breath and crack in the voice when he said please.

He listened to a mirror of himself, to ten-year-old Alesio pleading with Clef to please not hurt his father, please, he'd do anything, *anything!*

The reflection jarred him, suspending him out of his own body and history. It lifted Alesio out of Clef's machinations, out of that sense of the old strait's leader controlling him like a puppet.

I'm not enough to keep her grounded. She's going to drift away.

Clef's words sounded surreal and grasping now. No longer true. No longer right. Saida had teleported to him and nestled against him like a bird curling in a nest.

After all, Clef could not hear truths. He heard *lies.*

A thought surfaced, something he'd spun in the back of his mind like a coin on a bar top. He'd done so much to keep his own father safe. He used to mull over how to placate Clef in the cage matches, so the strait's leader wouldn't hurt his father. He'd deferred his dream of singing for years, because his father didn't have the capacity to plan for tangible things. Alesio had scraped money from his jobs at St.

Rina's and the Drinks De Capo for the privilege of hostel roofs and stale bread, while his father had tried to stop Alesio from 'ruining his young life.' They'd fought over what safety meant: food and notes and fighting for Clef in the now, or starvation coupled with freedom in the future—which, of course, translated to starvation first and freedom only in death.

He hadn't worried about protecting his father since he and Mona had become a couple. Something about their happy relationship had quieted that compulsion.

But then, it hadn't quieted at all, had it? Alesio had just switched over to protecting Saida. And not just that; he'd switched his position of thought, too: instead of focusing on surviving the tangible now, he'd begun to fear the abstract future, like his father used to. When had that happened? Was it just a natural progression when his life had stabilized the last year, no longer fighting for his worth in the cage matches, no longer fumbling for validation from his singing? But then, he still questioned his own value as he always had, it just manifested now in a different way, in his focus on Saida.

You're not enough.

There it was: the root of the lie he'd told himself his whole life. Clef had listened to it in Alesio's voice and repeated it aloud. All his fears, which were mostly about Saida leaving in various ways—Clef murdering her, her losing her memories, staying young while he aged, her losing interest in him—had all leaked from the same insecurity river, that fear of his own uselessness and incompetence.

He couldn't protect her from Clef. *He* couldn't figure out his own magic. *He* feared going to Flock and fighting hordes of cage fighters. *He* couldn't stop her from losing her memory, *he* would somehow lose access to the magic and grow old, *he* wasn't interesting enough for her to stay with him.

He wasn't enough.

He'd known that Saida did want to be with him from her words, but now, he felt it, too. She'd shifted in her own way, in the past few days. She'd become more certain of their relationship. She'd faced something in herself. He needed to move past his own fears, too. He'd worried so much about her that he hadn't listened to her, had pushed her away with his overprotectiveness, his need to prove his value to her.

He could help her stop the Hunger, now. He didn't have to keep listening to his fear, not when all evidence pointed to it being as false and manipulative as Clef himself.

Alesio left the message in the outhouse where it belonged and picked up Baylor's father.

"Let's get out of here."

25

FESTERING WOUNDS

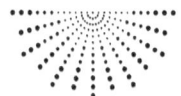

"**S**top!" Hestafon leapt towards Balt.

The Tastian delegate yelped and cowered, holding his hands over his head. Hestafon snatched the key out of his hand.

Clef remained inside; his hands manacled together.

Hestafon glared at Balt. "What in the name of the Sound were you about to do?"

The Tastian scuttled backwards. "He made me! He—he said he would send his cage fighters after me!"

Hestafon stepped forward. "When?"

"W-what?"

"*When* did he threaten you? How long have you planned on betraying us?"

"Don't blame the poor man." Before Hestafon had lost his magic, Clef's smooth voice had sounded like the scent of oil. "He's doing his best to survive, just like the rest of those poors shitting themselves out there."

Clef sat with his back to the bars on the far end of the cage. His cheeks had hollowed more so that his skin over his cheekbones

400

resembled a sheet draped over sharp rocks. The mottled stone-gray patches on his ears created a stark contrast to his bloodshot eyes.

He looked like—well, like how Hestafon used to imagine fox-people. Demented. Dangerous. Those eyes locked onto Hestafon now, and he tried not to shiver.

Balt tried to slink away, but Hestafon crowded him against the bars. He couldn't trust the Tastian delegate any longer. *What would Alesio do?*

He'd have to be quick.

He unlocked the cage. Clef narrowed his eyes and climbed to his feet. "Ah, you see the merits of—"

Hestafon shoved Balt into the cage, which only worked because neither of them understood his plan. The larger man staggered back and obstructed Clef, and Hestafon slammed the cage door shut. He turned the key in the lock and stepped away just as Clef ducked around Balt's bulk and crashed into the cage door.

Clef's eyes rolled, and froth bubbled around the corners of his mouth. Hestafon braced himself for a shout, but the old strait's leader gripped the bars and smiled at him with contrasting calmness.

Balt lumbered to his feet. "How *dare* you! I'm no criminal!"

"You just tried to let one free," Hestafon said. "I can't trust you. Not for now, anyway. We'll see what the rest of the Council says."

Balt sank down into the human version of a puddle, cradling his head.

Hestafon shook his head in disgust. "You're supposed to help your people in a crisis. Yet you came here on purpose and decided to help him."

"Usually, the faults we shame the most in others are what we hate the most in ourselves." Clef smiled at Hestafon, and his thin skin tore in little places around his lips as they stretched. "Don't tell me *you're* here on guard duty?"

Sign of severe ixor withdrawal. The doctor on Taste had mentioned that addicted people's skin around their lips and even their face broke down in withdrawal, as their skin couldn't align with continual slowed time. The symptom looked subtly different from Baylor's bleeding lips, which likely came from Shaping large amounts of ixor so often.

"Stop talking like you know me," Hestafon said.

"Ohhhh, you are guarding me. Strange that you've stooped so low, when you started so high. Usually that happens the other way around."

"That's not what I think. Not anymore."

"Maybe not. Maybe not. Your voice has altered its lies. Hmmm." Clef raised his bound hands and tapped his chin with a finger. "Ah. I hear it now. Aren't I supposed to help the people in this crisis? Can't I do more, as the leader of the largest city in all the worlds? I guard one person while all of Anthem panics, while I abandon Flock." He smiled, and more of his skin tore, creating a slight trickle of blood from his cheeks. "Did I get it right that time?"

Hestafon cleared his throat. He searched the room for sound cloths to block out the manipulative words, but they'd kept the room bare. Had Clef spoke the lies he'd Received from Hestafon's voice, or had he lied about what he'd Received?

Fatigue burned in Hestafon's eyes. How long had he stayed awake? All the world hopping had messed up his sense of time, but he estimated about eighteen hours.

Wait a minute. He stared at the old shadow leader of the straits. *How is his magic working? He shouldn't be able to do that.*

Had the magic returned? He closed his eyes and Received Clef's voice, and it swirled through his ears. He tried Shaping it and smelled traces of oil. He could just sense it, like a shy cat after someone had stepped on its tail, peeking around a corner towards him.

Relief washed over him, and now he didn't much care what Clef said. He still couldn't Shape very well, but he could Receive. That chasm inside himself had begun to fill in again.

Clef's magic, on the other hand—according to the many times Alesio had expounded on the subject in Council meetings— relied on a kind of super-Receiving. The old strait's leader couldn't Shape, but he could Receive better than most anyone.

Could Clef hear his *own* lies? The lies he told himself? He didn't seem like the type open to changing himself or trying to become a better person. But then again, the people around Hestafon might have said the same thing about him just a few months ago.

Hestafon slid to the ground. The sound of his cotton shirt sliding against the stone wall wafted faint traces of dried sweat, and his hair had loosened from its ponytail. He tied it back up.

The night had waned on, and now, after all the chaos and maneuvering through the city, he just wanted to close his eyes. But he had promised Alesio, and he would do his best.

His eyes drooped.

He forced himself to rise and pace, slapping his cheeks to keep awake. Both Clef and Balt dozed. Or at least, they pretended to.

After maybe two hours of this, when Hestafon had had to slap himself three times in a row to stop his eyes from closing, voices drifted from outside the cellar.

Maybe it's Naya. Or Muey, ready to take a guard shift. He yawned and listened at the door.

"In here! He's in here!" The doorknob rattled.

Hestafon didn't recognize that voice. He tensed, adrenaline snapping him awake, and brought out one of the bells in his battered case. The cellar had no windows.

Hestafon lowered his voice as deep as he could. "Leave at once!"

Silence.

His heart pounded. He didn't have the instincts or reactions of a fighter. *Alesio! Why did you trust me with this?*

Someone kicked the door open. Three young men rushed in, armed with knives. Sound-scars ridged their shoulders and necks.

His magic hadn't refilled all the way, but he could Shape again; he could sense it like a limb that had begun to regrow itself.

He stepped back and rang the bell hard, hoping the same thing would happen as before, calling for a brash magic in the manner that he rang it. He Received the sound and sure enough, it wanted to change its form, but not its timbre, not its loudness. He Shaped it into the smell of a just-cut onion, and the intruders cringed and scrubbed at their eyes.

He ran at one with his hands out in front of him, shoving one of them into the other room, and they stumbled backwards.

"Hey!" The one he'd pushed narrowed his eyes at him. "It's Hestafon!"

"Who?"

"The one in charge of Anthem, bugrat!"

Sounddamn it.

"Get him!"

Another one, stockier than the others and wearing the whisper of a mustache, grasped Hestafon, blinking tears from his eyes from the onion scent.

The one who had recognized him grabbed his bell case. "Ooh, what's in this fancy box?" The young man yanked it open and spilled the bells across the floor.

Hestafon had used the little magic that had refilled inside him, or he could have Shaped the ringing. If he tried to use more, he'd just drain himself, and he never, ever wanted that nonexistence in himself, ever again.

Hestafon tried to yank out of the stocky one's grasp, but he and the third person stepped with him. Hestafon ducked, but they both anticipated his movement and grabbed his arms, pulling them behind him.

"We got us a delegate! Look at this, Almid!"

Almid, the one who had upended the bell case, glared at the others. "You beat a freaking piper. I'm so proud."

"Aw, shut up, Almid," the third one said in a raspy voice. He had a Sound scar across his neck like someone had tried to strangle him. He looked sixteen at most.

"You shut up. What about what we came here for?"

Hestafon grimaced. Alesio had warned him about cage fighters that would try to free Clef. These people seemed a bit juvenile to have fighting experience, but Clef had recruited Baylor, so perhaps he targeted the young to train them early.

"Don't open the cage," Hestafon said. "Clef works with the Hunger!"

"You think we'd let him *out?*" Almid snorted, then rubbed his eyes again.

From his place sitting on the far end of the cage, Clef's eyes glittered bloodred in the flickering lamp light. Balt had sputtered awake near the front of the cage, and he scrambled backwards now, bumping into Clef, who cursed at him.

"The big one's in the way." The third one with the disturbing Sound scar released Hestafon, drew out a knife, and flung it at Clef through the bars. It clattered to the ground, almost hitting Balt instead, who screamed. Almid laughed and aimed his knife through the bars.

"Stop!" Hestafon lurched, trying to upset their aim. The stocky youth holding him cursed and slammed his fist down on Hestafon's head.

A bright light flashed in his mind's eye. He slumped, and the boy dropped him on the ground.

Why are they trying to kill him? I thought they worked for him.

"Hey! You aren't so high and mighty, now, are you?"

Hestafon couldn't tell if they spoke to him or Clef. Bitterness and fear laced their voices, edged with old pain.

This hurt. This anger. This draught of a wound left to fester. As Anthem's leader, to remedy these emotions he needed to understand their cause, how they had come to be.

A whistle of air. Another clatter on the ground. Hestafon's eyes fluttered, his vision blurry. If they killed Clef here, he would let Alesio down.

"Aww. I'm out of knives," the one with the neck scar said.

"That's what you get for throwing them around like that," Almid said. "You can't just summon more Sound knives, idiot."

"They're a lot harder to aim than Sound knives," the sturdy one said, as if defending Neck Scar.

"How did you find this place?" Hestafon asked, trying to distract them. *Good thing they can't sense their magic must have refilled at least a little.* They spoke with coherence instead of screaming glassy eyed at the sky.

Almid puffed out his chest. "We've known about this special cage for a while now. Pretty easy to figure out who it was for when search parties ask us every week if we've seen the old shadow leader."

"Yeah," Neck Scar said. "And we figured we'd come check it while everyone's screaming their heads off."

"Shut your shrikehole, Ponz," Almid said. "Don't just tell him everything. He's the Delegate and all."

"You said more than I did!"

"I did not."

The stockier boy handed something that glinted to Ponz. "Here. I have one left, you can try with mine."

"You're fighting the wrong man," Clef said. "The one you have on that side of the cage is the one with all the power."

"Shut up! You made my uncle fight in a cage match!"

Clef's voice seemed to oil the air in the room. "I've just done my best to survive, same as you. Look at him. He's the one in charge. He's the one who's supposed to make things better."

The silence stretched.

"He's got a point," Almid said at last.

Hestafon groaned. "Don't listen to him—"

"What if," Clef said, louder, drowning out Hestafon's weak voice, "You made *him* fight a cage match? Wouldn't that give you a sense of justice served? I've lived my life in the dirt and the mud, same as you. But him? He lives on the golden side of life. Eats fresh fruit. Wears silk pajamas to bed. Has comfortable shoes without holes in them. And yet, he's the one who keeps all those things for himself. Wouldn't it be grand to shove him in the dirt for once?"

Hestafon's head throbbed. Spots flickered across his vision. He could almost smell the youths wheeling on him like hounds scenting a hotrat.

And for some reason, he couldn't think of a single damn reason why they shouldn't listen to Clef.

"Yeah," Almid said. "That's a real interesting idea."

They dragged him through the door.

The sounds of chaos increased. People rushed by. He smelled blood without having to Shape it from a sound.

How long can a city panic? How long can people scream? They must collapse from physical exhaustion soon.

Hestafon fought his eyes closing into unconsciousness as the sights spun. Had that been the back alley where Naya had shown him how to reach the cellar?

He had to stay awake. He had to protect Clef. He had to . . . escape.

His eyes drifted shut without his consent, imprudent things. Blurred sounds merged into blurred odors. Cuffs on the side of his head blurred subsequent thoughts.

With the last of his strength, he gathered the little bit of magic that had trickled back to him in the last few minutes. He Received the screams around him. They wanted to stay caustic, and sharp. He Shaped them into the smell of wasabi, a pungent, sharp smell, and sent them into the noses of those holding him. They released him at once, covering their mouths and nose, coughing.

He rolled into the alley that he'd glimpsed. Before his assailants could force themselves back through the flow of the crowd and find him again, he stumbled over to the tunnel cover and all but threw himself into the darkness, and the darkness Received him and Shaped him into unconsciousness.

SAIDA LOPED AHEAD of Alesio as a foxan towards the Garden. Alesio cradled Baylor's father in his arms behind her. She'd given him her cracked mask to help with the smell at least a little.

She slipped Fecal Air into her fur pocket. They'd screamed for trimming: "I want to diffuse into an open space! I want to spread out and break all apart! I should not stay so dense; I am meant to merge with other Air! I did not wish to hurt this living man!"

Clef's message to Alesio had managed to rattle her, too. She couldn't imagine how much it had terrified him.

But something had shifted in Alesio in the past few hours. He hadn't crumpled into a ball of himself or even glared for several minutes at the message, as she'd assumed he would. Shock and horror had sailed across his face but hadn't moored at the dock. He'd straightened with a sense of obstinate determination and carried the young man's father out of there. And earlier, he'd also had that idea of using Clef's unique Receiving ability to try and figure out the Hunger's weakness.

Pride washed through her. When fear held her in its talons, she tended to fold herself smaller or run away. It took a lot of courage to grow larger instead, and bark back at that fear.

Marik waited for them at the entrance to the Garden, his ears drooping.

"I'm so sorry," he said to Saida. "I should've stayed to help you—" He blanched at the sight and smell of Baylor's father.

"Are you here to play again?" The Garden said. "Can you do it backwards? Can . . . you . . .?"

The mixture of Spatial and Scent magic, which manifested to Saida as pockets of haze she could locate with her nose, floated upwards. That strange yet familiar sensation came over her again, the excitement when gazing down into a vast forest from on top of a mountain, or up into a clear night sky on the night of a full moon. It had a startling similarity to the restless, aching anticipation she had before kissing Alesio, and that same shiver of happiness whenever she called up her own portals . . .

The Garden's voice faltered. Had Saida lost her connection to Magic Ear again?

But then it continued: "I can't portal anymore."

"What?" Saida said.

"*I can't portal anymore!*" The pockets of haze shot upwards, tearing off from the Garden like paper ripping out of a book.

"QUIT SCURRYING AROUND," the huge voice from the sky rumbled, and one of the five tendrils stretched closer, blocking out the stars, the other planets, the moon, everything. "HOLD STILL TILL I'M READY FOR YOU!"

The Hunger had woken from their food-induced nap.

That didn't take long. Saida flattened her ears against her head.

The tendril loomed over them, and opened that massive, ridged throat, and bared those massive fangs. They pulled magic for just a moment but didn't pull the rest of the Garden up. They closed their giant snake mouth.

"MMMM. NOTHING LIKE SPATIAL MAGIC."

Just like when the Hunger had ripped out the Epitaph trees, this reminded Saida of when Watthe had eaten many of her transplants the year before. Back then, though, the box that the Hunger had spoken through hadn't wanted him to.

"I thought doing that would corrupt you!" she shouted upward. "If you don't stop eating mixed magic, you'll just end up like your servant!"

A horrible laugh from above, though the Hunger didn't deign to respond with words, of course.

The tendril snaked back upwards, retreating. The spots inside of the Hunger swelled up to twice their size, occupying more space inside of the entity like swollen leeches.

Baylor hovered by his father's head, collecting shattered words like broken pottery and trying to arrange them into a sentence.

Alesio clenched his jaw. "Saida, the Portal Station . . ."

She and Alesio shared a look, then they both stepped into the Garden.

Nothing happened. No maze magic teleported them to a different area in the strip of plant and flower life.

"Marik," Saida said. "Go on ahead and warn the villagers what to expect. Tell them to bring out water and cloths." She hesitated. "You can just walk through the Garden. It's . . . disconnected from its magic."

The Lunnite's eyes widened. He tottered on ahead as she had asked, gaining speed as he recovered from the overwhelming volume of the Hunger's voice.

"Disconnected," the Garden whimpered, the voice faint. *"What is happening to me?"*

"The Hunger drained your magic," Alesio said. "But you're still here. You're still talking. It didn't consume you all the way."

"Will my magic come back?"

"I hope so," Saida said. She sidled against Alesio, connecting her body to his to reassure him with her warmth, with her words, like he always did for her. "For all of us."

They shuffled together at a slow pace to keep Baylor's father stable, Baylor staying near his father's head.

Saida frowned, knowing how the villagers would react to something like this. But they couldn't clean or attend the man's injuries without access to water, lots of bandages, and other supplies they didn't have.

Alesio laid the man down on a stretch of crushed grass beside a trampled field. Baylor ripped grass out of the ground, trying to wipe some of the filth off his father. "Wake up," he kept saying. "Dad, please, please . . ."

Lights bobbed towards them. Villagers holding lanterns. Marik appeared, then Tener, along with Verrity, Ishira, and Raos, who had guided them through the Garden. Beside them, five villagers toted a wooden stretcher, a bag full of nonflowers, soap, and washcloths.

Everyone stopped and covered their mouths. The Scentians probably couldn't smell him as well as normal, but for many of them, their magic had at least somewhat refilled. The squalid odor of the fecal matter clung to Saida's tongue like an aftertaste of the Scent magic. Did Taste and Scent have stronger transplants linking their two worlds, or were their magics so similar that they echoed each other like two people shouting across a chasm?

"They tortured him in a hole of waste," Saida said. "I know it's offensive for you all, but—"

"You don't have to ask," Verrity said, through bouts of gagging. "What this man endured is the worst offense. We will help him."

She snapped her fingers, and the Scentians wrapped their hands and arms in cloth, then paused. Alesio picked up the hint and the man, then laid him down again on the stretcher.

"What happened to the otherworlders?" Verrity asked.

"They're unconscious," Alesio said. "Someone should tie them up. The entire area smells horrible, though." He wiped his hands on a proffered cloth. Filth caked his whole front from carrying Baylor's father. He pulled off his cracked mask to give it to the delegate. Part of the mask caught on the dark locks of hair curling around his ears, and he winced, trying to detangle it. Saida stepped forward and did it for him, drawing his head down to her level. Alesio continued, "Anyone who goes in there will need masks as protection, especially as their magic refills."

"Interesting contraption. I'd heard Tastians had these." Verrity accepted the mask with a cloth covered hand, wiping it down several times. "Thank you for stopping those monsters. I am just ashamed it happened right under my nose."

Ishira looked at her, then away.

Saida pulled off her mask and handed it over as well, and after some coaxing, Baylor did the same. Verrity delegated two of the Scentians, along with Marik, who volunteered, to brave the horrifying stench-house and tie up Clef's followers before they could wake up. The three of them cleaned the masks with several cloths, then donned the facial protection and left.

"We will wash this poor man in the stream," Verrity said.

Verrity, Ishira, Raos, and another villager gripped the handles and carried him to a gurgling brook a half mile south from Tremain. The rest of them—six more villagers who had gathered, Saida, and Alesio —trailed after, while Baylor stayed at the front of the procession, close to his father's head.

Verrity and the other three lowered the injured man into a shallow part of the stream, then the rest of the Scentians swarmed over the filthy, unconscious human, wetting the cloths, rubbing them with the bars of soap, and sloughing the worst of the filth off with gentle motions.

Alesio and Saida immersed themselves, too, cleaning the slime and smells off with soap and determination. Alesio stripped off his filthy shirt, laying it on the bank. Saida did so as well with her human clothing, which she'd worn way too long anyway. Underwater, she grew all her foxan fur back over her human body. Before Saida could appreciate Alesio's shirtlessness, someone handed him a clean cotton one.

One of the Scentians gathered the garments in a basket, along with the clothing they peeled off Baylor's father, and covered the basket with a lid. Saida wondered what they'd do with the offending clothing. Bury it, probably.

Baylor bathed his father with a mutilated expression of hope, a mangled and distorted relief that brought lumps of tears to Saida's throat.

"Verrity." Saida's eyes dragged as the adrenaline of the last crisis faded. Her foxan form tugged on her bones, tapping on her to hide in a safe place, to curl up in a ball, to sleep somewhere for a very long time. She conceded her legs and her hands, struggling to keep her human face on around the Scentian villagers. "I assume you heard the Hunger a little while ago. We don't know if they spoke to everyone."

"We'd have to be deaf not to." Verrity wrung out her cloth further downstream. "No offense."

Alesio waved his hand. "None taken. It's helpful in some situations. As you saw."

"Well," Saida said, "We sensed that the Portal Station may have stopped working. Do you know if this is true?"

Almost as if she had summoned them with her words, a Soundian volunteer, recognizable by the cloth tied around his arm and the faint mottling of gray on his ears, sprinted along the path that led to the stream.

"Delegate!" He was a middle-aged man with sound-scars on his arms. An ex-cage fighter, perhaps. Alesio's hand, which she realized she held, tensed in hers, and he shifted his feet for a wider, lower stance. "Both arrival and departure portals have shut down at the Station."

"Sounddamn it," Alesio muttered. His hand relaxed in hers even as he lifted his other to rub at his eyes, stopped himself with a frown, and scrubbed at a bit of filth under his nails.

Ah, that's right. They needed to reach Anthem to pick up Clef, then teleport him to either the small Hunger in the Primal Plane or one of the Goddess Heads. But without the Portal Station, they'd have to wait till her portals recharged.

How long would the Hunger's satiety last before they woke again and drained more magic? They had already snapped up the Epitaph and drained the humans' Shape magic in all the worlds. Then they had woken for a late-night snack and drained the Garden's portal magic and that of the Portal Stations.

How long had the entity slept from the first feeding to the second? Seven hours? Six? Would they consume the humans, bones and all, before they moved on to foxans? Or would they suck up trees, and dirt, and rocks, the frame and substance of the worlds before then?

Those spots like islands had grown inside of the Hunger after they had fed. She bet that they absorbed the magic over time, and waited to digest all of it, storing it perhaps like a spider stored bellbugs in its web.

Saida's eyes burned, needing to close. The frigid water of the brook had chilled her at first, jolting her awake, but now, even the cold temperature had begun to lose its potency. She and Marik had uncovered the Hunger's secret and had triggered them to eat the Epitaph tree in the evening, their time. Then had come the panicked crowds, trying to rescue people on Vision, the portal to Scent, and finally, rescuing Baylor's father. Time, for her, had marched into the morning of the next day.

And what about Alesio? He'd had a full day of hauling Clef to the cellar before everything else that had happened. He'd remained in his fighting stance the past few minutes—not, she suspected, because he expected to fight, but because he would sway on his feet from fatigue without the lower, half-crouching posture.

Verrity raised her eyebrows. "Thank you, Volunteer. Tell those at the Station to rotate a two-person watch in case the portals start working again. Otherwise, tell the rest to return and rest." The volunteer nodded and jogged back towards the Portal Station.

Meanwhile, Ishira had knelt beside Baylor and placed a bar of soap in his hands. Her braided hair had fallen from its crown, and part of the braid had unraveled at the ends. He tried to pull away from her, jerking his head. Ishira pointed at his hands. "It is not possible or safe to clean with dirty hands."

Baylor stared at her a moment before he lowered his hands, and then his arms and legs, in the water, scouring himself with the soap.

"How did you know about the Portal Station?" Verrity asked Alesio and Saida.

"The Garden," Saida said. "The Hunger consumed their magic as we came back through." She hesitated. "They're a Spatial magic mixed with Scent, so we figured if they couldn't teleport, then the Portal Station might have stopped working, too."

The Hunger had mentioned Spatial magic. Maybe that was what the Hunger called Primal magic?

"I don't envy Hestafon's position as delegate right now," Verrity said. Saida didn't comprehend most of her words, her brain fuzzing out. "If Anthem citizens heard what we did, it will drive them into more of a frenzy." The Scentian delegate shook her head. "At least we're forced to relax here for now."

At the word, 'relax,' exhaustion struck Saida like a bell striking its clapper. She swayed on her hind legs, shrinking down to all fours, a sharp ache in her temples, her eyes burning like scorching coals in her head.

Her foxan side took the reins of her body gently, folding her humanness like a shirt on a shelf for when she had the mental capacity to think again.

Verrity gasped a bit, the sound coming from what seemed a distance.

"For now." Alesio lowered his voice. He scratched between Saida's ears, and she leaned into the touch. "I wish we could help calm the people on the other worlds, too, but I'm worried. If . . . the Hunger wakes up again as fast as they did from the first draining, we have maybe six hours before . . ."

"Before it feeds again," Verrity said.

"But we . . . *have* to sleep." He stopped scratching Saida's ears. "Even for just a few hours. If either of us tried to do anything right now, we'd just . . ." he trailed off. A thud sounded next to her. "Sounddamn it."

"Trip on flat ground?" Verrity said.

Why are they still talking? Saida rolled over and nipped at Alesio's fresh, borrowed shirt with her teeth.

He giggled at her impatience, struggling to speak in his drowsy hysteria. "Do . . . do you know how long before you can teleport?"

The words hardly made sense to her. She summoned the strength to respond, his ridiculous chortles infecting her so that she started to laugh, too. "They won't recharge . . . for another hour or so."

Alesio cocked his head. *"They?"*

"I can teleport twice a day now . . . unless it was a one-time thing."

"Well, that makes things a little easier, for once. Just once!" He raised his hands as he laid on the ground and sang out of key, and for that matter, without a lock. "There once was a lady, who did enjoy her pickles—"

Saida broke in, singing much worse and higher, almost a howl. "But she fairly loved peaches the most!"

"I'm going to get you both a place to sleep," Verrity said.

They continued the song together, sounding like feral dogs, rolling and crying in their laughter in the grass. "The pickle did try—" a break here for several seconds. "—her palate to please, but she only ever—" another span of seconds where they cackled and wiped at their eyes. "—licked her peaches clean!"

26

IT MIGHT NOT LAST

Tshira had insisted on hosting them, ushering them into a side room in her house to rest in, her head hanging and her hands clasped in front of her. She hadn't said anything beyond, "Please rest well."

Almost before her head hit the pillow, Saida had already plummeted into the portal of slumber.

At some point, her teleportation returned to her with a ping, her portals scuttling through the cracks of the world around her like mice pitter-pattering in the walls of a house. She blinked awake for a moment, but Alesio's arms surrounded her like a nest she'd curled into, and sleep dragged her under again, barricading her from reality, a fatigue so strong it held a faint echo of death.

The smell of food woke her the second time. Someone had placed a small, lit lantern on a table next to the bed, along with plates of food and clay mugs of clear water. Her mouth had dried out and her stomach rumbled.

She dragged herself from Alesio's warmth and reached for the mug, shifting at the last moment to grab it with a human hand instead of a paw with claws. She quaffed the whole thing without pausing. The fuzz in her mind cleared somewhat, though the headache and fatigue persisted. She dug into the food with gusto, shoveling in purple purpatoes slathered in a kind of gravy, but had to slow down to balance it all on her lap in the bed.

Next to her, Alesio groaned, rubbing at his eyes. His black, curly hair flipped upwards in the back from sleeping on it, and his beard had escaped its tidy pen, roaming out onto his cheeks. "Please let that be food."

"Sure tastes like it." She handed him a mug of water from the table and the other plate. He gulped it all down even faster than she had.

"How long did we sleep?"

They had collapsed around nine in the evening in Tremain, and Verrity had promised to wake them after five hours had passed. "Less than five hours, I guess."

"The ground and the sky and the trees all still there?" His voice had a raspy quality, and it made her shivery on the inside. In a good way.

She squinted out the window. "Well. That tree is still outside, unless I'm imagining it."

"You don't imagine things." He clasped her hands. He seemed to have regained his Receiving all the way, from how he hadn't needed to read her lips while she'd faced the window. "Saida, I want to apologize again. I knew how much you cherished your magic, and that they spoke to you, but I didn't . . . understand. Not until the voices spoke to me, too."

"Now you're as insane as me." She raised her eyebrows. "Sure you wanna join the group? We're very particular. Well, I am. The group is me."

"I very much want to join the group." He propped the pillows to support his back and crossed his legs in front of him. She scooted over and nestled in a circle as a foxan, laying on his legs. He scratched behind her ears like she liked, and she *murred* with simple pleasure.

She could sense his silvery voice again, the natural way a tiny amount of Sound magic accompanied his voice without him Shaping it, like a sprinkle of sugar on a pastry.

"There's something else I've wanted to tell you," he said. "I think . . . I've always felt like I've needed to protect people. To help people, if

417

they're in trouble. I think it was because of how Clef used my dad to force me to do things. But Mona's with my dad now, and she cares for him. So, I—I changed it to you."

Saida gazed up at him, tilting her ears forward at the catch in his voice.

"But . . . I didn't do it for you. I wanted you to feel safe with me . . . so you would stay. So you wouldn't leave me." He ducked his head. "But yesterday, when we found Baylor's father in that cesspit, I realized something. You teleported to me and said I was your favorite place. I worried so much about you that I didn't listen to you. You told me the magic would slow everyone's age, and I didn't believe you. I knew you didn't want to move in with me when I asked. I could tell, but that just made me more afraid. And so, I pushed you, and I'm sorry."

She trembled. She wanted to tell him. But now, she couldn't. Not after what he'd just said.

His greatest fear was that she would leave? How could she explain it was hers, as well? It would terrify him.

She'd run to him yet again, despite trying to distance herself, despite everything she'd tried to hold back. It hadn't mattered. Her body, her Spatial magic, had reached out to him in that moment.

"I do feel safe with you," she told him. "I do want to stay."

She'd wanted to tell him that for a long time.

"Is it real if it might not last?" Her Fear whispered to her.

"Saida?" The muscles tensed in his encircling arms.

Her love for him was real *now*. It had been real for the past year. What if she remained the same in the future, and still loved and cared for Alesio? Or what if she did change, but just that she fell more in love? What if they had a lasting relationship for however long they lived? She didn't know anything for sure, except that she loved him now, and she wanted to show him that. She wanted to strengthen their bond; not let it fade.

Receive. Shape. Communication. The symbols flashed through her mind. She wanted to communicate what she'd decided, but how could she explain something like that without telling him about her reservations in the first place?

"You should tell him," Difficult Truth said. "Communicate, Saida."

I can't tell him that! I'll just overcome the Fear and we'll be happy because I'm staying!

"Saida, you're shaking! Are you—"

She shifted, wrapping human legs around him and pressing her lips to his. He huffed in surprise and kissed her back, hesitantly, then just as passionately. She ran her hands along his arms and the muscles flexed under her touch. "Starlight," he breathed against her, then speared her mouth with his tongue, and her eyes rolled back in her head, her body felt like it liquefied on top of his. He hovered his hands by her sides, and she shivered, and retracted all her foxan fur clothing from her sides and back, guiding his hand with hers to brush her bare skin. His breathing gained heft, and she smiled. Kissing her was the only time he lost control of his breath.

She paused in the haze of pleasure. "Oh. Oh, we don't have time for this. We should go—"

He gripped her closer. "I think we're allowed a few sounddamned minutes."

She sputtered a laugh and splayed her hands over his stocky, muscled torso. He stroked her sides up and down with the backs of his knuckles. She held herself up on her palms and brushed herself over him, rolling his shirt up so she touched his skin as she did.

He groaned, his dark-brown eyes darkening further. "What are you doing to me?" He shucked his shirt off and embraced her, pulling her even closer, so their heartbeat frenzied as one. "Are you sure you can't use Touch magic, Miss Foxan?"

Her breath shallowed into panting. She tried to invent some witty quip, but her thoughts had dissolved, and her core had heated to a roaring flame. Silver threads from the magic of his voice, unShaped yet clinging to his breath and his words, looped around them like constellations, parts of them coalescing into brighter points when the magic touched their skin.

And he called *her* Starlight.

She pressed herself against him and retracted all her fur at once, so they pressed against each other skin to skin, and thrust her hands into his hair as she kissed him. He growled and his hands stroked down her sides, then down further over her hips and under her bottom, teasing at the edge. She scooted back so his hands filled with her backside, and it was his turn for his eyes to roll to the back of his head. "Oh, by the God of Sound—"

"You like this, then?"

"*Like* this?" He sat up and tugged her to straddle him. She rode against his hardness. "I've dreamed of this."

She blushed. "I have, too. Thought about it a lot."

He stared at her breasts. "By the Sound, you're beautiful." He paused. "Though it's a little unfair that you can undress just by thinking about it. Not that I'm complaining."

"Oh no," she said. "Guess you'll have to stay this way. Dressed."

She rubbed her body over his, back and forth, inching her chest closer to him each time. When he bent towards her, she arched away and grinned.

He stroked where her inner thighs met. "You think you're playing with me. And you're right. Please keep moving like that. Just like that. I don't care if the world's ending, please don't stop—"

He bent up and licked around her nipple. Sweet fire shuddered through her, and she trembled, staying close this time. He trailed his tongue down her breast, then over to the other side. She bucked on his lap, and his fingers kept stroking closer to that heat at her core. He sucked the nipple all the way in, and she yelped with the intensity. It felt like they were on Touch. He skimmed one finger along her heated folds, and her breath shortened with anticipation.

"You think I need to be undressed to do this?" He dipped the finger down, lifting the folds, and found something she didn't know existed. A bright spot of color flashed through her eyes. She almost screamed but muffled it.

"Alesio!"

"Told you."

He trailed his finger around the spot and stars burst in her eyes again. She arched her back, and his eyes snagged on her breasts. "Sound, you're beautiful."

"Al-Alesio! What is—that—"

He grazed the center of the nub, and then color and light suffused her. She might have shifted into a rainbow. Her mouth had dried out again because she'd panted for so long. But she didn't care. She writhed and gasped, and he laved her breast all around, then brushed the nipple and the nub at the same time and kept his hand over them, rubbing back and forth, and the colors and the light and the *feeling* shuddered all at once, and she cried out.

Everything faded again, and her vision returned.

He grinned. "I was the one playing with you, after all."

Aftershocks of pleasure rocked her. He pressed soft kisses to her open mouth. She trembled against him.

"Thank you for trusting me," he said. "To do that."

His hardness still poked her in the thigh through his pants, and she shimmied them off, one leg at a time. They giggled at the awkwardness until they pressed together again, and he paused, his voice turning serious. "Are you sure? With Carn, it must've—"

She pressed her fingers to his lips. "I want you to listen very closely. And don't move."

"Okay. Yes."

"You." She angled her hips over his. "Don't." She trailed his cock with one finger. He sucked in an involuntary breath. "Need." She hovered closer over him, then lowered herself an inch onto his shaft, and tensed, his arms straining with effort not to move.

"To worry." She lowered herself another inch, and her eyes fluttered with pleasure at the rubbing sensation against her inner walls. Sex had never delighted her before, not like this, or even close.

"Saida—!"

"Because I." She slid another inch of him inside her, and the veins in his neck ridged. Senses, she hadn't done anything like this before. Being the one in control felt *good,* almost as good as how his shaft pulsed like that. She had worried a little. His throat bobbed as he swallowed.

"Have never felt." She pushed him all the way in, and they gasped together at the slick friction, rocking back on the bed.

"So." She pulled herself back, almost to his tip, and he groaned, his hands clenching the sheets.

"Damn." She held herself there a moment, trembling with want herself.

"Saida!"

"*Good!*" She slid him all the way in, all at once, and he roared, his eyes rolling back to the ceiling. He grasped her bottom and held her to him, shuddering.

"Does that mean I can move now?" He said in her ear, his breath hot.

"Yes—"

He drew himself back and forth, back and forth, and the friction banked her like a fire, slow at first, then pumping faster and faster until her insides quivered for release. Then she clenched around him as that pleasure blinded her again, and he shouted, then rolled out of her right and into the sheets before his climax hit, holding her against him.

He flopped back on his back, shuddering with the aftershocks. "I think. I'm seeing stars."

She sagged on top of him, spent, her body flooding with languorous delight. "I want to do that. Every. Day."

"I would definitely be okay with that." He pulled her against him, hugging her and wrapping his legs around her. She snuggled into him, a profound and dreamy satisfaction blanketing her whole body.

"You did it," Fear said. "Even though—"

No. She would not let the negative voice ruin this moment. She didn't believe it any longer. She drove it out of her mind.

Alesio held her, humming into her hair, singing little phrases of the melody to the song he'd started for them. "I used to dream of brighter places, of playing for the crowds . . ."

Anthem was probably still in chaos, and the Cloves. And she just wanted to stay right here.

"We should go," Saida said.

"Nooooo," Alesio said.

She swung her legs off the bed. The movement chilled her, and she shifted to foxan to regrow her foxan fur all at once, licking herself for a few moments at the smelliest parts.

Behind her, Alesio rolled out of bed with a pouting expression and slithered to the floor. "I don't have any shirts."

Her muzzle twitched, pausing mid-lick. "You have that one right there."

"The one I just peeled off my sweaty body?"

She grinned at him. "You sure you're not a Scentian?"

He puffed up at her, ruffling her ears. "Not all of us can lick ourselves clean."

She barked a foxan laugh. "I'm kidding. It's Scent, of *course* someone left a washbasin, some nonflowers, and two sets of clean clothing folded on the other side of the dresser."

He rose, and, smirking at her, stalked stark naked past her to the washbasin.

She flushed. He used the provided soaps and clean cloths to wash himself, using unfair, distracting methods.

"Shut up," she said.

"I didn't say anything."

She shifted back to human, receding her fur all the way, and sauntered over to him. He paused in his movements, his jaw slackening. She bent and grabbed a handful of pale pink nonflowers from the basket next to the washbasin and rubbed herself with them.

"Shut up," he said.

"I didn't say anything."

"If you're trying to cloak our pheromones, that is *decidedly* counterproductive."

"You started it."

"I'm ready to finish it, too."

She chortled, but regretfully clothed herself with her foxan furs again, growing her standard shirt and shorts. Then she pulled on the other set of human clothes to ward off the winter cold in Anthem. He followed suit, muttering things about "later" and "just you wait."

Alesio scrubbed scooped a handful of pale pink nonflowers out of the bowl and rubbed them over his armpits. After some deliberation, she stuffed some in her fur pockets to cloak her emanating pheromones. The smells of their attraction dissipated.

Saida bit her lip, then she sprinkled the rest of the nonflowers on the bed. Ishira would appreciate that, especially if her Receiving had returned like Alesio's.

She opened the door. It faced out into a hallway with a stone floor. They strode down it and entered a room with some wooden chairs arranged around a table. Saida had left the trimming that had named themself Fecal Air there, instead of keeping them on her person. They didn't smell outside the vial, of course, but she still hadn't wanted to bring them into bed with her. She scooped them up and tucked them in one of her pockets.

"Hello! I would like to be released in an open area!" They said out loud, not just to her. "I don't want all my parts together like this!"

"I know, I know," Saida said. "I promise, I'll transplant you."

"I was stuck in there for so looooooong. Can I go today?"

"We just have a few other things we have to do first," Alesio said. "Shouldn't take long. Just some Planar-level housekeeping. Nothing big."

"Oh, good!" Fecal Air settled down in her pocket.

Saida fought down a laugh and bumped Alesio's side with her shoulder. They skulked outside in the dark. Silence laid over everything like a layer of dense, dark cake, and most had returned to their houses to sleep.

"Do you suppose anyone's up?" Saida asked. "We should let someone know we're leaving."

"Maybe at the Portal Station."

They followed the clean dirt street to the outside of Tremain, then hurried past the fields towards the Portal Station. Soft yellow lantern light bobbed there, illuminating Verrity and Ishira and a small crew of volunteer Soundians, working on shoring up the makeshift barriers around Scent's Portal Station. Marik worked along with them, and Saida cringed. Would the Lunnite keep hanging around her on the chance that she changed her mind? His words to her the other night —just twelve hours ago? — echoed in her mind: *I'm just saying, if you wanted to love more than one person, I would be here.*

She squeezed Alesio's hand. She refused to let fear of herself direct her actions. Alesio squeezed her hand back.

Verrity hurried over. Both she and Ishira had fresh, clean dresses on. Verrity wore a worn blue-gray dress that pulled at her wide shoulders and under her arms. The two Scentians' nostrils flared as they approached, probably sensing the pheromones on her and Alesio. Once that might have embarrassed Saida, but she didn't care at this point.

"Right on time," Verrity said. "I was just about to send someone to wake you."

Now that Saida had had a few hours of sleep, she noticed that the Scentian delegate had a stronger, more certain air about her.

"Do you know where Baylor is?" Alesio asked her. "And how did his father do overnight?"

Right. Baylor's father. She could still smell that horrifying stench, and those wounds . . . if he had died, his son could still snap and lose control.

"The young man hasn't left his father's side," Verrity said. "His father sleeps and seems to be doing better."

"Then he's better than how we found him," Alesio said. "I'm glad to hear it."

Marik joined them, and Saida bit her lip. They could use his help in securing Clef, but she didn't want to worry Alesio with his presence. She opened her mouth to tell the Lunnite to stay in Tremain.

"Saida explained that you can use Touch magic," Alesio told Marik. "It'd be helpful if you came with us."

Marik's eyebrows raised. He bounced a look back and forth from between them. Saida kept her face neutral to convey her neutrality.

". . . of course," Marik said.

"Good." Alesio bowed his head to Verrity. "Thank you for your hospitality. We need to leave now."

"Do we need to worry about Clef sending people here?" Verrity asked. "I mean . . . when the portals open back up?"

"We're heading out to find about the Hunger's weaknesses," Alesio said. "I plan to also find Clef's force of cage fighters." He bowed his head. "We will do better at protecting your village in the future. I've tried to protect many people, but in all the wrong ways. I was blind to how Clef used you. I am sorry for that."

Ishira cleared her throat. "It is difficult to see something hidden from you."

"And it's hard to combat fear when you feel powerless," Alesio said. "Clef manipulated me for a long time."

Tears shimmered in Ishira's eyes. She turned to the Scentian delegate. "Mother Verrity, I wanted to tell you many times. But I didn't know—I kept imagining those otherworlders coming here and . . ."

Verrity took a deep breath. "No one knows what's best all the time. You were just trying to protect the village." She touched the other woman's shoulder, then turned to Saida. "I forgot to mention in all the tumult, but Tener, your father, and I all visited the small Hunger again, and Tener figured out how to speak to a friendly portion of it."

Saida raised her eyebrows. "What did they say?"

"Something about needing to find a city named Kollu Or. Or something similar to that. We didn't have much time, and there was more, but so much has happened." The Scentian shook her head. "I'm sorry I don't remember more. I'm sure Tener or Darrow would know, they were closer to it."

"Thank you, Verrity."

"I hope you find what you're looking for," the delegate said. She lowered her voice. "For all our sakes."

Alesio covered a yawn. Five hours had not restored their energy, but it would have to do. He raised his eyebrows at Saida. "So. Can you still portal twice a day?"

Saida closed her eyes. Her portals skittered under them in the world's crust. Two of them responded to her initial inspection instead of one, scampering upwards towards her, and they gleamed brighter in her senses. "Yes."

"Wonderful. That means we can portal to Clef's holding room, then take him straight to one of those Goddess statues."

"I'm going, too!" Baylor ran into the circle of lantern light, his fists clenched.

He or someone else had wrapped his mouth all the way around his head, leaving an opening for him to eat or drink but covering the sores on his lips. His irises had returned to their normal brown, though some crimson still veined the white parts around them.

Saida tensed. Baylor had almost lost his control the day before and she didn't trust that he wouldn't misplace it again, especially around Clef.

Alesio did not change his stance as he usually did when confronted with danger. Did he think Baylor didn't pose a threat anymore, or did exhaustion cloud his judgment?

Wait. Was this how Alesio felt about her being in danger? The strength of the emotion surprised her, and she breathed through it with effort.

"Baylor," Alesio said, in a low tone, the kind that one used on small human children when they went red in the face.

"No! Please! You know how this feels, right? I *need* to see this through. I have to face him!"

"I need him alive for this," Alesio said. "You can't kill him. I would have to stop you."

Baylor's eyes glittered. "I don't . . . I don't need to kill him." His voice lowered to a whisper, his eyes darting around to the Soundian volunteers nearby. "I just need to show him he doesn't control me. Not anymore."

Alesio studied him for a long moment. Saida wished Hestafon were here so they could gauge the merit of the young man's words.

"Can you take off the amplifier?" Alesio asked quietly.

Baylor shook his head. He opened his mouth and pulled at the silver cap on his teeth. "It won't budge. Clef had me keep it on for over a month, and the little buttons don't work anymore." He swallowed, his throat bobbing. "Believe me. I don't want it."

Alesio considered that. Even if Baylor were lying, he wasn't about to reach into the young man's mouth and start yanking. That seemed like a quick way to lose a finger. And if Baylor were lying, the young man would just slow him with ixor the second he tried.

Alesio glanced at Saida, raising a questioning brow that creased like a Lunnite script she could suddenly read.

He knew it might not be the best plan to bring the damaged Baylor along, but empathy did not always take best ideas into account. However, Alesio was asking her if *she* felt comfortable going along with a lower standard plan—mediocre perhaps, downright abysmal at the worst.

Well. She didn't like it. Baylor could still flip his personality at any moment in his unhinged state.

But she couldn't unsee the soft sorrow in how Alesio regarded Baylor, how he saw the young man like a shattered, alternate version of himself that he could try and do right by.

She nodded.

Alesio let out a small breath. "Alright. You can come. Just remember," he added, when Baylor balled his fists and his eyes shimmered in victory, "That we need him. If we killed him now, he'd win."

"Alright." Baylor lowered those crimson-veined eyes.

Saida summoned a portal, and they strode through to the prison on Sound.

27

THE ONLY FEAR SHE HAD

After the Lunnites had made rubbings of as many carvings as they could hold in their packs, Tosn portaled Paras and the rest of them to Anthem.

They might as well have landed in a languid hornet's nest. People wandered through the streets in swarms, passing others who stood there sobbing. A few of them sprinted and shouted with the vigor of winged insects catching a whiff of an intoxicating flower.

"What happened?" Paras asked the nearest crying woman.

The Soundian gawped at her through splayed fingers. "Didn't you *feel* it? Our magic! Our magic!" Her speech decayed into incomprehensible sobs.

Mother Rean had suffered something similar once when attempting to Shape too large of a smoke cloud from a nearby forest fire. Here, some people had passed into the later stages where exhaustion won out, and they laid where their bodies had shut down in the snow-sludge, their lips and fingers blue with the cold. Most people still wandered in the middle stage—no energy left to run, but still stumbling—grasping with their hands for something intangible. A few still screamed at the sky, caught in the worst throes of the affliction.

429

Dawn had just arrived. How long had they been like this? And how had so many people been affected?

Paras wished she could step back into Tosn's portal. Back to the wonderful adventure of where she'd never been, the luring aroma of nobody to worry about.

The Lunnites crowded after her and paused, then huddled around *her*, as if she could protect them. As if, in the short time she'd been their guide, they'd upgraded her to guardian.

Had the Soundians trampled Tremain again? Was Verrity alright?

She clenched the two amplifiers in her pocket. Linia would want it to stop the otherworlders from overrunning her estate. Paras couldn't do much against a mob, but Linia might. She'd said she could sway the entire group of Soundians and force them to return to their homes. That would protect everyone, including the huddled group of Lunnites that had begun to depend on her.

A group of five people sprinted along close to them, then stopped and glared at the group of Lunnites. "Damn fur-mixes!" One of them spat.

The Lunnites huddled closer, recoiling as one. If there hadn't been fifty or so of them, the Soundians might have tried something, but the cohesive collection of them warded off physical attacks, it seemed.

One of the five Soundians tore in a random direction away from them, his legs pumping as if on their own volition through the slushy snow on the ground. The others followed.

"I have to do something important." Paras debated for a second. "Come with me. It's not safe for you here."

She dashed through the city, and they followed in a tight knot behind her that tangled and untangled at various points, dodging one still-active group—Tastians, not Soundians, from their darker complexions and textured hair—with their fists in the air, shaking them at the sky. One chanted, "Give it back! Give it back!"

She led them at a fast pace. If someone spat at them, or pointed, or shouted "fox-people!" she sped up, and soon, they all gasped for air.

They jogged into the streets protected by trees on the corners, muting some of the intense shouting and screaming. The barren fields had a massive bonfire set in the middle, and it flared high, fed by the wheat grain from the bins in the barn. A ring of Soundians in ragged and worn clothing cheered around it, seemingly past the stage of draining where they dashed around without autonomy; but now they perpetrated purposeful destruction.

Such violence. Such wanton waste. This is why we must stop them.

Paras turned down the winding brick road lined with hedges and ran along it till they all reached the massive house at the end of it. The Lunnites stared up at the massive, three-layered house with the golden pipe at the top. She smiled at them, searching for Higa and locking eyes with her. She would drop off the amplifier, and then, when Linia had calmed the Soundians, she would lead the Lunnites back to Scent. She'd have to convince her fellow villagers that Lunnites weren't a threat like in the stories, but once they met, it wouldn't take long. It hadn't for her, after all. And if any Soundians slipped through—well, she'd keep the second amplifier. Just in case. She could Shape now, after all, and Raos could Shape, too. Between the two of them, they could figure out a way to use magic to protect the village.

"Just follow me. I know who lives here." She strode up to the wall in front of the house and rang the little bell.

The guard appeared on top of the stone wall. He quirked an eyebrow at the Lunnites. "State your name and word of invitation."

"Paras. The word is 'amplifier.'"

"You may pass. They may not."

She glanced back at Tosn and the others, sweat from the run chilling on her skin in the frigid cold. The older Lunnite motioned her forward, paw outstretched. "We are much safer here than in the other part of the city. We can stay."

The guard swung the stone gate open, and Paras hesitated. "If a mob comes up here, though, you'll be trapped."

"We can see them coming." Higa pointed at the hedged road. "And hear them. They're not quiet."

"The door will close in five seconds," The guard said.

Paras hustled through the stone door, and it closed behind her without a sound. She dashed to the front door, and as before, it opened without her having to knock.

Linia waited there instead of one of the servants. She wore her white dress with the pastel blue jewels at her throat and ears. The whiteness of the room hurt Paras's eyes.

"I am pleased you are back." The gems she wore matched her eyes, which narrowed in on Paras like the hottest part of a fire despite their gentle shade. "Though you made the trip much quicker than expected. How did you manage to do so?"

Paras swallowed hard. "Oh, it wasn't that far."

Linia cocked her head, then lifted her lips in a small smile. "I see. Did you locate what I sent you for, then?"

Something in the piper's face paused Paras's urgency, urging caution.

Something cold and numb lived there, behind Linia's eyes, a senseless, callous thing, and something she had said echoed in Paras's mind. *People like you and I tremble in our homes and deal with the ramifications from those animals!*

Paras had come to know a set of people that she used to fear from afar. And even in all the chaos of the Soundians running rampant, deep down, they were just frightened people. Not animals. That seemed an important clarification, at least to that numbness scrutinizing her from behind the curtain of Linia's face.

"I don't want anyone to get hurt," Paras said.

"I promise to help everyone that I can." Linia held out her hand, her lips thinning, her eyebrows twitching. She'd plucked them even thinner than before into the width of a pen stroke.

Why am I hesitating? Paras frowned and gripped the smaller, box-shaped amplifier and the chunk of the Goddess Head amplifier. Her sweaty palms slicked their cool surfaces even in the cold air of Anthem's winter. "The Soundians have panicked again, and they're running all over the city, and maybe the other worlds, too—"

"Give the amplifier to me." Linia's voice sounded different, a layer of command laced inside the words.

Paras handed over the box-shaped amplifier to her, palm up in her tanned hand, out of place in all the whiteness.

Wait. Why am I—

The piper plucked it like a diamond from a pit of mud. Her eyes caressed the small square, and without any preamble, she pressed the silver box on all sides at once. A whirring sounded, and four little clamps popped out, one each side.

How did she know how to do that?

The Soundian opened her mouth and stuck it on her front tooth, and the device fastened onto it. She sucked air in and swayed for a few moments, closing her eyes.

"Linia?"

Her eyes peeled open, and she might have washed her expression in a stream, it was scrubbed so clean of emotion.

Then she gulped another breath. She pursed her lips. "Everything is alright."

Paras blinked. Linia's voice had a sharp quality that it hadn't had before.

"Can you stop the mobs in the streets, now?"

"I must acclimate to this power." Linia's voice smoothed, then sharpened again, like she sang to find the right key.

"How long will you need?"

Linia angled her head to the side. Her mouth bulged, as if she'd vomited and held the mess locked behind her lips.

"As. Long. As. It. Takes." Each word formed a Shaped Sound arrow and smacked into the carpeted floor so that the tufts of the carpet splayed apart.

Paras backed away through the still-open front door.

Linia jerked her head back to her and Paras flinched. The piper's blue eyes darkened as if a cloud had passed over them, and veins of red grew in the white parts. Her face contorted, and from her lips, instead of a sharpness, a sweet bell rang. "Stay . . ."

Paras blinked, swaying, her vision blurring a little, her hair falling over her shoulders. "O-okay?"

"Tell me again. How did you manage to make the trip so quickly?"

She didn't want to say for some reason. What was the reason? Her mouth moved of its own accord. "Tosn," she said. "One of the Lunnites can teleport."

"Ah." Linia's thin eyebrow arched. She stepped closer to Paras. "How interesting. Where are they now?"

"Outside. By your gate."

Linia stopped inches from her. "My dear." Her coy smile reminded Paras of a swanseize eyeing a root before they tore it from the ground. "I can hear silver ore ringing in your pocket."

"I—I thought I could use it. To protect my own world."

"Give it to me for now." The words shimmered in the air, sweet, soft. Paras's vision blurred more, and a pressure started in the back of her head. Her hand drifted down, and she reached in her pocket, lifted out the sliver of silver, and placed it in Linia's hand.

Linia regarded it as if she had just tasted cake for the first time and eyed another slice. She pressed on four places of the shard, but nothing happened.

A slight relief eased through Paras's mind, though she couldn't quite hold onto why. Linia would save Tremain. She needed the amplifiers to do it. Both amplifiers.

The piper tried different tapping sequences, and different spots on the shard, all to no avail. Then she narrowed her eyes, opened her mouth, and tapped the sliver shard against the amplifier she'd already clamped onto her teeth.

It sounded like a giant bell rang from inside Linia's body. She jerked forward, and gripped the shard of the Goddess Head, and it cut her palm, and some blood dripped down. Her body shook, and from her mouth poured a stream of sound so thick and strong, Paras could *see* it. The air wavered around them like heated air in a desert, and Paras stumbled back.

Then Linia stopped and closed her mouth. Sweat beaded on her forehead.

"I need to test this power," Linia said, and her words had a density to them, so thick they didn't register as words to Paras, just pure sound folded into meaning. When she opened her mouth, the wavering air flowed to the sliver in her hand, then back up again in a figure eight circuit. "Do come in and let me try it out on you. It won't hurt. But I need to ensure it works so that I can sway the mobs, you know."

"Yes . . ." Paras staggered back inside. Her vision blurred. She needed to help Linia. She needed to help Linia, so she could help . . . Tremain.

Linia closed the front door behind her. "Now, let's try out some simple commands first. Walk down the hallway and back again for me, would you dear?"

SAIDA STEPPED through the portal and two hands closed around her neck.

Clef had reached through the bars and grabbed her. His bound wrists just fit through the bars, but his hands could still squeeze.

She couldn't breathe. He shouted something. He spit in her face. "—*YOUR FAULT!*"

Alesio, Baylor, and Marik all sprang forward, Marik almost dropping the lantern he had brought along. Alesio grabbed Clef's hands and wrenched them back. Baylor snatched a knife from the sheathe at his side and menaced Clef with it, the brown dust of ixor trickling through his grimace and forcing the strait's leader to loosen his grip. Saida could sense, in that frozen moment, how the young man's amplifier extended his Tastian magic to affect people through their skin, not just if they breathed it.

"Ahhh." Clef's eyes rolled back in his head. "*Finally.*"

Saida dropped, rasping for breath, and Alesio caught her before she hit the floor, his muscled arms like a bouncy pillow. "Are you alright?"

She managed to nod, coughing, curling on the floor, shifting to foxan as her defensive instincts took over.

Muffled sounds from outside the storage building filtered through. Crashing, banging, and screaming.

"Give us back our magic!"

"The fox-people did this! They must have brought it here!"

Balt cowered inside the cage. He raised his head and whimpered at the group. "Let me out! I was shoved in here like some kind of criminal!"

"Where's Hestafon?" Alesio asked.

"Oho!" Clef's lips stretched up, tearing at the corners. His bloodshot eyes glowed like embers in a skull. Ixor had slowed his voice. "Did you . . . get my message, dear Alesio?" He giggled as if in slow motion, and the cadence teetered in unexpected directions.

Saida ground her teeth, wishing her breath didn't shudder in her tender throat. A year ago, when Alesio had found out what Carn had done to her, a grim dark had pooled in his eyes, an anger she didn't quite understand.

Now, she did. She wanted to tear Clef's lips off his face, so he couldn't use his voice any longer to torture Alesio, or any other vulnerable people, ever again. She tried to growl at the strait's leader but ended up coughing instead, which had a much lower intimidation effect.

Alesio gripped her tighter, then strode away from the cage and set her down against the other wall. "He's not worth it. Focus on breathing. Just like that."

She rose and rubbed her cheek against his neck as her foxan form desired, breathing in the moment, in his scent, in his sound, in his grounding warmth. How could everything be so wrong, yet so right at the same time? She used to believe that love was like a cage that forced people to stay when they didn't want to. But now, she thought of love as more like a sky: limitless. The only fear she had was falling out of it.

Alesio cradled the back of her head for a few more moments, then turned and strode back to the cage. Marik had helped Baylor push Clef backwards, and he'd stumbled, but stayed on his feet.

"Let me out!" Balt cried again.

"Someone put you in there," Alesio said. "Who?"

"Hestafon! He was crazy! He accused me of—" he glanced at Clef. "Uh, terrible things, which I did not do!"

Clef grinned, and Alesio faced the old leader of the straits. "Where. Is. Hestafon?"

"Was the kid's daddy dead when you got there? I told them . . . to make it slow."

Baylor started forward. Alesio laid a hand on the young man's shoulder. "You can't mess with us like that. We won't fall for it anymore."

Clef bowed his head. He smiled a wide, wide smile, tearing the paper-thin skin around his cheeks further. "Sounds . . . like a challenge."

Alesio shook his head and advanced to where the key hung on the wall outside to open the cage.

Clef pointed. "I told you. I told you . . . didn't I, Balt? *He came crawling back.*"

Balt spit on the floor of the cage and pointed at Alesio. "I knew it! You've been in league with him all along!"

Saida tried to speak, but it came out as more coughing.

"*What?*" Alesio stared at the Tastian. "I'm the one who hunted him down!"

"Exactly!" Balt pointed at him, his finger trembling, his double chin quivering. "The one who's talked about him the most! Your words reveal your betrayal!"

Clef cackled and the sound resembled a tangle of gravity shifts given speech. The effect both disturbed and disoriented Saida, as if one could get dizzy by listening.

"He's just trying to mess with you," Saida croaked to Alesio. Senses, speaking felt like trying to grate cheese out of her own throat. "Balt's an idiot, he'll believe anything."

"YOU SHUT UP!" Clef lunged at the bars, and Saida jerked back against the wall, almost hitting her head.

Clef paused, then his eyes snapped to Baylor. "Breathe."

The young man flinched. He pressed his bandaged lips tight together.

"Give it up, Clef," Alesio said. The lack of silver magic drifting from his lips indicated he held his breath. He crouched in his ready stance for combat, knees bent, balancing on the balls of his feet. "His father's safe. Your leverage is gone."

"I have fighters everywhere! I can have both your fathers killed at any time! You think any of you are safe?" Blood trickled down from his flesh-gouged cheeks. "You think you can protect everyone, Alesio? You know you can't!"

"We should gag him," Marik said.

Baylor hesitated, then pursed his lips and sent another thin stream of ixor at Clef.

"Ahhhh." The strait's leader sucked in the brown fog, then slumped down cross-legged on the floor, slowing even further than before.

Saida frowned. Clef had *wanted* Baylor to do that. Did he not care about ixor slowing his body? Or . . .

Oh.

Now that she could breathe easier, some things fell into place. Obvious things, like the fact that Clef was addicted to ixor.

She'd supposed at first that the Hunger's draining had deteriorated his skin, but maybe ixor had caused it, or worsened it, at least. They didn't know as much about ixor or its effects as they perhaps should, considering it could both alter someone's sense of time and intensify pain or pleasure. It would explain how his physical frame looked—not aged but *thinned*. His face had frayed almost to a skeletal degree, and his skin stretched, a threadbare coat spread too thin over the angles of his cheekbones.

Why hadn't that happened to Baylor? Then she remembered that the young man was immune to certain physical symptoms of his own ixor. Except the scarring and bleeding of his lips.

"In here!"

Tener's voice echoed from outside the cellar. Falrie slammed open the door, followed by Tener, both in their foxan forms. The cellar had become crowded. Mud smeared their fur coats and dried blood spotted Tener's muzzle.

A tightness in Saida's chest eased at seeing them alive and mostly unharmed.

"Thank the Senses you're alright!" Falrie started towards Saida and twined around her, both of them foxans. "Hestafon said you were on Scent." She scanned their group. "Where is he?"

Clef waved his hand, the movement slowed. "Probablyy . . . polishing his silverware . . . hiding awayy like this one." He inclined his head at Balt, beside him and near the front of the cage.

"I'm trapped in here!" Balt shrilled. "Why won't anyone listen? Let me out this instant!"

"That's not true," Tener said, speaking over Balt. "He said he needed to be here. He said it was important. Aunt Naya brought him here. Now that things have calmed down, Mom and I were coming to help guard Clef."

Clef clapped his hands, though the slowed motion made it appear like he was praying. "Who would havve thought . . . that Testy Hesty would've turned a leaf. Wworking for you . . . instead of the other way around?"

She and Alesio glanced at each other. Without Hestafon around to verify Clef's words, this plan might all be for nothing.

Clef continued, "Welll, it's . . . toooo late now! My cage fighters . . . alreadyy control the portals!"

Alesio stilled. Saida growled low in her throat, then shifted to human to gain height and to help her think more like a human. She needed all her human wits about her with Clef around.

"That isn't true, either," Falrie said.

"What do you mean?" Alesio asked.

"There's no fighters at Sound's Portal Station." Falrie sat back on her haunches, her tail curling around her paws. "Terrified people running around, yes. But no fighters taking over."

Clef bared his teeth at the older foxan. "I diddn't sayy . . . which portals . . . fur-mix."

Falrie bared her fangs back. "It wouldn't matter even if they had. The portals stopped working."

"Hah! That you know of!" White froth formed at the corners of his mouth, mixing with the blood on his cheeks.

Tener sidled up to Saida by her place on the wall, shifting to human so that they grew taller. They still just reached her shoulder, so they gestured for her to bend to their level, their dark brown eyes still reflecting in the darkness. She bent down close.

"Saida, there's something else you need to know. Dad, Verrity, and I visited the small Hunger—"

Falrie's ears flicked backwards. "You *what?*" She spun and glared at the young foxan. "I told you to stay away from it! Did *you* cause all this?" She flung her arms out, indicating the muffled bedlam of shouts from outside. She glared at Balt. "And you! Aren't you supposed to be out there helping calm your people?"

"They'll just trample me! They might as well be bloodthirsty animals!"

"Excuse me?" Falrie narrowed her eyes at the Tastian.

"Well," Balt said. "I wasn't referring to you." He looked at Marik. "Or you. Or any of the fur—uh, fox-people."

Falrie growled, her snout wrinkling, and Balt whimpered and backed up as far as he could to the far end of the cage. Clef, still sitting cross legged by the front of the cage, didn't even glance back at him.

"Saida," Tener said. "We talked to the baby Hunger, to the part that merged with the tree. We heard them."

Saida smiled at them. "Verrity told me. I'm so happy for you!"

Falrie whirled around again. "*What?*"

"The magic spoke, like you always said it could. They spoke to all of us." Tener perched a hand on Saida's arm. Their freckles had faded on their cheeks, leaving smooth, dark brown skin, and this somehow lifted the veil of their youth, revealing the seriousness in their eyes.

"You all could have died!" If Falrie could've Shaped Vision magic, Saida worried about how her mother's glare might have generated actual knifes. "We're having a serious talk about your obedience after all this!"

"It was important. I'm a part of these worlds, too, I want to save them like the rest of you!"

"Tener, what did the Hunger say? Verrity couldn't remember."

"You need to find a city called Kolsuv Mor. They said everything started there, and that you have to 'break the circle and destroy the tree.'"

"You can't trust anything the Hunger says!" Falrie raked her claws on the dirt ground of the storage room. "I can't *believe* Darrow deceived me like this! And Verrity, too!"

Saida's head reeled. Falrie's eyes had edges as sharp as her claws. Would she look like that someday, when she spoke to Alesio? "Falrie—"

"I've had enough of this! Why doesn't he *listen* to me?" Falrie shifted her paws to hands and gripped Tener's wrist. "He keeps undermining my decisions! He's supposed to be my partner!"

"You're the one not listening to us!" Tener flung her hand away. They shifted in and out of foxan in their face, but not their body, as if trying to hide their expressions. "Stop! You're tearing your bond with Dad!"

Falrie paused.

Clef had slumped to the floor under Baylor's ixor cloud. His shoulders shook in silent laughter and his eyes glittered like rubies. "Are *you* the one breaking it? Really? You just said . . . he's the one who doesn't listen."

"Stop that," Falrie said to Clef.

Clef's scrutinizing stare landed on Saida. "Say something else," he whispered to her. "Even a scream . . . a whimper will do. You're afraid of something like this . . . tearing?"

Cold fear skittered down Saida's neck and back.

"Shut up." Alesio unlocked the cage. "Baylor, can you slow Balt? I don't trust him."

The young man blew a stream of ixor at the Tastian delegate, who had begun heaving himself to his feet, then slumped against the back of the cage. Then Alesio, Baylor, and Marik crowded in, grabbed the strait's leader, and dragged him out with some might have considered an excessive use of force, but that Saida approved of. Alesio gagged him with a strip of cloth he tore from his own shirt, using quick, harsh motions.

"What are you doing?" Falrie asked.

"We're trying something," Saida said, her voice raspy, grating more cheese from her throat. "We're going to use him to try and stop the Hunger."

Hopefully their plan would work without Hestafon. But they couldn't delay any longer to try and find him. The next time the Hunger woke, the entity might just devour their entire Plane.

2 8

THE PART LEFT UNSAID

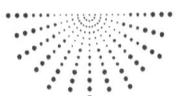

F irst, Linia ordered Paras to march across the hallway ten times. Paras did so, her mind blank, like when she adventured and her body just wanted to go.

Then, Linia asked her, with that sweet, ringing voice that morphed into a song-like tone, to show her to the Lunnites outside her estate.

"You know, those Lunnites feel just as strongly about keeping to themselves as you and I do," she said. "It's only fair that they help us, don't you think?"

"Only fair," Paras mumbled back. For some reason, the old Tremain phrase *you find the stink by going upriver* echoed in the back of her mind, but Linia's song drowned it out.

Tosn and Higa greeted her with glad voices, but Linia hadn't told her to respond, so she stood there, unmoving, as Linia sang with a larger voice, "Protect me, protect me, ring yourselves around me," and they had all done it, of course. How could anyone not do whatever such a beautiful voice asked?

The melody sang through their bones, infused into their muscles. Linia was doing what she'd promised. She would force everyone back into their homes. Paras and the Lunnites ringed around her, and they tramped down that hedge-lined brick road, curving around, and reached the barren, snow-covered fields.

More Soundians had gathered there, burning more wheat, and Linia sang out louder, "Protect me, protect me," and they stopped and stumbled up to her, and she sang, "Make a ring around me," and they did so.

Then they all marched in time to the melody in their hearts, each of their feet hitting the road at the same time, their hands swinging at the same pace as the others. More Soundians dashed towards them down the street, shouting and angry, but Linia's group sang Linia's song, and the approaching Soundians stopped, and their arms dropped.

Linia sang, "Protect me, protect me, form ahead of me," and the new Soundians did, spinning and swinging their arms and legs in time with everyone else. They trooped on like that for a while, and Paras was glad, so glad they had stopped running around with fear and anger in their faces. Everyone smiled, and sang, and they collected more and more people. Every voice in the mass added to Linia's volume, their voices sounding like hers. Each new person added power to her song in a compound effect, so that the sound of it became a huge wave sweeping over entire blocks of the city. Some people even exited their houses, drawn like bees to honey, their eyes sweet and their mouths lax, and something about that seemed strange, but no, it didn't matter, not when Linia would force all of Sound to stop its violence.

ALESIO STEPPED through the portal Saida had summoned, and there before him, five stone pillars surrounded a large carving of a woman's head, just as Saida had described. Overhead, a dark ceiling covered the night sky.

The Hunger? So close? He flinched.

Nothing happened, though, and when he squinted, he realized a tree canopy closed off their view above. Nothing except for a moss growing over all the tree trunks lit up the night, each of which cast an eerie neon green glow for a short range around them like giant phosphorescent mushrooms. One such tree grew nearby, illuminating the area for a short way. The air sweltered here, covering him a like a hot, wet blanket, and sweat trickled down his back within moments, the sense enhanced on Touch without a buoy suit.

He hoped this worked.

He and Marik hauled Clef inside the circle of pillars, Alesio checking every other minute that the manacles he'd Shaped with Touch magic still bound the old shadow leader's hands. He'd brought a rope along, too, just in case. Baylor stayed beside Alesio, ready to slow Clef with ixor should he try to escape. Tener rambled ahead alongside Saida, murmuring to her. They both had shifted, as if to mimic each other, to foxan hind legs and human torsos, arms, and heads. Saida had washed her braid-tail in the stream last night, but it remained straggly on the ends from her nervous habit of picking at it.

Falrie trailed behind as a full foxan. She hadn't expressed anything else after Tener's outburst, though she'd waited back in the cellar in Anthem till the last second before Saida's portal closed. She had jutted out her chin and marched through with a small measure of her customary assertiveness.

The Hunger would wake up, soon, after their late-night snack of the Portal Stations' magic and the Garden in Scent, and who else knew what other portal-based magic transplants.

When they woke, Alesio didn't count on them holding back.

Flowing symbols and circle-based foreign script covered the Goddess Head like strange hair. The same symbols wrapped around each of the pillars, and around a circle connecting each of the pillars, and in grooves leading towards the head likes the spokes of a wheel. Then the silver on the Goddess Head shone through the ambient moss-green tinged air.

The same exact silver as what Baylor had in his mouth.

"Saida," Alesio said. "That's—that's an *amplifier.*"

She bit her lip, reaching for her braid, but stopped herself. "With everything else happening it slipped my mind. I'm sorry. I should have warned you."

Alesio didn't even know how to process the information. He glanced at Baylor, who gaped at the thing, his eyes dilating with the enormity of possible power and inherent danger. "Do you know, uh, I mean, are they safe to interact with?" Alesio asked.

"I spoke to them," Saida said. "They didn't have an overwhelming power on their own. They're . . . I'm pretty sure these large ones used to be actual people, people from Transmutation who transformed themselves into the Goddess Heads. But they aren't transplants. They didn't merge with the magic of our worlds, like the Epitaphs did. Amplifiers probably only work when attached to something, or someone, that can Receive magic." She inclined her head to Baylor, who stepped back from the statue, shuddering.

At least he doesn't seem interested, Alesio thought. The tiny amplifier Baylor already possessed had caused the young man so much anguish, so that made sense.

Saida had her hand on the statue, her ears pricked towards it, also listening. Tears dripped down her reddish-brown cheeks.

She'd reconnected to her magic after all this time. He now knew some of what she'd experienced these past few weeks, that ache, that loss, and that her magic had returned to her made him so happy. Tener laid their head against her shoulder and wrapped their arms around her.

Alesio closed his eyes for a moment and listened for the Goddess Head's voice, connecting to them as both Hestafon and Saida had taught him.

"Hello. My name is Amplify. I am one of hundreds of Transmuters who died to become an Amplifier. Over the past several centuries, our Plane of Change has helped hundreds of worlds across thirty-five Planes and counting, building them magic technologies like electricity, forges, and sprinkler systems for crops."

Hundreds? *Hundreds* of Goddess Head Amplifiers?!

He controlled his breathing. Several hundred worlds, the magic had said. Thirty-five Planes and counting. When would Alesio's universe stop expanding?

As for Amplify themselves, their magic seemed small. Much smaller than he would have expected, considering their size, but they existed. They didn't seem hostile or dangerous, and their message seemed . . . stale, somehow. Not the same as other magical voices when he Received. But he couldn't help but wonder what would happen if he tried to utilize their power.

Then he swung his gaze to check on Clef again, and his heart guttered at the unrestrained hunger on the old shadow leader's face.

Baylor might not want to use the giant amplifier, but Clef might try to force the young man to do so.

This next part would have to be *very* delicate.

After a few moments of deliberation, Alesio propped Clef's limp, slowed body against one of the pillars.

Clef regarded Alesio with a bleary but triumphant smile, the skin of his face like crumpled paper, tinged green from the light of the luminescent moss.

Sweat slicked Alesio's palms.

Why is he happy right now? He couldn't have planned this!

Falrie pulled Alesio aside. She had shifted to her human form except for her back legs. "Even if he can do something like this, he'll just lie about the lies he hears! You'll wonder what he actually knows and what he says for his own ends."

She had a point. Alesio had planned to have Hestafon here to test the sound of Clef's words, but Hestafon had disappeared. He hoped the piper was alright.

But something had bothered him about the way Clef talked about the Hunger, and about how he'd acted around Baylor. Addiction had always held sway over the strait's leader, after all, in the form of a compulsive need to control and manipulate others.

Now, Clef had a new kind of addiction.

He placed a hand on Clef's shoulder and descended inside himself, into his Touch magic room. He located the ixor that had slowed Clef after several moments on the floor in the corner. He Received it by asking the ixor which parts of them wanted to become a different form, a ball, for a few moments. Most of the ixor magic streamed through, and he Shaped them into a ball, which he tossed away from Clef. The magic squealed in delight as they sailed through the air, breaking into powder again once they hit the ground several yards away.

"Alright," Alesio said. "Tell us the lies this statue believes."

Clef spit on Alesio. "And why should I do anything for you? Especially when you stole my ixor away?"

Alesio wiped the spit off his shirt. He knelt in front of the strait's leader and spoke under his breath, watching the man's manacled hands in case he tried anything. "If you do this, we might stop the Hunger. That's what you want, too, isn't it? You were loyal to Watthe, *not* the Hunger. Watthe rebelled against the Hunger, in the end."

Clef paused. Then he scoffed. "You want me to listen to a statue? I can't hear something that doesn't speak."

"Every magic has a consciousness and a voice if you listen well enough, and if anyone can, you can listen well enough."

Clef's glittering bloodshot eyes narrowed on Alesio's face. "Huh. You believe it." He shrugged, then his eyes rolled around to Baylor. "I get to keep him."

The young man stiffened.

"You misunderstand your situation," Alesio said. "You don't get to 'keep' Baylor like he's an object. You will never see him or his father again."

"You always were good at making deals," Clef said. "Look at me, jumping up to help you."

". . . I will ensure you receive a small portion of ixor each day." The words nauseated Alesio, but he couldn't lie, or Clef would know. "You stop the Hunger from ending it in the next few days, or however long before they consume our Plane." He paused. "You get to keep living, Clef. That's my deal."

Clef's face contorted. More blood seeped from several tears in his skin.

Beside him, Baylor studied Alesio's face, but kept his mouth shut.

They'd talked this over before, what they'd say. What precise wording to use.

"Fine. I'll fix what your damn fur-mix broke." Clef laughed. "Will they call me the Voice of Salvation next?"

Alesio worked his jaw, controlling the tremble in his sweaty hands. "Do it. Now."

Clef snickered, then focused his gaze on the Goddess Head. His eyes flickered shut, then opened again.

"I can't hear shit," Clef said. "There's . . . there's a lot of layers. This magic is old. Centuries old. I have to use the amplifier to Receive well enough."

"I'm *not* letting you—"

"Then I can't help." Clef shrugged. "Kill me now. It'll save me the agony of waiting the next thirty minutes without ixor, or however long we have."

Alesio ground his teeth. He glanced back at Saida, who shrugged. "His power is listening to lies, right? It's not like an amplifier will make him able to fight us."

"Baylor?" Alesio asked. "Is it safe? You'd know more than anyone."

Baylor stared at the Goddess Head. "The one I have is a lot to handle. I don't know what that's capable of." He raised his head. "But . . . it's sending those arms out again."

Gooseflesh rose the hairs on Alesio's arms. They all jerked their faces upwards. The Hunger's tendrils had crept outwards again towards the different worlds. *Sounddamn. We're really running out of time.*

"Alright," he snapped. He yanked Clef closer to the Goddess Head so he could place his manacled hands on it. "Can you even use it? It's not like you can stick it on over a tooth. Marik, do you know how to activate it?"

The Lunnite shook his head, eyes wide. "We did not know it could be used in such a way. Or we would have, long ago."

"As the official Voice of Salvation," Clef said, "I know how to activate these things. I *did* figure out how to unlock the one for Brezeek. You just need to scratch out the right runes that's stopping

from using it. All codes are lies, if you think about it. They veil truth."
He squinted at the Goddess Head, then grabbed a piece of jagged
stone off the ground and scraped one of the circular parts that created
the effect of curly hair, his manacled hands flashing in quick, darting
motions.

Marik let out a startled growl. "Don't—don't let him do that!"

The Head began to glow with a silver light.

In Alesio's mind, Amplify spoke again. Their speech still had a
recorded, stale quality, like what the small Hunger had repeated over
the last year. But the speech went on for much longer than it had
before, like Clef had managed to pull more of their thoughts to the
surface.

"Hello. My name is Amplify. I am one of hundreds of Transmuters
who volunteered to become an Amplifier. Over the past several
centuries, our Plane of Change has helped hundreds of worlds across
thirty-five Planes and counting, building them magic technologies
like electricity, forges, and sprinkler systems for crops.

"But the Bridges between Planes are failing, and we must find a
way to fix them, or no one will be able to travel between the Planes, or
perhaps even the worlds of their own Plane. Change's three worlds of
Transmutation, Divination, and Consumption will work together to
keep the Planes connected. Combining Divination's silver ore with
Consumption's ingesting magic, then Transmutation magic, many of
us have Shaped ourselves into Amplifiers. We will do everything we
can to power our ship to find Lunne and force her to reconnect what
she has neglected. We need to siphon unique magics from each world,
purify them all to raw Spatial magic, then teleport it back to the world
of Transmutation to power our ship. The combined drain to the
Planes will refill after Lunne reconnects the Bridges. All that matters
is finding Lunne."

Clef raised his head. Sweat beaded on his forehead and he stared at
the Goddess Head with an open mouth. Could the old strait's leader
hear magic voices as well, or just the lies the magic believed?

The strait's leader shuddered, then laughed. He reared back and
spat on the Goddess Head. "The lies and corruption and twisted

things this creature managed to do put my whole life and criminal enterprise to shame. *Shame!*"

Marik started forward, his hands out as if to strangle the old strait's leader, his human teeth bared in a foxan way. He'd wrapped his hair-tail in a long and wide strip of those plant fibers, and it lashed back and forth.

Falrie grabbed the Lunnite's arms and yanked him back. "Stop that. Many people wish to hurt that man, and they have greater cause than you."

Alesio offered Falrie a grateful look. The last thing he needed now was a scuffle in which he had to defend, of all people, Clef.

"What is it?" Alesio prodded him. "What did you hear in that message?"

"You are all so stupid and deaf!" Clef's laugh skittered and scrabbled up to a fever pitch. "Every syllable is a deathbed confession. Every breath a biography of mistakes. If you would shut up and let me listen, I could unravel the secrets of the world. The message you heard was just a note of what I hear, one note in a dirge, an elegy for all of us!"

Saida knelt before one of the pillars, watching Clef's face and keeping her distance. "The Goddess Head on Taste said some of that," she said. "The Transmuters must have all tried to think the same thing when they died. Or maybe they just believed the same thing as the other Transmuters." She shifted her face to a foxan muzzle, showing her fangs, flashing her claws. "So, the Goddess Head is lying to themself. Which part was the lie?"

Clef leered, and more of his skin tore off, revealing the red muscle of his jaw. "The part left unsaid. That's how it goes. It's true for you, too, isn't it?"

"Answer her!" Alesio stepped between them, blocking those mocking eyes. "If you don't use your voice to help us, you'll lose it. I will cut out your tongue."

"I'll lose everything in another few hours or so. There's no way to stop it. I tried to warn you—"

Alesio pulled his knife from its sheath, but Clef had paused, his hand still splayed on the Goddess Head. "That was a lie? Apparently, there is a way to stop it, now. A path forward." Clef cackled and his hands shook. "Fine, you want to know so bad before we all die?" He pointed at Amplify, the Goddess Head. "Here's what I'm Receiving from that sounddamned mantra. All the stuff about them helping the Planes with magic and the Bridges failing and them transforming themselves, that's all true, true in that they believed it and didn't try to lie, and it was also true in that they weren't wrong.

"But the lies started when they said, 'We will do everything we can to find Lunne and force her to reconnect what she has neglected.' They didn't believe that, not this Transmuter, anyway. I heard this underneath that message, their true thoughts:

"We must give up on finding Lunne. It is a lost cause. Perhaps she has died. We must find a way to save the Bridges ourselves."

Clef shook his head. "And though this Transmuter believed they needed to give up, part of it wasn't true. Finding Lunne wasn't a lost cause, at least, not back then."

Alesio would have suspected Clef put on an act, except for the sudden rain of sweat from his skeletal face.

Clef would never humiliate himself like this on purpose, even for a trick.

Beyond that, Alesio hadn't known that Clef could distinguish between the *kinds* of lies people told, like whether the lies they believed were factually true or not. How did Clef know the arbitrary truth about something that had happened over 800 years ago? Had the giant amplifier allowed him to access not just the differentiations between lies and truth, but *facts about the universe?* The implications of that . . . Alesio didn't want to ask and interrupt the revelations.

"The next part has several lies layered into it. 'We need to siphon unique magics from each world' has a lie of omission before it even takes that breath on the recording. Here's what I heard in that breath:

"First, we tried using the foxans' portal magic, or Shaped Spatial magic. But there are not enough foxans to create the amount of magic we need, especially not after the ones we experimented on fled.

Clef's thin skin tore over his cheeks, so that the remaining patches resembled islands on a sea of red. Using the Goddess Head seemed to exacerbate his condition, intensifying the symptoms.

"Anyway! On to the next one. 'We need to siphon unique magics from each world' leaves out way too many truths, creating more lies of omission. Here's what I heard underneath that phrase. *We convinced foxans ready to transplant, from our Plane and other Planes, to transform into a specific kind of transplant: portal trees, or Transplant Trees, that would draw the lesser magics from each world through their portals and store them in the trees.'* Ha! And there's a deeper layer of lies inside of that! The core falsehood is in the word 'lesser,' as mixed magics are actually more potent and volatile, just not the Spatial magic they believed was best."

Alesio's mouth hung open like an inefficient flytrap, then he closed it. Saida, Falrie, Tener, and Marik kept theirs open.

Alesio could somewhat follow this. Saida had at least mentioned that the five of the Epitaphs they'd searched ended up connected by portal magic. It made sense that those portals could pull in magic from the five worlds. The Hunger had consumed that Epitaph and kicked off the draining . . . yesterday?

Had it only been *yesterday* that that had happened? It felt like a week had stuffed itself inside the span of a few hours, like he'd been on ixor the whole time.

"The rest of this sentence goes on with more layered lies. 'Purify them all to raw Spatial magic' is a lie, but it's one they believed. *'When the time is right, I and the other Amplifiers will activate, increasing the intensity of the mixed magics stored in the Transplant Trees. This will purify them back to Spatial magic.'* Yeah . . . mixed magics do not purify backwards very well."

"Did *you* know that?" Marik asked. "How are you—how do you know that?"

"Try to keep up, fur-mix," Clef said. "I'm listening to the lies this magic believed. That includes false truths they assumed about the way this whole mess of a universe works. I may not know why mixed magic doesn't purify backwards, but I just know it doesn't, because my Receiving tells me it's a lie." His glistening, raw muscle twitched in his jaw.

Alesio winced. On Touch, that had to hurt beyond anything he could imagine.

Then he remembered what Clef had done to Balor's father, and his empathy evaporated.

"Go on," he said to Clef, with the voice that Clef had always used to force him to fight in cage matches.

The old strait's leader presented him with a glare, a prescient promise of future pain. Then his glare flipped into a grin. "You're becoming more like me in every moment. Threatening to cut my tongue out. Forcing me to work while in pain."

Alesio shook his head. "You can't shake me up anymore, Clef." He jerked his head up at the Hunger. "We don't have much time."

Clef growled, and Alesio couldn't help but thrill at that sound of frustration. For once, he controlled the situation. He pulled the strings. And that control had come to him, ironically enough, only after he had stopped fearing his own incompetence.

When he didn't fear himself, Clef couldn't use that fear against him.

"The part that goes, 'then teleport it back to the world of Transmutation to power our ship' is a lie because they didn't intend on powering a ship to search for Lunne at all. Here's what I Received. *We will then transfer the influx of Spatial magic back to the matching Amplifier on our world of Transmutation, mix with the runes we set, and Transmute our Plane and everyone on it into one being—a god.'* And in case this isn't obvious to you, this was also untrue because the mixed magics didn't purify, they imploded from the sheer power of too many magics forced together. Oh, and the Lunnites didn't deify. In case you didn't catch that either."

"A—a god?" Saida whispered. "They planned to amass enough power to become a god?"

"Am I done? Can I be done?" Clef rolled his neck around, sweat dripping off the exposed muscle of his jaw. The rest of his skin had peeled away from his face, even down his neck. "I mean, the rest of it is just common sense," Clef said. "You don't need a lie detector to understand that 'The combined drain to the Planes will refill after Lunne reconnects the Bridges' is a load of shrikeshit that they believed. 'All that matters is finding Lunne'? Hah! Here's what I hear: *We will power all the worlds' magics. We will refill what we took once we are god.*"

Clef filched a shaky breath from the humidity around him. Sweat ran down the exposed musculature of his face in rivulets. How he remained conscious while in such pain, and on Touch, did force a certain awe from Alesio.

Clef removed his hand from the Goddess Head and stumbled backwards, leaning against one of the pillars.

"That's why the box that the Hunger sent wanted Watthe to consume foxans," Saida said. Her foxan ears had slanted backwards. Her hind legs shifted to human legs and back again.

"– don't understand," Tener said on Alesio's left. Alesio craned his head around to hear them better. "What's Spatial magic?"

"They called it Spatial magic; we call it Primal. It's the same thing." Saida spoke as if in a trance. "Foxans are birthed from the Primal Plane, or the Spatial Plane. It's . . . it's a better name than Primal, don't you think, Tener? Doesn't the Primal Plane, and our magic, *feel* like space? When we shift, we Shape our own Space, when we create portals, we Shape the Space around us. That's why the Hunger wanted our Plane to become a Primal, or Spatial, magic overgrowth. Because before they mutated into the Hunger, the ancient Lunnites were obsessed with Spatial magic."

"Those bastards," Alesio muttered. He couldn't understand it all. Saida had told him other Planes existed, but with everything else happening, he hadn't considered what that meant. These Lunnites had come from another Plane. They'd had incredible knowledge and advancements, at least compared to the Sensory Plane. They'd built colony cities and connected them across the worlds, and perhaps even across other Planes. And then in a step of colossal misjudgment and overgrown ego, a splinter group had destroyed all those connections to try to become a god themselves.

Falrie had sunk onto the stone floor around the Goddess Head in her foxan form.

"This can't be." Marik had his head in his hands, staring at the ground. "This can't be . . ."

"Ixor?" Clef asked.

"You want ixor *now?*" Alesio blinked. "Won't that hurt, with your skin . . . uh, that way?"

"Please."

Alesio almost expected the old strait's leader to burst into flame after uttering such a vulnerable world. He glanced at Baylor.

Baylor folded his arms. "Might need him to listen to something else, you know? Like a . . . cloud. Or my fist."

"Alesio, you said 'every day.'"

"I didn't say when you'd get it." Alesio shrugged. "Baylor's the one in charge of that. And technically, he already gave you some today. Maybe you should have thought twice before torturing his father."

Clef lunged at him, but they'd been ready for such a thing. Baylor grabbed him and forced him to his knees. The young man didn't even have to tie him up with the rope they'd brought. The man's body wasted away, frail from using the Goddess Head and his addiction.

That fact, more than anything, would have made Alesio pity him. Addiction controlled people in unfair ways. Alesio knew what that was like.

But Clef had long ago spent anything that could have bought Alesio's pity.

Tener settled their hands on their hips. They'd grown taller than just a few days ago, and their dark hair curling around their ears brought out more mature angles in their face: a more defined jaw, highlighting higher cheekbones. Their eyes didn't seem too big for their face anymore. "Didn't the Hunger want twisted, fermented magic? I thought they disconnected the Planes so that the Primal Plane would create a big overgrowth."

Huh, Alesio thought. *They're right. That doesn't make sense.*

"That's what the Hunger prefers the most now." Saida's foxan ears flicked back. She shifted to her muzzle, then back to her human face.

"But if they tried to make an overgrowth by severing our Planes again, it would take centuries to form. I don't think they want to wait that long to consume us."

Tener glanced up at the canopy overhead, the blackness of the trees lit by patches of luminescent moss like green stars. "I don't think so, either."

Saida continued in almost a monotone voice, though her physical form fluctuated back and forth from moment to moment. "But the Hunger also likes Spatial magic, because the old Lunnites—the Transmuters—wanted Spatial magic. They went through all that trouble to purify mixed magics back to Spatial magic. And the Hunger mentioned something about wanting to save Spatial magic, or the foxans, for last."

"But how does knowing this help us now?" Tener asked.

That's the question, huh.

Falrie still huddled on the ground, not speaking, her eyes glassy and vacant, much like how she used to before the Reconnection. Perhaps Tener processed everything a little easier since they didn't have preconceived notions about how the worlds and Planes worked.

Saida stared at Amplify. Her whole form flickered to foxan, then to human, then back again.

Then what she had said earlier clicked into place. *When we shift, we Shape our own Space, when we create portals, we Shape the Space around us.*

Saida could Shape, too.

"No," he said. "Saida, it's too dangerous!"

"What's too dangerous?" Falrie jerked her head up, her speckled gray fur blending in somewhat with the weathered stone ground.

"Clef," Saida said, "My magic of teleporting, of shifting, of trimming. It's Shaped Spatial magic. Did I speak a lie?"

Baylor still watched over the kneeling Clef, ready to slow him or tie him up if he needed to. Clef tilted his head at her, then spat blood. "Now or before this?"

Alesio stepped between them, pressing the knife to Clef's throat. "Stop playing games."

The strait's leader cackled. "Neither of you can make up your mind. You should thank me, Requiem! You were right to have reservations about her. Isn't that right, fur-mix? You don't know if you'll stay with him."

SAIDA HUNCHED OVER, curling her tail around herself, terrified to meet Alesio's eyes. She struggled against the urge to retreat into her foxan self, that floating place that reacted based on sheer instinct, where her human emotions seemed less potent, like nonflowers had sprinkled over them.

She didn't want him to see the truth.

She'd solidified that she wanted to stay with him, but she could not *promise* him that she would. All her attempts to try could still end in failure. She could not promise they would stay in the same house together. She could not promise that they would grow old together. She could not promise that she would always, always stay the same, because history had shown that she had already changed so much, that she could not with truth in her heart say that the future would remain unchanged no matter what. That she would never grow to resent him. That she wouldn't shout at him, as her mother and father did to each other. That she wouldn't want to be somewhere else. With someone else.

She sputtered back and forth between her foxan and human selves, her paws growing fingers, then her fingers sprouting claws, her mouth blooming with fangs, then fading back into the flat squares of human teeth, her front legs lengthening into arms, then back again on all fours.

"That's Fear talking, Saida," Difficult Truth said. "That's what's hurting your bond."

She had to let him know. He deserved to know.

And she had to do it now, before she left. Because she had known —the knowledge had lain inside her heart like a seed since yesterday, when she'd recognized the Garden's magic as portal magic.

Spatial magic. That aching sense of wanderlust, that need to ramble into the sky and reach the stars—that was *her* magic. She hadn't wanted to explore what it meant when Marik had observed back on Taste that she could Shape magic, too. All of it had added up to the knowledge that, if she used the Goddess Head to amplify her Spatial magic, they could empower her to teleport all the way to the Hunger.

"Alesio," she said, and lifted her eyes to meet his. Her shifting paused in its constant reverberation, settling on a mixture of fangs in her human face, cutting her lips in its truth, in its pain. It hurt more here, on Touch. She grabbed her braid, gripping the bedraggled end with shaking hands.

Sweat dripped down his face, tinged green in the light of the mossy tree nearby. "I don't believe it. It's not true. Clef is lying! Tell me that he's lying!"

Clef snickered. "Why should I lie when the truth is so gratifying?"

"I *do* want to stay. I . . . I decided to try, even when I was afraid of myself, of changing."

"Isn't that nice," Clef said. "She'll try to stay with you. Try to love you. It must be hard for her, because you're such a piece of shit. But she'll *try*."

"It's not like that!" Saida cried out. "Alesio, he's twisting my words! Don't listen to him!"

Alesio's arms had sagged, and his facial muscles slackened.

"She's lying. She's leaving you because she's a fickle thing. Fur-mixes shift on the inside just as much as the outside."

All around them, it seemed like everyone had breathed in ixor, their expressions frozen. Her mom, Tener, Baylor, even the muscles glistening in Clef's face.

"I don't want to leave. Please believe me," Saida whispered. "But I can't stay now. Not when I have the chance to save you."

Something frayed in the space between them, and she didn't dare glance at Tener, fearing they would see her bond tearing, and their expression would confirm it.

Clef chuckled, tears of pain flowing down his skinned face. Alesio's head jerked towards him.

"In the end, you weren't enough. Not enough to save her, and not even enough to stay for."

Alesio's nostrils flared, his lips smashing into a thin line. Saida hated Clef more than she'd hated even Carn in that moment.

Clef began to laugh, and laugh, and the red, exposed muscles of his cheeks flexed like death itself cackled at her. "You activated the box. You led the Hunger to us, when we'd hidden from it for hundreds of years. You think you can stop it? That? What's your plan? It'll tear you apart the second you get there!"

"I have to try," Saida said.

"You'll just make it worse!" Clef tried to stand up, and Baylor shoved him back down. This physical action seemed to help Baylor remember they had brought a rope for this and grabbed it to gag him. "You'll feed it your Spatial magic and strengthen it, so it just consumes us faster! I've done everything I can to slow it down! Everything! Baylor! Wait! You know it, too! You've helped me slow it down!"

"What?" The young man paused, the rope in his hands, and looked to Alesio. "I swear, I don't know what he's—"

"Liar!" Clef screamed and wrenched away from the young man. "You're lying to yourself! I just can't hear it because of the ixor! Alesio. Alesio, listen to me. All those boxes in that warehouse? Fakes! You thought I had hundreds of amplifiers, didn't you? Hundreds of cage fighters?"

Saida trailed towards the Goddess Head. She released her braid and whispered to Fecal Air, "Looks like you get your wish today."

"Oh, good! I've waited so long!"

"I was toying with you the whole time." Clef laughed a jabbering laugh, high and shrill. "I did it just to boil your guts. I wanted more time to do it, though. Why do you think I gave this idiot one? So he could produce more ixor! So, I could breathe it and slow my time! Because she—" he pointed at Saida— "destroyed any chance we had the second she discovered that sounddamned beacon! That's what triggered it to come here! Alesio, are you not listening to me?! She drew its attention to that foxan transplant that was hiding us! The only shit-mix that ever did anything good for this Plane, and she ruined it! I just wanted a place where I had more time than the rest of you before that monster drained us all dry!"

Alesio just kept staring at Saida, his hands shaking, as if hoping he would read something different on her lips. Saida wanted to hold those hands, to deny everything, to stay.

But she couldn't delude herself any longer about what she had to do.

She didn't know if she made the right decision, or if her idea would work at all. But something similar had worked in the past. Watthe had consumed a lot of magic when he had terrorized the worlds a year ago, and transplanting magic into his body had worked to transplant him into the Primal Plane—or the Spatial Plane, as she thought of it now—killing him and reconnecting the Planes. If she understood what Clef had said—and believed him—the people of Transmutation had believed they could amplify and purify magic without understanding all the ins and outs of those magics. They had believed that lie. Because of that, the magic from all the different Planes had imploded and changed their Plane not into some benevolent god, but into the Hunger. The story sounded like how Watthe had gathered multiple magics and twisted himself into something bigger. So, transplanting magic into the Hunger might undo what the Hunger had become.

She touched the Goddess Head with foxan claws on human hands, closed her eyes, and Received her magic.

At first, she didn't sense any; she'd already used up her portals. But the Goddess Head, Amplify, expanded her ability across all the worlds. Hundreds of portals drew to her like moths to a flame, skittering up from the deep spaces of the Glass Sea under Sedella, clamoring for her to Shape them.

Because that is what she did when she called portals. She Shaped doorways to other places.

She told them, *For those of you who want to help me, I would like to journey to the Hunger.*

Many of them shuddered. Before they could leave, she added, *I am trying to stop them. I cannot promise they won't eat you now, but I will stop them from eating all of us in the next day or so.*

At that, most of them obliged, enough for her purpose. She began to Shape them into one long portal, a bridge crossing the divide to the place she asked. Amplify helped direct them. They hadn't transplanted here, hadn't merged with the Sensory Plane, but they remembered where they had come from.

It happened in less than a millisecond, though forever and a day passed by. Maybe her attempt would just flood or drain her. She had become a tiny river branching off from Amplify's vast ocean—or maybe more like a thousand oceans. Time shuddered around her and slowed, like she'd inhaled an incredible amount of ixor. Had she somehow always done this? Perhaps in the background of her whole life, part of herself had always Shaped this portal. But for all the time that passed, she had the distinct impression that Spatial magic liked doing this, that it flowed through her without dams or barriers or walls or rooms.

Maybe doing this would help feed the Hunger as Clef had said. But if she didn't try, then they would destroy everything anyway. She'd lose more than just Alesio. Her parents. Tener, and all her friends—human and fox-person—she'd made in the past year.

The Goddess Head shimmered as if infused with silver light, silver even in the filter of florescent green light around them, and she returned from that expanse, that infinite sea. The bridge stretched out before her, a hundred or more portals coupled like the links of a chain. How could a chain have two contrasting purposes; one to restrain and isolate, one to connect, to open, to unite?

"What is happening?" Baylor crouched, pale brown ixor shading the pink of his lips and the black skin of his hands.

"Saida!"

Alesio didn't try to run to her. Even now, he didn't want to chain her with their bond, to wrap it around her like a cage. He just reached for her with his voice like a hand she could hold, and that was what nearly undid her.

"Saida! Please, stay! Or at least let me come with you!"

Something inside her had crumpled. It hurt to swallow. "Love is caring for the other person, right? I want to do everything I can to keep you alive. Because I do love you, Alesio."

She stepped forward, even as she looked back.

Their faces lost color. Their mouths opened in screams, but no sound reached her. Clef had somehow managed to free himself in the chaos, and he stumbled towards Saida, knife drawn. Alesio didn't see him, focusing on Saida. If Clef couldn't reach her, he might try and kill Alesio—

Baylor blurred in from the side and buried a knife in Clef's neck.

The faces lost their features, smearing as space shifted. The city of Sedella faded.

She stepped further into the portal, and they all disappeared.

29

SMALLER THAN WE THINK

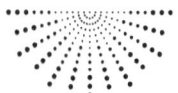

S *he left.*

She'd left to protect the worlds. She'd left to stop the Hunger. Though how she planned to do it, Alesio didn't know. Maybe she didn't know. She'd left, not knowing if she could come back, and she hadn't taken him with her.

"I can't protect you where you're going," he said, aloud, but he meant, *I want you to stay.* And that was the selfish part of him, the part that wanted to prove his worth by saving her from herself and others.

Something shivered between them and dimmed.

She'd said she feared herself, that she would change. And there it was, a bald admission of all his fears, that she might just up and float away one day, that he wouldn't protect her well enough from her own restless nature. That, as he aged, she'd forget him, uproot herself from him, and transplant somewhere else. With someone else. That he wouldn't be enough.

Alesio knelt where she'd disappeared and just cried.

At some point, Falrie curled up next to him, laying her head on his hands. She let out a whine, a keen that matched the pitch of his cries, as if singing with him. The intense silver light radiating from the

Goddess Head statue had faded, and the incandescent green glow from the moss tinged everything again.

He didn't move.

She'd wanted to stay. Her longing had showed in her face and thrummed along that invisible thread between them. Through all her fear about relationships, she'd wanted to try. But in the end, she'd still decided to leave, to potentially sacrifice herself to save him and all the rest of the worlds from the Hunger.

Does it matter why she left? She still left. The result is the same.

Something quivered inside him like a tortured mandolin string.

It did matter. He'd have done the same for her, given the chance and the ability. She hadn't done it to run away because of his incompetence or anything about him lacking, she'd done it to save him. That changed the results of his heart.

He loved her more than he'd ever loved anyone or anything before, but she'd loved him enough to let him go.

"—to go. Alesio."

He blinked. Sounds seemed unimportant. Falrie's form blurred in front of him.

"Now! We must go now! I can't portal much longer!"

Falrie and Tener pulled at him, unable to budge him. He stumbled up, not understanding.

"Baylor!" Tener shouted. "C'mon!"

The young man trembled, hovering over Clef's body. His bandages had loosened around his face, showing the glistening, open wounds on his lips.

Alesio reached out to him. "He can't hurt us anymore."

Baylor jerked his head up, then back down in a sharp nod. He gripped Alesio's hand, and the foxans hurried them along through Falrie's portal.

While traveling with Hestafon, three truths about Clef had revealed themselves to Alesio. The first truth, and most fundamental: Clef didn't control everything. He couldn't foresee and manipulate what Alesio would do all the time. He hadn't predicted that Hestafon could overcome Baylor's amplifier-infused abilities. He hadn't predicted that Alesio would overcome his rage and decide to use Clef instead of killing him. He wasn't—hadn't been—all powerful.

The second truth: Clef's words hurt the most because his lies *felt* like truth. He'd had the ability to pick out a grain of truth on a beach of lies. He had found echoes of a truth long ago spoken, a deep truth that had once formed an important chord, but that had changed in key. Like an overgrowth, they no longer reflected the purpose of the original magic, but that memory of the lie's origins lent it credibility. Made it feel real.

Clef's translation of the Goddess Head's lies had put on display the layered complexity and disparities between belief and fact. He had demonstrated how lies could hide in someone's fervent truth, and how undiscovered truths could hide in someone's fervent lie. And that had helped Alesio understand the third truth about Clef:

Even if he had truly believed Alesio wasn't worth anything, that didn't have to be true.

Clef's authority and influence fell apart in his head like a crumbling building. It had taken so long to build and to cage him in that place, to make him doubt himself in so many ways, to lie to himself over and over again. *You're not enough. You never will be. You're only worth a few notes when you're under my control.*

The schemes and psychotic manipulations of the straits' old shadow leader seemed petty to him, now, like a bird puffed up to appear bigger. Clef hadn't engineered hundreds of amplifiers to boost his followers. He hadn't gathered and trained some great army of cage fighters to infiltrate the Council and take over the worlds.

He'd hid.

He'd brainwashed and blackmailed Baylor, a youth tiptoeing into adulthood, to ensure a personal getaway from reality, and he'd hid. He'd always used and manipulated the most vulnerable people. He hadn't schemed with the Hunger at all; he'd tried to escape them by drugging himself into oblivion, just to give himself the fantasy of more time. And he'd squandered the actual moments he'd had left to screw with Alesio in the pettiest of ways.

Alesio's fear of the old strait's leader diminished moment by moment—not just because he'd died, but because the space and energy he'd taken up, the maze of insecurity Clef had established in him from a young age, fell in real time like gravity shifts untangling, and Alesio could see the way clear now, could see the man clear now. He was a lot smaller than Alesio remembered.

I wonder if all fears are like that. Smaller than we think.

Saida *was* their best chance to stop the Hunger. He couldn't save her from that. He zeroed in on that thought, and imagined he opened the window in one of his magic rooms for it. He let that concept in and Received it. The sharpness of her leaving dulled a bit.

Maybe he couldn't protect her anymore. But he would do all he could to support her, even worlds apart.

SAIDA TUMBLED through the multiple portals to the other side. Grayness surrounded her in a vacuum, and other indistinct floating pieces of wrecked buildings hung in the air, suspended as if on strings.

She did not fall, but she drifted down to a colorless mass of twisted stone, about as large as the Cadenza, which floated in the air. It blurred in her vision, a wavering like a heat mirage.

The moment she touched down, a spike of pain lanced through her. She arched her back, and something wrenched the cry from her; siphoning the noise even as it left her lips, almost before it reached her own ears. The mass of stone extended under her feet.

It had transmuted her sound into more of itself.

She clamped her lips shut, though she wanted to scream again. Her body vibrated, like her blood boiled and created friction. The stone touching her pulled at her and tore at her paws, at the fur and the skin, but the physical pull didn't pain her. She almost couldn't feel at all. But something yanked at the very foundation of her sense of self, a deterioration of identity that had her curling into a ball in agony.

The stonework around her had detailing, the haziness deteriorating as she neared it, but that reminded her—

A tree. The stone consisted of the Epitaph's trees the Hunger had consumed not too long ago but smashed into mangled bits and pieces of torn bark and crushed leaves. She could almost see the individual trees that used to manifest in each world: a smaller leaf here, a bit of apple there. Now, the Epitaph embodied agony in physical form.

She screamed again, and the sound flung through the air as if it tried to escape the muted stone-gray of the landscape, the fuzziness of her vision. Again, the jumbled Epitaph pulled her sound down, merged with it, and assembled a tiny bit more of the stone.

The Goddess Head in Sedella must have linked to the Epitaph, or what was left of them. Though it seemed as if the two beings hadn't agreed with each other, they had still lain next to each other for centuries and must have formed something of a bond.

Her throat swelled with grief. She forced the tears down to avoid giving the Hunger any more of her magic. Whatever sentience the foxan transplant had retained before, it had vanished. No voice spoke to her, even a recording, from what they had become.

The ends of a branch twisted up towards her, like a snake, and opened the end into a mouth. It had fangs, and it struck at her in slow motion, wavering through the air.

Saida pushed off the mass of stone to avoid the strike, and the vibration of her body lessened for the moment. The air still pulled at her skin and fur, but it didn't tear at them. Blood from her torn paws trickled down onto the lifeless and mangled Epitaph as she floated upwards, and the branch-mouth absorbed the drops and transformed into gray stone, so that it grew larger and almost four times as long. It settled back down, winding around part of the trunk, and stuck up towards her, like a horrible flower angling for the sun.

"MMMM." The Hunger's voice reverberated so loud, Saida had to clamp her hands over her ears. "SPATIAL MAGIC? I KNOW YOU'RE HERE SOMEWHERE, FOXAN."

I can't stay here long.

She paddled away, peering around her. From far off, everything seemed bigger and unclear like hills obscured by morning fog, but when she neared them, the larger picture gained detail and less haziness and dissembled as smaller fragments of strange, thorny fronds and – were those *hands?* With suction cups on the palms? – twisted and merged with each other, all of it stone.

The floating stone pieces were the spots inside the Hunger they'd observed before, which had swelled when the Hunger had consumed magic from the Sensory Plane. These foreign flora and bizarre bits of people had to be the victims of the last Plane the entity had consumed. The Hunger must keep them in reserve to fuel their passage—their ship—through the vast reaches of space from Plane to Plane.

She drifted in the direction of a pillar. Before she touched it, though, she pulled out Fecal Air. They didn't say anything. Had the Hunger severed her bond with Magic Ear? Or maybe the Hunger just drained her ability here, instead of severing it. Her senses felt continually diminished, as if her eyes strained, but only worked so far. The noise of her pushing off stone earlier sounded like the faint brushing of carpet.

What would Tener see, right now? Would all her bonds have severed, or had their glow just dimmed?

Here goes nothing.

She uncorked the vial, waved it next to the pillar, and held her breath.

A tree branch twisted around the pillar opened at the end into another snake mouth. It unhinged its jaw and snapped the air where she had waved the vial, then settled back down again, sticking out towards Saida. It grew, but much less than when she'd dripped blood, perhaps half as large again instead of four times its size. Nothing else happened.

I don't think that worked. Fecal Air had not transplanted and spread outward in any way. The Hunger had just consumed them. *Sounddamn it.*

Saida clenched her paws, then unclenched them. Her claws had already pierced her paw-pads, but she felt just the barest tickle. *It's draining my senses. My ability to Receive not just magic, but normal touch, or sound. It's why everything looks so foggy in the distance.* She gasped, her breath rushing out.

If they tasted more of her, the Hunger might figure out that a foxan had infiltrated their Plane. She had to figure out what to do, or they would consume her piece by piece.

———

MORNING LIGHT SIFTED down from a cloudy sky, obscuring not just the sun, but the reflected light from the worlds of Vision and Scent. Hestafon blinked his eyes open. He had curled up in the doorframe inside an alley, and numbness weighed down his feet and fingertips. He grimaced and flexed his extremities. Sensation shot back into his fingers, but not all the way to his toes, pins and needles stabbing at him. He kept himself from crying out and waited out the pain.

Memories from the previous night stumbled through his head like drunks trying to navigate a dance floor at three in the morning.

Clef. Those angry straiter kids had forced him away from his charge. They'd wanted to hurt Clef, maybe to kill him. And they'd recognized Hestafon . . . they'd dragged him into the streets . . . how had he escaped?

He had to get back to that cellar!

He maneuvered his legs out of the doorframe, wincing as more pins and needles stabbed through his thighs. What had happened out there? He peered out towards the street.

Someone lay there a few yards away in the gray slurry of mud and snow, face turned sideways. Hestafon gasped and staggered to his feet. His head reeled, and he clutched at it, waiting till everything stopped spinning.

He stumbled over to the person, a young woman with long brown hair, and crouched down, shaking her shoulder. "Miss! Miss?"

No response.

He pried her out of the muck, and she came free with a sucking sound. A slight fog emitted from her frost-blue lips. A strong sleep had claimed her, but laying out in the cold like this could kill her. He chafed at her hands and arms.

"Miss! Please wake up!"

She lolled in his arms.

"What do I do?" Hestafon gasped. His toes were still numb. The familiar panic rose in him. "What do I *do*?"

Tears rolled down his cheeks, slowing as they chilled. A shout pierced the quiet, and someone ran past the alley. How could anyone still be running? Did all the citizens of Anthem have the stamina of a trumpet player with five lungs?

Hestafon swallowed. Alesio had given him a job to do. With now determined quickness, he dragged the young woman out of the slush and into the doorframe, at least propped up and more protected from the elements. Then he hobbled out and peered into the street.

Many people slumped on the sidewalks, propped up against buildings. A few more lay in the slurry in the middle of the street. Here and there, groups of two and three shouted and dashed about, but in a different way than before. They didn't reach ahead of them in a physical attempt to reconnect to their magic, and they reacted to the shouts of their fellows. They avoided the people laying on the ground with more awareness, but still, they ran, anger contorting their faces. These, then, had recovered at least somewhat from the Hunger's draining. A couple of them had darker complexions and graying around their mouth instead of their ears, marking them as Tastians.

By reflex, he Shaped their shouting, because he could tell the sound *wanted* that, they wanted someone to identify them in a new way. Their yelling smelled like fire, like a flash of burning wood from a superheated flame.

His head pounded. He must have hit it falling in the alley.

Another group of three ran past. They shouted, "Find the fur-mixes! They can teleport us!"

People in Anthem didn't use that slur much anymore, but fear did that to people—brought back old beliefs. The same emotion rose in his own throat, but now he feared *for* the foxans and fox-people. What would the humans do if they did find a fox-person, or a Lunnite? They couldn't teleport, not like foxans, though the average Soundian might not know the difference.

Hestafon gritted his teeth. He didn't want to let Alesio down. At the same time, he couldn't just leave those poor people lying down in the slush. He waited till the shouting group had disappeared down the street and ran out to flip over the first prone person, an old man.

Cold. Stiff.

Hestafon swallowed, his hands shaking.

I must save as many as possible on my way.

He ran and flipped over the other two. They still lived. He dragged them over and propped them up against the buildings to keep their faces upward and out of the sludge. He slipped more than once. He stumbled, awkward without the control of his toes, still numb.

But he ruled this Senses-damned city. He had to do better.

He was supposed to be the delegate for this whole world, and he hadn't been able to handle one city.

I wish I could apologize to the people of Flock.

He hid from another group of shouters, their faces red and enraged. Did they know their magic had refilled at least some by now? Interesting how the absence of magic shook everyone to their foundation, but then they adjusted to that absence enough to not notice when their magic partially returned. Or did some of them use it as a subconscious excuse to act in such a way?

Smoke curled in the air ahead. He kept going. Less people laid in the sludge as he progressed towards the piper side, so he made better time.

The Hunger rotated in the sky again, and he kept his gaze from it, from those arm-tendril-snakes, those horrible vacuities that would suck him dry, cut him off from his magic. The fear drove him forward, faster, and faster, so that he dashed alongside another group.

He careened around a corner and almost smacked straight into a straiter mob. They had built a fire in the street from piles of trash. Hestafon stopped his headlong charge and shrank back from the light. He tried to double back, but another group of chanting, sweaty men cut him off. They'd lugged an old wire cage from the time of cage matches and set it next to the fire. Their shouts carried the scent of sweat and desperate denial.

"The world's ending, folks! Who wants to go out with some fun?"

"Fight! Fight! Fight!"

Hestafon edged around the corners of the firelight, trying to maneuver by using the broken stone houses as cover. But the commotion from the noise and the fire attracted more people, who swarmed through in front of him. He ducked in an alley and crouched there, caught between the cage match and the people drawn in by the cage match. Sounds of meaty fists and crunching bone carried the copper tang of blood.

How would Alesio have reacted to this? The singer had tried so hard to eradicate even the mention of cage matches on Anthem, but it seemed that when some people felt trapped, they liked trapping others to feel safer by comparison.

Hestafon peeked out. One man slammed into another, breaking his leg with an audible crack. The crowd gasped and Hestafon used the moment to sneak around the corner and behind the next house.

From there, he found a small, tiny ledge farther up that he sidled along, a fox-person way. The next house had two privacy fences, creating a makeshift tunnel open to the sky. He kept finding new places to twist through and sneak around, as if, by accepting the fox-people as people in his mind, their pathways opened to him.

Shouts arose from farther up the road, followed by thudding and banging sounds. Most of those who had recovered from the Hunger's draining had congregated in this part of Anthem, more on the piper side. Hestafon swallowed, but he needed to go that way to reach the cellar. He tried to keep to the hidden paths.

People ran everywhere back and forth, but a small group of straiters crowded outside an herbal remedy store, one which Hestafon had frequented before. These people, too, had wrested their mental control back, they could speak beyond babbling and screaming.

"Let us in! Please!" A woman shouted. "My daughter is sick!"

"Psst!"

The voice came from his left. A silhouette had cracked the store's window open. "Hestafon? Is that you?"

He knew that voice. Sturov, a noble in the piper district, who owned this store.

"Get in here! Those looters will kill you!"

Hestafon frowned and studied the 'looters.' They wore the dirty clothing of poorer straiters, the homeless who lived in the mud and the snow and begged on streetcorners. But they seemed to have regained their mental capacities, and violence didn't hold them in its grasp. *Interesting how different people react in different ways to threats and fear.*

The man standing next to the woman banged on the store's door again. "Please! Her fever keeps climbing, and none of the other stores are open!"

"Go away!" Sturov said from inside. "We aren't open, either!" His voice stank of fear, a sharp, acidic odor, and fear, fear, it was always fear that cut like a knife, inside a person and out!

Hestafon squared his shoulders. He strode through the running crowd. His voice didn't shake, which surprised him. "Open the door, Sturov."

The group of straiters whirled and surveyed his rumpled and bloodied cotton clothing.

Sturov cleared his throat. "Hestafon, why would you—"

"Delegate?" The woman outside the store covered her mouth with her hand. She and the others had the same thousand-eye stare as when Alesio had woken up in the infirmary on Taste. "We don't want to hurt anyone! We swear! But we need medicine!"

"Sturov." Hestafon struggled to keep his words, his *sound*, from becoming unpleasant, imagining he had a caramel in his mouth. "I'll pay for it. Just open the door. You all, wait till he brings it out."

"What are you doing?" Sturov hissed from behind the door. "Why're you helping those straiters? They're animals! They've set up cage matches in the middle of the streets!"

The store owner opened the door, and the straiters all stepped back, as if they hadn't believed it would happen. Sturov had bloodshot eyes and sweat-soaked gray hair, and he brandished a knife in his age-spotted hand. "No sudden moves! Hestafon, where—there you are. Come in quickly." He grabbed at Hestafon's arm, who pulled back.

Sturov paused, then narrowed his eyes.

"Give them some medicine," Hestafon said through gritted teeth.

The imagined caramel in his mouth helped a little, forcing him to take his time on his tone, to measure out his rhythm. "On my tab. Everyone's just scared, just like you. But we don't have to treat each other this way."

The straiters had their mouths open, watching this exchange. Sturov flipped his gaze back and forth between Hestafon and the group, then growled, "Give me a moment," and slammed the door. After a few tense minutes, he returned with a small basket full of bandages, vials, and cleaning wipes. "I'll remember this next year. I won't endorse your reelection!"

"That's fine," Hestafon said.

Sturov regarded the silent group of straiters. "The vials will bring down fevers." He thrust the basket at the nearest man and woman. The woman grabbed it and almost dropped it in her haste.

"Thank you," she mumbled, staring at Hestafon. The others all murmured their gratitude, too, glancing at him as they snatched various items from the basket, then shuffled away into the alley nearby.

Hestafon hands trembled.

Listening to Sturov felt like gawking at a tonal mirror. So condescending. So fearful of the unknown. How had he not heard it such a short time ago? How did Sturov not hear it? He'd spent his whole life tuning and perfecting how he rang bells to sound pure and on key, all the while his words sounded and smelled like that, like bitter knives flung in the dark? How had he been so ethically deaf?

Another scream sounded, high and shrill. He jerked his head up, and from the corner of his eye, a tendril of the Hunger moved closer. A jolt of primal fear rushed through him, and he gasped with the urge to run, to escape, but he controlled his breathing as he'd learned helped his panic attacks.

Another knot of people with silk clothing had gathered from the general stream of rushing humans. Pipers. They'd cornered two people in the street against the side of a building. A foxan, and another with foxan ears and human face, perhaps a fox-person. Then he recognized the four faded red stripes on the foxan's cheeks as Darrow, Saida's father.

Hestafon clenched his jaw and strode forward again, shoving through the chaos. Someone clipped him in the side with an elbow, knocking some breath out of him.

"Let them go!"

Two of the pipers pivoted. Their faces brightened. "Hestafon! Look! They can teleport us!"

At the word 'teleport', a group of people running past slowed, then clustered around them.

"I can't!" The other captive, a fox-person Hestafon didn't recognize, struggled in their grip. "I'm a Lunnite! I can't use portals!"

"We're trapped here! The Portal Station isn't working!" Another of the pipers shoved the Lunnite up against the wall, his arm against their throat. "Do it! Do it now!"

"They can't!" Hestafon tried to step forward, but the press of other people had become too great. They'd increased to fifteen or twenty people. The Lunnite's face reddened.

"Wait!" Darrow wheezed. The crowd had him pinned on the ground in his smallest foxan form. "I have one left! Let them go!"

Everyone jerked to stare at the foxan.

"Well, do it then!"

"Yeah! Do it!"

With a grim face, Darrow closed his eyes, calling up a portal a few feet away. A forest showed on the other side, the trees caressed by a warm, gentle breeze that smelled of evergreens and loam. Scent.

The safest world as we know it, Hestafon thought. *As long as they're in the woods, instead of Tremain.*

The people holding Darrow and the Lunnite released them and rushed through. Darrow coughed and stumbled to his feet, remaining in his foxan form. The Lunnite slumped against the wall they'd shoved him against.

More people clustered around the portal in moments, desperation on their faces, exhaustion running them ragged. They had more edges to their faces, angles in their cheeks that spoke of a life of constant hunger and wore cotton clothing that rustled instead of swishing with silk. Straiters.

"Let me go!"

"I have to get out of here!"

The fear rose in him, then, too, that sense of a cage descending. That tendril approached closer in the sky. People shoved each other, and a young man fell in the tumult and the others stepped on his torso.

"I can't hold it open much longer!" Darrow shouted; his voice strained.

The portal shrank, but still people shoved through, clambered over others, reaching towards it. It closed with a snap, forcing people out of itself every which way, depending on how far they'd gotten through.

The rest of the people turned back to Darrow, eyes full of sharpness.

"I can't open another," Darrow said.

"He's lying!"

"Let's cut an ear or two off. I bet he'll magically find another!"

Hestafon swallowed, and shouted out, "Hey, you bunch of—of—dirty straiters! I have my own personal portal station! Come this way if you want to use it!"

The rush towards the portal slowed. Faces slid towards him. Eyes narrowed. Lips thinned.

Hestafon gulped.

And ran.

FALRIE PORTALED Alesio and the rest of them to Anthem, close to the Portal Station.

People from multiple worlds ran every which way, but with a different kind of urgency than they had before. Exhaustion lined their faces, showing the effects of the Hunger's draining, but they didn't reach with clawed, desperate hands for their lost magic. They ran *from* the absence in the sky, instead of trying to find what they had lost. Although they may not have fathomed it, their magic had begun to refill.

Indeed, the Hunger rotated again, and one snake-tendril-arm-thing unfurled, grasping for them, blotting out half the entire sky. Even through Alesio's numbness, terror jolted through him, at the need to escape that void, to never, *ever*, let them steal his magic again.

A glow lit up the piper side, where people had lit fires in the streets. A child cried in the road for their mother; their face smudged with dirt. A few people had slumped against the buildings, still drained and sleeping off the Hunger's draining. One large group gathered farther off, and their chanting reached Alesio:

"Cage match! Cage match!"

I'm so tired. Alesio wanted to just lay down and let the worlds burn. He expected a rush of anger, or sadness, or really any emotion, but Saida might be dying, so did he care? She fought that abject horror, and he could do nothing to help her.

Don't think about it. Don't think about it. Just try and do what you can. She's still fighting, isn't she?

Baylor stood in front of him, his textured hair casting a larger shadow on the ground. He spoke without ixor muddying his voice. "Hey, bug-ass. Stay with me."

Alesio blinked. He'd decided to let her protect herself, to believe that she could keep herself together. He'd decided to allow her to reach out to him instead of him keeping her in a bubble Shaped out of fear. To let go of the need to feel needed.

He had. He'd decided.

It was hard to keep deciding, though. It was one thing to have an epiphany while Saida curled in his arms, safe and warm. It was another to cling to that understanding in her absence, while she dashed into danger, while she might drift cold in a dark place, forgetting herself, forgetting him . . .

He shook his head and swallowed his misery. He had to trust that she could handle herself without him by her side. Meanwhile, he would do what he could to help from afar, in the way best for her. For them.

Help from afar . . .

An idea sprang to his mind. An idea so outlandish he laughed at his own audacity.

"Alesio?" Baylor said.

Alesio straightened his shoulders. "Everyone, follow me. There's a way we could help Saida. But we need all the people together and listening."

It's the end of the worlds!" A man shouted. "Come and watch a piper fight!"

Alesio wended towards that voice, and the rest of them followed. On the way there, Darrow ran up to them in his human form, though, as usual, his foxan muzzle remained. His face and arms had scratches on them. He pointed at the fighting. "They have Hestafon!"

"By the Senses," Alesio cursed. He dashed through the streets, elbowing his way through the denser part of the crowds that had gathered around the displayed violence.

Behind him, Darrow gasped out in a strained, raspy voice, "He led them away from me! They would've run me down, but he led them away!"

Hestafon huddled in the cage, holding his arms over his head. His ponytail had fallen out, and his straight blonde hair had clumped at the ends with dried blood. More blood ran down the side of his face, and his arm bent at a bad angle. A straiter menaced him with a raised fist.

Alesio entered his house of Sound magic and listened. He listened to the sound of his own breathing, to the rhythm of his shoes on the street, to the shape of the words that he wanted to say before he said them. Everything joined into a chord. A tiny bit of Sound magic had returned to him.

"Please, just don't make me a knife! I know lots of humans use Sound for those, but I don't want to cut or stab. I want to flow, to feel a rush of wind!"

Alesio smiled. *I can work with that.* He sang, "Let him go!"

479

He Shaped the Sound magic inside him into a forceful sound wave that shoved the straiter back against the cage. Alesio barreled through the crowd, spun, and stretched his arms in front of it. "Listen to me—"

"It's the Voice! The Voice of Reconnection!"

"No, it's Requiem!"

"Save us! Save us from the Hunger!"

He spread his arms in his performer's pose, that upright, reaching posture that enchanted attention like moths to light. The raucous cheering quieted for a moment. Darrow and Baylor watched from further back in the crowd, elbowing their way closer.

"You have to listen," he said. "Cage matches won't stop the Hunger. You can't do this to people just because you're afraid—"

"Shut up!"

"He works with Hestafon! He's a straiter traitor!"

Everyone started shouting again, this time at him. No one could hear him, now. Performing music for an audience that had already given themselves to violence almost never worked, but at least he'd tried. Several people seized his arms, and they shoved him inside the cage, which had become cramped with three people inside it.

He tried not to let the cage Shape a cage of fear inside him. He couldn't let that happen. He couldn't shut down right now. Hestafon needed his help.

He had to fight.

The other straiter fighter leered at him, a man Alesio had fought and won against while fighting for Clef. Sneering faces stuck their tongues out at him from the crowd. He backed the few feet of space towards Hestafon.

"You didn't have to do that," Hestafon said. "Now you might get hurt, too."

"I can hold my own."

"I know that. I meant—"

The straiter threw a punch at him, and Alesio crouched, placed a hand on the floor for balance, and swung his leg in an arc, tripping him so he fell face-first. Alesio dove on his back, trying to pin him to the ground, but the man arced back and head-butted Alesio. Stars exploded in his sight. Alesio rolled off and staggered back against the cage. Clef's voice echoed in his head, what his brain imagined Clef would have said. *She left you. This is all you're good for.*

No. *That's not true.*

Someone grabbed his arm, and he almost fought back, but the heavy breathing and pained gasp sounded like Hestafon, so he let the piper drag him to the left, stumbling as he did. Something *zinged* next to him and clanged against the metal bars. A Sound knife.

He opened his eyes. The straiter grinned.

Did Saida do something to stop the Hunger? Or is that just his magic refilling like mine? He tried to peer upwards, but the top of the cage blocked his view of the sky, and too many people thronged around the cage.

"Straiter Traitor! Straiter Traitor!"

The fighter rushed with a heavy swing. Alesio ducked under the attack, grabbed the man's arm, and used his own momentum to throw him to the ground.

"Stop!" Alesio said. "I don't want to fight. You win! Just let us leave!"

The fighter rolled away from him and spit on the ground. "You ain't getting away that easy. You've gone soft, everyone knows it. It's time to pay you back."

"Alesio!" Baylor's voice. The young man rushed towards him from outside the cage, and Darrow chased Baylor, but couldn't keep up. "I can stop him!"

"No," he said. "Stay away."

The man had climbed to his feet. He rushed Alesio again. Alesio tried to dodge but slipped on a patch of ice. The man slammed into him. They tangled and twisted on the ground, both trying to gain the better position. The man inhaled and let loose a Sound knife at Alesio's shoulder. Alesio shoved the man's head to the side, so the knife hit the ground next to him. Alesio headbutted the man in the face to give him a matching bloody nose and kicked the man away.

The fighter rolled to his feet and released a Sound knife as he did so, trying to catch Alesio before he regained his footing. The shot flew wide by a few feet.

Hestafon cried out behind Alesio, and the crowd gasped as one. The cage fighter's eyes widened, and he stopped.

Alesio whirled around.

Red bloomed on Hestafon's chest. He blinked at Alesio, then fell sideways. Alesio lunged forward and caught him.

"Wait," Alesio said. "Wait. Hold on."

The piper coughed, and blood trickled from his mouth. "Sorry . . . I couldn't . . . guard Clef."

"It's fine! It's fine!" Alesio lowered Hestafon to the ground and pressed his hands over the wound. Blood gushed out around his fingers. "Oh, by the Senses. Hestafon. Hestafon, don't close your eyes!"

The crowd had gone quiet.

"Your voice . . . smells nice. . . like a soft rain."

"Someone get a doctor!" Alesio screamed.

The cage fighter lowered his eyes. "It's too late."

Hestafon had obeyed Alesio's request to keep his eyes open. He stared upwards at the cage top, unseeing.

Alesio bent his head over the piper's chest and bit his tongue to keep from crying out. If he released any noise, he felt it would sharpen on the razor in his throat and fly as a sword into the crowd. His hands shook, and hot tears dropped on Hestafon's face.

"Don't leave." Alesio bent over him. "Don't leave. I didn't get a chance—I didn't take the chance to tell you. You're going to be a great leader." His fingernails bit into his palms. "You're already a great friend."

"He jumped in front of the knife," someone said in the crowd, one of the young men that had shoved Alesio inside. "It would have hit me, but he just . . ."

Murmurs floated through the crowd like seeds on the wind, planting at random, growing in spurts.

"It's true, I saw it!"

"The piper saved him!"

Baylor opened the door to the cage, and Alesio's vision glazed with tears.

Saida, I couldn't protect him, either.

30

HEADING UPRIVER

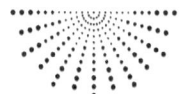

Saida jerked awake.

She'd drifted. She couldn't stay on any of the physical pieces of the Hunger, or they would tear her body apart. At some point the stress must have overwhelmed her and she'd fallen unconscious, her body deciding to shut down for her. She had reverted to her foxan form, that instinctual side of her that took over in times of distress, folding her as small as possible to avoid detection.

What had woken her?

The bond between her and Alesio twanged, like a plucked mandolin string.

Regret. Grief.

She sucked in a breath. The emotion quivered faint between them, but still there. *He* was still there, but suffering, somehow. Had the Hunger consumed more magic from the worlds? She reached out and wished she could cup her hand against his cheek.

Something in the endless gray landscape had shifted. Her vision hadn't cleared up—distant objects remained blurry and hazy. Her base Receiving had not refilled while she slept, even avoiding those snake mouths that had gulped at her senses. The air seemed a slow drain to her very being. However, five large, indistinct circles showed in the sky, now, colored the same as the five planets of her Plane. The part of the Hunger that she had teleported to must have rotated around so Saida's side faced the Sensory worlds.

She'd never viewed them like this altogether, and they formed a sort of interlocking pattern, like a fuzzy five-point star, the same pattern as on the back of the Epitaph: large, lavender Vision, small, azure Touch, the two similar light blue sapphires and emeralds of Scent and Sound, and the darker cobalt blue and russet Taste.

The Spatial Plane sat underneath the five circles. like a giant bowl, and something misty rose from it – Spatial magic feeding into the Sensory Plane.

Her vision blurred more. She'd floated into a space that pulled at her more and tore at her skin even while not touching one of the physical "buildings" and avoiding those snakes. She winced and managed to swim back to where the air itself didn't try to yank her apart.

But the Hunger had woken from their satiated sleepiness. The stone platforms, instead of just floating, had a sort of drive to them, a restlessness, and one glided towards her now, some of the snake mouths opening and hissing for her. She swam away from them, and they seemed to lose interest when she drifted far enough away.

How long did she have? Soon the Hunger would want to feed again. She needed to figure out a plan, now that her idea to transplant something here had failed.

Tener's words echoed in her mind. *"The baby Hunger said you need to find a city called Kolsuv Mor. They said it was where everything started, and that you have to 'break the circle and destroy the tree.'"*

On Vision, the damaged rings of ancient Lunnite script had choked the flow of energy to the Epitaph tree, so it hadn't functioned at full capacity.

She needed to damage the runes, in a specific place, where, according to Tener, "everything started." And destroy a tree. Another Epitaph tree? But where? How could she find them?

Wait. If everything had started in this city named Kolsuv Mor, the logic upstream meant that it'd be a Transmutation city, and that the

Hunger would be strongest there. It'd be where the air tried to tear her apart the most.

Saida swallowed, straightened her shoulders, and swam back towards the area she'd just escaped from.

LINIA HAD GATHERED MORE people from the houses. Those that paced inside their kitchens instead of the streets, those that sobbed into their doorframes rather than wander outside – she'd collected them and added them to her entourage. Children toddled out, and old ones with fragile skin, all of them marched in time, and that didn't seem like a thing that should happen. A burr in the smoothness of Linia's song itched at Paras, and she rubbed at her eyes.

Then Linia sang, "Sing louder!" And the wavering circuit in the air in front of her pulsed out, and everyone obeyed, and the song overtook everything else once again, and Paras could only move forward, and hadn't she always wanted that, anyway—to just explore new places? To avoid responsibility, to not have to plant the fields in Tremain, or do whatever Verrity wanted her to do?

Verrity.

The thought of her sister jarred her out of the song. She raised her head. How many people had Linia amassed? Hundreds. Maybe a thousand. They strode down the streets, now multiple streets at a time, streaming like so many drops of water in a river, like the river that her sister had pulled her out of all those years ago. They headed upriver, and something about the journey stank like a rancid fish, something slippery she couldn't grab hold of in her mind, and why would she want to do that, anyway?

Did Verrity march in this crowd, too, somehow pulled out of Tremain? Sweat slicked Paras's whole body, as if she'd run a long way, and grit caked the corners of her eyes, like she just awakened from a deep sleep and had forgotten to wash her face.

People far ahead of them had roamed away from bonfires in the street, and the company flowed around some cages in the middle.

Some of the caged people watched, their eyes all sweet and longing to join. No sign of her sister, though there marched Higa, her yellow green foxan irises dilated, her lips parted.

Higa!

Paras didn't want this – *what do I mean by 'this'?* – for Higa, or for Tosn, or for any of the Lunnites. What would Linia do with them? She had herded anyone and everyone out in the streets, and what if—what if they didn't have homes to return to? What then? What about the Lunnites, who hailed from another world? Would she just leave them out in the ice and the snow?

Linia stopped then and sang something new. "All but pipers, far and near, come this way, gather here!"

A pulse reverberated out from their huge group, the circuit of magic having grown large enough to encircle them all. Her song strengthened and resounded louder than the immediate group. The whole city started to sing, and repeat:

"All but pipers . . . far and near . . ."

Paras struggled to keep her mind apart, but the power of it overwhelmed her. The song had become a living thing, and Paras could not help but amplify it with her own voice.

BAYLOR HELPED Alesio out of the cage into the quietness of the crowd.

Hestafon had died.

Alesio couldn't process it, not when Saida had just left, not when Saida could have died too.

A little Touch magic tapped on the wall of his room, something like a bird's beak on a window, or the click of a claw on glass. He opened a window for the magic, and he swore Saida's hand brushed his cheek.

Their bond still existed. She still lived.

I know she can do this. I know that she loves me. He swallowed the lump of tears in his throat. *I will protect her in the way she needs me to.*

Sounds of rioting from far off still drifted into the street, but from moment to moment, new groups joined, Soundians, and Tastians, too, chaotic and loud, and the crowd shushed them, and brought them in, and whispered to them of a piper who had sacrificed themself to save a straiter. Tears ran down his cheeks, and everything seemed muffled again, except his emotions had drained, not his magic.

The ground began to shake, and a different sound reached him. A huge, swelling song. His mind blanked, and his mouth moved on its own.

"All but pipers, near and far . . ."

Alesio straightened, his thoughts dwindling. He clutched at them in his mind, but they sifted through his head like sand. He wanted to fight against it, but he also *didn't*. Too much had happened. A part of him wanted to let the song fill his mind instead of the pain of losing Saida, then Hestafon . . .

He marched, along with everyone else, flowing like a well-controlled river down the street.

LINIA SANG a different line to Tosn. "Open a portal, open it now, to where the Summit Wave looms!"

The rest of the people continued to sing the main melody, including Paras, independent of her wishes. Something about that song itched at her, but she could not move to scratch. She could not move unless the song willed it.

Tosn shook his head. "I cannot, I cannot, I used my portal already today." Tears dripped down his cheeks and into his gray, grizzled beard.

Linia gripped the older Lunnite's arm, something silver in her hand—*why is that important*—her knuckles white against where his skin changed to fur. "With my power and yours, open this door!"

Tosn's eyes flashed silver. He reached out and a huge portal appeared.

Ice cold water streamed out around their ankles, mixing with the slush of the snow, and a towering wave—*the Summit Wave*, Paras thought in some part of her outside of the song—waited for them, soaring towards them.

Higa strode past Paras towards the portal, towards that wall of impending water, her black fur slick and glistening wet from the spray, her yellow-green eyes vacant.

The spray wafted the scent of summer, the rich loam of a forest floor, into Paras's nose. She'd sat there under the rala trees, the thrill of hope blooming in her chest. Her heart had raced as the young blonde Scentian woman had scooted closer, had let her hand trail over hers . . . no woman in Sedella had shown interest, but this slip of a woman, though she appeared small, had such *drive,* such passion!

Paras blinked. She'd Received Scent magic. She'd lived in someone else's memory for a short time. Higa's memory . . . of her.

She blushed.

Then she refocused. The magic had snapped her out of the trance. Higa still marched towards that portal. Linia held the second amplifier in her hand, and she pressed it against Tosn's neck. She shared the amplifier's power with the Lunnite so he could keep the huge portal up.

Paras seized Linia's arm, trying to pull her away from Tosn. "You can't do this!"

Mud had spattered Linia's white silk dress, and silver coated her pastel blue eyes. She stopped singing, but the city continued to sing, luring more people towards them from across Anthem like a pot of honey calling to a trail of ants. Not just Soundians, either, but many darker-skinned people from the Cloves joined the masses. Linia's song had called for *all but pipers, near and far . . .*

"Dear Paras," Linia said. "I thought you wanted safety for your village."

"Not like this! You're sending them to their deaths!"

"Do you fault me for clearing the city of trash?" Linia wore a smile of callous beauty, the wrinkles around her lips pushing up to her cheeks, though her eyes did not change. "For putting them in their place? Clef might be a dirty straiter, but at least he kept his people in line with those cage matches. With all these portals opened to all the worlds, we need more stability. More safety. We need the dangerous people gone. You hear me? All those dangerous, filthy people will be *gone*."

She pointed at a young man with ridged sound scars on his cheek, knuckles bloody. "Gone." She jutted her chin at another, older man, with even more sound scars crisscrossing his arms like spiderwebs, still singing the song with the rest. "Gone. And when they're gone, that thing in the sky will leave, too, because it won't need to purge our world of detritus."

"That's—that's not right." Paras pushed against the weight of the song holding her tongue. "People can change! And what about that little boy?" She pointed at a toddler, who had just a grimy scrap of cloth over his rear end, hesitant in the shallow water.

"You can't grow fruit from bad soil," Linia said. "They all grow up to be criminals."

Linia's words reeked, stripped of their outer sweet perfume to reveal the rancid reasoning underneath.

The Hunger revolved overhead like an emptying drain, and one of its tendrils had reached towards Anthem like a massive arm. The Hunger loomed so large it had blocked out the sun.

Paras reached to peel the shard out of Linia's hand—

What am I doing? Linia is helping us all. Linia gathers all . . .

The people marched through the massive portal to Touch, cramming through twenty to thirty at a time. She had to think strong thoughts and focus on her own emotions to avoid letting the horde's singing assert authority over her mind again.

Paras dashed around Linia and covered her mouth with one hand, while trying to pull the piper's grip free of Tosn with the other. The intense power of the song flagged as Linia's voice paused, though the rest of the people continued to sing.

Linia didn't try to fight her, which surprised Paras. She stood there rigid as a plank. Maybe she could only do so many things at a time while controlling this many people.

"Tosn, can you hear me? Tosn!" Paras screamed in his ear.

The Lunnite didn't blink. Linia still pressed the clump of the

Goddess Head to his neck. He sang the song for the portal, keeping it open. The people flowed through, so many every second.

"Stop this!" She cried out. "It's not right!"

She couldn't think what else to say. Verrity would've known what to say. Paras missed her sister. Her mother's singsong words fluttered through her mind. *My Ver, my Par, the very pair of daring!*

Paras tried to grasp at the silver in the piper's hand, to try and shove it away from Tosn's neck, but Linia hummed something, and Paras's mind blanked for a moment.

What was I doing?

Higa had already passed through the portal, waiting on the other side with a growing number of Soundians. Sweet, excited Higa, who had wanted to adventure just like Paras. The Lunnite faced the Summit with the same glazed eyes and stiff expression as everyone else. Rounded up with as much respect as a bad batch of tomatoes, ready to be mixed with the fertilizer.

Why had Paras ever thought of fox-people or Lunnites as primitive or savage? She hadn't known any before, so why had she assumed? And these straiters—so many of them, wearing ragged, worn-out clothing and premature stress lines around their mouths and eyes— perhaps she'd misjudged them, too, because she hadn't known any before this?

Something pierced her side. She screamed. A silver knife jutted out of her hip.

Linia had taken advantage of Paras's slackened grasp and stuck her with a real knife from a hidden pocket in her dress.

"Grab her!" Linia sang the words and three of the closest people from the masses restrained Paras's arms, pulling her off Linia.

Paras shouted and thrashed, trying to wrench herself free. The knife in her hip scraped against the bone, and she screamed.

"What a shame," Linia said. "I planned to head to Tremain next, you know. I would have rid your village of those thugs Clef sent to control you."

Paras started. "How do you—"

"Of course I know about that. I know all about the deal you made with his men, to protect your people."

"They forced me!" Paras swallowed. Had someone from the village blabbered to Verrity? They'd all agreed to stay quiet.

"You and I are alike, my dear. I must protect my town from these dangerous people."

"No one's forcing you to do this! These are people, right here! There are children here! Part of your town! Some of them are even from other worlds!"

Linia donated Paras a smile, though her eyes did not volunteer for the charity work. "My dear Paras. I simply have a higher standard for what I consider 'people' than you do." She flicked her fingers as if ridding herself of a speck under her nails. "Take her along with you, my dears."

The water rose around their ankles, surging through the portal, knocking some of the people off their feet. Some of them blinked and shook their heads like they tried to get water out of their ears, but Linia's song caught them again in its net, and they lurched to their feet and continued their march.

Through the portal, the Wave of blue gray craned its neck down at them, its muddy feet foaming in front of it.

31
IN ALL THE VASTNESS OF
THE SKY

Alesio couldn't form thoughts. The shape of them eluded him, tangling in his mind like an intricate bar of music he tried to perform in a dream. Each time the notes—the words— snarled in a knot that snarled at him instead, with a not-face that sang the song, the song, the song!

He marched with a flood of others, but no one dashed around in a frenzy or screamed or shouted. Everyone sang, and everyone strode with a slow yet steady purpose, closer to where the song issued from.

A wind sprayed him with a fine mist, and he blinked. *Cold.* He shivered, and beside him, so did . . . he couldn't turn his head. The song snarled at him again to keep going, a cord of chords that anchored him to its host. He slogged along without pause.

The rim of a giant portal appeared in the middle of the street, and people marched through it into darkness. Water flowed around his ankles, then his calves. *Cold.*

Someone sang off key. No, someone sang the wrong song all together. A slender blonde woman screamed and kicked as three others dragged her towards the portal. Her tone clashed, like the background of patrons ordering another round at the Drinks De Capo while he performed. Like then, he tuned out the words and focused on his song, the words becoming an annoying sound in the background.

"Voice! Alesio!" The woman screamed, "You need to wake up! You have to stop Linia!"

Alesio continued his singing and steady march towards into the cold flowing water. The woman mere feet from him, her thrashing about kicking up the icy water onto his face. He didn't let him ruin his performance.

"Let go of me! Alesio!"

He just wanted his mind numb. It was so easy to keep walking. So, so easy.

"Senses! I hope this works," the woman said.

Alesio splashed through the water. The smell reminded him of something. A memory of another time wading through shallow water—

crouching around grey, teardrop shaped structures

three water ships searching for Saida

One ship sent ripples back to him. It had hit something. Then Saida gasped.

Alesio smiled. He circled around the pod to fall into her ambush. She dove into him, and they crashed into the water, she kissed him, and her lips pillowed over his.

He stared into her eyes. They joked and laughed, the words soft and blurry to his ears. His heart ached. He wanted to stay in this memory because he now recognized it as such, like becoming aware of a dream.

Now she's off risking her life to stop the Hunger, and I'm . . . Where am I? What am I doing?

The haunting echoes of music waited for him past this memory, muffled, the water under them vibrating with its controlling sound. Saida began to dissipate like smoke.

I may not be able to protect you against the Hunger, but I sure as hell can make sure you have a life to return to once you've dealt with it. Because you will come back. I believe in you, and I love you too.

He surfaced from both the memory and the song as if he breached a wave. Gasping, he dragged in more breath.

The song weighed on him like a dome of pressure, the magic from everyone around him amplified to a massive scale. Bodies shoved him as they marched, streaming around him without pause. He might be out from under the song's control now, but he didn't know how long he would last. Not to mention, those three people still dragged the shouting Paras away.

He descended into his Sound house and asked the strains of magic drifting outside the walls, "Who wants to push outward?"

A few bars of music streamed into the room—their name was Pulse! Pulse! Pulse! and he Shaped them into a Sound shield all around him to protect him from the mind controlling song.

He pushed his way to Paras and the people holding her. Once the Sound shield covered them, the people holding Paras released her and otherwise steadied themselves like people stumbling up from the bar after last call.

"Are you okay?" he asked the Scentian.

She held her head, groaning. "Thank the Senses you stopped the song. I was losing control again."

"Did you Shape that memory for me? With Scent magic?"

"I . . . yes. Sorry, having magic is new for me." She straightened. "We must stop Linia! She has two amplifiers, and she wants to kill all these people with the Summit Wave!"

"*What?* She's controlling everyone? I thought the Hunger had done something."

Not far away, Darrow trotted in a trance on all fours. Alesio asked if more magic wanted to join him, and Pulse! Pulse! Pulse! swelled into Da Da Dum PULSE, Da de Dum PULSE! pushing outwards to create a larger shield of silence. As with air magic, he had to keep feeding the shield with new magic or it would dissipate as the opposing song did not retreat but kept trying to wriggle into the melody line.

Darrow's eyes lost their glaze, and he stopped, too, shaking his head as if he had water in his ears.

What is going on? Did Linia plan this with Clef all along?

No. Clef had devolved into someone who couldn't do something like this. This threat had manifested from somewhere he hadn't foreseen, but perhaps he should have. Linia was one of the five shadow leaders of Anthem, after all.

Alesio checked his magic. Some Sound and Touch magic hovered behind the walls of both rooms, perhaps a third of his normal amount. He couldn't keep up this shield for longer than ten minutes, tops.

People flowed around them like water around rocks in a stream. Most seemed able to avoid unmoving objects, so they didn't trample him or Darrow. Many Tastians had joined the press of native Soundians, and a few Touchians as well, those who had come through the Portal Station before the Hunger had shut it down.

Falrie, Tener, and Baylor all trudged ahead, close to the giant portal. Naya had joined too, in a different cluster of people. They all marched with a collective uncanny serenity that veiled a tangle of trapped and fragmentary thoughts, like a pen filled with confused sheep for the slaughter.

It opened to Touch, where the fading light of sunset displayed . . .

The Summit Wave. It roared under ten miles away, headed straight towards them. It cast a long, long shadow, all the way through the portal into Anthem itself, where the brighter light of midmorning from Anthem's sunlight cut it off. Water from Touch flowed through the portal, streaming underfoot.

He froze. The wind and the spray of the Summit Wave screamed through the portal. He'd wondered what it would sound like, if the Summit Wave could thunder on Sound, and now it approached. Pressure built again outside his Sound shield, the weight of the loudness pushing on him like he'd swam deep underwater.

At least a thousand people had advanced to the Touch side. Perhaps half or more of the city of Anthem.

More people stumbled into Alesio's Sound shield, pausing, and piling up around them. Alesio splashed to a different spot to avoid a tangle of limbs. "Alright," he said to Paras. "Where is she?"

Paras pointed back towards the dwindling crowd on the Anthem side. He squinted. Linia's smaller frame stood next to a Lunnite. The older male one who had met with Alesio and Saida at the Cadenza.

Silver flashed in Linia's mouth, and then a stream of silver arced towards her other hand, which gripped another gleaming bit of silver. The stream arced back, creating a revolving figure eight of silver around her.

He clenched his fists. He didn't have time to ask or puzzle out why she had brainwashed these people to commit suicide by the Summit Wave. He had to stop her. He had to wake the city up, but his shield wouldn't extend that far. He didn't have enough magical power for that.

He asked the magic again, "Who wants to push outwards as far as you can, as loud as you can?"

A few harmonies streamed through. He Shaped them and the shield's identity shifted into a longer phrase: DA DE dum PULSE de DUM de Dum, DA de DUM PULSE, DA DE dum PULSE! The shield caught up to the other two foxans and Baylor, and the stretch of people between them.

They paused, blinking, obstructing the people around them and forcing them to divert their path.

"Baylor!"

The young man met his eyes. The skin around his mouth resembled a peeled fruit. Alesio pointed at Linia. "Stop her!"

Baylor tried to shoot an ixor dart at her, but too many people blocked the way, and he couldn't get a clear shot. He charged against both the current of people and that of the Glass Sea snaking under their feet. He breathed out ixor so he could cut through the marching crowd. Around him, people slowed, and stopped, slack-jawed in front of the portal.

For his part, Alesio had to shove his way through the crowd. His shield moved with him, restoring peoples' autonomy in swaths. This caused them to scream with fear as they comprehended the Summit Wave hurtling towards them, like a lighthouse revealing a sudden jagged reef to nearby ships.

He hadn't reached enough people. He had affected maybe fifty.

Not only that, but as his shield left them, Linia's song could seize their minds once again.

Linia sang louder, and the rest of her controlled crowd bulled forward, creating a stronger press and towing both the ixor-slowed people and the ones Alesio had woken up through the portal at a faster pace.

The wedge of people almost trampled Baylor in their rush. His face contorted and his hands clenched, but he shook his head and stared down, perhaps afraid of losing control and slowing someone enough to kill them. He breathed ixor in a circle around him, causing those who would have smashed into him to slow. Then, he bent down to and Shaped a path of ixor into the water, not slowing the people, but the liquid itself, so the sloshing waves did not displace as quickly, creating a semi-solid surface. This allowed Baylor and Alesio to run on top of the water, creating a straight path to Linia.

Magic pulsed outward from Linia's two-amplifier circuit at the back of the crowd, farther away from the portal. The sound of the song overpowered even the Summit Wave's roar, and Alesio's Sound shield trembled. He had maybe three minutes left where he could keep this up, or less, if he had to expand it.

As the two of them raced closer to Linia, Alesio could make out more detail. The circuit of magic from Linia's hand to her mouth spun faster with each rotation, until it pulsed with a new wave outward.

Could amplifiers amplify *each other*?

That would mean more than a simple increase of magic. It multiplied a person's normal abilities with each amplifier.

She had to use some of that power to increase the intensity considering she controlled people's very thoughts and bodies, not just the quality of her sound like he did during a performance at the Cadenza. He hadn't known Sound magic could do that. Unease prickled him at the implications of that.

Linia grimaced. "Form up, form up!" she called to the remaining people on the Anthem side of the portal. "Form a wall!"

The people clustered around her like bees protecting their queen, forming solid rings, linking their arms. Baylor could slow them, but they'd both still have to fight through several layers of tangled limbs, and by then.

Alesio closed his eyes and concentrated, finding the ground in his house of Touch magic. He imagined peeling up a tiny plank on the floor, and sludge bubbled up out of the opening.

"Do you have a name?" he asked. "What do you want to become?"

"I am Mire, but I want to fly! I want to try the high, high sky!"

Alesio could work with that. He formed Mire with his hands into a tall pole and solidified them so they would remain that shape. He'd called up just a little bit, so the magic didn't require nearly as long as if he'd asked an entire cliffside to Shape.

Alesio left the magic room, and a pole appeared in his hands. He dashed and vaulted over the press of bodies back towards Linia, pressing his Sound shield forward and down, so the people under him had a chance to become aware and scatter out of the way before he landed.

The water sloshed around his toes, a little shallower here, further from the portal. He ran again, and jumped again, straight for Linia.

Mire, the mud Shaped into a pole, whooped and sang. "Up so high! Up so high! How I love the new blue sky!"

Linia pointed at him and sang a low, deep note. A Sound javelin thicker than his arm shot up at him. It broke his Sound shield, but the impact threw the weapon off course enough that it rushed past his right ear.

He landed next to her.

Her song, amplified a thousandfold from the crowd, crashed into his ears, and he fought to keep his senses. He tried to swing Mire at her, but his limbs stopped of their own accord.

Wait. What was I doing?

She sang a Sound hammer, and did not swing it with her arms, but the weapon swung in the air as if on her command. It—well, *they*— knocked Mire from his hands, and her song reached for him with claws, ready to burrow into his ears like a large insect.

Mire melted back into mud, but the Sound hammer flew wide and slammed into the ground, hitting someone in the foot. The person screamed.

He clapped his hands over both ears. He Received and Shaped a Sound shield just around himself—the magic called themselves Small Wall—and silence blessed his ears once again.

She frowned and Shaped another Sound javelin, aiming at him from an awkward angle when he stepped inside her reach. Did she have trouble Shaping anything smaller than that, with all that power? Without stopping to enter a magic space and create something, he simply swung his fist and cracked her on the head.

She crumpled like a cut flower, her thin frame splashing into the shallow water. Maybe he should feel bad about hitting a woman, but she'd used a lot more force than he had. Also, she'd attempted a genocide.

Beside her, the older Lunnite shook his grizzled head and lowered his hand. The huge portal began to fold in on the edges.

Had the Lunnite created that portal? That didn't match what he knew about their abilities, but everything had turned so topsy-turvy, he couldn't afford to focus on the inconsistency. He knelt and grabbed the silvery shard from Linia in case she regained consciousness quicker than he imagined. It wouldn't fit over a tooth, like Baylor's or Brezeeks' had. It had a jagged edge, like it had broken off something. A Goddess Head statue, perhaps?

He clasped it in his hand. Would it amplify his magic?

Nothing happened. He slipped it in his pocket.

The portal continued to pleat at the edges like a tailor gathering in a hem. All of Anthem had reached the Touch side, and the Summit Wave would hit before they could funnel back through. They had maybe five minutes before that happened, and maybe a minute before the portal closed all the way.

The people on Touch, freed from Linia's song, began screaming and shoving each other as the spray and wind lashed their faces, and they became aware of their impending deaths.

Above them, the Hunger stretched the heavens, twisting them, with those empty snake-like arms full of fangs. The spots inside the entity had shrunk almost to the size from before the Hunger had drained everyone.

It would probably steal more than just their magic next time it came for them. If the Summit Wave didn't drown them first.

Baylor puffed up to him, his lips bleeding again from his usage of ixor. Darrow, Falrie, Naya, and Tener followed in his wake of slowed people. The portal shrank faster, cutting off the peoples' escape. It seemed to happen in slow motion as Alesio's heart crumbled.

Hestafon had died. Right after he'd tried to accept that Saida had left, Hestafon had protected a straiter, and died doing it. Just as Alesio had learned how to get along with him. After Hestafon had taught him so much about magic. After fighting with him against Clef's men, after saving his life the first time by Shaping the ixor inside the piper . . .

Wait.

Something about that caught his attention. Hadn't he transferred the ixor inside of Hestafon out of the piper and into his own magic room?

Didn't that mean that people could share magic in some way?

He faced Baylor and the foxans. "I have an idea to save the people and slow the Hunger, but I'm going to need everyone's help!"

Baylor winced at the Wave spray lashing them. Was Baylor immune to the ixor's pain increase? The young man tried to say something back, but the Summit Wave drowned him out.

Alesio closed his eyes. He'd almost depleted his Sound magic, and his Touch magic didn't have much, either. He could sense the magic on the other side, through the glass, but he didn't have enough energy to Receive them. He needed something that would allow him to speak to all the people, all at once.

The silver in Linia's mouth glinted.

Alesio had to do something, and he had to overcome what he couldn't manage. At least with that amplifier, he knew he had to stick it over his teeth. He reached into the unconscious Linia's mouth and gripped the amplifier, trying to tug it out, but it stuck.

The water lapped at his calves, now, even back here on Sound, and the portal had almost closed.

Baylor knocked his hand aside, then reached in and tapped something on Linia's amplifier, and it loosened. He thrust it at Alesio, and shouted, "Don't try to Receive too much magic too fast, before your capacity expands! It can still flood you!"

Alesio stuck the amplifier onto a tooth, and it clamped on. A cold ache radiated into his jaw.

A magic room opened inside the tooth, somehow separate from himself, but attached to his magic house like a tacked-on storage room. He couldn't quite tell where the boundary of his normal magic house ended, and the amplifier began.

Except . . . no. The space kept expanding. It wasn't a storage room. It was another house.

He forced himself to keep waiting, and the size of the extra space expanded again into, more like a whole field and his normal magic house sat in the middle.

Magic surged outside the walls of this strange dimension, the pressure building. Had Brezeek experienced this when Alesio had faced the cage fighter last year? Did Baylor feel like this *all* the time? Even with the amplified area surrounding his body like a giant bubble, it made him nauseous. He waited again, but this seemed as large as the space would inflate to.

He surfaced from the magic space's time-delay and studied that towering mass of water reaching into the clouds. He didn't just need area, he needed intensity. He needed to Receive more magic to accomplish both.

A second or two had passed. He grimaced and reached into his pocket, brushing against the coolness of the shard there. *I have to be sure.*

Alesio gripped the shard, not sure what to do. Nothing happened. He couldn't stand around trying to figure it out. He sloshed towards the portal, and the others followed him with grim faces. Maybe they thought they waded to their death. Well, maybe they did. He didn't know if this plan would work.

He brought out the shard, shaking it as he ran.

Nothing happened. Should he put it in his mouth? He didn't want to accidentally swallow it.

The closer he neared the portal, the higher the water level rose. To his knees, then his thighs. People shoved against him, trying to get through the portal before it closed.

Once through, the wind whipped around him like a lash, and cuts opened on his arms and legs from the power of it. People cried and screamed. The Hunger twisted the sky like someone wringing out a giant dishrag. The amplifier in his mouth ached with cold, and pulled his hand up like a magnet, drawing them together.

Expanse.

The 'storage room,' or 'field'— that separate, alien area that had attached to him— expanded far, far beyond him, growing his magic space exponentially. He waited.

He was a bird skimming over a forest.

He was a single leaf on a tree.

He was a wave rolling in the ocean.

He could draw either Sound or Touch magic into this massive space, but not both, not at the same time. He decided on Sound, and opened the tiniest window he could imagine, asking for magic that would want to reach out, to move through the air.

Someone crashed through it.

"My name is Rush! I am just a whisper of Rushing Thunder! I am the Sound of the Summit in this second! I would like to rush in many new directions, not just the one Rushing Thunder wants!"

Alesio almost reeled from the immensity of the twice-amplified Rush.

"Okay," he said. "Okay . . ." *What's something that would let me speak to lots of people?* "How about a tree? A . . . a hollow tree, with lots of branches, that sends your Sound out on many paths?"

"A tree? Oh, yes! I've seen those from afar on my travels!"

He began to Shape Rush as per their agreement, crafting a large tree of Sound magic that arched up and then down, towards the crowd, frozen in the time-delay. An entire day passed for him, as he, the size of a mouse in comparison, skittered up and down the branches, Shaping them as he went.

At one point, taking a small break to catch his breath, he trotted a bit away, trying to explore the insane space of this dimension. The rippling of time distortion shivered against him in waves.

Behind him, the tree shrank.

Alarmed, he returned to the tree, but it grew back just as when he had left.

He paced back and forth a few times to confirm his suspicions. It seemed, with the power of the amplifiers, time had slowed so much inside this strange dimension of his magical capacity that he could travel back or forward a few minutes as a physical distance.

Such a power didn't make much sense to him. He didn't have the mental faculties to understand it. His thoughts meandered in circles, as if in a time loop, or a dream.

He returned to the tree and Shaped it until he had finished.

Then, when he left his magic house and re-entered reality, a tree had appeared as if growing out of the air right in front of him. He almost shouted into the tree, but recalled his amplifier just in time, and spoke just above a whisper.

His words reverberated down to the panicking crowd, through the various hollow branches he'd Shaped Rush from, reaching them all. Because of his amplifier, it boomed louder than the Summit Wave.

"Everyone, listen up. We have a few minutes, maybe. If we work together, we can stop both the Summit Wave and slow the Hunger at the same time."

The crowd's screaming stopped, and they stared up at the giant tree that had appeared over their heads. They knew his voice, the Voice of Reconnection.

"The Hunger has not drained all our magic. Not yet. If you all help me Receive the magic of the Summit Wave, I could maybe Shape them into something else. Something the Hunger will take."

When he said his idea aloud, though, it became abhorrent to him. Now that he heard the voices in magic, he understood all magic had identities, just in a different way than people did. Even if the magic had shorter lifespans, even a few seconds long, that didn't mean their sentience had less meaning or importance. He couldn't—no, he wouldn't—just Shape magic as bait for the Hunger without their consent.

But how could he convince magic to give itself—themself—up like that?

Hestafon's words echoed back to him as they'd trudged back to Anthem with Clef.

Instead of Receiving and then Shaping magic into what I wanted, I rang the bell a specific way to attract the magic that wanted to be a syrup.

Maybe he couldn't convince magic that he'd already Received, but he could try to draw just the magic from the Primal Plane willing to sacrifice themself. Or themselves.

"We can't Shape Touch magic!" someone shouted back. "We're Soundians!"

"That's alright," he managed to say. "I'll take care of the Shaping part. I just need everyone to Receive the Touch magic along with me. Help me hold it all. I just need you to think these words:"

He began to sing, keeping his voice soft through the tree he had Shaped out of Sound magic, which remained a tree, even though the people reached to press their palms against the branches:

CLASP YOUR NEIGHBOR'S hand
    And close your eyes as one
    A room exists
    Where magic flows
    Inside of everyone
    We call forth this Waves' magics
    All those with a protective urge
    We call forth that magic
    That understands the heavens' Scourge
    We call forth all magic
    Who knows the potential price,
    We call all forth to try, to try

To save people and magics' lives.
Behind the wall, do we feel?
Can we Receive their voice?
Listen well, and listen close,
We must Receive their choice.

EVERYONE LISTENED AND RECEIVED. They showed up around him in that magical place. He couldn't see them, but he could sense them all through their linked hands. Each of them increased the capacity of the space, adding to the area as far as the world, as far and wide as the Summit Wave traveled around Touch each week. Even the foxans joined in, since they could Receive Sensory magic, they just couldn't Shape it. He gripped Baylor's hand, and another Soundian's, connecting him to the crowd, to the masses and to their magical ability to Receive as one, and Baylor added his amplifier to Alesio's two, again expanding, again increasing, compounding that magical space.

Alesio was a drop in an ocean. He was a grain of sand on a beach. He was a star in all the vastness of the sky. But he wasn't *alone*, this time. He still held everyone's hand, and they gave him their strength as more drops of water, more grains of sand, and more stars in the sky.

He didn't know if this would work. Maybe none of the magic would want to. And if they did, this could flood him or drain him too far and kill him either way. He had played a massive gambit. But he had to try.

He touched the walls of this space, on the edge of that ocean, and the Summit Wave waited. For him to Receive all of them, he had to open a door as large as he could open. Two double doors, like at the Cadenza.

All of them together threw open the doors.

Touch magic smashed through as soon as they touched the door, throwing them backwards. Water poured in like a dam had burst that had held back an ocean. They panicked, wondering if they had pulled too much through after all, more than they could handle. But it leveled out, and they gripped each other's hands and found their footing.

The magic rumbled, "My name is Summit Wave. I have answered your summons, for every week I race around this world, and I lose parts of myself along the way until I can collect them again. The *Tagizal* pushes me every week, so I am forced to run roughshod over stone and earth. I want to protect the others of my world from losing themselves, from knowing this pain." They paused, then added. "If I might make one request . . ."

"Anything," Alesio—no, the crowd said. They'd become something different in this magical place, connected in this way. They used Alesio's voice, as the voice of Reconnection, and they trusted him to do this.

"For this last form I take, I would like to rest. Like the *Tagizal*, unmoving. I want to be like the stones. I want to be a mountain."

The Crowd considered. "We cannot make you into stone. That'd change you into something else, that's not what Touch magic does. But . . . how do you feel about ice? You would still become a mountain."

A pause passed, and the Summit Wave accepted The Crowd's counter proposal.

Alesio separated himself from the rest of them. He began to Shape the Summit, condensing the water to create ice. The amplifier sucked in their magic and rose around the Wave as it towered over them, about to drown them all, and he began to freeze it. He had to do this by himself, as they could not Shape Touch magic. They could only add their time-delay to his, their capacity to Receive to his.

He squeezed the water and created pressure to cool and freeze it. The Summit Wave, as water tended to do, flowed around so that he had to freeze from the top down, to avoid the unShaped water wearing away the base.

In the time-delay, as earlier when he'd Shaped Rush, and when Baylor had poisoned him with ixor, time slowed and even stopped long enough that he could travel backwards or forwards hours, or days, or months, the further out into the expanse he went. As he Shaped the mountain, starting at the top and working his way down to the larger base, he journeyed further. On the leeward side of the mountain, time looped backwards, and on the other side, it wound forwards. The mountain grew and shrank accordingly.

He wondered if time had always warped this way when he Shaped, that it just hadn't been apparent in the milliseconds he might have traveled backwards or forwards in his smaller magic room or even his house he'd just expanded it to before this. It was more obvious because he had so much more space than he'd ever had—and therefore, much farther in time to travel. And that included the crowd adding their time-delay to his, allowing him to stay here as long as he needed while mere seconds passed in real time.

Saida had used the Goddess Head, an infinitely more powerful resource than even the three amplifiers altogether. How long had her journey taken, through the stars, to reach the Hunger?

On the future side of the mountain, his beard grew down to his shoulders, then his chest, and his hands cramped from Shaping day after day. On the past side, he lost some of the breadth in his shoulders, and he felt younger, perhaps in his mid-twenties instead of his thirties.

At some points, he wondered. Was this all a dream? Perhaps he had died. Or had he always worked on this mountain?

Then the tug of Saida's connection would reassure him, ground him. He hadn't lost years with her. Time had moved, but not forward very much at all.

Even using the two amplifiers' power to expand his capacity to Receive, his body, frozen on the physical side, could not have endured the strain of the inconceivable time distortion. The people didn't just add their Receiving and therefore their time-delay to his, but they shared the burden of it among them all, each of them experiencing years in a matter of moments.

Next to him, in a parallel world, his real body still gripped Baylor's hand. The young man blended a huge mixture of ixor into the hardening slush.

Smart, Alesio thought, one of the few thoughts he could manage in this dreamlike state. Infusing ixor into the Summit Wave would help to slow the Hunger down even more.

He created the crest of the mountain, then kept sloping it down, down, larger and larger, until he reached the massive base, which took another six months, at least what he could gather from the state of his beard on the future side of the mountain. Frozen Mountain. That was what they wanted to be called.

Then he let himself exit that planet-sized space inside himself, and he opened his eyes.

The Wave's feet of muddy, churning foam had almost reached them, about to envelope them all, but he had frozen them just in time. They had become a glittering blue-white mountain in front of them, radiating a freezing chill. Ice had formed under their feet, too from the strength of it, covering the Glass Sea for a long ways. Particles floated inside the ice in front of them like millions of bubbles. Brown particles.

Ixor.

Baylor had filled the whole ice mountain with it.

32
KOLSUV MOR

The air vibrated Saida's blood and ground her bones against each other. It tugged at the ragged end of her tail she had picked at almost into baldness, as if it sensed what she had already begun tearing apart.

As she traveled further into the hostile area, the floating world crumbs the Hunger digested appeared more frequent and closer to each other. This helped in that when she leapt off one, she could reach the next before she lost momentum.

A cliff from far off floated ahead and she maneuvered towards it. Her foxan legs had fatigued from "swimming" through the air. But the cliff, consisting of twisted bits of both organic and inorganic matter, propelled towards her, as well, so she didn't have to swim far.

As soon as she neared the cliff, two snake heads stuck out, reaching for her, one out of a large animal's leg, and the other a plank from a fence.

She dodged around them and touched down on the street a few feet away, braced, and then launched off again with her strong foxan hind legs, speeding through the air away from it and towards another nearby floating building. She didn't know which direction to aim for except for wherever it hurt the most. Her body shivered in

510

protest, and the friction of the movement shifted her tendons inside her.

Something in her left foot paw loosened. The numbness made it hard to tell, but it flopped in a decidedly unsettling motion when she increased her speed. Had she broken it, and just couldn't feel the pain?

Her quickened pace lasted her till she reached her chosen launch pad, a house from far away, but as she neared it, she realized its bricks were compressed stone eyes, as if all the eyes that this monstrous Plane had absorbed had gathered in one place. Then, ancient Lunnite symbols flowed through the stone like ripples of water, and this seemed to activate the eyes. They formed snake heads from the pupils, peeling themselves up and wavering towards her.

Saida shuddered and avoided the snake heads that rose out of the eyes, more of them, this time, but smaller. The snake heads bubbled upwards at her, faster, and she stumbled and rolled, her left foot paw unable to support her weight. She crouched on all fours and pushed off, launching before any of them could snick her with their fangs. In her haste, she flew at an angle that missed her next targeted jump, a tower with a sundial at the top.

She slowed, and swam towards it, but this time, the circular symbols flowed faster, activating four snake heads to rear up, too close. She backpedaled but couldn't stop herself in time. One of them, its body a lick of flame that had hardened to stone, struck her in the foot, the same foot that ached so much, and then coiled around it, becoming larger as it did so. It didn't gnaw at her physical body, but at something deeper.

Saida screamed, and the tower swallowed the sound of her pain at once. She braced, and launched, and something tore in her foot, at the ankle.

Saida flinched and shot a glance backwards.

Her foot paw had *snapped off!*

No blood accompanied the separation, almost like her body didn't believe it had happened. The pain jarred her, contrasted with her loss of feeling that had become so muted in the last hour. A forest of snake heads swarmed toward her floating foot, but it pulled away from them, tugging after her as if on an invisible string. The snake heads stretched further, but this attempt seemed to crack the ancient Lunnite circles underneath them, and they fell apart into segments.

The place where her foot had been reminded her of when she'd dislocated parts of her mind and placed them into Tricksy Stone and Goosefeather.

"Hello," a new voice said, in her mind. It sounded distinctly foot-like, in that it had a rhythmic cadence to its speech.

What had happened? Why hadn't her foot drifted away? What kept it attached? She twisted to stare at her leg. From the agony, she expected the snakes to have eaten part of it. But a nub remained down to her ankle, a clean break as if someone had sliced her foot paw off with a sword.

"My name is Left Foot Paw. I'm still a part of you! I haven't integrated with any other magic. I'll follow you as long as you know who you are!"

She had a bond with her foot. Her bond with her own body, her connection to herself, pulled them along. A faint outline of a golden tether showed.

She suppressed a hysterical laugh. *So, I just keep myself together? Wonderful. Not like I've struggled with that before.*

ALESIO SLUMPED TO THE GROUND. The people all stared up at the giant ice mountain they had created.

They'd stayed with him through it all. Three and a half years had passed in that time warped space, but he hadn't done it alone. Existing as a crowd, as an amalgamation of identities, seemed normal now, and it felt strangely isolating to possess just one personality, one concept of self.

That strangeness faded, however, like a dream he tried to hold onto, but had already lost the substance of.

The Hunger still reached down, twisting their reality, their sky, like a giant hand wringing out a towel, except the towel had a disturbing number of teeth in it. One of its five tendrils stretched towards them, towards Touch, and opened its maw around the top of the ice mountain.

"I DIDN'T KNOW THIS PLANE HAD SUCH A LEVEL OF TAINTED MAGIC."

The snake distended its jaw and swallowed the mountain all the way down to the base like the reverse motion of shedding its skin, and massive fangs flashed right in front of them.

A horrible crack sounded, and a colossal lump ascended the tendril's throat, disappearing into the Hunger.

All that work, all that time Shaping Frozen Mountain. He knew every facet of it, like he knew every note of a well-loved song. Gone in an instant.

"I'm sorry," Alesio whispered.

He had begun to understand, more than ever, the attachment Saida had to her magic items. Her friends. To communicate with something identified them into *someone,* and he'd just sacrificed a someone to save the humans of the Sensory worlds. Even though the Summit Wave had chosen to filter through at the Crowd's call for aid, and had chosen their fate, it still hurt. The lashing spray of the waves did not comprise all the wetness on his face.

Quiet sobbing sounded around him, and the people of Anthem and the Cloves and a sprinkle of Touchians knelt on the stones of the bottom of the Glass Sea, any water a mere trickle around the rocks. All other water had decided to become the mountain.

"WHAT IS THIS? WHAT DID ... YOU ... DO ..."

The Hunger settled back in the sky, the snake-arm coiling back up in extremely slow motion. The spots inside of them bulged to four times as large as before, so they more resembled landmasses instead of islands.

It worked. A hollow sensation filled Alesio, like the Sound tree he'd crafted, which the Hunger had snatched up along with Frozen Mountain. At least it had worked. He'd done what he could to help Saida.

A hand on his shoulder. One of the straiter men who had shoved him into the cage with Hestafon.

Hestafon. Had he found the piper dead less than thirty minutes ago? The shadow of three and a half years weighed in his body—faded in his memory, but not in his bones.

The crowd still waited around him, Baylor, Naya, and the foxans, hushed and respectful.

His father and Mona rushed up to him. Red lashes and bruises marred both their arms and legs from the spray and stones thrown from the Summit Wave's frothing current.

"You did it," his father said, in the quiet.

Alesio's limbs sagged with heaviness. He'd had to read his father's lips. Had Alesio gone deaf in his other ear from all the rushing wind and roar of the Summit Wave?

Wait. Water sloshed in his right ear, his good ear. He tilted his head to drain it out.

Too much had happened. He couldn't concentrate on what he—they—had just done. It had taken so long. He folded his legs under him, and they shook.

"What—what happened to you?" He asked his father. "Before all . . . this."

His father and Mona blinked back at him.

"We hid in the Drinks De Capo," Mona said. Mud smeared her short, strawberry blonde hair. Maybe they understood, because they had worked there with him, that he needed the small details right now. He needed someone to ground him with the mundane. With reality. "Until some pipers tried to hide there, too. And straiters followed them inside."

"It feels so long ago . . ." Luca held his head in his hand, as if trying to touch his thoughts and check they were still there. "That's right. The straiters dragged the pipers out to force them to fight in a cage match. We tried to stop them, but then that horrible song started. That's the last thing I remember, before you woke us all up, and we stood here in front of that horrible sound, and we spent . . . years in that strange space." His father turned to Mona. "It *was* years, right? It's so fuzzy, now."

Luca's cataracts had blinded him almost completely. The Summit Wave's roar and the lash of its water without seeing anything must have terrified him.

"I'm sorry you had to go through that," Alesio said.

"You saved us," someone murmured from a knot of people around them. Paras, Verrity's sister, stood there. Beside Paras, Naya busied herself by wrapping a tourniquet around a bleeding straiter woman's arm with someone's torn off shirt. Evidence of her healthcare dotted other peoples' bandaged hands nearby.

Alesio surveyed the crowd. They gazed at him with awe in their faces. He found himself searching for Saida, only to catch himself.

"*We* saved us," Alesio said. "I couldn't have done it without all of you listening to me and lending me your magic."

Jagged lines formed in the ice under their feet, and then it cracked, and everyone stumbled into the shallow ice water. A few shrieks sounded from the coldness and the increased sensitivity to that coldness, on Touch. Of course, none of them except the few Touchians there wore buoy suits.

They would have to stay here till one of the foxans regained their portaling ability. None of them wanted to touch an amplifier to force a portal from themselves. The foxans had joined the humans in that magical space of time dilation and had existed in that space along with everyone else for all those years.

"I couldn't handle spending days or weeks in there. Not right now." Darrow shuddered and the other foxans had said much the same.

Alesio couldn't blame them. The idea of spending any more time in that dreamy, half-awake state repelled him.

That meant this whole crowd would need to stay calm and patient for a while yet. He needed to take control of the situation before panic could spread again.

The idea exhausted him. He didn't want to do anything, ever again.

SENSORY MAGIC STREAMED into the Hunger. It lifted off the Sensory worlds like morning mist from a valley, sucked towards the Hunger through one of their massive snake-arms.

As the large magical shape—a mountain? —landed, the Hunger began to tear them apart, piece by piece, unraveling them like the weave of a blanket.

Did the magic scream, and she was just too far away to hear? Or did the Hunger steal the sound of their agony as well?

Though the magic the Hunger had absorbed was far off, it seemed to create an effect on the twisted material portions near her. The sections of floating substance swelled taller, wider. She had to maneuver around them, so they didn't crush her.

How much Sensory magic had the Hunger consumed? Was Alesio safe?

Wait. The air grew sluggish, as if the Hunger had just eaten such an enormous amount, they had become comatose. A muskiness lurked on her lips, the first taste she'd had in a long time in this barren place besides the potency of her own sweat and blood.

Ixor?!

Before it could affect her too much, she ripped off the edge of her shirt and tied it over her mouth.

As she did so, she identified a second type of magic in the spice; one that she hadn't discerned before. The way the Hunger fragmented everything made it easier to classify types of magic. Perhaps because the Hunger tried to break everything apart, she could recognize their base components?

Regardless, ixor consisted of more than just a Sensory based magic —she couldn't touch it or taste it. It had elements of what Alesio and other human Shapers had described when using magic: that of time slowing down inside themselves.

Of course. Of course! Other worlds existed, after all, with other, new magics beyond. The recipe for ixor included both Taste and Time magic.

At one point, a foxan must have placed a Time transplant inside the ixor plant on Taste. That explained ixor's strange properties, unlike most magics on the Sensory worlds.

Her mind had sped up, even as her body had slowed a little. But the Hunger had absorbed a huge dose of ixor, along with that mountain.

Baylor must have done it using his amplifier, though she had no idea how. Somehow, they had tricked the Hunger into eating a massive amount of ixor. Buying her time.

Thank the Senses.

She tested her next jump, angling towards a waterfall with drops of stone water forever hovering off an edge.

She drifted closer, Left Foot Paw still trailing behind her like a faithful puppy. What would happen if she shifted to human? Would her foot paw still change? She'd remained in her foxan form since she'd arrived. Her terror kept her on much too high alert to allow her to be human, without fangs or claws.

The water had fragments of humans in them and bushes and other world-bits, just like all the other pieces. No ancient ring symbols skulked around her. The ends of the rock did not rise towards her or transform into stone snake mouths. They persisted in their stone configurations in the waterfall, muddled and twisted into a mosaic of pain and suffering. The ixor had worked on them.

This close, without the fear of the snakes striking at her, she examined this section of the Hunger. Had this once flowed as a real waterfall, before the Severing? Lunnite circle script scrawled across the stone, matching what she and Marik had found in the ruins of the ancient Lunnite cities they'd visited.

She could imagine their world breaking apart, the people and parts of nature around the waterfall washing down its face, and then the implosion of magic had twisted, merged, and petrified everything. Shattered glass from a windowpane had merged with a bird's wing. A tree branch had warped around a human child's leg. She wondered if that child had worshipped Lunne, or if they had been too young to understand. The leg was small.

Her stomach performed a series of extensive flips. She closed her eyes, focusing on what she needed to do.

That ixor cloud had slowed the Hunger at the right time. She wouldn't have infiltrated much further if her limbs kept falling off.

She landed, braced herself, positioned towards the next building, and launched off in a strong leap, albeit a bit off balance on her three legs. She soared through the still air with much less resistance. The tiny bit of ixor she'd tasted had dissipated already, and whatever had grated at her bones and battered at her identity had stopped. Her vision began to improve, the closer stone formations becoming less hazy.

Ahead of her, the larger drifting stone sections had clumped, like a cosmic giant had scooped an entire city and kneaded it like dough in their hand, crumpling everything and mashing everything together into a dense ball.

That had to be Kolsuv Mor. The center mass that resembled the pupil of an eye from the perspective of the Sensory worlds.

The city where everything had started. The transmutation city where the Transmuters had created a base of operations. There, she could try to figure out how to stop the Hunger. At its heart.

Without the danger of the snakes and her body falling apart, she could dart around quicker and with less caution. Her foot paw still trailing after her, she landed on her leg stump instead. Her pain spiked a bit, the sense of Touch returning to her.

She didn't give herself time to think about it. Who knew how long the ixor would slow the Hunger? She jumped, soared, vaulted, and careened at a feverish pace, and finally, she arrived at the edge of that dense, crushed city.

Up close, more of the stone bits here contained a mixture of city and human parts rather than human and nature. Eyes gaped at her next to a fence post. Some kind of organ, a gray, veined lump that had once functioned in a body, squashed against a windowpane like some kind of tiny store display. Openings showed through the tangles of stone, and some of them resembled caves and tunnels like paths through the most horrific sphere-shaped mountain. She couldn't have wriggled through such chaos without losing all of herself if the Hunger hadn't been slowed. The snakes would have lunged and struck from all angles at every point, and she couldn't have dodged so many. They would have ripped her apart in moments. And over it all, that spherical script of the Lunnites, connecting and overlapping circles like ripples from a never-ending rain.

The pain had worsened, an ache below her left leg stump. It ached the most where it *wasn't*, in the absence. Even though Left Foot Paw stayed connected via that invisible string, their bond to her had torn. Her tail hurt, too, on the end. The ravenous strength of the air and the "buildings" around her, before the ixor had lulled them, must have yanked out more of her fur around the bald spot in her tail, sensing weakness.

What would her tail say to her, if they produced a magic voice? Would they scold her for her unconscious bad habit? Would they cry at how she had soothed herself using pain, to distract herself from the potency of her emotions by causing them both physical hurt?

She'd needed to extract *something*, and since she'd tried to break her initial bad habit of letting her animal side absorb all her extra feelings because it made her too forgetful, she'd instead taken it out on her poor hair and fur.

I'm sorry, Tail-Braid, she thought, trying to imagine what they might call themself. *I'll try to stop. I'm trying to stop a lot of things.*

She limped along on her foot paws and stump, picking through a tunnel of twisted branches which had pierced through hundreds of skulls, creating the effect of a new and horrifying tree canopy and foliage underfoot. Left Foot Paw kept catching on corners until she just picked them up in her mouth and carried them that way. Gravity, almost nonexistent before, had increased, drawing her inward, toward the center of the balled-up city.

If this was Kolsuv Mor, she witnessed the frozen tableau of the Hunger becoming the Hunger; the mixed magics imploding on Transmutation.

She trembled while imagining the scene in the time it had occurred; the wind from the initial implosion sucking people into the woods, impaling them on broken spars of trees. Her ears pricked forward on instinct, swiveling around to listen for anything, keeping her muzzle slightly ajar to better sniff and taste the air. Though no sound, scent, or smell issued forth, she could tell the force's direction from the petrified scene; the heart of the city had sucked everything inward.

The tunnel wound on and on, with several turnings and cutaway paths, and more than once she picked a path that ended, and she had to double back. She picked her way down a slope of mashed up bricks, bushes, and roofs, only to understand halfway down that it wound down into closed off, well-like structure, and she had to climb the slope again to escape. Saida found another route, a tunnel filled with the Lunnite's circle script. The symbols overlapped more, in denser patterns. Evidence that she neared the center.

Then, the tunnel opened, and a cliff wall rose ahead of her, studded with thousands of eyes.

She cowered in involuntary fear, shuddering until nothing happened for several seconds, and imagining her courage like magic that she just had to wait till it refilled, peeked out again.

The eyes protruded out from a cliff wall ahead of her, once a city street, now yanked upwards into a sheer bluff. The stone eyes stared at her with an ancient terror. The implosion had sucked them out of those skulls from the twisted woods.

Saida panted and her hands trembled. Tears pricked at her eyes.

Divination. Consumption. Transmutation.

Eyes. Mouths. Hands.

It all made sense in one horrifying moment. The Lunnites had drawn their plans on Kolsuv Mor, the origin city on Transmutation, engraved their script circles on every possible surface. The magic had transmuted everyone and everything in moments, imploding, tearing apart, rearranging, and then pulling everything into itself.

However, when it had transmuted everyone and everything in the Plane into stone, the magic had, of course, utilized the three worlds' magic to do so, and metonymizing them into the various incarnations around her.

Eyes for Divination. Mouths for Consumption. Hands for Transmutation.

That was why an inordinate amount of those body parts threaded through the Hunger.

The tunnel had emptied her out to the bottom of it, and the street walls surrounded her. No other way out presented itself, unless she retraced her steps and tried to find another path through the skull woods. She had to climb.

She needed to shift to human.

She prepared for a few moments, shivering. She would need to convince her foxan side to let her human side go. And she knew, now, how to do it: she conjured up her magic room inside of Magic Ear.

Her foxan side appeared, manifesting as her shifted self, hunched over Saida, the human, much like a swanseize would crouch over her nest of eggs. Her human side huddled there, her hands wrapped around her torso, kneeling, but she gazed up at Saida the foxan with a pleading expression.

Saida's consciousness hovered there without a form, almost like she watched a play between two halves of herself.

"Why do you want to change now?" Foxan-Saida said, their voice oddly familiar. "It's dangerous. Not a good place for humans. And you're very sad about leaving him there, when you might never see him again. Not to mention, you still miss your magic friends. Do you really want to feel that all right now?"

Human-Saida laid her palm on her foxan's chest, slowly, slowly, deliberately. Foxan-Saida eyed her with wariness but remained still.

"We need to do this," Human-Saida said. "We need to climb that wall to save him. We want to be with him, and we can't be with him if he dies."

"You were afraid, before, though. You still are afraid of how you might change." Foxan-Saida bent their head. "Afraid of my nature, how I shift. Afraid of . . . me."

In that moment, Saida's consciousness placed the voice. She spoke as her human side, eyes wide, unfolding her legs to stand.

"You're who's talked in my head. You're my Fear!"

Foxan-Saida's ears flattened, and they hunched their shoulders.

"You're who has frayed my bond with Alesio! You've tried to convince me that I'll hurt him!"

Her foxan side backed away as her human side clenched their fists, their face contorting. Consciousness-Saida caught her mental breath. Falrie had looked like that, screaming at Tener about how Darrow had betrayed her.

She couldn't let her human side drive her foxan self away. She could sense the bond between her halves fraying, so fragile in this place, the fibers ripping out one by one like the ends of her tail braid.

Receive. Shape. Conversation.

Her human side took a deep breath and blinked, her expression softening. She held out her palm face up. "I just . . . I want to know why. Why are you . . . why are you so afraid? Why is your name Fear, when you're my foxan? You're so much more than that."

"That wasn't always my name."

Human-Saida cocked her head along with Consciousness-Saida doing it mentally. "What?"

"You have so many emotions, when you're human," Foxan-Saida said. "And you didn't know what to do with them. They were too much. So, you brought them to me to absorb, which was fine at first." They shook their head, their ears angling back and forth. "But you had so many *fears*. Fear of humans. Fear of Carn. Fear of Touch. Fear of the place under Vision you fell into. Fear of Watthe, and of losing your magic friends. Fear of twisted love, the wrong kind of love, which you did learn wasn't love at all." Foxan-Saida sighed. "But then you changed to having fears about the future, about *me*. About how I could mess up *your* life. How my nature, my changing, shifting-ness, could hurt the people you love. And . . . all that fear . . . it's changed *me*, it's changed my name to Fear."

Consciousness Saida let out an "Ohhhhh" that Human-Saida echoed. "Is that why you are trying to convince me I'll hurt Alesio?"

Fur-mixes shift on the inside as much as the outside.

She'd wondered if Clef had lied about that, but he hadn't. It was true. And as much as Clef had intended it as a criticism . . .

"Change doesn't have to be a bad thing," Difficult Truth whispered beside her consciousness.

"How could I speak to you without fear," Foxan-Saida said, "When that is all I ever Receive from you?"

Her human side bowed her head.

"I'm sorry," Human-Saida said, after several moments. "I'm working on how to manage my feelings. How to feel them, instead of putting them in other places. Tricksy Stone would have called me out on hurting you like that. On hurting *us* like that."

"Tricksy Stone would have called you a lot of things."

Human-Saida let out a choked laugh. More silence passed inside of Magic Ear, that strange subliminal space with rows of shelves. It wasn't empty anymore. It was filled with the trimmings that Alesio had filled their new den with.

Their den.

Human-Saida revolved, gazing at all the trimmings.

"Alright. I'll handle some of it now. To show you that I don't want to just push my hardest emotions onto you." Human-Saida inhaled deeply. "We've learned we can Shape space, right? Well, that includes how we shift—on the outside, *and* inside. We might change, yes. But we already have, haven't we, this past year? We like kissing and even more than that. We never liked those things with Carn. We're learning how to read. And we're changing in how we miss people, like we missed our magic friends."

The fear rose in her, but she kept it, somehow, on her human side, instead of shoving it towards Foxan-Saida. Her consciousness bled into both of her other selves, now, merging with them, leaving the inner room of her Magic Ear.

But she kept that fear and rode the wave of it, instead of portaling it away, instead of shoving it into a separate part of herself, instead of trimming a piece of it and stuffing it into a magical stone.

"We can choose how we change," she said, returning to herself in front of the cliff of eyes. "Just like we can choose where we can teleport to. It all comes down to Shaping where we want to go, and who we want to be."

She had shifted to human.

"Thank you," she whispered to her foxan self. "Thank you for always being the strong side. Let me handle this one."

33
THE HEART OF THE HUNGER

L eft Foot remained detached, but they had shifted to human. Before she attempted the climb up the wall of eyes, she tried to tighten the bond with her foot and reattach them. Left Foot wound closer on their bond till they hovered a few inches away from the nub of her ankle but refused to pop back on.

"Please? Don't you want to be part of my leg again?"

"I'm sorry," Left Foot said. "The bond isn't strong enough."

Saida sucked in a breath. "It's okay. I can still make this work. I think."

She had some control over their movement, now. She could wiggle her toes and flex the foot. Perhaps because she'd tightened their bond? She practiced walking around on Left Foot as if they had attached. Doing so increased her height on one side, but that made it easier than hopping on one foot as a human.

She tottered over to the nearest part of the street cliff and grasped the first eye, jutting out like a handhold. Its smoothness made it difficult to grip. She almost slipped more than once on Left Foot. Gravity didn't weigh on her here as much as on her home planets, which helped her the most. But the place where Left Foot should have attached still ached, and fatigue crept in around her eyes again like shadows around a campfire. But she lugged her way up and hauled herself on top of the street, shaking from relief.

In front of her, a river lay tangled in segments with the planks of wagons, pillars of a large bridge, and more stone parts of people. It comprised her sky, as well; she'd journeyed deep enough into the city that it blocked her view of the free space.

What if I trap myself in here? What if I fall through some crack in a street and get wedged in?

No. She refused to let the fear overcome her. Knowing what she'd done to her foxan side provided her motivation to breath deeper, to take the next step. She wished, now, to change herself enough that she could change her foxan side's name to something besides Fear.

She didn't try to avoid imagining what could happen to her. She could only try and process those thoughts and then let them pass through her and out of her, instead of allowing them to sprout and grow. She recalled the fox-person's words, a year ago, the one from Anthem: *Fear paralyzes us all. The trick is not to let it keep hold of you. You escape by moving a little at a time.*

She surveyed the scene ahead.

Here, too, a story revealed itself: the bridge had collapsed with people still on it, and the wind and force of the implosion had flung them and everything else into the air, caught in a timeless free-fall.

At first, the way seemed blocked, until she crawled underneath a wagon wheel. From there, she edged around hundreds of specks of stone spray, which remained stuck in their positions no matter how hard she pushed.

At one point, she'd squeezed herself too tight between five of them, and she breathed through her pants of terror and shifted her torso just a little bit to foxan, just enough to slip between the two that had blocked her way.

She clambered up a bit of the river as big as a boulder, and from there, jumped across to another broken wagon wheel. The jagged spoke scratched her cheek, but she'd made it. She had crossed the "river."

On the other side, she faced once-buildings of crushed and twisted steel. They now resembled the snarl and underbrush of an untended forest. No tunnel or path showed itself, she had to wriggle around paralyzed explosions of brick and bas-relief open mouths, caught in their eternal screams.

Nearby, a branch wrapped like a ribbon around a lantern post. She could tell where the implosion had ripped each branch based on the immobile scene, and she reconstructed them in her head. Those two branches had once connected to that central trunk over there. And following the trajectory of that branch entwined in the spokes of a wagon wheel, it had belonged to another tree on her right.

She shuddered at its form in her mind—the branches seemed more bendy, almost rubbery, almost like the snakes that grew out of every bit of stone when they sensed her. They reminded her of the Hunger's limbs—*wait.*

That can't be a coincidence.

She combed around for more of those stone arms. She found five still attached to half of a trunk-like body holding the tattered stone pages of a book. The pages of the book displayed Lunnite script. She had to squeeze past their arms to reach a wider space.

A stone portal floated, suspended in front of her. A foxan's tail and their two back legs protruded out of it, as they must have attempted to flee. Where had they tried to escape to, in the end? Had they known that their entire Plane would become fodder for the Lunnites' Directive?

Too many of those trees with snake-like branches and mouths had the same base form. The tendrils in the sky, the arm-mouth-snakes that had attacked her, here, on the Hunger's Plane, all pointed to the same conclusion.

The magic, when asked to transform the Plane into the new Goddess, hadn't just used the three worlds' magic as a model for the Hunger's general appearance and eerie incorporations of eyes, mouths, and hands.

The Transmuters themselves had once resembled trees with fluid branches for arms. Not every Plane would have human life forms. The Plane of Change with the three worlds probably all had variations of tree-peoples, like the Sensory Plane had slight variations of humans.

Hadn't the Goddess Head's lies mentioned asking the foxans to become Transplant Trees? Had the ancient Lunnites planned for the foxans to become trees to . . . subtly worship them? Or, maybe, the people of Transmutation had comprehended that form the best, and worked their magic through them easier? Trees did draw from the earth and share nutrients between them.

It's interesting, too, she thought. *That when these tree-beings transmuted themselves into Amplifiers, they Shaped themselves into the form of the Goddess.*

The ancient followers of Lunne had wanted to become the next god, so that did make sense. They had wanted to replace Lunne. That put a different spin on the fact that they had called themselves Lunnites.

She studied the Transmuter with the five remaining arms. Had they known about the secret scheme? Or had they tried to change their fellow Transmuters' minds even as their world crumbled around them, and their plan imploded in their faces?

The voices of magic didn't speak here, but her connection to Magic Ear hadn't faded or been broken. The Hunger had squeezed the magic out of everything, juiced people and foxans and fox-people like lemons into the deepest part of the Hunger's maw to fuel their journey from Plane to Plane. Anything she might have heard would have sprung from the throats of the animated snake mouths, those tiny tendrils like the entity's arms and fingers, their sensory organs they used for searching out more magic.

The Lunnite's spherical writings appeared everywhere at this point—scrawled around pillars, or on a stone page in a book. She tried to follow where the circles became more concentrated, hoping they would lead her where she needed to go.

A circular symbol drifted towards her on the ground, sleepy and slow, awakening a single snake mouth that yawned and didn't seem aware of her. She gave it a wide berth, and it settled back down. She gritted her teeth and continued at a faster pace.

The forest of crumpled buildings and their inhabitants continued, and with every step she had to pass through a new tragedy. A small ribcage shielded by two larger arms with wrinkled skin, the arms propped up by a torn apart torso and shoulders, without a head. Just the outline of a flock of birds, smashed into the churned-up street like they had flown into a wave of cobblestone. She ducked under the "wave" as it gave her a few feet of clear path deeper into the debris, instead of journeying across it. More ancient Lunnite symbols flowed through the stone overhead, and snake arms uncoiled from the stone like fast-forming icicles dripping towards her, and fear thudded in her throat.

Keep moving. Just keep moving.

An image of Anthem torn apart like this flashed through her imagination—St. Rina's cathedral, all the instruments, the little bowls of sticky rice, the Cadenza, the *people!* She shuddered and almost whimpered but confined the sound. She didn't know when the Hunger would wake from their ixor-induced haze, and she didn't want to rouse them before then. She had triggered them before, as Clef had said she'd activated the box in the Primal Plane in the first place, which had signaled the Hunger and brought them here.

Before she could direct her mind somewhere else, an image of Alesio bleeding, his magic drained, his arms and legs and torso all twisted, torn apart, and flung across a vast expanse and formed into stone, blazed into her mind, and she crimped her lips to keep from crying out and feeding the Hunger with her sound.

She breathed through her nose. In and out. In and out.

She could not let that happen. She would not!

"You got this," her foxan side whispered to her.

Something inside her flashed, and she became aware of the bond between her and Alesio, the strand that connected them glowing again with a bright, bright light, *"like sunrises,"* Tener had described them, and she could portal to Alesio right now, and lean against him, and stroke her fingers through his hair.

But she loved him more than she needed him. She loved him by caring that the Hunger would tear him apart if she couldn't stop them!

She would give him a future where he could sing wherever he wished, and where his magic flowed, and where he wouldn't fear for her safety or his own.

She gritted her teeth and edged through a tiny area between a lantern merged with a foxan leg as its post. She followed a line of overlapping circles that led her through a forest of twisted human limbs.

Her stump ached. She had to crawl through a tunnel consisting of doors and toes and windows and fingers.

Those circles crept towards her, and fingers elongated out of them into the snake tendrils, growing out of the tunnel. They formed mouths on the ends, snapping up the sounds of her passing, and she couldn't avoid them in the tight quarters. They bit at her waist, at her cheek, and her sense of identity began to grate again inside her, juddering and shaking loose. She jerked herself away from them, stumbling out of the tunnel's end, and they wavered there, bulges in their throats moving as they swallowed. The stone inside the tunnel increased from their feast. All around her, underneath her, and above her, more snakes uncoiled from the centers of ancient Lunnite script, wavering, opening their mouths, revealing eyes inside instead of throats. Saida's heart quaked in her chest, as if the snakes had jarred it loose, too. Would it slosh out of her body like an egg slopping out of the shell?

Don't stop now! Run!

How long had she journeyed through these scenes of frozen horror? Exhaustion weighed like a gravity shift, pushing her down. Her eyes flickered, and she fought to keep her head up and her hands steady.

More of the ancient Lunnite script showed ahead, scrawled all over a wall blocking her way. She maneuvered around it, not wanting to waste time climbing, but as she did, the largest circle became an eye, blinking open, as large as her.

She screamed.

The sound did not reach far. Four snake mouths the size of her human leg wove up from the ground in front of her and snapped it up. She dodged them as they stopped to grow thicker, longer, and the massive eye tracked her movement, the pupil narrowing. The wall ended fifteen feet away. She dashed for it, and twenty or more snake mouths formed on it like ripples in a lake, gibbering, extending on tendrils. She careened around the corner, and the giant eye flowed over the wall to the other side like a curtain with those ghostly snake-arms and mouths on the ends, reaching, reaching! She kept running. Left Foot caught on a corner of stone, and she snatched them in her arms, sobbing with terror. The Lunnite script became even denser, like engravings of tangled curls, and stone and eyes and hands surrounded her.

There! A path, through the vestiges of a hallway, twisting downward, the direction she needed. She shoved her way inside, trying to quiet herself, though that infernal eye followed her, so it likely didn't matter.

She cringed, and her blood heated again, and where her one foot and stump touched the hallway floor, snakes hissed and rose from the human mouths like the pollen-heavy knob on the end of a flower.

The hallway walls flowered with mouths. She muffled her scream this time, her whole body shaking. The mouths crunched at her head, her waist, her thigh, grinding away not her physical body, but that which connected her to herself. Physically, it felt like she had cracked her knuckles, a slight popping sensation, but the pain on the inside compared to someone skinning her alive and then shredding the skin. The snake mouths swallowed her magic, sending it back into the hallway itself, lengthening it by a few feet, growing more stone.

She loosened as a whole, no longer just Saida, but becoming Parts of Saida, and the agony almost blacked out her vision. But the gravity of the place allowed her to slide down, tearing away from the mouths, the growing hallway not quite able to keep up with her slow fall, the mouths disconnecting once their tendrils reached too far for her.

Her body had disconnected into six parts like a shattered mirror. Both arms had snapped off. As had her head. Her torso had separated from her legs. And of course, Left Foot remained detached. The pieces of her remained inches away on their own bonded strings.

The logic of it hurt her head. How had she not died?

Even though it seemed at first that she had broken in pieces, the Hunger had assaulted and weakened her bonds with her physical body. They hadn't broken her apart all the way, not yet, or those pieces would not float after her. They still considered themselves a part of her, but not as close as they had before. *The bond isn't strong enough*, Left Foot had said to her, when she'd asked to reconnect.

The Hunger didn't just consume peoples' physical bodies or magic, but the bonds she knew tied them together. The Hunger broke people and magic and things down into the most basic of identities, and then they absorbed those pieces. She would run out of time, and pieces, to separate into, and then the Hunger could digest her.

She hopped along one leg. Her head and arms and torso did not fall to the ground but floated near where they used to attach like kites on a string, as if operating on memories of how they used to attach. She tried to keep thinking of herself as Saida, not as segments, to keep the bonds short and her fragments close together, but that felt like lying to those parts of herself. Themselves.

Ahead of her, three large pillars ringed a floating sphere, a core of pure numbness as large as a house. It hovered above several concentric Lunnite circles and a single tree.

The sphere looked like the absence of her foot, the absence of where things should've been, except worse. It felt like severed bonds, not just faded ones. It sounded like silence, not the kind of silence that rang in the ears, but pure and utter dead sound.

The heart of the Hunger.

She/They'd reached it. Now she needed to 'break the circle and destroy the tree' according to Tener.

There are lots of circles! Which one?

She figured it was the circles surrounding the tree, and the Hunger's spherical heart that floated near the tree's branches.

The sphere drew her towards it, the source of the gravitational pull. She/they'd fall into it if she didn't stop her/themselves. She wedged her fingers in the grooves of the engraved circles, tucked her torso around a corner. She could still move the parts of her/themselves, though she had to concentrate to do so, focusing on one at a time. Perhaps, since they were larger parts of her than a foot, they identified more with her sense of self?

She allowed Left Foot Paw and her other leg, still attached to her foot, to slide closer. She'd try to claw at the symbols of the outer circle, the big one that connected the pillars, first.

Underneath her, a large circle of Lunnite script morphed into a mouth, a giant mouth that yawned open. She tried to leap away, and the tongue and teeth of the mouth lifted out of it on fifty or more snake tendrils and crashed over like a wave, washing around her and twining around her leg and Left Foot Paw, forming more small mouths on the ends, swarming over her.

"I HAVE YOU NOW, FOXAN!" the Hunger roared.

The snake mouths crunched and champed and chewed, lapped and slurped and pulled her/them apart, so she segmented into such small pieces that she/they became little cubes, each named—

Blood and Bones and Laughter and Tail and Craving for Adventure and Fangs and Fear of Crowds and Foxan Side and Paws and Hands and Love for Tener and Fur Pockets and Sense for Portals and Ears and Love for Parents and Magic Ear and Love for Alesio and Ability to Trim Overgrowths and Love of How He Held Her and Restlessness and—

They drifted.

The snakes slithered off Them, having done their job, channeling Their magic into the stone pillars around the floating sphere, thickening the Hunger, deepening and broadening the grooves of the script underneath Them. The Hunger had broken Them apart into Their smallest pieces of identity. The snakes functioned as the teeth, and now the Hunger could digest those parts of Them; absorb Them and transmute Them into the stone or perhaps drawn into that sphere of numb nothing. The invisible bonds that connected Them must resemble such a complicated web
. . .

Wait. They could see the bonds, now. One of them glowed gold. Their bond with Alesio. Others glowed reddish brown, Their bonds with Darrow, and Falrie, and Tener. Did Tener see this with their bondsight?

All the bits of Them still existed. They were parts of a whole, components in a larger frame. Their eye floated and the rest of Them followed, pulled down, down, towards that sphere.

They needed to stop Themselves. But how? They felt so . . . distant.

They resembled hundreds of floating cubes, or small blocks like the foundation of a house, and each of those cubes had a name, and all together, those cubes created the whole pattern of Saida. Their bonds, those strands, held those blocks together. They knew this like They knew Their name, and all the names of each cube.

One of Their strands stood out from the others. *Part* of the strand had dulled to gray. They'd disconnected that bond from Magic Ear. But new strands had formed around the gray one to resecure it, climbing around it like vines around a trellis. The new strands had reforged Their bond with Magic Ear. This had thickened and brightened the bond, so it shone almost as golden bright as Their bond with Alesio.

Other, older bonds of friends They'd lost trailed off Magic Ear like limp strands of gray hair: the bonds that used to lead to Goosefeather, Tricksy Stone, Crinkle Leaf Pile, Jar of Sky . . .

When They'd created Tricksy Stone and Goosefeather, They'd accessed parts of Themselves, Their thoughts, and feelings, and trimmed them, and transplanted them with magic from the worlds. They'd placed Their vulnerable, soft feelings within Goosefeather, and Their logical, problem-solving side within Tricksy Stone.

When They'd lost them—using Goosefeather as a teleport and then Tricksy Stone as a transplant—Tricksy Stone had merged back to Their mind as Difficult Truth. Their bond with Difficult Truth glowed and connected to Magic Ear.

Some of Their bricks flickered with little light and most did not connect to Magic Ear. One of them, Sense of Time, connected to adjacent bricks named Vision, and Sound, and the other senses.

They'd stopped Themselves from hearing the voices in the magic, and Their loss of those bonds had caused Them to have those episodes of dissociation, of lost time. Difficult Truth had not lied to Them.

They willed the strands connecting Magic Ear to the rest of the other bricks. It was easy, now that They could see them. They had never individualized the parts of Themselves down so far. The Hunger had ironically given Them the capacity to see Themselves.

"It's kind of funny," Difficult Truth said. "We used to sever human bonds because we feared what they'd do to us. Then we moved on to severing or letting magic bonds fade because we feared losing them again. Both times it just disconnected what made us, us."

The voice, so reminiscent of Tricksy Stone, but missing some of their sarcasm and bite, almost broke Them down more, but They stopped that. If They did break down to smaller parts, the Hunger would absorb Them. A quivering in all of Them told Them so; that breaking any further would disintegrate Them and Their bonds would Sever.

Just a few moments had passed after the snake mouths had torn Them apart. They'd drifted mentally, losing precious seconds. They had to focus.

What had Left Foot Paw said? *I will stay with you as long as you know who you are.*

They gathered Themselves closer, tightening the bonds between all Their parts, physical and non-physical, like someone collecting all the shattered pieces of a windowpane, finding where They'd broken. She/They couldn't reattach Themselves into one person, not so near that stretching pull of the Hunger that continually unfolded her/Them, but They could focus on one part of her/Themselves at a time and think of those pieces as one. She/They concentrated on her/Their fingers, tightening the bonds between fingernails and knuckles and palms. She/They concentrated on her/Themselves having a hand—not a finger, not three fingers, not five fingers without a palm—but a hand.

She/They had to pull her/themselves together. Literally. She/They'd promised Alesio she could do this, and she'd had almost just fallen straight into the Hunger!

Alesio! A sudden panic filled her. How much time had passed? She had no way of knowing, but it felt like she'd wandered through the skull forest for months and struggled up the cliff of eyes for days. Had she always picked her way through cities containing twisted people?

Her bond with Alesio flashed like a golden river, tugging on her, as she yearned to know—what if he were dying? What if the Hunger had dragged all the people towards it? What if he unraveled like that mountain, losing himself?

What if he never had a future at all, let alone with her/them?

"Alesio!" Her voice traveled down their bond, twanging it like a mandolin string.

34
MIXED MAGICS

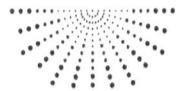

Alesio sat cross-legged on a larger rock. The fall sun had warmed the ice just enough in the past three hours to melt any un-cracked portions into slush, and people perched on anything above the cold shallows. Some had slogged a little way just to see how far the ice had formed, but it stretched for miles.

Over a thousand people, about seven hundred from Anthem, had traversed over to the Touch side. Groups of ten or more huddled together for warmth, cold and exhausted. They had no way of reaching Sound until the next day, for Tosn, the Lunnite who had teleported everyone, had used his teleport already to get them there. Well, Linia had amplified his ability, wringing another portal out of him even though he'd already used one that day. Her amplification had also enlarged the portal to her specifications, to shove as many straiters through as possible for her attempted psychotic killing spree.

Some of Alesio's suspicions about the Lunnites had turned out at least somewhat correct. Apparently, a few among them could Shape like humans, and the one called Tosn, their leader, could teleport like foxans. Tosn had portaled them close to the Summit Wave as per Linia's instructions, far from the Portal Station on Touch. Until one of the foxans or Tosn recharged their portals, they were stuck there, trying to stay above the shallow ice-water. Tosn, like the foxans, had said he didn't want anything to do with an amplifier for a long while, unless he had no other choice.

Fatigued and cold, Alesio didn't recognize the creeping danger at first. He'd just solved the immediate, massive concern of impending death, and like a kind of magic, his sense for danger had not yet refilled itself.

Tak comprehended their predicament first, a mere ten minutes or so after the Hunger had taken the bait of Frozen Mountain. The piper slogged over to Alesio.

"I hate to bother you and the other magic users," Tak said, "But we are all going to freeze our collective derrieres off if we do not warm up somehow. Especially the children."

Alesio looked up at him in a haze. The cold had a strange contrasting effect. Touch's increased sensation also caused frostbite faster than normal, which then produced numbness. An ironic outcome.

"Oh," Alesio said. "Right."

He knew this, of course. He'd taught the survival tactics in the expedition to Touch just a couple weeks ago—*a couple weeks ago?!*—though the cold hadn't become so bitter then. People had to keep their blood flowing unless they had access to a Touch shield.

Alesio surveyed the people. His own toes had started to numb. He stomped in place, cracking the ice under him. His thoughts had slowed, or numbed, as well. How could he Shape a Touch shield around this whole group without draining himself? He hadn't drained himself from Shaping the mountain thanks to everyone's participation, but he also didn't have much left. And fatigue held everyone in its grasp. No one would tramp around in circles in the frigid water. Most of the straiters' shoes consisted of thin flaps of leather or nothing at all, and schlepping through the slush could do just as much damage as staying still.

Baylor, the foxans, Naya, and Paras had all located various jutting rocks above the ice and crouched on them in precarious ways, the foxans shifted to their smallest selves with all their fur on, damp and looking as miserable as musicians who had accrued a considerable amount of rotten fruit on their stage.

Alesio could have tried using the amplifier in some way, perhaps Shaping a Touch shield by asking everyone to donate to his magic again, but the concept repulsed him. He'd plucked the device out of his mouth and dropped it in his pocket beside the other one. He didn't want to spend a second longer in that ocean of time-space. If he went back there . . . he didn't know if he could handle that.

But he'd learned more about magic than just the power of amplifiers in the last few days.

"Where's Muey?" Alesio asked.

They found the Touchian guide trying to hoist a group's spirits nearby and lead them to march in place. She remained one of the few still standing and moving around.

"Muey," Alesio said. "Do you have any magic left?"

The Touchian shook her head, standing in the frigid water herself so a young couple could huddle on a flat rock nearby. "Not enough to freeze the ice back to a thick sheet, which is what I want to do. I've saved the rest of it for emergencies."

"We can make that happen," Alesio said.

With a sense of urgency he dragged from the dregs of his being, he taught Muey how to utilize her magic better. Then, they worked together, calling forth only that which wished to do as they asked, and listened if the magic had any modifications.

After several minutes of intense concentration, he and Muey had Shaped the ice a good fifty yards wide and fifty yards long into a flat blanket of ice, which resembled the pearl-gray clouds floating above as the magic wished. Then they'd coaxed a different portion of ice to form into a pod-shaped dome around the ice, cutting off the wind. They had to fashion it smaller than they liked, since they had almost no magic, but it would shelter the most vulnerable.

"This is incredible!" The Touchian studied her hands, placing her palms on the thick ice. The people crowded into the large ice-pod around her, escaping the isolated rocks and huddling together for warmth. About half the people fit inside. "We did so much with so little magic."

Alesio sighed, staring at the people still shivering outside the dome. At least they didn't stand in ice-cold water any longer. But the wind cut sharp and frigid.

Muey and Tak looked to Alesio, as if he could conjure a miracle, as if he had accomplished all these things instead of them. They needed to understand that they had achieved so much on their own. He just passed on information.

His fatigue would have to wait in line before he addressed it.

"Listen up," he told the group of huddled people nearby who didn't fit in the shelter but waited on the flat patch of ice beside it. His voice carried in the cold, and more poked their heads up. "We'll have to rotate people in and out. To help you pass the time, and keep you awake so you don't freeze, I can teach you how to Receive and Shape better. I'll start with groups of ten. Who wants to go first?"

A field of hands bloomed like flowers popping up in spring. He gestured for ten of them to dislodge themselves from the others and forced them to trot in a circle around the others, getting their blood moving as he taught them the basics of what Hestafon had taught him.

No one had much magic after freezing the Summit Wave, but they could do more with their depleted store when Alesio taught them, as he had for Muey, how to Receive a certain amount of magic and listen to what it wanted to do. Those who could not Shape practiced Receiving magic, which helped with any lingering effects of the Hunger's draining.

The Soundians who could Shape generated a Sound shield large enough to keep the sound of the wind out, if not the cold and lash of it. The Tastians who could Shape practiced as well, enhancing the flavor of the icy water and sweetening the air. These magics served to keep them alert and awake, if not fed and warm. While working together, the Soundians could maintain a shield for as long as they wished.

What they had done with the Summit Wave had altered their understanding of Shaping forever.

Not everyone could Shape, of course, but after their fellows stopped jogging and slid back into the huddle with red cheeks and smiling faces, more joined in the exercise, moving their bodies to keep themselves from going numb in their extremities.

Those that could Shape constructed various shapes with their voices or breath, such as Sound birds, plates, windows, or plants, all things that dissipated after something touched them or they touched something else. None of the magic wished to become knives.

One young girl Shaped a blanket that wrapped around her, which then vanished. "It sounded so real, in my own mind," she whispered.

"They are real," Alesio said, crouching down to her level. He'd paused his exertions, allowing himself to rest and huddle with the others in their warmth. Muey was already teaching the next group. "They live shorter lives than us, but that doesn't mean they aren't real. We don't understand everything about them, yet, but the magic has their own wants and desires and identities."

"Voice," an old woman nearby spoke up. "I heard a rumor that before everything happened with Linia, the Council delegate sacrificed himself for a straiter. Do you know if this is true?"

Alesio bowed his head.

"It's true." Darrow flopped down next to Alesio, his arms human, his legs foxan and crossed under him. "I saw it happen. Some angry straiters forced Hestafon into a cage match. He threw himself in front of a Sound blade so it wouldn't hit someone outside the cage."

The group that had rotated outside murmured among themselves. A profound exhaustion settled over Alesio. He napped on and off in the ice-pod for about an hour or so, jarred awake every so often by people trading places with others, his sense of risk not quite drained. Or perhaps he'd stayed on such high alert for so long, it was difficult to stop, like a fighter who had curled his hands into fists and could uncurl them.

He levered himself up from his nap and went back outside. The wind had died down a little. The little girl patted his arm and conjured another Shaped Sound blanket so that it wrapped it around him but didn't touch him or the ice. It remained, hovering in the air, until she lost concentration and it fell to the icy ground and dissipated.

Tak settled next to him and whispered in his ear. Part of his handlebar mustache had been ripped out. "Alesio, the Hunger ate Frozen Mountain *extremely* quickly. How long do you think we have?"

"I ... I don't know."

Had it helped Saida? Had it made any difference? At least he had stayed true to his earlier convictions—helping how she wanted, instead of trying to put her in a bubble Shaped out of his own fear.

The bond between them jerked taut, like a rope pulled tight. *"Alesio!"*

He reeled back from the terror of her scream. It pounded on the walls of his Sound room. His heart raced.

Receive first.

He opened a door in the wall, tracing it with his fingers. Saida's scream shot into the room, bouncing off the ceiling, the floor, the other walls. It changed to a song, their song, the one he had sung for her.

"Hello! My name is Saida's Love. I would like to be with you!"

Alesio's breath almost left him. "How ... how do you want me to be with you?"

"I would like to be a door! I would like to open up and bring you to the rest of me!"

With trembling fingers, Alesio Shaped the Sound of the song of Love into a door in front of him, right there on Touch. It wasn't a physical door, but a door of Sound, a door that allowed her Spatial portal magic to connect to his Sound magic.

He understood, in that moment, that the bond between them *was* her Shaped Spatial magic, a kind of Portal Station that let the two of them find each other.

The door resembled the front door of the house he had bought for them, and its bright red had the exact hue of Saida's hair. He motioned everyone away, and the Soundians backed off.

"You're portaling to Saida, aren't you?" Naya stood nearby, her pants torn at the ends, showing the reddish-brown fur around her ankles.

"It's not safe—" Alesio began.

"We don't have time to debate this," Naya said. "Try to stop me."

"I'm going too," Baylor said, from behind Alesio.

It seemed that Alesio's stumbling from hearing Saida's voice had wakened more than a few people, including Falrie and Tener, who trotted over to him.

Falrie shifted her ears to foxan, and half lowered them. Tener gazed at her, and she stared at the icy ground. "If . . . if you feel like you need to go . . . I won't stop you."

Tener considered her. Then, instead of bouncing with excitement at their mother's thin permission, trotted over and nuzzled her cheek with theirs, also as a foxan.

"You go. I'll stay here and help the Soundians."

"Oh, Tener." Falrie buried her face in their side. "You've grown up already. You've grown more than I have in centuries."

"Alright," Alesio said. "Be ready for anything. Bring any weapon you have. We're teleporting to the Hunger." He gripped the two amplifiers in his pocket, then fit the smaller box-shaped one in his mouth with a grimace. "Here goes . . . everything." He gripped the doorknob and turned it.

The door dissipated, revealing a portal, and a twisted world beyond.

ALESIO DUCKED through the portal and crept between two pillars of stone, carved to resemble large, twisted arms. That sounddamned circle language surrounded them. The ends of the arms rose out of the stone and formed snake mouths, hissing at him. What felt like a thousand Sound knives began sawing at his soul.

He almost fell to his knees but staggered on past the pillars. Was Saida close? She had to be.

"COMING STRAIGHT TO ME?" The Hunger's voice slammed

into him, and he cried out. One of the snakes struck at the air near his mouth and a bulge showed in its throat, or arm, or whatever the hell it was.

The sound of his cry ceased. The snake-arm-thing had *absorbed* it.

And then it *grew longer.*

"HOW INCREDIBLY GRACIOUS OF YOU!"

More snakes lunged for him, and he scrambled to the left, then jumped over a part of a street that had warped around twenty or thirty feet together to create a cobblestone-like effect. Darrow, Falrie, Baylor, and Naya followed behind him. He seemed lighter, here, but gravity still tugged at him, towing him towards something, picking him a few feet off the "ground."

All around them, parts of bodies and city laced together in bizarre and tortuous fusions. Grey darkness filtered down through an unholy canopy of eyes, lampposts, windows, ears, bricks, and mouths, mouths everywhere, many of them on the ends of tentacle-like arms.

The air, the stones and eyes and hands all around them, this place grated and ripped at his bones, at his sense of self. Had Saida endured this agony since she'd teleported here? How could she—

Saida hovered a few feet away, beside another of the large twisted-arms pillars. Or . . . part of her did.

Her hands, and legs, and paws, and ears, and torso, and tail all floated in sections, like someone had cut her into tiny pieces. She crawled, her eye fixed on something past the pillar, and all her parts followed as if connected by invisible strands. This place had literally torn her apart.

Alesio cried out, reaching for her. *Is she alive? —How can she still be moving—?*

One of her eyes flicked in his direction, and then something drew him to her, pulling him like a string. Their bond. She reached out with half a palm, then her hands formed with all the fingers, and then her hands joined with her arm, and her shoulder, then all her parts formed together, and she hugged him, her face buried in his chest. Then she looked up at him.

"I thought I'd never see you again," she whispered, and the very air absorbed the sound, though he could read her lips. His sense of touch had decreased, again; her hug wrapped around him like a blanket, and his vision blurred to indistinct details after a hundred yards or so. He was being drained.

If he stayed here too long, he'd rip apart and merge into the stone around him, the tortured pieces of death, never to see another sunset.

But none of that mattered. She was alive.

"Don't you remember?" he said, just moving his lips, not feeding the Hunger any of his sound. "I can always find you. As long as that's what you want, too."

Something behind him broke him away her. More snakes had animated around them like a disturbed nest and had bitten into Falrie and Darrow. The foxans had their mouths open in screams, but the snakes swallowed the sound before it reached Alesio's ears.

Saida pointed. "We need to scratch the runes and break through the outer circle defenses to destroy the tree! If we get too close without breaking the magic of the circles, we fall apart!"

Alesio followed where she indicated. That strange, circular script crawled over three pillars, and three concentric rings surrounded a tree. A sphere hovered over that tree like a moon caught in its branches, and the sphere was so empty, so filled with nothing at all, he understood at once.

This was the heart of the Hunger, the place where the Transmuters must have begun their ritual to become a god.

The inside of it hurt Alesio's eyes, not because it shone too bright, but because it dimmed too dark. At the same time, it was not black, not dark, at all. He had no color to reference it because he did not see anything. He understood it as the vague concept of gray, the feeling of touching dead flesh, the negative ring of silence. His senses did not comprehend how to translate something that did not give off sound, touch, or color. It did not exist in how he understood existence, and his mind and body and soul shuddered, quivering like leaves in the summer viewing a vagary of fall, when they will fall, about to fall—!

That not-place tugged on him like a slight gravity shift. It drew him along at a steady pace, and even made him hover a little, since the sphere floated off the "ground." If he fell in there, or even neared it, he would never, ever return. He wouldn't just twist apart over minutes or hours, he'd feed the Hunger like wood in a furnace.

The little magic that had refilled inside Alesio depleted fast here. He clung to the pillars in the air to keep himself from drifting towards the sphere. He Received the Sounds of his internal organs, that of his beating heart, his filling lungs, his grating teeth. He warned the magic about sacrifice.

The grating teeth accepted, allowing him to Receive them. They wanted identity just for a moment, anyway, and to become something that could bite, like the grating sound they'd originated from.

He Shaped them into a Sound knife and flung them at the tree underneath the hovering sphere. The knife disintegrated before they even reached the tree, the magic absorbed and pulled apart.

No one could get close before weakening the circles, like Saida had said. He'd needed to see it before he understood it fully. People were made of magic, and if he tried to just go over there, he'd disintegrate.

Baylor's ixor slowed the snakes, instead of letting them just absorb the magic. Alesio motioned to Darrow, Falrie, and Naya, then pointed at the outer circle, and mimed scratching at it with his knife. Then he pointed to Baylor and motioned with a broad sweep all at the snake mouths advancing on them all.

They all nodded, remembering not to speak. Baylor, his lips bleeding once more, laid a wide swath of ixor down on the ground, slowing the snake mouths. Darrow, Falrie, and Naya clambered over and began to dig with knife and claws at one section near the three pillars. Alesio joined them, sliding out his knife he always kept on him, and scratched at the same part of the stone, trying to focus as much damage as possible in one place. Saida stumped over and scratched madly with her claws. Alesio had to keep one hand on the pillar to stop himself from floating away, which made using his knife even more difficult, costing him strength.

After six or seven strikes with his knife, one of the symbols seemed scratched enough that it stopped working, and the others had done similar amounts of damage. The pulling gravity towards the Hunger lessened in power, and the sense of their bodies shuddering apart lost a little intensity.

"STOP!" The Hunger roared. "STOP THAT RIGHT NOW!"

Several snakes burst out of the stone pillar next to him. He dodged and avoided all but two that bit his hand.

He screamed, and his hand *disconnected*. He lost sensation there, like his hand had fallen asleep. He could still control it, though it floated a little away his body, just as Saida's limbs did. He kept his footing against the pillar to his right. Baylor grimaced and laid down another layer of ixor so that the snakelike tendrils slowed.

Alesio tried another Sound knife, flicking it towards the tree underneath the Hunger's heart. The knife still dissipated, though it took longer to do so. Still not something he wanted to charge towards. He stepped towards the second concentric ring, still sensing that juddering of his sense of self shaking like a baby bird in someone's hand, and began scoring at the stone with his knife again. At least the pull of gravity had lessened, so he didn't have to brace himself.

Controlling his disconnected hand expended more precision and thought, as if his mental directions took a little more time to travel through the physical detachment. He grabbed the knife with his off hand and dug awkwardly at a thinner squiggle of script.

The rest of the group joined at other places around the circle, scraping at the runes a little way from each other with any random bits of architecture they could find, now that the stone had stopped sprouting snake tendrils.

Naya shouted in triumph, and no snakes leapt to swallow the sound. She'd managed her side of the second circle.

Saida and Alesio redoubled their efforts. An eye the size of a house winked open above them, dilated black with scrawled, crawling runes. It reached down to them, growing towards them, and sprouted more snake-arms with mouths on the ends out of it. Baylor sent a large cloud of ixor at it, slowing the sprouted layer of snake-arms, but the eye remained above them.

The rune under Alesio's knife scratched out, and the second circle ceased functioning. Once again, the pull of the Hunger lessened, and the ripping sensation at the core of his soul reduced. It seemed they needed to destroy a certain number runes per circle before it lost its absorbing magic.

"STOP! I MUST CONSUME; I MUST GO ON! LUNNE IS MISSING!"

Hundreds of snakes outside of where Baylor had laid ixor peeled up and out and down from the twisted stones. They hissed all around them like dancing flames in a huge fire and struck and bit with flashing fangs. The young man shouted and shot more ixor out, but they emerged from too many different directions, even overhead, dropping down on them.

Alesio learned in moments that he could not direct multiple pieces of himself at once. The composition of his being had disassembled into a chaotic mess of eighth notes, hands and feet and face and torso. He focused on just his arm and hand that gripped the knife and scraping at the third circle. He didn't want to waste any more magic testing the tree's strength. He had to ensure it would pierce the barrier.

Another snake grew up from the pillar next to him, too close. He had to dodge, moving to another part of the grooved circle. *Sounddamn it.* He'd wounded that area. But now a nest of snakes teemed over it.

The snakes had struck the other parts of him as he'd focused on the arm and hand he needed. His other hand separated into fingers and palms, his torso became ribs and heart and lungs, his face disjointed into a mouth and nose and ears. His skin popped off like an eggshell, floating nearby like a horrific outer shell of himself, leaving the rest of his body parts just muscle and sinew. Baylor slowed everyone's fragments, so they did not drift towards the Hunger. The young man had fragmented, too, into head and torso and legs.

Alesio worked on another area of the script, the thinnest symbol he could find. Another snake lunged at him from the ground, from a stone eye layered into the floor, catching his skinned arm, disconnecting it from his hand. He winced reflexively—he couldn't feel much of anything anymore—and kept going, but another snake reared up from the script itself, like a word had awakened, and bit *back* at the knife he held.

The knife disjointed into pieces, and he had to hold onto the point of it with his thumb and forefinger, like the smallest knife.

He dodged a second, slower attack from the word-snake, and surveyed the scene around him. The others fared the same as him, the hems of their lips unraveling, their eyes disjointing from their sockets. Falrie and Darrow tore at the stone with just their teeth and claws across the circle, the rest of their bodies trying to hide from the snakes behind the pillars, same as him. But the snakes had wound around those parts, biting, and biting them into smaller pieces, dividing fingers into fingernails and knuckles and tendons. Those pieces could escape, but since he didn't direct them, the snake-tendrils would curl around them and strike again.

Then the Hunger seemed to shudder, and the last bit of pulling magic ceased. The others had managed to damage enough runes to destroy the third circle's functioning.

Alesio needed to find the pieces of the two amplifiers. He wasn't part of the amplifier, so he couldn't sense those pieces, but the parts of himself that ripped near them. He gathered one amplifier chunk, the larger one, that had ripped along with a section of his hip, and another part of his upper thigh. He concentrated, directing those pieces of himself back closer together, and the amplifier snapped back together easier than he did. Then he found the small box in two pieces, one with half his tongue, the other connected to the tooth he'd fitted it over. That one came together as well.

Alesio connected the two, as he had done before.

Then he descended into that space inside himself, which had once again enlarged. Without all of Anthem adding their Receiving to his, he wasn't a drop of water in an entire sea, but he was more like a drop of water in a lake.

He decided on Sound magic. The idea of trying to use the already twisted stones around him repulsed him. Trying to Shape the script into a flat surface might feel like trying to wrestle snakes.

Not much Sound magic existed for him to Receive, here, even with the aid of both amplifiers. He opened a large window, calling for magic once more that were willing to sacrifice themselves to save the worlds, and who wanted to become a weapon. Small bits streamed through, not just because his requests filtered many out. The Hunger consumed magic from the very air, and not much could escape their pull. But the panting sound of the foxans, Alesio's own breathing, the sound of their scratching claws and knifes still created something, and he Received them in that moment, asking them what they wanted to be.

"M-my name is Quick Breaths," the magic said. "A weapon? You need a weapon, right? I want to dig at things like claws! Only bigger!"

He Shaped them into a javelin, like what Linia had used against him back on Sound. He launched them with his thoughts instead of his hands at the tree.

Quick Breath Javelin hit something that flickered like a Sound shield, then instantly disintegrated.

Shit.

What could he do against that? A kind of anti-magic shield?

Saida's hand found his. Just her hand, just his hand. All their other parts had fragmented, many of them to the smallest phase as tiny cubes.

"Meet me in your magic house," she said through their bond.

Alesio didn't bother telling her they couldn't do enough magic to puncture the Hunger's shield. These would be their last moments together. He descended once more to that vast, amplified space and Saida joined him there.

He'd never considered such a thing, before, but he'd managed it with all of Anthem, so of course *she* could meet him there. She even showed up physically, while the people of Anthem had just joined him mentally.

They were both still shattered, which surprised him. He hadn't noticed that, when he'd Shaped Quick Breaths. But now that he desperately wanted to hold Saida, he could only wrap his hand around her hand, same as in the physical world.

"We can't stay long," he warned her, speaking through their bond. "Maybe a couple minutes, because we're not Shaping magic. The amplifiers give us more time, or we'd already have had to go back."

"Who says we won't be doing magic?"

"Saida, you saw what happened—"

"I have an idea." Her hand released his and waved excitedly. "Make the biggest Sound javelin you can! Use all the magic you have! Trust me!"

He got to work.

She Shaped a portal. It pulled at the space around them, like folding in the corners of a piece of paper.

She was Shaping the *Space of magic,* the extra space that the amplifiers lent.

"Holy Sound," he said.

"I Shape too," she said, and parts of her lips quirked up at him. "I just didn't realize it, before."

"I need to tell you something," he said, as Sound magic slowly streamed into the space from his Receiving. "I need you to know. It's alright if you're not sure about the future, or if you'll change. By the Senses, I'm counting on it."

Tears flowed down parts of her cheeks like rain on a shattered window. Her identity shone out of her like a key signature in a song. She held the edges of the portal like a curtain she pulled open with her hand.

"I pushed you to need me, because that's what I thought I wanted. But I think it's better to be with each other just because we want to." He began Shaping the Sound magic into another javelin. He couldn't find her eyes, so he placed his hand over hers as he mixed the magic against the portal she'd crafted. "Is that what you want?"

A bit of water splashed down from an eye. The blocks of her fur and her hair and nose and mouth moved up and down in a nod like the stars in a sky making a constellation. "Even though it's selfish. I'm sorry about leaving. I really didn't want to. I really, really didn't."

"Selfish?" He wished he could stroke her hair. "You know, part of you spoke to me, the part of you that opened the door and crossed the distance between us. And they didn't name themselves Selfishness, but Love. Your *Love* told me they wanted to be with me."

More tears.

"How about this? If you want to separate at any point, you just need to tell me. And I'll accept it. I'd rather be with you for even a day and know I might lose you, than to stop being with you when we both want to be."

"I love that, and I love you," she whispered.

The magic had completed what they'd asked, and the space forced them both out, back into the Hunger.

Alesio launched the javelin towards the Hunger, letting out a disembodied howl. The Sound weapon would have spanned twice as long as he was tall, if he'd still had a body.

He didn't know how Saida had planned to make this work but he he didn't need to. He trusted her.

The javelin hurtled towards the twisted tree that held the Hunger together. Alesio tried to suck in air and hold his breath out of habit but had no mouth or lungs to do so.

Mere feet before the javelin reached the magic forcefield, the tip of glowed then flashed open into a portal.

Saida had Shaped a portal on the end of his javelin.

The weapon disappeared into the portal as if cast into a lake. The portal rippled then disappeared.

A fraction of a second later, the other end of the portal materialized a dozen feet ahead of the path of the javelin between the magic barrier and the tree. The javelin jettisoned out of the portal and pierced deep into the tree. The trunk of the tree cracked.

Everything seemed to *snap*.

A pulse emanated from the numb, gray, not-place like distant thunder. The tiny saw blades that had ripped into Alesio's bones and blood stopped, and all his cubes linked back up into eyes, his knees, his toes, then they joined and became his face, his legs, his feet, his torso, and then he was himself again.

Around him, Baylor materialized, and Naya, and Falrie, and Darrow, and Saida. It was like watching drops of rain coalesce on a window, becoming streams of water, then joining with rivulets along the ground to become a river.

"Everyone, hold hands!" Saida said, and the snake mouths did not swallow the sound of her words. A wind rushed out of the Hunger's center, gaining strength by the second. All around them, the stone formations unformed, untwisted, and broke down into their base materials, though they remained stone.

Arms unwound from the pillars. Fences dropped the stone human eyes that had dotted their posts. Overhead, what had created the low ceiling in this chamber released a swarm of wings, which fluttered in the wind away from the center.

"What is happening?" Naya asked, but the wind and the pushing force became stronger, and stronger, and they had to brace themselves against the untangling chaos. They reached out and huddled around each other.

THE HUNGER'S pulling power had reversed and no longer siphoned off Saida's magic abilities. In fact, it returned them, tenfold, hundredfold, all the magic they hadn't yet digested and changed into fuel for themselves.

She glowed.

All the parts of the Hunger showed themselves to her, and she understood how they had changed from one substance—organic tree —to another of stone, an Amplifier, just like all the others had done. One of their worlds used to have the magic of Transmutation, after all.

Then a part of her zoomed out, like a bird flying high in the sky, and the five Sensory worlds and their Primal Plane hove into view, then several other Planes, like the rock constellations on Vision. She zoomed out even more, and in a split second, perhaps a hundred Planes and all their different worlds spread out under her like patches on a quilt, and about a third of them were absent, nonexistent, more like jagged holes in space. Those had to be the Planes that the Hunger had consumed. Gray, broken lines ran between all the Planes. The Bridges? She looked behind her.

Close to the Sensory Plane shone a glow so bright, a beacon of magic so powerful and blinding, she flinched and shrank back down into her body again.

What in the Senses was that?

Lunne.

A single source of magic so brilliant could only be the Goddess.

But she had more urgent, immediate things to think about. Everything in the Hunger crumbled and pushed apart. She still held Alesio's hand. Her vision had lasted perhaps a second.

Her portals, pulled towards her from the power of her vision, perhaps, had followed her even into this twisted mass of pulling force, and she called one of them to her. They slipped through the churning torrent of wind and unraveling stone like a fish in an ocean and popped up behind them all in the space of a moment.

She held Alesio's hand, and his silver magic from his breath coiled with the gold in the bond between them, thickening the strand and suffusing it with a gradient of moonlight twining with the sunrise yellow.

He felt selfish this whole time?

She couldn't believe it. He wanted a relationship with her, even knowing the risks she presented. He had accepted her in every way; that she could shift both her physical body and her identity, and he still wanted to be with her.

And she wanted to be with him. Her Love had said that, not her Selfishness.

The force of the Hunger's explosion blew them through the portal, and they landed on Sound, next to Alesio's house, where she'd told the portal to go.

Above them, the Hunger crumbled. The hole of madness that had eaten up most of the sky, that had twisted it like a cloth, had changed. The spots inside of the entity grew, and grew, filling the absence. The central city of Kolsuv Mor, of course, but others, too. Bodies of water joined each other and created parts of an ocean, hovering like a shell of frosting over a nonexistent cake. Sections of land joined each other, pitted and cratered and with sheer edges as if something had sliced into them, but they formed into other chunks of one . . . two . . . three worlds. One had perhaps a third remaining, and two were just slivers, like the waning phases of a moon.

"What are they?" Baylor asked.

"The last Plane that the Hunger consumed," Naya said, "that it hadn't finished breaking down and digesting yet."

Saida nodded. Of course, Naya had figured it out.

From far away, all the horrifying disjointed bits of humans and animals showed as a twisting mass, but already they had started dissembling into disparate parts, untwisting, unmerging, unwinding, and some of them perhaps finding other bits stolen from them.

She imagined the stone eyes wedging into their stone skulls, the stone leaves curling around their stone branches, the stone droplets hailing into their stone river, rolling into where they'd sprayed up from. The last Plane that the Hunger had consumed, and perhaps tiny remnants of others, exploded outward, shooting back to their original places in the universe and settling there like eggs in a carton. She knew, somehow, that they could never turn back from stone, that their lives and identities remained stolen, but at least they would find rest as they unraveled from other magics and lives and buildings and animals they had not wished to merge with, a forced transplant that had mangled their souls.

How many Planes had the Hunger consumed? Perhaps thirty? The strange vision had shown her that the Hunger seemed to have destroyed about a third of the Planes in the universe. What had those people and magics looked like? What names might they have had?

She might never know the answer. They'd fed the void, that not-place inside of Kolsuv Mor.

These people didn't just lose their physical bodies. They lost their bonds with each other, and themselves.

The slivers of worlds shrank smaller in their sky, and smaller. The push from the center of the Hunger would carry them back to where they had originated from, like a spring wound for a long time finally released.

35
THEY WANT TO CHANGE

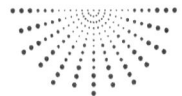

S aida trudged up the steps to the Cadenza, her heart pounding. What if she still couldn't hear their voice?

She and Alesio had had a lot of damage control to do, and they hadn't had time before now to visit. Well, maybe they could have swung by a few days ago. Three weeks had already passed since they'd defeated the Hunger. Old habits sometimes reared their heads, but she'd had practice dealing with a lot of snake-based imagery lately.

She would face the fear, though. And breathe through it instead of avoiding it any longer. She fingered her braid. The hair had just started to grow back around the end of her tail.

Alesio, ambling next to her, wove his arm through the open front of her human coat and around her waist. Winter had ascended to its peak in Anthem, and his hands warmed her skin under her fur. "Want me to wait outside?"

He wore a human coat over one of his new shirts for the performance tonight, a silver shirt with golden trim on the cuffs and the buttons. He'd shaved, but at her request, had allowed more of his beard along his lower cheeks to remain like an outline of attraction she could trace.

"I want you there with me," she said.

He skated his hand along her arm. She shivered at the contact, and he chuckled low in his throat, his eyes darkening, and whispered in her ear, "Later."

They strode through the big main doors, and through the echoing vaulted hallway. Saida appreciated the instant relief from the wind. A fire crackled in a large hearth, heating the foyer. Estro bowed to them, taking their coats.

"Are you and Tak coming to the De Capo tonight?" Alesio asked. "Should be wild, though not as wild as it *could* be. Baylor promised not to drug us all."

"I'd not miss an opportunity to wear my blue and gold dress pants." Estro opened the door to the main concert hall for them.

Alesio grinned. "My friend, every day is an opportunity for blue and gold dress pants."

Saida tugged at his coat, and Alesio laughed and let her tow him.

"Be good, you two," Estro called. "I'd like to keep the seats clean!"

Saida didn't listen. She listened to the ceiling. The huge gem that Tricksy Stone had become revolved above them like a miniature sun, changing colors from butter-yellow to auburn, then to indigo and mauve.

She closed her eyes and let herself Receive.

All magic had a voice, if someone listened for it, and every human possessed Received magic when they felt, tasted, touched, heard, or saw magic on each of their worlds. They just hadn't learned how to Receive the voices inside of the magic itself. She'd had to re-teach herself how to do it after disconnecting that part of her for so long. She'd had to accept that part of her told the truth, difficult as it might be.

"Hello. My name is Trickster Sky."

Their voice had a regal element, and she blinked. She had not expected the different voice, though she should have. They had changed, after all, when they had transplanted into the Cadenza's ceiling.

"Hello," she said, her voice trembling. "Hi. Um. Do you . . . do you remember me?"

"You don't know me, but I know you. I am not Tricksy Stone, but a part of Tricksy Stone is a part of me."

Tears slid down her face. Their voice had changed. She couldn't get over that.

"I want to learn the new you, and I hope you want to learn the new me," they said. "I think you may have changed more than I have."

Trickster Sky's gradation purpled, like Vision's lavender sky. The part of them sourced from Vision revolved, a mesmerizing jewel, and as always, she wanted to crane her neck to follow the pattern. That part of them remained the same.

"I tried to speak to you every time you visited, but you couldn't hear me," Trickster Sky said. "It saddened me."

Alesio squeezed her hand. He could hear them, too, of course, now that he knew how to Receive magic voices. Tricksy Stone had lied to her when they'd told her she imagined them, and she'd readily believed them to handle the grief of losing them. It was the only way she would've sacrificed them back then.

"They're right, you know," Alesio said. "You have changed. Etha told me that you had to sing to open the portals in that Epitaph. Making it as a big shot performer and everything!"

She shoved against him, bubbling out both laughter and a little sob.

Alesio smiled and released her hand. "I'll let you both get reacquainted."

After a long time, she exited the main concert hall and shut the doors behind her.

"… that amplifier out of his mouth?" Estro asked.

"It was tricky," Alesio said. "It had become a part of Baylor after he'd worn it so long. The ancient Lunnites—pre-Hunger, of course— manufactured the small amplifiers to help our societies build and create large structures, but they aren't meant to be worn for months at a time, or even for a full day, really. Falrie managed to trim it away, little by little, and Marik helped translate the runes to ensure safety. A Tastian doctor helped with the physical removal."

Saida slipped her hand back into his. He smiled at her, handing her human coat back, and she wanted to kiss him for mentioning Marik without hesitation in the silver stream of his voice.

The Lunnite hadn't stuck around much after the Hunger had dissipated from all their skies. He'd gone to work helping translate the sets of scripts in the colony ruins on the other Sensory worlds in painstaking detail. He'd also volunteered to lead another expedition team on Scent. Saida hoped he found love with someone who wanted him back.

She and Alesio sauntered through Anthem together side by side. She grew her fur as thick as she could against the elements.

A line of people waited outside the permanent portal to Vision. The Council had appointed certain interested Soundians into rotating teams that lived and learned about the other worlds and how the magic affected them, to stop the fearful mobs rampaging if disaster struck again. Those who agreed to it also trained in magic deprivation exposure, to help lessen the devastating effects of draining.

"Can we check on Baylor?" Alesio asked her. "I'd like to watch the next training session."

"What a wonderful idea," she said, shivering. She called up a portal in a moment, drawing it up from the ground. After the vision and out-of-body experience on the Hunger, teleporting had become easier. When everything had connected at such a high level, she'd learned to Receive her own kind of magic better, too, like a map that pointed her in the right direction. She could teleport three times a day now.

That vision echoed in her mind as if in a canyon on Sound: all those disconnected Planes, like people ripped from each other's arms, and that bright, bright light so close to the Sensory Plane, her Plane.

The Goddess, Lunne, was real. Both the ancient Lunnites and their modern followers had been right. They needed to find her and figure out why all the Planes had frayed and decayed so long ago, before the Hunger had Severed them for good. The world of Transmutation had tried to fix the issue—they had just landed on the wrong solution. She could relate.

Alesio hummed the song he'd sing tonight, and through their bond, he'd feel her anxiety spiking as she wandered off to the "what if" area of her mind. Their bond connected their emotions now; they each could sense the other. His voice was like a silver anchor she could hold onto in a strong wind, and she gripped his hand in gratitude. She let herself feel the worries, instead of ignoring them, sharing them through the bond. He Received them, and sent back reassurance, understanding, validation. He didn't say anything out loud, just kept humming the tune.

And her worries . . . dissipated once she let herself feel them, once she communicated them. Like a Sound object that someone touched.

They just wanted to be understood. They wanted their identities acknowledged like everyone else in existence, and her foxan side didn't want to cage them.

They didn't want to stay as worries. They wanted to shift. They wanted to change. They wanted to portal through her heart, be named like any other magic, then wave to her and travel to other places.

She'd figure out the mystery around Lunne another day.

The Scentians received them with smiles and nonflower chains they crafted, draping the muting scent over their heads. She and Alesio strolled towards the village; their coats flung over their arms.

Harvest time had arrived, and Verrity, Paras, and Ishira, along with a group of Scentians, directed one of the teams of Soundians in the fields on how to cut wheat with scythes, and how to gather the chaff off the end and separate the two. The Soundians worked with a quiet diligence, and they did not narrow their eyes or hunch their shoulders against advice. Tremain's simple life had a calming way about it.

Saida waved to the sisters. While Saida had fallen apart searching for a solution inside the Hunger, terrible things had happened on Sound. Alesio had filled her in on Linia's plot to use an amplifier and mass control all the straiters to march straight into the Summit Wave.

Linia hadn't counted on people like Paras, who she'd manipulated to bring her the amplifier in the first place, or Alesio with his partial deafness and mixed magics, breaking through her control.

Baylor's father, Aaer, worked alongside the Soundians. Shadows crept inside his eyes, and he had covered himself in chain after chain of nonflowers. He had opted to live in the village, with the Scentians' permission, after they had brought him in from the torture he'd endured at the hands of Clef's men. Saida would've supposed that he'd want to leave that world after what had happened to him, but even normal fecal smells proved too much for him to handle on other worlds, and the Scentian village had the ability to eliminate the scent altogether.

She and Alesio roamed a little way along a new path and found Baylor in the forest, gesturing in front of five Scentians. Each stood in front of a different tree or flower. "Now, the trick that I find helpful is, to think of your magic as like a room inside yourself. Can you all picture that?"

They all murmured assent; their eyes already closed. Many of them had heard this before, but regular training helped ensure that people didn't try to use too much magic and drain themselves into mania.

Baylor waved to them without speaking to avoid distracting his trainees. He had a brightness to his face. The peeling around his mouth had almost healed and the overgrowth that Saida had noted inside him had since retreated once they'd removed the amplifier.

"Okay, everyone. Now, focus on a small section of your room, the size of your hand, and trace a window open there." The five people traced with their hands a small square in front of them in the air. "Alright, do you hear the magic speaking to you? One by one, tell me if they want to change, and if so, what they want to change to."

A few moments later, one of the women spoke. "They say their name is Lily's Sigh. They say they want to ride along with the bees."

"Alright. How will you help them?"

The woman furrowed her brow in concentration, and lifted her hands, Shaping the Scent magic, and Saida sensed Lily's Sigh change from a wavering scent line into a flattened sheet, pulled down at the corners. The Scent magic lifted higher, much higher, and a nearby bee maneuvered towards them, running through them in search of the nectar they smelled.

"Very good," Baylor said.

"Looks like he's doing well," Saida said in a low voice.

"He does." Their bond, that link between them like a constant open portal, flickered with power. She understood, she *Received*, in a way, how Baylor mirrored his younger self, and how much it meant for him to know the young man was healing.

They left before the trainees opened their eyes so as not to disturb their concentration and wandered in the Garden. They played hide-and-seek tag in the portal maze, who delighted at their visit and reset the puzzle each time they figured it out, until the sun set. Then they rambled back to the Portal Station and left for Sound.

"BE CAREFUL WITH THE BLUESTAR HERB." Ishira paced up and down the line of people—interspersed with Soundian and Scentian, so that every otherworlder had a guide. "It has a tough root, and its thorns can slice deep."

The Soundians already had gloves on, but they stopped using their hands and remembered they had trowels. Verrity smiled from the side, her hands on her hips. She wore her good dress today, the one that propped up her breasts better and hid her thicker waist with how the layers fell. She elbowed Paras beside her. "What do you think? Do we tell her now?"

Paras had her hands in her pockets. "Sure. Yeah, that'd be good."

"Hey." Verrity narrowed her eyes at her sister. "Do we need to go over this again? I'm not mad at you."

Paras stooped her shoulders, her blonde hair curtaining around her. "You should be."

"I've had enough of people telling me what I should or shouldn't be. Don't you start."

"That's not—"

Verrity laughed. "Finally got you to look up." She grabbed her sister's shoulders. "I. Don't. Blame. You." She tilted her head. "Although, the next time you try and not tell me something, I *will* send Tener to go with you on an expedition. That foxan is relentless. They will not stop until you eat olos with them."

Paras started to cry.

"You do know what olos are? You know they're not, like, rocks or anything? I would think out of everyone in Scent, you'd know that—"

Paras squeezed her sister around the waist. "I don't deserve you. I don't deserve to leave on any expeditions for a year."

Verrity snorted. "It's been a month, and you've apologized approximately five hundred times. Really, if you don't leave on an expedition soon, I might go on one myself just to avoid you."

Paras didn't answer with a sarcastic rejoinder. That, more than anything, made Verrity sigh.

"Two very powerful people manipulated you," Verrity said. "The most powerful people we know of. Linia is—was—the richest person in all the worlds, and she used Sound magic against you."

"I let them manipulate me. Linia especially. All so I could go off— adventuring—" her words broke off into sobs.

Verrity allowed herself a moment's satisfaction at the punishment the Council had agreed on for Linia: working under heavy supervision out in the salt-flats of Taste, cutting the salt out of the ground and hauling it out to Liranel. A hard job, and one that she'd not wriggle out of any time soon, as her entire notes savings had all gone to reparations for the straiters she had injured and the families of those she had killed in her genocidal madness. She wouldn't buy her way out of this one.

Apparently, she'd used subtle Sound magic her whole life to attain her status and wealth, persuading with little whispers here and there. She'd managed to hide it until now, and once people knew she tried to manipulate them, they could defend themselves much easier. The Council had also ruled that Touch workers she'd bribed would return and finish the houses in the straits.

Paras let out another sob and Verrity patted her sister on the back. "Well, if there's one thing I've learned from all this, it's that people flourish best when they let themselves be where they want to be and do what they want to do." She raised her voice. "Ishira! Can you come over here for a moment?"

The young blonde woman hurried over. She eyed Paras's red,

blotchy face. "They're doing very well! Look, the little Soundian girl over there is playing with my Miera."

"Ishira," Verrity said. "I'm stepping down as Mother tonight. And I'm going to announce you as my replacement, if you agree."

The young woman's mouth dropped like a trapdoor. The end of her braid had unwound and lay in crimped curls on her shoulders. Her gaze darted over to Paras, then back to Verrity. "W-what?"

"You're ready," Verrity said. "And Paras doesn't want it. She wants to gallivant off into the sunset, as she told me once. With her new Lunnite girlfriend."

"She's not my girlfriend—"

"Could have fooled me, since you held hands yesterday. And both your pheromones smelled—"

"*Yet.*" Paras's tan cheeks had flushed red. "She's not my girlfriend *yet.* We haven't really talked about it. But yes, we—we want to be, I think."

"With a—" Ishira stopped herself. "Sorry. I mean . . . you do whatever makes you happy."

"Speaking of decisions," Verrity said. "Ishira. Do you want the job?"

"I—yes! I have so many ideas to strengthen the town, and work with the Soundians. I promise I'll work with the otherworlders."

"I know you will. That's why I said you're ready. I've watched you care for the new groups."

Verrity surveyed the field of chatting Scentians and Soundians, harvesting faster as they spoke to each other. The Harvest Dance would overflow the barn this year. She couldn't wait for the next set of Tastians would acclimate. They tended to bring goodies with them.

"I'm going to stay in Tremain, but I'll also travel to Suln and any other discovered Scentian towns, so the people across the world recognize and know me as Scent's delegate and trust me to convey their wishes to the Council. It'd be best I don't also tell them what to do or how to live their lives. From now on, I plan on representing all Scentians to the Council: what they want, what they need."

Paras and Ishira stared at her, the two bright suns of their blonde heads setting to the side.

"You seem . . . different," Ishira said.

Verrity smiled. "I feel different."

She'd decided, and it felt right to be decisive, to change. Tremain had grown, after all. Some people wanted to settle here from other places, especially Anthem or the Cloves, to escape the hustle and bustle of a large city. She couldn't keep up with that as Mother and commit to representing all of Scent.

That was who she wanted to be, and what she wanted to do.

"I just have one more thing I want to do, before I step down," Verrity said.

"What's that?" Ishira bit her lip, like she feared Verrity might decide to reverse her decision.

"I want," Verrity said, "To go to Anthem, and buy a special dress."

"You don't have to," Dad said.

Tener smiled at him. He had such a good heart. "I know I don't have to. I want to."

Mom shifted her hair to fur along the nape of her neck but didn't say anything out loud. She didn't reach out for their arm to hold them back, either.

They knew what she wanted to say. Their bond trembled with the unsaid words, like an echo of a whisper. "We weren't there for Saida when she grew up, and we want to be there for you."

They gripped her hands. "You did good, Mom."

She swallowed, and her bond that connected to her own emotions glowed brighter, then dimmed. She looked away, wrestling with her expressions. Falrie struggled to shift on the inside, but she had tried to, for Tener. She'd stepped back and let them do this.

They patted her on the back. They'd passed her in height, now. They'd grown another few inches in the past few weeks. Pointing this out to her might make her cry, so Tener did not. They didn't want to force things.

Dad reached out to hug his partner around the shoulders, but then pulled back, his forehead furrowing.

The bond between their parents shimmered for a moment. They both tried to mend things, just in different ways.

It would take time, if it happened. Their bond had almost broken when Mom had lost it back in the cellar. Tener didn't know what would happen if it snapped. Could they reconnect such a thing, like Alesio and Saida had reconnected the Planes, and Saida had reconnected to parts of herself? Tener didn't know for sure. Certainly, their parents would have to want to. For now, they stayed together.

They just . . . didn't thrive. Their bond didn't glow.

Tener couldn't imagine separating from the one person they had known and loved all their lives. To lose the one clear person out of a fugue of hazy memories. Tener had just existed for a bit over a year, and already their bonds anchored them, grounded them so much that just the idea of their connections fading—or, Senses forbid, disconnecting—set their heart pounding and turned their palms clammy. They didn't want that to happen to their parents. But Tener couldn't force them to stay together, just like Mom couldn't force Tener to stay away from this Guiding Ceremony.

They all passed through the Portal Station from Sound to Vision and stepped out into a fading lavender sky.

The foxans didn't have to navigate any of the outside maze-like gravity shifts, just the signposted, downhill slant that deposited them in front of the grieving family: a little boy and his mother in front of the pyre, where a middle-aged man lay dead.

The rest of Lavoa's villagers had showed up, as well, but stayed a respectful distance, some watching from their balconies, others from gravity shifts a little above the ground, but several yards away. This man had stayed in critical condition for over a month until succumbing to his injuries from the events after the Hunger's draining. They had dressed him in a simple cotton shirt and trousers, covering the cracked ribs from falling from a great height. He had been gathering vegetables for a stew when the Hunger had drained everyone. He'd floated into the sky after a startled movement and had kept floating upwards at a slow pace. His magic had refilled after a day or two, and he'd fallen back to the ground. Other Visionians had found him unconscious. Only two other people from Lavoa had died.

Yashalis nodded to the foxans as they halted next to the family. The village elder stood in front of the pyre with the traditional torch.

Tener surveyed the site, searching.

The few deaths Tener had witnessed had happened too quick to check for sure. But when that little boy had fallen up into the Hunger, her bonds had snapped, and the glow of her bonds had faded. All except one.

There. Still attached, but not glowing. A thin, fraying bond, like an old gray rope, trailed from the man's chest and into the ground.

But that wasn't what held their attention.

"What is it?" Dad asked, leaning towards them. "What do you see?"

Cut bonds hung from the little boy and the mother, bonds that used to attach to the man. These cut bonds hovered around the connected gray one in a ring and touched the ground around it like the torn off petals of a flower, but their bonds did not attach. Or could not attach.

Tener shook their head, not sure of what to say, and not wanting to interrupt the ceremony.

"We are here today," Yashalis said, "to commemorate Kiers back to the soil, so that he might one day grow again as someone, or something, new. May he see his first sunrise soon in his next life, on this world or another." She paused. "May you say your last respects."

The boy stayed back, lips unmoving, just staring. The woman stumbled forward, as if drawn to the still face of her husband. She whispered things that Tener did not try and listen to but watched as the gray bond between them glowed faintly, like a sparked match.

Then the woman stepped back in line with her son. His eyes glazed with tears. Her face did not move or change, portraying another kind of death.

"Are you ready?" Yashalis asked her. The woman dipped her head down, then up. The Council leader glanced to the foxans. "And are you?"

"We are," Mom said for the group, her voice smooth and strong. "We will guide Kiers's soul to the afterlife, as best as we know how."

Tener watched their Mom with a sense of interest. She showed so much strength on the outside, but the voice she spoke with did not connect to her confidence, but to her fear of the humans, of the outside worlds. She shifted to a facade of strength, a puffing up of the chest, a baring of the fangs. But humans couldn't seem to tell the difference.

At first, the foxans had all rejected the idea of this practice, Falrie most of all. But they had acquiesced at the obvious relief on the peoples' faces to have them there, performing this ritual. No one wanted to fall into an endless void in the sky. More hungry entities could wait to snap them up on their long journey.

The foxans all raised their hands as the ritual prescribed. Yashalis touched the burning torch to the oil-soaked pyre, and it flared up. The air heated around the grieving with the smell of burning flesh, and Falrie tossed a quick glance over at Tener, her eyes bloated with concern.

Tener kept their gaze glued to the pyre, for the man's bond to the ground had begun to glow, and so did the cut bonds of his wife and son. They sparked and held that spark, shining brighter, the match catching. Then the glow of all three traveled towards the ground—but stopped.

Tener stepped forward, then froze.

They didn't know what to do. Their parents had warned them about this, that the ritual simply fulfilled the humans' need for a mystical resolution and safety of unknowable reverence, but this . . . this seemed wrong, somehow. The soul didn't wander around lost and confused. The bond *wanted* to connect to the ground, but it couldn't.

They stepped forward, passing their parents, and Falrie inhaled sharply. But she didn't try and stop them.

They needed to do something, here. They just didn't know what. No one guided *them* on what to do. They held their hands towards the pyre, stretching their Empathy bond outward, that part of Tener that connected to others within seconds of meeting them and felt what they felt.

Their Empathy reached out like a long loop, and pulsed with glowing light, surrounding the three. The son and mother watched Tener, now, looking back over their shoulders. The pyre crackled, and the smell of burning hair and charred flesh pervaded the area. The little glow of the man's bond faded out.

Tener sobbed and fell to their knees. Their Empathy bond wrapped around the mother and son for a long moment. Five moments. Ten.

Then they released it, and stepped back, bowing their head. They dared not shake it and say, "I failed," in front of them. What good would such a statement do for these people? They had just wanted a ceremony, a vague spiritual reassurance. Tener didn't even know what they had failed at.

Something was wrong with how people died—and it had been wrong for a long, long time.

36

THE BRIDGES BETWEEN US

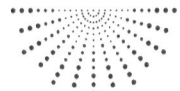

Tosn, Higa, Marik, and Paras labored with a select group of five Lunnites and three citizens of Vision.

Saida had portaled them to the now-ripped up site of Vision's Epitaph portal tree. They'd combed through the ruins with a slow precision for more of the ancient Lunnite script. Marik had showed them how the rocks formed the vision of the interlocking Planes the first day, and Tosn had spent most of his time tracing each circle and studying them.

Higa had found a few lines of Lunnite script the second day farther out, and on the third day, Paras had discovered a small pile of leaves from the portal tree that had fallen off long ago, tucked inside one of the rotating, hollow boulders. The leaves had adjusted to losing the rest of themselves, and instead of displaying a tiny portion of large portraits of other places, they showed the portraits, miniaturized.

The leaves presented many different places but returned to a specific one often: that of a Goddess Head statue on top of a tower.

Saida had begun helping the fox-people and the Lunnites differentiate magic as they couldn't before, sensing other magics that had transplanted here long ago from other Planes. It was like tasting a cake and parsing out the different ingredients: almond and aliberry, nutmeg and peppermint. Identifying the flavor she knew best—Touch magic—was easiest. Higa had learned to classify the other Sensory based magics with more difficulty.

The Goddess Head here on Vision had a magic not of this Plane, as well—it had an aura she had learned was Transmutation, that sense of substance changing into something else, but the silver ore had a mixture of another magic, as well. It had magic that stretched, that contracted, that waited, that speeded.

Amplified ore, those creations of the ancient Lunnites, were mixed with *time* magic. This concurred with the circle script they had translated on the five Sensory worlds, filling in the blanks they'd guessed at before.

For herself, Higa had not lost herself in a kind of trance when told the news about what the ancient Lunnites had done. Tosn and Etha, the oldest of their city, had taken to bed, their minds refusing to accept the difficult truths for several days.

She, Paras, and the rest of the Lunnites had confirmed these truths by piecing together the ancient scripts into a portrait of how the Hunger had come to be. Higa began writing down her analysis of the histories at night, after most of the other Lunnites had gone to sleep.

We Lunnites are not, after all, descended from the ancient Lunnites, she wrote. *Most of the ancient Lunnites were also Transmuters from the world of Transmutation, though some of them also came from the other two worlds of the Change Plane. Transmuters were beings that resembled trees and were not, as our people believed, foxans.*

These revelations had fascinated Higa instead of debilitating her like the elders. She had worshipped Lunne, not the ancient Lunnites, after all. But her easier adjustment could also be attributed to Paras. They'd kissed the other day.

The Transmuters/ancient Lunnites started, as far as I can tell, with the best of intentions, spreading their advanced machinery and magic across the Planes in a vast expedition to use their abilities to help others. They created wonders such as 'electricity' an energy that supposedly that traveled through the air that they could harness. This energy was somehow different from their magic, though we do not understand how. They traveled between Planes via the Bridges, an ancient Lunnite term. Apparently, portals used to span not just between worlds of the same Plane, but from Plane to Plane, and anyone could use them.

Higa thought the term 'Bridges' unnecessarily confusing. Why not just call the longer portals Plane Portals? But history was like that. A millennium of hindsight gave her a significant advantage on naming conventions.

The ancient Lunnites' electricity and their Transmutation magic, that of changing a substance into something else, worked well on multiple worlds, and many cultures and worlds welcomed them.

However, the ancient Lunnites of all three Change worlds began to realize something as they built their many colonies. The Bridges had begun to fray, taking longer and longer for people to travel them. Some people had even fallen into 'space.'

The word for 'space' still confused Higa, which was why she put quotes around it.

This word does not necessarily translate to the word for space between worlds or that of the blackness of the sky. But so far, I have no other word to describe it.

Translation, like history, was a finicky fellow in that minute details only mattered to the original person. Why describe the color blue when everyone could see it? How could these Lunnites have known that the color blue would lose its hue to everyone a thousand years later?

That was why Higa was so meticulous in her notes as she translated. Marik tended to flit around the ancient sites like a dragonfly, excited to find the newest and most interesting tidbit of information. But that wasn't how to translate. Word by word, cross-reference, double check. Next word.

Marik, to his credit, may have tried to distract himself from the fact that Saida had rebuffed his advances. His actions had mildly scandalized even Higa—trying to date an Envoy of Lunne? Had the Summit's spray gotten into his brain? — but having just started a relationship with Paras, she somewhat understood. When Paras loitered around her, well . . . her notes became less meticulous.

Speaking of. She needed to keep writing down her analysis and records of the Lunnites' history. Paras waited for her in her tent. To . . . talk.

Lunne, the foxan Goddess, is supposed to garden all connections, tending to them and keeping them strong. The ancient Lunnites decided to seek the Goddess and petition her to save the Bridges. They intended on sailing a massive ship through space once the Bridges failed so they could continue their search. To power this space sailing ship, however, they needed a massive amount of magic.

Unbeknownst to most of the ancient Lunnites, those in power on Transmutation had given up on finding the Goddess, and in their hubris, believed they could fix the problem themselves. They directed the ancient Lunnites below them in rank to follow a set of instructions to generate enough magic to fuel the space sailing ship, but that those in charge meant for another purpose.

Marik had helped compile the data around the space sailing ship section, having found the initial scripts about it on Vision when he had visited with Saida. Around the time that Higa had tromped through the Scent wilds for several days, he had flitted from world to world via the Transplant Tree.

She couldn't be too mad at him for that, though. Not when the time she'd spent had allowed her to get to know Paras. In Sedella, no other Lunnites had been . . . interested. Marik had long since given up trying to convince her that she could be bisexual.

As the Lunnites' dedicated archivist, Higa considered herself a thorough and detailed person. She'd employed these traits in other ways than her work, however. She'd never found someone like Paras; someone she'd wanted intimacy with—a female—and who also wanted that same kind of intimacy with her.

This splinter group of ancient Lunnites attempted godhood in several stages. The first was their failed attempts at utilizing Spatial magic. Again, I will explain in case this is read by someone centuries after me. What we used to call the Primal Plane, was called the Spatial Plane. The foxans of our time have adopted this term, as they feel it more accurately describes the raw magic in that place. Apparently, each Plane like our Sensory Plane has a respective Spatial Plane that feeds it raw magic. This magic transforms into the variety of unique yet similar magics of that Plane, like varieties of the same fruit. Ours is the Sensory, which increases the potency of the various Senses.

The ancient Lunnites wanted to use Spatial magic to power their 'ship', or secret purpose, because Lunne's foxans are born from the Spatial Planes, and because foxan magic, or Shaped Spatial magic, is what powered the Bridges and portals between worlds.

This logic did make sense to Higa. She probably would have tried the same thing at first, given the natural progression: Foxan magic equaled Bridge magic. Bridge magic was failing. Ergo, fix with foxan magic.

But *how* the ancient Lunnites had gone about the fixing irked her. They had no idea how the Goddess tended the magical connections between worlds and Planes, and no idea why she had stopped, and they had just tried to amass power, assuming that when they had enough, they would magically know what to do with it and how to fix the problem.

Typical of a powerful person, she mused. Power was a blinding thing, the more of it a person had, the less they considered others around them. Linia and the people of Anthem were prime examples. Linia had presumed that using an amplifier would solve all her fears. But when someone feared other people, removing the source of that fear had an unsettling conclusion.

However, she continued in her notes, *Spatial magic refused to funnel into the ancient Lunnites' runes. Spatial magic was too shapeless and changing in its raw form to settle into the grooves of their script.*

So, instead, the ancient Lunnites of the splinter group convinced foxans from the Change Plane to transplant into other Planes with specific forms and goals in mind. These foxans hadn't known the Lunnites' secret plan but simply wished at the end of their lives to strengthen other Planes with their magic. They were told to become Transplant Trees by merging with a transplant of each world in that Plane, and to use their portal magic to link those worlds together.

That was why the Transplant Tree on our Sensory Plane—what Saida used to term the 'Epitaph' and that we Lunnites used to call 'The Directive'—had five different powerful magics that matched the individual world they'd transplanted to.

The Transplant Trees didn't just store the magic of each world individually; but of all the worlds from the Plane they'd transplanted to. By doing this across several Planes, the plan was in motion to use hundreds of worlds' magics.

"Higa," Paras's soft voice called to her from inside the tent. "Are you almost done?"

Higa grinned. Paras brought out a kind of urgency in her. A restlessness to observe things in different ways. There was a benefit, sometimes, to leaving your hidden city and journey many miles. That was how you found new ruins to analyze, and breathtaking scenes like a cloud of swanseizes over gorgeous lakes that you couldn't wait to describe later. New people to study. In the best kind of ways.

"Almost," she said. "Give me ten minutes."

"I'll give you five!"

Higa blushed and worked to keep her writing neat and proper as she scratched her quill faster across the page.

The next stage involved the creation and use of the Goddess Heads. The ancient Lunnites did this by utilizing not just Transmutation magic, but the magic of the two other worlds in their Plane: Divination and Consumption.

Divination's magic could predict the potential change of a substance. Their people had discovered a silver ore deep in their ground, in which they predicted amplified power. Transmuters in the splinter group figured out how to merge their own magic with that of the world of Consumption's, in which the citizens could consume a substance and change their own bodies for a short time.

Combining these magics allowed select Transmuters, willing to end life as they knew it for their cause, to ingest the silver ore and transmute their physical bodies into huge amplifiers, becoming the Goddess Heads.

These Goddess Heads were stationed on hundreds of worlds across at least thirty-five Planes in preparation for their grand plan to siphon all the magic in the worlds through the Transplant Trees and become the Goddess.

Paras slipped out of the tent. Dusk had settled over Vision like a blanket with holes in it, letting the stars shine through.

The Scentian trailed her fingers along Higa's parchment paper, close to her pen, then up the pen as Higa stopped writing, then along Higa's hands, up her arms, around her shoulders. Paras's hands squeezed there, finding the knot of tense muscle and working at it.

"It's been five minutes," Paras said in her ear.

"Has it?" Higa breathed.

"Go on. Finish." She paused, and Higa could almost smell the grin on her. "Your writing."

Higa wrote with furious abandon, ink splattering the page.

The Hunger was then born out of the twisted backwash of a mixture of hundreds of magics too powerful to purify back into Spatial magic imploding in the Change Plane. The Change Plane, with its Consumption world—the world of ingesting and consuming of substances; the Divination world—the world of seeing the potential change in an object; and the Transmutation world—the world of changing one substance into another. Paras, you're so distracting –

Paras huffed. She'd kneaded Higa's shoulders farther and farther down until it wasn't her shoulders any longer. "Do you want me to be less distracting?" she lifted her hands from Higa's chest, and Higa looked over her shoulder at her, the pen dropping from her fingers, giving in to her urgent, needful side, the side that she'd never found before.

Has it really only been a month?

The Hunger had loomed in the Sensory worlds' skies around twelve days, give or take a few hours. It felt like several years to Alesio, like he'd inhaled a lot of ixor, or spent too long or wandered too far in a magic room. But something about walking into Flock gave him a different perspective.

The people watched them with the same suspicion as straiters watched pipers, scanning them up and down as if sizing them up for a fight. Instead of having a "piper" side, they all lived in thatch roofs and mud-filled streets. They didn't have running water in most of the houses. They spoke with a sharper tongue, as if ready to send out Sound knives at any moment.

That had jarred him out of his warped sense of time, reminding him of the one short trip he'd taken here with Saida, so Saida could portal the other foxans there and establish it as a place they could also teleport to.

That Saida had come this time as well showed how much she had grown in the past year. He had feared Flock before this, of course, but she had a more legitimate reason than he, considering several people in the crowd murmured the word "fur-mix" several times.

He pulled Saida closer to him. She squeezed his hand, sending reassuring feelings through their bond like Liranel water, cool and refreshing.

Alesio couldn't help but pick out a tall, larger man with twelve tattoos of cage match kills on his cheek and forced himself to peel his gaze away.

He felt like such a hypocrite. He couldn't keep himself from holding his breath. He'd saved his magic too, just in case the worst happened.

This was probably how Hestafon and pipers felt when they dared to show their faces in the straits. Fear. A hard to control fear that rose like vomit in the stomach.

Thinking of Hestafon still caused an ache in his chest. The piper had started to see the disparities, the unfairness between the city's two sides. His magic had helped Alesio understand the hurt he'd caused others. He'd even begun to perceive what Alesio had not: that Flock was hurting as much or more than the strait's side of Anthem. His memory inspired Alesio to be better, to keep his voice kind. To continue using his voice for good, instead of violence—especially when speaking to misunderstood and mistreated people.

It was funny, not in a laughing way, how blind he'd been about Flock, when he'd undergone similar harm. In fact, Clef's abuse and the straiters' downtrodden position in life seemed destined to spawn mistrust, violence, and disparity much the same way watered seeds sprouted easier. The phenomenon seemed cyclical, and he'd almost watered those seeds himself.

That he'd needed such a lesson had further reinforced his earlier decision. He had refused the clamor for him to become Anthem's next leader and nominated Mona in his stead. She had always excelled at crossing divides, after all.

At first, she'd stated that she absolutely would not, that she belonged in her beloved Drinks De Capo. But Alesio had sung her praises of how she brought the two sides of Anthem together, and how the city needed her discerning eye and diplomatic abilities, and how much she'd enjoy giving clean water to the straits and better housing, and her eyes had gone all thoughtful, and then she flicked a bar towel at him and sighed, and said that if the people would have her, she'd have music in her office at least.

The people had accepted Mona at once, since both sides knew of her and liked her. She'd seemed taken aback by that, as if she hadn't believed it would happen, but she kept her word. She ceded the day-to-day management of the Drinks De Capo to his father, who despite his now complete blindness, had become quite sufficient at slinging drinks.

She had refused, however, to become the delegate of Sound as well. "It's too much power for a world with two huge cities," she'd said. "Verrity has the right idea—the leader of a city shouldn't also represent that whole world. Have someone else do that. Maybe someone from Flock, so they feel more included. They're not happy there, and for good reason."

Indeed, as Alesio marched up to the dais where the Portal Station would appear, a low whistle veined through the crowd from multiple throats. The sources of the sound Alesio spotted all had shriker tattoos on their arms, marking them as the citizens who had overpowered Clef's group and reclaimed the shriker symbol.

These people had had to fight on their own, to make the best of their lives without the aid of anyone. They had expressed strong feelings to the Council last week about the Portal Station—frustration that it had taken so long to build one here, and the fear that they'd lose their newfound freedom they'd fought so hard for.

Alesio and Saida reached the dais, and Saida opened a fur pocket on her waist. She pulled out a clump of soft, glowing neon moss from Sedella, the last transplant needed to complete the Portal Station. She smiled at it, and their voice sounded in his mind, too, since they both knew how to listen.

"Hmmm, are you sure about this place? There are edges in peoples' eyes."

She whispered back on Alesio's right side. "You don't have to. But I can tell you that some places need a soft touch, before they can soften themselves."

The moss considered this, and Alesio held his breath. Another transplant had refused earlier this week, citing the same reasons.

The other transplants waited on the dais, already settled and placed at the four corners: a bit of water from Taste, a jar of the night sky from Vision—overjoyed that the Hunger had disappeared, clearing the view once more! — and a little bottle of the scent of the tomatoes growing in Tremain. The volunteers from Anthem had planted too many in one spot.

"Hmmm, I *am* good at being soft. Alright!"

Alesio took a quick breath. Saida did, too. She smiled at the moss and placed it on the dais on the fourth corner.

The transplants all glowed golden, merging, the threads of their growing bonds becoming visible to everyone in that moment. The low whistling in the crowd stopped, and everyone craned their necks and rose on tiptoe. The wonder in their faces softened the skepticism and anger.

Last year, when Saida had arranged for Alesio to sing in front of Tremain, that warmth had suffused him, and his perspective had changed. To change others' minds, he had to stop fearing them and how they could hurt those he loved, and start reaching out, instead.

Like Hestafon had. Like Saida had.

The transplants merged and stopped glowing. Four portals

glimmered at the four corners: two arrival portals from Tremain and Lavoa, and two departure portals leading to Touch and the Cloves.

They couldn't control which portals decided to become arrivals or departures, but somehow, it always seemed right for the city. Tremain remained somewhat vulnerable to outsiders, and Vision's gravity shifts made them the most dangerous to visit, at least at first, while people still learned. The Summit Wave had much decreased after Alesio and the crowd had formed the ice mountain, while the food in the Cloves had a way of allaying and diffusing tension.

The mixture of Scent and Vision magic on the dais submersed Alesio with that now familiar small boost of energy. He could breathe just a little easier, like his lungs had more space. The blended magic diffused through the surrounding streets. The crowd seemed to inhale as one, the people straightening like wilted plants receiving water.

"Flockians." Alesio spread his arms wide in his stage stance. "Thank you for your patience." He paused, struggling to find the right words. Even if Hestafon had not intended harm, the Delegate's fears about Flock had led to neglect and harm just the same. "I won't pretend to know what you all have gone through this past year, protecting your city alone. You've done a fantastic job of it."

The crowd quieted even further. Sweat beaded on the back of Alesio's neck.

"To be frank with you, the city of Anthem, my city, didn't do as well as you when the Hunger drained everyone. Hundreds of people were injured, and over . . ." his throat swelled, and his voice broke. "Forty-six people died. Our citizens also caused the deaths of twelve people on other worlds."

Silence held the reins on everyone's voices. They all knew this, of course. But Alesio knew his influence as the Voice of Reconnection, and how much it meant to have him say it out loud. To acknowledge mistakes, instead of pretending they hadn't happened.

To communicate.

"So, when I tell you," he continued, "that I value your strength, and your patience, I mean it. I am stepping down as Sound's temporary delegate in a week, and the Council has agreed to nominate someone from Flock as the next delegate."

There was a communal gasp of indrawn air, and then the people cried, laughed, and trilled with their tongues, a distinctive, loud sound that Alesio had never heard but didn't need translation for. Joy flooded the square like a sudden summer shower, a sweet relief of pressure.

Several minutes passed before the cheering calmed enough for Alesio to speak again.

"The Council has ruled that the delegates for Sound will switch between the cities once every two years, so neither one is ever neglected."

More cheering and trilling. Saida smiled at him, and he gripped her hand, raising it along with his.

"We present to you your Portal Station!"

At his declaration, as if waiting for the official words, a fifth portal shimmered into existence, in the center, bigger than all the others. The crowd gasped and everyone stepped back, as if afraid something would leap out at them from inside the portal.

A magic voice rang out from the center to them both. "Hello? Hello! Oh, you can hear me now? How grand, how grand! Well, come on then, jump in, it's been too long now, hasn't it?"

Saida's galaxy eyes shone. Her body bobbed like a cork in the water, unable to bottle her delight. Alesio Received her emotions: excitement to go to a new place.

She still had her teleport today. They could just portal back if they ended up in a dangerous spot.

Alesio bowed to the crowd. "And here we must leave you. Thank you for your hospitality!"

They jumped into the portal.

THEY'D PORTALED INTO BETWEEN, to that familiar hallway world she had known all her young life.

Saida deflated.

She hadn't visited Between in a while. She hadn't needed to; her parents had begun living in the Spatial Plane. It had always felt so cramped when she had all the wonderful, different worlds she could travel and explore on.

There was the small hill in the forest where she used to keep her den full of trimmings. The lake shimmered in the distance. The same vague brightness that could be a sun shone in the sky like a giant veiled lantern.

Wait.

That tree was new.

She knew each tree in Between. She'd counted them all several times — and that one, next to her den, was new.

She ran over to it, shifting to foxan because it felt right, here, and Alesio followed. "What is it?"

She didn't have words. More unknown trees presented past that one. The forest had grown larger, enough that no end presented itself.

"Do you like them?" The voice said. That same voice that had spoken to them on the dais back in Flock. Now, it came from all around, and one of the glowing bonds trailing from her chest connected to the air around them. "You always wanted more."

Saida paused. ". . . Between? Am I talking to Between?"

"Of course! Who did you think you were talking to? Tell me, though, do you like them?"

"I—I do," Saida said. "I do like them. They're wonderful trees."

"Oh, how grand! I'm so happy! And now you're here, I can tell you, I'm strong enough to Reconnect you!"

"Wait, what?" Alesio glanced this way and that, as if trying to pinpoint where the voice came from. "Reconnect where?"

The Between's voice turned a bit shy. "Just to one Plane. The closest one. I don't have enough strength to do anything more than that yet. Are you ready? You listened to me and Received my magic well enough. You're ready to Shape!"

Still confused, Saida closed her eyes, listened, and Received.

All the portals that lived in the Between, including those that recharged there at the time, and those scurrying through the worlds' crusts, seemed to perk up like people in Anthem hearing a giant, tolling bell, and they scurried towards her.

She Shaped hundreds of them, joining each one's ability to span a certain amount of space like links in a chain, creating one long, stable portal. Together, they reached much farther than she'd ever traveled before. She could do it without the aid of an amplifier because she followed the markings of an old, faded trail, an ancient portal that had existed before but had crumbled.

To help her Shape this extended portal, all the trees in the forest, and all the rocks in the ground, and all the water in the lake had unformed and become portals as well.

She understood, then, who Between was.

Between gave her the same impression as the Garden had back on Scent. That same sense of crisp adventure. Spatial magic. Magic she could Shape. Magic that she had already Shaped. Every time she had ever called a portal; she'd Shaped them from the Spatial Plane, and they had lived afterwards in Between.

This hallway world between the five Sensory worlds consisted entirely of portals. They comprised all the portals Saida and the other foxans had ever Shaped, like millions of drops of water made up a wave, like millions of bonds made up a person, like millions of stars made up the night sky.

The tether she'd Shaped landed on the new world like a bridge settling over a chasm. The opening, which appeared in front of her and Alesio, displayed a shining golden path, a long, long bond stretching into space, but she could sense a world on the other side where she'd connected to a world from a different Plane.

A Bridge.

Saida lifted her paw to her mouth, a distinctly human gesture as she sat on her foxan haunches. Everything clicked into place, even as her portals fastened closer together.

The Lunnites had discovered this part, that there used to be portals that stretched between Planes. They'd called these portals Bridges.

She and Alesio stood on a bit of ground she'd kept there for . . . peace of mind, but space, the kind of space between worlds, encompassed everything else around them, save for the glowing golden path leading beyond where they could see.

"How . . . how did I do that?" Saida whispered. "I mean . . . why did it happen now?"

"Well, you created a fifth Portal Station!" Between giggled from the portal. "That's what you call them, right? After your chosen person here Reconnected our Plane, I just needed five working Portal Stations to make a Bridge that would reach the next Plane! Because our Plane has five worlds!"

The two of them stood in front of the golden path, trying to process all of this. Saida counted in her head. "But we finished the fifth Portal Station awhile ago. This was the sixth—*oh.*" She slapped her hand to her face. "I wasn't listening, was I?"

Between nodded, which had the effect of shifting Saida's point of view up and down. "I tried to tell you. You couldn't hear me. It made me very sad. But when you created the Portal Station just now, you were listening to the magics when they added themselves to me, so I shouted to you again."

So, now she and others could travel to a different set of worlds. To some of those stars that glittered in the far-away sky.

Alesio gathered enough wits to ask, "So . . . what Plane did you connect to?"

"Well, just the closest world of the closest Plane. And that's Gravity! It's super close to us because it bonded to Vision a long, long time ago."

Alesio raised a hand as if asking to speak in a classroom. "There's a world called Gravity?"

"Well, of course! That's its magic. Why did you think the world of Vision has special kinds of gravity?"

They both stood there stupidly.

"I—I thought the gravity creates complex . . . patterns . . ." Saida said.

There was a moment of polite silence. Then Between laughed.

"I'm sorry. I'm sorry, that was rude. Oh, my Goddess, you're funny." They cleared their throat. "Anyway, are you ready to go? Do you want to use the Bridge we made? You do, right?"

Saida and Alesio stared at each other. Their lips twitched.

"I—I do, so *very* much," Saida said, forcing down a laugh. "I can't right at this second. I have to—you know, say goodbye to some people first."

"Oh. Right." The Bridge decreased a bit, creating some ground under their feet again. A few trees winked back into existence nearby and their leaves curled in a little on the edges. "Okay."

Saida blinked. "Between?"

"Yeah?"

"I love what you've done with yourself, here."

"Yeah?"

"Is the hill bigger, too?"

"Yeah, it is! And the lake! And there's more fish in the lake, since you all left, and . . . and no one's eating them . . ."

Saida hugged the new tree, shifting her foxan front legs into arms to better span its width. "I'm sorry I didn't come back before. You're a wonderful, amazing, beautiful magic. You take me to new places! Without you, I wouldn't have met Alesio, or anyone else!"

The trees bent their branches towards the two of them, patting them on their shoulders. Alesio's lips twitched even more, but he managed to hold in his laughter.

"I'm happy to hear that. I thought you didn't like me, you know, back then. And I tried to keep your trimmings safe for you, but that horrible, nasty foxan destroyed them. And then . . . you stopped visiting, and Darrow and Falrie left, too."

"I didn't appreciate what you did for me," Saida said. "I couldn't hear you speaking. I'm sorry."

"It's not your fault; the Planes disconnected a long time ago. It was a terrible time. Lonely. I felt so small." Between paused for a few seconds. More trees appeared, and more of the ground, and her little hill where Saida had once made her den. "But now everything is grand again! Go and say your goodbyes, then! I can't wait till I show you what I can do! How long till you come back?"

"Um . . ." Saida swallowed and raised her eyebrows at Alesio, her foxan ears pricked forward.

He grinned back at her, then addressed the tree she had hugged. "Not long. Can you give us a week—no, two weeks, to prepare? I've promised to perform at some places, and I don't want to skip out."

"Two weeks. Hmm. Yeah, that's not long at all! Okay! Yes!" The portal shimmered and shrank down to a normal portal size. "How about this one just takes you back to Anthem then, huh?"

"Thank you, Between." Saida blew a kiss at the air. "See you again soon."

3 7

TRANSPLANTED

While Alesio set up on stage at the Drinks De Capo, Saida wound her way through the audience, human except for her foxan ears and the fur mixing in her braid. Her parents sat together in their human forms, though with space between them. Their bond had strained, but it existed, the strands frayed but not broken.

She had bondsight, now, the same as Tener. She guessed that the vision of Lunne had given her the ability. The strands connected in hundreds of ways between the various people at the De Capo, like a net that everyone walked through. If she focused on one person, more of their bonds emerged to her that connected to various parts of themselves, like their gumption, their fear, or their self-confidence.

For their part, Tener had built bonds with almost everyone at the bar. Considering their ability, of course they'd known how to build friendships and connect as well as they had.

Now that she could see the bonds, now that she *listened* to the magic, she understood how to connect a little better, too. It reminded her of transplanting magic, in a way. She trimmed some of herself and shared it with someone, and that created a bond. An anchor. Something that kept her close even when distance separated them.

Estro and Tak held hands at the bar. Estro wore blue and gold dress-striped pants with a white shirt. Tak wore a golden shirt and blue pants. Their bond shone the brightest and thickest of all. Mona and Alesio's father, Luca, had a growing bond that twinkled between them like the tail of a star, the most like hers and Alesio's. Not as bright but still glowing. She trailed over to the two of them.

"Hello, Saida," Mona said, sliding her a piece of cheese and nut bread to pair it with from under the bar. She may have become the new leader of Anthem, but she still relaxed here at night with Luca as he managed the bar. "So, has he sung this song to you before?"

She grinned. "He's had a hard time keeping it from me. I know parts of the melody because he's always humming it." And he'd sung a bit of it to her that one night at his house.

Luca danced his fingers on the bar top. "I know parts of it, too. And I know who it's about." He winked one of his white eyes in her general vicinity.

"So, when will you follow in your son's footsteps and write me a song, eh?" Mona brushed his knuckles with her hand.

"Why, I thought you knew, my dear! I've composed it already." He sang in a steady baritone, "It's the rhythm of your footsteps when you stalk into the room, and the creak of your voice when you sing out of—"

Mona snatched a sound cloth and sent it flying in his face, and he chuckled and chased her around the bar. Estro used the moment to press his lips to Tak's.

Saida watched the two happy couples with a strange tightness in her chest, and then, of course, Tak chose to glance back at her at that moment.

The piper kissed his husband again then sidled over to her. "You gonna tell us the reason for your upside-down smile?"

Saida laced her fingers in front of her, then unlaced them. Breathed through the fear. The background sound in the bar had increased in volume, and she had lean close for them to hear. "Have any of you guys ever had a fight?"

The two couples stared at her, then Estro coughed. Mona let out a guffaw. "A few. A few."

"How do you know . . . you know."

Luca cocked his head. "There's a lot of outcomes for what that could mean."

Saida shifted her hands to paws. "If the fighting hurts you both too much." Through her bond, Alesio sensed her anxiety, even as he tuned his mandolin on stage, and he twanged the melody to what he'd hummed earlier. Her emotions had a place to go, now, instead of being stuffed inside her foxan self. She could breathe so much easier, like she had more space in her body, in her heart.

"Everyone fights," Luca said. "It's a good thing. It shows you both still have your own identity and will. It's *how* you fight that matters."

Mona slipped her arm around his waist. "The old hotrat's right."

"Hotrat, huh?" Luca tapped his chin. "Well, I *can* make you burn—"

Saida flattened her ears against her head. They all chuckled, and Mona clapped her hand over Luca's mouth. "Don't traumatize the poor girl!" She paused. "How *much* do you fight? Because that can be a sign. If you've tried fighting the right way but can't find a path forward . . . it's not a bad thing to end it. Believe me, having owned a bar for as long as I have, you see the signs."

They all swiveled towards Saida. She'd picked up the end of her braid. She forced herself to let it drop. "We don't—um, we don't fight a lot. I just don't want to, um, in the future."

"Ah," Tak said, wiggling his mustache. It hadn't grown back in all the way yet, so he'd trimmed the other side to match the ripped off bit. His face thinned without the handlebar effect. "Things make some sense at last." He stepped forward. "Here's the thing. I've been with that tall glass of whiskey over there for over ten years now. We've had our ups and downs. It doesn't help that I'm a bit of a firebrand myself."

"A bit?" Estro quirked his lips.

"But I can tell you something." Tak clapped his hand on Saida's shoulder. "What Luca said earlier is right. How you talk to your partner when you're angry or scared says everything. When you're hurt and upset, will you try to hurt them on purpose to prove a point, or can you still speak with love? That's the real way to fight."

Mona grabbed a mug off the bar and held it up, her strawberry blonde hair swinging around her shoulders. "De Capo that. If people learned how to stop making knives out of their words, less of them would cut themselves."

Tener raced by them, gripping a bag of cinnamon olos. Baylor chased after them. "Don't you dare teleport! You know that's cheating! Hey! Hey, don't eat *as* you're running!"

"I said I'd give them to you if you caught me! If I eat them before, too bad for you!"

Saida smiled. Tener had grown taller, about as tall as Baylor. But a maturity displayed itself, too, in the way that they dashed and chortled and played, a calculated immaturity.

Tener drew out the broken childishness of Baylor, unfolding it like a crumpled flower. In that moment, Baylor looked more sixteen or seventeen than nineteen or twenty, and Tener possessed a smooth *agelessness,* with their glossy hair curling around their ears, and their baggy shirt and pants.

She had waited over a hundred years before she'd left Between. Her parents had reached middle age when they had turned 500. Neither Falrie nor Darrow knew why or how Tener had aged so fast in a year, though they guessed that the Spatial Plane's magic played catch up after the Severing.

Across the room, Falrie almost reached out to Tener as they dashed past her and Darrow's table. She stopped and said something to Darrow. Her father leaned his muzzle close and whispered in Falrie's ear, and she laughed. A single strand of the frayed rope of their bond reconnected.

She hadn't understood why they'd had trouble in the first place. She'd feared *that* the most, the not knowing, the uncertainty.

But she'd begun to understand. They'd been together for so long in Between, knowing only each other—and, for half of those centuries, her—that the worlds had overwhelmed them both. They'd reacted in

591

different ways, however: Falrie, overprotective. Darrow, insecure. In that way, she and Alesio had mirrored their struggles.

Maybe they wouldn't stay together. Maybe they would. Saida couldn't force them to, but even if they separated, that didn't mean that she and Alesio would do the same.

She needed to stop focusing on what *could* happen and instead focus on what she *wanted* to happen. She didn't have to fear her own chaotic nature, because it would listen to her on important things. It was a part of her, after all.

"Go on, take a seat." Tak slid onto a barstool next to her and pulled out his harmonica. "He's about to start." He grinned. "I'm going to try and match pitches with him like he used to do to Hestafon. Let me know if he notices."

She fought off a grin. "I think he sees you already. He's giving you a special gesture."

"He what?" Tak squinted at the stage. "Oh, that's just him encouraging me. He's holding up that finger to say I'm number one!"

———

ALESIO ASCENDED the stage at the Drinks De Capo and felt once again like a different person. He wore his new silver shirt with gold trim and buttons, the one Saida said matched their bond colors.

He didn't worry about Saida leaving him, or about someone hurting her, or that he'd age while she remained young. He felt light as a bird. Even with the knowledge that they would leave on a trip to another Plane just filled him with excitement.

He singled out where Saida had landed next to Tak, who held his harmonica in his hands and a twinkle in his eyes. Alesio chuckled. The old rascal.

He started with a new De Capo favorite, a song called "Of All the Places" that had started in the Cloves detailing the wonders of the different worlds. Though it favored the world of Taste, no one seemed to begrudge the ranking.

· · ·

Oₕ, the hue of blue on Vision
    Is a sight the worlds over
    And the Glassy Sea on Touch
    Does brush one like a lover

Bᴜᴛ ᴀʟʟ ᴛʜᴇ places everywhere
    Cannot compare to simple water
    The flavor of Liranel on Taste
    Makes even Touchians falter.

Oₕ, the trace of sage and ginger
    On Scent can curl the toes,
    And the songs they sing on Anthem
    Do ring, peal, and crescendo

Bᴜᴛ ᴏꜰ ᴀʟʟ ᴛʜᴇ places in the Senses,
    Simple butter on a slice
    Of the Cloves' fresh baked bread
    Could fetch a piper's dowry price.

Rᴀᴜᴄᴏᴜs ʟᴀᴜɢʜᴛᴇʀ ᴀᴄᴄᴏᴍᴘᴀɴɪᴇᴅ the song's end line. Musicians in Anthem had already started riffing on it, creating other versions where Sound was the best world. Alesio had no doubt that each world would have their own version soon.

Using the momentum of the first song, he launched into "The Song of the Street," and the place clapped along faster and faster until they couldn't keep up, and the audience, as always, dissolved in laughter.

The last song waited in his throat.

He strummed the mandolin, listening for anything off key. He'd tuned it earlier, but standard practice dictated to always check on stage. Sure enough, he needed to tweak one of the strings.

Do instruments feel nervous? Now that he understood more about how magic worked, he could imagine that his mandolin could have stage fright just like him. He strummed again, and this time the chord rang true.

Inside his house of Sound, he Received the chord.

"I am called Pianissimo," the chord said in his mind. "I am soft. I am tremulous. I want to become louder. I want to be tall and strong!"

I can do that, he told them. Aloud, he said, "This one's an original called "Transplanted", and it's dedicated to the foxan who once again, has managed to save us all."

He began with Pianissimo, pre-Shaped, just playing music without enhancing the Sound with magic. He Shaped Pianissimo's crescendo with each stanza, with each repetition of the chorus. Pianissimo became Piano, or just soft, then Mezzo Piano, medium soft, then Mezzo Forte, medium loud, then Forte! Loud! Grand! Resplende

I USED to dream of brighter places
    Of playing for the crowd,
    I thought the waves of all those faces
    Would drown the darkness in my sound.

YOU TUNED my ear to hear through the lies
    that hid and tried to seize me
    You are my brightest place,
    your name's a euphony,
    Oh, you've transplanted me.

I USED to want to be needed
    To prove my worth and stop the worst
    Things that could happen to you, keeping

You safe and never leaving me

YOU TUNED my ear to hear through the lies
    that hid and tried to seize me
    You are my brightest place
    You've transplanted me.

HOW HAD he played before without listening to what the magic wanted to become? Magic changed eternally, it shifted and shone with so many different facets in the space of a breath. How had he charged forward with just what he wanted them to do and be, instead of asking and helping them what they wanted? This constant asking and shifting gave both so much more. Gave Saida so much more. Allowed them both to become, instead of forcing them into a preconceived thing.

Communication, as Saida had put it. A free-flowing, never-ending stream of questions and answers, of Receiving and Shaping, between them.

THAT NIGHT, as she had every night since the Hunger had disappeared from their skies, Saida spent the night at Alesio's house—though lately, she'd begun thinking of it more as their house, and their kitchen, and their bed. It helped that she'd begun trimming magic again and had placed some her trimmings into the room that Alesio had saved for them. She had Dusk in a Bottle, and Velvet Rainbow, and Ever-Tasty Muffin all up in a row on a shelf, and plenty more shelves waited, ready for her to fill them up with magic.

That night, as he had every night, Alesio asked her, "Do you want to stay with me tonight?"

And she answered the same as she had every night since.

"Yes."

ABOUT THE AUTHOR

Emmie Christie's work includes practical subjects, like feminism and mental health, and speculative subjects, like unicorns and affordable healthcare. She is a novelist, short story writer, and narrator. *All the Skies So Hungry* is the second installment in her fantasy romance trilogy, *Transplanted*. The first book in the series, *A Caged and Restless Magic*, debuted in Feb 2024.

Christie's short fiction and poetry has appeared in over 120 magazines and anthologies, including notable publications such as *Factor Four, Small Wonders*, and *Flash Fiction Online*. She has also narrated several pieces for the magazine *Strange Horizons*. Find her at www.emmiechristie.com, her monthly newsletter, or on BlueSky.

If you enjoyed this novel, please rate and review on on Amazon or Goodreads. Attention is good protein, and this author is always hungry.